# Praise for *In the F*

"The appearance in English of this new version of Aleksandr Solzhenitsyn's best novel, mistranslated as *The First Circle* when it appeared in Britain and America more than forty years ago, is an exciting literary event. . . . This is a great and important book, whose qualities are finally fully available to English-speaking readers. *In the First Circle*, containing ninety-six chapters, is about a fifth longer than the original English translation, and it is a vastly better novel, though the earlier one was hailed as a masterpiece and contributed significantly to the Nobel Prize for Literature that Solzhenitsyn won in 1970. . . . This new version is magnificent. Like all great Russian novels, it is a study of the human condition, wise and insightful and startlingly universal."

—*Washington Post*

"The new edition of Aleksandr Solzhenitsyn's epic novel, *In the First Circle*, captures better than any other work of fiction the quintessence of communist rule at its Stalinist peak: all-pervasive, paranoid, oppressive, incompetent, lethal. . . . The new edition of the novel differs subtly but importantly from the version published in English in 1968. That was based on a self-censored text that the author had prepared in the hope of getting it published in the Soviet Union. It left out the hero's espionage for America, the Christian faith of his friend, and other details that the Soviet authorities would have found utterly intolerable. The longer text is deeper and darker."

—*The Economist*

"Solzhenitsyn's Cold War masterpiece. . . . A new radically retranslated edition, which is greatly expanded." —*The Times* (London)

"Solzhenitsyn's Soviet-censored masterpiece. . . . In this many-voiced, flashback-rich, philosophical, suspenseful, ironic, and wrenching tale, Solzhenitsyn interleaves the stories of a grand matrix of compelling characters (women are accorded particular compassion) trapped in a maze of toxic lies, torturous absurdities, and stark brutality. . . . [An] indelible novel of towering artistry, cuastic wit, moral clarity, and spiritual fire."

—*Booklist* (starred review)

"A gripping novel in the best tradition of Russian realism. . . . Masterfully translated by Harry T. Willets, it is rich with memorable characters, finely crafted episodes, and beautiful language."

—Paul E. Richardson, *Russian Life*

"The publication by HarperCollins of *In the First Circle* (the book's original title) in a restored ninety-six-chapter version, is therefore a publishing event of the first order. . . . With the publication of the restored version of *In the First Circle*, we have an opportunity to rise to Solzhenitsyn's challenge and again to take him seriously as an artist and thinker of the first rank."

—Daniel J. Mahoney, *First Things*

# IN THE First Circle

Also by Aleksandr I. Solzhenitsyn

## Fiction

*One Day in the Life of Ivan Denisovich* (1963)
*Cancer Ward* (1968)
*Stories and Prose Poems* (1971)
*August 1914 (The Red Wheel: Knot I)* (1972)
*November 1916 (The Red Wheel: Knot II)* (1999)

## Nonfiction

*Nobel Lecture* (1972)
*Letter to the Soviet Leaders* (1974)
*The Gulag Archipelago, 1918–1956: An Experiment in Literary Investigation* (1974)
*From Under the Rubble* (1975)
*Warning to the West* (1976)
*A World Split Apart* (1978)
*The Oak and the Calf: Sketches of Literary Life in the Soviet Union* (1980)
*The Mortal Danger* (1980)
*Rebuilding Russia: Reflections and Tentative Proposals* (1991)
*Invisible Allies* (1995)
*"The Russian Question" at the End of the Twentieth Century* (1995)

## Poetry

*Prussian Nights: A Poem* (1977)

## Drama

*The Love-Girl and the Innocent: A Play* (1969)
*Candle in the Wind* (1973)
*Prisoners: A Tragedy* (1983)
*Victory Celebrations: A Comedy in Four Acts* (1983)

# IN THE First Circle

A NOVEL

THE RESTORED TEXT

Aleksandr I. Solzhenitsyn

*Translated by Harry T. Willetts*

HARPER PERENNIAL

NEW YORK • LONDON • TORONTO • SYDNEY • NEW DELHI • AUCKLAND

HARPER PERENNIAL



HarperCollins books may be purchased for educational, business, or sales promotional use. For information, please e-mail the Special Markets Department at SPsales@harpercollins.com.

FIRST EDITION

*Designed by Joy O'Meara*

Library of Congress Cataloging-in-Publication Data

Solzhenitsyn, Aleksandr Isaevich, 1918–2008.
[V kruge pervom. English]
In the first circle : a novel / Aleksandr I. Solzhenitsyn ; translated by Harry T. Willetts.—1st Harper Perennial ed.
p. cm.
ISBN 978-0-06-147901-4
1. Soviet Union—Politics and government—1917–1936—Fiction. 2. Soviet Union—Politics and government—1936–1953—Fiction. 3. Political persecution—Soviet Union—Fiction. I. Willetts, H. T. II. Title.
PG3488.O4V23 2009
891.73'44—dc22 2008039336

16 17 18 OV/RRD 10 9

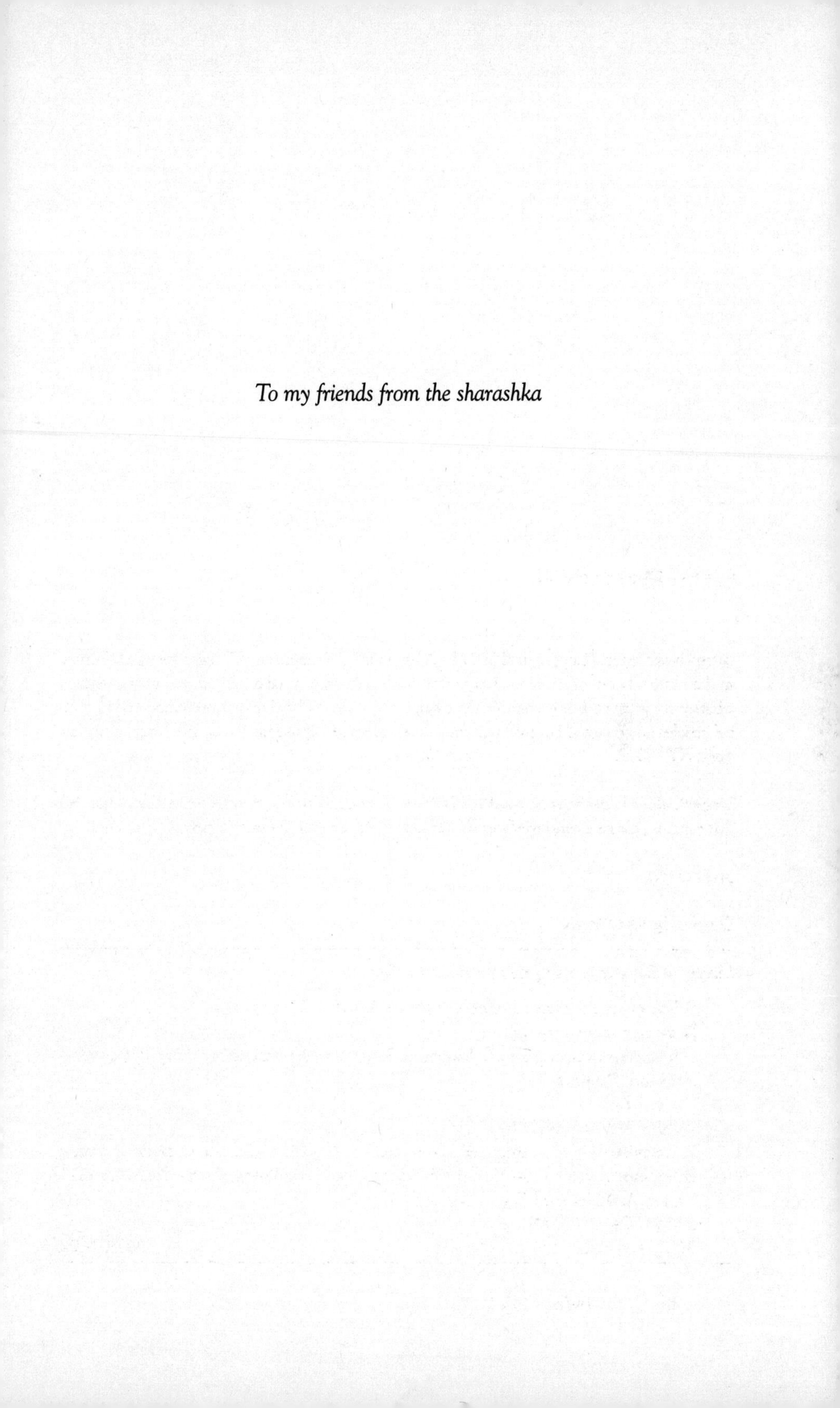

*To my friends from the sharashka*

# Contents

*Foreword by Edward E. Ericson, Jr.* XIII
*Cast of Characters* XXVII
*Author's Note* XXXI
1 Torpedo 1
2 A Miscue 6
3 Sharashka 9
4 A Protestant Christmas 13
5 Boogie-Woogie 18
6 A Peaceful Existence 23
7 A Woman's Heart 28
8 "Oh, Moment, Stay!" 34
9 The Fifth Year in Harness 39
10 The Rosicrucians 44
11 The Enchanted Castle 51
12 Number Seven 57
13 He Should Have Lied 64
14 The Blue Light 69
15 A Girl! A Girl! 74
16 A Troika of Liars 80
17 Hot Water 89
18 "Oh, Wonder-Working Steed" 93
19 The Birthday Hero 97

20 A Study of a Great Life 105
21 Give Us Back the Death Penalty! 129
22 The Emperor of the Earth 144
23 Language as an Instrument of Production 150
24 The Abyss Beckons Again 156
25 The Church of Nikita the Martyr 162
26 Sawing Wood 171
27 A Bit of Methodology 180
28 The Junior Lieutenant's Job 185
29 The Lieutenant Colonel's Job 193
30 A Puzzled Robot 201
31 How to Darn Socks 207
32 On the Path to a Million 217
33 Penalty Marks 224
34 Voiceprints 233
35 Kissing Is Forbidden 239
36 Phonoscopy 243
37 The Silent Alarm 248
38 Be Unfaithful to Me! 257
39 Fine Words, Those, "To the Taiga!" 262
40 A Rendezvous 269
41 And Another One 277
42 And Among the Kids 283
43 A Woman Was Washing the Staircase 289
44 Out in the Open 297
45 The Running Dogs of Imperialism 315
46 The Castle of the Holy Grail 324
47 Top-Secret Conversation 335
48 The Double Agent 342
49 Life Is Not a Novel 347

50 The Old Maid 359
51 Fire and Hay 368
52 To the Resurrection of the Dead! 373
53 The Ark 378
54 Leisure Amusements 381
55 Prince Igor 388
56 Winding Up the Twentieth 397
57 Prisoners' Petty Matters 402
58 A Banquet of Friends 408
59 The Buddha's Smile 420
60 But We Are Given Only One Conscience, Too 431
61 The Uncle at Tver 443
62 Two Sons-in-Law 456
63 The Diehard 466
64 Entered Cities First 474
65 A Duel Not by the Rules 483
66 Going to the People 493
67 Spiridon 497
68 Spiridon's Criterion 506
69 Behind a Closed Visor 512
70 Dotty 522
71 Let's Agree That This Didn't Happen 525
72 Civic Temples 533
73 A Circle of Wrongs 537
74 Monday Dawn 543
75 Four Nails 551
76 Favorite Profession 556
77 The Decision Taken 564
78 The Professional Party Secretary 569
79 The Decision Explained 578

80 One Hundred Forty-Seven Rubles 587
81 The Scientific Elite 597
82 Indoctrination in Optimism 601
83 The King of Stool Pigeons 607
84 As for Shooting . . . 611
85 Prince Kurbsky 620
86 No Fisher of Men 626
87 At the Fount of Science 634
88 The Leading Ideology 643
89 Little Quail 654
90 On the Back Stairway 662
91 Abandon Hope, All Ye Who Enter Here 672
92 Keep Forever 683
93 Second Wind 697
94 Always Caught Off Guard 711
95 Farewell, Sharashka 716
96 Meat 729

# Foreword

IT HAS TAKEN a half century for English-language readers to receive the definitive text of the best novel by the man who may well be the most famous author of our times. Such is the fate of art created under a totalitarian regime. In a desperate attempt to get his literary artifact published at all, the author took it upon himself to sever some of its parts, a gruesome act of sacrifice. Yet the work's artistic power was so great that even in its wounded condition it drew much praise. The authentic version of the novel traveled an extraordinarily rough road from composition to publication, and the dramatic story of the unkind cuts inflicted on it along the way deserves to be known in all its details. For the restored work's appearance in the present volume is a major publishing event.

Aleksandr Solzhenitsyn initially composed *In the First Circle* from 1955 to 1958, when he was in his thirties. In 1968 an expurgated version titled *The First Circle* came out in many languages. The loss in English of the preposition *In*, doubtless through an innocent decision, subtly shifts the novel's focus from people in a place to the place itself; the present version eliminates this distortion. Before the author died in 2008, four months short of his ninetieth birthday, he knew that the novel as he intended it was finally scheduled to appear in English a year thereafter. The years between 1958 and 2009 left plenty of time for the novel to endure a tortured textual history. Compared with the version previously available in English, the plot has been altered, depictions of some major characters have been substantially modified, new characters have been introduced, and many entirely excised chapters have been reinstated. For readers familiar with the previously available English version, *In the First Circle* will be a revelation.

Solzhenitsyn wrote the book under exceptionally difficult circumstances. In 1953, as he was about to emerge from the Gulag after eight years of incarceration, he contracted cancer, which brought him near death's door in the months that followed. Consigned to "perpetual" internal exile in Kazakhstan after prison and camp, he found work as a village schoolteacher. In every spare moment he wrote. *In the First Circle* was his largest project, and he lavished great care on it. No sooner had he finished the first draft in 1958 than he put it through two revisions.

The drama of his life story took a quantum leap forward when in 1962, as a total unknown, he made his sensational entry onto the world's stage with the publication of *One Day in the Life of Ivan Denisovich*, a story about life in the Soviet prison camps. While that short work was under consideration by the prestigious Moscow journal *Novy Mir*, Solzhenitsyn wrote a fourth draft of *In the First Circle* in 1962. *One Day* appeared with the imprimatur of no less a personage than Premier Nikita Khrushchev and electrified readers in the Soviet Union and around the world.

Hoping to parlay one success into another, Solzhenitsyn decided to try to squeeze *In the First Circle* through the censors' sieve. Yet, anticipating that its themes transgressed strict Soviet limits, he tempered his hopes with realism and in 1964 put the manuscript through a process of "lightening." The pruned and politically toned-down result of this act of self-censorship was what he later called an "ersatz, truncated" version; the number of chapters dropped from ninety-six to eighty-seven. In an augury that Solzhenitsyn's sacrificial pragmatism was doomed to fail, the KGB in 1965 broke into the apartment of a friend of his and made off with a copy of the novel, which then circulated among selected officials. Although *Novy Mir* had agreed to publish the novel in its eighty-seven-chapter form, higher authorities kept withholding their approval. (Fascinating insights into the Soviet regime's hostility toward *In the First Circle* became available in 1995 when formerly secret government documents were published under the title *The Solzhenitsyn Files*.) Another major work of his, *Cancer Ward*, came closer to receiving the backing of the official Soviet Writers Union, but it, too, remained blocked. Solzhenitsyn's window of opportunity had closed.

The 1960s established Solzhenitsyn's reputation as a courageous hero. He checked with defiant resistance every move by the Soviet regime to stifle him, as if he were a chess master playing a game with life-and-death stakes. Meanwhile the Western press closely watched the unfolding struggle, and the free world rooted for him. In 1968, with official harassment relentlessly constricting his options, he took the desperate step of authorizing the publication in the West of the "lightened version" of *In the First Circle*, a copy of which he had been able to send out. The secretiveness required for this transmission from East to West meant that he lost control over the book and could not see it through press. Almost simultaneously *Cancer Ward* also appeared in the West, though without the author's permission. And when he was expelled from the Writers Union in 1969, prominent Western writers signed letters of vociferous protest.

Both long novels, like the short *One Day in the Life of Ivan Denisovich* before them, were widely hailed as major literary achievements. The double-barreled evidence led one American scholar to declare, "No longer can there be the slightest question about his literary stature or doubt of its permanence." Another established American critic called *The First Circle* "the greatest Russian novel of the last half of the century." British critics joined the chorus, one describing it as "a majestic work of genius" and another judging it "arguably the greatest Russian novel of the twentieth century." A handful of years later, when the Soviet authorities forced Solzhenitsyn into Western exile and he began to make speeches, political controversies would come to color, or discolor, assessments of his fiction, but the broadly appreciative opening round of reactions rested solidly on artistic criteria. In the meantime, unknown to anyone outside the tight-knit circle of helpers whom he later dubbed his "invisible allies," he was holding in reserve a nearly finished blockbuster nonfiction work, *The Gulag Archipelago*, which was ready to be released when it would do the most good in his ongoing campaign against the ideological state—and which had the potential to become the checkmate move in his chess game with the regime.

Not until 1978, as Solzhenitsyn—by then living in Vermont—put together his first, twenty-volume *Collected Works*, did he return *In the First Circle* to its authentic form of ninety-six chapters, each of which was refined to take on an aesthetic unity of its own. In the version now reaching us, nine chapters are entirely new to English-language readers, and a dozen more are substantially altered. It is a testament to Solzhenitsyn's artistic power that an unperfected version of *In the First Circle* not only received high praise from the start but retained a wide readership through four decades. He died secure in the conviction that the book he left to posterity was even better.

The English translator of the canonical text is Harry T. Willetts, renowned for combining fidelity to Solzhenitsyn's rich, complex Russian with supple equivalents in English prose, and the only person Solzhenitsyn fully trusted to render his fiction in English. Willetts was pressing to finish his work right up to the time of his death at age eighty-two in 2005. The editing of the English text entailed filling in a few blanks left by Willetts, tying up loose ends, regularizing punctuation and other mechanical details, and replacing Briticisms with American diction and idiom.

"In the First Circle" fairly represents Solzhenitsyn's theory of literature. He adheres closely to the canons of the realistic tradition of Russia's nineteenth-century masters of fiction, starting with Dostoevsky and Tolstoy. Rather than invent characters and strands of plot out of his imagination, he takes actual, verifiable events that transpired in places that can be located on maps, and his characters are based on real-life prototypes, a number of whom are known through historical sources. His process of transmuting reality into fiction entails imaginatively delving into the inner lives of the characters and reconstructing the motives behind their actions. Despite starting with actual people, events, and locations, Solzhenitsyn in his Gulag writings—the fiction and *The Gulag Archipelago*—succeeds in creating a literary world that is as distinctly his own as are the signature literary worlds created by such authors as Dostoevsky, Dickens, Kafka, and Faulkner.

Solzhenitsyn's commitment to the Russian literary tradition is also revealed in his embracing a sense of continuity between literary art and the realm of moral values. Shunning the moral relativism that permeates modern thought, he unapologetically treats good and evil and the human soul as metaphysical realities. Instead of camouflaging the didactic impulse, he accepts the age-old definition of literature as delightful instruction. Like his great predecessors Dostoevsky and Tolstoy, he allows his characters to engage in colloquies about big ideas. His literary theory is laid out most clearly, if briefly, in the opening section of his *Nobel Lecture*, in which he contrasts two kinds of artists. One kind starts with subjectivity and "imagines himself the creator of an autonomous spiritual world." The other starts with the objective order and "recognizes above himself a higher power and joyfully works as a humble apprentice under God's heaven," accepting that "it was not he who created this world" and that "there can be no doubt about its foundations."

Solzhenitsyn's Gulag-based fiction typically originates in autobiography. The works are populated largely by characters he knew, and he does not hesitate to use himself as a prototype. He typically presents one constricted place as the primary setting and concentrates the time of the action into a brief period. *In the First Circle* is based on Solzhenitsyn's own time in a prison research institute, the slang term for which is *sharashka.* It is located in a Moscow suburb named Marfino (slightly disguised as Mavrino in the eighty-seven-chapter version), specifically in a former seminary building that the Soviet authorities turned into a place of incarceration, a metamorphosis that has both historical and symbolic significance. The approximately three years Solzhenitsyn spent there, 1947–50, are compressed in the novel into four days, December 24–27, 1949, the symbolically charged period of Western Christmastide, which in that year followed the extravagant national celebrations of Stalin's seventieth birthday on December 21. At times the focus switches to settings and characters located outside the sharashka; these shifts establish an inside-outside dialectic that impels readers to contemplate the integral relationship between the restrictive institutions of the penal system and the oppressive realities of the Soviet Union as a whole. Similarly the compressed time frame is supplemented by many episodes of flashback. The gallery of characters is huge, constituting a top-to-bottom cross section of Soviet society. Inside the Marfino institute are the *zeks* (slang for "prisoners") plus their keepers and civilian employees. Among the numerous characters who reside outside the sharashka, many have either working or personal relationships with the zeks. Solzhenitsyn brings in such historical personages as Stalin himself and his powerful Minister of State Security, Viktor Abakumov. Even Eleanor Roosevelt comes onstage for a hilarious cameo appearance (chapter 59).

The denizens of this sharashka are charged with the state project of developing a telephone encryption device designed to identify the voices of individuals whose telephone conversations are monitored by the state's omnipresent recording system; they are forced to play the lead role in the detective story. To prop up the morale of these imprisoned scientists and technicians, the Gulag administration permits them amenities forbidden to run-of-the-mill zeks stuck in the conventional labor camps. The sharashka zeks enjoy adequate food, access to tobacco and books, space to walk, and time to talk, so that a prisoner newly arrived from the camps wonders if he has died and gone to heaven. But no, he is told, he has reached the "first circle" of hell, which in Dante's *Inferno* spared virtuous pagans the active torments of hell's lower circles. The Dantean title enables Solzhenitsyn to employ one of his favorite literary devices: understatement. The title character of *One Day in the Life of*

*Ivan Denisovich* experiences a long workday in forbiddingly cold weather as almost a good day. *In the First Circle* places zeks in the mildest precinct of the Gulag. Paradoxically readers vicariously experience Ivan Denisovich's day as unbearable and the zeks' loss of freedom as the essence of hell.

THE NARRATIVE POINT OF VIEW used in this novel is both sophisticated and, as will become clear, perfectly suited to the novelist's purposes. Solzhenitsyn follows what he has called the "polyphonic" principle of novelistic construction. This is a method by which characters take their turns as the central character of a chapter or a series of chapters, and in each of these units the narrative is presented from the point of view and in the language of the given character. In each case the basic account retains the third-person format combined with the subjectivity that the first-person mode would normally feature. The technical term for this type of narrative is *erlebte Rede*, a German phrase that means "experienced speech," sometimes rendered in English as "narrated monologue." The "polyphonic" aspect simply points to the presence of many such individual viewpoints and voices. In principle, no single character dominates; whereas one character, Gleb Nerzhin, is identifiably the author's alter ego, three others (Rubin, Volodin, Stalin) are on center stage for about as many pages. Polyphony has much in common with the method of drama, and the writing of plays occupied Solzhenitsyn in the years preceding the writing of this novel. Moreover polyphony is a highly effective technique for bringing out the fundamental worldview of each character. Sometimes the respective worldviews are refined through dialogical engagement, and sometimes they simply clash; either way the juxtaposition of competing worldviews is a vital function of the novel.

Although Solzhenitsyn's self-inflicted cuts injured the novel, it would be understandable if readers of a well-received text that they did not know was truncated were to feel twinges of loss over certain deviations from the novel they cherished. One should not, of course, overstate the differences between the intended and doctored versions; after all, Solzhenitsyn was trying to get as much of his design as possible into print. Thus characters who are modified remain recognizably the same persons, and the detective-story plot retains its basic structure. The primary moral themes also survive intact, though politically sensitive subsidiary themes, such as whether the Soviet Union should have the atomic bomb and whether Stalin had served the tsarist secret police as a double agent, fell victim to the scalpel.

In no aspect of the novelist's craft is the superiority of the uncut version on clearer display than in the treatment of character; indeed this novel is so thoroughly steeped in characterization that a discussion of its themes must be interwoven with an account of its cast. Of the five individuals who rise to the top level of importance—Gleb Nerzhin, Lev Rubin, Dmitri Sologdin, Innokenty Volodin, and Joseph Stalin—all of them, with the possible exception of Rubin, the unwavering Marxist, are richer, fuller characters in the uncensored text, and the two characters who are arguably the most important, Nerzhin and Volodin, undergo the type of change that distinguishes dynamic fictional characters from static ones.

As important as characterization is, however, plot is the fictional element that crystallizes at a stroke the contrast between the two versions. The instigating action in the opening chapter sets the terms for the episodes and thematic developments to come. In the eighty-seven-chapter version Volodin, an up-and-coming Soviet diplomat, makes a risky call from a public telephone to warn his well-placed family doctor against sharing with Western colleagues information about an experimental drug, because the paranoid Soviet authorities would consider such an act a betrayal of a state secret. The phones are disconnected, and the accompanying click signals to Volodin that the secret police were monitoring the call. The recorded phone call brings together the world of the sharashka and the circumambient Soviet setting, when the Marfino zeks are instructed to discover the identity of the audiotaped voice. Their investigative work succeeds, and Innokenty takes his first step toward the brutal world of the Gulag. The ninety-six-chapter version retains the recorded phone call, but everything else is different. Volodin places the call to the U.S. Embassy in Moscow to warn of an impending espionage operation in New York at which a Soviet spy will pick up secrets about atomic bomb technology. (This episode, unlike the invented one about the family doctor, is taken from real life, as befits Solzhenitsyn's penchant; the Soviet spy's name is Georgy Koval.) It is no wonder that Solzhenitsyn softened Volodin's overtly anti-Soviet act by turning it into a gesture of basic human decency. Official Moscow would never let an author tell the story of Koval the spy. Yet this softening lowers significantly the moral stakes involved in Volodin's action. That diminution of the novel was the high price Solzhenitsyn felt compelled to pay in order to try to get the bulk of the book published.

In the opening chapter, faced with the moral dilemma of what to do about the stunning secret that has fallen into his possession, Innokenty Volodin asks himself, "If we live in a state of constant fear, can we remain human?" This rhetorical question implicitly establishes the ideal of "humanity," which reverberates throughout the novel. Volodin the innocent answers the question with an action: He makes the phone call. And he changes his life. No character is more radically altered from one version of the novel to the other than Volodin. In the shortened form he is a jaded young member of the privileged Soviet elite. In the full form he is a young functionary in the state apparatus whose moral evolution leads him to commit treason against the regime of which he is a part. Readers are left to ponder, along with him, the ethics of betraying the worst sort of regime—or a modern variation on the long-standing theme of the legitimacy of tyrannicide.

Solzhenitsyn achieves Volodin's transformation by restoring extended flashback sequences. Chapter 44, titled "In the Open," traces a walking day trip by Volodin and his young sister-in-law Klara. The countryside they traverse comes to symbolize for Volodin the now-disfigured face of perennial, persevering Russia. He is deeply moved by the boundless and majestic vistas, tragically besmirched as they have become by abandoned villages and desecrated churches. Later, in another flashback (chapter 61), Volodin travels to visit his mother's brother, Uncle Avenir, a character not present in the trimmed-down version. Volodin decides to make this trip after stumbling upon letters written by his now-dead mother. As a boy he was thrilled by tales of his absent father's bold actions on the Bolshevik side of the Civil War, considering his mother weak by comparison. But her letters reveal that she was independent-minded and knowledgeably dedicated to traditional Russian culture. Volodin hopes his uncle can illuminate him further. Avenir, who leads a reclusive life in an out-of-the-way village, has managed to accumulate a huge collection of old newspapers documenting the flagrant Soviet lies about the actual course of events in twentieth-century Russia. The list of cover-ups and deliberate misrepresentations is utterly overwhelming, and Volodin is impressed by his uncle's thought that a regime capable of such massive deception must not have access to the atom bomb. Volodin's new insights propel him toward the previously unimaginable decision to make his fateful phone call.

Whereas Nerzhin remains recognizably the author's alter ego, the uncut version demonstrates the considerable extent to which Volodin also stands in for the author. Volodin's arrest, interrogation, and imprisonment mirror the author's experiences so closely as almost to merge fact and fiction. As Nerzhin and Volodin confront the apparatus of the totalitarian state, they move through parallel stages of intellectual and moral development. Both characters are marked by an early phase of unthinking conformity with Soviet ideology. Both reinforce a love of country through their profound appreciation of its natural beauty. Both find their minds opened by suffering. Both move through a philosophical phase of skepticism, which in Volodin's case centers on Epicurus's thought and in Nerzhin's case is akin to Socratic questioning rather than to a cynicism rooted in relativism. In Volodin, we glimpse the author before he became a zek; in Nerzhin, the author afterward.

The process of "lightening" the novel left Rubin, for all his intrinsic interest as a character, essentially unchanged. In sharp contrast, it short-circuited Sologdin's characterization more than anyone else's except Volodin's. A brilliant engineer and powerful polemicist, Sologdin is Rubin's main ideological adversary, and he relishes reciting the evils of the Soviet system. In the abbreviated version, however, his critique of collectivism tends to make him sound like an eccentric contrarian, whereas in the complete version his iconoclasm stems from his Christian convictions. As the zeks' conversations proceed, Sologdin predicts that Nerzhin will move beyond his current skepticism and "will come to God"—by which he specifies that he means "a concrete Christian God," along with the full accompaniment of classic Christian doctrines. Of the three argumentative friends at Marfino, Nerzhin is the most dynamic character. Numerous attributes of his—his birth date, education in mathematics, status as a married man, even physical appearance—faithfully mirror his literary creator. Solzhenitsyn's three years at Marfino were crucial to his moral and spiritual development; and Dimitri Panin, the prototype of Sologdin, writes that Nerzhin conveys "an extraordinarily truthful and accurate picture" of Solzhenitsyn's inner being, as well.

The world of *In the First Circle* is a radically inhuman world, whether one resides inside or outside the Gulag system. The ideal of "humanity" derived from Volodin's early rhetorical question comes to function as the criterion for judging human quality in every character. The concept of humanity includes both normal human desires and the kind of simple decency that needs no theoretical explanation; it applies to quotidian and life-changing decisions alike. Positive characters either are drawn instinctively to this ideal or else, like Nerzhin, aspire to it consciously, while negative characters suppress it in themselves and wish to destroy it in others. The paradoxical presence of authentically humane instincts in the ideologically fixated Rubin is precisely what makes him such an interesting, often appealing, figure. Minor figures, too, are judged by the criterion of genuine humanity; they, too, are imbued with a moral seriousness that makes them intriguing and significant. What does it mean to be a human being? The novel's central theme can be defined no more narrowly than that, though that definition also could be no broader than it is.

The pursuit of this ideal of true humanity finds its focal point in Nerzhin. For this thinking man, however, realizing his full humanity requires not only moral behavior but also the construction of a worldview supportive of such behavior, a comprehensive philosophy of life that takes into account the eternal questions of human nature, the nature of the universe, and the source of meaning. Solzhenitsyn entered adulthood as a loyal Communist, had his ideological faith shaken by prison, and retreated into skepticism for the time being. Chapter 47, which the author deleted because it wrestles with the question of whether it is morally acceptable for the Soviet state to have access to nuclear weaponry, contains a description of a key step in his alter ego's philosophical odyssey: Nerzhin has definitively broken with his youthful Marxism. He now denies that justice is class based, asserting instead that justice is "the foundation of the universe" and that human beings are "born with a sense of justice in our souls." Thus he begins to believe that an objective moral order is built into the universe and that there is an absolute distinction between justice and injustice, good and evil. This change of mind prepares him to try "going to the people" (in chapter 66), not with Marxist shibboleths in mind but in the spirit of the long-standing Russian idea that the folk wisdom of the peasantry provides a reliable moral compass. He is drawn to the humble janitor, Spiridon, whose homespun but rock-solid moral sense provides a welcome contrast to the abstract philosophizing of Nerzhin's intellectual friends. When Nerzhin, after sufficient observation, concludes nevertheless that "the people" are not in all ways morally superior, he decides that his only route to becoming a fully actualized human being is to fashion his soul by thinking for himself. By virtue of his unrelenting search for a principled moral point of view, Nerzhin's odyssey carries him beyond not only Marxism but also skepticism. His open-ended journey has brought him to the edge of religious belief. Evidence external to the text reveals that Solzhenitsyn himself did embrace in adulthood the religious belief in which he had been reared as a boy; but that destination of his spiritual odyssey lies beyond the Marfino years, and fidelity to the facts forbade his transferring it to Nerzhin.

One major character in the canonical version stands apart from all others, just as he did in real life: Iosif Vissarionovich Djugashvili, alias Stalin,

Man of Steel. The four consecutive chapters about him in the trimmed-down version grow to five (chapters 19–23), and the average length of each chapter increases. Augmenting historical information with artistic license, the author imagines the inner workings of the dictator's mind, in the same way that he sought to characterize Lenin in eleven chapters scattered through the four volumes of his epic *The Red Wheel.* From one version to the other Solzhenitsyn's Stalin does not change his mind about anything; rather, his mind is explored in greater detail. Stalin is measured by the same criterion of "humanity" that applies to all people, and by dint of a lifetime of antihuman actions, he fails the test utterly. Stalin is a creature of darkness, and readers will remember the indelible picture of his nocturnal lucubrations, which yield little satisfaction for himself and only torment for the millions under his control. Imagining himself the guardian of the abstract masses, he actually views "the people" as the principal impediment to his megalomaniacal fantasies. In Dantean terms he is as distant in spirit from the denizens of the first circle as possible; Solzhenitsyn places him in the pit of hell alongside Satan, where the greatest of malefactors are not consumed by fire but encased in ice, frozen in isolation, utterly immobilized. According to Christian tradition the greatest torment of hell is eternal separation from God, with all hope of divine fellowship abandoned. Djugashvili the onetime seminarian has turned himself into Stalin the ruler, but also the greatest victim, of the infernal empire. His only social relationships are those with his henchmen, little Stalins who have allowed him to shape them in his image and who carry out his diabolical will in the evanescent kingdom of hell on earth. Solzhenitsyn gained his worldwide fame by defiantly opposing the Soviet regime and undermining its legitimacy. The Dantean metaphors of *In the First Circle* cinch the indictment as only art can do.

Beyond the literary elements of setting, plot, theme, and especially character, language per se rises to the level of being a theme in its own right. Language is not only the medium of literature but also the most basic attribute of the human condition, traditionally understood as the sine qua non that distinguishes human beings from animals. It is profoundly symbolic that the inhuman state described in these pages is bent on suppressing, distorting, and perverting all aspects of language. Volodin's warning phone call is cut off. Stalin commissions work on a device that will scramble speech. Everyone must constantly be on guard against potential informers who might be listening in on their talk. Harsh restrictions concerning what is allowed to be discussed during spouses' prison meetings aim to reduce the conversation between man and wife to little more than an exchange of platitudes. Nerzhin and his wife, Nadya, must resort to hints and phonetic masking in an achingly inadequate attempt to communicate their complex feelings.

The state even requires prisoners to write optimistic lies to their loved ones. In fact, lies pervade all levels of the system, from the false reports presented to Stalin by his ministers to the gross misrepresentations of Soviet propaganda about history and such mundane things as the true contents of a truck conveying prisoners but labeled "Meat." The same mendacity infuses the carnival of deception in which Mrs. Roosevelt and her entourage of Quaker matrons visit a prison cell that has been hurriedly beautified to look like a vacation resort with extravagant amenities. Thus, Solzhenitsyn's last words to his fellow countrymen as he departed into exile were titled "Live Not by Lies!" And, in a real sense, the assault on language amounts to a recognition of its crucial importance, and Stalin accordingly labors to compose an essay on linguistics. The same acknowledgment of the centrality of language can be seen in Rubin's attempts to buttress his Marxist faith by far-fetched etymological comparisons, as well as in Sologdin's equally eccentric project to purify Russian by inventing substitutes for foreign words. In contrast to these problematic undertakings, Nerzhin's fact-based study of phonetics is presented as scientifically valid.

IN THE HISTORY OF LITERATURE, justice delayed need not be justice denied. The day of *In the First Circle* has come. The timing of its unveiling may be particularly propitious. This is the first work by Solzhenitsyn to go to press in English since he died. A major author's death fosters reflection on his overall achievement. Long gone are the distractions of celebrity and controversy that once beclouded Solzhenitsyn. This is the perfect time for fresh eyes. This is also a time to wonder how well *In the First Circle* will hold up through the reckoning to come. Remembering that from antiquity a literary classic has been defined as a book still read a century after appearing, one might say that the approval since 1968 of a novel that had not yet been revealed in its whole glory has easily given it a forty-year head start toward fulfilling that definition. An intriguing intimation of the prospects for the canonical text in English translation comes from the Russian experience with the canonical text itself, which has undergone only minor touching up during its three decades of availability. In 2006 a Russian television network presented its versions of six classic Russian novels: Dostoevsky's *Idiot* and *Brothers Karamazov*, Tolstoy's *War and Peace*, Bulgakov's *Master and Margarita*, Pasternak's *Doctor Zhivago*, and one more, the only one by a then-living author, Solzhenitsyn's *In the First Circle*. That is fitting company for the novel to keep.

*Edward E. Ericson, Jr.*
*October 2008*

## Cast of Characters

*Viktor Semyonovich Abakumov*—Colonel General; Minister of State Security; formerly head of SMERSH.

*Grigory Borisovich Abramson* (Grigory Borisych, Borisych)—Zek (prisoner) at Marfino sharashka (special prison); serving second consecutive term; engineer; Trotskyist.

*Agnia*—Girlfriend of Anton Yakonov in his youth.

*Avenir*—Uncle of Innokenty Volodin.

*Aleksandr Yevdokimovich Bobynin*—Zek; senior engineer; assigned to Number Seven Lab; age forty-two.

*Amantai Bulatov*—Zek; Kazan Tatar; assigned to Number Seven Lab; formerly POW under the Germans.

*Bulbanyuk*—General; one of the officials overseeing the experiment in voice identification.

*Vladimir Erastovich Chelnov*—Zek; serving eighteenth year of incarceration; formerly professor of mathematics and corresponding member of the Academy of Sciences; lists nationality as "zek."

*Iosif Vissarionovich Djugashvili* (Soso, Koba, Iossarionych)—Real name of Stalin.

*Rostislav Vadimovich Doronin* (Ruska, Rusya, Rostislav Vadimych)—Zek; sentenced to twenty-five years; mechanic; assigned to Vacuum Lab; adventurist; age twenty-three; designated for shipment out of Marfino.

*Konstantin Dvoetyosov*—Zek; assigned to Vacuum Lab; gigantic man.

*Ivan Feofanovich Dyrsin* (Vanya)—Zek; in tenth and last year of his sentence; engineer; assigned to Number Seven Lab.

*Nikolai Arkadievich Galakhov* (Kolya)—Husband of Dinera; famous young Soviet author; age thirty-seven.

*Dinera Petrovna Galakhova* (Nera)—Daughter of Pyotr Makarygin; sister of Dotnara and Klara; wife of Nikolai Galakhov.

*Illarion Pavlovich Gerasimovich* (Larik, Illarion Palych)—Zek; serving second term of incarceration; engineer, optics expert; designated for shipment out of Marfino.

*Natalia Pavlovna Gerasimovich* (Natasha)—Wife of Illarion; jobless; age thirty-seven.

*Ernst Golovanov* (Erik, Erik Saunkin-Golovanov)—Real name Saunkin, pseudonym Golovanov; literary critic; acquaintance of Klara Makarygina.

*Isaak Kagan*—Zek; directs battery room; stool pigeon.

*Ilya Terentievich Khorobrov* (Ilya Terentich, Terentich)—Zek; arrested for defacing election ballot with an obscenity; engineer, radio expert; assigned to Number Seven Lab; designated for shipment out of Marfino.

*Klimentiev*—Lieutenant Colonel; commandant of Marfino, supervisor of the guards; authorized visit of Nerzhin and wife.

*Klykachev*—Lieutenant; predecessor, then assistant, to Boris Stepanov as Communist Party organizer at Marfino.

*Ippolit Mikhailovich Kondrashov-Ivanov* (Ippolit Mikhalych)—Zek; resident painter of art works; age fifty.

*Kuleshov*—Lieutenant, Ministry of State Security.

*Viktor Lyubimichev*—Zek; electrician; assigned to Number Seven Lab; stool pigeon.

*Pyotr Afanasievich Makarygin*—Public prosecutor in Moscow; father of Dinera, Dotnara, and Klara.

*Alevtina Nikanorovna Makarygina*—Wife of Pyotr Makarygin; stepmother of Dinera, Dotnara, and Klara.

*Klara Petrovna Makarygina*—Youngest daughter of Pyotr Makarygin; free worker at Marfino; friendly with Ruska Doronin.

*Yakov Ivanovich Mamurin*—Zek; formerly director of Communications Department, Ministry of the Interior; placed in charge of Number Seven Lab.

*Myshin*—Major; Operations Officer at Marfino, responsible for security.

*Nadelashin*—Junior Lieutenant; guard at Marfino.

*Gleb Vikentievich Nerzhin* (Glebka, Glebochka, Gleb Vikentich, Vikentich)—Zek; mathematician; assigned to Acoustics Lab; interlocutor of Rubin and Sologdin; age thirty-one; designated for shipment out of Marfino.

*Nadezhda Ilyinichna Nerzhina* (Nadya)—Wife of Nerzhin; graduate student.

*Foma Guryanovich Oskolupov*—Major General; head of Special Technology Department, Ministry of State Security.

*Aleksandr Nikolaevich Poskryobyshev* (Sasha)—Lieutenant General; head of Stalin's personal secretariat; gatekeeper and spokesman for Stalin.

*Andrei Andreevich Potapov* (Andrei, Andreich)—Zek; electrical engineer; assigned to Number Seven Lab; formerly POW under the Germans; age forty.

*Valentin Martynovich Pryanchikov* (Val, Valentulya, Valentin Martynych, Pryanchik)—Zek; engineer, radio expert; assigned to Acoustics Lab; formerly POW under the Germans; age thirty-one.

*Dushan Radovich*—Serb; faithful Marxist; acquaintance of Makarygin.

*Adam Veniaminovich Roitman*—Engineer Major; senior deputy of Yakonov; supervisor of Acoustics Lab; winner of a Stalin Prize; age thirty.

*Lev Grigorievich Rubin* (Levka, Lyova, Lyovka, Lyovochka, Lyovushka)—Zek; linguist; assigned to Acoustics Lab; steadfast Communist; interlocutor of Nerzhin and Sologdin; age thirty-six.

*Mikhail Dmitrievich Ryumin* (Minka, Mikhail Dmitrich)—Senior MGB interrogator; formerly SMERSH investigator.

*Selivanovsky*—Deputy Minister of State Security.

*Serafima Vitalievna* (Sima, Simochka)—Free worker at Marfino; worked alongside Gleb Nerzhin, developed amorous interest in him.

*Rakhmankul Shamsetdinov*—Staff member of Moscow Oblast Communist Party Committee; guest lecturer in political propaganda at Marfino.

*Shchagov*—Engineer Captain; soldier in Red Army during World War II; friend of Nadya Nerzhina.

*Shikin*—Major; security operations officer at Marfino; rival of Myshin.

*Shusterman*—Senior Lieutenant; guard at Marfino.

*Artur Siromakha*—Zek; electrician; assigned to Number Seven Lab; king of stool pigeons.

*Smolosidov*—Lieutenant; MGB officer at Marfino; entrusted with physical property for top-secret project.

*Dmitri Aleksandrovich Sologdin* (Mitya, Mityai, Dmitri Aleksandrych)—Zek; engineer, designer; assigned to Design Office; serving second term and twelfth year of incarceration; interlocutor of Nerzhin and Rubin; Christian; age thrity-six.

*Boris Sergeevich Stepanov* (Boris Sergeich)—Secretary of Communist Party at Marfino; age forty-nine.

*Gennady Tyukin* (Genka)—Lieutenant, Ministry of State Security.

*Pyotr Trofimovich Verenyov*—Before World War II a senior lecturer in mathematics at Rostov University; Nerzhin's former teacher.

*Innokenty Artemievich Volodin* (Ini, Ink, Inok)—Diplomat, State Counselor Grade Two in Ministry of Foreign Affairs (equivalent in rank to lieutenant colonel); age thirty.

*Dotnara Petrovna Volodina* (Dotty, Nara)—Wife of Innokenty Volodin; daughter of Pyotr Makarygin.

*Anton Nikolaevich Yakonov* (Anton Nikolaich)—Engineer Colonel; chief engineer, Special Technology Department; head of operations at Marfino.

*Spiridon Danilovich Yegorov* (Spiridon Danilych, Danilych)—Zek; of peasant stock; yardman; age fifty.

*Larisa Nikolaevna Yemina*—Free worker at Marfino; copyist; worked alongside Dmitri Sologdin; married; age thirty.

*Zemelya*—Zek; engineer, vacuum-tube expert; assigned to Vacuum Lab.

*Zhvakun*—Lieutenant; guard at Marfino.

## Author's Note

Such is the fate of Russian books today: They bob up to the surface, if ever they do, plucked down to the skin. So it was recently with Bulgakov's *Master*—its feathers floated over only later. So also with this novel of mine: In order to give it even a feeble life, to dare show it, and to bring it to a publisher, I myself shortened and distorted it—or, rather, took it apart and put it together anew, and it was in that form that it became known.

And even though it is too late now, and the past cannot be undone—here it is, the authentic one. By the by, while restoring the novel, there were parts that I refined: after all, I was forty then, but am fifty now.

*Written: 1955–58*
*Distorted: 1964*
*Restored: 1968*

# IN THE
# First Circle

I

# Torpedo

THE FILIGREED HANDS POINTED to five minutes past four.

The bronze of the clock was lusterless in the dying light of a December day.

A high window, beginning at floor level, looked down on bustling Kuznetsky Most. Yardmen trudged doggedly to and fro, scraping up fresh snow that was already caking and turning brown under the feet of pedestrians.

State Counselor Grade Two Innokenty Volodin surveyed all this unseeingly, lolling against the edge of the embrasure and whistling something long drawn out and elusive. His fingertips flipped through the pages of a glossy foreign magazine, but he had no eyes for them.

Volodin State Counselor Grade Two—the diplomatic-service equivalent of lieutenant colonel—was tall and narrow-shouldered and wore a suit of some silky material instead of his uniform, looking more like a well-off young drone than an official of some importance in the Ministry of Foreign Affairs.

It was time to switch the lights on or go home, but he stayed where he was.

Four o'clock was not the end of the working day but only of its daytime part. Everyone would now go home, have something to eat, and take a nap; then at 10:00 p.m. the thousands and thousands of windows in forty-five All-Union and twenty Union-Republican ministries would light up again. A single individual ringed by a dozen fortress walls could not sleep at night, and he had trained the whole of official Moscow to stay awake with him until three or four in the morning. Knowing the peculiar nocturnal habits of their lord and master, all sixty-odd ministers kept vigil, like schoolboys awaiting a summons from the headmaster. To fight off sleep they would summon their deputies; then deputy ministers would rouse department heads, research officers would erect ladders and swarm over card indexes, clerks would charge along hallways, and stenographers would break their pencil points.

Today was no exception. It was Christmas Eve on Western calendars. All the embassies had fallen silent and given up calling two days ago, but the ministry would be staying up through the night just the same.

They—the Western diplomats—had two weeks of vacation ahead of them. Trusting babes! Stupid donkeys!

The young man's nervous fingers paged through the magazine hastily, mechanically, while hot waves of terror welled up inside him, then subsided, leaving him cold.

Innokenty flung the magazine away and began pacing the room, shuddering.

Should he call or shouldn't he? Did it have to be now? Would Thursday or Friday be too late over there?

Too late. . . . There was so little time to think about it, and absolutely nobody to ask for advice!

Surely there was no way of finding out who had made a call from a phone booth? If he spoke only in Russian? If he didn't hang around but walked away quickly? Surely they couldn't identify a muffled voice over the telephone? It must be a technical impossibility.

In three or four days' time he would be flying there himself. It would be more logical to wait. More sensible.

But it would be too late.

Oh, hell! His shoulders, unused to such burdens, hunched in a shiver. It would have been better if he had never found out. Better not to know.

He scooped up all the papers on his desk and carried them to the safe. His agitation grew. Innokenty lowered his brow onto the dull-painted iron of the safe and rested there with closed eyes.

Then suddenly, as though he felt his last chance slipping away from him, without calling for a car, without so much as closing his inkwell, Innokenty rushed for the door, locked it, handed his key to the guard at the end of the hallway, almost ran down the stairs, overtaking the usual gold-braided personages, dived into his overcoat, planted his hat on his head, and ran out into the damp twilight.

Rapid motion brought him some relief.

His low French shoes, worn fashionably without galoshes, sank into the slush.

As he passed the Vorovsky Monument in the ministry courtyard, Innokenty looked up and shuddered. The building of the Great Lubyanka, which looked out on Furkasov Passage, suddenly took on a new significance for him. This gray-black nine-storied hulk was a battleship, and the eighteen pilasters loomed like eighteen gun turrets on its starboard side. And Innokenty's tiny craft was being helplessly sucked into its path, under the bows of the swift, heavy vessel.

Or no—he wasn't a helpless captive canoe; he was deliberately heading toward the battleship like a torpedo!

He could hold out no longer! He turned right onto Kuznetsky Most. A taxi was about to pull away from the curb. Innokenty grabbed it, hurried the driver downhill, then told him to turn left, under the newly lit streetlights of the Petrovka.

He still couldn't decide where to make his call—where he could be sure that no one would be hovering impatiently, distracting him, peering through the door. But if he looked for a single phone booth in some quiet spot, he would make himself more conspicuous. Wouldn't it be better to pick one in the thick of it all, as long as it had soundproof brick or stone walls? And how stupid he had been to chase around in a taxi and make the driver a witness. He dug into his pocket, hoping not to find the fifteen kopecks for the call. If he didn't, he could obviously put it off.

At the traffic light on Okhotny Ryad, his fingers felt and drew out two fifteen-kopeck pieces simultaneously. So that was that.

It seemed to calm him down. Dangerous or not, he had no alternative.

If we live in a state of constant fear, can we remain human?

Without intending it, Innokenty now found himself riding along the Mokhovaya past the embassy. Fate was taking a hand. He pressed his face against the window, craning his neck, trying unsuccessfully to make out which windows were lit up.

They passed the university, and Innokenty motioned to the right. It was as though he were circling on his torpedo to position it properly.

They sped up to the Arbat; Innokenty gave the driver two bills, stepped out, and crossed the square, trying to moderate his pace.

His throat and his mouth were dry with the dryness that no drink can help.

By now the Arbat was all lit up. In front of the Khudozhestvenny Cinema, there was a long line for *The Ballerina's Romance*. A faint bluish mist clouded the red M above the metro station. A woman with a dark southern complexion was selling little yellow flowers. The doomed man could no longer see the battleship, but his breast was bursting with desperate resolve.

Remember, though: not a word in English. Let alone French. Mustn't leave the smallest clue for the tracker dogs.

Innokenty walked on, erect and no longer hurrying. A girl eyed him as he passed.

And another one. Very pretty, too. Wish me well out of it!

How big the world is and how full of opportunities! But all that's left for you is this narrow passage.

One of the wooden booths outside the station was empty but seemed to have a broken window. Innokenty walked on, into the station.

Here the four booths set into the wall were all occupied. But in the one to the left, a rough-looking character, not quite sober, was finishing his call and hanging up the receiver. He smiled at Innokenty and started to say something. Innokenty took his place in the booth, carefully pulled the thick-paned door closed, and held it shut with one hand; the other, still gloved, trembled as it dropped a coin into the slot and dialed a number.

After several prolonged buzzes the receiver was lifted at the other end.

"Is this the secretariat?" Innokenty asked, trying to disguise his voice.

"Yes."

"Please put me through to the ambassador immediately."

The answer came in very good Russian.

"I can't call the ambassador. What is your business?"

"Give me the chargé then! Or the military attaché! Please be quick!"

There was a pause for thought at the other end. Innokenty put himself in fate's hands: If they refused—let it go at that, don't try a second time.

"Very well, I'm connecting you with the attaché."

He heard them making the connection.

Through the thick glass he saw people passing, within inches of the row of phone booths, hurrying, overtaking one another. One person peeled off and stood impatiently waiting his turn outside Innokenty's booth.

Somebody with a thick accent and a well-fed, indolent voice spoke into the telephone:

"Hello. What did you want?"

"Is this the military attaché?" Innokenty asked brusquely.

"Yes, air attaché," drawled the voice at the other end.

What next? Shielding the receiver with his hand, Innokenty spoke in a low but urgent voice:

"Mr. Air Attaché! Please write this down and pass it to the ambassador immediately."

"Just a moment," the leisurely voice answered, "I'll call an interpreter."

"I can't wait!" Innokenty was seething. And he had dropped his attempt to disguise his voice. "And I will not talk to any Soviet person! Do not put the receiver down! This is a life-and-death matter for your country! And not only your country! Listen! Within the next few days a Soviet agent called Georgy Koval will pick something up at a shop selling radio parts; the address is—"

"I don't quite understand," the attaché calmly replied in halting Russian. He, of course, was sitting on a comfortable sofa, and no one was on his trail. Animated female voices could be heard in the background.

"Call the Canadian Embassy. They have good Russian speakers there."

The phone booth floor was burning under Innokenty's feet, and the black receiver with its heavy steel chain melting in his hand. But a single foreign word could destroy him!

"Listen! Listen!" he cried in despair. "In a few days' time the Soviet agent Koval will be given important technological information about the production of the atomic bomb, at a radio shop—"

"What? Which avenue?" The attaché sounded surprised. He thought a moment.

"Who are you, anyway? How do I know you're speaking the truth?"

"Do you know what a risk I'm taking?" Innokenty shot back. Somebody seemed to be knocking on the glass behind him. The attaché was silent. Perhaps taking a long puff at his cigarette.

"The atomic bomb?" he repeated dubiously. "But who are you? Tell me your name."

There was a muffled click, and dead silence followed, unbroken by crackling or buzzing.

They had been cut off.

## 2

# A Miscue

THERE ARE ESTABLISHMENTS in which you suddenly come across a dull red lamp over a door marked "Staff Only." Or, more recently, it may be an imposing plate-glass sign: "Strictly No Entrance for Unauthorized Persons." There may even be a grim security guard sitting at a little table and inspecting passes. As always, when confronted with the forbidden, your imagination runs away with you.

In reality, the door opens onto another unremarkable corridor, perhaps a bit cleaner. A strip of cheap red carpet, standard government issue, runs down the middle. The parquet floor has been more or less polished. Spittoons are stationed at fairly frequent intervals.

But there are no people. There is no movement out of one door and into another. And these doors are all covered with black leather, black leather stuffed with padding, pinned down by white studs, and bearing shiny oval number plates.

Even those who work in one such room know less about what goes on in the room next door than they do about the day's gossip on the island of Madagascar.

On the same gloomy frost-free December evening, in the building of the Moscow Central Automatic Telephone Exchange, on one of those forbidden corridors and in one of those inaccessible rooms, known to the superintendent of the building as Room 194 and to Department XI of the Sixth Administration of the Ministry of State Security as Post A-1, two lieutenants were on duty. Not in uniform, however: They could enter and leave the telephone exchange with greater anonymity in civilian dress. One wall was occupied by a switchboard and acoustic apparatus—black plastic and shiny metal. A long schedule of instructions, on dingy paper, hung on the other.

These instructions anticipated and warned against every imaginable breach of or departure from routine in monitoring and recording calls to and from the U.S. Embassy, stipulating that two persons should be on duty at all times, one listening in continuously, never removing the earphones, while the other should never leave the room except to go to the bathroom, and that they should alternate duties at half-hour intervals.

If you followed these instructions, mistakes were impossible.

But such is the fatal incompatibility of officialdom's perfectionism with man's pitiful imperfection that these instructions had for once been disobeyed. Not because the men on duty were novices, but because they were experienced enough to know that nothing special ever happened, least of all on the Western Christmas Eve.

One of them, the flat-nosed Lieutenant Tyukin, was certain to be asked in next Monday's politics class "who are 'the friends of the people' and how do they fight against the social democrats," why we had to break with the Mensheviks at the Second Congress and had been right to do so, why we had reunited at the Fifth Congress, again acting correctly, then at the Sixth Congress had again gone our separate ways and yet again had been right to do so.

Tyukin wouldn't have dreamed of starting his reading on Saturday, with little hope of memorizing anything then, except that after duty on Sunday he and his sister's husband intended to do some serious drinking. He would never be able to take in any of that crap with a hangover on Monday morning, and the Party organizer had already rebuked him and threatened to bring him before the Party bureau. The important thing was not answering in class but being able to present a written summary. Tyukin hadn't been able to find time all that week and had been putting it off all day, but now he had asked his colleague to keep working for a while, made himself comfortable in a corner by the light of a desk lamp, and started copying into his exercise notebook selected passages from the *Short Course*.*

They hadn't yet gotten around to switching on the overhead light. The auxiliary lamp by the tape recorders was on. Kuleshov, the curly-haired lieutenant with the chubby chin, sat with his earphones on, feeling bored. The embassy had phoned in its shopping orders in the morning, and from lunchtime onward seemed to have fallen asleep. There hadn't been a single call.

After sitting like this for some time, Kuleshov decided to take a look at the sores on his left leg. They kept breaking out again and again for unknown reasons. They had been dressed with "brilliant green" zinc ointment and a

* *Short Course: The History of the All-Union Communist Party (Bolsheviks)—Short Course*. The central catechism under Stalin, required reading for all Soviet citizens from 1938 to 1956, allegedly authored by Stalin.

streptocidal preparation, but instead of healing, the sores had spread under the scabs. The pain had begun to make walking uncomfortable. The MGB clinic had made an appointment for him with a professor. Kuleshov had recently been given a new flat, and his wife was expecting a child. And now these ulcers were poisoning what should have been a comfortable life.

Kuleshov removed the tight earphones, which pressed on his ears, moved to a brighter spot, rolled up the left leg of his trousers and his long underwear, and began cautiously feeling and picking at the edges of the scabs. Dark pus oozed out under the pressure of his fingers. The pain made his head spin and blotted out all other thoughts. For the first time the thought shot through his mind that perhaps these were not just sores but . . . he tried to remember a terrible word he had heard somewhere: gangrene? . . . And . . . what was that other thing?

So he did not immediately notice the bobbins start noiselessly spinning as the tape recorder automatically switched itself on. Without taking his bare leg from its support, Kuleshov reached for the earphones, put one ear to them, and heard:

"How do I know you're speaking the truth?"

"Do you know what a risk I'm taking?"

"The atomic bomb? But who are you? Tell me your name."

*The atomic bomb!* Obeying an impulse as instinctive as that of a man who grabs the nearest object to break his fall, Kuleshov tore the plug from the switchboard, disconnecting the two telephones—and only then realizing that, contrary to instructions, he had not intercepted the caller's number.

The first thing he did was look over his shoulder. Tyukin was scribbling his summary and had eyes for nothing else. Tyukin was a friend, but Kuleshov had been warned to keep an eye on him, which meant that Tyukin had received similar instructions. As he turned the Rewind knob of the recorder and plugged the spare recorder in to the embassy loop, Kuleshov thought at first of erasing the recorded message to conceal his blunder. But he remembered at once that his chief had often said that the work of their post was duplicated by automatic recording in another place, and he dropped that silly idea. Of course the recording was duplicated, and for suppressing a conversation like that you'd be shot!

The tape had rewound itself. He turned the Play knob. The criminal was in a great hurry and very agitated. Where could he have been speaking from? Obviously not from a private apartment. And hardly from his place of work. It was always from public phone booths that people tried to get through to embassies.

Opening his directory of phone booth numbers, Kuleshov hurriedly dialed a telephone located on the steps of the entrance to the Sokolniki metro station.

"*Genka! Genka!*" he croaked. "Emergency! Call the operations room! They may still be able to catch him!"

## 3

## Sharashka

"NEW BOYS!"

"They've brought us some new boys!"

"Where are you from, comrades?"

"Friends, then, where are you from?"

"What are those patches on your chests and on your caps?"

"That's where our numbers were. We had them on our backs and our knees as well. They ripped them off when they sent us out of the camp."

"What do you mean, numbers?"

"What century are we living in? Numbers sewn on human beings? Tell me, Lev Grigorievich, is this what you call progress?"

"Valentin, old buddy, don't try starting anything; go and get your supper."

"I don't feel like supper when I know that people are walking around somewhere with numbers on their foreheads!"

"Friends! You're getting nine packs of Belomors apiece for the second half of December. You're in luck."

"What sort of Belomors? Java or Ducat?"

"Half and half."

"Dirty bums. It's poison gas, that Ducat. I'll complain to the minister—I give you my word I will."

"What are those overalls you're wearing? Why are you all decked out like parachutists?"

"It's a sort of uniform they've introduced. They used to issue worsted suits and good overcoats, but the bastards are cutting back on us now."

"Look! New boys!"

"They've brought us a new batch!"

"What's the matter with you supermen? Never seen a real live *zek* before? What are you blocking the hallway for?"

"Well, well! Who's this I see? Dof-Donskoy!? Where've you been all this time, Dof? I looked all over Vienna for you in '45—all over Vienna!"

"Never seen such a ragged, unshaven lot. Which camp have you come from, friends?"

"From different camps. Rechlag . . ."

". . . Dubrovlag. . . ."

"Never heard of them, and I've been inside nine years."

"They're new ones—special camps, they're called. They were only started in '48."

"They grabbed me and slung me into the meat wagon right outside the entrance to the Prater in Vienna."

"Hang on, Mitya, let's hear what the new boys have to say."

"No, let's get some exercise! And a breath of fresh air! Lev will debrief the new boys, never fear."

"Second shift! Suppertime!"

"Ozerlag, Luglag, Steplag, Kamyshlag. . . ."

"Makes you think there's some unrecognized poet sitting in the Ministry of State Security. He hasn't got the stamina for whole poems, can't get it together, so he thinks up poetic names for prison camps."

"Ha-ha-ha! It's a funny world, men, a mighty funny world! What century are we living in?"

"Keep it down a bit, Valentin, boy!"

"Excuse me—what's your name?"

"Lev Grigorievich."

"Are you an engineer as well?"

"No, I'm a linguist."

"Linguist? They even have linguists in this place?"

"Better ask who they don't have here. There are mathematicians, physicists, chemists, radio engineers, telephone engineers, designers, artists, translators, bookbinders—they even shipped in a geologist by mistake."

"So what does he do?"

"He's all right; he got himself fixed up in the photography lab. There's even an architect. A pretty special one at that! Stalin's personal architect. Built all his dachas for him. Now he's inside with us."

"Lev! You pose as a materialist, but you're always ramming spiritual pabulum down people's throats! Listen, friends! When they march you into the mess hall, we've set out about thirty plates for you on the last table by the window. Chow down all you can hold; just make sure your bellies don't burst!"

"Thanks very much, but aren't you robbing yourselves?"

"Costs us nothing. Anyway, who eats pickled herring and millet mush nowadays? Too, too common!"

"What did you say? Millet mush common? It's five years since I saw any!"

"It probably isn't millet but magara."

"Magara? Are you crazy? Just let them try magara on us, and see what we'd do to them!"

"What's the food like in transit prisons nowadays?"

"Well, in Chelyabinsk—"

"The old prison or the new one?"

"I can see you're an expert. The new one—"

"Are they still economizing on bathrooms upstairs? Do they still make the zeks carry garbage buckets three stories down?"

"Yes, it's just the same."

"You said this place is a sharashka? What's that mean—sharashka?"

"How much bread do you get here?"

"Who hasn't had supper yet? Second sitting!"

"We get four hundred grams of white bread per man, and there's black bread on the tables."

"What d'you mean, on the tables?"

"What I say. It's there on the tables, ready cut. If you want it you can take it; if you don't you needn't."

"You mean we're in Europe here or what?"

"Not quite Europe. You get white bread on the table there, not black."

"Ah, but we break our backs working twelve or fourteen hours a day for those Belomor cigarettes and a bit of butter."

"Sitting at a desk all day? Call that backbreaking work? Swinging a pick, now that'll give you a backache!"

"Sitting in this sharashka, God knows, is like being stuck in a swamp. You're cut off from the land of the living. Did you hear that, gentlemen? It seems they've taken a firm line with the baddies, and you don't get mugged even in Krasnaya Presnya nowadays."

"Professors get forty grams of the best butter, engineers twenty. From each according to his ability, to each according to what is available."

"So you worked on the Dnieper Dam?"

"Yes, I worked for Winter. It's the Dnieper Dam that landed me inside."

"How did that happen, then?"

"Well, I'll tell you. I sold it to the Germans."

"The Dnieper Hydroelectric Station?"

"Come on—it was blown up!"

"So what? I sold it to them after it was blown up."

"Honestly, it's like a breath of fresh air! Transit camps! Prison trucks! Camps! Keep moving! Sovietskaya Gavan, here I come!"

"And back again. Val boy, right back here."

"Yes! Back in a hurry, of course!"

"Do you know, Lev Grigorievich, this rush of impressions, this change of scenery is making my head spin. I've lived fifty-two years, recovered twice from fatal illnesses, been married twice to rather pretty women, fathered sons, been published in seven languages, received academic prizes, and never have I been so blissfully happy as today! What a place! To think that tomorrow I won't be driven into icy water! I'll get forty grams of butter! There'll be black bread on the tables! Books aren't forbidden! You can shave yourself! Guards don't beat zeks! What a great day! What radiant heights! Maybe I'm dead? Maybe I'm dreaming? I feel as though I am in heaven!"

"No, my dear sir, you are still in hell, only you've ascended to its highest and best circle—the first. You were asking what a sharashka is. You could say it was invented by Dante. He was at his wits' end as to where to put the ancient sages. It was his Christian duty to consign those heathens to hell. But a Renaissance conscience couldn't reconcile itself to lumping those luminaries in with the rest of the sinners and condemning them to physical torment. So Dante imagined a special place for them in hell. Let's see. . . . It goes something like this:

*"We reached the base of a great Citadel . . .*

"Look around at the old arches here!

*"Circled by seven towering battlements . . .*
*Through seven gates I entered with those sages. . . .*

"You came here in the Black Marias, so you didn't see the gates—"

*"There with a solemn and majestic poise*
*stood many people gathered in the light . . .*
*with neither joy nor sorrow in their bearing. . . .*
*I half-saw, half-sensed,*
*what quality of souls lived in that light. . . .*
*What souls are these whose merit lights their way*
*even in Hell? What joy sets them apart?"*

"Ach, Lev Grigorievich, I can explain it in a way that the professor will much more readily understand. You need only read *Pravda*'s front page: 'It has been shown that a good fleece of wool depends on the feeding and general care of the sheep.'"

# 4

# A Protestant Christmas

THE CHRISTMAS TREE was a pine twig stuck in a crack in the top of a stool. A multicolored string of low-wattage bulbs was wound around it twice. Milk white vinyl-covered wires connected them to an accumulator on the floor.

The stool stood in a corner of the room, in the passage between two double bunks. The mattress from one of the upper bunks screened the whole corner and the tiny Christmas tree from the glare of the overhead lights.

Six men in thick dark blue denims, of the sort worn by parachutists, had taken their stand by the tree and were listening gravely, heads bowed, as one of their number, brisk Max Adam, said a Protestant Christmas prayer.

There was no one else in the whole large room, which was densely furnished with identical double bunks, welded together by the frames. After supper and an hour to stretch their legs, all the others had gone to work the evening shift.

Max finished his prayer, and all six sat down. Five of them were overwhelmed by bittersweet nostalgia for their homeland—their beloved, orderly, and reliable Germany, under whose tiled roofs this first festival of the year was so joyous and so moving. The sixth, a big man with a bushy black beard, was a Jew and a Communist.

Fate had intertwined Lev Rubin's fortunes with those of Germany, in peace and war.

In peacetime he had been an expert on the German language; he spoke impeccable modern Hoch Deutsch, but could when necessary have recourse to several dialects. Every German who had ever put his name to a published work he remembered as effortlessly as if he had been a personal acquaintance. He spoke of little towns on the Rhine as though he had often strolled about their well-washed shady streets.

In fact, he had been only in Prussia, and only with the army.

As a major in the Department of Psychological Warfare, he had singled out in prisoner-of-war camps Germans reluctant to remain behind barbed wire and willing to assist him. He carried them off and housed them comfortably in a special school. Some of them would be passed back through the lines equipped with TNT and forged reichsmarks, leave passes, and army paybooks. They might blow up bridges, or they might just roll on home and enjoy themselves until they were caught. With others he talked about Goethe and Schiller and discussed the broadcasts they would make through megaphones, urging their brothers-in-arms to turn their weapons against Hitler. Some of his collaborators with a flair for ideology found it particularly easy to switch from Nazism to Communism, and they were transferred in due course to various "Free German Committees," where they prepared themselves for the socialist Germany of the future. The simple soldiers among them—and Rubin himself with them—by the end of the war had twice crossed the ruptured front lines and taken fortified positions by force of persuasion, so as to save Soviet manpower.

But in his efforts to convert Germans, he had inevitably begun to feel close to them, gotten to like them, and, once Germany was prostrate, to pity them. That was what had landed Rubin in prison. His enemies in the administration accused him of speaking out against the slogan "Blood for blood, a death for a death" after the offensive of January 1945.

It was more or less true. Rubin did not try to refute it. It was infinitely more complicated than it might appear from a newspaper report or the wording of the charge against him.

By the stool with the illuminated Christmas tree, two lockers had been pushed together to serve as a table. They began serving one another. There was canned fish (prisoners in the sharashka were allowed to make purchases from Moscow shops), there was lukewarm coffee, and there was homemade cake. The conversation was sober and subdued. Max steered it onto peaceful subjects: old folk customs, sentimental Christmas Eve stories. Alfred, the bespectacled Viennese physics student whose course had been interrupted by the war, spoke with a comical Austrian accent. Gustav, a moonfaced youngster with a piglet's pink transparent ears, stared wide-eyed at the Christmas lights, scarcely daring to join in the conversation of his elders. (A member of the Hitler Jugend, he had become a prisoner of war one week after the war ended.)

The conversation, however, took a wrong turn. Somebody mentioned Christmas 1944, five years back, and the Ardennes offensive. The Germans, to a man, were proud of this glorious piece of ancient history: The vanquished had routed the victors. And they remembered how on that Christmas Eve Germany had listened to Goebbels.

Rubin, one hand toying with a strand of his bristly black beard, confirmed what they said. He remembered that speech. It had been a great success. Goebbels had spoken as though it cost him a great mental effort, as though he bore on his own shoulders all the burdens that were bringing Germany to its knees. He probably had already a presentiment of his own end.

SS Obersturmbannführer Simmel, whose long body could scarcely fit in between the table and the double bunk, did not appreciate Rubin's politeness. He couldn't bear the idea that this Jew would dare to express any opinion of Goebbels at all. He would never have demeaned himself by sitting at the same table with Rubin if he had felt able to forgo Christmas Eve with his compatriots. But the other Germans were all insistent that Rubin should be there. For this little group of German exiles, storm blown into the gilded cage of a sharashka in the heart of barbarous and chaotic Muscovy, there was only one person with whom they felt any kinship, only one they understood: this major in the enemy's army, who had spent the whole war sowing the seeds of discord and moral collapse among them. Only he could make comprehensible the customs and mentality of the natives, advise on behavior, and translate the latest international news from Russian.

Casting around for a remark that would really sting Rubin, Simmel said that, anyway, there were hundreds of pyrotechnic orators in Germany—why, he wondered, was it the rule with the Bolsheviks to read out speeches submitted for approval beforehand?

The taunt was all the more hurtful for being justified. There was no point in trying to explain to an enemy and a murderer that oratory, wonderful oratory, had once existed in Russia but that Party Committees had stamped it out. Rubin felt only disgust for Simmel, nothing more. He remembered Simmel's arrival in the sharashka after years in Butyrki Prison, wearing a creaking leather tunic: There were still marks on the sleeve where the insignia of the SS (the civilian SS, the worst of the lot) had been picked off. Even prison had not softened the expression of hardened cruelty on Simmel's face. Simmel was the reason why Rubin had not wanted to come to tonight's supper party. But the others had begged him so earnestly, and he felt so sorry for them, lost and lonely as they were, that he could not cast a cloud on their celebration by refusing.

Rubin suppressed his urge to explode and translated into German Pushkin's advice not to judge a shoe by its uppers.

Max mildly interrupted what might have developed into a quarrel with his own version of a dubiously relevant line from Pushkin. Under Lev's guidance, he said, he could now spell out poems by Pushkin in the original. But why hadn't Reinhold taken any whipped cream with his cake? Where, though, had Lev been that Christmas Eve? Lev recalled that he had been in his dugout near Rozhan in the Narev bridgehead.

And just as the five Germans recalled their torn and trampled Germany, piously painting it in the brightest colors, Rubin, too, found vivid memories returning of the Narev bridgehead, then of the sodden forests along the Ilmen.

The Christmas tree lights were reflected in moist eyes.

As usual, they asked Rubin for the latest news. But he would have felt awkward offering a review of the past month. He could not let himself become a neutral purveyor of information, could not give up hope of reeducating these people. Yet he could not convince them that in our complicated age socialist truth sometimes forces its way forward by a tortuous path. All he could do was to select for them, as he did for History (and, without realizing it, for himself), only those current events that confirmed that the high road had been accurately predicted, ignoring those that seemed likely to divert it into a quagmire. But December had been a month in which, apart from the Sino-Soviet negotiations and the Boss's seventieth birthday, nothing positive seemed to have happened. He would feel ashamed—and it would serve no educational purpose—to tell the Germans about Traicho Kostov's trial, at which the foreign correspondents had been confronted rather late in the day with a sham recantation, allegedly written by Kostov in his death cell, so that the whole crude judicial farce had come apart at the seams.

On this occasion, Rubin dwelled mostly on the historic victory of the Chinese Communists. The amiable Max listened to Rubin and nodded encouragement. His eyes were guileless. He was attached to Rubin but, since the Berlin blockade, had begun to distrust much of what he said, and (unknown to Rubin) in the shortwave lab where he worked, he had occasionally risked his neck by assembling, listening to, and then dismantling a miniature receiver that looked nothing at all like a receiver. He had heard, from Cologne and on the German service of the BBC, not only how Kostov had retracted the self-incriminating statements that his interrogators had obtained by torture but also about the consolidation of the Atlantic alliance and the new prosperity of West Germany. He had, of course, passed all this on to the other Germans, and they lived for the day when Adenauer would free them.

Still, they nodded politely as Rubin talked.

Anyway, it was high time for him to be gone; he had not been released from the evening shift. He praised the cake (Hildemuth, the fitter, bowed in gratification) and asked the company to excuse him. His hosts politely delayed his departure; then they thanked him for coming, and he thanked them for having him. After which the Germans settled down to sing Christmas carols sotto voce.

Just as he was, with a Mongolian-Finnish dictionary and a slim volume of Hemingway in English under his arm, Rubin went out into the hallway. The hallway was broad, with an unpainted and scuffed wooden floor. There were no windows, and the electric light was on day and night. It was the same hallway in which, during the supper break an hour earlier, other lovers of novelty had interviewed the new zeks fresh from the camps. Of the doors along the hallway, one opened onto the inner prison stairway, and several others belonged to "room-cells." They were "rooms" because the doors had no locks, but they were also "cells" because spy holes, little glass windows, had been set in the doors. The guards here had no use for these peepholes, but they had been adopted in accordance with the regulations for real prisons, simply because the name given to the sharashka in official documents was "Ministry of State Special Prison No. 1."

Through one such peephole could be seen a Christmas Eve party like the one he had left, for the Latvian fraternity, who had also been given time off.

All the other zeks were at work, and Rubin was worried that he might be stopped at the exit and dragged off to the security officer to give an explanation in writing. At both ends of the hallway there were doors that filled its whole width: At one end a wooden four-paneled folding door under a semicircular arch led to what had once been the sanctuary of the seminary's church, and was now also a "room-cell." At the other there was a locked two-panel door reinforced from top to bottom with sheet iron. This door, which led to their place of work, the prisoners called the "royal gates."

Rubin walked up to the iron door and knocked on the Judas window. A guard's face pressed against the glass on the other side.

The key turned quietly in the lock. As luck would have it, the guard was easygoing.

Rubin went out onto the grand stairway of the ancient structure, crossed the marble landing, walked past two ornate wrought-iron lamps, which no longer gave light. Still on the second story, he entered a hallway and pushed open a door marked "Acoustics Laboratory."

## 5

# Boogie-Woogie

THE ACOUSTICS LABORATORY occupied a lofty, spacious room with several windows that was chaotically cluttered with wooden racks and dazzling bright white aluminum counters loaded with apparatus, assembly benches, newish plywood cabinets from Moscow workshops, and comfortable writing desks that had seen better days in the Berlin building of the Lorenz Radio Company.

Big bulbs in frosted fixtures shed a pleasant, diffused white light.

There was a soundproof acoustic chamber, with sides short of the ceiling, in the far corner of the room. It looked unfinished: Its exterior was upholstered with ordinary sacking stuffed with straw. The door, which was a yard thick but hollow, like a circus clown's dumbbells, was open at present, and the cloth door curtain was thrown back to air the booth. Near the booth, rows of copper sockets gleamed in the black lacquered panel of the central switchboard.

A diminutive fragile girl with a pale unsmiling face sat at a desk with her back to the booth, holding a goat's-hair shawl tight around her narrow shoulders.

There were perhaps ten other people in the room, all men, all in identical blue overalls, busying themselves by the light of the overhead fixtures and the pools of brightness from swivel desk lamps (also of German origin), walking back and forth, hammering, soldering, sitting at assembly benches and writing desks. Three makeshift receivers mounted on aluminum panels, without casing, provided a medley of jazz, piano music, and songs from the Eastern European democracies.

Rubin walked slowly across the laboratory to his desk, holding the Mongolian-Finnish dictionary and Hemingway down low. White cake crumbs had lodged in his wavy beard.

The overalls issued to the prisoners were all cut from the same pattern, but there were different ways of wearing them. One of Rubin's buttons was missing, his belt was slack, and loose folds sagged over his belly. A young prisoner stood in his way. He was wearing exactly similar overalls but was something of a dandy. His blue cloth belt was drawn tight around his slim waist, and the top button of his overalls was undone to reveal a light blue silk shirt, faded after many washes but held together around his neck by a bright tie. This young man occupied the whole width of the side passageway on Rubin's route. His right hand lightly waved a hot soldering iron; he had rested his left foot on a chair and his left elbow on his knee as he pored over the diagram of a radio in an English-language journal that lay open on his bench, simultaneously singing

*Boogie-woogie, boogie-woogie.*
*Samba! Samba!*

Rubin could not get by and stood there for a moment with an exaggeratedly meek look on his face. The young man appeared not to notice him.

"Val, my friend, do you think you could pull in your rear foot a bit?"

Val answered, without looking up from his diagram, in short, sharp bursts.

"Lev Grigorievich! Back off! Get lost! Why do you turn up here in the evening? What is there for you to do?"

He raised his light, boyish eyes to look at Rubin wonderingly. "What the hell do we need a philologist for, anyway? Ha! ha! ha!" (three carefully separated syllables). "You're no engineer, after all! It's a scandal!"

Comically protruding his fleshy lips and widening his eyes, Rubin lisped: "Baby mine! I've known engineers who kept a soda-pop stall."

"Not me!" Valentulya snapped. "I'm a first-class engineer, and don't you forget it!" He laid his soldering iron down on its wire stand and straightened up, tossing back an unruly mass of silky hair the same color as the lump of rosin on his bench. He was fresh complexioned, his face was unmarked by experience, and his movements were boyish. It was impossible to believe that he had graduated before the war, been in a German POW camp, spent some time in Europe, and was now in his fifth year of imprisonment back in his homeland.

Rubin sighed. "Without a duly witnessed reference from your Belgian boss, our administration cannot—"

"Reference, nothing." Valentin made a convincing show of indignation. "How dense can you be? Surely you realize I'm mad about women!"

The grave little girl couldn't help smiling.

Another prisoner in the place by the window to which Rubin was trying to make his way stopped work and listened to Valentin approvingly.

"Your love, I think, is purely theoretical," answered Rubin, his jaws moving as though languidly chewing.

"And I madly love spending money!"

"Of which, however, you have—"

"So how can I be a bad engineer? Just think: To love women—different ones all the time—you have to have a lot of money! To have a lot of money, you have to earn a lot! To earn a lot of money, if you're an engineer, you must have a brilliant command of your special field! Ha-ha! You grow pale!"

Valentin's elongated face was tilted provocatively at Rubin.

"Got it!" exclaimed the zek by the window, whose desk faced the young woman's.

"Got it, Lyovka! I've finally caught Valentin's voice! It's bell-like, that's what it is! I'll write it down, shall I? A voice like that you could recognize over any telephone. However much interference there was."

He opened out a big sheet of paper, on which there were columns of names with ruled squares beside them, and a tree diagram.

"God, what a load of bull!" Valentin made a gesture of disgust, seized his soldering iron, and set the rosin smoking.

The passageway was clear. Rubin took his seat and also applied himself to the classification of voices.

For some time they examined the chart together without speaking.

"We're making progress, Glebka," Rubin said at last. "Used in conjunction with 'visible speech,' we've got a useful weapon here. Before very long we shall know, you and I, what determines the quality of a voice on the telephone. . . . What's that on the radio?"

The loudest noise in the room was jazz, but where they were, a torrent of piano music from the homemade receiver on the windowsill could be heard above it. A single melody surfaced repeatedly, was swept away in the flood, and reemerged only to be overwhelmed again.

"Beethoven's Sonata No. 17," Gleb replied. "One I've never really . . . Just listen."

They bent their heads toward the receiver, but the jazz made listening very difficult.

"Valen-*tine*!" Gleb said. "Do us a favor! Show us how bighearted you are!"

"I've shown you already," Valentin snapped. "Who set up that receiver for you? If I unsolder your coil, that'll be the end of it!"

The slip of a girl raised her eyebrows sternly and intervened. "Valentin Martynych! It really is impossible! We can't listen to three radios at once. Switch yours off—please."

(As it happened, Valentin's radio was playing a slow foxtrot, and the girl was enjoying it.)

"Serafima Vitalievna! This is monstrous!" Valentin bumped into an empty chair, tilted it at an angle, and gesticulated as if he were addressing a public meeting. "How can a normal healthy human being not like lively, invigorating Western popular music? You are poisoned here with all sorts of rubbish. You must, surely, have danced the "Blue Tango"? Surely you've seen Arkady Raikin's reviews? Ah, but you've never been in Europe either! How could you possibly learn how to live? I do most earnestly advise you to fall in love with somebody soon!"

He held forth over the chair back, not noticing the bitter lines round the young woman's mouth. "Somebody, anybody—*ça dépend!* Lights twinkling in the night! The rustle of silken gowns!"

"He's out of sync again!" Rubin said in alarm. "We must exercise our authority."

He reached behind Valentin's back and switched off his radio.

Valentin spun around as if he had been stung.

"Lev Grigorievich! What gives you the right—?"

The limpid melody of Sonata No. 17 poured out unhindered, competing now only with the rather crude song from the far corner.

Rubin's frame was blissfully relaxed; his face was a pair of mild hazel eyes over a beard with cake crumbs.

"Engineer Pryanchikov! Do you remember the Atlantic Charter? Have you made your will yet? To whom have you left your bedroom slippers?"

Valentin's face grew serious. He stared into Rubin's eyes and asked quietly: "Listen, what the hell d'you think you're doing? Can't a man feel free even in prison? If there's no freedom there, where can he expect to find it?"

One of the fitters called him over, and he went off despondently.

Rubin sank noiselessly into his chair, back-to-back with Gleb, and settled down to listen, but the soothing cadences broke off suddenly, like a speech interrupted in mid-sentence—and that was the modest and unostentatious conclusion of Sonata No. 17.

Rubin swore obscenely, for Gleb's ears only.

"Spell it," Gleb answered, still sitting with his back to Rubin. "I can't hear you."

"I said just my luck," Rubin answered hoarsely, also without turning round. "Now I've missed that sonata. I'd never heard it before."

"Because you're so disorganized, shall I ever get it into your head!" his friend grumbled. "And a very good sonata it is, too! Did you notice how it ends? No noise, not a whisper. It breaks off abruptly—and that's that. Just like in real life. . . . Where were you earlier?"

"With the Germans. Christmas party," said Rubin with a laugh.

They carried on their conversation, invisible to each other, but almost resting the backs of their heads on each other's shoulders.

"Good for you." Gleb thought a while. "I like your attitude to them. You spend hours teaching Max Russian, though you'd be perfectly entitled to hate them."

"Hate them? No. But of course, the love I used to feel for them is clouded. Max is a gentle chap, and no Nazi, but doesn't even he share responsibility with the hangmen? After all, he didn't try to stop them, did he?"

"No. Just as you and I do nothing to stop Abakumov or Shishkin-Myshkin."

"You know, Glebka, when you come to think of it, I'm as much Russian as Jew. And as much a citizen of the world as I am a Russian."

"I like that. Citizens of the world! It has a clean, unbloodied sound!"

"In other words we're cosmopolitans. So they were right to lock us up."

"Of course they were. Although you keep trying to convince the Supreme Court of the opposite."

The radio on the windowsill announced: "Logbook of Socialist Emulation in half a minute."

Half a minute was long enough for Gleb's hand to move with unhurried efficiency to the receiver and, before the announcer could get a single croak out, switch it off as though wringing his neck. His face, no longer animated, looked gray and tired.

Pryanchikov was grappling with another problem, calculating how to mount a serial amplifier—and lightheartedly singing, "Boogie-woogie, boogie-woogie. Samba! Samba!"

# 6

## A Peaceful Existence

GLEB NERZHIN WAS THE SAME AGE as Pryanchikov but looked older. His auburn hair, parted in the middle, was still thick, but there were crow's feet around his eyes, little wrinkles around his mouth, and furrows across his brow. His skin was affected by the lack of fresh air, and his face had a wilted look. But what above all made him seem older was the economy of his movements: that economy by which nature conserves the flagging strength of prisoners in the camp. In the sharashka, with meat on the menu and work that overstrained no one's muscles, Nerzhin, with the length of his sentence in mind, was nonetheless trying to make a habit of minimal movement.

At present, Nerzhin's desk was barricaded with piles of books and files, and the working space in between had also been taken over by files, typescripts, books, and journals, Russian and foreign, all left open. Any unsuspecting outsider would have seen the stillness after a hurricane of scientific thought.

But it was all camouflage. Nerzhin always put up a front in the evening in case one of the bosses looked in.

In fact, he had no eyes for anything before him. He had pulled back the light silk curtain and was staring through the dark windowpane. In the depths of the vast night, big patches of light marked the outskirts of Moscow, and from the city itself, hidden behind a hill, rose an immense haze of diffused, pale light, which gave the sky above it a dull reddish glow.

Nerzhin's special chair, with its flexible back, his rolltop desk—something not made in the Soviet Union—and his comfortable place by the south window would have revealed him to anyone familiar with the history of the Marfino sharashka as one of its founding members.

The sharashka had taken its name from what had once been the village of Marfino but was now territory within the city limits. The sharashka had been inaugurated some three years ago on a July evening. A dozen or so zeks, summoned from the camps, were driven to what had once been a seminary, just outside Moscow. The building had been fenced around with barbed wire in readiness. That was remembered as an idyllic age: You could switch on the BBC loud in the prisoners' living quarters (no one yet knew how to jam it), you could stroll about the "zone" in the evening without asking permission, you could lie in the dewy grass, left uncut, contrary to regulations (it is supposed to be cropped close so that *you* cannot crawl through it to the wire), and you could observe the eternal stars or the perishable Sergeant Major Zhvakun on night duty and all in a sweat, steal timber from a building under repair and slide it under the barbed wire to take home for firewood.

The sharashka did not yet know what direction its research was to take and occupied itself unpacking numerous crates, three trainloads of them from Germany, staking claims to comfortable German chairs and desks, and sorting out equipment for telecommunications, ultrashortwave radio, and acoustics. Much of it was obsolete or had been damaged in transit. And the sharashka gradually realized that the Germans had purloined or destroyed the best of the equipment and the most recent documentation, while the MVD* captain sent to "relocate" the Lorenz factory, an expert on furniture but not on radio or the German language, spent his time in and around Berlin searching out elegant pieces for his own Moscow apartment and those of his superiors.

* MVD: MVD, MGB, NKVD, GPU, and KGB, all of which are mentioned in the present novel, are acronyms for the Soviet security agencies at different periods and are successors to the Cheka, instituted by Lenin in 1917. More alike than unlike, they represent the fundamental continuity of the system of political police and intelligence services throughout the Soviet period.

The grass had been mowed long ago, the doors now opened for the prisoners to take exercise only when a bell rang, and the sharashka, transferred from Beria's to Abakumov's jurisdiction, had been put to work on scrambler telephones. They had hoped to complete the assignment within a year, but it had dragged on for two years, expanding and becoming more and more complicated as new lines of inquiry multiplied. On Rubin's and Nerzhin's desks it had reduced itself to the problem of identifying voices on the telephone, which meant determining what makes a person's voice unique. Apparently no one had done anything of the sort before. At any rate, they had come across no relevant published work. They had been given six months to complete their task, then another six, but they had still made little progress, and the deadline was alarmingly close.

Uncomfortably aware as he was of this pressure, Rubin nonetheless grumbled over his shoulder: "I somehow don't feel a bit like working today."

"You amaze me," Nerzhin retorted. "A mere four years at the front and not quite five in jail, am I right? And already you're tired! Better put in for a Crimean rest cure."

They were silent for a while.

"Working on your own thing, aren't you?" Rubin asked quietly.

"Uh-huh."

"So who's going to work on the voices?"

"To tell the truth, I was counting on you."

"What a coincidence. I was counting on *you*."

"You have no conscience. How many books have you checked out of the Lenin Library, supposedly for this job? Speeches of famous lawyers. Koni's memoirs. *Improve Your Acting*. And to crown it all you brazenly called for a work on Princess Turandot. Can any other zek in the Gulag boast of such a varied collection of books?"

Rubin's thick lips protruded, which always made him look stupid:

"Strange. With whom did I read all those books during working hours—including the one about Princess Turandot? Could it have been you?"

"Well, I do want to work. I could lose myself completely in my work today but for two little things. Number one, I'm agonizing over the parquet floors question."

"What parquet floors?"

"In the MVD house, on Kaluzhskaya Zastava, the semicircular building with the tower. Our camp helped build it in '45, and I was employed as a parquet floor layer's apprentice. I learned today that Roitman happens to live in that very house. And I began to feel an artist's pangs of conscience, or maybe I'm just worried about my reputation. What I wonder is whether my floorboards creak or not. If they do, it may mean that I did a slovenly job. And I'm powerless to put it right!"

"D'you know, that would make a good play!"

"For a socialist-realist playwright. The second thing is: Isn't it infuriating to be working on Saturday evening when you know that only the free employees get Sunday off?"

Rubin sighed. "The frees have already peeled off to various places of entertainment. Making pigs of themselves."

"But do they choose the right places of entertainment? Do they get more out of life than we do? That's a moot point."

Prisoners, of necessity, learn to talk quietly, and even Serafima Vitalievna, sitting opposite Nerzhin, was not supposed to hear them. They had both turned their backs to the room and sat facing the window, the lights in the prison grounds, the guard tower dimly discernible in the darkness, scattered lights in distant greenhouses, and the whitish haze over Moscow.

Nerzhin was a mathematician but no stranger to linguistics, and ever since the phonology of Russian speech had become the subject of the Marfino sharashka's research, he had been paired with Rubin, the only linguist in the place. For two years they had sat together, back-to-back, twelve hours a day. They had discovered at once that they had both fought at the same time first on the northwestern front, then on the Belorussian front; both possessed the "gentleman's junior medal set"; both had been arrested in the same month by the very same SMERSH*; both of them had been charged under the universally popular point Ten; and both had been given a "tenner" (not that this made them different from anyone else). There was a slight age difference—six years—and Nerzhin, a captain, was one step lower in rank.

Rubin was favorably disposed to Nerzhin because he had not been jailed as a former prisoner of war and so was not infected with the anti-Soviet spirit of "abroad." Nerzhin was "one of us," a Soviet man, only he had spent his whole youth poring over books, reading himself silly, and had got it into his muddled head that Stalin had distorted Leninism. No sooner had Nerzhin

* SMERSH: The acronym for SMERt SHpionam (Death to Spies), the Soviet agency for military intelligence during World War II.

recorded this conclusion on a scrap of paper than he was arrested. Shell-shocked by jail and labor camp, Nerzhin had nonetheless remained at bottom "one of us," and so Rubin had the patience to listen to the confused and nonsensical thoughts that were all he had for the time being.

They looked out into the darkness again.

Rubin made an impatient noise.

"You really are an intellectual pauper. It worries me."

"I'm not competing. There's a lot of cleverness in the world but not much goodness."

"Well, here's a good book for you. Read it."

"Another one about the poor bamboozled bulls?"

"No."

"About stalking lions, then?"

"Certainly not."

"I can't make sense of people. What do I want with bulls?"

"You have to read it!"

"I don't have to do anything! For anybody! For you or anybody else! Duties duly discharged, as Spiridon says."

"You pathetic person! It's one of the best books of the twentieth century!"

"And will it really tell me what we all need to know? Where humanity went wrong?"

"He's a clever, goodhearted, infinitely honest writer—soldier, hunter, fisherman, drunk, womanizer—coolly and sincerely contemptuous of all that's false, a stickler for simplicity, utterly humane, with the naïveté of genius. . . ."

"Spare me the rest!" Nerzhin said with a laugh. "You'll give me an earache with your spiel. I've lived for thirty years without Hemingway, and I expect to go on a bit longer. My life's in tatters anyway. I need to limit myself! Find my own way. . . ."

He turned back toward his own desk.

Rubin sighed. He still did not feel like working.

He began studying a map of China propped up against a shelf at the back of his desk. He had cut this map out of a newspaper and pasted it onto a piece of cardboard. Throughout the past year, he had marked with a red pencil the advance of the Communist forces, and now that their victory was complete, he kept the map upright before him to cheer him at moments of weariness and depression.

But today Rubin was in the grip of a sadness so acute that not even the enormous red expanse of victorious China could overcome it.

Meanwhile Nerzhin, pausing now and then for a thoughtful suck at the sharp tip of his plastic pen, was writing, in a script so minute that it looked more like the work of a needle, on a tiny page lost in the camouflaging billows of learned paper.

"The history of 1917 holds no surprises for a mathematician. A tangent soaring at ninety degrees toward infinity at once plunges into the abyss of minus infinity. In the same way, Russia, taking off for the first time toward a freedom never before seen, immediately came to an abrupt stop and plunged into the worst of tyrannies. No one has ever managed it at the first attempt."

The big room of the Acoustics Laboratory was living its peaceful everyday life. The electrician fitter's little engine hummed. Orders were shouted: "Switch on!" "Switch off!" The radio was dishing out the usual sentimental pap. Somebody loudly demanded a "6-K-7" valve.

Taking advantage of moments when no one could see her, Serafima Vitalievna looked intently at Nerzhin, who was still covering his scrap of paper with writing like tiny embroidery.

Major Shikin, the security officer, had instructed her to keep an eye on this prisoner.

## 7

# A Woman's Heart

Serafima Vitalievna, a young woman so small that it was difficult not to call her Simochka, was an MGB lieutenant. She wore an orange blouse and a warm shawl around her shoulders.

The free personnel in this building were all MGB officers.

In accordance with the Constitution, free personnel had a great variety of rights, among them the right to work. This right, however, was limited by the eight-hour day and by the fact that their labor created no added value, consisting solely in watching prisoners. Whereas the prisoners, though deprived of all other rights, had an ampler right to work—up to twelve hours a day. During the additional hours—from 6:00 to 11:00 p.m., including the supper break—the free personnel of each lab had to take turns supervising the prisoners' work.

Today it was Simochka's turn. All power and all authority in the Acoustics Lab was for the present vested in this small, sparrowlike girl.

She was supposed to see to it that the prisoners worked and did not slacken, that they did not make use of the workplace to manufacture weapons or try to tunnel out, and that they did not avail themselves of the radio parts abundantly provided to rig up shortwave transmitters. At 10:50 she had to take all secret documentation from them, put it in a big safe, and seal the door of the laboratory.

It was not quite six months since Simochka had graduated from the Institute of Communications Engineering and, on the strength of her spotless record, been appointed to this special, secret scientific research institute, known only by a number but called by prisoners in their irreverent vernacular a "sharashka." Free personnel were given officer's rank as soon as they were taken on and paid twice the salary of an ordinary engineer (in recognition of their rank and for their uniform), and all that was asked was devotion to duty and vigilance, literacy and professional skills being of secondary importance.

This suited Simochka very well. She, and many of her classmates with her, had carried away no knowledge when she left the institute. For a number of reasons. The girls had arrived from school knowing no mathematics and no physics (they had found out in the higher classes that teachers who gave low marks were upbraided by the headmaster at staff meetings, so that you could get your graduation certificate without studying at all). Then, in the institute, if there was ever time for it, the girls sat down to work at their math and radio technology as if they were lost in a bewildering, pathless, alien forest. More often than not, there just wasn't time to study. For a month and more every autumn, students were whisked off to collective farms to dig potatoes, so that for the rest of the year they had eight or even ten lectures a day, with no time to go over their notes. Monday was political education day, and there would be another compulsory meeting of some sort later in the week. Then "social work": wall newspapers, amateur concerts . . . help out at home, do the shopping, wash, change your clothes . . . an evening at the movies, the theater, the club. If you can't have fun, can't dance a bit in your student days, you may never get another chance. Young people aren't meant to work themselves to death.

To Simochka and her friends, preparation for exams meant preparing a lot of crib sheets, hiding them in articles of female attire inaccessible to males, then retrieving the necessary piece of paper in the exam room, smoothing it out, and pretending that it was rough work produced on the spot. The examiners could, of course, have shown up the inadequacy of their students' knowledge by supplementary questions, but they were overburdened themselves with committee work, open meetings, proliferating plans, progress reports to the dean and to the rector, so that redoing the exam would have been one chore too many. What is more, they would have been under attack for a high failure rate, just as though they had turned out defective goods in a factory: Someone would have quoted Krupskaya* (was it?) to the effect that there are no bad pupils, only bad teachers. The examiners therefore did their best not to shoot the candidates down but to bring the exam to the quickest and most favorable conclusion.

As senior students, Simochka and her friends admitted to themselves with dismay that they still had no great liking for their chosen profession and indeed found it tiresome. But it was too late to change. Simochka shuddered at the thought of working in a factory.

Then, suddenly, she found herself at Marfino. What pleased her about the place from the start was that she was given no independent work assignment.

But you didn't have to be a frail little thing like Simochka to feel uneasy entering the confines of this isolated fortress beyond the city limits, where handpicked guards and security officers kept watch over major political offenders.

They had all been briefed together—all ten girl graduates of the Institute of Communications Engineering. They were informed that they had landed in a place worse than any battlefield—a snake pit, in which one careless move could mean disaster. They were told that they would be meeting the dregs of humanity, people unworthy of the Russian language that they so unfortunately spoke. They were warned that these people were especially dangerous because they never bared their fangs but invariably wore a false mask of politeness and good breeding. And if you questioned them about their crimes (which was expressly prohibited!), they would try by an ingenious tissue of lies to represent themselves as innocent victims. The girls were instructed that they in turn should not vent their hatred on these reptiles but make an outward show of politeness—without, however, entering into discussions of anything except

* Krupskaya: Nadezhda Krupskaya, Lenin's wife and an active revolutionary in her own right.

the work at hand, never accepting messages for the outside world. And at the very first breach of regulations, suspicion of a breach, or possibility of suspecting a breach, they must hurry along to the security officer, Major Shikin.

Major Shikin—a short, dark-complexioned, self-important man with bristly graying hair on his large head and small feet in boy-size shoes—added the thought that although the reptilian interior of these malefactors was as clear as could be to experienced people like himself, there might possibly be among inexperienced girls like these new arrivals one who in the mistaken kindness of her heart could commit a breach of regulations by, for instance, lending a prisoner a book from the employees' library. (Not to mention mailing a letter, because any letter, whatever Maria Ivanovna it was addressed to, would inevitably be sent on to an American spy center.) Major Shikin earnestly begged the girls, if they saw one of their number fall, to come to her rescue like true friends by frankly informing Major Shikin what had happened.

In conclusion, the major did not conceal the fact that a liaison with a prisoner was punishable under the criminal code, which, as everyone knows, is sufficiently elastic to include sentences of twenty-five years' hard labor.

It was impossible to contemplate the joyless years ahead of them without a shudder. Some of the girls indeed had tears in their eyes. But the seeds of distrust had been sown, and as they left the briefing session they talked about other matters, not about what they had just heard.

More dead than alive, Simochka had followed Engineer Major Roitman into the Acoustics Lab, at first hardly daring to open her eyes.

That was six months ago, and since then something strange had happened to Simochka. No, her belief in the dark machinations of imperialism had not been shaken. Nor was it any less easy for her to suppose that the prisoners working in all the other rooms were bloodstained criminals. But in the dozen zeks whom she met daily in the Acoustics Lab—people gloomily indifferent to freedom, to their own lot, to the ten years or the quarter-century of imprisonment before them, the scholars, the engineers, and designer-fitters preoccupied day in and day out with nothing but the work that was not their own, pointless work, which would bring them not a penny in earnings or a smidgen of fame—in these people she strove in vain to detect the notorious international criminals so easily recognized by the moviegoer and so deftly ferreted out by Soviet counterespionage.

Simochka had no fear of them. Nor could she find it in herself to hate them. These people inspired in her nothing but unqualified respect—for the range of their knowledge and the stoicism with which they bore their misfortune. And for all the alarm bells of her Komsomol conscience,* however much love of the fatherland nagged at her to report every trick and misdemeanor on the part of prisoners to the security officer—for some inexplicable reason Simochka had begun to feel that it would be unthinkably mean to do so.

It was even more obviously impossible where her nearest neighbor and fellow worker was concerned—Gleb Nerzhin, who sat facing her over their two desktops. Simochka had worked closely with him ever since her arrival, assigned to assist him in carrying out experiments on articulation. The Marfino sharashka was required from time to time to assess the quality of voice reproduction over particular telephone circuits. Excellent as their equipment was, no instrument had yet been invented which would indicate this by the movement of a needle. Only the voice of a speaker reading out separate syllables, words, and phrases, and the ears of listeners trying to pick up the text at the other end of the line, could provide a measurement in terms of the incidence of error. These experiments were what they called "articulation tests."

Nerzhin was busy—at least he was meant by his superiors to be busy—looking for the optimum mathematical programming of these tests. They were going well, and Nerzhin had even put together a three-volume monograph on their methodology. When he and Simochka had a great accumulation of work to get through, Nerzhin would establish priorities and give firm instructions. His face looked so youthful as he did so that Simochka, who thought of war as it was shown in the movies, pictured Nerzhin at such moments in his captain's uniform, in the midst of cannon smoke, his light brown hair windblown, shouting out "Fire!" to his battery. A scene seldom omitted in war movies.

But if Nerzhin wanted things done in a hurry, it was in order to put the obvious tasks behind him and avoid further effort for as long as possible. He had once said as much to Simochka: "I'm active because I hate activity."

"What do you like, then?" she asked timidly.

"Thinking."

And, in fact, once the flurry of work abated, he would sit for hours, hardly changing his position, looking old, gray-faced, and haggard.

---

* Komsomol: The League of Young Communists, the youth arm of the Communist Party.

Where was his self-assurance now? He was slow and irresolute; he pondered lengthily before adding a sentence or two to the minutely written notes that Simochka could, not for the first time, see among the untidy heap of reference books and technical articles. She had even noticed that he tucked them away somewhere on the left-hand side of his desk but not, apparently, in a drawer. Simochka felt faint with curiosity: What was he writing, and for whom? Nerzhin had unwittingly become the focus of her compassion and rapt admiration.

Simochka's girlhood had held nothing but unhappiness so far. She was not pretty: Her looks were spoiled by a nose much too long and hair that had refused to grow out, gathered now into a skimpy bun at the back. She was not just small, she was extremely small, and her figure was that of a fourteen-year-old schoolgirl rather than a grown woman. She was, moreover, straitlaced, averse to jokes and frivolity, which made her still less attractive to young men. So it was that in her twenty-third year no one had ever courted her, hugged her, or kissed her.

Then, just a month ago, something had gone wrong with the microphone in the testing booth; Nerzhin called Simochka over to fix it, and she had come into the booth holding a screwdriver. In the soundproof and airless confined space, where there was scarcely room for two people, she had bent over the microphone that Nerzhin was already inspecting, and her cheek had brushed against his. Their cheeks touched—and she froze in horror: What would happen next? She should have pulled away from him, but she continued stupidly inspecting the microphone. It dragged on and on, this most terrifying moment in her life—their cheeks, close together, were burning—and he didn't move! Then, suddenly, he took her head in his hands and kissed her on the lips. A blissful weakness flooded Simochka's body. What she said at the moment had nothing to do with the Komsomol or the motherland. . . .

"The door isn't locked!" A flimsy blue blind fluttered between them and the noise outside, the people walking about and talking, who might draw the blind aside and walk in. The prisoner Nerzhin was risking nothing except ten days in the punishment cells, but the girl was putting at risk her clean record, her career, perhaps even her freedom; yet she hadn't the strength to break loose from the hands that tilted back her head.

For the first time in her life she had been kissed by a man!

So the steel chain forged with such reptilian cunning snapped at the link that had been fashioned from a woman's heart.

# 8

## "Oh, Moment, Stay!"

"WHOSE BALD HEAD IS THAT, rubbing the back of mine?"

"I'm in a poetic mood, my child. Let's have a chat."

"Actually, I'm busy."

"Come off it! Busy! I'm upset, Glebochka! Sitting by that improvised German Christmas tree, I started talking about my dugout in the bridgehead north of Pultusk, and suddenly it all came rushing back. The war! Life at the front! So vivid! So nostalgic! . . . Listen, war has its good points. . . . Wouldn't you say?"

"You aren't the first I've heard say so. I've read in those magazines for German soldiers that sometimes came our way: the cleansing of the soul, *Soldatentreue*.*

"Swine. But if you like, there's a rational kernel in all that—"

"I refuse to believe it. The Taoist ethic says that 'weapons are the instruments of misfortune, not honor. The wise man wins reluctantly.'"

"What's this I hear? The ex-skeptic has signed up with the Taoists now?"

"I haven't quite decided."

"I started by remembering my favorite Fritzes—how we used to make up captions for leaflets. A mother embracing her children, a flaxen-haired Margarita weeping, that was our main leaflet, with the message in verse."

"I remember it. I used to come across them."

"And suddenly it all came back in a rush. . . . Did I ever tell you about Milka? She graduated from the Institute of Foreign Languages in '41, and they posted her to our unit as a translator. A snub-nosed girl, moved a bit awkwardly—"

"Hold on. . . . Was she the one who went with you to receive the surrender of Graudenz?"

"Aha! Extraordinarily vain little thing she was. Loved being complimented on her work, and woe betide anyone who told her off—loved being recommended for decorations. Remember the woods just beyond Lovat, to the south of Podtsepochie as you go from Rachlitsy toward Novo-Svinukhovo?"

---

* *Soldatentreue*: Soldierly loyalty; a military ethic of commitment to one's comrades in arms.

"It's all woods around there. This side of the Redya or the other?"

"This side."

"Right, got it."

"Well, she and I went rambling in those woods. We were there all day. It wasn't spring yet. March. You squished about in water, sloshed through the puddles in your felt boots, your head was drenched with sweat under your fur cap, but there was that wonderful smell—you know—that air. We wandered about like young lovers, like newlyweds. Well, if a woman's new to you, you relive it all together from the very beginning, you blossom and ripen like a young lad, and . . . you know. . . . That never-ending forest! Just occasionally smoke from a dugout, a battery of seventy-sixes in a clearing. We avoided them. We went on wandering till evening, a damp, pink sunset. I'd been aching for her all day. And suddenly a 'crate' started circling overhead. And Milka decided she didn't want to see it shot down—'It's doing no harm, and if it isn't shot down, fine, we'll spend the night out here in the forest.'"

"That meant she'd surrendered! Who ever saw our antiaircraft gunners hit a crate?"

"Right. . . . Every ack-ack gun on either side of the Lovat blazed away at it for a good hour—and never touched it. So we found an empty bunker."

"A surface bunker?"

"Yes. Remember them? They'd built a lot of them the year before, like dens for wild animals."

"The ground was too wet to dig in."

"Right. The floor inside was strewn with pine branches; there was a smell of resin from the walls, and of smoke from previous fires. There were no stoves; you had to make your fire right there on the floor. There was a little hole in the roof. No light, of course. As long as the fire was burning, it cast shadows on the timbered walls. . . . That's living, eh, Gleb?"

"I've noticed that if one of the characters in a story told by a prisoner is a maiden, all the listeners, including me, are desperately anxious for her to be a maiden no longer when the story ends. In fact, that constitutes the main interest of the story for the zek. This shows a need to know that there is justice in the world, don't you think? A blind man needs to be reassured by the sighted that the sky is still blue and the grass still green. The zek needs to believe that, theoretically, there are still real, live attractive women in this world and that they give themselves to lucky men. . . . Some evening you've remembered! Making love, and in a pine-scented shelter at that, with no shooting going on. Some kind of war that is! Only that same evening your wife was changing her sugar coupons for a sticky mess of sweets squashed into the paper and planning to ration them so that they'd last your daughters thirty days."

"Go on, then, reproach me. . . . A man mustn't know just one woman, Glebka; if he does, he knows nothing at all about them. It impoverishes the human spirit."

"The spirit as well? Didn't somebody say 'If you've really known one woman . . .'"

"That's rubbish."

"What about two, then?"

"Two will get you nowhere either. Only by comparing many can you begin to understand. It's no vice, no sin—it's nature's design."

"Coming back to the war. In cell No. 73 in Butyrki . . ."

". . . along a narrow corridor on the second floor . . ."

"Just so! A young Moscow historian, Professor Razvodovsky, who had just been put inside and had never of course been at the front, argued cleverly, passionately, and cogently, on social, historical, and ethical grounds, that war has its good side. There were ten front-line soldiers in the cell, some ours, some Vlasovites,* but all desperate characters, wild cats. They'd fought in every spot you can think of, and they almost tore that professor apart; they furiously denied that there was the least little smidgen of good in war! I listened—and said nothing. Razvodovsky's arguments were strong ones; at moments I thought he was right, and my own recollections sometimes suggested that there was good there, but I didn't dare argue with those soldiers: the 'something' on which I was ready to agree with a civilian professor was the same something which made me, a heavy artilleryman, different from the infantry. Just think, Lev, except for the time when you took that fortress you were just a desk soldier at the front, never in a close engagement from which retreat would have been more than your life was worth. I wasn't much more of a soldier myself; I was never in the first wave of an offensive, and I never had to rally the men. You know how it is: Memory is treacherous, and all the honors sink to the bottom —"

"Look, I'm not saying—"

"—and only the pleasant things remain. But ever since Junker dive-

* Vlasovites: Followers of General Andrei Vlasov, the Soviet commander who defected to the Germans in World War II and fought against the Soviet regime.

bombers nearly made mincemeat of me one fine day at Orel—sorry, I just can't recapture the pleasure. No, Lyovka, war is best when it's farthest away."

"Well, I'm not saying that war itself is good, only that we can have good memories of it."

"So maybe we'll have good memories of the camps one of these days. And of the transit prisons."

"Transit prisons? Gorky? Kirov? N-n-no. . . ."

"Just because the administration there swiped your suitcase, you refuse to look at it objectively. Ask a VIP—with a job in the clothes storeroom, say, or the bathhouse, and shacked up with a love-girl. He'll tell you there's no place like a transit prison. What it comes down to is that happiness is a relative concept; it's all in the mind."

"Etymologically the Russian word for happiness has unmistakable connotations of 'transience' and 'insubstantiality.' *Schast'e* comes from *se-chas'e*, meaning 'this hour,' 'this moment.' "

"Sorry, my learned friend, it doesn't. Look it up in Dahl. It comes from *so-chast'e*, the share a person wrests from life. Its peculiar etymology gives us a pretty sordid conception of happiness."

"Just a minute. My explanation also comes from Dahl."

"You surprise me. So does mine, I tell you."

"This calls for research in all languages. I'll make a note!"

"Madman!"

"It's an idiot who says so! Let's do a bit of comparative philology."

"Like Marr, you mean? Everything derives from the word for 'hand'?"

"You bum, you! Listen, have you ever read Goethe's *Faust*, part 2?"

"Why don't you ask whether I've read part 1? Everybody says it's a work of genius, but nobody reads it. Some people rely on Gounod's version!

"No, part 1 is quite straightforward. What's the problem?"

" '*Of sons and worlds I cannot speak;*
*human toil is all I see.*'

"Now that does something for me!

"Or there's this:

" '*What we don't know is just what we needed;*
*What we know is no use to us.*' "

"That's great!"

"Part 2, I admit, is heavy going. But what a profound idea. You know the contract between Faust and Mephistopheles: Mephistopheles will take possession of Faust's soul only when Faust cries: 'Stay, fleeting moment, thou art beautiful!' But whatever Mephistopheles lays before him—the return of his youth, Margarita's love, easy victory over his rival, boundless wealth, knowledge of all the secrets of existence—nothing can wring from Faust's breast the fateful exclamation. Many years have passed; by now Mephistopheles himself is worn-out, trailing after this insatiable being; he sees that there is no way of making the man happy and is ready to abandon this barren sport. Faust, by now aged and blind all over again, gives orders for thousands of workers to be summoned to dig canals and drain the marshes. His brain, senile for the second time and—or so the cynic Mephistopheles thinks—crazed and clouded, is aglow with a grand idea: to make mankind happy. At a signal from Mephistopheles, hell's servants appear and start digging Faust's grave. Mephistopheles has lost all hope of winning his soul and simply wants to bury him, to be rid of him. Faust hears the sound of many shovels. 'What is that?' he asks. The spirit of mockery has not deserted Mephistopheles. He paints Faust a false picture of the draining of the marshes. Soviet critics like to interpret this passage in the spirit of socialist optimism: As they would have it, Faust, feeling that he has benefited mankind, and finding in this his supreme joy, exclaims: 'Stay, fleeting moment, thou art beautiful!' But we have to ask ourselves whether Goethe was not ridiculing the idea of human happiness. Because in reality nothing whatsoever has been done for mankind. Faust pronounces the long-awaited sacramental phrase one step from the grave, deluded and perhaps truly insane, and the lemurs immediately hustle him into the hole. Is this Goethe's hymn to happiness, or is he ridiculing it?"

"Ah, this is the Lyovochka I love—reasoning from the heart, talking wisely, and not sticking abusive labels on things."

"You miserable latter-day Pyrrho! I knew I would make you happy! And I haven't finished yet. In one of my prewar lectures—they were devilishly daring!—I developed this excerpt from Goethe into the elegiac idea that there is no such thing as happiness, that it is either unattainable or illusory. Then, suddenly, a note was passed to me, a page torn out of a miniature notebook—squared paper:

" 'But I'm in love—and I am happy! What do you say to that?' "

"What did you say?"

"What can anybody say?"

# 9

## The Fifth Year in Harness

THEY WERE SO carried away that they no longer heard the noise of the laboratory and the tiresome radio in the far corner. Nerzhin on his revolving chair had turned his back on the laboratory again. Rubin leaned sideways, folded his hands on the back of his chair, and rested his beard on them.

Nerzhin spoke, evidently delivering thoughts long pondered.

"When I was outside and read what wise men had to say about the meaning of life, or happiness, I always found it difficult to understand. I treated them with respect: They were sages, doing what they were supposed to do. But the meaning of life? We are alive, and that's what it means. Happiness? When life is very good to us, that's happiness, everybody knows. . . . Prison has my blessing! It's made me think. To understand what happiness means, let us first consider being full. Remember the Lubyanka or your time in counterintelligence. Remember that thin, watery porridge of oats or barley, without a single sparkle of fat. Do you just eat it? Just dine on it? No—it's Holy Communion! You receive it with awed reverence, as though it were the life's breath of the yogis! You eat it slowly, eat it from the tip of a wooden spoon, eat it utterly absorbed in the process of eating, the thought of eating—and the pleasurable feeling suffuses your whole body, like nectar; you are dizzy with the sweetness which you discover in these mushy boiled grains and the dishwater that holds them together. And—lo and behold!—you live six months, live twelve months on a diet of next to nothing! Pigging out on choice chops can't compare!"

Rubin could not and never did listen for long. His idea of conversation (and this was how it usually went) was to strew before his friends the intellectual booty captured by his quick mind. As usual, he was eager to interrupt, but Nerzhin gripped the front of his overalls with five fingers and shook him to prevent him from speaking.

"So in our own wretched persons and from our unhappy comrades, we learn what it means to eat our fill. It doesn't depend on how much we eat, not at all, but on how we eat! It's the same with happiness, Lyovushka, it's exactly the same; it doesn't depend at all on the size of the good things we've wrested from life. It depends solely on our attitude to them! As the Taoist ethic has it: 'He who knows how to be content will always be content.'"

Rubin laughed.

"You're an eclectic. You pluck pretty feathers from every bird to beautify your own tail!"

Nerzhin's head and hand peremptorily denied it. His hair had slipped down over his forehead. He found the argument very interesting, and he looked like a boy of eighteen.

"Don't try to confuse the issue, Lyovka, it isn't like that at all! I draw my conclusions not from the philosophical works I've read but from the life stories I hear in prison. When I need to formulate my own views, why should I set out to discover America all over again? There are no unexplored countries on the planet Philosophy. I turn the pages of the wise men of old, and I find my own most recent thoughts. Don't interrupt! I was about to give you an example. In the camp—and it's even more true here in the sharashka—if a miracle happens and I get a quiet Sunday off, and in the course of the day my soul thaws out and is at ease, there may not have been any change for the better in my objective situation, but the prison yoke lies more lightly on me. And then suppose I have a really satisfying conversation or read an honest page—there I am, on the crest of the wave! I've had no real life for many years, but I forget it! I'm weightless, I'm suspended in space, I'm disembodied! I lie there on my top bunk, I look at the ceiling just above me, it's bare, the plaster's peeling, but I shudder with the sheer bliss of being! I fall asleep on the wings of happiness! No president or prime minister can go to sleep as content with the Sunday behind him!"

Rubin grinned good-naturedly. His grin expressed a measure of agreement and a measure of indulgence for a deluded young friend.

"And what do the great books of the Vedas have to say on the subject?" he asked, his lips protruding in a humorous funnel.

"The Vedas—I don't know," Nerzhin retorted, quite sure of himself. "But the books of Sankhya say that 'human happiness is ranked with suffering by the discerning.'"

"I can see you're an adept," Rubin muttered into his beard.

"Adept in what? Idealism? Metaphysics? Why aren't you sticking labels on it?"

"Is it Mityai who's leading you astray?"

"No, Mityai's angle is quite different. Listen, shaggy beard! The happiness of continual victory, the happiness of desire triumphantly gratified, the happiness of total satisfaction . . . is suffering! It is the death of the soul; it is a sort of permanent moral dyspepsia! Never mind the philosophers of the Vedas and the Sankhya. I, Gleb Nerzhin, I myself, a prisoner in harness for five years, have risen by my own efforts to a level of development at which the bad can also be seen as the good, and it is my firm belief that people do not know themselves what they should aspire to. They squander their strength in the pointless scramble for a handful of material goods and die without even discovering their own spiritual riches. When Lev Tolstoy dreamed of being put in prison, he was thinking like a genuinely clear-sighted man with a healthy spiritual life."

Rubin guffawed. He always guffawed when he completely rejected the views of his opponent in a debate (and that was his normal experience in prison).

"Harken, child! Your words come from an unformed youthful mind. You prefer your own experience to the collective experience of mankind. You are poisoned by the odors of the prison night bucket, and you expect to see the world clearly through its exhalations. We ourselves have come to grief; our own fate is all awry. But how can a man allow his convictions to be changed or swayed one little bit just by that?"

"So you're proud of your consistency?"

"I am! *'Hier stehe ich und kann nicht anders.'*"

"Of all the pigheadedness! That's what I call metaphysics. Instead of learning from prison, instead of absorbing this new life . . ."

"Absorbing what? The toxic bile secreted by life's losers?"

". . . you have willfully sealed your eyes, stopped your ears, adopted a pose—and you think that shows intelligence? Is refusal to develop intelligent? You struggle to believe in the triumph of your infernal Communism, but try as you may, you don't believe—"

"It isn't a matter of belief, you dunderhead, but of scientific knowledge! And objectivity!"

"What? You call yourself objective?"

"Ab-solutely!" Rubin said loftily.

"Never in my life have I known a more biased man than you!"

"Just try to rise above your own molehill! Try to look at things in historical perspective! Historical necessity. Do you know the meaning of it? The inevitability of conforming to the inherent laws of history. Everything goes the way it must! Historical materialism could not cease to be true just because you and I are in prison. Don't root in the mud, just to grub up the moldering corpse of skepticism."

"Try to understand, Lev! It gave me no pleasure, it made me sick at heart to part with that doctrine! It was the clarion call, the ruling passion of my youth; I forsook and cursed all other things for its sake! Now I'm like a blade of grass in the crater where a bomb has uprooted the tree of faith. I've lost so many arguments since I've been in prison—"

"Because you weren't clever enough, fathead."

"—that I was bound in all honesty to jettison your rickety constructions and look for others. It isn't easy. My skepticism may be a shelter by the wayside, to sit out the storm—"

"Bunk! Absolute garbage! You'll never make a real skeptic! Skeptics are supposed to suspend judgment, and you're in a hurry to pronounce on everything! Skeptics are supposed to cultivate ataraxia, imperturbability, and you boil over at the slightest excuse!"

"Yes, you're right." Gleb buried his head in his hands. "I train my mind to soar above it all . . . but the world around me makes me giddy, I lose control, I snap at people, get indignant."

"Above it all? And you're at my throat because there's a shortage of drinkable water at Dzhezkazgan."

"I would like to see you packed off to Dzhezkazgan! You might change your tune there!"

"Fathead, idiot! You might at least try reading what great men have to say about skepticism. Lenin, for instance."

"Well? What about Lenin?" Nerzhin had lowered his voice.

"Lenin said: 'To the paladins of liberal logorrhea *à la russe*, skepticism is a stage on the way from democracy to vile lackey liberalism.' "

"What, what, what? Sure you aren't misquoting?"

"His precise words. It's from *Remembering Herzen* and it refers to . . ."

Nerzhin hid his head in his hands, as though conceding defeat.

"Well," said Rubin mildly. "Satisfied?"

"Oh yes." Nerzhin's whole body rocked. "You couldn't have found anything better. To think that I once worshipped him!"

"What do you mean?"

"What do I mean? Is that the language of a great philosopher? That's simply the sort of wild abuse people go in for when they have no arguments! 'Paladins of logorrhea'! It makes you sick to say it. Liberalism means love of freedom, so it has to be slavish and dirty. Whereas applause on command is a leap into the realm of freedom, I suppose?"

In the heat of argument, the friends had forgotten the need for caution, and their exclamations were now loud enough for Simochka to hear. She had been darting glances of stern disapproval at Nerzhin for some time. The late shift was drawing to an end, and she felt hurt that Nerzhin wasn't taking advantage of these convenient evening hours and hadn't even looked around at her.

"No, your brain is simply out of kilter," Rubin said in despair. "Can't you put it more clearly?"

"Well, it might make more sense this way: Skepticism is a way of silencing fanaticism; skepticism is a way of liberating dogmatic minds."

"And who's the dogmatist here? Me, I suppose? Am I really a dogmatist?" Rubin's big warm eyes looked at him reproachfully. "I'm a prisoner, one of the 1945 intake, like you. I've got four years of war lodged like shrapnel in my side and five years of prison around my neck, so I can see things just as clearly as you. And if I was convinced that the whole thing was rotten to the core, I would be the first to say we must publish another *Kolokol*! We must sound the alarm! We must destroy! You wouldn't find me hiding in the shrubbery, refusing to pass judgment! Covering my nakedness with the fig leaf of skepticism! . . . But I know that the decay is only apparent, only superficial, that the root is sound, the stem is sound, so that we must come to the rescue, not destroy!"

The internal telephone rang on the vacant desk of Engineer Major Roitman, head of the Acoustics Lab. Simochka rose and went over to it.

"Try to understand, try to get the iron law of our age into your head: There are two worlds, two systems! And there is no third way! There can be no *Kolokol* uselessly ringing into the wind. It's impossible! You cannot avoid choosing: Which of the two world forces are you for?"

"Be off with you! It just suits the Big Chief to reason that way. That 'two worlds' nonsense has helped him to make doormats of us all."

"Gleb Vikentich!"

"Listen to me now!" It was Rubin's turn to seize Nerzhin by his overalls with a commanding hand. "He is a very great man!"

"Blockhead! Hog's brain!"

"One of these days you'll understand! He is at once the Robespierre and the Napoleon of our Revolution. He is . . . wise! He is truly wise! He sees further than our blunted vision can reach—"

"And has the nerve to consider us all fools! He foists his ready-chewed cud on us. . . ."

"Gleb Vikentich."

"Eh?" Nerzhin came to himself and abandoned Rubin.

"Didn't you hear? There was a phone call." It was the third time Simochka had called him, standing at her desk stern and frowning, her folded arms drawing the brown mohair shawl tight around her shoulders. "Anton Nikolaevich wants you in his office."

"Oh?" The excitement of argument had faded from Nerzhin's face, and the wrinkles had returned. "Right, thank you, Serafima Vitalievna. Hear that, Lyovka? Anton wants me. Wonder what for?"

A summons to the office of the director of the institute at ten o'clock on Saturday evening was an extraordinary event. Although Simochka was trying to look official and indifferent, Nerzhin could see that she was alarmed.

Their heated exchanges were forgotten. Rubin looked at his friend with concern. When his eyes were not dilated by polemical passion, they were almost feminine in their gentleness.

"I don't like it when the top brass starts taking an interest in us," he said.

Nerzhin shrugged. "Why worry? Ours is such an unimportant piffling little job, all this voice business—"

"We will get it in the neck from Anton before long. We will live to regret Stanislavsky's memoirs and the speeches of famous lawyers!" said Rubin with a laugh. "Maybe it's Number Seven's articulation tests?"

"The results have been signed already; there's no going back on them. Anyway, if I don't come back—"

"Don't be silly!"

"What's silly about it? Life here is like that. But burn you-know-what." Gleb pulled down the rolltop quietly, put the keys in Rubin's hand, and went off at his usual leisurely pace. A prisoner five years between the shafts never hurries. He knows that what comes next can only be worse.

# 10

## The Rosicrucians

NERZHIN MADE HIS WAY UP THE BROAD, red-carpeted stairway, deserted at this hour, with bronze candlesticks and an ornate stucco ceiling overhead, to the third floor. Trying to look carefree, he strolled past the desk of the "free employee" manning the outside telephones and knocked at the door of the director of research, MGB Engineer Colonel Anton Nikolaevich Yakonov.

The office was spacious, carpeted wall to wall, and furnished with armchairs and sofas. The azure patch in the middle was the dazzling cloth on a long conference table, contrasting with the brownness of Yakonov's elegant desk and armchair in the far corner. Nerzhin had viewed this magnificence before, but not very often, and usually not alone but in group discussions.

Engineer Colonel Yakonov was over fifty but still in his prime. His stature, the hint of powder on his face after shaving, his gold-rimmed pince-nez, his soft, princely plumpness—an Obolensky or a Dolgoruky?* —his majestic, self-assured movements, made him a conspicuous figure among the grandees of his ministry.

"Take a seat, Gleb Vikentich!" An expansive wave accompanied the invitation. He sat hunched in his outsize armchair, twiddling a fat colored pencil over the polished brown desktop.

Addressing him by his first name and patronymic was a mark of courtesy and goodwill that cost the engineer colonel no effort, since he had a list of all the prisoners, with their full names, under glass on his desk. (Those unaware of this were amazed at Yakonov's memory.) Nerzhin bowed silently. (He did not hold his hands along the seams of his trousers but did not wave them about either.) He sat down expectantly at the imposing, highly polished desk.

Yakonov's voice was a rich rumble. It always seemed strange that this fine gentleman did not cultivate an exquisite lisp.

"Do you know, Gleb Vikentich, I happened to think of you half an hour ago, and I started wondering what wind exactly had blown you into the Acoustics Lab, to—er—Roitman?"

Yakonov pronounced this name with undisguised contempt and, in the presence of Roitman's subordinate, didn't even prefix it with the word "Major." Relations between the head of the Research Institute and his senior deputy had deteriorated so far that there was no longer any point in concealing it.

Nerzhin tensed. Instinct told him that the conversation was off to a bad start. It was with the same contemptuous and ironical curve of his not-exactly-thin and not-exactly-thick lips that Yakonov had told Nerzhin some days back that he, Nerzhin, was perhaps objective about the results of the

* Obolensky or Dolgoruky: Noble families of long-standing eminence.

voice tests but that he treated Number Seven not like a dear departed relative but like an unidentified drunk found dead under the Marfino fence. Number Seven was Yakonov's hobbyhorse, but it was going very badly.

". . . I, of course, greatly appreciate your personal contribution to the science of voice classification . . . " (he was being sarcastic!) ". . . and I'm dreadfully sorry that your original monograph was printed only in a small, classified edition, which denied you the fame of a sort of Russian George Fletcher . . . " (brutally sarcastic!) ". . . but I should still like to see a little more . . . profit, as the Anglo-Saxons put it, from your activities. I pay homage to the abstract sciences, but I am a practical man."

Engineer Colonel Yakonov had risen high enough, yet was still at a sufficient distance from the Leader of the Peoples, to permit himself the luxury of not disguising his cleverness or refraining from idiosyncratic pronouncements.

"Well, now, let me ask you frankly, what is going on right now in the Acoustics Lab?"

The most ruthless question imaginable! Yakonov simply didn't have time to keep up with everything, or he would have gotten their number long ago.

"Why the devil do you waste your time on that gibberish? '*Styr . . . smyr . . .*' You're a mathematician, aren't you? A university man? Look behind you."

Nerzhin looked and rose from his chair. There were three of them in the office, not two! An unremarkable man in dark civilian clothes rose from a sofa to face him. His round spectacles flashed as he moved his head. In the lavish light from overhead, Nerzhin recognized Pyotr Trofimovich Verenyov, a senior lecturer in his university before the war. But true to his prison training, he remained silent and made no movement, assuming that the man before him was a prisoner and fearing to compromise him by premature recognition. Verenyov smiled but also looked embarrassed. Yakonov rumbled reassuringly.

"I must say, this ritual restraint is one of the things I envy about the mathematical fraternity. All my life I've thought of mathematicians as a sort of Rosicrucian brotherhood, and I've always regretted that it was never my luck to be initiated into their mysteries. Don't be shy. Shake hands and make yourselves comfortable. I shall leave you for half an hour. You can exchange fond memories, and Professor Verenyov can explain the tasks that the Sixth Administration has set us."

With this, Yakonov lifted himself out of his oversize chair and made light work of carrying his far-from-light frame—made more imposing by his silver-

and-blue epaulets—to the exit. When Nerzhin's hand met Verenyov's, they were alone.

To Nerzhin, set as he was in his prison ways, this pale man in the twinkling glasses was like a ghost unlawfully returning from a forgotten world, separated from today's world by the forests around Lake Ilmen, the hills and ravines of the Orel region, the sands and marshes of Belorussia, prosperous Polish farms, the tiled roofs of little German towns. Other memories were engraved on this nine-year interval between meetings: the bright, bare boxes and cells of the Lubyanka, the grime and stench of transit prisons, stifling compartments in prisoner-transport trains, cold and hungry zeks out in the biting wind of the steppes. It was impossible to think back beyond all this and relive how it felt to see the formula for the functions of an independent variable written out on the pliant oilcloth surface of a blackboard.

They lit cigarettes, Nerzhin unsteadily, and sat facing each other across a small table.

It was not Verenyov's first encounter with a former student—from Moscow or from Rostov, where he had been sent before the war to draw a firm line between conflicting schools of thought. But this meeting with Nerzhin was something out of the ordinary for him, too: this establishment so near to and so remote from Moscow, shrouded in a smokescreen of supersecrecy, wound around with ring after ring of barbed wire, those unfamiliar blue overalls instead of normal human dress. . . .

The younger of the two, with the lines around his mouth more pronounced than ever, apparently had the right to ask the questions, while the older man answered as though ashamed of his modest academic career: evacuation, return from reevacuation, three years working with K——, successful doctoral thesis on topology. . . . Nerzhin, boorishly casual, did not even ask the subject of his contribution to this austere field of study in which he had once himself intended to choose his degree project. He suddenly felt sorry for Verenyov. . . . Ordered magnitudes, incompletely ordered magnitudes, finite magnitudes. . . . Topology! The stratosphere of human thought! In the twenty-fourth century it might just possibly be of use to somebody, but for the present . . . For the present. . . .

*Why should I speak of suns and worlds,*
*I have eyes for man's suffering alone.*

But why had Verenyov left the university and landed in this department? Posted here, of course. But couldn't he have refused? Well, yes, he could, only. . . . In this job his salary was doubled. . . . Did he have children? . . . Four of them. . . .

For some reason, they started going over the students who had graduated with Nerzhin. Their final examination had taken place on the day war broke out. The most gifted of them had been killed or shell-shocked. They're the ones who always stick their necks out, never look after themselves. While those of whom you would never have expected it were completing a higher-degree course or held lectureships. Well, and what about the pride of the department, Dmitri Dmitrich! Goryainov-Shakhovskoy! A little old man, so very old that he had become slovenly in his habits, his black velvet jacket was always smothered in chalk, and he often put the blackboard duster into his pocket instead of his handkerchief. A walking anecdote, a compendium of innumerable professorial jokes, the life and soul of the Imperial University of Warsaw, which in 1915 had moved to the commercial town of Rostov as though to a graveyard. On his golden jubilee as a scientist, he was honored with congratulatory telegrams from Milwaukee, Cape Town, Yokohama. . . . Then in 1930, when the university was revamped as an "Industrial-Pedagogical Institute," he had been "purged" by a proletarian commission as a "hostile bourgeois element." Nothing could have saved him had he not known Kalinin personally. It was said that Kalinin's father had been one of the professor's father's serfs. Whether that was so or not, Goryainov took a trip to Moscow and brought back an order to "keep your hands off this man."

And they did. They took such good care not to touch him that those not in the know were sometimes quite alarmed. One minute he would be writing a scientific paper with a mathematical proof of God's existence. The next, in a public lecture on his idol, Newton, the droning voice from under the yellowing mustache would announce that somebody had sent up a note saying, "According to Marx, Newton is a materialist, but you say that he is an idealist. My answer is that Marx misrepresented the facts. Newton believed in God, as all great scientists do."

Recording his lectures was a nightmare! The stenographers were in despair! Because his legs were weak, he would sit right by the blackboard, facing it, with his back to his audience, writing with his right hand, erasing with his left, and mumbling to himself incessantly. It was hopeless trying to understand his ideas during a lecture. But Nerzhin and a fellow student, taking it in turns, sometimes managed to write it all down and went over it in the evening. They were awestruck, as though they were gazing into a sky filled with twinkling stars.

So what had become of the old man? He had been concussed in an air raid on Rostov and evacuated half-dead to Kirghizia. Then there was some story about his sons, both lecturers—Verenyov didn't know the details, some dirty business, something treasonable. Stivka, the younger one, was now a longshoreman on the New York waterfront, so they said.

Nerzhin studied Verenyov closely while he was talking. Strange that good scientific minds, so agile in multidimensional space, should look at life itself with tunnel vision. A thinker is insulted by thugs and louts—that is just a symptom of immaturity, a momentary lapse; if his children remember their father's humiliation—that is obscene, that is treason. And who really knew whether Stivka was actually a New York longshoreman or not? The secret police shape public opinion.

What, Verenyov asked, had Nerzhin done to . . . find himself inside?

Nerzhin laughed.

No, really, what had he done?

"Thought the wrong thoughts, Pyotr Trofimovich. The Japanese have a law that a man can be put on trial for his unspoken thoughts."

"The Japanese! But we have no such law, do we?"

"Oh yes we do; it's called 58 slash 10."

After this, Nerzhin listened with one ear as Verenyov told him Yakonov's real reason for bringing them together. The Sixth Administration had sent Verenyov to intensify and systematize the work they were doing on encoding. Mathematicians were needed, lots of them, and Verenyov was delighted to see among them a former student for whom he had had high hopes.

Nerzhin mechanically asked for details, and Pyotr Trofimovich, in a fine mathematical frenzy, set about explaining the object of the research and detailing the experiments to be made and the formulas to be reconsidered. Nerzhin's mind, meanwhile, was on those scraps of paper which he covered with his tiny handwriting, secure and at peace behind his camouflaged defenses, while Simochka stole loving glances at him, and Lev good-naturedly bumbled.

Those tiny pages were the first fruits of his maturity. It was preferable, of course, to reach maturity before your thirties—and in your original subject. Why, it might be asked, should he stick his head into those jaws from which historians themselves had scuttled away to ages safely over and done with?

Why was he so fascinated by the riddle of the grim inflated giant who had only to flutter an eyelash and Nerzhin's head would fly off?

Should he, then, surrender to the tentacles of the cryptographic octopus? For fourteen hours a day they would crush him, never relaxing even during rest periods. Probability theory, number theory, the theory of error, would monopolize his thoughts. It would be brain death. Desiccation of the soul. What room would there be for meditation? For trying to make sense of life?

Still, this was a sharashka. Not a camp. There was meat for dinner. Butter in the morning. The skin on your hands was not lacerated and callused. Your fingers weren't frostbitten. You didn't slump onto the bed-planks like an insensate log in your filthy rope sandals—no, you got into bed happily, under a clean white comforter.

So what was the point of just living all your life? Living for the sake of living? With no concern beyond your physical comfort?

Lovely comfort! But what is the point if there is nothing more?

Reason told him to agree.

His heart said, Get thee behind me, Satan!

"Pyotr Trofimovich, do you know how to make shoes?"

"What was that?"

"I mean, can you teach me to make shoes? I want to learn to make shoes."

"I'm sorry, I don't understand. . . ."

"Pyotr Trofimovich! You live in a shell! When I've served my sentence, I will be going into the depths of the taiga into permanent exile. I can't do any sort of work with my hands, so how am I going to live? There are brown bears out there. Another three Mesozoic eras will come and go before anybody out there needs Leonard Euler's functions."

"What are you talking about, Nerzhin? If your work as a cryptographer is successful, you will be released early; your conviction will be annulled; you'll be given an apartment in Moscow."

"My dear Pyotr Trofimovich, I don't want any thanks from them, I don't want their forgiveness, and I'm not interested in catching minnows for them. . . ."

The door opened, and in came the great panjandrum with the gold-rimmed pince-nez on his fleshy nose.

"How goes it, my Rosicrucian friends? All settled?"

Still seated, Nerzhin looked Yakonov straight in the eye and replied:

"With respect, Anton Nikolaevich, I consider that my work in the Acoustics Laboratory is not yet complete."

By now Yakonov was standing behind his desk, the knuckles of his pudgy hands resting on its glass top to take his weight. Only those who knew him well would have realized from his words that he was angry.

"Mathematics! And articulation. You've traded the food of the gods for a mess of pottage. You can go."

And with the two-colored lead of his fat pencil, he made a note on his memo pad: "Write off Nerzhin."

# 11

# The Enchanted Castle

YAKONOV HAD HELD his position of trust as chief engineer of the Special Technology Department of the MGB for several years now, during and since the war. He wore with dignity the insignia of an engineer colonel, silver epaulets with blue borders and three big stars, which his knowledge had earned him. His position was such that he could exercise general supervision from a distance, make an occasional erudite report to an audience of high officeholders, indulge in an occasional clever and colorful conversation with some engineer over his finished model, and in general enjoy the reputation of an expert, bear no responsibility, and pick up a good few thousand rubles a month. It was a post in which Yakonov had graciously bestowed his eloquence on all the department's ingenious technical schemes in their infancy, stayed aloof from them in the days of growing pains and adolescent maladies, and honored once again with his presence the pauper's funeral of a failure or the coronation of a hero with a crown of gold.

Anton Nikolaevich was not young or self-confident enough to chase after the treacherous glitter of a Golden Star or the badge of a Stalin Prize winner, to snap up for himself every task set by the ministry or by the Boss himself. Anton Nikolaevich was sufficiently advanced in years and experience to avoid such excitement—and the soaring exultation and plunges into despair inseparable from it.

Clinging to these principles, he had survived without unpleasant incidents until January 1948. Then, that January, somebody had suggested to the Father of the Peoples of East and West the idea of creating a special secret telephone. Nobody who intercepted his telephone conversations would be able to understand them! He could sit in his country home at Kuntsevo and converse with Molotov in New York! The Generalissimo's august finger, yellowed around the nail by nicotine, picked out the Marfino establishment, which had previously been concerned with developing walkie-talkie sets for the militia. The historic words spoken on the occasion were, "Why do I need these transmitters? To catch burglars?"

He set a deadline—January 1, 1949. Then he thought a bit and added: "Well, all right, make it May 1."

The job was an extremely responsible one and the schedule extraordinarily tight. After some thought, the ministry decided that Yakonov personally must bring Marfino up to snuff. He tried hard to prove that he was overloaded already and could not take on another commitment, but in vain. The head of his department, Foma Guryanovich Oskolupov, had only to turn those green cat's eyes on him, and Yakonov remembered the blots on his record (he had been in prison for six years) and fell silent.

That was almost two years ago, and the chief engineer's office in the ministry building had been unoccupied ever since. The chief engineer spent his days and nights at the far end of town in the former seminary building with the hexagonal tower over its redundant sanctuary.

At first he quite enjoyed running things personally: wearily slamming the door of his personal Pobeda, speeding to Marfino lulled by its purring engine, driving through the barbed-wire-festooned gates past a saluting sentry, walking with an entourage of majors and captains under the century-old limes of the Marfino copse. Yakonov's superiors had demanded nothing of him except plan after plan after plan, and "socialist obligations." And the MGB's horn of plenty was inverted over the Marfino institute: equipment purchased from Britain and America; equipment captured from the Germans; homegrown convicts summoned from the camps; a technical library for twenty thousand new acquisitions; the best security officers and archivists, the old bulls of the MGB herd; and finally prison guards with the finest Lubyanka education. The old building of the seminary had to be converted, and new buildings put up for the prison staff and for the experimental workshops; so when the yellow flowers on the limes sweetened the air, you could hear in the shade of those giants the sad voices of slow-moving German war prisoners in bedraggled gray-green tunics. These slothful fascists had no appetite for work after four years of postwar imprisonment. No Russian eye could bear to watch them unloading bricks from a truck: each brick slowly passed from hand to hand, as carefully as if it were crystal, and gently stacked. While they were installing radiators under the windows and re-laying rotten floors, the Germans sauntered through super-secret rooms, squinted sullenly at the labels on equipment, some in German, some in English—a German schoolboy could have guessed what sort of work these laboratories would be doing. All of which was dealt with in a report submitted by prisoner Rubin to the engineer colonel. He was right to do so, but security officers Shikin and Myshin ("Shishkin-Myshkin" in prison vernacular) did not find the report at all helpful: What were they supposed to do about it? Report their own oversight to their superiors? In any case it was too late, because the prisoners of war had been repatriated, and those who had gone to West Germany could, if anyone was interested, report on the location of the institute and of its individual laboratories. Yet when officers from other MGB directorates had business with the engineer colonel, he was not allowed to give them the address of his outfit, and rather than risk the least little chink in his curtain of secrecy, he would travel to the Lubyanka to talk to them.

The Germans were dismissed and replaced by zeks just like those already in the sharashka, except that their clothes were ragged and dirty and they were not given white bread. What could be heard under the limes now, in and out of season, was the steady buzz of healthy Gulag obscenities, reminding the zeks in the sharashka of their unchanging motherland and their inescapable fate. Bricks flew from trucks like leaves in the wind, so that scarcely one reached the ground whole. Zeks chanting, "One, two, and down she comes" tipped the plywood cover over the back of the truck and saved the guards work by crawling under it themselves, merrily embraced the foully swearing wenches, and were carried away through the streets of Moscow back to their camp for the night.

So in this enchanted castle, separated from the capital and its unwitting inhabitants by barbed wire and bullets, ghosts in black quilted jackets wrought fabulous changes: Marfino acquired piped water, sanitation, central heating, and neat flower beds.

Meanwhile the establishment so auspiciously founded grew and expanded. Another institute, already engaged in similar work, was merged with Marfino, arriving with its own desks, chairs, cabinets, loose-leaf files, apparatus that would be obsolete in a matter of months, not of years, and its own head, Engineer Major Roitman, who became Yakonov's deputy. Alas, the creator of the newly arrived institute, its inspirer and protector, Colonel Yakov Ivanovich Mamurin, head of Special and Secret Communications in the Ministry of the Interior, an outstanding servant of the state, had met his end in tragic circumstances before all this.

One day the Leader of All Progressive Mankind, on the telephone to the Chinese province of Yenan, had been annoyed by interference and crackling in the receiver. He called Beria and said in Georgian:

"Lavrenty! What sort of idiot is in charge of communications in your department? Remove him."

Mamurin was duly removed, but only as far as the Lubyanka. No one knew what to do with him next. The usual instructions were missing. Was he to be put on trial? If so, on what charge? And how long should his sentence be? If he had been an outsider, they could have slapped a "quarter" (of a century!) on him and packed him off to Norilsk. But the big wheels of the MVD knew how true it was that "where you go today I may follow tomorrow," and held on to Mamurin until they felt sure that Stalin had forgotten him. So there was no investigation and no trial. He was simply relegated to his country home outside Moscow.

One summer evening in 1948, a new zek was delivered to the Marfino sharashka. Everything about his arrival was unusual: He was brought in a passenger car, not in a prison car; he was escorted not by a common guard but by the head of the Prisons Department of the MVD; and to cap it all, his first supper was served under a butter-cloth cover in the office of the prison governor.

They heard the new arrival (zeks are supposed to hear nothing but hear everything) say that he "didn't want any sausage" and the head of the Prisons Department urging him to "take nourishment." A zek who had gone to the doctor for some medicine overheard this through a partition. After discussing this hair-raising news, the basic population of the sharashka decided that the new arrival was nevertheless a prisoner and went to bed satisfied.

Where the new man spent that first night is a question that historians of the sharashka have not resolved. But one rather primitive zek, a ham-fisted fitter, came face-to-face with the newcomer in the small hours on the wide marble porch (later out-of-bounds to prisoners).

"Hi there, pal," he said, with a friendly punch in the chest, "where've you come from? What did you get done for? Sit down and let's have a smoke."

But the new arrival shied away from the fitter in disgust. His pale, lemony face twisted in a grimace. The fitter looked hard at the pale eyes, the thinning fair hair on the balding skull and said angrily: "The hell with you, then! Vermin! Like something out of a lab jar! You'll be locked up with the rest of us after lights out, and you'll sure as hell find your tongue then!"

But the "creature out of a lab jar" never was in fact shut up in the main prison. They found him a little third-floor room, on the same hallway as the laboratories, and wedged into it a bed, a table, a cupboard, a flowering plant in a pot, and a hotplate, and tore down the cardboard blocking the barred window, which however looked out not on God's world but on a landing on the rear stairway. The stairway itself was on the northern side of the building, so that even in the daytime there was scarcely a glimmer of light in the privileged prisoner's cell. The bars could of course have been removed, but after some hesitation the prison staff decided to leave them there. They themselves did not understand this mysterious affair and could not decide on the safest line to take.

The newcomer was promptly christened "the Man in the Iron Mask." For quite a time no one knew his name. Nor could anyone talk to him. They saw him through the window, sitting dejectedly in his solitary cell, or wandering like a pale ghost under the lime trees, at times when ordinary zeks were not allowed out. The Man in the Iron Mask was as sallow and emaciated as any "goner" after two good years of processing by interrogation officers, but his foolhardy rejection of sausage made that scenario improbable.

Much later, when the Man in the Iron Mask started turning up for work in Number Seven, the zeks learned from the free workers that he was in fact the very same Colonel Mamurin who had forbidden his subordinates in the Communications Department of the Ministry of the Interior to put their heels down when they walked along the corridor: If anyone failed to walk on tiptoe, he would rush out through his secretary's room in a fury yelling: "Do you know whose office you're stamping past, you oaf? What's your name?"

Much later they learned the reason for Mamurin's sufferings. The world of free men had rejected him, and he was too fastidious to join the world of zeks. At first, he read a great deal in his solitude: *The Struggle for Peace; Knight of the Golden Star; Russia's Glorious Sons*; then the verses of Prokofiev and Gribachev and . . . he underwent a miraculous transformation: He began writing verse himself! It is well known that poets are born of unhappiness and spiritual torment, and Mamurin's torments were more agonizing than those of any other prisoner. After two years inside, without examination or trial, the latest Party directives were still his meat and drink, and the Wise Leader was still his god. Mamurin confided to Rubin that the really terrible thing was not prison food (his meals, incidentally, were prepared separately), or separation from his family (he was, incidentally, driven home once a month to spend a night in his own apartment), or the denial of primitive animal needs—no, it grieved him to think that he had forfeited the trust of Iosif Vissarionovich; it hurt to feel himself no longer a colonel but cashiered and dishonored. That was what made imprisonment so much harder to bear for Communists like themselves than for the unprincipled scum around them.

Rubin was indeed a Communist. But after receiving the confidences of his would-be kindred spirit and reading his verses, Rubin recoiled from this happy find and began avoiding Mamurin, hiding from him in fact, spending his time among people who unfairly attacked him but were his equals in misfortune.

Mamurin was nagged by an ambition as importunate as toothache: to vindicate himself in the eyes of the Party and the government. Alas, what this director of communications knew about communications went no further than the handling of a telephone receiver. Strictly speaking he was not capable of work but only of management. But as manager of an operation patently doomed to failure, he would hardly return to favor with the Communications Engineers' Best Friend.

He must manage something assured of success. By then two such promising projects had taken shape in the Marfino institute: the Scrambler and Number Seven. People either take to each other or line up against each other at first sight, obeying some impulse that defies logic. Yakonov and his deputy Roitman had not taken to each other. Month by month they found each other more and more insufferable. Harnessed as they were to the same chariot, by some heavier hand, they could not break free; all they could do was pull in opposite directions. When work on the secret telephone reached a stage at which alternative experimental programs were possible, Roitman conscripted everyone he could get for the Acoustics Laboratory to work on the "vocoder." (The name was derived from the English "voice coder." An attempt was made to substitute a Russian name meaning "artificial speech apparatus," but it had not caught on.) Yakonov's riposte was to denude all the other groups: The cleverest engineers and the finest imported equipment were concentrated in Number Seven. Other projects wilted and died in the unequal struggle.

Mamurin had chosen Number Seven for two reasons. For one thing, he could not subordinate himself to his own former subordinate, Roitman. And for another, the ministry, too, thought it was just as well that Yakonov, a non-Party man with a past, should have an unsleeping fiery eye at his back.

From that day on, Yakonov could please himself whether or not he spent the night in the institute. The cashiered MVD colonel, suppressing his poetic passion for the sake of his country's technical progress, the lonely prisoner with the feverish pale eyes and the hideously sunken cheeks renouncing food and sleep, burning himself out like a candle, kept Number Seven on a fifteen-hour day and remained at his post till 2:00 a.m. Such a conveniently long working day was possible only in Number Seven, for there was no need for free employees to work nights in order to supervise Mamurin.

It was to Number Seven that Yakonov had gone when he left Verenyov and Nerzhin together in his office.

# 12

# Number Seven

JUST AS ORDINARY SOLDIERS KNOW, without being shown the battle orders from headquarters, whether they are part of the main offensive or a supporting action, so the three hundred zeks in the Marfino sharashka had correctly deduced that Number Seven was the decisive sector.

No one was supposed to know Number Seven's real name, but everybody in the institute did. It was the "Clipped Speech Laboratory." "Clipped" was an English word. Not only the engineers and translators in the institute but the fitters, the turners, the grinders, perhaps even the deaf and slow-witted carpenter, knew that the original models for the installation were American, though officially they were "ours." This was why American journals with diagrams and theoretical articles about clipping, which were on sale on newsstands in New York, were here given serial numbers, stapled, classified, and, to frustrate American spies, sealed up in fireproof safes.

Clipping, damping, amplitude compression, electronic differentiation, and integration of random speech—it produced an engineer's parody of human speech. It was as if someone had taken it into his head to dismantle New Athos or Gurzuf, put the material in little cubes in matchboxes, mix them all up, fly the lot to Nerchinsk, sort them out, and reassemble them precisely as they were before, reproducing the subtropics, the sound of the surf, the southern air, and moonlight.

This was just what had to be done with the speech reduced to little packages of electrical impulses, and what is more, it had to be reproduced not only so that it could be understood but so that the Boss could recognize the voice at the other end.

While prisoners in the camps gritted their teeth in the struggle for existence, those in the sharashkas lived in something like luxury. And the authorities had long ago made it a rule that if a project was successful, the zeks most closely concerned with it received all that they could desire—their freedom, a clean passport, an apartment in Moscow—while the others received nothing, not a single day's remission of sentence, not even a hundred grams of vodka in honor of the victors.

There was nothing in between.

So those prisoners who had successfully acquired that special tenacity that seems to enable a prisoner to cling to a mirror with his fingernails tried to get into Number Seven as a springboard to freedom.

One who succeeded was the brutal engineer Markushev, whose knobbly face radiated readiness to die for the ideas of Engineer Colonel Yakonov. Others of the same stripe also found their way there.

But the perspicacious Yakonov also recruited zeks who had not volunteered. One such was Amantai Bulatov, a guileless Kazan Tatar with big horn-rimmed glasses and a deafening laugh who was serving ten years as an ex-POW and for his alleged link with Musa Dzhalil, an "enemy of the people." (They jokingly called Amantai the firm's oldest employee. After graduating from the Radio Institute in June 1941, he was tossed into the Smolensk debacle. Because he was a Tatar, the Germans extracted him from the POW camp, and he began his practical work on the shop floor of the Lorenz company when its management was still signing letters with a "Heil Hitler!" Then there was Andrei Andreevich Potapov, an expert on ultrahigh voltages and the construction of power stations. He had landed in Marfino because an incompetent bureaucrat had made a mistake when consulting the Gulag's card index. But Potapov, a real engineer and an indefatigable workhorse, soon found his way around at Marfino and was irreplaceable in the handling of apparatus for the precise measurement of radio frequencies.

There was also engineer Khorobrov, an outstanding radio expert. He had been assigned to Number Seven at its inception, when it was just one team among others. He had wearied of it recently and made no effort to keep up with its furious tempo. Mamurin was getting just as tired of him.

Finally a special order as swift and urgent as a lightning flash had produced from a punitive brigade in a hard-labor camp near Salekharda a gloomy prisoner and engineer of genius, Aleksandr Bobynin, who was immediately set over all the others. Bobynin had been plucked from the jaws of death. And now Bobynin was first in line for release if their project succeeded. So Bobynin worked hard, keeping it up after midnight, but with such an air of dignified disdain that Mamurin was afraid of him and did not dare make the sort of remarks to him that no one else was spared.

Number Seven was the same sort of room as the Acoustics Lab, but on the floor above it. It, too, was littered with apparatus and a medley of furniture, but there was no ramshackle soundproof box in a corner.

Since Yakonov appeared in Number Seven several times a day, it did not treat his arrival as a descent from on high. All that happened was that Markushev and other toadies made sure that he saw them and bustled around more briskly and cheerfully than ever, while Potapov, to make himself invisible, used a frequency meter to stop a gap among the apparatus on a rack that screened him from the rest of the laboratory. He had worked without a break, paid all his debts, and was now quietly fashioning a lump of transparent red plastic into a cigarette case, intended as a Christmas present for someone.

Mamurin rose to meet Yakonov as his equal. He was not wearing blue overalls like the other zeks but a suit of expensive cloth, yet even this made his haggard features and his bony frame no handsomer.

The expression on his sallow brow and his bloodless lips, the lips of one not long for this world, was meant to signify pleasure, and Yakonov read it right.

"Anton Nikolaich! We've readjusted to every sixteenth impulse, and it's much better. Come and listen in. I'll read you something."

"Reading" and "listening in" were the usual way of testing the quality of a telephone circuit: The circuit would be changed several times a day by the addition or subtraction of a unit, and adjusting the articulation every time was laborious, too slow to keep up with the ideas of the engineers on design, and it was not worth trying to get rough figures from the forbidding science now monopolized by Roitman's foster child Nerzhin.

Mamurin and Yakonov, obedient as usual to a single thought, had no need of questions or explanations. Mamurin went first to the far corner of the room, turned his back, pressed the receiver to his cheekbone, and started reading from a newspaper into the telephone, while Yakonov stood by the stand with the control panels, put on the earphones plugged in to the other end of the circuit, and started listening. Something dreadful was going on in the earphones; the sounds made by Mamurin were fragmented by crackling, rumbling, and howling. But just as a mother gazes lovingly at her ill-favored babe, Yakonov, instead of tearing the earphones from his tortured ears, listened harder and decided that this new horrible noise seemed rather better than the horrible noise he had heard before dinner. The new noise was not live colloquial speech but a measured and exaggeratedly precise recital: Mamurin was reading an article about the high-handedness of Yugoslav frontier guards and the effrontery of the butcher Rankovich, who had turned a freedom-loving country into one great dungeon, so that Yakonov easily guessed the bits he couldn't hear, realized and as quickly forgot that he was guessing, and became more and more certain that audibility had improved since dinner.

He naturally wanted to share his joy with Bobynin. The heavily built, thickset prisoner with the defiantly shaved head (you could please yourself how you wore your hair in the sharashka) was sitting nearby. He had not turned around when Yakonov entered the lab, but instead crouched over a long strip of photo-oscillogram film, measuring something with a pair of dividers.

This Bobynin was the least of God's creatures, a nonexistent zek, the lowest of the low, with fewer rights than a kolkhoznik.* And Yakonov was a bigwig.

Yet Yakonov could not bring himself to distract Bobynin, however much he wanted to.

You can build the Empire State Building. Train the Prussian army. Elevate

* Kolkhoznik: A kolkhoz is a Soviet collective farm; a worker on it was known as a kolkhoznik.

the hierarchy of a totalitarian state higher than the throne of the Most High.

But there are still people whose moral superiority defeats you.

There are common soldiers whose company commanders fear them. Laborers whose foremen tremble before them. Prisoners who strike fear into their interrogators.

Bobynin knew all this and deliberately took such a stand with his superiors. Whenever Yakonov talked to him, he felt a cowardly urge to pander to this zek, to avoid upsetting him. He was angry with himself, but he noticed that everybody who talked to Bobynin behaved in the same way.

Yakonov interrupted Mamurin and took off his earphones.

"It's better, Yakov Ivanovich, definitely better! I would like Rubin to listen in a bit; he has a good ear."

Somebody, once upon a time, had gotten from Rubin the answer he wanted and had remarked upon his "good ear." Others had repeated this unthinkingly and come to believe it. Rubin had landed in the sharashka by chance and earned his salt as a translator. His left ear was like everybody else's, but he was a little deaf in his right as a result of shell shock; he had to conceal this after his hearing had been praised. The fame of his "good ear" had given him a firm footing in the sharashka, and he had subsequently dug himself in still more securely with his magisterial work on "The Audio-Synthetic and Electro-Acoustic Aspects of Russian Speech."

Rubin was summoned from the Acoustics Laboratory by telephone. While they were waiting, they listened in again, some of them for the tenth time. Markushev, eyes strained, brow knitted, held the receiver briefly and abruptly pronounced it "better, much better." (He had known it would be: Readjusting to every sixteenth impulse had been his idea.) Bulatov could be heard all over the lab shouting that they must arrange with the encoders to readjust to thirty-two impulses. Two obliging electricians, Lyubimichev and Siromakha, shared a pair of earphones, almost pulling them apart: Each of them listened with one ear and enthusiastically confirmed that it had indeed become more distinct.

Bobynin went on measuring his oscillogram without raising his head.

The black hand of the big electric clock on the wall jumped to 10:30. In every lab except Number Seven, they would shortly be finishing work and handing in secret journals to be put in safes; the zeks would be going off to bed and the free employees running to catch buses, which were infrequent at this late hour.

Ilya Terentievich Khorobrov, keeping to the back of the lab where the bosses could not see him, lumbered over to Potapov behind his shelf-rack. Khorobrov was a native of Vyatka, from its most godforsaken corner, near Kai, bordering on the land of the Gulag, thousands upon thousands of versts* of marsh and forest, an expanse greater than France. He had seen and understood more than most, and things had sometimes become so unbearable that he felt like standing under one of the loudspeakers out in the street and banging his hand on the iron post. The unremitting need to conceal his thoughts, to stifle his sense of injustice, had bowed him, given him a forbidding look, etched deep lines around his mouth. The time came when he could no longer suppress his longing to speak his mind: At the first postwar elections he had crossed out the candidate's name and written a crude obscenity on the ballot form. That was a time when houses could not be rebuilt and fields went unsowed for lack of working hands. But a whole team of ace sleuths spent a month studying the handwriting of every elector in the district, and Khorobrov was arrested. He went off to the camp naively rejoicing that there at any rate he would be able to speak his mind. But the camp was no free republic either! With stool pigeons all around him, Khorobrov learned to hold his tongue there, too.

Common sense demanded that he should bustle about as busily as the others in the anthill that was Number Seven and earn, if not his release, at least a comfortable existence. But the loathing inspired in him by injustice, even when it did not affect him directly, had reached such a pitch that he no longer wanted to live.

He slipped behind Potapov's shelf-rack, bent over his table, and quietly suggested that they should leave.

"Andreich! It's time we cleared off. It's Saturday."

Just at that moment Potapov was fixing a pale pink catch to the translucent red cigarette case. Head on one side, he admired his work and asked:

"What do you think, Terentich? Do the colors match?"

Receiving no reply, neither approving nor negative, Potapov gave Khorobrov a grandmotherly look over his wire-framed spectacles.

"Why tease the dragon?" he asked. "Time is on our side; any *Pravda* lead article will tell you that. We'll evaporate as soon as Anton leaves."

He had a habit of separating his syllables and reinforcing the important word in a sentence with a gesture.

* Verst: Pre-Revolutionary unit of distance equal to 0.6629 miles.

By this time Rubin had arrived in the lab. Rubin had not been in the mood for work all evening, and right then, at 11:00 p.m., the only thing he wanted was to get back to the prison as quickly as possible and to lap up some more Hemingway. But he arranged his features to express keen interest in the improved quality of Number Seven's circuit and would have no one but Markushev as his reader, because his high-pitched voice with its basic tone of 160 hertz would come across less clearly. (This approach put his expertise beyond doubt.) Rubin donned the earphones and repeatedly commanded Markushev to read louder or more quietly or to repeat phrases that he himself had invented to check particular sound sequences. In the end he gave it as his verdict that by and large there was a tendency to improvement, that the vowels came across just marvelously, that the unvoiced dentals were not quite so good, that he was still worried about the fuzzy edges of *zh*, and that the consonant group *vsp*, so characteristic of the Slavic languages, didn't come across at all and needed a bit more work.

There was an immediate chorus of delighted voices. So the circuit was an improvement. But Bobynin looked up from his oscillogram, and his deep voice boomed a mocking comment.

"Nonsense! It's one step forward, one step back! What we need is method!"

His unwavering stare reduced them all to embarrassed silence.

Behind his shelf-rack Potapov was gluing the pink catch to the cigarette case. Potapov had spent every day of his three years in Germany in prison camps. He had survived mainly thanks to his skill in making attractive lighters, cigarette cases, and holders from garbage and without tools.

Nobody was in any hurry to leave work! And this on the eve of their stolen Sunday!

Khorobrov straightened up. He placed on Potapov's table the things that had to be put in the safe, emerged from behind the rack, and moved unhurriedly toward the door, passing the crowd around the clipper.

Mamurin paled and barked angrily after him.

"Ilya Terentich! Why don't you have a listen? Where do you think you're going, anyway?"

Khorobrov, just as unhurriedly, turned around and answered with a twisted smile, stressing each syllable. "I would have preferred not to mention it out loud. But since you insist, I am at present on my way to the lavatory, or shall I say the john. If all goes well there, I shall proceed to the prison and go to bed."

In the scared silence that followed, Bobynin, who was hardly ever heard to laugh, guffawed.

This was mutiny on the high seas! Mamurin took a step toward Khorobrov, as though about to strike him.

"What do you mean, sleep?" he shrilled. "Everybody else is working, and you want to sleep?"

With his hand on the door handle, and scarcely containing himself, Khorobrov answered, "That's right. I just want to sleep! I've worked my twelve hours according to the Constitution, and that's enough!" He was about to explode and add something irremediable, when the door opened and the duty officer addressed Yakonov.

"Anton Nikolaich! You're wanted urgently on the outside phone."

Yakonov rose hurriedly and went out ahead of Khorobrov.

Shortly afterward, Potapov also turned off his desk lamp, transferred his own and Khorobrov's confidential papers to Bulatov's desk, and limped neither quickly nor slowly toward the door. A motorcycle accident before the war had left him lame in his right leg.

The call for Yakonov was from Vice Minister Selivanovsky summoning him to the ministry, to the Lubyanka, at twelve o'clock, midnight.

A dog's life!

Yakonov went back to his office, dismissed Nerzhin, offered Verenyov a lift, put on his street clothes, returned to his desk with his gloves on, and under "Nerzhin—write off" added "Khorobrov ditto."

# 13

# He Should Have Lied

NERZHIN WALKED BACK to the Acoustics Laboratory knowing that something irreparable had happened but unaware as yet how serious it was. When he got there, Rubin was missing. The others were all there, and Valentin, who was busy in the passageway with a panel studded with dozens of radio valves, flashed a glance at him.

"Steady there!" he said, one hand up, palm outward, like a policeman stopping a car. "Why is there no current in my third stage? Maybe you can tell me."

Then he remembered: "Ah, yes, why did they send for you? *Qu'est-ce qu'est passé?*"

Nerzhin was sullenly unforthcoming. "Cut the clowning, Valentin." He could not confess to this single-minded devotee of his own science that he had just that moment renounced mathematics.

"If you have worries, let me prescribe dance music! Anyway, what have we got to be miserable about? You've read that guy . . . what's his name? The one with the cigarette between his teeth—smoke a yard, throw two away . . . never handles a spade himself, but urges everybody else to dig . . . you know who I mean.

*With police of my own to keep watch over me*
*Safe behind bars is the best place to be.*

But another thought had claimed Val's attention, and he was already giving orders.

"Vadka! Plug in the oscilloscope, quick!"

Nerzhin went to his desk. He noticed, before sitting down, that Simochka was agitated. She stared at him openly, and her faint eyebrows twitched.

"Where's the Beard, then, Serafima Vitalievna?"

"Anton Nikolaevich sent for him as well. He wanted him in Number Seven," Simochka answered out loud. She moved over to the switchboard and spoke still louder, so that everyone could hear: "Gleb Vikentich, come and check the new word lists with me; we've still got half an hour."

Simochka was one of the readers on the articulation project. There was a standard measurement of audibility, and they were supposed to ensure that all readers kept to it.

"How can I check you in all this noise?"

"Let's go into the box." She gave Nerzhin a significant look, picked up her lists, which were written on drawing paper in India ink, and went over to the box.

Nerzhin followed her.

He bolted the hollow yard-thick door, then squeezed through the little inner door, and before he could pull down the blinds, Sima had thrown her arms around his neck and was standing on tiptoe to kiss his lips.

He picked her up—she was very light; there was so little room that the toes of her shoes knocked against the wall—sat on the only chair, in front of the microphone, and lowered her onto his knees.

"Why did Anton send for you? What was wrong? How bad was it?"

"The amplifier isn't on, is it? We don't want this relayed over the loudspeaker."

"How bad was it?"

"What makes you think it was something bad?"

"I felt it must be the moment they rang for you. And I can tell by your face."

"When are you going to call me Gleb?"

"I haven't got used to the idea yet."

The warmth of her unknown body flowed into his knees, through his hands, and upward. Unknown, mysterious as any woman's body would be to him after so many years of soldiering and prison. And not everyone has a wealth of youthful memories.

Simochka was remarkably light: Her bones might have been filled with air; she could have been made of wax—she was as weightless as a bird that looks bigger because of its feathers.

"Yes, my little girl. It looks as if . . . I will be moving shortly."

She twisted around in his arms, letting her shawl slip from her shoulders, and hugged him as hard as she could.

"Where to?"

"Why ask? We are people of the abyss. We disappear into the hole from which we surfaced . . . back to the camp," Gleb explained, as though teaching a child.

"But *why-y-y?*" she wailed.

Gleb looked wonderingly into the eyes of this plain little girl whose love he had won so unexpectedly and with so little effort. She was more anxious for him than he was himself.

"Maybe I could have stayed on. But it would have been in another lab. We still wouldn't be together."

As though this had been his reason for refusing in Anton's office! But he was stringing sounds together as mechanically as the Scrambler. In reality a prisoner's situation was so desperate that if Gleb had been transferred to another lab, he would have tried to form a relationship with some other woman working beside him, and if he had remained in the Acoustics Lab, any other woman at the next desk, whatever she looked like, would have done just as well as Simochka.

She, poor thing, pressed her little body to his and kissed him.

Why, all those weeks since their first kiss, had he spared Simochka, begrudged her the illusion of future happiness? She was unlikely to find anyone to marry her, and someone was sure to take advantage of her. She had thrown herself at him . . . afraid and eager at once. Why shouldn't he . . . before he plunged back into the camps, where there would never be the slightest chance . . .

"I wouldn't like to go away without. . . . I want to take with me the memory of. . . . What I mean is, I want to leave you with my child. . . ."

Embarrassed, she lowered her head and resisted his efforts to raise it with his fingers.

"Little bird . . . don't hide from me. Look up. Say something. Don't you want that?"

She threw back her head and spoke from deep inside herself. "I'll wait for you. How many years have you still got to do? Five? Well, I'll wait five years for you! But will you come back to me when you're released?"

She was deliberately misunderstanding him, speaking as though he were not already married. The long-nosed little thing was determined to marry him!

Gleb's wife was living right there. In Moscow somewhere, but it might as well have been on Mars.

Gleb had something else to think of, as well as Simochka, there on his knees, and his wife on Mars—those reflections on the Russian Revolution hidden away in his desk. They had cost him so much labor. Tentative sketches, but they had evoked some of his finest thoughts.

They didn't allow the smallest scrap of paper with writing on it to be taken out of the sharashka. And if anything was found when they frisked him in transit prison, he was bound to get an extra few years.

He had to lie. Make lying promises, as people always do. Then when he left Marfino, he could leave his notes with Simochka for safekeeping.

But with those eyes fixed hopefully on him, he could not lie. He ignored her question, avoided her gaze, opened her blouse, and began kissing her angular shoulders.

"You asked me once what I keep writing all the time," he said hesitantly.

"What is it, then?" Simochka asked curiously.

If she hadn't chimed in, hadn't seemed so eager, he would probably have confided in her then and there. But her eagerness put him on guard. He had lived so long in a world full of booby traps with cunningly concealed tripwires.

Those loving, trustful eyes might well be working for the security officer.

He remembered how it had all started. She had put her cheek to his! It could all be a put-up job!

"It's just history," he answered. "About the days of Peter the Great. But it's precious to me. I will carry on writing till Anton slings me out. But where can I put it all when I leave?"

His eyes searched hers suspiciously.

"Why do you ask? You can give it to me. I'll keep it safe. Keep on writing, my dear."

She had another question for him. "Tell me, is your wife very beautiful?"

The magneto-telephone connecting the booth with the lab rang suddenly. Sima pressed the knob so that she could be heard at the other end but held the receiver away from her mouth. Flushed, and with her clothes in disarray, she began reading from the test card in a flat, expressionless voice.

"*D'yer . . . fskop . . . shtap. . . .* Yes, hello, what is it, Valentin Martynych? Double diode-triode? There aren't any G-G-7s, but I think there's a 6-G-2. Let me just finish this list, and I'll be out there."

She put down the phone and snuggled up to Gleb.

"I must go. Somebody will notice. Please let me go."

But her plea was halfhearted.

He tightened his hold and pressed her whole body to his own.

"No! I let you go before, and I shouldn't have. This time I'm not going to!"

"Please! They're waiting for me! I have to close the lab!"

"I want you now! Right here!"

He kissed her.

"Not today, though!"

"So when?"

"Monday," she said submissively. "I will be on duty, instead of Lira. Come during the supper break. We will have a whole hour together. . . ."

By the time Gleb had opened the inner and unbolted the outer door, Sima had buttoned herself up and combed her hair.

She went out first, looking cold and remote.

# 14

## The Blue Light

"I WILL THROW a shoe at that blue bulb one of these days. It gets on my nerves."

"You'll miss."

"At five meters? Couldn't if I tried. Bet you tomorrow's compote?"

"You take your shoes off on the bottom bunk. Add another meter."

"Six meters, then. The things those swine think up just to aggravate the zeks. I can feel it pressing on my eyeballs all night long."

"What, the blue light?"

"Blue or not blue, light exerts pressure. Lebedev proved that. Aristipp Ivanych, you asleep? Do me a favor, hand up one of my shoes."

"I can pass you a shoe, Vyacheslav Petrovich, but tell me first what you've got against the blue light."

"For one thing it has a short wavelength and so more quanta. The quanta hit me in the eye."

"It sheds a gentle light and reminds me personally of the blue nightlight my mother used to put on for me when I was little."

"Mama's got blue shoulder boards now! But let me ask you, can people ever be trusted with real democracy? In every cell I've been in, whenever a problem arises, if it's only about washing the mess tins or sweeping the floor, every imaginable shade of opinion is expressed. Freedom would be the ruin of human beings. Only the big stick, alas, can teach us the truth."

"D'you know what ? An icon lamp would be just right here. After all, that used to be an altar."

"Not an altar, the baldachin over the altar. They've built over the altar."

"Dmitri Aleksandrych! What are you doing? Opening windows in December! Give us a break!"

"Gentlemen! It's oxygen that makes the zek immortal! In this room there are twenty-four people, and outside it's neither freezing nor blowing. See this book? It's an Ehrenburg. I'll open the window just one Ehrenburg."

"Make it one and a half! It's suffocating on these top bunks."

"When you say one Ehrenburg, do you mean sideways?"

"No, lengthwise. It fits the frame beautifully."

"It's enough to drive anybody crazy. Where's my camp overcoat?"

"I'd send all these oxygen fiends to Oy-Myakon. After twelve hours' hard labor at sixty below, they'd crawl into a goat pen as long as it was warm."

"I have nothing against oxygen in principle, but why does it always have to be cold? I'm all for warmed-up oxygen."

"Why the devil is it always so dark in this room? Why do they switch the white light off so early?"

"Valentulya, you're a twit! If you had your way, you'd be wandering around till one o'clock. Who needs light at midnight?"

"And you're a fop!

*"In a cobalt jumpsuit*
*Above me's a fop.*
*In the cozy camp zone*
*Everything's so good."*

"Who's smoking again? Why do you all smoke? Filthy habit. . . . Damn, the teapot's cold as well."

"Val, where's Lev?"

"Isn't he on his bunk?"

"I can see a couple of dozen books, but no Lev."

"So he'll be by the bathroom."

"Why by?"

"They've screwed a white bulb in, and the wall is warm from the kitchen. I dare say he's there reading. I'm just going for a wash. Any messages?"

". . . Yes, well, she puts some bedclothes on the floor for me, and lies on the bed herself. She was a juicy piece, I can tell you. Really juicy!"

"Friends, I beg you, talk about something else, anything except women. With all the meat we eat in the sharashka, that's antisocial talk."

"Now then, all you heroes! Leave it off! Lights out has sounded!"

"Never mind lights out, I think I hear the national anthem somewhere."

"I dare say you'll sleep when you're ready."

"Where's their sense of humor? They've been blaring out that anthem for five solid minutes. It's gut-wrenching! When will it ever end? Why on earth couldn't they make do with one verse?"

"One verse and the call sign, for a country like Russia?"

". . . I fought in Africa. Under Rommel. What was bad about that? Well, it was very hot, and there was no water."

"There's an island in the Arctic Ocean, Makhotkin Island. It's named after the polar aviator Makhotkin, who is now doing a stretch for anti-Soviet agitation."

"Mikhail Kuzmich, why do you keep tossing and turning?"

"Can't I turn over if I want to?"

"Of course you can, but just remember that every little turn down below is enormously amplified when it reaches me up here."

"You've managed to miss the camps so far, Ivan Ivanych. They sleep four to a bunk there. When one man turns over, the other three are seasick. Sometimes a man down below rigs up a curtain and brings a woman in, and you get a magnitude-twelve earthquake! People still manage to sleep."

"Grigory Borisych, when did you first land in a sharashka?"

"I'm thinking of putting in a pentode and a little rheostat there."

"He was a man who knew how to look after himself, a methodical man. When he kicked his shoes off at night, he wouldn't leave them on the floor; he'd put them under the pillow."

"You couldn't leave anything on the floor in those days!"

"I was in Auschwitz. The terrible thing there was that they marched people straight from the train to the gas chambers with a band playing."

"The fishing there is marvelous, and so is the hunting. Go out for an hour in the autumn, and you can come back adorned with pheasants. Step into the reed beds, and you've got boar. Walk out onto the plain, and you've got rabbits."

"All these sharashkas date from 1930, when they started rounding up engineers in droves. The first was on Furkasov. That's where they planned the White Sea Canal. Then there was the Ramzin outfit. The experiment caught on. Outside, you can never get two great engineers or two great scientists to work together on the same project. They're rivals for fame, for a Stalin Prize, and sooner or later one of them will squeeze out the other. That's why outside every project planning team is a pale penumbra around one brilliant head. But what happens in a sharashka? Nobody needs to worry about fame or money. If Nikolai Nikolaich gets half a glass of sour cream, Pyotr Petrovich gets the other half. A dozen bears can live amicably in the same den because there's nowhere else for them to go. They play a little chess, smoke a few cigarettes, and when they get bored, somebody says, 'I know, let's invent something!' 'Good idea!' Many of our scientific advances were made that way. And that's the whole point of the sharashkas."

"I've got news for you, boys! Bobynin's been driven off somewhere!"

"What d'you mean, driven off?"

"The junior lieutenant came and said, 'Get your hat and coat on.' "

"Did he have to take his gear?"

"No gear."

"One of the top brass must have sent for him."

"Foma, maybe?"

"Foma would have come here. Aim a bit higher!"

"The tea's gone cold. It's a dog's life!"

"Val, boy, you're always rattling that spoon in your glass after lights out! I'm sick and tired of it!"

"So how am I supposed to stir my tea?"

"Noiselessly."

"Nothing happens noiselessly. Except cosmic catastrophes, because sound doesn't travel in outer space. If a nova exploded right behind us, we wouldn't hear it. Ruska, your blanket's falling off. Why don't you tuck it in? You asleep? Do you realize that our sun is a nova and that the earth is doomed to destruction in the very near future?"

"I refuse to believe it. I'm still young, and I want to live!"

"Ha-ha! How primitive! . . . Such cold tea! *C'est le mot!* . . . Wants to live!"

"Val, boy, where've they taken Bobynin?

"How should I know? To see Stalin, maybe."

"What would you do if Stalin sent for you, Val?"

"Me? Boy, oh boy! I would present him with a full list of complaints."

"Such as?"

"I've told you—every single one. *Par exemple*, why do we have to do without women? It cramps our creative potential."

"Pryanchik! Put a sock in it! Everybody's fast asleep. Why are you shouting your head off?"

"What if I don't want to sleep?"

"Anybody smoking? Keep it out of sight. The junior lieutenant's coming."

"What's the bastard want now? . . . Mind you, don't trip, Citizen Junior Lieutenant; you might get a bloody nose!"

"Pryanchikov!"

"Eh?"

"Where are you? Not asleep yet?"

"Yes, I'm asleep."

"Get dressed quickly."

"What for? I want my sleep."

"I said get dressed. Get your hat and coat on."

"What about my things?"

"Never mind your things. Transport's waiting. Hurry up."

"Am I going with Bobynin?"

"Bobynin's gone already. Another one's come for you."

"Another what, lieutenant? Meat wagon?"

"Come on, hurry up. No, it's a Pobeda."

"Who's sent for me?"

"Come on, Pryanchikov. That's enough questions. I don't know the answer myself. Get a move on."

"Give them an earful, Val!"

"Tell them about visits!"

"Shouldn't Section 58 prisoners get one visit a year?"

"Tell them about exercise periods."

"And letters!"

"And our uniforms!"

"Workers of the world, unite! Ha-ha! Adieu!"

". . . Comrade Junior Lieutenant, where on earth is Pryanchikov?"

"I'm bringing him, Comrade Major! Here he is!"

"Sock it to them, Val boy. Every bit of it! Don't be shy!"

"The filth are mighty busy in the middle of the night!"

"Wonder what's happened?"

"Never saw anything like this before!"

"Maybe war's broken out? Maybe they're taking them to be shot?"

"Idiot! D'you think they'd take us one at a time? When war comes, they'll mow us down wholesale. Or put something in the mush to infect us with plague, like the Germans did in concentration camps in '45."

"Leave it now, let's get some sleep. We'll hear all about it in the morning."

"I remember Beria sending for Boris Sergeevich Stechkin in 1939–40. He never came back to the sharashka empty-handed. Either the prison governor would be replaced, or exercise periods would be prolonged. . . . Stechkin couldn't stand the differential rationing system: Academicians were bribed with cream and eggs, professors got forty grams of the best butter, and ordinary workhorses only twenty. . . . A good man, Boris Sergeevich, God rest him."

"Is he dead, then?"

"No. He was released. He got a Stalin Prize."

## 15

# A Girl! A Girl!

At last even Abramson, who had served two sentences and learned all about sharashkas the first time around, tired of murmuring. In two places whispered stories were nearing their end. Somebody was snoring loudly, horribly, sounding at times as if he was about to burst.

The blue light over the four-paneled door set in the vaulted entrance shed a dim light on a dozen double bunks, fastened together in pairs and arranged fanwise around the large semicircular room. This room, probably the only one of its kind in Moscow, was twelve good masculine strides in diameter. Up above, there was a spacious dome, at the base of a hexagonal tower. Around the dome there were five elegant arched windows. The windows were barred but not "muzzled" (fitted with inverted awnings), so that in daytime you could see the wilderness that passed for a park on the other side of the highway, and on summer evenings the plaintive singing of husbandless girls in a Moscow suburb troubled the prisoners' minds.

Nerzhin, on the top bunk by the central window, was not even trying to sleep. Down below, Potapov, the engineer, had been sleeping the untroubled sleep of an honest workingman for some time. On the next bunk to the left, the moonfaced vacuum-tube expert, Zemelya, sprawled and snuffled contentedly, with Pryanchikov's empty bed beneath him, while to the right, on a bunk set right against Nerzhin's own, Ruska Doronin, one of the youngest zeks in the sharashka, was sleeplessly tossing and turning.

As the conversation in Yakonov's office receded, Nerzhin saw more and more clearly that his refusal to join the cryptographic group was not just an episode in his professional career but the turning point in his life as a whole.

It was bound to earn him, probably very soon, a long and grueling trek to somewhere in Siberia or the Arctic. It would mean death—or victory over death.

He needed to think about this abrupt change of direction. What had he achieved during this three-year breathing space in the sharashka? Was he now tough enough to stand being tossed back into the abyss of the camps?

As it happened, the following day was Gleb's thirty-first birthday. (He did not, of course, feel like reminding his friends of it.) Was he at the midpoint of his life? Near the end? Just beginning?

His thoughts blurred. At one minute he found himself weakly imagining that it was not too late; he could put things right, agree to join the cryptographers. Then he began remembering his grievance—that they had kept postponing his wife's visit for eleven months now—and wondering whether they would let him see her before he left.

But then his other self awoke and flexed its muscles. The breadlines of the First Five-Year Plan had transformed a diffident boy into a different Nerzhin, brash and defiant, and the life he had led since, especially in the camps, had left him still tougher. His sturdy inner self was already busily calculating how often he would be searched—as he left Marfino, on admission to Butyrki, on admission to Krasnaya Presnya; how to conceal fragments of pencil lead in his jacket; how to smuggle his old overalls out of the sharashka (every extra layer is precious to a working stiff); how to prove that the aluminum teaspoon he had carried around ever since he had been inside was his own, not stolen from the sharashka, which had almost identical ones.

He even felt a restless urge to get up then and there, in the dim light, and begin his preparations, start rearranging and hiding.

All this time Ruska Doronin kept impatiently changing his position. One minute he was lying on his stomach, burying himself in his pillow, and pulling the blanket over his head so that his feet were uncovered; the next he would be flat on his back, flinging off the blanket and exposing a white bedspread and a dingy sheet. (One of the two sheets was changed every bath day, but by December the sharashka had overspent its yearly soap allowance, and bath day was delayed.) Suddenly he sat up in bed, hoisted himself, pillow and all, up against the iron back, and opened a hefty volume of Mommsen's *History of Rome*. Noticing that Nerzhin was awake and staring up at the blue bulb, Ruska asked in a hoarse whisper:

"Gleb, have you got any cigarettes handy? Give me one."

Ruska did not smoke as a rule. Nerzhin reached over to the pocket of his overalls, which was hanging on the back of the bunk. He took out two cigarettes, and they both lit up.

Ruska concentrated on his smoking and did not look at Nerzhin. His face, which was always changing its expression—at one moment it was naive and boyish, at the next the face of a trickster of genius—under its mop of unruly dark-blond hair looked attractive even in the ghastly light from the blue bulb.

"Here," said Nerzhin, putting an empty Belomor pack where Ruska could use it as an ashtray.

They tapped their ash into it.

Ruska had been in the sharashka since summer. Nerzhin took an immediate liking to him and felt an urge to protect him.

But it was soon evident that Ruska, though only twenty-three (and with twenty-five years of imprisonment hanging over him), needed no protector. His character and outlook had been fully formed by the vicissitudes of a short but turbulent life—not so much by his four weeks of university education, two in Moscow, two in Leningrad, as by two years on the run, with forged documents and the whole Soviet police force on his trail (he had sworn Gleb to absolute secrecy when he told him), and most recently by two years of prison. With his gift of instant mimicry, he had quickly mastered the wolfish law of the Gulag: He was always on his guard and confided in very few people, though on the surface he was childishly candid. He was feverishly active and tried to pack a great deal into a short time. Reading was just one of his many activities.

Gleb, wearying of his muddled thoughts, was still not ready for sleep and judged that Ruska was even less so. He whispered a question in the hushed room:

"Well, how's the theory of cycles going?"

They had been discussing this theory not long ago, and Ruska had meant to look for confirmation of it in Mommsen.

Ruska turned around at Nerzhin's whisper but looked blank. He wrinkled his brow, struggling to make sense of the question.

"I mean, how's the theory of historical cycles going?"

Ruska sighed, and as he released his breath, his face and his restless mind also relaxed. He leaned sideways, shifted his weight onto his elbow, tossed his cigarette, which had gone out half smoked, into the empty pack Nerzhin had put next to him, and said dully: "I'm sick of everything. Books and theories included."

They were silent again. Nerzhin was about to turn onto his other side when Ruska gave a laugh and began whispering, gathering speed as he warmed to his subject:

"History is so monotonous that it makes you sick to read it. It's as bad as *Pravda*. The nobler and more honorable a man is, the dirtier the treatment his fellow countrymen hand out to him. Spurius Cassius wanted to get land for the common people, and the common people let him be put to death. Spurius Melius wanted to give bread to the hungry people, was suspected of wanting to be king, and was executed. Marcus Manlius, the one who was awakened by the cackling of the geese in all the schoolbooks and saved the Capitol, was executed for treason! What do you think of that?"

"You amaze me!"

"Read enough history, and you'll want to be a villain yourself. It pays better. If it hadn't been for the great Hannibal, we would never have heard of Carthage, but the wretched place banished him, confiscated his property, and razed his dwelling to the ground! There's nothing new under the sun. All that time ago, Gnaeus Naevius was put in the stocks for writing daring plays. The Aetolians, long before we thought of it, proclaimed a false amnesty to entice émigrés back home and put them to death. The Romans had already arrived at a truth that the Gulag keeps forgetting: It's uneconomic to let a slave go hungry; you must feed him. The whole of history is one unmitigated fuck-up. It's every man for himself and the devil take the hindmost. There's neither truth nor error, no progress, no future."

The ghastly blue light made the disillusionment trembling on those young lips more painful to see.

It was partly Nerzhin's doing that Ruska had begun to think this way, but hearing it from Ruska now made him want to protest. Among his older friends Gleb's role was destructive criticism, but he felt some responsibility toward this young prisoner.

"A word to the wise, Rostislav," he replied very quietly, leaning over so that he was almost speaking into his neighbor's ear. "However clever and ungainsayable such philosophical systems as skepticism or agnosticism or pessimism may be, you must remember that they are in their very nature condemned to impotence. They cannot govern human activity, because people cannot stand still and so cannot do without systems that affirm something, that point to some destination."

"Even if the goal is a quagmire? Anywhere, just as long as we press on?" Ruska retorted.

"Even if . . ." Gleb hesitated. "Hell, I don't know. Look, I myself think that mankind has a great need of skepticism. We need it to crack open rock-hard heads, to choke fanatical throats. It is needed here more than anywhere, yet it establishes itself on Russian soil with more than usual difficulty. But skepticism cannot give a man a firm footing. And that is something he must have."

"Give me another cigarette."

Ruska lit up and puffed nervously.

"You know, it's a good thing the MGB didn't let me go on studying. And end up as a historian."

He pronounced each word distinctly, in a loud whisper.

"Suppose I'd graduated, and gone on to do postgraduate work, like an idiot. Say I had become a scholar, and maybe not a venal hack, though that's a big maybe. Say I'd written a fat book taking a fresh look (the eight hundred and third) at ancient Novgorod's administrative system, or Caesar's war with the Helvetians. . . . There are so many cultures in the world! So many languages! So many countries! So many clever people, and still more clever books, in every one of them! What sort of idiot would want to read it all? What was that quotation of yours? 'The conclusions arrived at by experts with such difficulty will be shown by other, still greater, experts to be illusory.' Was that it?"

"Steady now," Nerzhin admonished him. "You're cutting the ground from under your feet. You're leaving yourself nothing to aim at. We can doubt, we must doubt. But we must have something to love, don't you think?"

Ruska seized on the word. "To love! Yes, something to love," he crowed. "But not history, not theory—a girl." He leaned over toward Nerzhin's bed and seized his elbow. "What is the most important thing they've deprived us of, would you say? The right to attend meetings? Politics classes? The right to subscribe to State Loans? The one and only thing that the Big Chief could do to hurt us was to deprive us of women! So that's what he has done. For twenty-five years! The swine! I wonder if anybody realizes," he said, beating his breast, "what a woman means to a prisoner?"

"You can go mad that way!" Nerzhin protested, but a sudden warmth welled up in him when he thought of Sima and her promise for Monday evening. . . . "Get it out of your head! Or your mind will black out altogether." (Ah, but on Monday . . . the thing that comfortable married people take for granted, but that becomes a raging, feverish animal need in a desperate prisoner!) "What does Freud call it?" His voice was getting weaker as his own thoughts grew muddled. "Sublimation—that's it! Switch your energy to other matters! Study philosophy, and you'll need neither bread nor water nor a woman's caresses."

(But he shivered as he pictured in detail what it would be like the day after tomorrow. This unbearably delicious thought robbed him of speech.)

"My mind is fogged already! I won't get to sleep all night! A girl! Everybody needs a girl! To hold her in your arms. To . . . oh, what's the use?" Ruska carelessly dropped his cigarette onto the bedding, turned over abruptly, flopped on his belly, and tugged the blanket over his head, exposing his feet.

Nerzhin grabbed the smoldering cigarette just as it was about to slip between the bunks onto Potapov down below and stubbed it out.

He had recommended philosophy to Ruska as a refuge, but it was one in which he heard himself howling like a caged animal. Ruska's youth had been spent on the run with the whole Soviet police force behind him, and now prison had him in its clutches. But what about me? Gleb asked himself. What held me back when I was seventeen, or nineteen, and hot gales of passion darkened my mind? He had curbed himself, suppressed his urges, wallowed in the dialectic like a piglet burying its snout in muck, grunting and guzzling, afraid of missing something. The years before his marriage, his irrecoverable misspent youth, were now, in prison after prison, his bitterest memory. He had been helplessly ignorant, had no idea how to relieve his fits of madness, lacked the words with which to draw someone close, the tone of voice that women yield to. He was also inhibited by an old-fashioned concern for female virtue, and there was no older and wiser woman to lay a gentle hand on his shoulder. Or rather, one such woman had called to him, and he had not understood. Later, on the floor of a prison cell, he had gone over it all in his mind, remembered that lost chance and all those wasted years, and these memories were like red-hot needles in his brain.

Never mind—less than forty-eight hours to get through until Monday evening.

Gleb leaned over and whispered in his neighbor's ear. "Ruska! What about you? Is there somebody?"

"Yes, there is." He spoke in a painful whisper, lying flat on his back and clutching his pillow. He was breathing into it, and the heat returned by the pillow, and all the heat of his youth that was wasting away so uselessly in prison fevered the trapped young body that cried out for and had no hope of relief. He had said, "Yes, there is," and he wanted to believe that there was a girl; but what he had was something elusive, indefinable . . . not a kiss, not even a promise, only the memory of how one evening a girl had listened to his stories about himself with a look of compassion and fascination, and her look had made Ruska for the first time feel that he was a hero and his life story a remarkable one. Nothing had happened between them as yet, but enough had happened for him to say that he did indeed have a girl.

Gleb continued questioning him. "So who is she?"

Rostislav peeked from under the blanket and answered in the darkness.

"It's . . . it's Klara."

"Klara? The prosecutor's daughter?"

## 16

# A Troika of Liars

THE HEAD OF the Department of Special Assignments was near the end of his report to Minister Abakumov. It dealt with the timing of lethal acts abroad in the coming year, 1950, and who exactly should carry them out. The program of political assassinations had been approved in principle by Stalin before he went on vacation.

Abakumov, a tall man made taller by elevator shoes, with black hair slicked back from his brow, was wearing the shoulder boards of a colonel general. He sat with his elbows planted masterfully on his imposing desk. He was large but not fat (he took care of his figure and even played tennis from time to time). His eyes were quick, shrewd, and suspicious.

He dictated the necessary corrections to the department head, who hastened to write them down.

Abakumov's office, though not quite a hall, was more than just a room. There was a disused marble fireplace and a tall mirror, the ceiling was high and molded, nymphs and amoretti chased each other across it, and there was a chandelier (the minister had ordained that all should remain as before, except that the green parts were painted over, since that was a color he couldn't stand). There was a balcony door, bolted and barred winter and summer. Nor were the big windows looking out on the square ever opened. Timepieces on view were one grandfather clock with an exquisite case, one chiming mantelpiece clock with a figurine, one electric wall clock of the sort seen at railway stations. These were somewhat at odds as to the time, but Abakumov was never misled, because he also had two gold watches on his person: one on his hairy wrist and one (with an alarm) in his pocket.

Offices in this building grew larger as occupants rose in rank. So did desks. So did the conference tables with their dark blue, scarlet, or blush pink cloths. But nothing grew with such zealous haste as the portraits of the Inspirer and Organizer of Victories. Even in the offices of simple investigators he was portrayed much larger than life, and in Abakumov's office the Leader of Mankind had been painted by a member of the school of Kremlin realists on a canvas five meters high, full length from his shoes to his marshal's cap, ablaze with all his decorations, which in real life he never wore, most of them conferred on himself by himself, some few the gift of kings and presidents, no longer, however, including the Yugoslav orders, which had been skillfully dabbed out with paint matching his tunic.

It appeared, however, that Abakumov found this five-meter image inadequate, that he felt a need to be inspired at every minute by the sight of the Counterespionage Agent's Best Friend, even when he had his eyes on his papers, for on his desk he also had an upright slab of rhodonite with a bas-relief of Stalin.

Furthermore, a portrait of Abakumov's immediate superior, a simpering person in pince-nez, was roomily accommodated on one wall.

When the head of the Death Department had left, three men entered in single file, and in single file they crossed the patterned carpet: Deputy Minister Selivanovsky, the head of the Special Technology Department; Major General Oskolupov; and the chief engineer of that department, Engineer Colonel Yakonov.

In strict order of seniority, and with a meticulous show of respect for the occupant of the office, they marched forward in step, so that only Selivanovsky's feet were heard.

Selivanovsky, a lean old man with close-cropped grizzled hair, wearing a gray suit of unmilitary cut, occupied a unique position among the minister's ten deputies: He was in charge not of security officers or investigators but of communications and delicate secret technology. This meant that his master's anger was less frequently visited on him, in conference and in ministerial orders. He was more at ease in this office than the others and promptly sat down in the overstuffed leather armchair facing Abakumov's desk.

With Selivanovsky seated, Oskolupov was front man. Yakonov stood close behind him, apparently trying to conceal his bulk.

Abakumov saw Oskolupov thus suddenly revealed to him, perhaps for the third time in his life, and found the man rather to his liking. Oskolupov was on the plump side, his neck strained at the collar of his tunic, and his chin, obsequiously drawn in, would soon be a double one. His leathery face, more heavily pockmarked than that of the Leader himself, was the simple, honest face of a man who carries out orders, not that of a know-it-all intellectual with crackpot ideas.

Abakumov squinted over Oskolupov's shoulder at Yakonov and asked who he was.

"Me?" Oskolupov was dismayed to find himself unrecognized.

"Me?" Yakonov said, bending slightly sideways. He drew in his rebellious soft belly as best he could—for all his efforts it kept growing—and his big blue eyes were blank as he presented himself.

"Yes, you," the minister said sniffily. "Marfino's your outfit, is it? Right, sit down."

They sat.

The minister picked up a ruby red Plexiglas paper knife, scratched himself behind the ear with it, and spoke again.

"Let's see . . . how long have you been pulling the wool over my eyes? Two years, is it? And the plan allowed you fifteen months, was it? When will the two prototypes be ready?" He shook his fist in warning. "No lies! I don't like lies!"

This was the very question for which the three high-placed liars had prepared themselves when they learned that they were to appear together. Oskolupov spoke first, as they had arranged. Bracing his shoulders as though to catapult himself at the all-powerful minister, and gazing triumphantly into his eyes, Oskolupov said: "Comrade Minister! Comrade Colonel General!" (Abakumov preferred this to "Commissar General.") "Permit me to assure you that the personnel of my department will spare no efforts—"

"What do you think this is? A public meeting? What am I supposed to do with your efforts? Wrap my backside in them? I'm asking you for a date."

He took out a gold-nibbed fountain pen and aimed it at a seven-day calendar.

Yakonov then intervened, according to plan, his subdued voice emphasizing that he spoke as a technician, not an administrator.

"Comrade Minister! Within a frequency range of up to 2,400 hertz, at an average transmission level of zero point nine nepers . . ."

"Hertz, hertz, hertz—that's all I ever get from you—zero point nine hertz, might as well be the square root of zilch. I want those instruments! Two of them! Whole ones! When do I get them? Eh?"

He eyed the three of them in turn.

Selivanovsky now took the floor, speaking slowly, stroking his gray-and-white crew cut.

"May I inquire what exactly you have in mind, Viktor Semyonovich? Two-way conversations can't yet be perfectly encoded. . . ."

The minister shot him a glance.

"Do you take me for an idiot? What's it mean, can't be encoded?"

Fifteen years ago, when Abakumov was not a minister, and neither he nor anyone else foresaw that he ever would be (he was in fact a sergeant major in the NKVD, being a big, strapping fellow with long arms and legs), his four years of elementary education had sufficed. He sought to improve his qualifications only in jujitsu. All his training was done in the gymnasiums of the Dynamo Sports Club.

Then, in the years when the ranks of the interrogation service were drastically thinned, while the need for interrogators grew just as rapidly, Abakumov was found to have a talent for the job, his long arms making deft and damaging contact with a prisoner's ugly mug. That was the beginning of a great career. Within seven years he was head of the counterespionage agency, SMERSH, now he was a minister, and not once in his steep ascent had he felt undereducated. And even here, at the top of the tree, he was too shrewd to be bamboozled by subordinates.

Abakumov was getting angry and was about to bring down on his desk a clenched fist the size of a cobblestone, when the high door opened and Mikhail Dmitrievich Ryumin came in without knocking. Ryumin was a short, rotund cherub with nice rosy cheeks whom everyone in the ministry called Minka—few of them, however, to his face.

He walked as noiselessly as a kitten. Drawing near, he turned his innocent light eyes on those seated there, shook hands with Selivanovsky (who rose slightly from his chair), went to the side of the minister's desk, and, inclining his head and lightly stroking the grooved edge of the desktop with his plump little hands, purred reflectively: "You know, Viktor Semyonovich, I think this is a job for Selivanovsky. We don't pay the Special Technical Department for nothing, do we? Surely they can identify a voice from a tape? If they can't, we should send them all packing."

He smiled as sweetly as if he were offering a little girl chocolate. And gave each of the department's three representatives an affectionate look.

Ryumin had lived for many years in complete obscurity as a bookkeeper in a consumers' cooperative in the Archangel oblast.* A pink and puffy man with a peevish mouth, he had needled his ledger clerks with every malicious remark he could think of, sucked fruit drops incessantly and offered them to the warehouse manager, talked to truck drivers diplomatically, to cart drivers arrogantly, and submitted documents for the chairman's signature on time.

But during the war he had been drafted into the navy and trained as a Special Department interrogator. That was where Ryumin had come into his own. He had eagerly and successfully mastered the art of the frame-up. (Perhaps he had always had half an eye on this great advance?) In fact, his zeal had once proved excessive. He had concocted such a crude case against a newspaper correspondent attached to the Northern Fleet that the prosecutor's office, always so subservient to the "Organs," balked—and did not, of course, put a stop to it but did get up the nerve to alert Abakumov. Abakumov summoned the little SMERSH investigator to discipline him. He entered the office timidly, expecting to lose his bulbous head. The door closed. When it opened again an hour later, Ryumin emerged full of importance, henceforth senior investigator of special cases at SMERSH headquarters. His star had risen steadily ever since (ominously for Abakumov, but neither of them knew that as yet).

"I'll send the lot of them packing anyway, Mikhail Dmitrich, believe you me! When I've finished with them, they'll wonder what hit them!" Abakumov said, looking angrily at all three.

They lowered their eyes guiltily.

"But," Abakumov went on, "I just don't understand. I mean, how can you identify somebody from a voice over the telephone? An unknown person? Where do you start looking?"

"Well, I'll give these three the taped call. They can play about with it, and compare it . . ."

"You mean you've made an arrest?"

* Oblast: A province, or area, that serves as a subnational administrative division of the state.

"What do you think?" Ryumin said with his sweet smile. "Four men were picked up near the Sokolniki metro station."

A shadow flitted over his face. He knew in his own mind that by the time they were picked up, it was too late. But once arrested, they couldn't just be released. One of them might have to be processed so that the case would not remain officially unsolved.

There was a hint of irritation in Ryumin's obsequious voice:

"What's more, I'll tape half the Ministry of Foreign Affairs for them if you like. But that would be overdoing it. We need only pick one of the five or perhaps seven people in the ministry who could have the information."

Abakumov was indignant.

"So arrest every one of the bastards. Why beat your brains out over it? What are seven people? Ours is a big country; we won't run out of population!"

"Can't be done, Viktor Semyonovich," Ryumin replied judiciously. "The Foreign Ministry isn't like the Ministry of the Food Industry. That way we would lose the trail completely, and besides, somebody in one of the embassies might skip out and join the non-returners. We simply have to find out exactly who it was. And as quickly as possible."

"Hmm," Abakumov said thoughtfully. "Only I don't understand what we're comparing with what."

"One tape with another."

"One tape with another? . . . Right, do you think you'll have the know-how sometime, Selivanovsky?"

"I still don't understand what this is all about, Viktor Semyonovich."

"What is there to understand? There's nothing hard about it. Some bastard, some dirty rat, probably a diplomat—otherwise he would have had no means of knowing about it—called the American embassy from a phone booth and ratted out our intelligence agents over there. It has to do with the atom bomb. Finger him and you'll be a hero."

Selivanovsky looked past Oskolupov at Yakonov. Yakonov met his gaze and raised his eyebrows slightly. This was intended to mean that the whole thing was unprecedented, that the methodology did not exist, that they had no background, that they had enough to worry about as it was, that they should leave this alone. Selivanovsky was intelligent enough to understand this twitch of Yakonov's eyebrows and the whole situation, and was preparing to muddy the waters.

But Foma Guryanovich Oskolupov had been doing some thinking of his own. As head of department he was determined not to be a mere figurehead. Since his appointment to that post, he had become more and more convinced of his superior merits, and he fully believed that he could master all the department's problems and solve them more easily than anyone else; otherwise he would not have been appointed. Although he had only an elementary education, he could not entertain the idea that any subordinate of his could understand their business better than he, except perhaps for matters of detail or situations where some minor adjustment was needed. He had recently been at a first-class health resort, where he had worn civilian dress instead of uniform and had passed himself off as a professor of electronics. He had met there the eminent writer Kazakevich, who had not been able to take his eyes off him. Kazakevich kept taking notes and said that in Foma Guryanovich he had found the model for his portrait of a modern scientist. After this stay in the sanatorium, Foma felt every inch a scientist.

On this occasion, too, he understood the problem instantly and took the bit between his teeth.

"Comrade Minister! Of course we can do it!"

Selivanovsky looked round at him in surprise.

"Which establishment can we do it in? Which laboratory?" he asked.

"The telephone lab at Marfino. You said it's a telephone call, didn't you? Right, then."

"But Marfino is working on a more important assignment."

"Never mind. We'll find somebody to do it. There are three hundred people there; surely we can find somebody?"

He stared with doglike eagerness at the minister.

Abakumov didn't quite smile, but his face again expressed approval of the general. He had been just the same on his way up: Show me the enemy, and I'll smash him to pulp. We all like juniors who resemble ourselves.

"Good man!" he said approvingly. "That's the way to look at it! The state's interests are what matter! Everything else is secondary. Right?"

"Precisely, Comrade Minister! Precisely, Comrade Colonel General!"

Ryumin was apparently not at all surprised or impressed by the selfless dedication of the pockmarked major general. With a casual glance at Selivanovsky, he said:

"I'll come and see you tomorrow, then."

He exchanged a look with Abakumov and left the room, treading softly.

The minister explored his teeth with a finger, removing remnants of the meat he had eaten for supper.

"Well, then, when is it going to be? You've led me on long enough—to begin with, it was the first of August, then it was the October holiday, then the New Year. . . . What about it?"

He looked hard at Yakonov, forcing him to answer for himself.

Yakonov seemed to have difficulty in finding a comfortable position for his neck. He bent it slightly to the right, then slightly to the left; he raised his chilly blue eyes to look at the minister, and then lowered them again.

Yakonov knew that he was very clever. Yakonov knew, too, that people even cleverer than himself, people whose minds were on their work for fourteen hours a day, all year round, with not a single day off, were concentrating on that accursed contrivance. . . . The recklessly generous Americans, who publicized their inventions in generally available journals, were also indirectly participating. Yakonov knew as well the thousands of difficulties already overcome and the fresh ones through which his engineers were struggling like swimmers in a heavy sea. Yes, the very last of the absolutely final deadlines for which they had pleaded with this lump of meat buttoned up in a tunic was only six days away. But they had been forced to plead for and agree to ridiculous deadlines only because the Coryphaeus of Sciences had at the very beginning allowed a single year for what was really ten years' work.

Now they had agreed, in Selivanovsky's office, to ask for a reprieve of ten days. They would promise two prototypes of the telephone device by January 10. This was what the deputy minister had insisted on. And what Oskolupov wanted. Their intention was to produce something, half finished but freshly painted. For the time being, nobody would test, indeed nobody would know how to test, the absolute reliability of the coding. Before it reached the stage of serial production, and before sets were dispatched to Soviet embassies abroad, another half year would have elapsed, and both the coding and the sound quality would have been put right.

But Yakonov also knew that inanimate objects ignore deadlines set by men, and that what would emerge from the apparatus on January 10 was not human speech but gibberish. And what had befallen Mamurin would inevitably be repeated with Yakonov: The Boss would call Beria in and ask, "What idiot made this machine? Get rid of him." And Yakonov would become at best another "Iron Mask," but more probably an ordinary zek once again.

With the minister's eyes on him, he felt the noose tightening round his neck. He fought down his craven fear and blurted out as if gasping for breath: "Another month! Just one more month! Till February the first!"

He looked imploringly, almost doglike, at Abakumov.

Talented people are sometimes unfair to mediocrities. Abakumov was cleverer than Yakonov supposed. It was just that prolonged lack of exercise had rendered the minister's brain useless to him. His whole career had worked out in such a way that thinking had always brought setbacks, whereas zealous subordination had always brought gain. Abakumov therefore tried to avoid mental exertion as far as possible.

He probably knew in his heart that ten days or even a month would not help when two years had already gone by. But in his eyes the blame rested on this trio of liars; Selivanovsky, Oskolupov, and Yakonov had only themselves to blame. If the job was so difficult, why, when they took it on twenty-three months ago, had they agreed to a year? Why hadn't they asked for three? (He had forgotten that he himself had put them under merciless pressure.) If they had dug their heels in with Abakumov, Abakumov would have dug his heels in with Stalin; they could have settled for two years and stretched it to three.

But the terror secreted in them during so many years of subjugation was so great that not one of them, then or now, had the courage to stand up to his superiors.

Abakumov's own practice was to allow himself some leeway, and when he was dealing with Stalin, he always added a couple of months. On this occasion Iosif Vissarionovich had been promised that one sample of a Scrambler telephone would be placed before him by March 1. So that in the last resort they could be allowed an extra month, but it must really be a month and no more.

Abakumov took up his fountain pen again and asked quite simply:

"When you say a month, are you using ordinary human language or bullshitting again?"

"Exactly one month! Exactly." Delighted by this happy outcome, Oskolupov beamed as though he were eager to take off directly for Marfino and seize a soldering iron himself.

Abakumov scribbled a note in his desk diary.

"That's it, then. By the Lenin anniversary. You'll all get Stalin Prizes. Selivanovsky, will it be ready?"

"It will! It will!"

"Oskolupov, I'll have your head, remember. Will it be ready?"

"Well, Comrade Minister, all it needs now is . . ."

"What about you, Yakonov? You know what you stand to lose? Will it be ready?"

Yakonov stuck to his guns.

"One month! By February first."

"And if it isn't? Think about it, Colonel. Colonel! You're lying, aren't you?"

Of course he was lying. And of course he should have asked for two months. But what was done could not be undone.

"It'll be there, Comrade Minister," he promised miserably.

"Remember, I didn't put the words in your mouth. I can forgive anything but not deception! Off you go now."

With lighter hearts they trooped out, as they had come, in single file, averting their eyes before the icon of the five-meter Stalin.

Their rejoicing was premature. They did not know that the minister had set a trap for them.

As soon as they had been shown out, a new arrival was announced: "Engineer Pryanchikov!"

## 17

## Hot Water

THAT NIGHT ABAKUMOV HAD BEGUN by ordering Selivanovsky to produce Yakonov. Then, without letting any of the others know, he had sent two telephoned telegrams to Marfino at fifteen-minute intervals, summoning to the ministry the zek Bobynin, then the zek Pryanchikov. The two were delivered in separate cars and made to wait in different rooms with no opportunity to concoct a story.

Pryanchikov was in any case hardly capable of doing so. His natural candor was such that many a sober child of the times considered him mentally deficient. "A phase shift" was their term for it in the sharashka.

Just now he was even less capable of collusion or prevarication than usual. He was still dazed by brilliant visions of Moscow speeding dizzily past the Pobeda's windows. After the suburban gloom surrounding the camp area at Marfino, driving out onto the brilliantly lit highway, then on toward the cheerful bustle of the station, and on again to the neon-lit shop windows of the Sretenka came as a shock. For Pryanchikov neither the driver nor his two companions in plainclothes existed; it was as though he were inhaling and exhaling flame, not air. He could not tear himself away from the window. He had never been driven through Moscow even in the daytime, and in the whole history of the sharashka not a single prisoner had ever seen Moscow by night.

At the Sretenka Gate the car was held up by the crowd leaving the cinema and then by a traffic light.

Prisoners in their millions imagined that in their absence life outside had come to a halt, that there were no men left, and that women were pining away with no one to share, no one needing their love. But Valentin saw the well-fed, animated metropolitan crowd surging past, caught glimpses of hats, veils, silver-fox furs; and his tingling senses were assailed through the frosty air, through the solid bodywork of the car, by wave after wave after wave of perfume from the women walking by. He heard laughter, the buzz of voices, tantalizing fragments of conversation, and he wanted to smash the plastic glass and cry out to those women, tell them that he was young, that he was full of longing, that he was in prison for no reason! After the monastic seclusion of the sharashka, this was a fairy-tale world, a taste of the high life that he had never had the luck to lead as a penniless student, then a prisoner of war, then a prisoner.

Afterward, waiting in a room of some sort, Pryanchikov looked right through the tables and chairs that stood there. The emotions and impressions that had him in their grip were reluctant to let him go.

A glossy young lieutenant colonel asked Pryanchikov to follow him. With his scraggy neck, his thin wrists, his narrow shoulders, and his skinny legs, he had never looked like such a weakling as when his escort left him at a door and he entered Abakumov's office.

He did not even realize that it was an office—it was so spacious—and that it belonged to the pair of golden shoulder boards at the end of the great room. Nor did he notice the five-meter Stalin at his back. Nocturnal Moscow and its women were still passing before his eyes. Valentin might have been drunk. He just could not conceive why he was in this hall and what sort of hall it was. He would not have been surprised if beautifully dressed women had come in and started dancing. How ludicrous to imagine that somewhere, in a semicircular room lit by a single blue lightbulb, though the war had ended five years ago, he had left unfinished a glass of cold tea and men were puttering around in their underwear.

His feet were treading on carpet, wastefully laid on the floor. The carpet had a soft, deep pile, and you just wanted to roll on it. There was a row of big windows in the right wall, and on the left side of the room a tall mirror reached down to the floor.

Free men don't appreciate things! To a zek, who cannot always get to a cheap little mirror smaller than the palm of his hand, looking at himself in a big mirror is a treat!

Pryanchikov halted, drawn to the mirror as if by a magnet. He went up close to it and examined his clean, fresh face with satisfaction. He adjusted his tie a little, then the collar of his blue shirt. Then he backed away slowly, inspecting himself *en face*, at an angle, and in profile. He concluded these evolutions with a sort of dance step. Then he went up close to the mirror again and examined himself thoroughly. Gratified to find himself quite handsome and elegant, in spite of his blue overalls, he moved on, not meaning to get down to business (he had forgotten all about that) but intending to continue his survey of the room.

Meanwhile, the man who could imprison anyone he pleased in one half of the world, and in the other half have anyone he pleased murdered, the all-powerful minister, in whose presence generals and marshals turned pale, was watching this puny zek with curiosity. He had arrested and condemned them by the million, but it was a long time since he had seen one at close quarters.

Pryanchikov minced toward the minister and looked at him inquiringly, as though he had not expected to find him there.

"You are Engineer . . . er . . . " Abakumov consulted his scrap of paper.

"Er, yes," said Valentin absently. "Pryanchikov."

"You're a senior engineer in the group working on the, er . . . " He glanced at his notes again. ". . . artificial speech device?"

"What? What d'you mean, artificial speech device?" Pryanchikov waved a hand dismissively. "Nobody at our place calls it that. They changed its name during the campaign against kowtowing to foreign science. It's a vocoder. Voice coder. Or scrambler."

"Anyway, you're the senior engineer."

"I suppose so. What about it?" said Pryanchikov warily.

"Sit down."

Pryanchikov sat down with alacrity, carefully hitching up his trousers with their knife-edge crease.

"Please speak quite frankly. You needn't be afraid that your immediate superiors will punish you for it. This scrambler, then, when will it be ready? Speak frankly, now! In a month's time? Or maybe you need two months? Speak up and don't be afraid."

"Ready? The scrambler? Ha-ha!"

Pryanchikov flung himself against the soft leather chairback, threw up his hands, and loud, youthful laughter rang out under that vaulted ceiling for the first time. "Whatever do you mean? I can see you just don't understand what the scrambler is. Let me explain it to you!"

He bounced out of the springy chair and darted over to Abakumov's desk. "Got a bit of paper? This will do!" He tore a leaf from a blank notepad on the minister's desk, grabbed the minister's meat-red pen, and began sketching a complex of sinusoids in hasty squiggles.

Abakumov was not alarmed. The strange engineer's speech and movements were so childishly honest and spontaneous that he put up with this encroachment and watched Pryanchikov curiously, without listening.

"You must realize that the human voice consists of many different harmonics," said Pryanchikov, sputtering in his eagerness to get it all said in a hurry. "Well, the idea of the scrambler is to reproduce the human voice by artificial means. . . . Blast! How do you manage to write with such a lousy pen? . . . to reproduce it by adding together at least the main harmonics, each transmitted by a separate set of impulses. You are familiar, of course, with Cartesian rectangular coordinates—every schoolboy is—but what about Fourier's series?"

"Hold on," Abakumov said, coming to his senses. "Just tell me one little thing: When will it be ready? And I mean ready."

"Ready? . . . Hmm. . . . Haven't really thought about it." The city by night was losing its fascination as his mind focused on the work he loved. "The interesting thing is this: The job gets easier if we make the timbre of the voice coarser. In that case the number of components . . ."

"I'm asking you for a date. First of March? First of April?"

"Are you serious? April? . . . Without the cryptographers we'll be through in, say, four or five months, no earlier. And what's it going to sound like when we get around to coding and decoding the impulses? The voice quality is bound to be even coarser. So let's not try to guess!" he urged Abakumov, tugging at his sleeve. "I'll explain the whole thing to you here and now. When you understand, you'll agree that haste will get us nowhere!"

But Abakumov, his gaze immobilized by the meaningless squiggles of Pryanchikov's sketch, had already pressed the button on his desk.

The glossy lieutenant colonel reappeared and invited Pryanchikov to leave.

He obeyed with a look of open-mouthed bewilderment on his face. What vexed him most was that he had not finished what he had to say. Then, on his way out, he realized with a shock to whom he had been talking. He was almost at the door before he remembered that the guys had asked him to make complaints . . . to demand. . . . He turned around sharply and started back.

"Here! Listen! I completely forgot to tell you. . . ."

But the lieutenant colonel barred his way and hustled him toward the door; the big boss at the desk wasn't listening. And in that brief awkward moment all the abuses, all the irregularities of prison life escaped the memory so long monopolized by the technicalities of radio engineering, and all that Pryanchikov could think of to shout as he went through the door was: "For one thing, there's no hot water! You get back from work late at night, and there's no hot water to make tea with."

"Hot water?" queried the big boss—a general, was he? "Right. We'll see to it."

# 18

## "Oh, Wonder-Working Steed"

IN CAME BOBYNIN. He wore blue overalls, like Pryanchikov, but was a hefty fellow with a prison-camp haircut.

Showing as little interest in his surroundings as if he visited this office a hundred times a day, he walked straight ahead, sat down, without speaking, in one of the comfortable armchairs near the minister's desk, and lengthily blew his nose into a not-very-white handkerchief, laundered by himself last bath day.

Abakumov, who had been somewhat disconcerted by Pryanchikov, though he had not taken that lightheaded young man too seriously, was glad to find that Bobynin looked more sensible. So instead of yelling "On your feet!" he assumed that Bobynin was no expert on shoulder boards and had not realized as he passed through a succession of antechambers just where he was going.

"Why," Abakumov asked almost mildly, "do you sit down without permission?"

Bobynin, with the merest sideways glance at the minister, went on cleaning his nose with the help of the handkerchief and answered simply: "Well, there's a Chinese saying that standing is better than walking, sitting is better than standing, and lying down is better still."

"Have you any idea who I might be?"

Resting his elbows comfortably on the arms of the chair he had chosen, Bobynin hazarded a lazy guess.

"Who you might be? Marshal Göring, or somebody like that?"

"Like who?"

"Marshal Göring. He once visited an aircraft factory near Halle, where I happened to be working in the designers' office. The generals there were all walking on tiptoe, but I turned my back on him. He took a good look and went off into the next room."

Something remotely resembling a smile passed over Abakumov's face, but it quickly became a frown as he studied this outrageously insolent prisoner.

"What do you mean? Don't you see any difference between us?"

"Us meaning you and him? Or you and me?" Bobynin's voice was like stage thunder. "I see the difference between us very clearly: You need me, and I don't need you!"

Abakumov could produce a peal of thunder and scare people himself. But on this occasion he felt that shouting would be useless and would only make him look silly. This prisoner was obviously a problem.

He contented himself with a warning.

"Listen, prisoner, just because I'm being easy on you, you mustn't forget yourself."

"If you were rough, I wouldn't talk to you at all, Citizen Minister. Shout at your colonels and your generals. They've got a lot to lose."

"We can make you toe the line if we have to."

"That's where you're wrong, Citizen Minister!" Bobynin's bold eyes flashed with undisguised hatred. "I've got nothing, understand, nothing at all! You can't get at my wife and child; a bomb got to them first. My parents are dead. All I own in this world is a handkerchief. These overalls and the buttonless shirt underneath them (he bared his chest to show it) belong to the state. You took my freedom from me long ago, and you can't give it back because you have no freedom yourself. I'm forty-two years old, and you've slapped a twenty-five-year sentence on me, I've been in hard-labor camps, walked about with number patches on my clothes, and wearing handcuffs, and with dogs around me, and I've been in a penal work brigade; so what else can you threaten me with? What else can you take away from me? My engineer's job, perhaps? That would be your loss, not mine. I'll have a cigarette."

Abakumov opened a pack of Troika cigarettes, special Kremlin issue, and pushed it over to Bobynin.

"Here, take some of these."

"No, thanks, I won't change my brand. Might make me cough." He took a Belomor from his homemade case. "In fact, you should get it into your head, and pass it on to whoever needs to know up above, that your power depends on not taking absolutely everything away from people. The man from whom you've taken everything is no longer in your power; he is free again."

Bobynin stopped talking and concentrated on his smoking. He was enjoying teasing the minister and reclining in such a comfortable chair. His only regret was that he had refused the deluxe cigarettes, just to show off.

The minister consulted his scrap of paper.

"Engineer Bobynin! You are a senior engineer working on the speech clipping apparatus?"

"I am."

"Please tell me precisely when it will be ready for use."

Bobynin's bushy eyebrows shot up.

"What's all this? Couldn't you find somebody senior to answer that question?"

"I want to hear it from you. Will it be ready by February?"

"February? Are you joking? If we cut all the corners, hurry now and worry later, it could be ready, say, half a year from now. But with perfect coding? I have no idea. A year maybe."

Abakumov was stunned. He remembered the menacing twitching of the Boss's mustache and shuddered to think of the promises he had made, echoing Selivanovsky. He had the sinking feeling of a man who goes to the clinic with a cold and finds he has cancer of the nasopharynx.

The minister supported his head on both hands and said feebly:

"Now, Bobynin. Weigh your words. I beg you. What can we do to hurry it up?"

"Hurry it up? Can't be done."

"But why? What's the reason? Whose fault is it? Don't be afraid, tell me!

Give me the names of those responsible, whatever sort of shoulder boards they wear! I'll soon have them off!"

Bobynin threw back his head and gazed at the Rossia Insurance Company's nymphs gamboling on the ceiling.

"That makes two and a half to three years, and the time limit you were given was one year."

At this Bobynin blew up.

"What do you mean, time limit? Do you think scientists are wizards with magic wands? 'Build me a palace by tomorrow'—and tomorrow a palace there will be. What if the problem is posed incorrectly? What if new phenomena come to light? Time limit! Don't you know that something more than an order is needed? You need free men with full bellies and minds at ease. And not this atmosphere of suspicion. Look, we shifted a little lathe from one place to another, and either while we were doing it or after, it got cracked. God knows how it happened. Repairing it was an hour's work for a welder. It's only fit for the scrap heap anyway. A hundred and fifty years old, no motor, an overhead belt drive. Well, because of that, Major Shikin, the security officer, has been badgering us all for two whole weeks, interrogating everybody, looking for somebody to pin a second sentence on for sabotage. That's one parasite, the security officer at the workplace; then there's the other parasite, the security officer in the prison block, making nervous wrecks of us with his conduct reports and dirty tricks. What the hell do you expect all these security operations to produce? Everybody says we're making a secret telephone for Stalin. Stalin personally is putting the pressure on, and even for an assignment like this you can't ensure regular supplies of equipment; either we haven't got the condensers we need, or the radio valves are the wrong kind, or there aren't enough electronic oscillographs. We're paupers! It's a disgrace. 'Who's to blame?' you ask. Do you ever spare the men a thought? We all work twelve hours a day for you, some of us sixteen, and you give meat only to the senior engineers and bare bones to the rest. Why don't you let the '58-ers* see their families? It's supposed to be once a month, and you allow it once a year. Do you think that helps to keep morale up? Maybe there aren't enough meat-wagons to transport prisoners? Or enough money to pay the guards overtime?

* '58-ers: Citizens who were arrested under Article 58 of the Russian (RSFSR) Penal Code, which targeted counter-revolutionary activities; its most notorious section was number 10, with its catchall terms "anti-Soviet and counter-revolutionary propaganda and agitation."

Regulations! You've got regulations on the brain. You'll drive yourselves mad with regulations. At one time Sunday was our day off. Now it's forbidden. Why? To make us work harder? Are you trying to skim cream from shit? It's not going to speed things up if we suffocate for lack of a breath of air. Now here we are again. Why did you send for me in the middle of the night? Isn't the day long enough? I have work to do tomorrow. I need sleep."

Bobynin sat up straight, looking big and angry.

Abakumov was breathing heavily, huddled over the desk. It was 1:25 a.m. In an hour's time he had to present himself at the Kuntsevo dacha and report to Stalin.

If this engineer was right, how could he wriggle out of it?

Stalin never forgave.

As he dismissed Bobynin, he remembered the trio of liars from the Special Technology Department, and hot rage blinded him.

He took up the receiver and sent for them.

## 19

# The Birthday Hero

THE ROOM WAS NOT VERY BIG and not very high. It had two doors, and what may once have been a window was now blocked up, flush with the wall. The air, however, was fresh and pleasant (a special engineer was responsible for its circulation and chemical purity).

A great deal of space was occupied by a low ottoman with flowery cushions. Twin lamps with pink shades were attached to the wall above it.

On the ottoman lay a man whose likeness has been more often sculpted, painted in oils, watercolors, gouache, and sepia; limned in charcoal, chalk, and powdered brick; pieced together in a mosaic of road maker's gravel, or seashells, or wheat grains, or soybeans; etched on ivory; grown in grass; woven into carpets; spelled out by planes flying in formation; recorded on film . . . than any other face ever has been in the three billion years since the earth's crust was formed.

Now he was just lying there, with his legs in soft Caucasian boots like thick stockings. He was wearing a service jacket with two big breast pockets and two big side pockets—an old, well-worn tunic of the sort he had worn, some of them khaki, some black, since the Civil War, perhaps in imitation of Napoleon, and had changed for a marshal's uniform only after Stalingrad.

The man's name was declaimed by all the newspapers of the terrestrial globe, mouthed by thousands of announcers in hundreds of languages, thundered by public speakers in their exordia and perorations, piped by the thin voices of Young Pioneers,* intoned in prayers for his health by bishops. This man's name burned on the parched lips of prisoners of war and the swollen gums of convicts. It had replaced the previous names of a multitude of cities and squares, streets and avenues, palaces, universities, schools, sanatoriums, mountain ranges, ship canals, factories, mines, state farms, collective farms, warships, icebreakers, fishing boats, cooperative cobblers' shops, nurseries—and a group of Moscow journalists had even suggested renaming the Volga and the moon after him.

Yet he was only a little yellow-eyed old man with gingery (not pitch black, as in his portraits), thinning (luxuriant according to his portraits) hair, with deep pockmarks in a gray face and a sagging dewlap (these last features were not portrayed at all), with uneven, blackened teeth, a mouth smelling of pipe tobacco, and fat, moist fingers that left marks on documents and books.

Moreover, he was not feeling very well today: He had gotten tired and had overeaten during the jubilee celebrations, there was a weight like a stone in his stomach, and belching left a sour taste in his mouth. Salol and belladonna had not helped, and he did not like taking purgatives. He hadn't dined at all today and had decided around midnight, quite early for him, to lie down for a bit. Although the air was warm, his back and shoulders felt cold, and he had covered them with a brown mohair shawl.

A deathly silence had flooded the house and grounds and all the world.

In this silence time seemed scarcely to stir, scarcely to crawl. It had to be lived through like an illness, and every night he had to invent some business or some distraction. It was easy enough to shut yourself off from the spatial universe, refuse to move about in it. But it was impossible to shut yourself off from time.

Right now he was paging through a little book in a stiff brown binding.

* Young Pioneers: A mass organization established in 1922 for Soviet youths from ten to fifteen years old.

He looked with satisfaction at the photographs, dipped into the text, which he knew almost by heart, and turned more pages. The book was designed to slip comfortably into an overcoat pocket without bending; it could accompany people wherever they went, whatever they did. It had a quarter of a thousand pages, but they were sparsely covered with bold print so that even the semiliterate and the aged could read them without fatigue. The title was stamped on the cover in gilt letters: *Iosif Vissarionovich Stalin: Short Biography*.

The honest and unpretentious words of this book sank irresistibly into the human heart, bringing peace. The strategist of genius. His wisdom and foresight. His iron will. From 1918 onward, he was in effect Lenin's deputy. (Yes, yes, I was!) When he became leader of the Revolutionary armies, he found chaos and panic at the front. Stalin's instructions formed the basis of Frunze's plan of operations. (True, true, that's just how it was!) It was our great good fortune that in the difficult years of the Fatherland War we were led by a wise and experienced Leader, the Great Stalin. (Yes, the people had been lucky!) Everybody knows the shattering power of Stalin's logic, the crystal clarity of his mind. (No need for false modesty, it's all true.) His love for the people. His sensitive concern for the people. His intolerance of pomp and publicity. His extraordinary modesty. (Modesty, yes, that's very true.)

His infallible knowledge of men had enabled the celebrant to collect a good team of authors for his biography. But however thorough they are, however they slave at it, no one else can write about your deeds, your leadership, your qualities as cleverly, with as much feeling, and as truthfully as you can yourself. So Stalin sometimes had to summon this or that member of the team for a leisurely talk in order to inspect their manuscript, gently indicating where they had gone wrong and suggesting improvements in the wording.

As a result the book was now a great success. This second edition had come out in five million copies. For such a huge country? Not nearly enough. The third edition must be boosted to ten million, or twenty. It must be on sale in factories, schools, collective farms. It should be distributed to them directly, according to the number of employees.

Nobody knew as well as Stalin did how much his people needed this book. His people could not be left without continual instruction and edification. His people must not be kept in uncertainty. The Revolution had left them orphaned and godless, and that was dangerous. Stalin had spent twenty years doing his best to correct that situation. This explained the millions of portraits throughout the country (it was not Stalin himself who needed them;

he was modest), the constant thunderous repetition of his glorious name, the unfailing mention of him in every article. The Leader himself had absolutely no need of all this; it no longer gave him any pleasure; he had grown sick of it long ago; it was his subjects who needed it, the simple Soviet people. As many portraits, as many repetitions of his name as possible. But he himself must appear seldom and say little: as though he were not always with them on this earth but at times in some other place. That way there was no limit to their rapturous adoration.

It was not nausea, but a sort of heavy upward pressure from the stomach. He took a feijoa from a bowl of peeled fruit.

Three days ago salvos had hailed his glorious seventieth birthday.

To the Caucasian way of thinking, a septuagenarian is still in his prime, able to tackle a mountain, a horse, or a woman. And Stalin was still perfectly fit. He simply had to live to ninety. He had set his heart on it. There was so much to be done. True, one doctor had warned him about . . . never mind what, the man had apparently been shot later. No, there was nothing seriously wrong with him. He refused injections and therapy of any sort. He knew enough about medicines to prescribe for himself. "Eat more fruit!" they told him. As if a Caucasian needed to be told about fruit!

He sucked the pulp of the feijoa, screwing up his eyes. It left a faint tang of iodine on his tongue.

Yes, he was perfectly fit, but he noticed certain changes as the years went by. He had lost his hearty appetite. There was nothing he savored; eating had begun to bore him. He no longer delighted in selecting wine for each dish. Tipsiness simply gave him a headache. If Stalin sometimes sat over a meal half the night with his minileaders, it was just to kill the long, empty hours, not because he enjoyed the food. Women, too, were something he needed rarely and never for long, although he had indulged himself freely after Nadya's death. They did not thrill him but left him feeling . . . dulled. Nor did sleep bring relief as it had when he was younger: He woke up feeling weak and muddleheaded and reluctant to rise.

Though he had decided to live to ninety, Stalin thought miserably, he personally could expect no pleasure from the years ahead: He must simply accept another twenty years of suffering for the sake of mankind at large.

This was how he had celebrated his birthday. On the evening of the twentieth, Traicho Kostov had been done to death. Only when the dog's eyes glazed over could the real celebrations begin. On the twenty-first, Stalin had been feted in the Bolshoi Theater, where Mao, Dolores, and other comrades had made speeches. Then there had been a great banquet. Still later, an intimate banquet. They had drunk old wine from Spanish cellars, wine once sent in payment for arms. Then he and Lavrenty privately had drunk Kakhetinskoye and sung Georgian songs. On the twenty-second, there was a big diplomatic reception. On the twenty-third, he had seen himself portrayed on screen in *The Battle of Stalingrad, Part II*, and on the stage in *The Unforgettable 1919*.

He had liked both productions, although they left him exhausted. His role not only in the Fatherland War but in the Civil War, too, was more and more truthfully portrayed nowadays. Everyone could see what a great man he had been even then. Stage and screen now showed people how often he had warned and corrected the rash and superficial Lenin. What noble words the playwright had put in his mouth: "Every toiler has the right to say what he thinks!" And how cleverly the scriptwriter had handled that night scene with his Friend. Although Stalin no longer had such a close and devoted friend, because people were always so insincere, so treacherous. And, as it happened, he had never had such a friend, no, never, but when he saw it on screen, Stalin felt a lump in his throat (what a writer! that's what I call a writer!): It was as if he had always wanted such a truthful and selfless Friend, someone to whom you could say out loud the thoughts that came to you in the long night hours.

But you couldn't possibly have such a Friend, because he would have to be very, very great. And if he were as great as that, where would he live? What would his job be?

As for all those others, from Vyacheslav Stone-Bottom to Nikita the Gopak-dancer,* how could anyone take them seriously? You could die of boredom sitting at the table with them. Not one of them ever came out with a clever remark, and whenever you made a point, they all agreed immediately. At one time Stalin had a soft spot for Voroshilov, because of Tsaritsyn and the Polish campaign and because he had reported the meeting of those traitors Zinoviev and Kamenev with Frunze in the cave at Kislovodsk. But

* Vyacheslav Stone-Bottom and Nikita the Gopak-dancer: Stalin refers to two of his principal deputies. Vyacheslav Molotov was known to sit working as long as his boss required; Nikita Khrushchev, of peasant stock, was alleged to have been repeatedly asked by Stalin to perform the Gopak squat dance.

Voroshilov was a stuffed dummy with an army cap and medals, not a human being.

There was no one he now remembered as a friend. No one of whom he could remember more good than bad.

He had, and could have, no friend, but the common people all loved their Leader and were ready to sacrifice life and soul for him. That was made clear by the newspapers, the cinema, and the exhibition of birthday presents. He rejoiced to think that the Leader's birthday had become a nationwide festival. So many birthday messages had arrived, greetings from institutions, from organizations, from factories, from individual citizens. *Pravda* had asked permission to publish them, not all at once but in two columns daily. Publication would extend over several years, but that was all to the good.

As for the presents, ten galleries in the Museum of the Revolution could not house them. So that the citizens of Moscow could view them freely in the daytime, Stalin paid a visit by night. The work of thousands and thousands of craftsmen, the finest gifts earth could offer, stood, lay, or hung before him, but here, too, the same cold indifference, the same apathy had gripped him. What good were all these presents to him? He was soon bored with them. Once again, there in the museum, an unpleasant memory stirred at the back of his mind, but as so often recently the thought remained vague. He knew only that it was unpleasant. Stalin walked through three galleries without choosing anything, pausing for a moment at the big television set with an engraved plate reading "To Great Stalin from the Chekists." This, the biggest of all Soviet television sets, and the only one of its kind, had been made at Marfino. Stalin inspected it briefly, turned on his heel, and left.

But by and large it had been a marvelous occasion. His proud record! his victories! achievements such as no political leader in the world could equal! Yet for him this triumphant occasion had been hollow.

It was as though something lodged in his chest nagged and galled him.

He took another bite of the feijoa and sucked it.

Yes, the people loved him, but the people's faults were innumerable. Left to itself, the people was good for nothing. You need only ask yourself who was to blame for the retreat in 1941. Who retreated? The people, who else?

That was why he ought not to be celebrating, or lying around, but getting down to work. Thinking.

Thinking—that was his duty. At once his lot and his punishment. He had to live another two decades, like a prisoner serving a twenty-year sentence, with no more than eight hours' sleep in the twenty-four; that was all he could manage. All those other hours he must struggle through, as though he were dragging his aging, vulnerable body over sharp stones.

Hardest of all for Stalin were morning and early afternoon. While the sun was rising, shining merrily, reaching its zenith, Stalin slept in darkness, shuttered, secluded, secret. He awoke when the sun was already declining, losing strength, toward the end of its short one-day life. Stalin had breakfast at about three o'clock in the afternoon but began to come to life only toward evening, when the sun was setting. In the hours between, his brain was warming up, waking sullenly, distrustfully; he could make only negative and prohibitive decisions. Dinner began at 10:00 p.m. A few favored members of the Politburo or foreign Communists were usually invited. Four or five hours were painlessly killed over a steady succession of dishes, drinks, jokes, and discussions, and at the same time his mind picked up speed and the impetus for the creative legislative thinking of the second half of the night was generated. All the major decrees that kept the great state on course took shape in Stalin's head after 2:00 a.m. and never later than dawn.

That time had come around again, and a decree conspicuously lacking in the body of the law was ripening. He had made fast forever almost everything in the land, stopped all movement, dammed all currents, all two hundred million knew their place, but the kolkhoz system had sprung a leak. This was all the stranger because the general situation on the farms was conspicuously good—witness the films and novels on the subject—and anyway Stalin often talked to collective farmers himself on the platforms of rallies and congresses. Nonetheless, like the perspicacious and unceasingly self-critical statesman he was, Stalin had forced himself to look still deeper. One of the obkom* secretaries (subsequently shot, he believed) had let slip that the farms had one dark side: Old men and women enrolled in the thirties worked ungrudgingly, but an unconscientious element among the young tried when they left school to obtain passports by fraud and to sneak off to the towns.

Education! What a mess they had got into with, first universal seven-year, then universal ten-year education, with those "children of cooks" who now went to university. Lenin in his irresponsible way had muddled matters,

* Obkom: Soviet shorthand for an Oblast Committee of the Communist Party.

recklessly littering the place with promises, which had since become a crippling burden to his successor, to Stalin. "Any cook must be able to administer the state," but how had Lenin pictured this in concrete terms? Did he mean that the cook, instead of cooking on Fridays, would take her seat on the oblast executive committee? A cook was a cook; her job was to prepare dinner. Governing people was a rare skill, a task that could be entrusted only to special cadres, cadres specially selected, trained, and tempered, highly disciplined. Management of the cadres themselves must rest in a single pair of hands, the practiced hands of the Leader.

Why not write it into the statutes of each collective farm that since the land belongs to it in perpetuity, everyone born in a particular village automatically acquires membership in the farm at birth? Represent this as a right and an honor. Launch a public-relations campaign immediately: "A Further Step Along the Road to Communism," "Youth's Inheritance—the Collective Granary," . . . well, the writers would find the best way to put it.

Somehow his mind was not on his work today. He felt unwell.

There were four short knocks, or rather not so much knocks as a muffled sound, as if a dog was pawing the door.

Stalin pulled a lever near his couch, the safety catch clicked, and the door opened slightly. No curtain hung in front of it (Stalin did not like anything that hung loosely, anything with folds in which someone could hide), and he could see the bare door opening just wide enough to admit a dog. It was, however, at the upper, not the lower, end of the gap that a head appeared; that of the bald though still-young-looking Poskryobyshev, who wore a permanent expression of honest devotion and unbounded eagerness to serve.

Though it worried him to see the Boss lying down, half covered with the mohair shawl, he did not ask about his health (Stalin disliked such questions), but said almost in a whisper: "Iosif Vissarionovich, you made an appointment with Abakumov for half past two. Will you be wanting to see him?"

Iosif Vissarionovich unbuttoned the flap of his breast pocket and pulled out a watch on a chain (like all those of his generation he detested wristwatches).

It was not yet 2:00 a.m.

The heavy lump was still there in his stomach. He didn't feel like getting up and changing his clothes. But he could not relax his grip on any of them; the slightest weakening would be felt at once.

"We'll see," said Stalin, wearily blinking. "I'm not sure."

"He might as well come. He can wait," Poskryobyshev said, nodded three or four times, then froze again, looking expectantly at the Boss. "Have you any further instructions, Iossarionych?" No instructions could be read into the languid, lifeless gaze that Stalin turned on him. But Poskryobyshev's question had struck a sudden spark from his erratic memory, and he asked something that he had intended to ask long ago but kept forgetting.

"What about the cypresses down in the Crimea? Are they being cut down?"

"They are, Iossarionych." Poskryobyshev nodded confidently, as though he had been expecting this very question and had just rung through to the Crimea to inquire. "Around Massandra and Livadia a lot of them have been felled already, Iossarionych!"

"Have a report sent in just the same. In code. Make sure there's no sabotage." The unhealthy yellow eyes of the All-Powerful looked troubled.

One of his doctors had told him earlier in the year that cypresses were bad for his health and that he needed air impregnated with the aroma of eucalyptuses. Whereupon Stalin had given orders for the Crimean cypresses to be felled, and eucalyptus saplings to be imported from Australia.

Poskryobyshev acknowledged his orders and also undertook to find out what was happening about the eucalyptuses.

"Right," said Stalin, satisfied. "You can go for now, Sasha."

Poskryobyshev nodded, backed toward the door, inclined his head once more, then withdrew it and closed the door. Iosif Vissarionovich operated the remote-control lock again. Clutching the shawl, he turned onto his other side. And continued paging through his *Biography*.

But recumbency, a slight chill, and indigestion had lowered his resistance, and he surrendered helplessly to dark thoughts. What rose before him now was not the dazzling and preordained success of his policies but his ill luck in life and all the enemies, all the obstacles with which fate had sought to bar his way.

## 20

# A Study of a Great Life

Two-thirds of a century. The beginnings lost in a blue haze. And who then could have imagined in his wildest dreams how it would end? Looking backward, it was difficult to resurrect and believe in the beginning.

He had been born to a life without hope. An illegitimate son, registered in the name of a drunken, penniless cobbler. An illiterate mother. Grubby little Soso forever splashing about in the puddles near Queen Tamara's hill. How could such a child ever escape from the depths of degradation, let alone become ruler of the world?

But the author of his existence had pulled strings; and, although he did not belong to a priestly family, the boy had been admitted, contrary to the established practice of the church, first to a church school, then, still more remarkably, to a seminary. From the highest point of the blackened iconostasis, the God of Sabaoth sternly summoned the novice prostrate on the cold stone flags. Oh, how zealously the boy had entered into the service of his God! How unreservedly he surrendered himself! In his six years of schooling he crammed into himself as best he could the Old and New Testaments, the Lives of the Saints, and church history, and he was a punctilious altar boy.

Yes, there it was in his *Biography*, a snapshot of Dzhugashvili wearing a gray cassock with a round, buttoned collar before he was expelled. There was no color in his boyishly oval face; he looked exhausted by prayer. His hair, grown long in readiness for his ordination, was carefully parted, humbly smeared with oil from the icon lamps, and combed down right over his ears. Only his eyes and his tense brows hinted that here was a novice who might someday be an archbishop.

But God had disappointed him. Time had left behind the odious, sleepy little town where the Medzhuda and the Liakhva meander among rounded green hills. In noisy Tiflis clever people had realized long ago that God was a joke. And the ladder up which Soso was so tenaciously climbing led, he now saw, not to Heaven but to a pauper's garret.

He was at a boisterous and bellicose age; he longed for action. Time was passing, and nothing had been achieved! He had no money to go to university, obtain a government post, or set up in business. Instead, there was socialism, which turned no one away, socialism, which was used to seminarians. He felt no inclination toward any art or science, he lacked the know-how to become an artisan or a thief, he was not successful enough with women to become the lover of a rich lady, but Revolution summoned all men, received them with open arms, and promised them a place.

At his own suggestion his favorite photograph of himself had been inserted at this point in the book. There he was, almost in profile. He was wearing . . . not exactly a beard or a mustache or sideburns; he simply hadn't shaved for quite a while, and beard, mustache, and sideburns had run together in a picturesque manly growth. He was all eagerness, all aspiration, but he did not yet know to what. What a likable young man! A frank, clever, energetic face, not a trace of the fanatical novice. Free now of the lamp oil, his hair had sprung up and flopped forward to conceal what was perhaps a rather unsatisfactory feature, his low, sloping forehead. He was poor; his jacket had been shabby when he bought it; a cheap checkered scarf was draped around his neck with bohemian abandon, covering his unhealthily narrow chest in lieu of a shirt. One of many such young men in Tiflis, surely doomed to tuberculosis.

Whenever Stalin looked at that photograph, his heart filled with pity (for no heart is altogether incapable of it). How difficult everything had been for him; the whole world was against that splendid young man, his only shelter a cold but rent-free closet at the observatory after his expulsion from the seminary. (He had wanted for safety's sake to combine the two things, and for four years had attended Social Democratic study groups while continuing to say his prayers and recite his catechism, but they had expelled him just the same.)

Eleven years of prayer and genuflection had gone for nothing. . . . All the more resolutely did he transfer his youthful energies to the Revolution!

But Revolution, too, had proved a disappointment.

What sort of Revolution was it, anyway, in Tiflis? Bigheaded braggarts playing games in a wine cellar. You could get lost in this anthill of nonentities. They had no concept of advancement by regular stages or of seniority. It was just a question of who could outtalk whom. The former seminarian came to hate those chatterers more than he hated provincial governors or policemen. (Why be angry with them? They earned their salary honestly and naturally had to defend themselves, but there was no excuse for these upstarts!) Revolution? Among Georgian shopkeepers? It would never happen! And now he had cut himself off from the seminary, lost what should have been his way in life.

The hell with it anyway, this so-called Revolution, all these paupers, workers who boozed their wages away, sick old women, people cheated of a few odd kopecks. . . . Why was he supposed to love them and not his young, clever, handsome, unappreciated self?

It was only in Batum, when he led a couple of hundred people (including the idly curious) along a street for the first time that Koba (his Revolutionary nickname) felt the thrill of power. People were following him! After that first experience he never forgot the taste of it. This was the life that he was made for, the only sort of life he could understand: You speak, and people have to do what you say; you show them where to go, and people have to go there. There is nothing better than this, nothing finer in the world. Riches are nothing in comparison.

A month later the police bestirred themselves and arrested him. Nobody feared arrest in those days. It meant very little. You were in custody for two months, and when you were let out, you were a martyr. Koba behaved admirably in the common cell and encouraged the others to treat their jailers with contempt.

But they hung on to him. All his cellmates went and were replaced by others. He was still inside. What, after all, had he done? No one was punished so severely for an insignificant demonstration.

A whole year went by! And he was transferred to a dark, damp, one-man cell in Kutaisi Jail. Here he began to despair. Life was going by, and instead of rising in the world, he was sinking even lower. The damp gave him a painful cough. And all this gave him even more reason to hate those professional loudmouths, fortune's favorites, it seemed: Why did they get away with "Revolution" so lightly; why weren't they kept inside as long?

Then one day a gendarme officer he knew from Batum arrived at Kutaisi Jail. "Well, Dzhugashvili, have you had time to think? This is only the beginning, Dzhugashvili. We shall keep you here until you either rot with consumption or correct your line of conduct. We want to save you and your soul. You were five minutes away from becoming a priest, Father Iosif! Why did you join that gang? You don't belong with them. Tell me that you're sorry."

He was indeed sorry, so very sorry! His second spring in jail was ending, his second dreary summer of jail lay ahead. Why, oh why had he thrown away a modest position in the church? How rash he had been! The wildest imagination could not conceive of Revolution in Russia in less than fifty years' time, when Iosif would be seventy-three. What good would Revolution be to him then?

But it wasn't just that. By now Iosif had gotten to know himself, to realize that he was by nature deliberate and methodical, a lover of order and stability. But these were the very qualities—order, stability, solidity, consistency—that sustained the Russian Empire. What was the point of trying to destabilize it?

The officer with the corn-colored mustache paid visit after visit. (Iosif found his trim gendarme's uniform with its handsome shoulder boards, neat buttons, piping, and buckles most attractive.) What I am offering you is after all an opportunity to serve the state. (Iosif was ready to transfer once and for all to the service of the state, but he had spoiled his chances at Tiflis and Batum.) You will receive an allowance from us. To begin with, you will help us by working among the Revolutionaries. Choose the most extreme faction. Start playing a leading role in it. We will always handle you carefully. You will communicate with us in such a way that no shadow of suspicion will fall on you. But first, so as not to compromise you, we will transport you under guard to a distant place of exile, and you will leave it immediately—that's what everybody does.

Dzhugashvili was not long in deciding. The third wager of his young life was laid on the secret police!

He was exiled to Irkutsk Province in November. Among other exiles there he read a letter from a certain Lenin, well known for his newspaper *Iskra.* Lenin had isolated himself at the outermost limit of the movement and was now writing around in quest of supporters. He was obviously the man to join.

Iosif left the dreadful frosts of Irkutsk toward Christmas and was in the sunny Caucasus before the war with Japan broke out.

From then on he enjoyed a long period of immunity. He met underground activists, composed leaflets, convened meetings. . . . Others were arrested (especially those he didn't like), but he escaped notice and was not on the wanted list. Nor was he called up for military service.

Then suddenly. . . ! Though nobody was expecting it so soon, no preparations had been made, nothing had been organized. It was upon them! Crowds marched through Petersburg bearing political petitions. Grand dukes and other bigwigs were assassinated, Ivanovo-Voznesensk was on strike, Lodz rebelled, the battleship *Potemkin* mutinied, a manifesto was squeezed out of the tsar, in spite of which machine guns were soon chattering in the Presnya district of Moscow, and the railways were brought to a standstill.

Koba was stunned, thunderstruck. Could he have made yet another mistake? Why was he so completely lacking in foresight?

The Okhranka* had misled him! He was a three-time loser! Give me back

* Okhranka: A slang term for the tsarist secret police, charged with monitoring the activities of Russian revolutionaries at home and abroad.

my uncompromised Revolutionary soul! Trapped in a vicious circle! Tumble Russia into a Revolution, and the day afterward your denunciations will come tumbling out of the Okhranka archives. But after all the shooting, the uproar, the hangings, they looked around and the Revolution had vanished!

This was when the Bolsheviks adopted the sound Revolutionary practice of "expropriation." Some Armenian moneybags would be sent a letter telling him where to bring along ten, fifteen, or twenty-five thousand rubles. And the moneybags would bring the money, to persuade them not to blow up his shop or kill his children. This was the real thing! This was what genuine Revolutionaries should be doing! Not wasting time on scholastic argument, leaflets, demonstrations. . . . This was real Revolutionary activity! The goody-goody Mensheviks grumbled that robbery and terrorism were incompatible with Marxism. Oh, how mercilessly Koba ridiculed them, hunting them down like cockroaches—it was for this that Lenin called him "the marvelous Georgian." The "ex-es" were robbery, but what else was Revolution? Wasn't that robbery? How ridiculous they were, those sanctimonious humbugs! Where else would you get money for the Party? Where? From the Revolutionaries themselves? A bird in hand is worth two in the bush.

The "ex-es" were in fact the form of Revolutionary activity that Koba liked most of all. And no one was as clever as Koba at recruiting uniquely reliable people like Kamo, who would unquestioningly obey his orders, brandish a revolver, snatch a sack of gold, and take it to Koba. When they snatched 340,000 rubles from the couriers of a Tiflis bank, that could be seen as a proletarian Revolution in miniature, and only idiots lived in expectation of the big one. This was one of the things that the police did not know about Koba, and the dividing line between police and Revolution remained as before. He was never short of money.

The Revolution now carried him around on Continental trains and on ships, showed him islands, canals, and medieval castles. All rather different from a stinking Kutaisi cell! In Tammerfors, Stockholm, and London, Koba was able to take a close look at the Bolsheviks and the manic Lenin.

They took good care of him. The more prominent, the better known he became in the Party, the nearer to home his places of exile were. He would be banished now not to Baikal but to Solvychegodsk, and for two years, not three. Between spells of banishment, he was allowed to play at Revolution unhindered. Finally, after he had walked away three times from exile in Siberia and the Urals, the implacable and indefatigable rebel was shunted off to Vologda, of all places, where he lodged in the police chief's apartment and could reach Petersburg by train overnight.

But one February evening in 1912, Ordzhonikidze, a junior colleague in the Baku days, arrived in Vologda from Prague, shook him by his shoulders, and shouted, "Soso! Soso! You've been co-opted to the C.C."

The moon shone on wreathing frozen mist as the thirty-two-year-old Koba, wrapped up in his fur coat, paced the yard for hours. He was vacillating yet again. Member of the Central Committee! Ah, but Malinovsky was both a member of the Bolshevik Central Committee and a deputy in the state Duma. Lenin was particularly fond of Malinovsky. So what? That was under the tsar. After the Revolution anyone in the C.C. today was sure to be a minister. No Revolution could be expected, of course, in his lifetime. But even without Revolution a Central Committee member had some sort of power. Whereas his prospects in the employment of the secret police were . . . what? He would always be an insignificant snooper. Instead of a member of the Central Committee! No, he must part company with the security police. Azef's hideous fate haunted him day and night.

The following morning they took the train to Petersburg. Where they were promptly arrested. The young and inexperienced Ordzhonikidze was given three years in the Schlüsselburg Fortress, with banishment to follow. Stalin, true to form, was merely banished for three years. True, it was to a rather distant place, the Narym region. This was meant as a warning. But communications in the Russian Empire were not too bad, and in late summer Stalin made his way safely back to Petersburg.

He now switched his efforts mainly to Party work. He visited Lenin in Krakow (no difficult matter even for an "exile"). He organized a printing press here, a May Day demonstration there, a leaflet campaign somewhere else, and suddenly, at an evening meeting in the Kalashnikov labor exchange, he was nabbed. The Okhranka had lost its temper, and this time he was sent packing to a real place of exile, Kureika, beyond the Arctic Circle. The tsar's government could dish out ruthless sentences when it wanted to, and he got—horror of horrors!—four years, four whole years!

Stalin faltered yet again. For what and for whom had he renounced his comfortable, uneventful life under state patronage and gotten himself banished to this godforsaken hole? "Member of the C.C." might tickle the ear of an idiot, but . . . Several hundred members of assorted parties shared Stalin's exile, and when he looked at them, he was horrified. What a loathsome breed these professional Revolutionaries were—empty show-offs, loudmouths, incapable of independent action, mentally bankrupt. Stalin, the Caucasian, dreaded the Arctic Circle less than the company of these flimsy, unstable, irresponsible, unserious people. To cut himself off from them once and for all—he would sooner have lived with the bears!—he married a Cheldonian, a mammoth of a woman with a squeaky voice. Better her tittering and the evil-smelling fat she cooked in than all those assemblies, debates, altercations, comrades' courts. . . . Stalin let it be known that he wanted nothing to do with these people, broke off relations with them—and with the Revolution, too. Enough was enough. At thirty-five he was not too old to start living honestly. There comes a time when you must stop drifting before the wind, with your empty pockets like billowing sails. He despised himself for wasting so many years with those pathetic hacks.

From then on he was a man apart, steering clear of Bolsheviks and anarchists alike. He had no thought now of escaping; his intention was to serve out his sentence like an honest exile. Besides, war had broken out, and only there in exile could he be sure of surviving. He stayed put with his Cheldonian woman, keeping his head down. A son was born to them. The war seemed never-ending. He would have fought tooth and nail for an extra year of exile! Russia had a tsar too feeble even to hand down a decent sentence!

The war went on and on. And the Police Department, with which he had once been on such good terms, handed his file card, and his soul with it, to a recruiting officer who didn't know the first thing about Social Democrats and their Central Committees and who called up Iosif Dzugashvili, born 1879, no previous military service, to serve as a private in the Imperial Russian Army. That was the beginning of the future great marshal's military career. He had tried three different careers one after another, and now he would be embarking on a fourth.

A sleepily gliding sled carried him along the Yenisei to Krasnoyarsk, and on to the barracks at Achinsk. He was in his thirty-eighth year, and he was . . . a nothing, a Georgian soldier, shivering in a skimpy greatcoat, cannon fodder for the front in transit across frozen Siberia. A great life was about to be cut short around some Belorussian farmstead or some Jewish shtetl.

But before he had learned to roll up a greatcoat or load a rifle (in later years, as a commissar and then a marshal, he still didn't know how and would have been embarrassed to ask), ticker-tape messages from Petrograd caused people to hug one another in the streets and shout steamily into the frosty air, "Christ is Risen!" The tsar had abdicated! The empire was no more!

How had it happened? Who had brought it about? They had given up hope, stopped counting on it. "Unknowable, O Lord, are Thy ways!" How true were these words Iosif remembered from his childhood.

No one could remember when the Russian public had last rejoiced so unanimously. But, until another telegram arrived, Stalin could not join in the general jubilation. Till then the specter of Azef, hanged by the neck, dangled importunately over his head.

The news he needed came one day later. The Okhranka's headquarters had been sacked and burned. All its documents had been destroyed!

They knew, those Revolutionaries, what to burn first! Stalin felt sure that there were others like himself in the files, quite a few of them.

(The Okhranka had gone up in flames, but for the rest of his life Stalin was watchful and suspicious. With his own hands he paged through tens of thousands of archival pages and pitched whole files into the flames without examining them. Still, he missed something, and in 1937 it very nearly saw the light of day. Whenever a member of his own Party was put on trial, Stalin invariably accused him of having been a police informer: He had learned how easy it is to fall and found it hard to imagine that others had failed to insure themselves as he had.)

Stalin later refused to speak of the "great" February Revolution, but he had forgotten how he himself had rejoiced and sung and winged his way from Achinsk (there was nothing now to stop him from deserting!) and done foolish things and handed in at a post office in the backwoods a telegram to Lenin in Switzerland.

Once in Petrograd, he had immediately agreed with Kamenev that this was it, all that they had dreamed of in their underground days. The Revolution was complete, and all they had to do was consolidate its achievement. This was a time for practical people (especially those who were already members of the C.C.). They must do all in their power to support the provisional government.

It was all so clear to them until that adventurer, who knew nothing about Russia, who lacked all-around practical experience, arrived and—spluttering, slurring, twitching—came out with his "April theses" and created total confusion! Yet somehow he cast a spell over the Party and dragged it into the July uprising! This desperate adventure failed, as Stalin had foretold, and the whole Party almost went under with it. And where did the strutting gamecock turn up next? He had saved his skin by fleeing to the Gulf of Finland, while the foulest abuse was heaped upon Bolsheviks back home. Was his liberty more valuable than the prestige of the Party? Stalin had posed the question candidly at the Sixth Congress but had not obtained a majority.

Altogether 1917 had been an unpleasant year: too many meetings, eloquent ranters were carried on the crowd's shoulders, Trotsky was never off the stage in the Circus building. Where had they all come from, these nimble-tongued ninnies, swarming like flies onto honey? He had never seen them in exile, never seen them when he was carrying out "ex-es"; they had been idling abroad, and now they had come back to yap their heads off and sneak into the front row. Whatever the subject under discussion, they hopped onto it as quick as fleas. They always knew the answer before the question was asked, before the problem arose. They laughed at Stalin openly, insultingly. True, he steered clear of their debates, never sat on platforms. For the time being he was keeping his own counsel. He did not like bandying words, trying to shout an opponent down, and he was no good at it. This was not how he had imagined the Revolution. Occupying important posts, doing a serious job—that was what he had looked forward to.

They laughed at him, all those pointy-beards, but why was it on Stalin that they loaded all the heaviest and most thankless tasks? They laughed at him, but why did all the others in Kschessinskaya's former palace suddenly develop stomachaches and send Stalin to Petropavlovka when the sailors had to be persuaded to surrender the fortress to Kerensky without a fight and themselves withdraw to Kronstadt? Why? Because the sailors would have stoned, say, Grishka Zinoviev. Because you had to know how to talk to the Russian people.

The October Revolution had been another reckless venture, but it had come off. Good. Full marks to Lenin there. Nobody knew what would follow, but for the time being, good. Commissariat of Nationalities? Very well, then, I don't mind. Draw up a constitution? Why not? Stalin was sizing up the situation.

Surprisingly, for a year the Revolution looked like a complete success. Nobody would ever have expected it, but there it was. That clown Trotsky even believed in world Revolution and opposed the Brest-Litovsk peace treaty. In fact, Lenin, too, believed in it. Pedants! Fantasists! Only an ass would believe in a European Revolution. They had lived there for years and learned nothing. Whereas Stalin had traveled across Europe once and understood it completely. They should thank Heaven that their own Revolution had been a success. And sit quietly. Pause for thought.

Stalin looked around with a sober and unprejudiced eye. Thought things over. And saw clearly that these phrasemongers would ruin this great Revolution. Only he, Stalin, could steer it in the right direction. In all honesty, in all conscience, he was the only real leader among them. He compared himself dispassionately with those poseurs, those mountebanks, and he saw clearly his own essential superiority, their instability, his own staying power. What set him apart from all the others was his understanding of people. He understood them at the point where they touched ground, at the base, understood that part of them without which they would not stand on their feet and remain standing: Everything higher than that—all the pretenses, all the boasts—was "superstructure" and of no importance.

Lenin, of course, could soar like an eagle. He could amaze you: turn right around overnight and say, "Let the peasants have the land!" (we can always change our minds later), think up the Brest-Litovsk treaty in a single day (even a Georgian, let alone a Russian, suffered when he saw half of Russia handed over to the Germans, but Lenin felt nothing!). As for the New Economic Policy, it went without saying, that was the neatest trick of the lot; nobody need be ashamed to learn from such maneuvers. Lenin's greatest gift, the most remarkable thing about him, was his ability to hold the real power very tightly in his own two hands. Slogans changed, the subjects of debate changed, allies and opponents changed, but all power remained in his hands and his hands alone!

But the man could not really be relied on. He was storing up a lot of grief for himself with his economic policy; he was bound to trip himself up with it. Stalin accurately sensed Lenin's volatility, his reckless impatience, and worst of all his poor understanding, or rather total lack of understanding, of people. (He had tested it on himself: Whichever side of himself he chose to show was the only one that Lenin saw.) The man was no good at infighting in the dark—in other words, real politics. Turukhan (66° latitude) was a tougher place than Shushenskoye (54°), and Stalin felt himself that much tougher than Lenin. Anyway, what experience of life had this bookworm theoretician ever acquired? Lowly birth, humiliations, poverty, actual hunger, had not been his lot: He had been a landowner, though a pretty small one. He had been a model exile and never once run away! He had never seen the inside of a real prison; indeed, he had seen nothing of the real Russia. He had idled away fourteen years in emigration. Stalin had read less than half of his writings, not expecting to learn a great deal from him. (He did, of course, sometimes produce remarkably apt definitions: "What is dictatorship? Unlimited government, unrestrained by laws." Stalin had written "Good!" in the margin.) If Lenin had had a sound, sober understanding, he would have made Stalin his closest associate from the start; he would have said, "Help me! I understand politics, I know about social classes, but real live people I don't understand!" But the best thing he could think of was to pack Stalin off to some far corner of Russia, where he was put in charge of grain requisitioning. Stalin was the man he needed most in Moscow, so he sent him to Tsaritsyn.

Lenin arranged things so that he sat in the Kremlin throughout the Civil War. While Stalin's lot for three whole years was that of a nomad, scouring the whole country, shaken to bits on horseback or in an unsprung cart, frozen half the time, trying to thaw out by a campfire. Stalin, of course, admired himself in those years: He was a sort of young general without formal rank, elegant and smart, wearing a leather cap with a star, a cavalry officer's double-breasted coat of fine cloth, unbuttoned, and soft leather riding boots, made to order. The clever young face was clean-shaven except for the flowing mustache. No woman could resist him (and his third wife was a beauty).

Of course, he never held a saber, never got in the way of bullets; he was too valuable to the Revolution. He was not like that muzhik Budenny. Whenever you arrived somewhere new—Tsaritsyn, Perm, or Petrograd—you would keep quiet for a while, then ask a few questions, stroke your mustache, write "to be shot" on a list or two, and people would soon begin to show you great respect.

Besides, if the truth be told, he had shown himself to be a great soldier and the architect of victories.

The whole gang who had scrambled to the top and crowded around Lenin, struggling for power, all thought themselves very clever, very subtle, very complex. Their complexity in fact was what they particularly boasted about. Where twice two clearly made four, they would shriek in a chorus that you were zero point one two short. The worst of the lot, the foulest of them all, was Trotsky. Stalin had simply never met such a loathsome person in all his life, with his insane conceit, his oratorical pretensions. And he never would argue honestly; there was never a straight yes or no; it always had to be both yes and no, or neither yes nor no. "Neither peace nor war"—what rational human being could make sense of that? And his arrogance? Rolling around like the tsar himself in a sitting room on wheels. What sort of Supreme Commander could he make, with no strategic flair at all?

This Trotsky's behavior so galled and annoyed him that Stalin at first lost control and broke rule no. 1 for all politicians: Never let a man see that you are his enemy; never let your irritation show. Stalin, instead, was openly insubordinate, abused Trotsky in letters and in conversation, and missed no opportunity to complain about him to Lenin. As soon as he heard about Trotsky's opinion or decision on any matter whatsoever, he would immediately put forward reasons for doing just the opposite. But that was no way to win. Trotsky bowled him over like a ninepin. Trotsky chased him out of Tsaritsyn and out of the Ukraine. And on one occasion Stalin was taught the harsh lesson that not all means of struggle are good, that some holds are barred. At a Politburo meeting he and Zinoviev joined in complaining about Trotsky's unauthorized executions. Whereupon Lenin took several blank sheets of paper, signed at the bottom of each page with the words "approved in advance," and in their presence handed these to Trotsky to fill in when he pleased.

He learned his lesson! He was ashamed! What had he been complaining about? Lenin was right, and so, just for once, was Trotsky: If you couldn't shoot people without trial, you would never be able to make history at all.

We are all human, and our senses are quicker to prompt us than our reason. Every man gives off a scent, and that scent tells you how to act before your head does. Stalin, of course, had made a mistake in openly opposing Trotsky too soon (it was a mistake he never made again). But he sensed correctly that he should stand up to Lenin. His reason would have told him to truckle to Lenin, always to say, "Oh, how right you are! I'm with you there!" But Stalin's unerring instinct found a very different way: to speak to Lenin as roughly as he could, to resist as stubbornly as a Georgian donkey. I'm an uneducated man, a rough diamond, a bit of a savage; you'll have to take me as I am or not at all. He wasn't just rough, but boorishly insolent. ("I can only stay another two weeks at the front, and then you'd better give me some leave." Would Lenin have forgiven anyone else for such a thing?) This inflexible, intransigent Stalin it was who won Lenin's respect. Lenin realized that this "marvelous Georgian" was a strong personality, that such people were much needed, and that as time went by, they would be needed more and more. Lenin listened readily to Trotsky, but he also gave Stalin a hearing. If he curbed Stalin, he reined in Trotsky, too. The first was to blame for Tsaritsyn, the second for Astrakhan. "You must learn to cooperate," he would urge, but he had to accept their inability to get along. Trotsky came running to complain that although prohibition was in force throughout the republic, Stalin was drinking his way through the tsar's cellar in the Kremlin; what if the soldiers at the front came to know of it? Stalin turned it into a joke; Lenin laughed; Trotsky stopped pointing his beard at them and went away empty-handed. When Stalin was removed from the Ukraine, he was given a second commissariat (Workers' and Peasants' Inspectorate) to make up for it.

That was in March 1919. Stalin was into his fortieth year. For anybody else the WPI would have been a shabby little snooping operation, but under Stalin it rose to become the most important people's commissariat! (That was just what Lenin wanted. He knew Stalin's firmness, his unswerving sense of purpose, his incorruptibility.) It was to Stalin that he entrusted the tasks of seeing justice done in the Republic, of keeping an eye on the morality of Party officials, even the most important of them. If Stalin understood the nature of his work correctly and was prepared to devote himself to it body and soul, with no thought for his health, he could now surreptitiously (but quite legally) gather incriminating evidence against all responsible officials, dispatch investigators, collect denunciations, and take charge of the ensuing purges. To do all this, he must create an apparatus, selecting from all over the country people as selfless, as unyielding, as himself, and who, like him, were prepared to toil in obscurity for no visible reward. It was slow, demanding, painstaking work, but Stalin welcomed it.

It is rightly said that we reach maturity at forty. Only then do we finally understand how to live and how to behave. Only then did Stalin become aware of his greatest strength: the power of the unspoken verdict. Your mind is made up, but the person whose head depends on your decision must not learn it too soon. Time enough for that when his head rolls! Another strength was his habit of disbelieving what others said and attaching no importance to his own words. Say not what you mean to do (you may not know it until the moment comes) but what puts the other person at ease. A third rule for the strong man is never to forgive anyone who betrays you, and if your teeth are in someone's throat, never to let go, though the sun rises in the west and portents appear in the heavens. A fourth rule for the strong man is not to rely on theory. Theory never helped anyone; you can always produce some sort of theoretical justification after the event. What you must always keep in mind is what fellow traveler you need for the present and at which milestone you must part company.

These rules helped him in due course to regularize the Trotsky situation. With the help of Zinoviev to begin with, and later that of Kamenev, too. (Cordial relations were established with both of them.) It became obvious to Stalin that he need not have worried so much about Trotsky: No need to shove him into the ditch; he would jump and land in it unassisted. Stalin knew his business and worked away quietly, unhurriedly selecting cadres, trying people out, committing every one of them to memory so that he would know who could be relied on, looking for opportunities to promote and place them. The time came when, just as he had expected, Trotsky took a tumble, unaided. In the trade union controversy. His exhibitionist ravings infuriated Lenin—he shows no respect for the Party!—and Stalin was, conveniently, in a position to replace Trotsky's people: Krestinsky with Zinoviev, Preobrazhensky with Molotov, Serebryakov with Yaroslavsky. Voroshilov and Ordzhonikidze, Stalin's own men, were hoisted into the Central Committee. The illustrious Commander in Chief was now unsteady on his heron's legs! And Lenin realized that Stalin was the unshakable defender of Party unity and that he asked for nothing, wanted nothing for himself. What won over all the leading comrades was the nice, guileless Georgian's refusal to join in the scramble for the platform, to court popularity, as all the others did. He never flaunted his knowledge of Marx; he worked away modestly, handpicking party apparatchiks, a solitary comrade, true as steel, honest as the day was long, self-denying, diligent, a little undereducated, perhaps, a bit crude, rather limited. . . . So when Lenin became ill, they elected Stalin secretary-general, rather as Mikhail Romanov was elected tsar.

That was in May 1922. Anybody else would have been satisfied with that much and sat silently rejoicing. Not Stalin, though. Anybody else might have set about reading *Das Kapital* and making excerpts. Stalin, though, sniffed the air and knew that it was now or never: The conquests of the Revolution were in danger; there was not a minute to lose. Lenin could not hang on to power and, left to himself, would not transfer it to safe hands. Lenin's health was precarious, and maybe that was for the best. If he survived as leader, there was no knowing what might happen; nothing was certain. Erratic, bad-tempered, and now sick into the bargain, he was more irritating every day; he was simply a hindrance. In everybody's way! He could abuse a man, make him feel small, dismiss him from an elected post for no reason at all.

Stalin's first idea was to dispatch Lenin to, say, the Caucasus for a rest cure. The air was good; there were out-of-the-way places which were without phone connections to Moscow and to which telegrams traveled slowly. A place like that, with no official business to be done, would steady his nerves. A tried and trusted comrade, the former expropriator (bank-raider Kamo), could be on hand to keep an eye on his health. Lenin was willing, and arrangements were discussed with Tiflis, but there were inexplicable delays. In the meantime, Kamo was run over and killed. (He had been talking too much about the "ex-es.")

Whereupon Stalin, concerned for his leader's life, raised the question with the Commissariat of Health and the professor of surgery: The bullet fired by Fanny Kaplan had never been extracted; it was poisoning Lenin's organism. Should he not have another operation for its removal? The doctors were persuaded. They said as one man that it was necessary, and Lenin consented. But once again there were delays. And all that happened was that Lenin went off to Gorky.

"We must be firm with Lenin," Stalin wrote to Kamenev. Kamenev and Zinoviev, his best friends at the time, agreed completely. Firm about his treatment, firm about his routine, firm about excluding him from official business, for the sake of his precious life. And of course firm about keeping him away from Trotsky. Krupskaya, too, must be curbed; she was only an ordinary Party member. Stalin was made officially "responsible for the health of Comrade Lenin," and he did not consider it beneath him to deal directly with the doctors in charge, and even with nurses, to give them instructions on the most beneficial regimen for Lenin, which was to say no to him and keep saying no even if he got upset. In political matters the prescription was the same: Lenin doesn't like the draft law on the Red Army—right, push it through; Lenin doesn't like what we're doing about the Central Executive Committee—right, push it through. Don't give way at any price; remember he's a sick man; he can't possibly know best. If he insists on something being done urgently, take your time over it, postpone it. The secretary-general can even answer back, very rudely—it just means he's a straight shooter; he can't force himself to behave unnaturally, to do violence to his own character.

Still, for all Stalin's exertions, Lenin made a slow recovery: His illness dragged on till autumn, when the argument about the Central Executive Committee grew heated, and dear Ilyich was up and about only briefly. He left his bed only to resurrect in December 1922 his entente cordiale with Trotsky, and against Stalin, of course. If that was all he had gotten up for, he had better go back to bed. Medical surveillance now became stricter. He was forbidden to read or write or be told anything about official business; he must just eat his gruel. But dear Ilyich took it into his head to write his political testament, behind the secretary-general's back, another move against Stalin. He dictated for five minutes a day, which was all he was allowed, all Stalin allowed him. But Stalin grinned into his mustache as the stenographer came clippety-clop along the corridor in her high heels, bringing him the obligatory copy. Next Krupskaya had to be pulled up sharply, as she deserved, whereupon dear Ilyich got overheated and suffered his third stroke! All Stalin's efforts had failed to save his life.

He had chosen a good time to die. Trotsky, as luck would have it, was in the Caucasus, and Stalin gave him the wrong date for the funeral, because there was no need for him to attend: It was much more fitting for the secretary-general to pronounce the oath of loyalty (and very important that he should).

But Lenin had left that will. It could set comrade against comrade; it might be misunderstood. Some people even wanted to replace the secretary-general. So Stalin drew even closer to Zinoviev, assuring him that he was now the obvious leader of the Party, and urging him as future leader to present the Central Committee's report to the Thirteenth Congress, while Stalin retained his humble post of secretary-general, which was all he wanted. So Zinoviev lorded it on the Congress platform, delivered his report and . . . and that was all. (He could hardly be elected to the nonexistent post of "leader of the Party.") But in return for this privilege, he persuaded the Central Committee that Lenin's testament would not even be read out at the Congress and that Stalin would not be dismissed, since he had now mended his ways.

The members of the Politburo were all of one mind at the time, all against Trotsky. They made a good job of rejecting his proposals and removing his supporters from their posts. Any other secretary-general might have been satisfied. But Stalin the indefatigable, the unblinking, knew that it was far too soon to relax.

Would it be a good thing if Kamenev took Lenin's place as chairman of the Council of People's Commissars? (When Stalin and Kamenev had visited the sick man together, reports in *Pravda* had made it appear that Stalin had gone alone. Just in case. He foresaw that Kamenev, too, was not eternal.) Maybe Rykov would be better? Well, Kamenev himself agreed, and so did Zinoviev, such was the harmony among them all!

But before long a great blow was struck at this friendship. It transpired that Zinoviev and Kamenev were humbugs and double-dealers: They were intent only on power; they did not cherish Lenin's ideas. They had to be cut down to size. They became the "new opposition" (and the garrulous Krupskaya found herself in their company), while Trotsky, after all the punishment he had taken, held his peace for the time being. The situation thus created was a very favorable one. The dawn of Stalin's friendship with the amiable Bukharin, the Party's leading theorist, conveniently supervened at this point. Dear little Bukharin did the speechmaking: Dear little Bukharin provided the theoretical foundations and justifications (the other lot called for "an offensive against the kulak," so our slogan was "Alliance Between Town and Country"). Stalin himself was not the least bit ambitious for fame, for authority; he just looked after the voting and made sure that the right man was in the right place. A lot of the right comrades were already in the posts where they were needed, and voting correctly. Zinoviev was dismissed from the Communist Internationale; Leningrad was taken away from the opposition.

You would have thought that they would have resigned themselves to the situation, but no: They now joined forces with Trotsky, and that poseur had one last inspiration, the slogan "Industrialization." So Stalin and dear little Bukharin came out with "Party unity!" For unity's sake all must knuckle under! Trotsky was banished; Zinoviev and Kamenev were gagged.

Another great help was the "Lenin draft": After that, the majority of the Party consisted of people untainted with the vices of the intelligentsia, uncontaminated by the squabbles which went on in the underground and in emigration, people to whom the former importance of Party leaders meant nothing and their current image everything. Sound people, dedicated people were rising from the depths of the Party to occupy important posts. Stalin had never doubted that he would find such people and that it was they who would save the conquests of the Revolution. But fate had another surprise in store: Bukharin, Tomsky, and Rykov also proved to be two-faced. They did not stand up for the unity of the Party! And Bukharin proved to be not the no. 1 theorist but the no. 1 muddlehead. His crafty slogan "Alliance Between Town and Country" had a hidden significance: It hinted at the restoration of the old order, capitulation to the kulak, the abandonment of industrialization!

Valid slogans were finally discovered. Only Stalin had been capable of formulating them: "Attack the Kulak and Force the Pace of Industrialization!" And of course "For Party Unity."

It was the turn of this vile rightist gang to be swept out of the leadership.

Bukharin, flattering himself, had once quoted some sage's dictum that "inferior minds make better administrators." Wide of the mark, Nikolai Ivanovich, you and your sage: sound minds, it should be, not inferior minds.

Your own mental capacity you demonstrated at your trials. Stalin had sat in a closed-off section of the gallery, watching them through a wire screen and smiling to himself. What orators they once were! How forceful they had once seemed! That they should come to this! Pathetic washouts!

His understanding of human nature and his sober good sense had always been Stalin's strengths. He understood those he saw with his own eyes. But he also understood people whom he had not seen for himself. When things were difficult in 1931–32 and the country was without food and clothing, one good push from outside might have toppled us, or so it seemed. The Party gave the command: Sound the alarm; there is a danger of intervention! But Stalin himself had never believed a word of it, because he had just as clear a picture of those other, Western windbags.

There was no way of measuring what it had cost, in health and strength and stamina, to cleanse the Party and the country of their enemies, to cleanse Leninism, that infallible doctrine to which Stalin had never been false: He was doing precisely what Lenin had envisaged, only somewhat less drastically and without unnecessary fuss.

So much effort! And yet things were never quiet; there was never a time when no one stood in the way. One minute it would be Tukhachevsky popping up to say that but for Stalin he would have taken Warsaw. Then Frunze stepped out of line, and the censor nodded. Or some trashy yarn pictured Stalin as a dead man upright on a mountain, and once again those idiots failed to spot it. Then the Ukraine let the crop rot in the fields; the Kuban opened fire from sawn-off shotguns. Ivanovo—yes, Ivanovo!—went on strike. . . .

Never once did Stalin lose his self-control. Not after the mistake he had made with Trotsky. He knew that the mills of history grind slow, but they never stop turning. No need for a noisy show of indignation; all those who were jealous of him would go away, die, be trodden into the dung heap. (Sorely wounded as Stalin was by those writers, he did not seek revenge, not for that; to do so would not have taught a lesson. He waited for another opportunity; there would always be an opportunity.)

And sure enough, everyone who in the Civil War had commanded so much as a battalion, so much as a company in units that were not loyal to Stalin, every last man of them went, disappeared. Delegates to the Twelfth, Thirteenth, Fourteenth, Fifteenth, Sixteenth, and Seventeenth Congresses, as though answering a roll call, departed to a place from which no votes are cast, no speeches made. Mutinous Leningrad, that dangerous place, was twice purged. Even friends like Sergo had to be sacrificed. Even such diligent helpers as Yagoda and Yezhov had to be taken out afterward. And in time the long arm reached Trotsky and split his skull open.

With no major enemy aboveground, he had surely earned a breathing space? Finland poisoned it. Marking time on the Karelian Isthmus, he had felt disgraced in the eyes of Hitler, who was strolling through France with his walking stick. An indelible blot on the military genius's reputation! Those Finns, that hostile nation of double-dyed bourgeois, ought to be deported, down to the smallest child, to the sands of the Karakum, and he himself would sit at the phone and keep the tally: so many shot and buried, so many still to go.

Disasters rained on him thick and fast. Hitler tricked him and invaded, a lovely alliance wrecked out of sheer stupidity! His lips had trembled at the microphone as he blurted out the words involuntarily, "Brothers and sisters"; there was no wiping them from the record now. But those brothers and sisters had fled like sheep; no one had been ready to fight to the death, although they had been given clear orders to do just that. Why didn't they stand and fight? Why had they not immediately stood and fought? . . . It was hurtful.

Then there was the evacuation to Kuibyshev, to the empty air-raid shelters. He had always been master of the situation; he had never once weakened . . . except that one time, when he had succumbed to panic, quite needlessly. He had paced his rooms for a week, had telephoned again and again: Has Moscow surrendered yet? No, it hasn't surrendered. It seemed incredible that the Germans would be halted! But our boys stopped them! Heroes, of course. Heroes. But many had to be taken out; it would be no victory if the rumor got around that the Commander in Chief had temporarily left the city. (This explained the photographs taken of a small parade on November 7.)

Meanwhile, Berlin radio was washing all that dirty linen—the murders of Lenin, Frunze, Dzherzhinsky, Kuibyshev, Gorky—why stop there! The old enemy, Churchill, who looked fat enough for a Georgian pork pot roast, flew in to smoke a couple of cigars in the Kremlin and gloat. The Ukrainians proved treacherous. (In 1944 he had dreamed of resettling the whole Ukrainian population in Siberia, but there were too many of them to replace.) There were other traitors: the Lithuanians, the Estonians, the Tatars, the Cossacks, the Kalmyks, the Chechens, the Ingush, the Latvians, yes, even the Revolution's sturdiest prop, the Latvians. Even his own kin, the Georgians, who were safe from mobilization—he couldn't help suspecting that even they would welcome Hitler. The only ones who remained loyal to their Father were the Russians and the Jews.

So even the "national question" became a joke at his expense in those trying years.

But those misfortunes, too, were in the past, thank God. Stalin had recovered a lot of ground by outwitting Churchill and the holier-than-thou Roosevelt. Since the twenties he had scored no success to compare with his triumph over that pair of fools. Answering their letters or returning to his quarters after a meeting at Yalta, he couldn't help laughing at them. These statesmen, who thought themselves so clever, were more stupid than babes in arms. They would keep asking what things would be like after the war. Well, just send us your planes, send us your canned food, and when the time comes, we'll see. Toss them a word, the idlest passing thought, and they would jump for joy and rush to get it down on paper. Feign an excess of loving kindness, and they would be twice as soft. He had got from them—free, gratis, for nothing—Poland, Saxony, Thuringia, the Vlasovites, the Krasnovites, the Kurile Islands, Sakhalin, Port Arthur, half of Korea. He had run rings around them on the Danube and in the Balkans. The "smallholders'" leaders triumphed in the elections and went straight to jail. Mikolajczyk was quickly toppled; Beneš's heart gave out, as did Jan Masaryk's; Cardinal Mindszenty confessed to his misdeeds; Dimitrov was admitted to the Kremlin heart clinic and there renounced his nonsensical plan for a Balkan federation.

All Soviet citizens returning home after living in Europe were sent to the camps. All prisoners who had served only one ten-year sentence were sent back to serve another.

In a word, things seemed to be coming right at last.

But when even the Siberian taiga no longer rustled with hints of an alternative socialism, the black dragon Tito crept into the open and blocked all roads ahead.

Stalin, like some legendary hero, was exhausting his strength, hacking away at the endlessly proliferating heads of the hydra. . . .

HOW COULD HE have let himself be misled? Failed to discern the scorpion soul of the man! He, the great expert on human psychology! In 1936 they had

Tito by the throat! And they had let him get away! . . . Ay . . . ay . . . ay . . . ay . . . ay!

Stalin groaned, swung his legs off the couch, and clutched his balding head. Vain regrets rankled in his bosom. He had toppled mountains, and he had tripped over a dunghill.

Iosif had tripped over Josip.

That Kerensky was still living out his days somewhere or other did not trouble Stalin at all. Nicholas II or Kolchak could return from the grave; Stalin had no personal animosity toward any of these: They were honest enemies who did not turn themselves inside out to offer some new, improved socialism of their own.

A better Socialism! Different from Stalin's! The pipsqueak! Socialism without Stalin was no different from fascism!

Not that Tito would get anywhere. Nothing could come of his efforts. As an old horse-doctor who has slit open any number of bellies, chopped off innumerable extremities in smoky peasant huts, looks at a lady medic in the making, come to do her practical work in spotless white, that was how Stalin looked at Tito.

But Tito made play with long-forgotten slogans from the early days of the Revolution: "workers' control," "land for the peasants." . . . Soap bubbles to fascinate idiots.

Lenin's *Collected Works* had gone through three revised editions, the works of the Founding Fathers through two. All those who had raised awkward questions, all who had been mentioned in obsolete footnotes, all who had thought of building Socialism differently had long ago fallen asleep. And now, when it was clear that there was no other way, and that not only Socialism but Communism would long ago have been constructed

—if it were not for grandees who got too big for their boots, lying reports, soulless bureaucrats, indifference to the public good, slackness in organizational and explanatory work among the masses, lack of direction in the indoctrination of Party members, deliberate delays in construction;

—if it were not for stoppages and absenteeism in industry, the production of substandard goods, poor planning, reluctance to adopt new technology, the nonperformance of scientific research institutes, the inadequate training of young specialists, the reluctance of young people to take jobs out in the wilds, sabotage by prisoners, loss of grain

> in the fields, the embezzlements by bookkeepers, pilfering at depots, thieving stockroom and shop managers, predatory truckers. . . .
> —if it were not for complacent local authorities! excessively tolerant and venal militiamen! criminal misuse of the housing stock! brazen black-marketing! greedy housewives! spoiled children! trolley-car gossips! nitpicking writers! cock-eyed filmmakers! . . .

When everyone could see that Communism was on the right road and not far from completion, that cretin Tito and his Talmudist Kardelj reared their ugly heads and declared that this was not the way to build Communism!

At this point Stalin realized that he was talking aloud, chopping the air; that his heart was beating furiously, his eyes were clouding, and an unpleasant urge to twitch had crept into his limbs.

He took a deep breath. Stroked his face and his mustache. Took another deep breath. He must not let it all get him down.

Ah, yes, he had to see Abakumov. He was about to rise, but his eyes had cleared, and he spotted a little black-and-red booklet, published in a cheap mass edition, on his telephone table. He reached for it in pleasurable anticipation, propped himself up on his cushions, and lay back for a few minutes more.

It was an advance copy of a work to be published in millions of copies in ten European languages, Renaud de Jouvenel's *Tito: Traitor in Chief.* (It was a happy circumstance that the author could approach the dispute impartially, being an objective Frenchman, and what was more, with an aristocratic "de" to his name.) Stalin had read the book carefully some days earlier (and indeed had given advice when it was being written), but he was always reluctant to part with an enjoyable book. It would help so many millions of people to see through that vainglorious, conceited, cruel, cowardly, loathsome, hypocritical, villainous tyrant! That vile traitor! That hopeless blockhead! Even the Western Communists had lost their bearings, didn't know whom to believe. Even that old fool André Marty would have to be expelled from the Party for defending Tito.

He paged through the book. There it was! Let nobody make a hero of Tito: On two occasions he had wanted, like the coward he was, to surrender to the Germans, but Arso Jovanovic, his chief of staff, had forced him to go on being commander in chief! Noble Arso! Murdered. And what about Petricevic? "Murdered simply because he loved Stalin." Noble Petricevic! The best people were always killed by somebody else; it fell to Stalin to finish off the worst.

It was all there—how Tito was probably a British spy, how vain he was about his underpants with a royal monogram, his physical ugliness, his resemblance to Göring, all those diamond rings on his fingers, his chestful of medals and decorations (what pathetic vanity in a man unendowed with strategic genius).

An objective, an ideologically sound book. Perhaps Tito was also sexually inadequate? That ought to be mentioned.

"The Yugoslav Communist Party is in the power of murderers and spies." "Tito was only able to take over the leadership because Béla Kun and Traicho Kostov vouched for him."

Kostov! Stalin felt a pang. The blood rushed furiously to his head; he stamped his foot; he kicked out violently, booting Traicho in the face, bloodying his ugly mug! Stalin's gray eyelids trembled with satisfaction that justice had been done.

That damned Kostov! That filthy swine!

Extraordinary how transparent the machinations of these scoundrels became in retrospect! They were all Trotskyists, but how cleverly they had disguised themselves! Kun at least had been polished off in '37, but it was only ten days since Kostov had stood before a Socialist court and reviled it. Stalin had managed so many trials successfully, compelled so many enemies to trample on themselves, and then the Kostov trial had gone disastrously wrong. It was a disgrace, with the whole world watching! The cunning of the man! To deceive experienced interrogators, grovel at their feet, then take it all back in open court! In the presence of foreign journalists! Where was his sense of decency? His Communist conscience? His proletarian solidarity? Appealing to the imperialists! All right, so you're not guilty, but die anyway, for the good of Communism!

Stalin flung the book away. No, he must not lie down! Battle called.

He rose. Straightened up, but not all the way. Unlocked (and locked behind him) the other door, not the one at which Poskryobyshev had knocked. His soft boots shuffled almost silently along a narrow, low-ceilinged, crooked hallway, also windowless. He went past the secret entrance to his underground driveway and stopped at a two-way mirror, through which he could see the waiting room.

He looked. Abakumov was already there. Sitting with a big notebook in his hand, looking strained, wondering when he would be summoned. Stepping more firmly, no longer shuffling, Stalin went into his bedroom, which was also low-ceilinged, cramped, windowless, and air-conditioned. Under the oak paneling there was armor plating, and only then stone wall.

With a little key that he carried in his waistband, Stalin unlocked the metal lid of a decanter, poured himself a glass of his favorite cordial, drank it, and locked the decanter again.

He went over to the mirror. The eyes that had outstared Western premiers gazed back at him, stern and incorruptible. He looked austere, simple, soldierly. He rang for his Georgian orderly, to get dressed.

Even to a henchman he would present himself as he would appear in the eyes of history.

His iron will. . . . His inflexible will.

Never for a moment, never for a moment, must he cease to be . . . a mountain eagle.

## 21

# Give Us Back the Death Penalty!

HARDLY ANYONE DARED CALL HIM SASHA to his face or even to think of him by that name. It had to be Aleksandr Nikolaevich. "Poskryobyshev rang" meant "The Boss rang." "Poskryobyshev has ordered" meant "The Boss has ordered." Poskryobyshev had lasted more than fifteen years as head of Stalin's personal secretariat. It was a long time, and anyone who did not know him well might marvel that his head had not rolled. His secret was simple: He was at heart an officer's servant, and he had entrenched himself in his job by acting accordingly. Even when he was made a lieutenant general, a member of the Central Committee, and head of the Special Department for Surveillance of Members of the Central Committee, he was incapable of imagining himself as less of a nonentity in comparison with the Boss. "To your native village, Soplyaki" ("Wimps' home"), the Boss would say, and he would clink glasses with a complacent giggle. Stalin's nose for such things never let him down, and in Poskryobyshev he scented neither doubt nor contumacy.

But in his dealings with his juniors, this homely, balding courtier acquired enormous importance. When he spoke to underlings over the telephone, his voice was the faintest whisper; you had to ram your head into the receiver to hear anything. You could occasionally share a little joke with him on matters of no moment, but ask how things were in there today? Your tongue would go on strike.

On this occasion Poskryobyshev told Abakumov:

"Iosif Vissarionovich is working. He may not want to see you. He gave orders for you to wait."

Relieving Abakumov of his briefcase (it had to be handed over before you went in to the Man), Poskryobyshev escorted him into the waiting room and went away.

Abakumov had not ventured to ask what he most wanted to know: what sort of mood the Boss was in today. He was left alone in the waiting room, his heart pounding.

This large, powerfully built, and strong-willed man, whenever he found himself there, felt faint with dread, just like any ordinary citizen at the height of the Terror listening in the night hours for footsteps on the stairs. His ears became ice cold, then filled with blood and became red hot, and whenever this happened, Abakumov feared that his continually burning ears would arouse the Boss's suspicion. The least little thing made Stalin suspicious. He did not, for instance, like people to put their hands into inside pockets in his presence. So Abakumov transferred to his breast pocket the two fountain pens he had ready to take notes.

Beria was the channel for day-to-day management of State Security, and it was from him that Abakumov generally received his instructions. But once a month the Autocrat liked to sample in the flesh the man to whom he entrusted the defense of the world's most advanced social order.

Those interviews, an hour at a time, were the heavy price which Abakumov paid for all his power, all his high-and-mightiness. He lived, he enjoyed life, only from one interview to the next. When the appointed time came, his heart died within him; his ears turned to ice; he handed over his briefcase not knowing whether he would ever get it back; he bowed his bull head at Stalin's office door, uncertain whether he would be able to raise it in an hour's time.

What made Stalin terrifying was that any slip in dealing with him was like mishandling a detonator: You would do it only once in your life; there was no chance to correct it. What made Stalin terrifying was that he never listened to excuses; he did not even make accusations. One end of his mustache twitched slightly, and sentence was passed somewhere inside there, but the condemned man was not informed of it; he went peacefully on his way, was arrested that night and shot before morning.

Worst of all was when Stalin said nothing and you were left to torment yourself with conjecture. If Stalin threw something heavy or sharp at you, stamped on your foot, spat at you, or blew hot tobacco ash in your face, his anger was not final; it would pass! If Stalin was rude and abused him, even in the most obscene language, Abakumov rejoiced; that meant that the Boss still hoped to reform his minister and to go on working with him.

By now, of course, Abakumov realized that excess of zeal had carried him too high for comfort; he would have been safer lower down. Stalin was always pleasant and affable when he talked to peripheral people. But you couldn't break out of the inner circle; there was no way back.

All you had to look forward to was death. Of natural causes. Or . . . best not to mention it.

So whenever he reported to Stalin, Abakumov lived in fear of being found out.

What if it became known that he had used his position in Germany to line his pockets? That thought alone kept him shivering in his shoes.

At the end of the war Abakumov had been head of SMERSH (the "Death to Spies" organization). All counterespionage units in all front-line army groups came under his command. For a time it was possible to enrich yourself undetected. To help finish Germany off completely, Stalin adopted Hitler's idea of permitting those at the front to send parcels home. Fight for the honor of the motherland? Fine. For Stalin? Better still. But shouldn't the fighting man be given some personal, material interest in victory? Say, the right to send home the spoils of war, rankers five kilograms a month, officers ten, generals a pood?* (This gradation was fair, because a soldier's pack must not weigh him down on the march, whereas a general always has his car.) But the counterespionage network was in a much more advantageous situation. It was out of reach of enemy shells. It was safe from enemy bombers. SMERSH's life was lived just behind the front line, in the zone that was no longer under fire but not yet invaded by treasury officials. Its officers were shrouded in a cloud of secrecy. Nobody would dare inquire what they had put in a sealed freight car, what they had removed from a sequestered estate, what

---

* Pood: Pre-Revolutionary unit of weight equal to 36.11 pounds.

their sentries were there to guard. Trucks, trains, and airplanes carried off the riches amassed by SMERSH's officers. Lieutenants shipped out thousands, colonels hundreds of thousands, and Abakumov raked in millions.

He did not, of course, imagine for a moment that gold, even deposited in a Swiss bank, would save him if he lost his ministerial post or if the regime he served collapsed. But he could not watch his subordinates getting rich while he took nothing for himself. Such self-denial was more than flesh and blood could bear. So he sent out search parties, one after another. Even two cases full of men's suspenders were more than he could resist. He looted automatically, like a man under hypnosis.

This treasure of the Nibelungs brought Abakumov not affluent ease but the constant dread of exposure. None of those in the know would dare denounce the all-powerful minister, but the merest chance might destroy him. He had derived no benefit from what he had taken, but he could hardly declare it to the Ministry of Finance now!

He had arrived at 2:30 a.m., but at 3:10 he was still pacing the waiting room restlessly, with his big empty notebook in his hand, faint with fear, and with those telltale burning ears. Only one thing could make him happy now: that Stalin would feel overworked and unable to see him. Abakumov was afraid that he would be punished for the secret telephone. He did not know what lie to tell next.

At last the heavy door slowly opened, halfway. Quietly, almost on tiptoe, Poskryobyshev stepped into the gap and speechlessly beckoned. Abakumov followed, trying not to put his big broad feet down heavily. He inserted his trunk into the next half-open door, steadying it with one hand on the polished bronze handle.

He paused on the threshold and said, "Good evening, Comrade Stalin! May I come in?"

He had foolishly forgotten to clear his throat, so that his voice sounded hoarse and insufficiently obsequious.

Stalin was writing at his desk, in a tunic with gilded buttons and several rows of ribboned medals but without epaulets. He finished a sentence and only then raised his head to look at the new arrival with owlish malignity. Without speaking.

A very bad sign! Not a word.

And he resumed his writing.

Abakumov closed the door behind him but dared go no farther without a nod or gesture of invitation. He stood with his long arms hanging straight at his sides, bending slightly forward, a respectful smile of greeting on his fleshy lips, but his ears were aflame.

No one had used this simplest of interrogator's ploys, greeting a man's entry with hostile silence, more often than the Minister of State Security. But familiar as it was, when Stalin received him like that, Abakumov was ready to collapse in terror.

In Stalin's night study, a small, low-ceilinged room, there were no pictures or ornaments, and the windows were tiny. The low walls were oak-paneled, and a few bookshelves ran along one of them. The desk stood near to but clear of one wall. There was a record player with a radio in one corner, with records on a set of shelves beside it. Stalin enjoyed listening to his old speeches in the night hours.

Abakumov waited, bent double in supplication.

Yes, he was completely in the hands of the Leader, but up to a point the Leader was in his hands, too. Just as in battle, if one side advances too impetuously, the armies interlock, each outflanks the other, and you cannot be sure who is surrounding whom, so here: Stalin had locked himself (and the whole Central Committee) into the State Security system; everything he wore, ate, drank, sat on, lay on was provided by MGB people, and the MGB alone now guarded him. So that in some freakish ironical sense, Stalin was Abakumov's subordinate. Only it was not very likely that Abakumov could successfully assert his authority first.

Bowed low, the hefty minister stood and waited. While Stalin went on writing. Whenever Abakumov entered that room, Stalin would be sitting and writing like that. It was as though he never left the spot, never stopped writing, imposingly, authoritatively, so that every word that flowed from his pen at once hardened into history. A desk lamp shed light on his papers; the rest of the room was only faintly lit by concealed overhead lights. This time Stalin paused occasionally, leaned back in his chair, and squinted sideways at the floor. He gave Abakumov a dark look, as though he were trying to hear something, although there was not a sound in the room.

Where does it come from, that commanding manner, that way of endowing every little movement with significance? The finger movements, the gestures, the raised eyebrows, the intent gaze, were no doubt those of the young Koba. But in him none of this had frightened people; no one had read into these movements a terrible meaning. Only when holes enough had been made in the backs of heads did people begin to see in the Leader's slightest movement a hint, a warning, a threat, an order. Noticing other people's reactions, Stalin started observing himself, discerned the latent menace in his gestures and glances, and began consciously cultivating them so that they became still more predictable in their effect on those around him.

At last Stalin looked grimly at Abakumov and showed him with a jab of his pipe where he was to sit.

Abakumov sprang happily to life, stepped lightly forward, and sat down, but only on the front half of the chair. He was not at all comfortable, but it would be easier to stand up should he need to.

"Well?" asked Stalin brusquely, glancing at his papers.

The moment had come! He must take care now not to lose the initiative.

Clearing his throat with a little cough, Abakumov began speaking rapidly, almost enthusiastically. He would curse himself later for his verbose eagerness to please, for the reckless promises made in Stalin's office, but he could not help it. It was always the same: The more unfriendly the reception, the rasher Abakumov was in his assurances to the Boss—and the more extravagant his promises.

The beauty of Abakumov's nocturnal reports, their main attraction for Stalin, was that they always uncovered some very important and widely ramified hostile group. Abakumov never turned up to report without the news that some such group had been rendered harmless. As usual, he had such a group (at the Frunze Academy) in readiness and could fill much of the time with details.

But he began by describing progress (real or fictitious he did not know himself) in the preparations to assassinate Tito. He said that a time bomb would be put on board Tito's yacht before it sailed for Brioni.

Stalin looked up, stuck his dead pipe in his mouth, and made it gurgle twice. He showed no further interest, but Abakumov, who could sometimes read his chief's mind, felt that he had hit the spot.

"What about Rankovich?" Stalin asked.

Of course, of course! They must choose a moment when Rankovich, Kardelj, Moshe Pijade—the whole gang—could be blown sky-high together! According to his calculations it was bound to happen no later than next spring! (When the bomb went off, the yacht's crew would die as well, but the minister did not mention this trivial fact, and his interlocutor did not inquire.)

But what were his thoughts as he sat blowing into his pipe and staring at his minister expressionlessly over his pendulous nose?

Not, of course, the thought that the Party he led had been born rejecting terrorist acts against individuals. Nor yet the thought that he himself had thrived on terrorism all his life. Breathing noisily into his pipe and staring at that overfed, rosy-cheeked bullyboy with the burning ears, Stalin was thinking what he always thought when he saw subordinates so mettlesome, so ready for anything, so eager to please. Indeed, it was not so much a thought as an instinctive reaction: How far can this man be trusted today? And with it, automatically: Has the time come to sacrifice this man?

Stalin knew very well that Abakumov had lined his pockets in 1945. But he was in no hurry to punish him. It suited Stalin that Abakumov was what he was. Such men were easier to manage. In the course of a lifetime Stalin had found that the people to be treated with the greatest caution were men of principle, so-called, like Bukharin. They were the nimblest of tricksters, difficult to trip up.

But even the transparent Abakumov was no more to be trusted than anyone else on this earth.

Stalin had not trusted his own mother. Nor God. Nor his Revolutionary comrades. Nor the peasants (you couldn't trust them to sow and get the harvest in unless you forced them). Nor the workers (who wouldn't work unless norms were set for them). Still less did he trust the engineers. He had not trusted his soldiers and generals to fight without punitive battalions and security detachments to cut off their retreat. He never trusted his henchmen. He had not trusted his wives and mistresses. Even his children he had not trusted. And he had always been proved right!

There was one man he had trusted, and only one, in a life free of trust and mistakes. In the eyes of the world, that man had seemed so firm in friendship and in enmity, he had swung around so sharply and held out his hand in friendship. This was no windbag; this was a man of action!

And Stalin had believed him!

That man was Adolf Hitler.

Stalin had looked on with approval and malicious glee while Hitler dismembered Poland, France, Belgium, while his planes blackened the skies over England. Molotov came back from Berlin in a fright. There were intelligence reports that Hitler was concentrating troops in the East. Hess fled to England. Churchill warned Stalin that he was about to be attacked. Every rook on the aspens of Belorussia and the poplars of Galicia screeched warnings of war. Every market woman in Stalin's own country prophesied war from one day to the next. Stalin alone was unperturbed. He went on sending trainloads of raw materials to Germany and did nothing to fortify his frontiers, for fear of offending his colleague.

Hitler he had believed!

And this faith had very nearly cost him his head.

Which was one more reason why he now believed absolutely nobody!

Abakumov could have answered this overbearing distrust with bitter words but dared not utter them. Stalin shouldn't have played at Trojan horses! He shouldn't have sent for that fathead Popivoda to discuss anti-Tito pamphlets. Shouldn't have turned down those splendid fellows handpicked by Abakumov to kill the bear, men who knew the language, knew the country's ways, even knew Tito by sight. Stalin shouldn't have turned them down after a look at their dossiers (anybody who's lived abroad is not one of us); he should have trusted them and given them the job. Abakumov himself was angered by this inertia.

But he knew his Boss! You must devote a proportion of your powers to his service, more than half but not the whole. Stalin would not tolerate open noncompliance. But excessively efficient performance he hated; he saw in it an insidious threat to his uniqueness. Nobody but he must know or understand or do things perfectly!

So Abakumov, like the other forty-five ministers, kept up a show of exertion in ministerial harness but pulled with only half his shoulder power.

Just as Midas turned all that he touched to gold, so Stalin turned all that he touched to lead.

Today, though, Stalin's face brightened as Abakumov proceeded with his report. After a detailed account of the proposed bomb blast, the minister went on to report arrests at the Ecclesiastical Academy, then with minute particularity the business at the Frunze Academy, then the results of espionage in South Korean ports.

Duty and common sense demanded that he should now report the telephone call to the American Embassy the day before. But he could say nothing. He could assume that Beria or Vyshinsky had already reported it. It might be best to behave as if he had not yet been told of it himself. It was precisely because Stalin trusted nobody and encouraged duplication that every draft animal pulled half-heartedly. For the moment it would pay him not to be in a hurry with promises to find the culprit with the aid of the new technology. He was doubly afraid to use the word "telephone" just then; it might remind Stalin of the secret telephone. Abakumov even tried not to look at the telephone on the desk, in case his eyes drew the Boss's attention to it.

Stalin was obviously trying to remember something right then! Perhaps the secret telephone! His brow puckered in deep folds, his fleshy nose tensed, he stared hard at Abakumov (the minister did his utmost to look honest and guileless), but he could not remember! The thought half glimpsed slipped back into a black hole. The creases in his gray brow relaxed impotently.

Stalin sighed, filled his pipe, and lit it.

"Oh, yes!" The first puff had reminded him of something, but something incidental, not the important thing he had been trying to recall. "Is Gomulka under arrest?"

Gomulka had recently been dismissed from all the posts he held in Poland, missed his footing and slid into the abyss.

Abakumov confirmed that Gomulka had indeed been arrested, rising slightly from his chair in his relief. (Stalin had in fact been informed earlier.)

Stalin pressed a button on his desk to switch from the overhead light to several wall-lights. He rose and began to pace the floor, puffing at his pipe. Abakumov understood that no further report was required and that instructions would now be dictated. He opened the big notebook on his knees, got out his pen, and prepared to write (the Boss liked his words to be taken down immediately).

But Stalin walked over to the record player and back, puffing away, without saying a word, as though he had completely forgotten Abakumov. His gray, pockmarked face grew grim in a tortured effort to remember. Looking at him in profile as he passed, Abakumov saw that the Boss's shoulders were bowed, that his back was hunching, which made him appear smaller than he was, quite small in fact. Abakumov found himself conjecturing (he usually suppressed such thoughts in this place, in case the Highest somehow sensed them) that the Boss would not live another ten years. He was going to die, and although it might not be very wise of him, Abakumov wanted it to be soon; for all of them, Stalin's henchmen, it would surely be the beginning of an easier, freer life.

Stalin meanwhile was depressed by yet another lapse of memory; his head was refusing to work for him! On the way here from his bedroom he had been thinking of one particular question he needed to ask Abakumov, and now he had forgotten it. Helplessly, he tried frown after frown, struggling to remember.

Then suddenly he threw back his head, looked at the top of the opposite wall, and remembered, not what he needed to remember now but what he had been unable to remember two nights ago in the Museum of the Revolution, much to his annoyance at the time.

. . . It had happened in '37. Before the twentieth anniversary of the Revolution, when so much had changed in the way it was presented, he had decided to inspect the exhibition for himself and make sure that they had gotten nothing wrong. In one room, the one in which a huge television set now stood, the scales suddenly fell from his eyes, and he saw high up on the wall facing him big portraits of Zhelyabov and Perovskaya. Their faces were bold, fearless, their gaze implacable: They called on all who entered to "kill the tyrant."

The gaze of the two "People's Will" leaders went through him, like two arrows through his throat. He recoiled, he croaked, he choked, and, choking, pointed a shaking finger at the pictures.

They were taken down at once. And in Leningrad the first holy relic of the Revolution, the wreckage of Alexander II's carriage, was removed from the museum.

Beginning that very day, Stalin ordered refuges and safe apartments to be built for him in various places, sometimes riddling whole mountains with passageways, as on the river Kholodnaya. Losing his taste for life in the middle of a thickly populated city, he had ended up in this out-of-town villa, this low-ceilinged night office close to his bodyguard's orderly room.

The more people he relieved of their lives, the more he feared for his own. His brain invented many valuable improvements in the security system, such as, for instance, that the names of those on guard duty should be posted only one hour before the guard was mounted, and that each squad should be made up of soldiers from different barracks at a considerable distance from one another; when they met on guard duty, they would be seeing each other for the first time, and for twenty-four hours only, so that they would not be able to plot anything. His villa had been built like a labyrinthine mousetrap. There were three stockades, and their gates were not in line with one another. He had arranged for himself a number of bedrooms, and his bed was made up at the last moment, immediately before he retired.

All these precautions were dictated not by cowardice but by prudence. Because his person was of inestimable value to the history of mankind. Other people, however, might not realize this. And so as not to make himself a conspicuous exception, he prescribed similar precautions for all the lesser leaders, in the capital and in the provinces, forbade them to go to the bathroom without attendants, ordered them to ride in a gaggle of three indistinguishable vehicles. . . .

Painfully reminded of the Populist Revolutionaries' portraits, he stood stock-still in the middle of the room, looked around at Abakumov, and said, wagging his pipe in the air: "What are you doing for the protection of Party cadres?"

Following it with a malignant look, a hostile look, screwing his head to one side.

With his blank notebook open, Abakumov raised his behind from his chair in deference to the Leader (but did not stand up, knowing that Stalin liked people to keep still when they talked to him), and succinctly (because the Boss considered lengthy explanations insincere) and unhesitatingly began talking about something that he had not been expecting to talk about. (Ever-readiness was most important in this context; Stalin might interpret any hesitation as proof of malicious intent.)

"Comrade Stalin!" Abakumov's feelings were hurt, and his voice trembled. He yearned to use the more intimate "Iosif Vissarionovich," but this form of address was discouraged as presumptuous; no one must claim intimacy with the Leader, put himself almost on the same level.

"What else do we, the security apparatus, exist for, what is our whole ministry for, if not to make sure that you, Comrade Stalin, can work and think and lead our country without anxiety?"

(Stalin had said "the safety of Party cadres," but he wanted to hear only about himself, and Abakumov knew it.)

"Not a day goes by without me checking, making the necessary arrests, taking a good look at the situation!"

Stalin was still studying him closely, head on one side, like a doubtful raven.

"Tell me," he asked thoughtfully. "Are there still cases of terrorism? Haven't we seen the end of them yet?"

Abakumov sighed deeply.

"I wish I could tell you that there are no cases of terrorism, Comrade

Stalin. But there are. We have to render them harmless . . . in the most unexpected places."

Stalin closed one eye, and his other expressed satisfaction.

"That's good," he said, nodding his head. "I can see you're doing your job."

"What is more, Comrade Stalin. . . ." Abakumov, rules or no rules, could not bear to remain seated while the Leader stood, and he rose halfway from his chair, without unbending his knees completely (he never went there in elevator shoes). "What is more, we never let these things mature to the stage of actual planning. We nip them in the bud while they're still just a notion! We use Section 19!"

"Good, good." With a soothing gesture Stalin waved Abakumov back to his seat (he didn't want that great hulk looming over him). "So you think there are still malcontents among the masses?"

Abakumov sighed again.

"Yes, Comrade Stalin. A certain percentage."

(He would have looked pretty foolish if he had said there were none! If there were none, who needed him and his entire organization?)

"You're right," Stalin said with feeling.

His voice was hoarse, wheezy, dull.

"I see you know your job at State Security. You know, some people tell me there's no discontent, everybody who votes in elections votes for us, so everybody's satisfied. What do you think of that?" Stalin grinned. "Political blindness! The enemy hides his face, votes for us, but he is not content! Five percent, would you say? Or maybe eight?"

(This perspicacity of his, this self-critical realism, this refusal to let the incense go to his head, were qualities which Stalin particularly prized in himself!)

"Yes, Comrade Stalin," Abakumov replied with conviction. "Five percent. Perhaps seven."

Stalin continued his journey round the study, circling the desk en route.

"That is a weakness of mine, Comrade Stalin." Abakumov was getting bolder. His ears had cooled down. "I am incapable of complacency."

Stalin gently tapped the ashtray with his pipe.

"What about the younger generation? What is their attitude?"

Answering these questions was like juggling with knives. . . . You only had to cut yourself once. . . . Say "good," and it would be "political blindness." Say "bad," and you "lack faith in our future."

Abakumov spread his fingers and refrained from speaking too soon.

Stalin did not wait for an answer. "We must show greater concern for the young," he said, his pipe tapping an emphatic accompaniment. "We must be particularly hard on the bad habits of young people!"

Abakumov sat up and started writing.

Stalin was carried away by this thought, and his eyes lit up with a tigerish gleam. He refilled his pipe, lit it, and began striding about the room much more vigorously than before.

"You must intensify your observation of student attitudes! Weed out whole groups, not just individuals! And you must go to the limit permitted by the law: twenty-five years, not just ten! Ten is like sending them to school, not to prison! Ten is fine for schoolboys. Once they start shaving, it's twenty-five! They're young enough! They'll survive!"

Abakumov scribbled. The first cogs in a complex machine began to turn.

"And you must put an end to the rest-cure conditions in political prisons! Is it true what Beria tells me, that political prisoners get food parcels?"

Abakumov was pained. "We'll eliminate them, Comrade Stalin! We'll put a stop to it!" he exclaimed, writing away. "That was a mistake on our part, Comrade Stalin! I'm sorry!"

(It was indeed a blunder! He should have raised it himself!)

Stalin faced Abakumov, feet wide apart.

"How many times do I have to tell you? You ought to know by now. . . ."

He spoke without anger. His eyes, stern no longer, expressed his confidence in Abakumov; he would learn the lesson, he would understand. Abakumov could not remember Stalin ever speaking to him so simply and so kindly. His feeling of apprehension had abandoned him; his brain was working like that of a normal man in normal conditions. A departmental matter had been causing him as much discomfort as a bone in his throat; out it came at last. His face brightened.

"We do understand, Comrade Stalin." (He spoke for the whole ministry). "We do understand: The class struggle will continue to grow more acute! All the more reason, then. . . . Put yourself in our position, Comrade Stalin. . . . We are tied hand and foot in our work by the abolition of capital punishment! We've been cudgeling our brains for two and a half years. . . . There's no way of documenting executions. So when somebody has to be shot, we must produce two versions of the sentence. Then again, we can't show the executioners' payment in the books, and our accounts get in a muddle. Besides, we've got nothing to threaten them with in the camps. We badly need capital punishment! Please, Comrade Stalin, give us back the death penalty!" A cry from a loving heart. Abakumov pressed his palm to his breast and gazed hopefully at his dark-faced Leader.

Stalin gave him perhaps the slightest of smiles. His bristling mustache trembled, but not alarmingly.

"I know," he said softly, understandingly. "I've been thinking about it."

Amazing man! He knew everything! He thought of everything before he was asked. Like a god hovering over them, he anticipated men's thoughts.

"One of these days I will give you back the death penalty," he said thoughtfully, looking deep into the future, perhaps years and years ahead. "It will be a useful educational measure."

Of course he had been thinking about it! This past two years or so he had regretted more than any of them that he had yielded to an impulse; to show off to the West, he had been false to himself, behaved as if people were not rotten through and through.

Yet all his life, that had been his distinctive characteristic as a statesman: Neither dismissal, nor systematic harassment, nor confinement in a madhouse, nor imprisonment for life, nor banishment, had ever seemed to him an adequate way of dealing with persons known to be dangerous. Death was the only fully reliable answer. Only the death of the criminal could confirm the reality and fullness of your power.

If the tip of his mustache twitched indignantly, there was only one possible sentence: death.

His scale included no lighter penalty.

Stalin withdrew his gaze from the bright distant future and turned it on Abakumov. Squinting from beneath lowered lids, he asked: "But aren't you afraid you might be the first to be shot?"

The word "shot" remained almost unspoken; his voice sank to a faint murmur, as if the thought went without saying.

But it chilled Abakumov to the core. His Dear Leader, his Beloved Leader, stood over him, just out of reach of a straight punch, studying every little line in the minister's face, to see how he would take the joke.

Not daring either to stand or to remain seated, Abakumov raised himself slightly on tensed legs, his knees trembling from the tension.

"Comrade Stalin! . . . If you think I deserve it. . . . If it's necessary. . . ."

Stalin's gaze was wise and penetrating. He was quietly turning over in his mind the inevitable second thought about any of his henchmen. Alas, there was a fatality which men could not defy: The most zealous of aides must sooner or later be disowned and cast off. Sooner or later they all compromise themselves.

"Quite right!" he said, with an indulgent smile, as though complimenting Abakumov on his ready understanding. "When you deserve it, that's when we'll shoot you."

He waved his hand, urging Abakumov to sit down. Abakumov made himself comfortable again.

Stalin thought awhile and then began speaking in a tone more friendly than the Minister of State Security had heard from him before.

"There will be plenty of work for you shortly, Abakumov. We shall be carrying out another exercise, like the one in 1937. The whole world is against us. War has long been inevitable. Ever since 1944 it has been inevitable. And before a great war there must be a great purge."

Abakumov ventured a protest.

"But Comrade Stalin, aren't we putting enough inside already?"

"You call that putting enough inside?" Stalin waved his hand, good-humoredly deprecating. "When we do start putting them away, you'll really see something! When the war comes and we move forward, we'll start putting Europe inside! Strengthen the Organs!* Strengthen the Organs! All the staff you need! Pay them what you like! I shall never refuse you!"

Then a benign dismissal.

"Right, off with you for now."

ABAKUMOV DIDN'T KNOW whether he was walking or flying as he crossed the waiting room to collect his briefcase from Poskryobyshev. He had a whole month of life before him, and it might even be the beginning of a new era in his relations with the Boss.

True, there had been a threat. He might be shot himself.

But of course that was only a joke.

* Organs: A nickname for the Soviet secret police, with its vulgar double entendre intended.

# 22

## The Emperor of the Earth

THE GREAT RULER, aroused by great thoughts, strode mightily about his night study. Music swelled within him; an enormous brass band provided the accompaniment to his march.

Discontented, eh? Let them be! They always had been discontented, and they always would be.

But Stalin had a passing acquaintance with an uncomplicated version of world history, and he knew that given time people will forgive all bad things, indeed forget them, or remember them as good. Whole nations behaved like Queen Anne in Shakespeare's *Richard III*: Their wrath was short-lived, their will infirm, their memory weak, and they would always be glad to give themselves to the victor.

The crowd was, as it were, the stuff from which history was made. (Make a note of it!) It shrank in one place only to swell in another. So there was no need to treat it gently.

The reason why he had to live to ninety was that the struggle was not over, the building was not finished, the times were uncertain, and there was no one to take his place.

He must wage and win the last world war. Exterminate like gophers the Western Social Democrats and all persistent pests throughout the world. Then, of course, he must raise the productivity of labor. Solve all those economic problems. In short, build Communism, as the phrase went.

In that context, by the way, completely incorrect ideas had entrenched themselves. Stalin had thought it over recently and reached clear conclusions. Naive and shortsighted people pictured Communism as a kingdom of plenty, of freedom from necessity. But that would be an impossible social order; at that rate Communism would be worse than bourgeois anarchy! The first and main characteristic of true Communism must be discipline, total subordination to authority, and strict execution of orders. (The intelligentsia must be kept under particularly firm control.) Second, "plenty" must be modest plenty, not even sufficiency in fact, because overprosperous people fell into ideological disarray, as could be seen in the West. If a man does not have to worry about food, he escapes the material pressure of history, being ceases to determine consciousness, and everything is topsy-turvy.

So, when you came to think of it, Stalin had built true Communism already.

This could not, however, be announced, or people would be asking, Where do we go next? Time went on; the whole world was in motion; one had to have somewhere to go.

Obviously it never would be possible to announce that the Communist society had been built. That would be a methodological error.

Now there was a man for you—Bonaparte! He was not frightened by the barking of Jacobin yard dogs; he declared himself emperor, and that was that.

There was nothing bad about the word "emperor." It meant "commander," the man who gave the orders. That was in no way incompatible with world Communism.

What a splendid ring it would have! Emperor of the Planet! Emperor of the Earth!

On and on he marched, while the brass bands played.

Someday, maybe, they would discover a preparation that would make him—him alone?—immortal. No, they would be too late.

But how could he abandon humanity? To whose care could he leave it? They would get in a muddle, make mistakes.

Very well, then. He would build more monuments to himself, bigger ones, higher ones (technology wouldn't stand still). Erect a statue on Kazbek, erect a statue on Elbrus, with their heads always above the clouds. And then, so be it, he could die, the Greatest of the Great; none was his equal; there was no one in the history of the earth to compare with him.

Suddenly he stopped.

On earth, yes, . . . but what about up there? He had no equal here, of course, but what if you raised your eyes higher, above the clouds; what about there?

He began pacing again, but more slowly.

This was the one doubt that sometimes insinuated itself into Stalin's mind.

On the face of it, the facts had been proven long ago, and all objections refuted.

All the same, there was some obscurity.

Especially if you had spent your childhood in the church. If you had gazed into the eyes of icons. If you had sung in the choir. If you could chant "now lettest thou thy servant . . ." right now without a slip.

Just lately these memories had for some reason become more vivid in Iosif's mind.

His mother, as she lay dying, had said, "It's a pity you didn't become a priest." He was the leader of the world proletariat, the unifier of Slavdom—and in his mother's eyes a failure.

Just in case, Stalin had never spoken out against God; there were plenty of orators without him. Lenin might spit on the cross and trample it; Bukharin and Trotsky might mock. Stalin held his tongue.

He had given orders that Abakadze, the inspector of seminaries who had expelled the young Dzhugashvili, should not be harmed. Let him live his life out.

And when, on July 3, 1941, his throat had dried up and tears had come into his eyes—tears not of terror but of pity, pity for himself—it was no accident that the words that forced their way from his lips were "brothers and sisters." Neither Lenin nor any of the others could have uttered those words, intentionally or otherwise.

His lips had spoken as they had been accustomed to speak in his youth.

Nobody saw him, nobody knew, he had told no one, but in those first days he had locked himself in his room and prayed, prayed properly, except that it was in a corner without icons, prayed on his knees. The first few months had been the hardest time of his life.

At that time he had made a vow to God: If the danger passed and he survived in his post, he would restore the church and church services in Russia and would not let believers be persecuted and imprisoned. (It should never have been allowed in the first place; it had started in Lenin's time.) And when the danger was over, when Stalingrad was behind him, Stalin had done all that he had vowed to do.

Whether or not God existed only God knew.

Most probably he did not. Because if he did, he was extraordinarily complacent. And lazy. To have such power . . . and put up with it all? Never once interfere in earthly matters? How could that be? Leaving aside the deliverance of 1941, Stalin had never noticed anyone but himself making things happen, never felt anyone at his side, elbow to elbow.

But suppose God did nonetheless exist, suppose he had power over souls. . . . Stalin must make his peace before it was too late. In spite of the heights he had reached. His need, in fact, was all the greater because of that. Because there was emptiness all about him—no one beside him, no one near him, the rest of mankind was somewhere far beneath him. So that God was, perhaps, nearer to him than anybody. And also lonely.

It had given Stalin real pleasure in recent years that the church in its prayers proclaimed him the Chosen of God. That was why the Monastery of Saint Sergius was maintained at the Kremlin's expense. No great power's prime minister got such a warm reception from Stalin as did his docile and doddering Patriarch; he went as far as the outer door to meet the old man and put a hand under his elbow when he took him in to dinner. He had even been thinking of looking perhaps for some little property, a little town house of some sort, and presenting it to the Patriarch. People used to make such gifts, to have prayers said for their souls.

Stalin knew that a certain writer was a priest's son but concealed the fact. He had asked him, when they were alone once, whether he was Orthodox. The man had turned pale and lost his tongue. "Come on, cross yourself! Do you know how?" The writer had crossed himself, thinking that he was done for. "Well done!" said Stalin, clapping him on the shoulder.

There was no getting away from it: In the course of a long and difficult struggle, Stalin had occasionally overdone things. It would be nice to get together a splendid choir and have them sing over his coffin, "Lord, now lettest thou they servant . . ."

In general, Stalin had begun to notice in himself a curious predilection not just for Orthodoxy. Now and again he felt the tug of a lingering attachment to the old world, the world from which he himself had come but which he had now spent forty years destroying in the service of Bolshevism.

In the thirties, for purely political reasons, he had revived the word "motherland," obsolete by then for fifteen years and almost obscene to the ear. But as the years went by, he had begun to take genuine pleasure in using the words "Russia" and "motherland." It somehow helped to put his own power on a firmer basis. To sanctify it, so to speak.

In earlier days he had carried out Party policy without counting how many of those Russians were expended. But gradually he had begun to take more notice of the Russian people and to like them, a people that had never betrayed him, had gone hungry for as long as it was necessary, had calmly faced all difficulties—even war, even the camps—and never once rebelled. They were devoted; they were pure in heart. Like Poskryobyshev, for instance.

After the victory Stalin had said quite sincerely that the Russian people had a clear mind, strength of character, and staying power.

In fact, as the years went by, Stalin's own wish was to be taken for a Russian himself.

He found some enjoyment, too, in playing with words reminiscent of the old world: instead of "school heads" let's have "directors"; instead of "command personnel" let's have "officer corps"; instead of All-Union Central Executive Committee, Supreme Soviet ("supreme" was a very fine word); let officers have orderlies; let secondary-school girls be educated separately from the boys, and wear aprons, and pay for their special lessons; let every civil service department have its own uniform and marks of distinction; let Russians rest, like all other Christians, on Sunday, and not on nondescript days that were just numbers; let only legal marriage be recognized, as under the tsar—never mind that he himself had once paid dearly for it, and never mind what Engels thought. And although he had been advised to shoot Bulgakov and burn his White Guardist play *The Days of the Turbins*, some power had jogged his elbow, and he had written, "Performance permitted in one Moscow theater."

Right there, in his night study, he had stood before the mirror to see how old-fashioned Russian epaulets went with his tunic—and had enjoyed doing it.

In the last analysis there was nothing intrinsically objectionable about a crown as the highest mark of distinction. The old world, after all, was a tried and tested world, a stable world that had lasted three hundred years. Why not borrow what was best in it?

At the time, the surrender of Port Arthur could only gladden the heart of the young Stalin, a Revolutionary on the run from exile in Irkutsk Province, but after the defeat of Japan in 1945 he had told a bit of a fib, claiming that the surrender of Port Arthur forty years earlier had always been a stain on the pride of older Russians like himself. Yes, yes, older Russians. It was no accident, Stalin sometimes reflected, that the man to establish himself as ruler of that country and win all hearts in it was Stalin and no other, not one of those illustrious loudmouths or pointy-bearded Talmudists, people without kin, without roots, without substance.

There they were, there they all were, on his shelves, unbound, in pamphlets dating from the twenties: those who had choked on their own eloquence, been shot or poisoned or burned, died in car crashes or committed suicide! Removed from all libraries, declared anathema, excluded from the canon—but there they all were, lined up for his inspection! Every night they offered their pages to him, wagging their little beards, wringing their hands, spitting at him, shouting themselves hoarse, yelling out from the shelves, "We warned you!" "You should have done things differently!" Nitpicking was easy; you didn't need brains for that! The reason why Stalin had assembled them there was to sharpen his temper at night when he had decisions to make. Somehow it always turned out that the opponents he had destroyed had not been altogether wrong. Stalin listened cautiously to those hostile voices from beyond the grave, and he occasionally adopted some of their ideas.

Their conqueror, in his generalissimo's uniform, with his low, retreating pithecanthropoid brow, shuffled along the shelves, clawing at his enemies, grabbing now one, now another, reordering their ranks.

The invisible band that had accompanied his marching played a few false notes and stopped.

By now his legs were aching and threatened to give way. A heavy surf pounded in his head. The chain of his thoughts slackened and snapped. He had quite forgotten why he had gone over to the bookshelves. What had he just been thinking about?

He sank onto the nearest chair and buried his face in his hands.

A dog's life. . . . Old age. Without friends. Without love. Without belief. Without desire.

Even his beloved daughter was useless to him, a stranger.

The feeling that his memory was impaired, that his mind was growing dim, that he was cut off from all living beings, filled him with impotent dread.

He looked around the room with clouded eyes and could not have said whether the walls were near or far away.

On the occasional table near him stood another locked decanter. Stalin felt for the key, which was attached to his belt by a long chain (when he was feeling faint, he might drop it and take a long time to find it), unlocked the decanter, poured, and drank his stimulant.

He sat for a while with closed eyes. He began to feel better in himself. Better still. Quite well.

His eyes cleared and fell upon the telephone, and the thing that had eluded him all night wriggled through his memory again. He caught a brief glimpse of it, like the vanishing tip of a snake's tail.

There was something he should have asked Abakumov. Whether Gomulka had been arrested? . . .

Aha! That was it! He rose, shuffled over the carpet, reached his desk, took a pen, and wrote on his desk diary "secret telephone."

They kept reporting that the best experts had been brought together, that they had all the necessary equipment, that morale was good, that there was keen competition between teams, so why couldn't they finish it? Abakumov, damn his insolence, had sat there a solid hour, the dog, and said not a word!

They were all the same, in every department, every one of them out to deceive his Leader! How could they possibly be trusted? How could he ever take a night off?

His breakfast was still more than ten hours away.

He rang for his dressing gown. His country could sleep, free from care, but there was no sleep for its Father!

## 23

# Language as an Instrument of Production

EVERYTHING, SURELY, had been done to ensure his immortality.

But to Stalin it seemed that his contemporaries, though they called him Wisest of the Wise, were less ecstatic in their praise than he deserved. Their enthusiasm was superficial; they had not appreciated the full depth of his genius.

Of late he had been nagged by the thought that, in addition to winning the third world war, he ought also to perform some great scientific feat, make his own brilliant contribution to a branch of learning other than history and philosophy.

He could, of course, make such a contribution to biology, but he had entrusted work in that area to that honest and energetic man of the people, Lysenko.* In any case, Stalin found mathematics or perhaps even physics more alluring. All the Founding Fathers had fearlessly tried their strength in those sciences. He could not help envying Engels when he read his bold

* Lysenko: Trofim Lysenko (1898-1976), an agronomist, developed a pseudoscientific theory of heredity that denied the existence of genes. Stalin put Lysenko in charge of Soviet science with the mission of stamping out genetics as an ideologically unacceptable approach in the study of biology.

ratiocinations on zero, or on the square of minus one. Stalin was equally enthralled by the resolute way in which Lenin had plunged into the thickets of physics and left neither hide nor hair of the scientists, proving that matter could not be converted into any form of energy.

He himself, though, however often he paged through Kiselev's *Algebra* or Sokolov's *Physics for Upper Forms*, found them uninspiring.

But just recently a happy inspiration, though in quite another field, that of philology, had been fortuitously provided by Professor Chikobava of Tiflis. Stalin vaguely remembered Chikobava, as he remembered all Georgians of any importance; he had frequented the house of the younger Ignatoshvili, the Tiflis lawyer, a Menshevik, and was himself the sort of awkward customer by now inconceivable except in Georgia.

Having reached an age, and a level of skepticism, at which a man begins to care little for the things of this world, Chikobava in his wisdom had written what appeared to be a heretical, anti-Marxist article arguing that language was certainly not "superstructural" and that there were no such things as bourgeois and proletarian languages but only national languages. And he had dared to attack Academician Marr himself by name.

Both Chikobava and Marr were Georgians, so the response came in a Georgian university bulletin, a dingy unbound copy of which, in ligatured Georgian script, now lay before Stalin. Several Marxist-Marrist philologists had assailed the impudent creature with accusations, after which all that remained for him was to await the MGB's knock in the night. It had already been hinted that Chikobava was an agent of American imperialism.

Nothing could have saved him if Stalin had not picked up the receiver and let him live. He let Chikobava live but decided to write an imperishable exposition of his homely provincial thoughts, perfected by a genius.

True, he would have caused more of a stir by refuting the reactionary theory of relativity, say, or wave mechanics. But affairs of state left him simply no time for that. Philology, after all, was next door to grammar, and grammar had always seemed to Stalin a near neighbor of mathematics in point of difficulty.

It could be written vividly, eloquently (he was already sitting and writing). "Take the language of any one of the Soviet nationalities—Russian, Ukrainian, Belorussian, Uzbek, Kazakh, Georgian, Armenian, Estonian, Latvian, Lithuanian, Moldavian, Tatar, Azerbaijani, Bashkir, Turkmen . . . ." (Damn! As time went by, it got more and more difficult for him to stop once he started listing things. Why stop, anyway? The reader would get the point more readily and wouldn't feel like arguing. . . .) "It is obvious to everybody that. . . ." And then say whatever was so obvious.

What, though, was it? The economy was the base, social phenomena the superstructure. And, as always in Marxism, there was no third possibility.

Stalin, however, had learned from experience that you couldn't manage without a third possibility. There were, after all, neutral countries (to be finished off piecemeal, later on) and neutral parties (not in our country, of course). In Lenin's time, if you'd said, "Who is not with us is not necessarily against us," or something of that sort, you would have been expelled from the Party that very minute.

Well . . . that was the Dialectic for you. It was the same here. Stalin had pondered over Chikobava's article, struck by a thought that had never occurred to him before: If language is superstructural, why does it not change from one social epoch to another? If it is not superstructural, what is it? Part of the base? Of the mode of production?

Strictly speaking, the mode of production consisted of "forces of production" and "relations of production." To call language a "relation of production" was probably wrong.

So, was language a "force of production"? The "forces of production" were tools, materials, and people. And although people used language, language was not people. It was a hell of a problem, a blind alley if ever there was one.

The most honest thing to do would be to recognize language as an instrument of production, like, say, machine tools, railways, the mails. And, of course, telecommunications. Lenin had said it: "Without the mails there can be no socialism." Nor, obviously, without language.

But come straight out with the thesis that language is an instrument of production, and the giggling would begin. Not here at home, of course.

There was no one he could consult about it.

It could, of course, be put cautiously, something like this: "In this respect language, which is essentially distinct from the superstructure, does not differ from the instruments of production, from, say, machines, which are as indifferent to class as is language."

"Indifferent to class!" Another thing you wouldn't have said earlier on. . . .

He wrote a period. Folded his hands behind his head, yawned, and stretched. He hadn't done very much thinking, but he was tired already.

Stalin rose and began walking about his study. He went over to a small window, which had two thicknesses of transparent yellowish bulletproof glass with a shield of compressed air between them. The windows looked out on a little walled garden, where the gardener puttered about under surveillance during the morning and no one else appeared at any hour of day or night.

Beyond the unbreakable glass, mist hovered in the garden. The country, the earth, the universe, were alike invisible.

In these night hours, when there was not a sound to be heard, not a human being in sight, Stalin could not be sure that his country existed at all.

He had traveled south several times since the war and seen nothing but one great dead-looking empty space. No sign of a living Russia, although he had journeyed thousands of kilometers overland (he did not trust planes). If he went by car, an empty highway unrolled before him, with an unpopulated zone beside it. If he went by train, the stations were lifeless, and at each stop only his retinue and very carefully vetted railwaymen (most probably security police) walked along the platform. He was beginning to feel that he was alone not only in his villa at Kuntsevo but in Russia as a whole, that the whole of Russia was a figment (extraordinary that foreigners believed in its existence). Luckily, though, this lifeless expanse regularly supplied the state with grain, vegetables, milk, coal, iron, all in the prescribed quantities and at the prescribed time. The same empty space provided excellent soldiers. (Stalin had never set eyes on these divisions, but to judge by the cities they took—which he hadn't seen either—they undoubtedly existed.)

Stalin felt so lonely because he had no one to try out his thoughts on, no one to measure himself against.

Still, half the universe was there in his breast, all order and clarity. Only the other half, what was called objective reality, was lost in the swirling mist that covered the world.

From where he now was, in his fortress-like, heavily guarded night study, Stalin had no fear at all of that other half; he felt that he had the power to twist it into any shape he liked. It was only when he had to step into objective reality on his own two legs, when, for instance, he had to attend a banquet in the Hall of Columns, where he had to cross on his own two legs the space between car and door, then on his own two legs go up a staircase, cross a much too spacious foyer, and see the guests standing to either side of him, thrilled, respectful, but far too numerous—that was when Stalin felt wretched and didn't even know what to do with his hands, which had long ceased to be of use for self-defense. He would fold them on his belly and smile. The guests thought that the Omnipotent One was smiling to be nice to them, but he was really smiling in embarrassment. . . .

Space he himself had called "the fundamental condition of the existence of matter." But having mastered one-sixth of the world's dry space, he had begun to fear it. The good thing about his night study was that there was no space.

Stalin closed the metal shutter and stomped back to his desk. He swallowed a tablet and sat down again.

He had been unlucky all his life, but he must keep working. Posterity would appreciate him.

How had it come about, this "Arakcheev regime" in philology? Nobody dared say a word against Marr. Strange people! Timid people! You spend your life teaching them the meaning of democracy, you chew it up for them, put it in their mouths, and they spit it out!

He had to do it all himself. Yet again.

In a fit of inspiration, he wrote a few sentences:

"The superstructure is created by the base precisely in order to. . . ." "Language is created precisely in order to. . . ."

In his eagerness to get the words down, he hung his ashen face with its big, burrowing nose low over the paper.

The wretched Lafargue, who also fancied himself a theorist, spoke of "the abrupt linguistic revolution in the years 1789–1794." (Had he checked with his father-in-law?)

Revolution? What revolution? The language spoken before was French. And French it remained.

It was time to put a stop to all this idle talk of revolutions!

"Comrades obsessed with explosions should note that the law of qualitative change by way of explosion is not only inapplicable to the evolution of language but rarely applicable to other social phenomena."

Stalin leaned back and read over what he had written. It looked pretty good. Agitators must elucidate this passage with particular care, making it clear that at a certain stage revolutions come to an end and things develop only in an evolutionary way. It might even be that quantity no longer passes into quality. But that could wait till another time.

"Rarely?" . . . No, it was still too soon to say that. Stalin crossed out "rarely" and wrote "not always." Think of a neat little example.

"We have progressed from the bourgeois individual peasant order" (a new term that, and a good one!) "to the socialist collective farm. . . ."

He used a peroid, as anybody else would, thought a bit, and added "order." This was the style he favored: Drive the nail home, then hit it again. If he repeated all the words, every sentence seemed somehow more easily understandable. His pen raced on: "However, this overturn was accomplished not by means of an explosion, that is to say, not by overthrowing the existing regime" (this was a passage which the agitators must explain with particular care) "and the creation of a new one" (no one must even think of that!) . . .

Because of Lenin's superficiality Soviet historians recognized only revolution from below and regarded revolution from above as imperfect, freakish, bad form. But the time had come to call things by their proper names.

"We succeeded in this because it was a Revolution from above, an overturn accomplished on the initiative of the existing regime."

Stop. That didn't look right. It suggested that the peasants had not taken the initiative in collectivizing.

Stalin leaned back in his chair, yawned, and suddenly forgot entirely what he had just been thinking. The investigative zeal that had flared up a little while ago flickered out.

Bent double, tripping over the long skirts of his dressing gown, the ruler of half the world shuffled through a second narrow door flush with the wall, into the narrow labyrinth again, and on to a narrow, windowless bedroom with concrete walls.

He lay down, groaning, and tried to cheer himself with the thought that while neither Napoleon nor Hitler had been able to take Britain, because they each had an enemy on the Continent, he would have none. He would sweep straight from the Elbe to the Channel. France would crumble like wormy timber (the French Communists would help); he would take the Pyrenees in his stride. Blitzkrieg, of course, was a gamble. But there was no alternative to a lightning strike.

We can start as soon as we have made enough atomic bombs and purged the home front thoroughly.

He snuggled into his pillow and tried to collect his wandering thoughts. . . . We shall need a blitzkrieg in Korea, too. . . . With our tanks, artillery, and air force, we may manage without world revolution. . . .

In fact the simplest route to world Communism was via a third world war: First unify the whole world; then establish Communism. Otherwise there were too many complications.

No need for any more revolutions! We'll put revolution behind us! Not a single revolution ahead!

He sank into sleep.

## 24

# The Abyss Beckons Again

ENGINEER COLONEL YAKONOV LEFT the ministry by the side entrance in Dzherzhinsky Street, rounded the black marble prow of the building, walked through the Furkasov Street colonnade, and recognized his own Pobeda only when he was about to grab the door handle of someone else's car. There had been thick fog all through the night. Snow had fallen fitfully and melted quickly. It had now stopped. Now, toward dawn, it was foggy only near the ground, and a film of brittle ice covered the puddles.

It was getting colder.

Nearly five o'clock, but the sky was still black. The only light was from the streetlamps.

A first-year student who had spent the night in a doorway with his sweetheart looked enviously at Yakonov as he got into his car. Would he ever have a car himself? Would he ever take a girl for a drive? He had only ridden in a truck so far. And only in the back. On the way to a kolkhoz to help with the harvest.

He couldn't know how little he had to envy.

"Home?" the driver asked.

Yakonov stared unseeingly at the pocket watch in the palm of his hand. "Home?" the driver repeated.

Yakonov started.

"Eh? No."

"Marfino?" The driver was surprised. He was wearing felt boots and a sheepskin coat, but he was chilled to the bone after his long wait and wanted to get to bed.

"No," the engineer colonel answered, pressing his hand to his chest just above his heart.

The driver looked at his chief's face in the dull lamplight filtering through the windshield.

This wasn't the chief he knew. Yakonov's lips, usually complacently relaxed, occasionally arrogantly pursed, were trembling helplessly.

And he was still holding the watch on the flat of his hand uncomprehendingly.

The driver had been waiting since midnight, furious with the colonel. Cursing into his sheepskin collar, remembering every dirty trick the colonel had played in the last two years. But he asked no more questions and drove off at random. His rage had subsided.

Late night had passed into early morning. Only occasional cars passed them on the empty streets. No policemen, no muggers, no one to mug. The trolleys would be running soon.

The driver looked round at the colonel several times, wondering what to do. By now he had sped as far as the Myasnitsky Gate, driven along the boulevards to Trubnaya Square, and turned into Neglinnaya Street. But he couldn't keep this up till morning!

Yakonov stared straight ahead, his eyes unblinkingly fixed on nothing.

He lived on Bolshaya Serpukhovka. Calculating that once he saw his own neighborhood the colonel would want to go home, the driver made for Zamoskvoreche. He turned out of Okhotny Ryad onto Red Square, which was deserted and forbidding.

There was frost on the battlements and the tops of fir trees along the Kremlin Wall. Mist clung to the roadway under the wheels of the car.

Two hundred meters from them, behind the battlements that poets insisted on calling sacred, beyond the guardhouses, sentry boxes, patrols, and lookouts, dwelled, so those same poets said, the man they called the Unsleeping One, no doubt now nearing the end of his solitary night's work. They drove past without giving him a thought.

It was only when they had driven downhill past Vasily Blazhenny and turned left along the embankment that the driver braked and asked again:

"Would you like to go home, Comrade Colonel?"

That was certainly what he ought to do. For all he knew, the nights he would be spending at home could be counted on his fingers. But just as a dog runs off to die alone, Yakonov felt that he must go somewhere else, get away from his family.

He drew the folds of his leather coat around him, got out of the Pobeda, and said to the driver: "Go home and get some sleep, old fellow. I'll walk from here."

It wasn't the first time he had called his driver "old fellow." But there was such sadness in his voice that he seemed to be saying good-bye forever.

Moscow River was shrouded in wreathing mist from bank to bank.

With his overcoat unbuttoned and his colonel's tall fur hat awry, Yakonov set off along the slippery embankment.

The driver thought of calling out to him, or even going with him, then thought, High-ups like him don't drown themselves, turned the car around, and drove away.

Yakonov walked along an unbroken stretch of the embankment, with the river on his right and an endless wooden fence on his left. He kept to the middle of the asphalted path, his eyes fixed unblinkingly on the distant street lamps.

When he had gone some way, he began to feel that this one-man funeral procession was giving him a simple enjoyment such as he had not experienced for a long time.

When they were summoned to the ministry for the second time, the worst had happened. It was as though all the ceilings above had caved in on them. Abakumov had raged like a wild beast, springing at them, chasing them round the office, swearing obscenely, spitting at them, and landing a punch on Yakonov's face that was obviously meant to hurt and that drew blood from his soft white nose.

He had demoted Selivanovsky to the rank of lieutenant and sent him to an outpost in the polar regions. Oskolupov he had sent back to Butyrki Prison, where he had begun in 1925, to resume his career as an ordinary guard. Yakonov himself had been put under arrest for deception and repeated sabotage but sent back to Number Seven, to put on blue overalls, work beside Bobynin, and put the Scrambler in working order with his own hands.

Then he had recovered his breath and given them a new, and final, deadline: the Lenin anniversary.

The big, tasteless office swam before Yakonov's eyes; the floor heaved. He tried to stem the nosebleed with a handkerchief. He stood before Abakumov helplessly, thinking of those with whom he spent only one hour in twenty-four but for whom alone he schemed and struggled and bullied every other hour of his waking day: two little girls, one eight, one nine, and his wife, Varyusha, who was all the more precious because it had been a late marriage. He had been thirty-six at the time and had barely emerged from the gates toward which the minister's iron fist was pushing him again.

After all this Selivanovsky had taken Oskolupov and Yakonov to his own office and threatened to put the two of them behind bars rather than incur demotion and relegation to the Far North.

And then Oskolupov had taken Yakonov to his office and declared that henceforth he would always be conscious of the connection between Yakonov's jailbird past and his present acts of sabotage.

By now Yakonov had reached a high concrete bridge, over which on the right bank lay Zamoskvoreche. But instead of taking this way out, he went on under the bridge, where a militiaman was walking up and down on guard. The militiaman's suspicious gaze followed the strange drunk wearing pince-nez and a colonel's tall hat.

Farther on, Yakonov crossed a short bridge over a narrow channel. He had reached the Yauza, where it falls into the Moskva, but he did not even look to see where he was going.

Yes, they had been caught up in a crazy game, and now it was coming to an end. It wasn't the first time Yakonov had witnessed and been drawn into an insane, an impossible scramble, in which the whole country—with its people's commissars and oblast secretaries, scientists, engineers, directors and site managers, shop foremen and team leaders, workmen and women on collective farms—was swept off its feet. Whoever you are and whatever you set out to do, you very soon find yourself in the grip, the stranglehold, of arbitrary, impossible, crippling schedules! Give us more! Faster! Faster still! Fulfill the norm! Overfulfill the norm! Fulfill it three times over! Work a voluntary shift! Beat the deadline! Beat it by a bigger margin! Buildings and bridges collapsed, crops rotted in the fields or never came up at all, and the man who found himself in this mad whirl, which meant every single person, had no escape except to fall sick, get caught in the machinery, go mad, get run over so that he could have a rest at last in a hospital or health resort, let them forget about him, breathe forest air—then again, yet again, gradually slip back into harness.

Only sick people alone with their illness (and not in a hospital!) could live an untroubled life in the Soviet Union.

Yakonov, however, had always managed so far to skip nimbly from projects doomed by over-haste to others where life was quieter or which were at an early stage.

Now, for the first time, he felt that he was trapped. The scrambler project couldn't be salvaged in such a hurry. He had nowhere else to go. And he'd left it too late to fall sick.

He stood at the parapet and looked over it. The fog had settled low on the ice, leaving it bare in places. Immediately below, Yakonov could see a dark patch where the ice had melted.

It was as if the black hole of his prison years had opened up to receive him again.

To Yakonov those six years were a hideous gap in his life, as if he had been stricken by plague, the greatest of catastrophes.

He had been jailed in 1932, as a young radio engineer, after two trips abroad on official business, which were the reason for his imprisonment.

He had then been one of the first convicts recruited by one of the early sharashkas.

How he had longed to forget his prison past! And for others to forget it! For fate to forget it! How anxiously he had shunned all who reminded him of that disastrous time, all who remembered him as a convict!

He tore himself away from the parapet, cut across the embankment, and for no good reason went up a steep rise. He came out onto a path that skirted the long fence around yet another construction site. A well-trodden path, where it was less slippery.

Only the central card index at the Ministry of State Security knew that the ministry's uniforms sometimes concealed former convicts.

There were two others in the Marfino Institute, as well as Yakonov.

He scrupulously avoided them, did his best not to get into conversation with them off duty, and never saw them alone in his office, in case people started imagining things.

One of them, Knyazhenetsky, a septuagenarian professor of chemistry, had been Mendeleev's favorite student. He had served the prescribed ten years and then, in recognition of a long list of scientific achievements, had been sent to Marfino. He had worked there as a "free" employee for three years, but then the whiplash of the "Instruction on the Reinforcement of the Rear" had caught even him. A telephone call summoned him to the ministry, and he did not return. Yakonov would always remember Knyazhenetsky descending the institute's red-carpeted stairway, shaking his silvery head, wondering why he had been called in for half an hour, while as soon as his back was turned, Shikin, the security officer, had taken out a penknife and removed a photograph of the professor from the institute's honors board on the upper landing.

The other one, Altynov, was not distinguished, just efficient. His first term of imprisonment had made him taciturn, distrustful, as quick to suspect the worst as only the convict clan can be. So as soon as the "Instruction" began insinuating itself into every nook and cranny of the city, Altynov wangled his way into a heart clinic. He played the part so realistically and for so long that the doctors gave up on him, and his friends no longer lowered their voices in his presence, realizing that after thirty years of excruciating anxiety, his heart had simply given out. And now Yakonov, doomed a year ago as an ex-convict, was doomed yet again as a saboteur.

The abyss was calling its children home.

. . . YAKONOV WAS CLIMBING a path over waste ground, not noticing where he was going or that it was uphill.

He stopped at last, out of breath. His tired feet ached from stumbling over uneven ground. As his vision cleared, he looked back downhill to take his bearings.

In the hour since he had left his car, the waning night had grown much colder. The mist had cleared. The ground underfoot, strewn with rubble and broken glass, the tumbledown shed or watchman's hut nearby, and a fence left standing around an abandoned building site down below were touched with white—frost or snow?

There were white steps set in this hillside, so close to the center of Moscow, yet so strangely desolate. Perhaps seven steps, then a gap, then more steps.

These steps stirred a vague recollection. Yakonov, wondering, climbed them, followed the cinder path above, then up more steps. The building to which the steps led was not clearly visible. Its shape was so strange that it seemed to be in ruins yet miraculously preserved.

Did it mark a spot where bombs had fallen? But all bomb damage in Moscow had been cleared away. What destructive force could have been at work here?

A paved terrace had once separated the two flights of steps. Now great fragments of flagstones lay on the steps, making it difficult to climb them.

The steps led up to wide iron doors, shut fast and blocked knee-deep by heaps of rubble.

Of course! Of course! Yakonov winced under the lash of memory. He looked about him. Its course marked by rows of streetlights, the river wound its way down below, disappearing with a strangely familiar bend under a bridge and on to the Kremlin.

But where was the bell tower? It was no longer there. Or were those heaps of stone what had been the bell tower?

Yakonov's eyes were smarting. He squinted.

He sat down on the broken stones that littered the porch.

Twenty-two years ago he had stood on this very spot with a girl named Agnia.

## 25

# The Church of Nikita the Martyr

HE SPOKE HER NAME, and his pampered body shivered with the onrush of forgotten sensations.

He had been twenty-six, Agnia twenty-one. She was a girl from some other world. Her misfortune was a sensitivity, a fastidiousness that made the normal life of human beings impossible for her. Sometimes, when she was talking, her brows and nostrils quivered as though she were about to take flight. No one had ever said so many harsh words to Yakonov, reproached him so sternly for behavior that might be thought perfectly ordinary but in which she, startlingly, discerned something base and ignoble. Strangely, the more faults she discovered in Anton, the more devoted to her he became.

He had to be cautious in argument with her. She was not very strong, and an uphill walk, hurried movement, or even animated discussion tired her out. The least little thing could upset her.

Nonetheless she found the strength to wander in the forest for days on end. She did not, as city girls out for a walk in the woods traditionally do, take a book with her; it would have interfered with her enjoyment of the forest. She simply wandered around, sitting down occasionally, studying the secrets of the forest. She always skipped descriptions of nature in Turgenev, which she thought superficial. When Anton went with her, he was astonished by her perceptiveness: She noticed how the trunk of a birch had bowed to the ground in memory of a snowfall; she noticed the changing tints of the forest grass in the evening. He never noticed anything of that sort himself; for him the forest was just forest, green trees, good air. . . .

The Forest Rill, Yakonov had called her in the summer of 1927, which they had spent in neighboring dachas. They went everywhere together, and everybody assumed that they were engaged.

But that was very far from being so.

Agnia was neither pretty nor plain. Her expression changed continually: At one moment she wore a winning smile; at the next she looked drawn and unattractive. She was above middle height but slender, fragile, and her step was so light that she seemed scarcely to touch the ground. Anton was quite experienced and liked best a woman with some flesh on her, but he was attracted to Agnia by something else, and when he had become used to her, he told himself that he also liked her as a woman and that she would ripen with time.

She shared the long summer days with him happily enough, walking verst after verst into the green depths, lying beside him in forest clearings, but she was reluctant even to let him stroke her hand.

"Must you?" she would say, trying to free herself.

It wasn't fear of what people might think, because as they returned to the holiday village she would gratify his amour propre and submit to walking arm in arm.

Having convinced himself that he loved her, Anton fell at her feet in one of those forest clearings and proposed. Agnia was deeply dismayed.

"I'm afraid I'm misleading you. I don't know what to say. I just don't feel anything. When I think about it, I just don't want to live. You are a clever man, a brilliant man, and I ought to be overjoyed; but, instead, it makes me want to die."

That's what she had said. But every morning she looked apprehensively for any change in the way he behaved toward her.

She had said that. But she also said, "There are lots of girls in Moscow. When autumn comes, you'll meet a pretty one and stop loving me."

She sometimes let him embrace her and even kiss her, but her lips and arms were unresponsive.

"I'm so unhappy," she said. "I used to believe that love was like a fiery angel descending from heaven. But here we are; you love me, and I'll never meet anyone better, yet I'm not happy about it; I just don't want to go on living."

There was something of the retarded child about her. She was afraid of the intimacies that bind husband and wife and would ask in a faint voice, "Is all that necessary?"

"It certainly isn't the most important thing," Anton would answer earnestly. "Most certainly not! It only supplements our spiritual union!"

That was when her lips first slackly responded to his kiss. "Thank you," she said. "If it weren't so, life wouldn't be worth living. I think I am beginning to love you. I shall try as hard as I can to love you."

That same autumn they were walking around the backstreets near Taganka Square, and Agnia said in the low voice she used in the forest, which was barely audible above the city traffic, "Do you want me to show you one of the loveliest places in Moscow?"

She led him to the railings of a little brick church. It was painted white and red, and its sanctuary abutted on a crooked lane without a name. There was very little room inside the railings, only a narrow path around the church for processionals, with barely room for priest and deacon side by side. The gentle glow of altar candles and colored lamps could be seen through the barred windows. In one corner of the precinct grew a huge old oak. Its yellowed branches overshadowed both the dome and the lane, making the church look tiny beside it.

"This is the Church of Nikita the Martyr," Agnia said.

"But not the most beautiful place in Moscow."

"Just wait."

She took him through the gate. Oak leaves, yellow and orange, lay on the flagstones of the yard. Almost in the shade of the oak stood an ancient campanile with a hipped roof. This, and a little house belonging to the church outside the precinct, obscured the low setting sun. An old beggar woman bowed low before the open double doors on the north side, crossing herself as the golden chant of evensong reached her.

"And that church was of wondrous beauty and radiance," Agnia quoted, almost in a whisper, her shoulder close to his.

"What century does it belong to?"

"Do you have to have a century? What do you think of it, anyway?"

"It's pretty, of course, but not all that—"

"Look now, then!" Agnia's outstretched hand quickly drew Anton farther on, to the portico outside the main door; they emerged from the shadow into the stream of light from the setting sun and sat on the low stone parapet, beside the churchyard gate.

Anton gasped. It was as though they had soared free from the narrow ravine of the city and come out on a steep eminence with an open view far into the distance. The portico swept down through the gap in the parapet to a long course of white stone steps, several flights of them, alternating with little landings and descending down the hillside to the Moscow River. The river was on fire in the light of the setting sun. To their left Zamoskvoreche dazzled them with the yellow brilliance of its windows; straight ahead the black chimneys of the Moscow Power Station poured smoke into the glowing sky; almost directly under them the glittering Yauza flowed into the Moscow, with the orphanage to the right beyond it, and beyond that the fretted contours of the Kremlin; while still farther away the five red-gold domes of the Church of Christ the Savior blazed in the sun.

And in all this golden radiance Agnia sat with a yellow shawl around her shoulders, screwing up her eyes at the sun and looking golden herself.

Anton, carried away, could only say, "Yes! That's . . . Moscow!"

"How cleverly Russians chose sites for churches and monasteries in ancient times," Agnia said with a catch in her voice. "I've been down the Oka and the Volga, and wherever you go, they're built in the most imposing places. The architects were God-fearing; the masons were righteous men."

"Yes . . . Yes . . . That's . . . Moscow. . . !"

"But it's going, Anton," she cried. "Moscow is going!"

"Going? Going where? You're imagining things."

"They're going to demolish this church, Anton," she insisted.

"How do you know?" he asked angrily. "It's an architectural monument; they'll let it stand."

He looked at the little bell tower and the oak branches peeking through its apertures.

"They'll pull it down!" Agnia prophesied confidently, still sitting motionless in her yellow shawl in the yellow light.

No one in Agnia's family had taught her to believe in God. On the contrary. In the days when churchgoing was the rule, Agnia's grandmother and mother had not gone, not observed fasts, had turned their noses up at priests, and whenever possible ridiculed the religion that had lived so cozily side by side with serfdom. Agnia's grandmother, mother, and aunts had their own sturdy creed: always to be on the side of those who are harried, hunted, oppressed, persecuted by the powers that be. Her grandmother, it seemed, had been known to all the Moscow members of the People's Will Party; she gave them shelter and helped them in every way she could. Her daughters had taken over from her and hidden underground Socialist Revolutionaries and Social Democrats. Little Agnia always felt for the hare that might be shot and the horse that might be whipped. But as she grew up, her sympathies took a direction that her elders could never have expected: She was for the church because it was persecuted.

She insisted that "in our day and age" it would be base in her to shun the church, and to the horror of her mother and grandmother, she began attending regularly and found herself enjoying the services.

"What makes you say the church is persecuted?" Anton asked in surprise. "Nobody stops them ringing their bells and baking their altar bread and having their processions. Let them carry on, by all means, but they aren't really wanted in the cities and the schools."

"Of course it's persecuted." Agnia's voice never rose above a murmur in disagreement. "When people say and print anything they like about the church and never give it a chance to defend itself, when they confiscate the altar furnishings and exile priests, don't you call that persecution?"

"Have you ever seen a priest banished?"

"It isn't something you see in the streets."

Anton pressed harder.

"And what if it is persecuted? Say the church has been persecuted for ten years. For how long did the church do the persecuting? Ten centuries?"

"I wasn't alive then," said Agnia, shrugging her narrow shoulders. "I have to live here and now. I see what is happening in my own lifetime."

"But everybody ought to know a little history! Ignorance is no excuse! Haven't you ever wondered why our church managed to survive the 250 years of the Tatar yoke?"

"Because its faith was deep? Because Orthodoxy proved spiritually stronger than Mohammedanism?"

It was a question, not an assertion.

Anton smiled indulgently.

"What a dreamer you are! Do you really think that the soul of our country was ever Christian? In the thousand years of its existence, did we ever really forgive our oppressors? Did we ever 'love them that hate us'? Our church endured because after the Tatar invasion Metropolitan Cyril paid homage to the khan—the first Russian to do so—and begged from him guarantees of safety for the clergy. How did the Russian clergy safeguard its lands, its slaves, and its cult? Why, with the Tatar sword! And, if you like, Metropolitan Cyril was right, a political realist. That's the way to be. That's the only way to come out on top."

Agnia never argued when she was challenged. She looked at her fiancé with wide-eyed bewilderment, as though she saw him for the first time.

"That's what all those beautiful churches with their cleverly chosen sites were built on!" Anton thundered. "And on schismatics burned at the stake! And on sectarians flogged to death! Persecuted church! Don't waste your sympathy on it!"

He sat down beside her on the sun-warmed stone of the parapet.

"And anyway, you aren't fair to the Bolsheviks. You've never taken the trouble to read their most important books. They show the greatest respect and concern for world culture. They stand for an end to the tyranny of man over man, for the empire of reason. Above all, they are for equality! Imagine it: universal, total, absolute equality. No one will be more privileged than anyone else. No one will enjoy special advantages, either in income or in position. What could be more attractive than a society like that? Isn't it worth making sacrifices for?"

(Attractions apart, Anton's origins had made it necessary to *join the right side* before it was too late.)

"All these frivolous notions of yours will stand in your way; you'll never get into an institute. And what's the use of your protests, anyway? What can you do?"

"What can a woman ever do?" Her thin braids (nobody wore braids anymore; everybody had bobbed hair, but she went on wearing them in the spirit of contradiction, although they did not suit her) had flown apart. One hung down her back; the other lay on her breast. "All that a woman is capable of is deterring a man from great deeds. Even women like Natasha Rostova. I can't stand her."

"Why?" Anton was staggered.

"Because she wouldn't let Pierre join the Decembrists!"* Her weak voice broke again.

She seemed to be made of nothing but surprises.

The transparent yellow shawl had slipped down over her bent elbows and looked like a pair of delicate golden wings.

Anton gently, as though afraid he might break it, clasped his hands around one elbow.

"And you? Would you have let him?"

---

* Decembrists: Revolutionaries who in December 1825 rebelled against Tsar Nicholas I as he succeeded Tsar Alexander I to the throne. Although they were easily routed in a showdown in St. Petersburg, their gesture of defiance inspired subsequent generations of Russian revolutionaries.

"Yes."

Anton, however, saw no heroic feat ahead of him for which he would need to seek release. It was the busiest time of his life, his work was interesting, and his prospects excellent.

Belated worshippers who had climbed from the embankment went past, crossing themselves when they saw the open door of the church. The men took their caps off as they entered the precinct. But there were far fewer men than women, and no young people.

"Aren't you afraid of being seen near a church?" Agnia had not meant it sarcastically, but that was how it sounded.

It was, indeed, already dangerous, as it would be for many years ahead, to be noticed by a colleague anywhere near a church, and Anton felt too conspicuous for comfort.

He was beginning to get irritated.

"You must be careful, Agnia," he warned her. "We must know how to recognize the new in good time. Anyone who doesn't will be hopelessly out of date. You have begun to feel drawn to the church because it sanctifies your aversion to life. Get a grip on yourself! Force yourself to take an interest in something, if it's only in the process of living."

Agnia drooped. The hand with Anton's gold ring hung limply. The girl's figure looked bonier, thinner than ever.

"Yes, yes," she said in a sinking voice. "I realize perfectly well at times that living is very difficult for me, that I just don't want to live. The world has no place for people like me."

Something snapped inside him. She was doing everything she could to make herself unattractive to him! His resolve to keep his promise and marry Agnia was weakening.

She looked up at him, searching his face, unsmiling.

And she isn't really pretty, Anton thought.

"You can probably look forward to fame and success and prosperity," she said sadly. "But will you be happy, Anton? You must take care, too. When we get interested in the process of living, we lose . . . we lose . . . how can I put it?" She rubbed fingers and thumb together, feeling for the word. She looked sick with anxiety.

"Once the bell stops ringing, once the tuneful sounds fade, you can never call them back. But all the music is in them. Do you understand?"

She was still struggling to find words.

"Imagine yourself dying and suddenly asking for an Orthodox funeral. . . ."

Then she insisted on going inside to pray. He couldn't walk off and leave her there alone. They went in. Under a vaulted ceiling a gallery with windows latticed in the Old Russian style ran around the church.

Through the little windows the setting sun flooded the church with light and spilled shimmering gold on the top of the icon stand and a mosaic of the Lord of Hosts.

There were few worshippers. Agnia set a thin candle on a big copper stand and stood, grave and still, except for a perfunctory sign of the cross, her hands folded over her chest, staring, rapt, before herself. The diffused glow of the sunset and the orange reflections of candlelight had brought life and warmth back to Agnia's cheeks.

It was two days before the Nativity of the Mother of God, and they were reciting the litany of the day. It was an inexhaustibly eloquent outpouring of praise for the Virgin, and Yakonov felt for the first time the overwhelming poetic power of such prayers. The canon had been written not by a soulless dogmatist but by some great poet immured in a monastery, and he had been moved not by a furious excess of male hunger for a female body but by the pure rapture that a woman can awake in us.

YAKONOV CAME TO HIS SENSES. He was sitting on a pile of sharp stone fragments from the portico of the Church of Nikita the Martyr, soiling his leather coat.

Yes, they had wantonly destroyed the bell tower with the hipped roof and smashed the stone steps down to the river. It was impossible to believe that the golden evening he had remembered and this December dawn had happened on the same few square meters of Moscow soil. But the view from the hill was as spacious as ever, and the river still wound its way between two (now dimmed) rows of streetlamps. . . .

. . . SHORTLY AFTERWARD HE HAD GONE ABROAD on official business. When he got back, he had been told to write—which meant little more than putting his name to—a newspaper article about the decadence of the West, its social system, its morals, its culture, about the disastrous condition of the Western intelligentsia, and about the impossibility of new scientific discoveries in that part of the world. It wasn't true, but it was not altogether false. There were facts to support these assertions, but there were other facts, too. The Party

Committee sent for him—he was not a Party member—and was very insistent. Hesitation on Yakonov's part could have aroused suspicion, left a blot on his reputation. And anyway, what harm could such a piece do to anyone? Europe would surely be none the worse for it.

His travel notes were written. Agnia sent his ring back in a postal package, to which she had tied with cotton thread a scrap of paper with the words "To Metropolitan Cyril."

And he had felt relieved.

HE ROSE, hauled himself up to a latticed window of the gallery, and peered in. From inside there was a smell of damp brickwork, cold, and decay. His eyes dimly discerned more heaps of broken stone and rubbish.

Yakonov drew back from the window. He felt his heartbeat slowing down and leaned against the jamb of a rusty iron door unopened for many years.

Abakumov's threat welled up in him like an icy wave of fear.

YAKONOV WAS AT THE SUMMIT of what looked like power. He was a high official of a mighty ministry. He was clever and talented, and his cleverness and talent were widely recognized. At home a loving wife and two charming little girls, rosily sleeping, awaited his return. The upper rooms, with balcony, of an old Moscow building constituted his excellent apartment.

His monthly salary came to many thousands. A personal Pobeda could always be summoned by phone.

But he stood there, his elbows resting on dead stones, and he did not want to live. His soul was so empty of hope that he had not the strength to stir hand or foot. He was not moved to look around at the beauty of the morning.

It was getting light.

There was a solemn purity in the chilly air. A shaggy coat of hoarfrost had furred the enormous stump of the felled oak, the cornices of the half-ruined church, the intricately patterned lattices of its windows, the wires that ran down to the little house nearby, and the top of the long fence circling the site of a future skyscraper.

# 26

## Sawing Wood

IT WAS GETTING LIGHT.

Thick frost had trimmed with white the fence posts of the prison area and the outer security zone, the barbed wire in tangles of twenty strands at a time, bristling with thousands of spiky asterisks, the sloping roof of the watchtower, and the weeds running wild on the wasteland beyond the wire.

Dmitri Sologdin admired this miracle with unshaded eyes. He was standing near the sawhorse. He was wearing a padded jacket, prison-camp issue, over blue overalls, and his head, on which the first traces of gray could be seen, was uncovered. He was a nonentity, a slave without rights. He had been inside for twelve years, but because he had been sentenced to a second term, there was no knowing when, if ever, his imprisonment would end. His wife had wasted her youth waiting in vain for him. To avoid dismissal from her present job, as from so many others, she had pretended that she had no husband and had stopped writing to him. Sologdin had never seen his only son—his wife had been pregnant when he was arrested. Sologdin had gone through the forests of Cherdynsk, the mines of Vorkuta, two periods under investigation, one of six months, one of a year, tormented by lack of sleep, drained of his strength, wasting away. His name and his future had long ago been trampled into the mud. All he possessed was a pair of well-worn padded trousers and a tarpaulin work jacket, kept at present in the storeroom in expectation of worse times to come. He was paid thirty rubles a month—enough for three kilos of sugar—but not in cash. He could breathe fresh air only at stated times authorized by the prison authorities.

And in his soul there was a peace that nothing could destroy. His eyes sparkled like those of a young man. His chest, bared to the frost, heaved as though he were experiencing life to the full.

LONG AGO, when he had been under interrogation, his muscles were shriveled ropes, but they had expanded and grown firm again, and they demanded exercise. That was why, quite voluntarily and for no reward, he went out every morning to chop and saw wood for the prison kitchen.

But ax and saw can be terrible weapons in a convict's hands, and they were not readily entrusted to him. The prison authorities were paid to suspect that the convict's most innocent act is a treacherous ruse; they judged others by themselves, refused to believe that a man would volunteer to work for nothing, stubbornly suspected Sologdin of planning his escape or armed mutiny, especially as there were hints of both in his record. Standing orders therefore provided that a guard should position himself five paces away from Sologdin while he worked, out of range of his ax but watching every movement. There were guards willing to perform this dangerous duty, and the prison authorities, reared in the admirable ways of the Gulag, did not think one watcher to one worker a waste of manpower. But Sologdin turned obstinate and aggravated their suspicions by declaring that he would not work in the presence of a "screw." That was the end of his woodchopping for a time. (The prison governor could not coerce prisoners. This was not a prison camp. The inmates here were engaged in intellectual labor and did not come under his ministry.) The real trouble was that the planners and accountants had made no provision for this work, and the women who came from outside to cook the prisoners' food refused to chop wood because they were not paid extra for it. The authorities tried detailing off-duty guards to do the job, tearing them away from their dominoes in the orderly room. The guards were all blockheads, handpicked as young men for their physical fitness. But during their years of service in prisons, they seemed to have lost the habit of work—their backs soon started aching, and the pull of the dominoes was strong. They just couldn't produce enough firewood, so the governor had to give in and authorize Sologdin and any other prisoners who turned up (usually Nerzhin and Rubin) to chop and saw without additional surveillance. The sentry on the watchtower could in any case see them clearly, and the duty officers, too, were told to keep an eye on them.

As darkness retreated and the waning lamplight merged with the light of day, the rotund figure of Spiridon the yardman appeared from around the corner of the building. He was wearing a fur hat with earflaps—no other prisoner had been given one—and a quilted jacket. The yardman was also a convict but one subordinate to the commandant of the institute, not to the prison authorities. To keep the peace, he sharpened the axes and saw for the prison, too. As he got nearer, Sologdin could see the missing saw in his hands.

Spiridon Yegorov walked around the yard, which was guarded by machine guns, at all hours from reveille to lights out, without escort. One reason why the authorities felt able to relax the rules was that Spiridon was blind in one eye and had only thirty percent vision in the other. The sharashka's budget provided for three yardmen because the yard was really several yards joined together, two hectares in area, but Spiridon, unaware of this, did the work of all three and felt none the worse for it. What mattered was that here he could "eat his bellyful," at least a kilo and a half of black bread, because there was plenty of bread and to spare, and the men let him have some of their gruel. Spiridon was conspicuously fitter, and plumper, than he had been in Sev-Ural-Lag, where he had acted as nanny to many thousands of logs.

"Hey, Spiridon!" Sologdin called out impatiently.

His face, with its graying ginger mustache and graying ginger eyebrows, was very mobile and, when he was answering someone, often expressed eagerness to oblige. As it did now. Sologdin did not know that this exaggerated show of helpfulness was often derisive.

"What d'you mean what's the matter? The saw won't cut!"

"I can't think why," Spiridon said, sounding surprised. "You've complained about it I don't know how many times this winter. Let's have a try."

He held the saw by one handle.

They began sawing. The saw jumped out once or twice, trying to change its place because it wasn't lying comfortably, but then it sank its teeth in and was on its way.

"You grip it awful hard," Spiridon cautiously advised him. "Just get three fingers around the handle like around a pen and move nice and easy, smooth like . . . that's it . . . you've got it! Only when you pull it toward you, don't tug at it."

Each man believed himself superior to the other: Sologdin because he knew all about mechanics, the resistance of metals, and other scientific matters, and also because of his broad grasp of social issues; Spiridon because material objects always obeyed him. Sologdin, however, patronized the yardman openly, whereas Spiridon hid his feelings.

Even halfway through the thick log, the saw never seemed to be sticking; it cut away with a thin whine, sputtering pine shavings onto the two men's overalls.

Sologdin burst out laughing.

"You're a wizard. Spiridon! You had me fooled. You sharpened the saw and set it yesterday."

Spiridon complacently chanted in time to the saw. "She chews and chews and never swallows, but all her sawdust gives to others."

And before the saw was through, the butt of the log fell off under the pressure of his hand.

"I didn't sharpen it at all," he said, turning the saw over so that Sologdin could see the cutting edge. "You can see the teeth are just the same today as they were yesterday."

Sologdin bent down to look at the saw and could see no file marks. But the rascal had certainly done something to it.

"Come on, Spiridon, let's cut another length."

Spiridon held his back. "No, I can't. I'm all worn-out. All the work my grandfathers and great-grandfathers didn't do has landed on me. Anyway, your pals will be here soon."

Sologdin's friends, however, were in no hurry.

It was now broad daylight. A morning magnificently adorned with hoarfrost stood revealed. Even the drainpipes, and the ground itself, were decked with hoarfrost, and in the distance the tops of the lime trees in the exercise yard wore splendid silvery gray manes.

"How did you land in the sharashka, Spiridon?" Sologdin asked, looking closely at the yardman.

He was killing time. In all his years in the camps, he had associated only with educated people, expecting to glean nothing worthwhile from less cultured prisoners.

Spiridon smacked his lips. "You may well ask. You're all learned folk, you and all the others they've lumped together in this place, and here am I thrown in with you. On my card it says I'm a glassblower. Well, I was a glassblower once, at our factory near Bryansk. But that's a long time ago, and now my eyesight's gone, and the work I did is no use in this place; what they want here is a really clever glassblower, like Ivan. There wasn't another like him in our whole factory, and never had been. But they just took a peek at my card and brought me here. Then they took a good look at me and were going to send me packing, but the commandant, God bless him, took me on as a yardman."

Nerzhin came around the corner from the direction of the exercise yard and the one-story staff building. He was wearing unbuttoned overalls, a padded jacket draped around his shoulders, and a towel, prison issue, as broad as it was long, around his neck.

He greeted them abruptly—"Morning, friends"—shedding garments, stripping off the upper part of his denims, and removing his undershirt as he came.

Sologdin looked askance at him. "Gleb, my boy, are you crazy? Where's the snow?"

"Right here," Nerzhin retorted, scrambling onto the roof of the woodshed, where there was a virgin layer of something fluffy that was partly snow and partly hoarfrost. He scooped up handfuls of it and began vigorously rubbing chest, back, and sides. He rubbed himself with snow down to the waist all through the winter, although any guard who chanced to be near would try to stop him.

Spiridon shook his head: "Look what a sweat you're in now."

"Still no letter, Spiridon Danilovich?" Nerzhin called out.

"This time there was a letter for me."

"So why haven't you brought it for me to read? Is everything all right?"

"There was a letter, but I can't get it. The Snake's kept it."

"Myshin? Won't he hand it over?" Nerzhin stopped rubbing himself.

"He put my name on the list, but the commandant had me cleaning out the attic, and before I knew it, the Snake had shut up shop. It'll be Monday now."

"The scoundrels!" Nerzhin sighed, baring his teeth.

Spiridon waved it away.

"Don't damn the priests—leave it to the devil," he said, with one eye on Sologdin, whom he didn't know well. "All right, I'm off."

In his big fur hat, with its flaps untied, Spiridon looked like a comically flop-eared mongrel as he set off for the guardroom, to which no other prisoner was admitted.

"Spiridon!"

Sologdin suddenly remembered and called after him. "What about the ax? Where's the ax?"

"The duty guard will bring it," Spiridon shouted back, and vanished.

"Well," said Nerzhin, vigorously rubbing his chest and back with his scrap of terry toweling. "I didn't come up to Anton's expectations. He says I treat Number Seven like 'a drunk's corpse under Marfino's fence.' Then yesterday evening he offered me a transfer to the cryptography group, but I refused."

A slight movement of Sologdin's head and a grin perhaps expressed disapproval. Between his neatly clipped graying ginger mustache and matching beard, his smile revealed sparkling white teeth, sound teeth untouched by decay. The gaps had been made by outside forces.

"You're behaving more like a bard than a reckoner," he said.

Nerzhin was not surprised: "Mathematician" and "poet" had been replaced, in accordance with Sologdin's well-known whimsical habit of speaking the Language of Ultimate Clarity and not using "bird language," that is, foreign words.

Still half naked, unhurriedly toweling himself, Nerzhin gloomily agreed.

"Yes, it's not like me. But I suddenly felt so sick of it all that I didn't care anymore. If I go to Siberia, I go to Siberia. . . . I'm sorry to find that Lyovka is right—I'm a failure as a skeptic. Obviously skepticism isn't just a system of ideas; it's mainly a matter of character. I want to intervene in what goes on. May even give somebody a smack in the chops."

Sologdin found a more comfortable position against the sawhorse.

"It gives me deep joy, my friend. Your hardened unbelief" (meaning what was called "skepticism" in the Language of Seeming Clarity) "was unavoidable on the road away from . . . the satanic drug" (he meant "Marxism," but he couldn't think of a Russian synonym for it) "to the world of truth. You are no longer a boy" (Sologdin was six years older); "you must find yourself spiritually, understand the relation between good and evil in human life. And you must choose."

Sologdin looked meaningfully at Nerzhin, who, however, showed no inclination to choose between good and evil then and there. He put on his shirt, which was too small, and answered back as he thrust his arms into his overall sleeves.

"That's a weighty statement. But shouldn't you also be reminding me that 'reason is feeble' and that I myself am the 'source of error'?"

He rounded on his friend as though struck by a new thought.

"Look, you're supposed to have the 'light of truth' in you, yet you say that prostitution is morally beneficial, and that Dantes was in the right when he fought his duel with Pushkin."

Sologdin smiled complacently, baring a defective set of longish teeth with rounded edges.

"Well, didn't I successfully defend those propositions?"

"Yes, but the thought that in the same skull, the same breast. . . ."

"That's life. You must get used to it. I freely admit that I'm like one of those wooden eggs you can take apart. I am made up of nine spheres, one inside the other."

"'Sphere' is bird talk!"

"Sorry. You see how uninventive I am. I am made of nine roundnesses. It is not often that I let anyone see the inner ones. Don't forget that we live with our visors down. We have been forced to. And anyway, we are more complex than the people depicted in novels. Writers try to explain people completely, but in real life we never get to know anyone completely. That's why I love Dostoevsky. Stavrogin, Svidrigailov, Kirillov. What are they really like? The closer you get, the less you understand them."

"Stavrogin? Which book is he in?"

"*The Possessed.* Haven't you read it?" Sologdin was astonished.

Nerzhin draped his damp, skimpy towel around his neck like a muffler and pulled on his officer's service cap, which was so old that it was coming apart at the seams.

"*The Possessed*? Come off it. Where d'you think my generation could get hold of it? It's counterrevolutionary literature! Too dangerous!"

He put on his jacket.

"Anyway, I don't agree. When a new arrival crosses the threshold of your cell, you hang down from your bunk and your eyes bore into him—is he friend or enemy? You size him up in a flash. And, surprisingly, you're never mistaken. Is it really as difficult as you say to understand a man? Remember how you and I first met. You arrived in the sharashka when the washbasin was still out on the main stairway, right?"

"Right."

"It was morning, and I was on my way downstairs, whistling some silly little tune. You were drying yourself, and you suddenly raised your face from the towel in the half darkness. I was rooted to the spot. It was like looking at the face in an icon. Later on I looked more closely, and you were by no means a saint—I don't mean to flatter you. . . ."

Sologdin laughed.

". . . Your face isn't at all gentle, but it is unusual. I felt at once that I could trust you, and after five minutes I was telling you. . . ."

"I was staggered by your rashness."

"But a man with eyes like yours can't be a stoolie!"

"It's too bad if I'm so easy to read. In a camp you need to look nondescript."

"Then that same day, when I'd been listening to your evangelical revelations, I tempted you with a question. . . ."

"Of the Karamazov variety."

"Ah, you remember! I asked you what should be done with professional criminals. Remember what you said? 'Shoot the lot!' Right?"

Nerzhin, now as then, looked hard at Sologdin, as though giving him a chance to retract.

But the bright blue of Dmitri Sologdin's eyes was untroubled. He folded his arms picturesquely over his chest, one of his most becoming poses, and loftily declared, "My friend! They who want to destroy Christianity, and only they, would have it become the creed of eunuchs. But Christianity is the faith of the strong in spirit. We must have the courage to see the evil in the world and to root it out. Wait a while—you, too, will come to God. Your refusal to believe in anything is no position for a thinking man; it's just spiritual poverty."

Nerzhin sighed.

"You know, I don't even mind acknowledging a Creator, some sort of Higher Reason in the universe. I'll even say that I feel it to be so, if you want me to. But supposing I found out that there is no God, would I be any less moral?"

"Undoubtedly!"

"I don't think so. And why do you have to insist, why do all of you always insist, that we must recognize not just God in some general sense but a concrete Christian God, plus the Trinity, plus the Immaculate Conception? Would my philosophical deism be the least bit shaken if I learn that not one of the Gospel miracles ever happened? Of course it wouldn't!"

Sologdin sternly raised a hand with an admonitory finger.

"There's no other way! If you begin to doubt a single dogma of the faith, a single word of the scriptures, all is lost! You are one of the godless!"

His hand slashed the air as though it held a saber.

"That's what repels people! All or nothing! No compromises, no allowances made. But suppose I can't accept it in toto? What can I be sure of? What can I rely on? I keep telling you—the one thing I know is that I know nothing."

Socrates' apprentice took hold of the saw and offered the other handle to Sologdin.

"Another time, then," Sologdin agreed. "Let's cut wood."

They had begun to feel the cold, and they sawed away briskly. Powdered brown bark sputtered from under the saw. The job had been done more skillfully with Spiridon at the other end of the saw, but after many mornings working together, the friends got along without recriminations. They sawed with the zeal and enjoyment of men whose work is not performed under duress or the lash of poverty.

Sologdin, flushed scarlet, growled once, when they were about to cut their fourth log: "Just try not to snag the saw."

And after the fourth log was cut, Nerzhin muttered: "It was a knotty one, all right, that bastard."

Fragrant shavings, some white, some yellow, fell on the trousers and shoes of the sawyers at each swish of the saw. This rhythmical work soothed them and re-tuned their thoughts.

Nerzhin had awakened in a bad mood, but now he was thinking that camp life had left him stunned only for the first year. Now that he had his second wind, he would not fight tooth and nail for a trusty's job, he would not be afraid of general duties; now that he knew better what really mattered, he would join the morning work parade in his padded jacket, smirched with plaster or fuel oil, and slowly stick at it for the whole twelve-hour day, day in and day out for the five remaining years of his sentence: Five years wasn't ten years; five years you could survive. You just had to keep reminding yourself that prison was not just a curse—it was also a blessing.

These were his thoughts as he took alternate pulls at the saw. He could not possibly imagine that his partner, as he pulled the saw his way, thought of prison only as an unmitigated curse, from which he must sooner or later break free.

Sologdin was thinking now about his great secret achievement of the past few months, which held the promise of freedom. He would learn the definitive verdict on his work after breakfast, and he knew in advance that it would be favorable. Sologdin swelled with pride at the thought that his brain, exhausted by so many years of interrogation, and then of hunger in the camps, starved for so many years of phosphorus, had still succeeded in mastering a major engineering problem! How often we notice it in men approaching their forties—that sudden uprush of vital forces! Especially if the surplus energy of the flesh is not expended in procreation but mysteriously transmuted into powerful thought.

## 27

# A Bit of Methodology

MEANWHILE THEY SAWED AWAY. Their bodies grew hot; their faces glowed; their jackets had long ago been tossed onto the unsawed timber; freshly cut logs were piling up around the sawhorse. And still there was no ax.

"Maybe that's enough?" Nerzhin asked. "We'll never chop all that."

Sologdin agreed. "Let's have a rest." The blade of the saw twanged as he put it aside.

They whipped their caps off. Steam rose from Nerzhin's mop and Sologdin's thinning hair. They took deep breaths. The air seemed to search out the mustiest corners of their insides.

"But if they send you off to a camp now," Sologdin asked, "how will that affect your work on the New Time of Troubles?" (He meant the Revolution.)

"How can it? I'm not exactly pampered here. Having a single line of it in my possession means risking the hole whether I'm there or here. I can't get a permit to use the public library here anyway. I probably won't be let into the archives as long as I live. As for clean paper, even in the taiga I can find birch bark or pine bark. And however often they frisk me, they can't confiscate my real assets; the suffering I've gone through and watched others experience provides a wealth of historical insights. Don't you agree?"

"Splendid!" Sologdin answered heartily. "I can see you're learning! So you've decided not to spend fifteen years reading all the books on the subject first?"

"More or less, and anyway where would I get them?"

"Let's have no 'more or less'!" Sologdin loudly admonished him. "Remember, the idea is the thing! A powerful initial idea determines the success of any activity. And the idea must be your own! An idea, like a living tree, bears fruit only if it develops naturally. Books, and other people's opinions, are scissors; they can cut through the life of your idea. You have to begin by thinking it through for yourself. Only then should you check it against what you find in books."

Sologdin looked searchingly at his friend.

"What about the thirty little red volumes—are you still going to read them from beginning to end?"

"Yes! To understand Lenin is to understand half the truth about the Revolution. And where did he reveal himself more clearly than in his books? Besides, I can find them anywhere, in any public reading room."

Sologdin looked dark, put his cap on, and perched awkwardly on the sawhorse.

"You are a madman. You'll fill your head with nonsense. It'll get you nowhere. It's my duty to warn you."

Nerzhin also took his cap from the sawhorse and perched on the pile of logs.

"Don't let your profession down. Think like a mathematician. Apply the nodal points method. How is any unknown phenomenon investigated? How is any undrawn curve plotted? All at once or point by point?"

"All right, all right!" Nerzhin didn't like beating about the bush. "I see what you mean."

"So why not apply this to a . . . person from real life?" (Nerzhin mentally translated it into the "Language of Apparent Clarity": a historical person.)

"Get an overall view of Lenin's life, spot the main breaks in gradualness, the sharp changes of direction, and read only what relates to them. How did he behave at *those* moments? And there you have the whole man. The rest you don't need at all."

"So when I asked you what should be done with professional criminals, I was inadvertently applying the nodal points method to you?"

An evasive grin narrowed Sologdin's bright eyes. He thoughtfully draped his jacket over his shoulders and changed his position on the sawhorse but looked no more comfortable.

"You have upset me, Gleb, my boy. You may have to leave here any day now. We will have to part. One of us will perish. Or both of us. Will we live to see the day when people can meet and talk openly? I would like to have time to share with you . . . at least some of the conclusions I have reached about ways of unifying the aim, the agent, and his work. They might be of use to you. Of course, my inarticulateness makes it very difficult for me; I'll put it rather clumsily. . . ."

That was typical of Sologdin! Before dazzling you with his ideas, he felt compelled to disparage himself.

Nerzhin took over, to speed things up.

"Don't forget your poor memory! And the fact that you are 'a vessel of error.'"

"Quite so," Sologdin confirmed with a fleeting smile. "Well, then, knowing my own imperfection, I have spent many years in prison forging rules for myself that gird my will with a band of iron. These rules are a sort of general survey of ways of approaching work."

Methodology, thought Nerzhin, translating as usual from the Language of Ultimate Clarity. His shoulders were getting cold, and he, too, draped his jacket around himself.

The light was growing stronger, and they could see that it would soon be time to leave the firewood and report for the morning roll call. In the distance, in front of the special prison's staff building, they caught glimpses of the Marfino exercise yard under a canopy of magically whitened limes. Towering over the other strollers were the thin, upright figure of the fifty-year-old artist Kondrashov-Ivanov and the bent but also very lanky Merzhanov, once Stalin's court architect but now forgotten. They also saw Lev Rubin, who had overslept, trying to break through to the woodpile. The guard barred his way because it was too late.

"Look, there's Lyovka with his beard in a tangle."

They both burst out laughing.

"Well, then, would you like me to tell you one or two of the rules each morning?"

"Go ahead. We can try it."

"Here's an example: How should one behave in the face of difficulties?"

"Not be downhearted?"

"That's not enough."

Sologdin gazed past Nerzhin and out beyond the prison zone at the low, thick underbrush, powdered with frost and faintly tinged with the uncertain pink light from the east. The sun was undecided whether to appear or not. Sologdin's face, grave and lean, with its fair, curly beard and fair, clipped mustache, was somehow reminiscent of Alexander Nevsky.*

"What should be our attitude to difficulties?" he said solemnly. "In the sphere of the unknown, we should regard difficulties as a hidden treasure! As a rule, the more difficult things are, the more they can help us. It is worth less

* Alexander Nevsky: A thirteenth-century Russian prince greatly esteemed for his military leadership and diplomatic wisdom that preserved Northeast Russia from destruction by the Mongols. He was canonized by the Russian Orthodox Church.

if the difficulties arise from your struggle with yourself. But when they come from the increasing resistance of the object, it's splendid!" (The rosy glow of dawn seemed to pass over Alexander Nevsky's face, carrying with it the reflection of difficulties as beautiful as the sun.)

"The most promising path for investigation is that on which the greatest external meets the smallest internal resistance. Setbacks must be regarded as showing the need for further application of effort and concentration of the will. If great exertions have already been made, setbacks are a still greater cause for rejoicing! They mean that our crowbar has struck the iron treasure chest! And overcoming increased difficulties is all the more valuable in that the agent grows in stature with each setback, grows in proportion to the difficulties he meets!"

"Bravo! Well said!" Nerzhin called out from his log pile.

"That doesn't mean that we can never forgo further effort. Our crowbar may have struck a stone instead. Once convinced of that, or if your resources are insufficient, or in violently hostile surroundings, you may even abandon the goal itself. But it is important to examine your reasons meticulously!"

"Now, there I'm not sure I'm with you," Nerzhin said slowly. "What surroundings are more hostile than prison? Where could our resources be less adequate? But we go on doing what we must. To give up now might mean giving up forever."

Dawn tints had lingered on the shrubs until unbroken gray cloud extinguished them.

Sologdin looked down absently at Nerzhin, as though withdrawing his eyes from a message graven on tablets of stone. Then he began to speak again, almost chanting:

"Now hear the rule of the last few inches! The region of the final inches! What that means is immediately obvious in the Language of Utter Clarity. The work is nearly completed, the goal is almost attained, everything seems to have been mastered and finalized, but the quality of the thing is not quite right. Finishing touches are necessary, perhaps further research. At that moment of weariness, the temptation to abandon the work without perfecting it is particularly strong. Work in the sector of the last few inches is very, very complicated but also particularly valuable because it is carried out by the most perfect means! The rule for the last few inches amounts to just this: Do not give up work at this point! Do not put it off, or the agent's current of thought will be diverted from the region of the last few inches! And do not begrudge time spent on it, knowing that the goal is not speedy completion but the achievement of perfection!"

"Good, very good," Nerzhin whispered.

In a quite different voice, a sarcastic voice, Sologdin said:

"What's the idea, Junior Lieutenant? This isn't like you. Why have you been so long with the ax? We won't have time to chop the wood now."

The moonfaced junior lieutenant, Nadelashin, had been a sergeant major not so long ago. After his promotion to officer rank, the prisoners in the sharashka, who were quite fond of him, had taken to calling him "junior."

Mincing toward them, panting comically, he handed over the ax with a guilty smile and said eagerly:

"No, please, Sologdin, please chop the wood! There's none at all in the kitchen; there's nothing to cook dinner with. You can't imagine how much work I have without your making me more."

Nerzhin snorted. "Eh? What? Work? Junior Lieutenant! You really call what you do work?"

The duty officer turned his moon face to Nerzhin. Knitting his brow, he recited from memory: "'Work is the overcoming of resistance.' When I walk around quickly, I'm overcoming air resistance, so I, too, work." He tried to look impassive, but his face lit up in a smile when Sologdin and Nerzhin both roared with laughter in the frosty air. "Please, please chop the wood!"

He turned and minced off toward the staff building, outside which at that very moment they caught a glimpse of the smart, overcoated figure of his superior, Lieutenant Colonel Klimentiev.

"Gleb, my boy," said Sologdin in surprise. "Do my eyes deceive me? Is that Klimentiadis?" (That year there had been a lot in the newspapers about Greek detainees who sent telegrams from their cells to parliaments everywhere and to the UN describing the hardships they were suffering. In the sharashka, where prisoners could not always send as much as a postcard to their wives, let alone write to foreign parliaments, it had become the practice to change the name of prison officers so that they sounded Greek—Myshinopoulos, Klimentiadis, Shikinidi.)

"What brings Klimentiadis here on a Sunday?"

"Don't you know? Six men are being taken to see family."

Nerzhin had heard about this earlier. Now his whole being, so full of light and joy while he was sawing wood, was suffused with bitterness again. It was nearly a year since he had been allowed a visit and eight months since he had put in an application, which had been neither approved nor rejected. One reason for this was that, not wanting his wife to lose her graduate student status, he had not given her address at the dormitory but instead asked for letters to be sent poste restante. The prison would not accept this. Because he was so intensely introspective, Nerzhin was free from envy. Neither the wages nor the rations of more deserving prisoners disturbed his peace of mind. But some people had visits every couple of months, while his vulnerable wife had pined and hovered outside the fortresslike walls of prisons, and the thought of this injustice was torture to him.

Moreover, today was his birthday.

"They are, are they?" Sologdin was just as bitterly envious. "They take the stoolies down there every month. And I will never see my Nina again. . . ."

(Sologdin never used the words "until the end of my sentence" because he had reason to know that prison sentences do not necessarily have an end.)

He watched Klimentiev stand talking to Nadelashin for a minute or two, then enter headquarters.

He spoke suddenly and rapidly: "Gleb! Look, your wife knows mine. When you go in to see her, try to ask Nadya to look Nina up and tell her just three little things from me: He loves you! he worships you! he adores you!"

"You know they've refused me a visit; what's gotten into you?" Nerzhin, taking careful aim to split a log clear in two, did not hide his annoyance.

"Just take a look!"

Nerzhin looked around. "Junior" was coming toward them and beckoning to him. Dropping the ax and brushing against the propped-up saw with his jacket so that it fell to the ground with a twang, Gleb ran like a little boy.

Sologdin's eyes followed them as Junior took Nerzhin into headquarters. Then he placed a log upright and swung at it with such bitter rage that he not only split it into two blocks but drove the ax into the ground.

The ax was government property anyway.

## 28

# The Junior Lieutenant's Job

WHEN HE HAD CITED his textbook definition of work, Junior Lieutenant Nadelashin had not been untruthful. He was on duty for only twelve hours every two days, but the work was exacting; it involved scurrying to and fro between floors, and it was extremely responsible.

His spell of duty the previous night had proved more than usually bothersome. He had reported for duty at 9:00 p.m., checked off the prisoners, 281 of them, as all present, supervised their exit to their places of work for the evening, stationed sentries on the landing of the main staircase and in the headquarters hallway, mounted a patrol under the windows of the special prison, and was about to feed and billet the new arrivals when he was torn away by a summons from the operations officer, Major Myshin, who for some reason had not gone home.

Nadelashin was an exceptional person not only among jailers (or "prison operatives," as they were now called) but among his compatriots in general. In a country where the words for "vodka" and "water" look as much alike as the liquids themselves, Nadelashin never took a drop, even for a cold. In a country where every other person has an advanced degree in obscene language from the army or the camps, where the foulest words are used in the presence of children, not only by drunks (and by children themselves at play), not only by people fighting to get onto a bus at an out-of-town stop, but in intimate conversation between friends, Nadelashin was not only unskilled in obscenity, he did not even use words like "devil" and "scum." He had just one little saying when he was angry—"A bull should toss you!"—and he usually said it under his breath.

On this occasion, too, he kept his "A bull should toss you" to himself as he hurried off to see the major.

Operations Officer Myshin, whom Bobynin in his conversation with the minister had unfairly described as a drone, the unhealthily obese, violet-complexioned major, detained at "work" that Saturday evening by the emergency, instructed Nadelashin

—to check whether the German and Latvian Christmas celebrations had begun;
—to list by groups all those celebrating Christmas;
—to observe personally, and also by dispatching rank-and-file guards every ten minutes, whether those celebrating drank wine, what they talked about among themselves, and above all whether they indulged in anti-Soviet agitation;
—to discover if possible some deviation from prison routine and put a stop to this unseemly religious debauch.

He did not say "put a stop to" but "as far as possible put a stop to. . . ." Peacefully celebrating Christmas was not specifically forbidden, but Myshin's Bolshevik heart could not endure it.

Junior Lieutenant Nadelashin, his face like an impassive winter moon, reminded the major that neither he nor, still less, his guards knew German, let alone Latvian (indeed, their Russian wasn't all that good).

Recalling that during his own four years of service as political officer of the guard company in a camp for German prisoners of war, he had learned only three German words (*Halt! Zurück!* and *Weg!*), Myshin abbreviated his instructions.

Having received his orders and saluted clumsily, Nadelashin went off to install the new arrivals, for which purpose he had a list, also from the operations officer, showing who was to be put in which room and which bunk. (Myshin attached great importance to centrally planned allocation of places in prison living quarters, where his informants were evenly distributed. He knew that the frankest conversations are held not amid the bustle of the working day but at bedtime, and that the most sullen anti-Soviet utterances were made in the early morning, so that it is particularly useful to have an observer in a nearby bed.)

Nadelashin next dutifully looked once into every room where Christmas was being celebrated, ostensibly to estimate the wattage of the lightbulbs hanging there. He also sent a guard to take just one look. And he made a list of the celebrants.

Then Major Myshin summoned him again, and Nadelashin delivered the list. Myshin was particularly interested to see that Rubin had been with the Germans and recorded this in a file.

By then it was time to change sentries and settle an argument between two guards as to which of them had been on duty longer last time and who owed whom how many hours.

Next it was time to sound lights-out, argue with Pryanchikov about hot water, make the rounds again, extinguish the white light, and switch on the blue. . . . After which he was sent for yet again by Major Myshin, who just wouldn't go home. (His wife was unwell, and he didn't want to listen to her grumblings all evening.)

Major Myshin, in his easy chair, kept Nadelashin standing while he interrogated him. Who, from what he had observed, were Rubin's usual leisure companions? Had he at any time spoken defiantly about the prison administration? Had he voiced demands in the name of the masses?

Nadelashin was unique among the MGB officers who supervised teams of guards. He had been severely reprimanded time and time again. His native kindheartedness had long been a handicap to him in his career. If he had not made an effort to conform, he would have been dismissed long ago and perhaps even jailed. It was not in his nature to be rude to prisoners. He smiled at them with genuine goodwill. Whenever he could show some slight indulgence, he did so. In return the prisoners liked him, did not complain about him, did not defy him, and talked uninhibitedly in his presence. He had sharp eyes and good ears, and he was quite literate, so he wrote it all down in a special little notebook to assist his memory and reported some of it to his superiors, thus compensating for various derelictions of duty.

So it was now. He took out his notebook and informed the major that on December 17 a gang of prisoners had been walking along the lower hallway on the way back from their after-dinner exercise, and he, Nadelashin, had been walking right behind them. The prisoners were bellyaching about tomorrow being Sunday and about not being able to get a day off, and Rubin had said to them, "Will you fellows never learn that it's hopeless expecting sympathy from those reptiles?" (the prison staff).

"He actually said that, 'those reptiles'?"

"His very words," the moonlike Nadelashin confirmed with a tolerant smile.

Myshin opened the file again, made a note, and ordered Nadelashin to put in a separate report.

Major Myshin hated Rubin and was accumulating incriminating evidence against him. When he started work at Marfino and learned that Rubin, an ex-Communist, went around boasting that, jail or no jail, he was still a Communist at heart, Myshin had called him in for a talk about life in general and about their future collaboration in particular. Myshin had confronted Rubin word for word, with the arguments recommended at Ministry of State Security briefing sessions:

—if you are a true Soviet citizen, you will help us;
—if you do not help us, you are not a true Soviet citizen;
—if you are not a true Soviet citizen, you are anti-Soviet and deserve a stiffer sentence.

But Rubin had asked, "Should I write my denunciations in ink or in pencil?" "Ink is better," Myshin advised him. "Only, you see, I've already proved my devotion to the Soviet regime with my blood, and I don't need to prove it in ink."

So Rubin had shown the major from the start the full extent of his disingenuousness and duplicity.

The major had made one more attempt. This time Rubin made the glaringly false excuse that, since he had been jailed, he was obviously considered politically unreliable, and, that being so, he could not collaborate with the operations officer.

Since then, Myshin had nursed his resentment and collected all the evidence he could for use against Rubin.

Before the major had finished with the junior lieutenant, a sedan arrived from the Ministry of State Security to pick up Bobynin. Taking advantage of this happy coincidence, Myshin dashed outside without his overcoat and hung around the car, inviting the accompanying officer to come in for a warm-up, advertising the fact that he, Myshin, stayed behind working at night, badgering Nadelashin, anxiously asking Bobynin whether he was warm enough (he was demonstratively wearing a padded jacket brought along from the camp, not the heavy overcoat issued at Marfino).

Immediately after Bobynin's departure, Pryanchikov was sent for, and the major could not possibly think of going home. To relieve the suspense while he waited to discover who else would be sent for and when they would all return, the major went to see how some of the guards were spending their rest period. They were playing a desperate game of dominoes. Myshin, who was responsible for their political education, set about examining them on the history of the Party. Although they were officially on duty, they answered the major's questions with understandable reluctance. Their performance was lamentable. Not only were these warriors unable to name a single work by Lenin or Stalin, they even said that Plekhanov was a tsarist minister and had shot down the Petersburg workers on January 9, 1905. Myshin told Nadelashin off for letting his shift get out of hand.

Bobynin and Pryanchikov returned together and went to bed without a word to the major. Disappointed and more worried than ever, he left in the same car, since the buses had stopped running.

The off-duty guards told the major what they thought of him—now that he had gone—and started getting ready for bed. Nadelashin, too, yearned for a catnap, but it was not to be; there was a telephone call from the guardhouse of the convoy troops who manned the towers around the Marfino complex.

The guard commander excitedly reported that he had been called up by the sentry in the tower at the southwest corner. In the thickening fog he had clearly seen someone lurking at the corner of the woodshed, then trying to crawl toward the wire between the prison yard and the outer security zone. The sentry's challenge had frightened the man, and he had run right back into the yard. The guard commander announced that he was about to call his own regimental HQ and write a report on this untoward occurrence, and he asked the duty officer at the special prison to organize a sweep of the yard in the meantime.

Although Nadelashin was firmly of the opinion that the sentry had been having hallucinations and that the prisoners were safely locked in behind new iron doors set in stout ancient walls four bricks thick, the mere fact that the guard commander was writing a report called for energetic action and a corresponding report from him, too. He therefore sounded the alarm and led the "resting" shift around the fogbound yard with "Bat" lanterns. After this he himself went around all the cells again. He considerately refrained from switching the white light on (to avoid unnecessary complaints) but could not see very well by the blue light and bumped his knee painfully on the corner of someone's bed before illuminating the heads of the sleeping prisoners with his flashlight and counting all 281 of them.

He then went into the office and, in the neat, round handwriting that mirrored his limpid soul, wrote a report on the night's events, addressing it to the commandant of the special prison, Lieutenant Colonel Klimentiev.

By then it was morning, time to check the kitchen and sound reveille.

That was how Junior Lieutenant Nadelashin had spent the night. He had every right to tell Nerzhin that he did not eat the bread of idleness.

Nadelashin was well over thirty, although the freshness of his whiskerless face made him look younger.

His father and grandfather had been tailors, not tailors deluxe but good craftsmen, serving people of modest means, not above taking orders for turning or shortening or for emergency repairs. The boy was meant to follow in their footsteps. He himself took a liking to this pleasant and undemanding work as a child and trained himself for it by watching and helping. But the NEP* came

* NEP: Instituted by Lenin in 1921, the so-called New Economic Policy reintroduced limited private enterprise into the Soviet economy. It was intended as a temporary measure to revitalize the Soviet system after the excesses of "war Communism."

to an end, and his father was presented with a twelve-month tax demand. He paid up. Two days later he was confronted with another twelve-month demand. Utterly shameless, they came again two days after this with a third demand, for three times the previous amount. Nadelashin's father tore up his license, took down his sign, and joined a cooperative workshop. Nadelashin himself was called up soon afterward, found himself serving with the Ministry of the Interior's forces, and was later transferred to the prison guard service.

During the fourteen years of his service, four waves of prison guards had passed him by. Some were already captains. He had been grudgingly awarded his first star just a month ago.

Nadelashin understood much more than he let on. He realized that these prisoners, deprived of basic human rights, were in fact often his superiors. But he also, as we all do, assumed that others were not essentially different in character from himself and could not imagine that they were such murderous villains as they were, each and every one, made out to be in politics classes.

He remembered, even more precisely than the definition of work in his night-school physics textbook, every bend in the five prison corridors of the Big Lubyanka and the interior of each of its 110 cells. In accordance with the Lubyanka's regulations, guards were moved from one part of the corridor to another every two hours. This was a precaution against their becoming too intimate with prisoners, thereby being won over or bribed by them. (Guards were in any case better paid than teachers or engineers.)

A guard had to peep through every spy hole at least once every three minutes. Nadelashin, with his exceptional memory for faces, thought that he could remember every single prisoner on his floor of the prison between 1935 and 1947 (when he had been transferred to Marfino), whether they were famous leaders like Bukharin or ordinary front-line officers like Nerzhin. He thought that even now he would recognize any one of them in the street, whatever he was wearing. In fact, they never reappeared in the street, and it was only here, in Marfino, that he had met again old acquaintances whom he had once had under lock and key, without, of course, letting them know that he recognized them. He remembered seeing this or that prisoner in a cataleptic trance from enforced sleeplessness in blindingly lit boxes, one meter square; slicing a four-hundred-gram ration of damp bread with a thread; absorbed in one of the beautiful old books with which the prison library was abundantly stocked; filing out to the latrine; holding his hands behind his back when called in for interrogation; suddenly cheerful and talkative in the last half hour before bedtime; lying under the bright light on a winter night, hands outside the blankets, swathed in towels to keep warm (there was a standing order that anybody who hid his hands under his blanket must be woken up and made to take them out).

Nadelashin liked best of all listening to arguments and conversations between these white-bearded academicians, priests, old Bolsheviks, generals, and funny foreigners. Eavesdropping was part of his duty, but he listened for his own edification, too. Nadelashin would have liked—if his official duties had ever allowed it—to listen to somebody's story from beginning to end without interruption, to hear how he had lived before and what he had been jailed for. He was astonished that these people, in the dreadful months when their lives had broken down and their future was in the balance, found the courage to talk not about their sufferings but about everything under the sun: Italian artists, the behavior of bees, wolf hunting, or the way some fellow—called Kar-bu-zi-ye, was it—built houses, though he wasn't building for them.

One day Nadelashin happened to overhear a conversation that particularly interested him. He was sitting in the back of a police truck, escorting the two prisoners locked in a cage inside it. They were being transferred from the Big Lubyanka to the Sukhanovo—the "country house"—a sinister, dead-end prison outside Moscow, from which many left for the grave or the madhouse. Nadelashin had not worked in the place himself, but he had heard that even the meals there were a form of refined torture; they did not prepare coarse and heavy food for the prisoners, like everywhere else, but brought delicate, savory dishes from the rest home nearby. The torture consisted in the size of the portions; they would bring a prisoner a small bowl half full of soup, one eighth of a rissole, two slivers of a roast potato. You weren't fed, merely reminded of what you had forfeited. Such "meals" were much more distressing than a bowl of watery gruel, and they helped to drive people mad.

Normally the two prisoners in the truck would have been separated, but on this occasion they were being moved together. Nadelashin could not hear the beginning of their conversation, but then something went wrong with the engine. The driver went off somewhere, the officer was sitting in the cab, and Nadelashin heard the prisoners' quiet conversation through the grating in the cage door. They were cursing the government and the tsar, but not the present government and not Stalin. They were vilifying the emperor Peter I. What harm could he have done them? For whatever reason, they were tearing him to pieces. One of them cursed Peter, among other things, for disfiguring or suppressing Russian national dress, and so making Russians indistinguishable from other peoples. This prisoner gave a detailed inventory of traditional garments, described their appearance, and said on what occasions they were worn. He asserted that it was not too late even now to resurrect some parts of these costumes, combining them in a comfortable and dignified fashion with modern dress, instead of blindly copying Paris. The other prisoner replied jokingly—they could still make jokes!—that you would need two men, a tailor of genius clever enough to put it all together and a fashionable tenor to wear these clothes and be photographed in them, after which all Russia would quickly adopt them.

This conversation particularly interested Nadelashin; tailoring had remained his private passion. After so many duty periods in the halls of the main political prison, where madness was at white heat, the rustle of cloth, the ease with which it let itself be folded, the innocuous character of the work, were soothing.

He clothed all his children, made dresses for his wife and suits for himself. But he kept it secret.

It would be thought demeaning in a member of the armed forces.

## 29

# The Lieutenant Colonel's Job

LIEUTENANT COLONEL KLIMENTIEV'S hair was what is called jet black: shiny black, lying smoothly on his head as though molded to it, divided by a part, and below his nose was slicked something like a handlebar mustache. He had no paunch and, at the age of forty-five, held himself like a trim young soldier. Also, he never smiled on duty, and this made him look darker and more somber still.

Although it was Sunday, he had arrived even earlier than usual. In the middle of the recreation period, he crossed the exercise yard, noting at a glance all that was amiss (without interfering—that was beneath his dignity), and went into the headquarters of the special prison, ordering Duty Officer Nadelashin in passing to summon prisoner Nerzhin and come along himself. Crossing the yard, the lieutenant colonel had taken special note of the way in which, as he approached, prisoners either tried to walk quickly by or slowed down and turned away, so as not to come face to face and have to greet him yet again. Klimentiev observed this coolly and was not offended. He knew that genuine contempt for his function was not the whole explanation and that fear of seeming obsequious in the eyes of comrades was more important. Almost every one of these prisoners, called to his office alone, behaved affably, and some of them ingratiatingly. There were all sorts of people behind bars, and some were worth more than others. Klimentiev had realized this long ago. He respected their right to be proud, and stood fast on his own right to be strict. A soldier at heart, he had, so he thought, brought into the prison rational military discipline instead of the sadistic discipline of torturers.

He unlocked his office. It was hot inside, and there was a stifling smell of paint blistering on the radiators. The lieutenant colonel opened the ventilation pane, took off his overcoat, sat down, armored in his tunic, and surveyed the uncluttered surface of his desk. He had not turned over Saturday's page on his desk calendar, it had a note saying, "Christmas tree?"

From this half-empty office, in which the "means of production" still consisted only of a safe containing prison "cases," half a dozen chairs, a telephone, and some buzzers, Lieutenant Colonel Klimentiev, without, as far as could be seen, clutch or driving belts or gears, exercised physical control over three hundred prisoners' lives and organized the work of fifty guards.

Though he had come in on Sunday (he would make up for it during the workweek) and half an hour early, Klimentiev had lost nothing of his customary coolness and poise.

Junior Lieutenant Nadelashin presented himself apprehensively. A round, red spot stood out on each cheek. The lieutenant colonel had recorded none of his numerous sins of omission, but Nadelashin was very much afraid of him. A comic figure, round-faced and unsoldierly, Nadelashin made a clumsy attempt to stand at attention.

He reported that everything had been in order during his night duty, there had been no breaches of regulations, but there had been two unusual incidents, one of which was dealt with in a report. (He laid it before Klimentiev on a corner of the desk, but the report immediately took off and corkscrewed to rest under a distant chair. Nadelashin dived after it and replaced it on the desk.) The second incident consisted of the summons to the Ministry of State Security of prisoners Bobynin and Pryanchikov.

The lieutenant colonel knitted his brow and inquired more closely into the circumstances of the summons and the prisoners' return. This news was, of course, disagreeable, indeed alarming. Being commandant of Special

Prison No. 1 meant living on the rim of a volcano, meant always being under the minister's eyes. This was no remote lumber camp, where the commandant could keep a harem and a troupe of clowns and pass sentence like a feudal lord. Here you had to keep to the letter of the law, take care not to step out of line, and never give the slightest indication of your own feelings, whether of anger or compassion. But Klimentiev was like that anyway. He did not think that Bobynin or Pryanchikov could have found any irregularity in his behavior to complain of last night. Long experience had taught him not to fear slander from prisoners. It was colleagues who were likely to slander you.

Then he ran through Nadelashin's report and saw that the whole thing was nonsense. That was why he kept Nadelashin on; the man was literate and sensible.

But he had so many faults! The lieutenant colonel gave him a dressing-down. He reminded Nadelashin at some length of all the things he had overlooked last time he had been on duty: The prisoners had been led out to work in the morning two minutes late, many beds in the cells had been made up hastily, and Nadelashin had, weakly, failed to recall the careless prisoners from their work and make them try again. He had been told about all this at the time. But you could talk as much as you liked to Nadelashin; it was water off a duck's back. And just now, at morning exercise? Young Doronin had stood stock-still right on the boundary line of the exercise area, carefully inspecting the restricted zone and the space beyond it in the direction of the greenhouses, broken ground with a gully running across it, which could be very convenient for escapers. Doronin had a twenty-five-year sentence; he had a history of forging documents and had eluded a nationwide dragnet for two whole years! Yet not one of the guard detail had told Doronin to stop dawdling and to circulate. Another thing—where had Gerasimovich taken his walk? He'd broken away from the rest and gone off behind the big lime trees in the direction of the engineering shops. Remember what Gerasimovich was in for! This was his second term, under Article 58, clauses 1a to 19, i.e., treasonable intent. He hadn't betrayed his country, but he had been unable to prove that his reason for going to Leningrad in the first days of the war was not to be there when the Germans arrived. Had Nadelashin forgotten that he must study the prisoners continually, both by direct observation and from their dossiers? Finally, what did Nadelashin think he looked like? His tunic was not pulled down (Nadelashin pulled it down); the star on his cap was crooked (Nadelashin straightened it); he saluted like an old woman.

Was it any wonder that, when Nadelashin was duty officer, prisoners didn't keep their beds tidy? Unmade beds meant a dangerous crack in prison discipline. Today they leave their beds untidy, and tomorrow they'll mutiny and refuse to go to work!

The lieutenant colonel then went on to give instructions: The guards escorting prisoners to meet relatives will assemble in the third room for briefing. Nerzhin is to remain standing in the corridor. You may go.

Nadelashin left the room perspiring. Listening to his superiors, he was always sincerely distressed by the justice of their reproaches and admonitions and vowed to offend no more. But once he resumed his routine and bumped into so many prisoners, each with a will of his own, all pulling different ways, every one of them wanting some little morsel of freedom, Nadelashin could not refuse them, hoping that with luck it would pass unnoticed.

Klimentiev picked up his pen and crossed out his "Christmas tree" note. He had made his decision the day before.

Christmas parties were unknown in special prisons. But this year some prisoners, and some of the best behaved among them, had begged for permission to hold one. Klimentiev had started thinking that there was perhaps no good reason to refuse permission. It could obviously do no harm, and there wouldn't be a fire; in matters electrical they were all professors. And it was very important, on New Year's Eve, when all the free employees went off to enjoy themselves in Moscow, to provide some relaxation back at the institute, too. He knew that the eve of a holiday was particularly hard for prisoners to bear. Who knows, one of them might decide to do something desperate, something stupid. So the day before, he had rung the Chief Administration of Prisons, to which he was directly subordinate, and sought their consent to a party. Prison regulations forbade musical instruments, but they could find nothing about seasonal parties and so neither expressly approved nor flatly forbade it. Long and impeccable service had given Lieutenant Colonel Klimentiev an infallibly sure touch in all his actions. So on his way home, on the escalator in the metro, he had reached his decision: All right, then, let them have their party!

As he entered the compartment, he thought with satisfaction that he was no mere rubber stamp but an intelligent, efficient, and indeed a kindhearted human being. Not that the prisoners would ever appreciate it or find out who had wanted to ban the party and to whom they owed it.

The decision, once made, made Klimentiev feel good. Instead of pushing and shoving his way into the compartment like the other Muscovites, he stepped in last just before the doors closed and made no attempt to grab a seat but clasped a stanchion and watched the blurred reflection of his gallant self in the mirroring window, beyond which the blackness of the tunnel and the endless pipes with cable sped past. Then he shifted his gaze to a young woman sitting near him. She was neatly but inexpensively dressed, in a black artificial astrakhan coat and a cap of the same material. A bulging briefcase lay on her knees. Klimentiev looked at her and thought that her face was pleasant but very tired and that she showed an indifference to her surroundings unusual in a young woman.

At that moment the woman glanced in his direction, and they looked at each other for some time without expression, as casual fellow travelers do. But suddenly the woman started, and Klimentiev glimpsed an anxious question in her eyes. As his profession required, he had a good memory for faces. He recognized the woman, and his look betrayed it. She noticed his hesitation and was obviously confirmed in her own conjecture.

She was the prisoner Nerzhin's wife, and Klimentiev had seen her on visiting days at the Taganka Prison.

She frowned, looked away, and glanced again at Klimentiev. He was now staring out into the tunnel, but out of the corner of his eye he saw her watching him. Suddenly, she made up her mind, rose, and moved so close to him that he was compelled to look at her again.

She had gotten up looking determined, but then her courage seemed to fail her. She had lost the independent air of an emancipated young woman riding in the metro. It looked as though, in spite of her heavy briefcase, she meant to give up her seat to the lieutenant colonel. Hers was the heavy lot of all political prisoners' wives, wives of "enemies of the people"; wherever they went, no matter to whom they turned, if their unfortunate marital status became known, they were branded with their husbands' indelible shame. In the eyes of the world such a woman shared the guilt of the double-dyed miscreant to whom she had rashly entrusted her future. Such women, indeed, often began to feel as guilty as the "enemies of the people" themselves, whereas their hardened husbands did not feel guilty at all.

The woman moved very close so that her question could be heard over the clatter of the train. "Comrade Colonel! Please forgive me! I believe that you are in charge of my husband? Am I mistaken?"

A great many women of all kinds had risen and stood before Klimentiev in the long years of his service, and he saw nothing unusual in their anxious timidity. But here, in the metro, although she had addressed him very circumspectly, there was something unseemly about the woman standing before him in supplication with all those eyes upon them.

"Why . . . why are you standing? Sit down, sit down."

"No, no, that doesn't matter," she said, her eyes fixed on the lieutenant colonel in urgent, almost fanatical entreaty.

"Tell me, please, why I haven't been allowed a vis . . . why I haven't been able to see him for a whole year? When will I be able to? Please tell me."

Their encounter was as improbable as that of one particular grain of sand with another forty paces away. A week earlier permission had been received from the Prisons Administration of the Ministry of State Security for certain prisoners, among them Nerzhin, to see their wives on Sunday, December 25, 1949, at the Lefortovo Prison. But there was a footnote forbidding notification of the prisoner Nerzhin's wife poste restante, as he had requested.

Nerzhin had then been called in and asked for his wife's real address. He mumbled that he did not know. Klimentiev, trained by prison regulations never to tell prisoners the whole truth, did not expect frankness from them. Nerzhin, of course, knew but wouldn't say, and it was obvious why he wouldn't—for the same reason that the Prisons Administration would not accept poste restante as an address, because notification was sent by postcard, with the words "You have been granted permission to visit your husband at such and such a prison. . . ." Not satisfied with having the wife's address in its records, the ministry did its best to reduce the number of candidates for such postcards by seeing to it that all the neighbors would recognize the wives of enemies of the people; they must be brought out into the open, isolated, hemmed in by the right-thinking public. This was what the wives feared. Nerzhin's wife did not even use his surname. She was obviously trying to hide from the Ministry of State Security. So Klimentiev had told Nerzhin that there would of course be no meeting. And had not notified his wife.

But now the silent attention of all around them was fixed on this woman who had demeaned herself by rising and standing before him.

"Writing poste restante is forbidden," he said, just loudly enough for her to hear above the racket of the train. "You have to give an address."

Her expression changed rapidly.

"But I'm leaving soon! I'm leaving very soon, and I have no permanent address now."

She was obviously lying.

Klimentiev's intention was to get out at the first stop and, if she followed him, to explain to her in the entrance hall, where there would be fewer people, that such discussions could not be permitted outside official premises. The wife of an enemy of the people seemed in fact to have forgotten her inexpiable guilt! She looked into the lieutenant colonel's eyes with a dry, hot, pleading look, a look inaccessible to reason. Klimentiev was astounded by that look. What force made her cling so obstinately and hopelessly to a man whom she didn't see for years at a time and who could only ruin her whole life?

"It is very, very important to me," she assured him, wide-eyed, trying to detect any sign of wavering in Klimentiev's face.

He remembered a piece of paper lying in the safe at the special prison. That piece of paper, developing the "Order on the Reinforcement of the Rear," aimed a fresh blow at relatives who declined to give addresses. Major Myshin intended to read this document to the prisoners on Monday. If this woman didn't see her husband tomorrow and didn't give her address, she might never see him again. Telling her here wouldn't amount to a formal notification; it wouldn't be on record. It might look as if she had turned up at Lefortovo just on the off chance.

The train was slowing down.

All these thoughts passed quickly through Lieutenant Colonel Klimentiev's head. He knew that the prisoner's worst enemy is the prisoner himself. And that every woman's worst enemy is the woman herself. People cannot keep quiet, even to save their skins. More than once in the course of his career, he had been foolishly soft, permitted something forbidden, and nobody would ever have known, except that the very people who had benefited from his indulgence had thought fit to tell the world about it.

He must not be weak, not this time!

All the same, as the train noise subsided and the colored marble of the station flashed into view, Klimentiev said to the woman:

"You have been granted permission to visit. Come at ten a.m. tomorrow." He did not say "to Lefortovo Prison" because passengers making for the door were too near.

"Do you know the Lefortovo wall?"

She nodded, overjoyed. "Yes, I do."

And suddenly her eyes, dry a moment ago, were full of tears.

Anxious to escape those tears, expressions of gratitude, and any other superfluous talk, Klimentiev stepped out onto the platform to await the next train.

He was surprised at himself and vexed. He need not have said it.

THE LIEUTENANT COLONEL kept Nerzhin waiting in the corridor of prison headquarters because he was an insubordinate prisoner, always the barrack-room lawyer.

After standing there so long, Nerzhin had indeed not only given up hope of a visit but, accustomed as he was to all sorts of misfortunes, had begun to expect some new horror. He was all the more surprised to learn that he would be going to meet his wife in an hour's time. The exalted code of conduct that he constantly inculcated in other prisoners forbade any sign of joy or even satisfaction. He should have casually inquired exactly when he should be ready and then left the room. He considered such behavior essential to prevent the authorities learning too much about the prisoner's mentality and gauging the effect on him of their actions. But this was such a sudden reversal of fortune and his joy was so great that Nerzhin could not help beaming and heartily thanking the lieutenant colonel.

He, by contrast, did not move a muscle. He went immediately to brief the guards who would be keeping the prisoners and their visitors company. The briefing included a reminder of the importance and top-secret status of their establishment, an explanation that the political offenders going to see relatives that day were inveterate criminals, and that, when allowed visits, they were solely and obstinately intent on passing the state secrets to which they had access directly to the United States of America, through the intermediacy of their wives. (The guards themselves had not even a rough idea of what was being developed within the walls of the laboratories, and it was easy to plant in them a holy dread that a single scrap of paper passed to an outsider might bring the whole country down in ruins.) Then followed an enumeration of the main possible places of concealment in clothing and shoes and the techniques of discovering them, though clothing (respectable, special clothing) was issued one hour before the visiting time. By means of question and answer, the lieutenant colonel made quite sure that the instructions on body searches had been firmly grasped. And in conclusion they studied, with examples, the turns that conversation between prisoner and visitor might take, practicing listening in and interrupting all subjects except personal and family matters.

Lieutenant Colonel Klimentiev knew the regulations and was a lover of order.

# 30

# A Puzzled Robot

NERZHIN ALMOST BOWLED Junior Lieutenant Nadelashin over in the dimly lit staff hallway as he rushed back to his quarters. The scrap of terry toweling was still tucked loosely around his neck and into his jacket.

Just five minutes earlier, when he was standing in the hallway waiting to be called in, the thirty years of his life had seemed to him one long, senseless, depressing chain of misfortunes from which he lacked the strength to struggle free. And the greatest of these misfortunes had been his departure for the army so soon after his marriage, then his arrest and his long separation from his wife. Their love, he saw clearly, was doomed to be trampled in the mud.

But now he had been told that he would be seeing her around noon today, and suddenly his life was like a taut bowstring—a life that made perfect sense, in the round and in detail; a life in which his war service, his arrest, and all those years apart from his wife were simply the most unlooked-for episodes in his progress toward his goal. Outwardly he might seem unhappy, but Gleb was secretly happy in his unhappiness. He drank from it as from a fresh spring. In this place he had gained an understanding of people and of events not to be had elsewhere, least of all in the sheltered comfort of a quiet family home. From his early years what Gleb had most feared was getting bogged down in a life of humdrum routine. As the proverb says, "It's not the sea that drowns you, it's the puddle."

But he would go back to his wife! They were soul mates! The ties that bound them were unbreakable! A visit! She was coming to see him! On his birthday!

And after yesterday's talk with Anton! It was the last visit he would ever be allowed in this place, but it could never have meant more to him.

Thoughts flashed through his mind like fiery arrows: Don't forget to say this! Remember to say that! Oh, yes, and that!

He rushed into the semicircular room, where prisoners were scurrying around, making a lot of noise. Some had just come back from breakfast, others were only just on their way to wash, and Valentulya had thrown back his blanket and was sitting up in his underclothes, laughing and gesticulating as he told them about his conversation with the bossy night owl who had turned out to be the minister. Valentulya was worth listening to! But this was, for Gleb, one of those amazing moments in life when the singing inside you threatens to burst your rib cage, and a century is not long enough to do everything you want to do! Still, he couldn't miss breakfast either; breakfast is a blessing that a prisoner is not always destined to enjoy. Anyway Valentulya's story was nearing its inglorious end; the whole room condemned him as a cheap little pipsqueak for his failure to tell Abakumov about the things prisoners so desperately needed. Now he was struggling and squealing while five volunteer torturers dragged his underpants off and, egged on by the whoops, howls, and guffaws of the rest, chased him round the room, warming his hide with their belts and splashing him with spoonfuls of hot tea.

Along the radial passageway to the central window, Andrei Andreevich Potapov was sitting on the bunk under Nerzhin's and facing the one Valentulya had vacated, drinking his tea, watching the fun, laughing until he cried, and dabbing at the tears under his glasses. No sooner was reveille sounded than Potapov's bedding was arranged in an uncompromisingly exact right-angled parallelepiped. The bread he was eating with his tea was very thinly buttered; he never bought extras in the prison shop but sent all the money he earned to his "old woman." (He was paid a lot by the sharashka's standards—150 rubles a month, a third as much as a free cleaning woman, because he was an irreplaceable expert and in good standing with the bosses.)

Nerzhin removed his jacket as he went, tossed it onto his still-unmade bed, said good morning to Potapov, without waiting for his answer, and rushed off to breakfast.

Potapov was that very engineer who had confessed under interrogation, attested in a signed deposition, and confirmed in court that he had sold to the Germans, and sold at a bargain price, the firstborn offspring of the Stalin Five-Year Plans, the Dnieper Hydroelectric Station, though only after it had been blown up. For this unimaginable, this incomparably heinous crime, Potapov's punishment, thanks to the clemency of a humane tribunal, was a mere ten years of imprisonment followed by deprivation of rights for five years—"ten and five on the horns," in prison slang. Nobody who knew Potapov when he was young, and certainly not he himself, could have dreamed that, nearing forty, he would be jailed for a political offense. Potapov's friends called him, with some justice, a robot. Life for Potapov meant only work; even three-day public holidays bored him, and he had gone on leave only once in his life, when he got married. In other years there was nobody around to stand in for him, and he had willingly given up his vacation. If there was a shortage of bread, vegetables, or sugar, he took little notice of such irrelevancies; he just tightened his belt and cheerfully continued work on the only thing that interested him, high-voltage transmission. Except when they told jokes, Potapov was only dimly aware of people who were not concerned with high-voltage transmission. Those who created nothing with their hands but merely sounded off at meetings or wrote for newspapers he did not regard as people at all. He had been in charge of all electrometric procedures at the Dnieper Hydroelectric Station and had sacrificed his wife's life as well as his own on the insatiable bonfire of the Five-Year Plans.

By 1941 they were building another power station, and Potapov was exempt from military service. But when he heard that the Dnieper Station had been blown up, he said to his wife, "I will have to go, Katya."

And her reply was, "Yes, Andrei, you must."

And off he went, wearing pebble glasses, an ill-fitting tunic, and, although he had one tab on his shoulder, an empty holster. (There was still a shortage of weapons for officers in the second year of the war for which we were so well prepared.) At Kastornaya, in the July heat and the smoke from burning rye, he was taken prisoner. He escaped but was recaptured before he could reach his own lines. He escaped again, but parachutists dropped around him on the open plain, and he was a prisoner for the third time.

He went through the cannibal camps of Novograd-Volyn and Czestochowa, where prisoners ate bark from the trees, grass, and dead comrades. The Germans suddenly transferred him from one such camp to Berlin, where someone who spoke excellent Russian ("a polite man but scum") asked whether he could possibly be Potapov, the Dnieproges engineer. By way of proof, could he draw a diagram, say, of the switch mechanism for the generator?

The diagram in question had already been published, and Potapov had no hesitation in drawing it. He told the story himself under interrogation, though he need not have done so.

This was what was described in his case history as "betraying the secret of the Dnieper Hydroelectric Station."

What followed, however, was not included in his dossier: The unknown Russian who had thus verified Potapov's identity invited him to sign a voluntary declaration of his willingness to restore Dnieproges, whereupon he would be released immediately and given ration cards, money, and any job he liked.

When this tempting offer was laid before him, the painful workings of the robot's mind showed in his heavily wrinkled face. Then, without striking his chest or shouting proud words, staking no claim to the posthumous title of Hero of the Soviet Union, Potapov humbly answered in his southern brogue:

"You must know that I've signed one oath of loyalty. If I sign this other now, it'll be a bit of a contradiction, won't it?"

In this mild and untheatrical fashion did Potapov express a preference for death rather than the good life.

"Well, I respect your convictions," the unknown Russian answered, and sent him back to the cannibalistic camp.

The Soviet court did not include this in the charges against him and so gave him only ten years.

Engineer Markushev, on the other hand, did sign such an undertaking and did go to work for the Germans, and the court sentenced him to ten years also.

There you see Stalin's hand! That purblind equation of friend and foe which made him unique in human history!

Nor did the court try Potapov for his behavior in 1945 when, mounted on a tank, wearing the same old cracked and wired-up spectacles, machine gun in hand, he burst into Berlin with the Soviet assault force.

So Potapov got off lightly, with a mere "ten and five."

NERZHIN GOT BACK FROM BREAKFAST, kicked off his shoes, and climbed on to his bunk, rocking both himself and Potapov. He now had to perform his daily acrobatic exercise: make his bed, leaving not a single wrinkle, while standing on it. But as soon as he tossed his pillow aside, he discovered a cigarette case made of dark red translucent plastic that contained a dozen "White Sea Canal" cigarettes tightly packed in a single layer and had a plain paper band around it, on which was written in a draftsman's neat hand:

*Ten years he spent thus, killing time:*
*His life suspended in his prime.*

There could be no mistake about it. In the whole sharashka no one but Potapov was capable at once of such craftsmanship and of quoting lines from *Yevgeny Onegin* remembered from his schooldays.

Gleb lowered his head over the side of his bunk and called to him. Potapov had finished his tea and unfolded his newspaper. He was reading it sitting up, so as not to make his bed untidy.

"What now?" he muttered.

"This is your work, isn't it?"

"I couldn't say. Did you find it somewhere?" He was trying not to smile.

"Andreich!" said Nerzhin reproachfully.

A smile of good-natured artfulness made Potapov's wrinkles deeper. Straightening his glasses, he answered.

"I was sharing a cell in the Lubyanka with Count Esterhazy once, carrying the night bucket out on even dates, you know how it goes, while he did it on odd ones, and teaching him Russian from the "Prison Rules" on the wall, and I gave him three buttons made out of bread as a birthday present—all his buttons had been cut off—and he swore that not one of the Hapsburgs had ever given him a more welcome present."

In the "Classification of Voices" Potapov's was described as "toneless and crackly."

Still hanging head down, Nerzhin gazed affectionately at Potapov's rugged face. With his glasses he looked no older than his forty years and still quite vigorous. But when he took them off, the dark hollows under his eyes were those of a death's-head.

"But you embarrass me, Andreich. I can't give you anything like this. I haven't got hands like yours. . . . How did you manage to remember my birthday?"

"Are there any other notable dates in our lives here?"

They sighed.

"Want some tea?" Potapov asked. "It's my special brew."

"No, Andreich, I haven't got time for tea. I'm getting a visit today."

"Great! Your old woman?"

"Uh-huh."

"Hey, you, Valentulya, stop generating smoke right by my ear."

"What right does one person have to bully other people?"

"What's in the paper, Andreich?" Nerzhin asked.

Potapov looked up at Nerzhin's suspended face with a crafty Ukrainian squint.

*Tall tales from the Britannic muse*
*The budding maiden's dreams confuse.*

"They have the bare-faced impudence to maintain that. . . ."

Nerzhin and Potapov had met in the second year after the war, nearly four years ago. In a restless, rackety, overcrowded Butyrki cell, half dark even in mid-July. There, and at that time, the most wildly different careers, the unlikeliest paths crossed. The latest influx was from Europe. Through the cell passed novices still cherishing faint memories of European freedom; sturdy Russian prisoners of war, exchanging a German *stalag* for their fatherland's Gulag; hammer-hardened and hot-forged veterans of the camps, in transit from the cave dwellings of the Gulag to the oases of the sharashkas. When he got into the cell, Nerzhin slid flat on his belly under the bedboards (they were close to the ground), and down there on the asphalt floor, before he could make anything out in the dark, cheerfully asked: "Who's last in the line, friends?"

A cracked, unmusical voice replied: "Cuckoo! You're after me."

After that they moved along, under the bedboards, from day to day, as men were pulled out for posting, "away from the pail and toward the window"; and in the third week they began the return journey back "from the window toward the pail," but by now on top of the bedboards. Later on they shuffled toward the window across the wooden boards once more. That was how Nerzhin and Potapov became firm friends, in spite of differences in age, background, and tastes.

There it was that Potapov, in the weary months of brooding after his trial, confessed to Nerzhin that he never had taken any interest in politics, and never would have, if politics hadn't laid about him and kicked his ribs in.

There, under the bedboards in the Butyrki Prison, the robot for the first time in his life began to wonder—which, as everybody knows, is bad for robots. No, he still did not regret refusing German rations; he did not regret the three lost years awaiting death from starvation in captivity. And as before he thought there should be no question of submitting our internal disorders to the judgment of foreigners.

But the spark of doubt had fallen into his mind and smoldered.

For the very first time the perplexed robot had asked himself, "What the hell was the Dnieper Power Station built for, anyway?"

# 31

# How to Darn Socks

THE ORDERLY OFFICERS made the rounds of the special prison at 8:55. This operation took hours in the camps, with the prisoners standing out in the cold, harried from place to place, counted and recounted—singly, in fives, in hundreds, by brigade—but here in the sharashka it went quickly and painlessly: The prisoners would be drinking tea at their lockers; two orderly officers, the one going off duty and his relief, would come in; prisoners would stand up (some of them!) while the relieving officer scrupulously counted heads, made announcements, and gave complaints a perfunctory hearing.

The officer coming on duty, Senior Lieutenant Shusterman, was tall, dark haired; and though not exactly grim, he took care, as all guards of the Lubyanka School are supposed to, not to show any human feeling at all. He had been sent, together with Nadelashin, from the Lubyanka to Marfino in order to stiffen prison discipline. Some of the prisoners in the sharashka remembered them both from the Lubyanka; as senior sergeants they had both served at one time as escorting officers. They would take charge of the newly arrived prisoner, who would be standing, facing the wall, and march him up the famous "worn steps" to the mezzanine between the fourth and fifth floors, where an opening had been knocked in the wall between the prison and the interrogation block. For a third of a century all those held in the central prison had been taken that way: monarchists, anarchists, Octobrists, Kadets, S-Rs, Mensheviks, Bolsheviks, Savinkov, Kutepov, the Exarch Pyotr, Shulgin, Bukharin, Rykov, Tukhachevsky, Professor Pletnyov, Academician Vavilov, Field Marshal Paulus, General Krasnov, scientists of world fame, and newly hatched poets—first the criminals themselves, then their wives and daughters. They were marched up to a uniformed woman with a Red Star on her chest, and every prisoner, as he passed, signed his name in her Book of Fates, writing in the one-line gap cut in a tin sheet so that he would not see the names before and after his own. They were then taken up some stairs where nets had been rigged in the stairwell like safety nets at the circus, in case a prisoner jumped. They were led through the long, long corridors of the ministry on Lubyanka Square, made stuffy by electricity and chilled by the gold of colonels' shoulder boards.

Though the prisoners under interrogation were in the depths of their initial despair, they quickly started noticing the difference: Shusterman (they didn't know his name then, of course) eyed the prisoner morosely from under his bushy brows, sank his fingers like talons into the man's arms, and brutally dragged the panting wretch upstairs. Moonfaced Nadelashin, who looked a little eunuchlike, always walked at a slight distance from the prisoner, never touched him, and told him politely which way to turn.

Shusterman, however, although the younger, now had three stars on his shoulder boards.

Nadelashin announced that those who were going to see visitors should report to the headquarters building at 10:00 a.m. Asked if there would be a film that day, he replied that there would not. A slight murmur of discontent was heard, but Khorobrov's comment from his corner was:

"No film at all is better than crap like *Cossacks of the Kuban*."

Shusterman turned around sharply to try to catch the speaker and as a result lost count and had to start again.

In the silence that followed, somebody invisible but quite audible said: "Now you've done it; they'll put that on your file."

Khorobrov's upper lip twitched as he answered, "Let them, damn and blast them. They've got so much on me there's no room left in my file."

Dvoetyosov, still unkempt and in his underwear, dangled his long hairy legs over the side of his top bunk and called out in an uncouth yell:

"Junior Lieutenant! What about the party? Will there be a party or not?"

"There will," Junior answered, obviously pleased to be giving good news. "We'll put the tree up here in the semicircular room."

"Can we make some toys, then?" Ruska shouted cheerfully from another top bunk. He was perched up there cross-legged, tying his tie with the aid of a mirror propped up against his pillow. He would be meeting Klara in five minutes. He had seen her already through the window, crossing the yard from the guardroom.

"We will have to ask about that. I haven't had any instructions."

"What do you need instructions for?"

"What's a New Year's tree without toys?"

"Friends! Let's make toys!"

"Steady there, boy! What about hot water?"

"Will the minister supply it?"

The room buzzed merrily, discussing the party. The orderly officers had already turned to leave, but Khorobrov's harsh Vyatka accent rose above the hubbub and called after them: "And you can tell them to leave us the tree until the Orthodox Christmas! It's a Christmas tree, not a New Year's tree!"

The officers pretended not to hear and left.

Everybody was talking at once. Before he had finished with the officers, Khorobrov was busily explaining himself in dumb show to someone invisible. He never used to observe Christmas or Easter but had started doing so in prison in a spirit of contradiction. At least those days were not marked by stricter searches and stricter discipline than usual. For the anniversaries of the Revolution and May Day, he usually found himself some washing or sewing to do.

Abramson, his neighbor, finished his tea, wiped his lips, polished a misted pair of glasses, square lenses in a plastic frame, and said:

"Ilya Terentich! You're forgetting the second commandment for prisoners: Thou shalt not stick thy neck out!"

Khorobrov woke up from his debate with the unseen partner and spun around as though he had been stung.

"That's the Old Testament; it belongs to your rotten generation. You were meek and mild, so they polished the lot of you off."

The taunt could not have been more unfair. It was men imprisoned at the same time as Abramson who had organized a strike, and a hunger strike, at Vorkuta. But it had made no difference in the end. The precept caught on because it made sense.

Abramson merely shrugged. "If you act up, they'll pack you off to a hard-labor camp."

"That's what I want, Grigory Borisych! I don't mind going to a blasted hard labor camp; at least I'll have good company. Maybe you can speak freely there, without stoolies all around you."

Rubin, with his beard disheveled and his tea unfinished, was standing by the bunk bed that held Potapov and Nerzhin and making a friendly speech to its upper story:

"Congratulations, my young Montaigne, my infant Pyrrhonist."

"I'm very touched, my dear Lev, but why. . . ?"

Nerzhin was kneeling on his top bunk holding a writing case. It was a prisoner's spare-time handiwork, which meant that it was the most carefully executed work in the world, since prisoners have nowhere to hurry to. Neatly tucked inside a deep-red calico cover were pockets, fastenings, press studs, and packets of excellent paper looted from Germany. All this, of course, had been made on the state's time and with the state's materials.

"Anyway, we aren't allowed to write anything much in this sharashka except denunciations."

"My birthday wish for you"—Rubin's large, thick lips shaped themselves into a comic trumpet—"is that the light of truth may illuminate your skeptical and eclectic brain."

"You and your truth! Who knows what truth is?" Gleb sighed. His face, which had looked youthful while he was busy preparing for his wife's visit, had become haggard and ashen. And his hair was all over the place again.

On the neighboring top bunk, above Pryanchikov, a plump, bald-headed, middle-aged engineer was using the last few seconds of free time to read the newspaper borrowed from Potapov. He held it wide open, at some distance from his eyes, occasionally frowning and moving his lips as he read. When the electric bell shrilled in the hallway, he looked annoyed and folded the newspaper untidily.

"What's all this damned nonsense about world domination? They keep blathering on about it all the time."

He looked round for a suitable place to fling the newspaper.

At the far end of the room, the enormous Dvoetyosov had struggled into his overalls and was standing with his enormous behind sticking out, smoothing and straightening his bed into shape on the top bunk.

"Who keeps on about it, Zemelya?" he called out in his bass voice.

"They all do."

"What about you? Are you out to dominate the world?"

"What, me?"

Zemelya sounded surprised, as though he took the question seriously. "No-o-o." He smiled broadly. "Why the hell would I want to? I have no such ambition." He climbed down, grunting.

"In that case, let's go and work ourselves sick!" Dvoetyosov said, launching his bulk from the bed and landing with a resounding thud. He was going to his Sunday work uncombed, unwashed, and unbuttoned.

The bell rang lengthily. It was ringing to announce that inspection was over and that the "royal gates" were open. Prisoners were already thronging through them onto the stairway of the institute.

Doronin was first out. Sologdin, who kept the window closed while he was getting up and having his tea, now wedged it open with the Ehrenburg volume and hurried into the hallway to catch Professor Chelnov as he emerged from the "professor's cell." Rubin, as usual, had managed to get nothing done in the early morning. He hurriedly put what he had not eaten and drunk into his locker, upsetting something inside it, and flapped around his lumpy, rumpled, impossible bed vainly trying to straighten it enough not to be brought back to make it again.

Nerzhin, meanwhile, was trying on his "fancy dress." At one time, long, long ago, prisoners in a sharashka wore smart suits and overcoats every day and went to meet their visitors in the same clothes. Now they had been made to wear blue overalls, so that the tower sentries could distinguish them from free workers. But the prison authorities made them change when they had visitors, handing out used shirts and suits confiscated, perhaps, from private wardrobes when an inventory was made upon arrest. Some prisoners liked seeing themselves well dressed, if only for a few brief hours; others would gladly have avoided this dressing up in dead men's clothes, but the authorities flatly refused to take them in overalls: Relatives must not get a bad impression of prison life. And no one was stiff-necked enough to forfeit a relative's visit. So dress up they did.

The semicircular room had emptied. Left behind were twelve pairs of beds welded into twelve double-decker bunks and made up hospital fashion, with the sheets turned back over the blankets to catch the dust and get dirty first. This system could only have been thought up by a bureaucratic and, surely, masculine brain; even the inventor's wife would not use it in her own home. However, this was what the Prison Health inspectorate demanded.

A pleasant silence, rare in this place, had settled on the room, and no one felt like breaking it.

There were four of them left behind. Nerzhin, costuming himself, Khorobrov, Abramson, and a balding designer.

The designer was one of those timid zeks who spend years inside without beginning to acquire the cool cheek a prisoner needs. He would never have dared to stay away from work even on Sunday, but, feeling poorly, he had armed himself in advance with permission from the prison doctor to take what in any case should be his day off. Now he had laid out on his bed a number of socks with holes, some darning wool, and a cardboard mushroom of his own making, and was wondering, with knitted brows, where to begin.

Grigory Borisovich Abramson, who had duly completed one ten-year sentence (not counting six years of banishment beforehand) and was now serving a second, couldn't always avoid turning out on Sundays, but he did his best. At one time, in his Komsomol days, wild horses couldn't have kept him away from voluntary work on Sundays. But Sunday shifts were thought of then as a headlong rush to get the economy right; in a year or two, everything would be going splendidly, and thereafter all gardens would bloom as one. But as the decades went by, voluntary work on Sundays ceased to be exciting and became mere drudgery. The trees that were planted refused to blossom and indeed were mostly pushed over and mangled by tractors. Long years of imprisonment and reflection had changed Abramson's mind; he had come to believe that man was by nature averse to work and would not do it unless poverty or a big stick compelled him to. So despite the fact that—all things considered, and keeping in mind the still-valid and only possible goal of mankind (Communism)—all these endeavors, including even Sunday shifts, were undoubtedly necessary, Abramson no longer felt strong enough to take part in them. He was one of the few men in the place who had served, and more than served, ten full, ten terrible years, and he knew that it was not a myth, not wild twaddle on the part of the court, not a bad joke till the first general amnesty (as new boys always believed); ten years meant ten, if not twelve or fifteen, exhausting years out of a man's life. He had learned long ago to economize on muscular movement, to cherish every minute of relaxation. And he knew that the best way to spend Sunday was to lie still in bed, stripped to your underwear.

So now he pulled out the book with which Sologdin had wedged the window open, shut the window, unhurriedly removed his overalls, lay down under the blanket, wrapped it around himself, cleaned his glasses with a scrap of chamois leather kept for the purpose, put a piece of hard candy in his mouth, straightened his pillow, and got out from under his mattress a rather fat book, wrapped in paper as a precaution. Just to look at him would make you feel comfortable.

Khorobrov, on the other hand, was in torment. He was lying fully dressed on top of his made bed, his feet, in shoes, resting on the bedrail, miserable in his idleness. He felt keenly, and took a long time to get over, things that others treated lightly. In accordance with the well-known voluntary principle, all prisoners were listed every Saturday, without necessarily being asked, as volunteers for Sunday work, and the prison was duly notified. If registration had indeed been voluntary, Khorobrov would have put his name down every time and gladly spent his days off at his workbench. But because registration was a blatant farce, he felt bound to stay in bed and vegetate in the locked prison.

Prisoners in camps can only dream of a Sunday spent lying down in a warm, closed room. But in a sharashka the prisoner's ache is not in his back.

There was absolutely nothing to do! Such newspapers as there were he had read the day before. Books from the special prison's library lay in a heap, open or shut, on the stool by his bed. One was a collection of articles by eminent writers. Khorobrov, after some hesitation, opened it at an article by the Tolstoy who, if he had had any conscience, would not have dared to publish under that name. The article, written in June 1941, said that "German soldiers, driven by terror and madness, have run up against a wall of iron and fire at the frontier." Khorobrov slammed the book shut with a whispered obscenity and put it aside. Whenever he looked into a book, he chanced on some sore point because his world was made up of nothing but sore points. These rulers of men's minds in their lavishly appointed out-of-town houses heard nothing except the radio and saw nothing but their flowerbeds. A semiliterate peasant knew more about life than they did.

The other books in the heap were "artistic literature," but reading them sickened Khorobrov just as much. One was a bestseller called *Far from Moscow*, which everybody outside was avidly reading. Khorobrov had read a bit of it the day before and tried again now, but it made him feel queasy. It was a pie without filling, a hollow egg, a stuffed bird. It was about the use of convict labor on building sites. But the camps were not given their proper names; the builders were not called zeks; nothing was said about short rations or punishment cells. The zeks became Komsomols, well dressed, well shod, and bursting with enthusiasm. An experienced reader sensed immediately that the author knew, had seen, had touched the truth, that he might well have been an operations officer in a camp himself, but that he was a barefaced liar.

His one and only oath turned up on schedule, with its three words differently arranged, and Khorobrov tossed the bestseller aside.

Another of the books was the *Selected Works* of the famous Galakhov. Vaguely remembering him and expecting something better, Khorobrov had started reading this volume but had given up, feeling that it was the same sort of insult as the list of Sunday "volunteers." Galakhov had written passable love stories but had long ago slipped into the approved manner, writing as though his readers were not normal people but imbeciles who could be kept happy with meretricious trash. Anything deeply troubling was missing from these books. Except for the war, their authors would have been left with nothing to write except hymns of praise. The war had given them access to feelings that all could understand. But even so they concocted unreal personal problems, like that of the Komsomol who derails munitions trains by the dozen behind enemy lines but agonizes day and night because he is not paying his dues and so may not be a genuine Komsomol.

Khorobrov rang the changes on his favorite oath again and felt a little better.

Another of the books on the locker was *American Short Stories* by progressive writers. Khorobrov could not check these stories against real life, but the selection surprised him; every story inevitably contained something very nasty about America. This poisonous collection, taken together, gave such a nightmarish picture of their country that you could only wonder why the Americans hadn't all fled or hanged themselves long ago.

No, there was nothing to read!

Khorobrov decided to have a smoke. He took out a cigarette and rolled it between his fingers. In the dead silence he could hear the tight-packed paper. He wanted to smoke without leaving the room, right there, with his feet up on the bedrail. Prisoners who smoke know that the cigarette you really enjoy is the one you smoke lying down, on your own strip of bedboard or your own bunk—a leisurely smoke, with your eyes fixed on the ceiling and the pictures from the irrecoverable past and the unattainable future that float across it.

But the bald-headed designer was a nonsmoker and didn't like smoke, and Abramson, though a smoker, subscribed to the fallacious theory that the air in the room should be fresh. While in prison Khorobrov had come to believe firmly that respect for the rights of others is the beginning of freedom, so he lowered his feet to the ground with a sigh and made for the door. On the way he saw the thick book in Abramson's hands, decided that it was not from the prison library and must have come from outside—and nobody would ask for rubbish to be brought in.

He was not foolish enough to ask Abramson out loud, "What are you reading?" or "Where did you get that from?" (The designer, or Nerzhin, might overhear the answer.) He went very close to Abramson and spoke quietly.

"Grigory Borisych, can I take a peek at the title page?"

"Go ahead," said Abramson, rather grudgingly.

Khorobrov opened the book and read, *The Count of Monte Cristo.*

He was so staggered he could only give a whistle.

"Borisych," he asked tenderly, "is there anybody after you? Can I have it later?"

Abramson took his glasses off and thought a bit.

"We'll see. Can you give me a haircut today?"

The prisoners didn't like the visiting Stakhanovite barber. Enthusiastic amateur barbers from among their own number would cater to every whim, taking their time because they had plenty of it ahead of them.

"Who can we get a pair of scissors from?"

"I'll get Zyablik's."

"All right, I'll do it."

"Good. The bit up to page 128 comes out. I'll give it to you shortly."

Noting that Abramson was on page 110, Khorobrov went into the hallway for his smoke in a more cheerful frame of mind.

Gleb was fuller all the time of the holiday spirit. Somewhere, probably in the student dormitory at Stromynka, Nadya, too, would be feeling excited in this last hour before their meeting. When you meet, you can't collect your thoughts; you forget all that you meant to say. Better write it down, memorize it, burn the scrap of paper; they wouldn't let me take it in with me. Just remember that there are eight points. Point 1: I may be going away. Point 2: My sentence won't end when it's supposed to; there will be a period of exile to follow. Point 3. . . .

He hurried down to the clothes storeroom and ironed his dickey. The dickey, Ruska Doronin's invention, had been adopted by many others. It was a piece of white material (obtained by tearing a sheet into sixteen pieces, but the orderly in charge of the linen closet did not know that) with a white collar stitched onto it. This bit of cloth was just big enough to fit into the opening at the neck of your overalls and conceal the "MGB Special Prison No. 1" stamp on your undershirt. There were, in addition, two strings, to be tied behind your back. The dickey helped to create the generally desired appearance of well-being. It was simple to wash, it served faithfully on workdays or holidays, and you were not ashamed to be seen in it by the females among the institute's free employees.

Next, Nerzhin stood on the stairs and tried in vain to give his scuffed shoes a shine, using somebody's dried-up and crumbling polish. (The prison did not provide a change of shoes on visiting days; shoes could not be seen under the table.)

When he went back into the room to shave (even straight razors were allowed in this place, so haphazard were the regulations), Khorobrov was already reading avidly. The designer's extensive darning operations had spread from the bed to the floor. Abramson, turning his head slightly away from his book, peered down from his pillow to give instructions.

"Darning is only effective when it is carried out conscientiously. God forbid that you should adopt a formal attitude to it. Don't hurry; keep your stitches close together; go over every place cross-darning twice. Another common error is using the broken stitches around the edges of a ragged hole. Don't try to do it on the cheap; don't worry about a few odd snippets; trim the edges of the hole neatly. Have you ever heard the name Berkalov?"

"Who? Berkalov? No."

"You do surprise me! Berkalov was an old-time artillery officer, the inventor of the BS-3 cannon—you know, that marvelous cannon with the simply crazy muzzle velocity. Well, then, Berkalov was sitting one Sunday, just as you are now, in a sharashka darning his socks. Somebody turned the radio on: 'Berkalov, Lieutenant General—Stalin Prize, First Class.' He'd only been a major general when he was arrested. Well, he finished darning his socks and started making himself some fritters on a hotplate. In came a guard, caught him at it, took the illegal hotplate away from him, and made out a report to the commandant recommending three days in the hole. But at that very moment the commandant himself ran in like an excited schoolboy: 'Berkalov! Get your things together! You're off to the Kremlin! Kalinin is asking for you!' That's the sort of thing that can happen to a man in Russia."

# 32

## On the Path to a Million

Old Professor Chelnov, a mathematician well known in many sharashkas, who used to enter in the "nationality" column not "Russian" but "zek" and who in 1950 was nearing the end of his eighteenth year of imprisonment, had applied the fine point of his pencil to many technical inventions, from the continuously operating boiler to the jet engine, and had invested a bit of his soul in some of them.

Incidentally, Professor Chelnov maintained that the expression "invest one's soul" should be used with care, since only zeks certainly had immortal souls, which were denied to "frees" because of their worldliness. In friendly conversation with other zeks over a bowl of ice-cold congealing porridge or a steaming glass of cocoa, Chelnov did not disguise the fact that he had borrowed this thought from Pierre Bezukhov. When the French soldier would not let Pierre cross the road, he, as everybody knows, burst out laughing. "Ha ha! The soldier wouldn't let me cross! Me? He wouldn't let my immortal soul cross!"

Professor Chelnov was the only prisoner at Marfino excused from wearing overalls. (Abakumov himself had been asked to authorize it.) The weightiest argument for this concession was that Chelnov was not a permanent Marfino zek but an itinerant zek; once a corresponding member of the Academy of Sciences and director of a mathematical institute, he took his orders from Beria in person and could be dispatched to any sharashka confronted by a particularly urgent mathematical problem. Having solved it in outline and showed his hosts how to complete the calculation, he would be transferred elsewhere.

Chelnov did not, as any normally vain person would, make the most of his freedom to dress as he pleased. He wore an inexpensive suit, and the jacket and trousers were not even identical in color. He always wore felt boots. Over the few gray hairs left to him he tugged a nondescript woolen cap, knitted perhaps for a skier or a little girl. But his most distinctive article of dress was a weird woolen traveling shawl, pinned in two thicknesses around his shoulders and his back and somewhat resembling a woman's warm shawl.

Chelnov, however, could wear that cap and that shawl in a way that made him not a ridiculous but a majestic figure. His long, oval face, his sharp profile, his authoritative way of speaking to the administration, and that faint blue haze in his faded eyes, which is peculiar to those capable of abstract thought, made Chelnov strangely like Descartes or perhaps Archimedes.

Chelnov had been sent to Marfino to work out the mathematical principles of a fully reliable Scrambler: an apparatus that by its automatic rotation would switch banks of relays on and off, and so confuse and distort normal speech that hundreds of people equipped with analogous mechanisms would not be able to decipher the conversation traveling along the wires. Research into the design problems of a mechanism of this sort was in progress in the design office. Two other designers, besides Sologdin, were working on it.

The moment he arrived in the sharashka from a camp on the Inta, Sologdin took a look around and promptly told them all that his memory was impaired by long starvation and his faculties, congenitally limited in any case, blunted, so that he was in no condition to do anything but subsidiary work. He could afford to take such a bold line because he had not been put on "general duties" in the camp but had been given a comfortable engineering job and was not afraid of being sent back. (For the same reason, when discussing work with his superiors in the sharashka, he could afford to keep them waiting while he thought up substitutes for such foreign words as "engineer" and "metal." This would have been impossible if he had aspired to promotion, or even to better rations.) He was not, however, sent away but kept at Marfino on probation. He had escaped from the mainstream, where tension, rush, and nervous strain prevailed, into a quiet backwater. There, without honor but without fear of censure, he was under very lax supervision, and he had enough free time in the evening, when no guard was watching, to begin working along his own lines on a fully efficient Scrambler.

He believed that great ideas dawned only in isolated minds.

Sure enough, during the last six months he had hit on the solution that completely eluded the ten engineers specially chosen—and incessantly pressured and harassed—to look for it. (He kept his ears open and heard how they were looking at the problem and where they had gone wrong.) Two days earlier Sologdin had given his work to Professor Chelnov for an opinion, also unofficially. Now he was climbing the stairs side by side with the professor, respectfully supporting him by the elbow and awaiting his verdict.

Chelnov, however, never let work and leisure interfere with each other.

During their brief journey along hallways and up stairways, he did not give away by so much as a word the appraisal that Sologdin so eagerly awaited. Instead he talked in a carefree way about his morning walk with Lev Rubin. When Rubin had been turned away from "the wood," he had recited to Chelnov a poem of his on a biblical subject. There were only a couple of metrical faults, there were original rhymes, such as "Osiris" and "oh see this," and on the whole he was bound to say that the poem wasn't bad. In ballad form it told the story of Moses leading the Jews for forty years through the wilderness, suffering hunger and thirst and other privations, until the people became delirious and rebelled—but they were not in the right; Moses was right, because he knew that in the end they would reach the promised land. Rubin was particularly anxious to impress on his listener that "it hasn't been forty years for us yet."

So what had Chelnov said to that?

He had directed Rubin's attention to the geography of Moses' transit. To get from the Nile to Jerusalem, the Jews had no need at all to walk more than four hundred kilometers, so that even resting on the Sabbath, they could easily have gotten there in three weeks! Must we not therefore suppose that for the remainder of the forty years Moses was leading them not *through* the Arabian desert but *around and around* in the Arabian desert, until all those who remembered their well-fed Egyptian servitude would have died off and the survivors would appreciate so much more the modest paradise that Moses would be able to offer them?

Professor Chelnov took the key to his room from the orderly at the door to Yakonov's office. No other prisoner, except the Iron Mask, was trusted that far. No zek had the right to remain in his working quarters for a single second unsupervised by a free employee, since an elementary concern for security suggested that a prisoner would inevitably take advantage of a single second free from surveillance to break open the safe with the aid of a pencil and photograph secret documents with the aid of a trouser button.

Chelnov, however, worked in a room where there was nothing but an unlocked cupboard and two bare desks. So they had decided (after consulting the ministry, of course) to sanction the issue of a key to Professor Chelnov personally. Ever since, his room had been the cause of perpetual anxiety to the institute's security officer, Major Shikin. During the hours when prisoners were locked in the prison behind a double steel-reinforced door, this highly paid comrade with the irregular working hours would come to the professor's room on his very own feet to sound the walls, jump up and down on the floorboards, peer into the dusty gap behind the cupboard, and shake his head somberly.

And just getting his own key wasn't the end of it. Four or five doors along the hallway on the third floor the Top-Secret Department had its sentry post. This consisted of a small table with a chair beside it and on the chair a cleaning woman, not just a woman to sweep the floor and make tea, but rather a special-purpose cleaning woman to check the passes of people on their way to the Top-Secret Department. These passes, printed in the ministry's main printshop, were of three kinds: permanent, weekly, and valid for one occasion, all designed by Major Shikin (whose idea it had been to make the dead end of the hallway top secret).

The work of the checkpoint was not easy; people didn't go by very often, but knitting socks was categorically forbidden, both by the regulations hanging there on the wall and by repeated oral instructions from Comrade Major Shikin. The cleaning women (there were two of them, each working a twelve-hour shift), spent their duty hours in an excruciating struggle against sleep. Colonel Yakonov himself also found this checkpoint a nuisance because people kept interrupting him all day long to sign their passes.

All the same, the checkpoint remained. To cover the wages of the two cleaning women, they kept not three yardmen, provided for in their budget, but one, the aforementioned Spiridon.

Although Chelnov knew that the woman now sitting at the checkpoint was called Maria Ivanovna, and although she let this gray-headed old man through several times a day, she started and said: "Your pass."

Chelnov showed his cardboard pass, and Sologdin produced a paper one.

They passed the checkpoint and a couple of doors—the first a glass door, nailed up and smeared with whitewash, which led to the back stairs and the serf-artist's studio, then the door of the Iron Mask's private room—and unlocked Chelnov's door.

It was a cozy little room with a single window giving a view of the prisoners' exercise yard and the clump of secular elms that fate had ruthlessly annexed to the zone guarded by machine-gun fire. The towering treetops were still lavishly frosted.

A dirty white sky hung over the earth.

To the left of the limes, outside the camp area, a house could be seen, gray with age but now also frost whitened, an old two-story house with a boat-shaped roof. It had been the home of the bishop who had once lived near the seminary, which was why the road leading to this place was called Bishop's Road. Farther on, the village roofs of little Marfino peeped out. Beyond that there was open field, and farther away still on the railway line, bright silvery steam from the Leningrad-Moscow train could be seen rising through the murk.

But Sologdin did not even glance through the window. Ignoring an invitation to sit down, feeling his legs firm and youthful beneath him, he leaned against the window frame and fastened his eyes on the roll of papers lying on Chelnov's desk.

Chelnov asked him to open the ventilation pane, sat down on a hard chair with a high, straight back, straightened the shawl around his shoulders, opened the list of points for discussion that he had written on a page from a scratch pad, picked up a long, sharp-pointed pencil like a lance, looked hard at Sologdin, and suddenly the flippant tone of their recent conversation was no longer possible.

To Sologdin it was as though great wings were beating the air in that little room. Chelnov spoke for no more than two minutes but so concisely that there was no breathing space between his thoughts.

The gist of it was that he had done more than Sologdin had asked. He had produced estimates of the theoretical and mathematical feasibility of Sologdin's design. The design, then, was promising, and close enough to what was required, at least until they could switch to purely electronic equipment. Sologdin must, however, find a way to make the device insensitive to low-energy impulses and determine the effect of the main inertial forces so as to ensure adequate flywheel momentum.

"And one thing more"—Chelnov's bright gaze dwelled briefly on Sologdin—"one thing you mustn't forget. Your encoding process is constructed on the random principle, and that's good. But a random process fixed once and for all becomes a system. To make it absolutely secure, you must improve your process so that the random sequence changes randomly."

Here the professor looked thoughtful, folded his sheet of paper in two, and fell silent. Sologdin lowered his eyelids as though dazzled and stood there unseeing.

With the professor's first words a hot wave of emotion had welled up in him. Now he felt that if he did not press shoulder and ribs firmly against the window frame, he would soar exulting to the ceiling. Perhaps his life was approaching its zenith!

He came from an old gentry family that had long been dwindling like a spent candle and had finally sputtered out in the fiery intensity of the Revolution. Some of his kin were shot; others emigrated; yet others lay low or even assumed false identities. The young Sologdin took a long time to make up his mind about the Revolution. The rebellion of an envious mob whipped up to a frenzy by agitators he hated, but he found something congenial in its ruthless single-mindedness and inexhaustible energy. He worshipped, with Old Russian fervor in his eyes, in decaying Moscow chapels. He also put on a leather jacket, open at the neck, proletarian fashion (everybody was wearing them in those days) and joined a primary Komsomol organization. Who could tell him the right thing to do: whether to look for bloody vengeance on this gang of criminals or work his way up into the Komsomol leadership? He was sincerely devout and also helplessly vain. He was capable of sacrifice but also fond of money. Is there any young heart that does not want the good things of this world? He shared the belief of the godless Democritus: "Happy is the man who has both wealth and intelligence." Intelligence he had been born with; wealth he lacked.

So at the age of eighteen (and in the last year of the NEP!), Sologdin made it his chief and unconditional object to acquire a million—no more and no less, but by hook or by crook he would have his million. It was not wealth for its own sake he was interested in, not just having means at his disposal. This was an examination he must pass to prove that he was no idle dreamer but a man of action who could set himself other practical tasks.

He proposed to reach his goal by way of a dazzling invention. But he was ready to take some other route—it need not have anything to do with engineering—if it was shorter. But no environment could have been more hostile to his ambition than that of Stalin's Five-Year Plans. All he managed to wring out of his engineering qualifications was a bread card and a pathetic wage. And if from one day to the next he had offered the state an amazing cross-country vehicle or a plan for the profitable restructuring of all Soviet industry, it would have brought him neither his million nor glory but quite probably would have invited distrust and harassment.

Doubts about his future were soon dispelled. The meshes of the net became tighter, and a big fish like Sologdin was inevitably caught in one of its periodic trawls. While serving his first sentence in a prison camp, he was given a second.

It was twelve years since he had seen anything of the world outside. He should by now have forgotten his ambition to make a million. But a strange, labyrinthine path had led him once again to the enchanted tower! And his trembling hands were selecting from the bunch a key to open its steel door.

Could it be to him that this Descartes in a girl's cap was saying such flattering things?

Chelnov had folded his list of talking points into four and then into eight.

"As you can see, there's still quite a lot of work to be done. But this design will be the best of all those so far submitted. It will mean your release and the quashing of your conviction. Not to mention a share in a Stalin Prize, if the bosses don't intercept it!"

Chelnov smiled. His smile was as sharp and thin as his features.

The smile was for himself. He, who at various times and in various sharashkas had done far more than Sologdin was about to do, ran no risk of winning a prize, or a clean sheet, or his freedom. He had in fact never been tried and convicted. He had once called the Wise Father a slimy reptile, and for that was now spending his eighteenth year inside without having been sentenced and without hope.

Sologdin opened his sparkling blue eyes, stood youthfully erect, and said rather theatrically: "Vladimir Erastovich! You have given me support and confidence! I have no words to thank you for your kindness. I am deeply indebted to you!"

But an absent-minded smile hovered on Sologdin's lips.

As he was returning Sologdin's roll of papers, the professor remembered something else.

"By the way, I owe you an apology. You asked me not to let Anton Nikolaevich see your drawing. But yesterday it just so happened that he came into the room in my absence, unrolled the drawing on my desk, as he always does, and realized at once what it was all about. I had to reveal your identity."

Sologdin's smile gave way to a frown.

"Does it really matter all that much? Why should it? One day sooner, one day later. . . ."

Sologdin was of two minds himself. Maybe it was time to take the drawing to Anton?

"I don't quite know how to put it, Vladimir Erastovich. . . . Don't you think there's something morally dubious about it? After all, it isn't a bridge or a crane or a machine tool. The order didn't come from industry but from the very people who put us inside. So far I've been doing it just to . . . to test my powers. Just for myself."

Just for himself.

That was something Chelnov understood very well. The best research was generally done that way.

"But in the circumstances isn't that a luxury you can't afford?"

With Chelnov's pale, calm eyes upon him, Sologdin pulled himself together.

"Forgive me. I was just thinking aloud. Please don't reproach yourself. I'm endlessly grateful to you!"

He held Chelnov's limp, fragile hand deferentially for a moment, then left with the roll of paper under his arm.

He had entered that room a little while ago a supplicant but unburdened. He was leaving it victorious but with heavy responsibilities, no longer master of his time, his plans, his labor. Chelnov, meanwhile, did not lean back in his chair but sat and sat, upright, eyes closed, lean featured, and wearing his pointed woolen cap.

# 33

## Penalty Marks

STILL EXULTING, Sologdin flung open the door with excessive force and went into the design office. But instead of the crowd he expected to find in this big room that was always abuzz, he saw a solitary plump female form over by the window.

"Alone, Larisa Nikolaevna?" he asked in surprise, striding across the room.

The copyist Larisa Nikolaevna Yemina, a woman of thirty, looked around from her drawing board by the window and smiled over her shoulder at Sologdin as he approached.

"It's you, Dmitri Aleksandrovich. I was beginning to think I was in for a whole boring day by myself."

Sologdin surveyed the overgenerous figure in the bright green knitted outfit—knitted skirt and knitted top—stepped briskly over to his desk without answering, and, before sitting down, made a mark on a sheet of pink paper lying by itself. After this, standing almost with his back to Yemina, he pinned the drawing he had brought to his adjustable drawing board.

The design office was a light and spacious room on the third floor with big windows facing south and ten such drawing boards—some horizontal, some inclined, some almost vertical—placed among the normal office desks. Sologdin's board, near the far window at which Yemina sat, was set up vertically and swung to an angle at which Sologdin was screened from the head of the office and the entrance, while daylight fell directly on the drawings pinned there.

After some time Sologdin asked curtly: "Where are they all?"

"I was going to ask you that," Yemina trilled.

He shot her a quick glance, moving only his head, and said sarcastically, "All I can tell you is where the four unpersons who work in this room are. Make the most of it. One of them has been taken to see a visitor. Hugo Leonardovich has got his Latvian Christmas party. I'm here, and Ivan Ivanovich has begged off to darn his socks. What I would like to know in return is where our sixteen free, and so much more important, comrades are."

He was standing in profile to Yemina, and she could see the condescending smile between his neat little mustache and his neat goatee.

"You mean you don't know that our major arranged with Anton Nikolaevich last night to give the design office a day off? Just my bad luck to be duty officer."

Sologdin frowned. "A day off? In honor of what?"

"Because it's Sunday, of course."

"Since when has Sunday been a nonworking day around here?"

"Well, the major said we have no urgent work at the moment."

Sologdin spun around to face her squarely.

"We have no urgent work?" he exclaimed almost angrily. "I like that! We have no urgent work!" Sologdin's pink lips twisted in an impatient grimace. "Would you like me to see to it that all sixteen of you sit here copying day and night from tomorrow onward? What do you say to that? All sixteen!" His voice rose to a shout of malicious glee.

Unmoved by the awful prospect of days and nights at the drawing board, Yemina preserved the calm that went so well with her placid large-scale beauty. That morning she hadn't even picked up the tracing paper that lay across her slightly inclined board. The key with which she had let herself in still lay on it. Propping herself comfortably against the desk (her knitted sleeve, pulled taut, emphasized the rounded fullness of her upper arm), Yemina rocked herself very gently and gazed at Sologdin with big, friendly eyes.

"God forbid! Are you really capable of anything so wicked?"

Sologdin stared at her coldly and asked: "Why do you use the word God? Aren't you the wife of a Chekist?"

"What of it?" She sounded surprised. "We bake Easter cakes, too. So what?"

"Easter cakes?"

"That's what I said!"

Sologdin gazed down at the seated Yemina. The green of her knitted two-piece attire was vivid, audacious. Skirt and jacket hugged and emphasized the lines of her opulent figure. The jacket was unbuttoned at the neck, and the collar of a flimsy white blouse was turned out over it.

Sologdin made a check on the sheet of pink paper and said aggressively: "I thought you said your husband was a lieutenant colonel in the MGB?"

"Well, that's my husband! But me and my mother are . . . well . . . just women!"

She smiled disarmingly. Her thick flaxen braids were wound into an imposing crown around her head. She smiled and was indeed like a peasant woman—as portrayed by a great actress.

Sologdin said no more but sat sideways at his board, so as not to see Yemina, and studied the drawing pinned to it, squinting. He felt as though he was still sprinkled with the flowers of triumph, as though they still clung to his shoulders and chest, and he did not want to dispel this blissful feeling.

He would, sometime, have to begin his real life, the Great Life.

And the time was now. He was at the very zenith.

Though there was still some lingering doubt. . . . Yes, that was it. Insensitivity to low-energy impulses and the shortfall in spin momentum could be taken care of, Sologdin felt instinctively, although of course he would have to double check. But Chelnov's last remark, about randomness becoming a fixed pattern, was worrying. It did not imply that there was anything intrinsically wrong with his work, only that it fell short of the ideal. At the same time, he had a vague awareness that somewhere in his work there was an imperfection, a neglected "final inch," which Chelnov had not sensed and he himself had not detected. It was important to locate it and start putting it right in the course of this quiet Sunday that had come around just when he needed it. Only then could he show his work to Anton and start using it to breach the concrete walls.

He made an effort to shut Yemina out of his mind and concentrate on Professor Chelnov's suggestions. Yemina had been sitting near him for six months, but they had never talked much. For that matter, they had never been alone together. Sologdin occasionally teased her a bit when his schedule allowed him a five-minute break. Her official position was that of copyist, so that she was his subordinate, but socially she belonged to the ruling class. The only natural and dignified relationship between them was enmity.

Sologdin looked at his drawing, and Yemina, still propped on her elbow and swaying slightly, looked at him. Suddenly she asked in a loud voice: "Dmitri Aleksandrovich! What about you? Who darns your socks?"

Sologdin's eyebrows rose. He didn't even understand.

"Socks?" He went on looking at his drawing. "Oh, I see. Ivan Ivanovich wears socks because he's still a new boy. Been in less than three years. Socks are a relic of what they call"—compelled to use "bird language," he choked on the word—"capitalism. I just don't wear socks!"

He made a mark on the white sheet.

"What do you wear, then?"

Sologdin couldn't help smiling.

"You are overstepping the bounds of modesty, Larisa Nikolaevna. I wear that proud article of Russian attire, the foot rag!"

He pronounced the words with relish, as though he was beginning to enjoy the conversation. His sudden transitions from sternness to jest always alarmed and amused Yemina.

"I thought it was soldiers who wore foot rags."

"Soldiers and two other groups: prisoners and collective farmers."

"Well, they have to be washed and mended, don't they?"

"You're mistaken! Who ever washes foot rags nowadays? People just wear them for a year without washing them, then throw them away and ask the authorities for new ones."

"Do they really?" Yemina looked almost alarmed.

Sologdin burst into carefree youthful laughter.

"At any rate that's one way of looking at it. And where would I get the cash to buy socks? You're an MGB tracing woman. How much do you get a month?"

"Fifteen hundred."

"Aha!" Sologdin exclaimed triumphantly. "Whereas I, a fashioner of things"—in the Language of Utter Clarity this meant "engineer"—"get thirty little old rubles! Can you see me splurging on socks?"

Sologdin's eyes twinkled merrily. It had nothing to do with Yemina, but she glowed.

Larisa Nikolaevna's husband was an oaf. His family had long ago become nothing more to him than a soft cushion, and he was nothing more to his wife than a piece of furniture. When he got home from work, he ate at length, with great enjoyment, then slept. After his snooze he read the papers and twiddled the knobs on the radio (he periodically sold his old set and bought one of the latest make). A soccer match (true to his calling, he was a Dynamo fan) might arouse some excitement and even passion in him, but nothing else could. He was as dim and as dull as could be. The other men in her circle were much the same: They spent their leisure boasting about their successes and their medals, playing cards, drinking themselves purple, then drunkenly pestering and pawing her. . . .

Sologdin fixed his eyes on his drawing again. Larisa Nikolaevna went on staring at his face, eyeing his mustache, his beard, his full lips. . . .

She would have liked to rub her face against his prickly beard.

She broke the silence again. "Dmitri Aleksandrovich! Am I disturbing you?"

"Yes, you are a bit. . . ," Sologdin answered. The "last few inches" required deep and uninterrupted thought. But her proximity was distracting him. He abandoned his drawing for the time being, turned around to his desk and toward Yemina, and began looking through unimportant papers.

He could hear the faint tick of her wristwatch.

A group of people walked along the hallway, talking quietly. Mamurin's sibilant voice was raised in Number Seven, next door. "How long's that transformer going to be?" Followed by an irate shout from Markushev: "You shouldn't have let them have it, Yakov Ivanovich!"

Larisa Nikolaevna folded her arms on the desk before her, rested her chin on them, and let her languishing gaze play on Sologdin.

Sologdin went on reading.

"Every day! Every hour!" She spoke reverently, almost in a whisper. "Working so hard . . . in prison! You're a remarkable man, Dmitri Aleksandrovich!"

This observation brought Sologdin's head up sharply.

"What has prison got to do with it, Larisa Nikolaevna! I've been inside since I was twenty-five, and I'm supposed to get out when I'm forty-two. But I don't believe it. They're sure to add another bit on. I will have spent the best part of my life in the camps, the years when my powers are at their height. A man shouldn't knuckle under to external circumstances—that's too humiliating."

"You seem to do everything according to plan!"

"Whether he's free or in prison, it makes no difference; man must cultivate firmness of purpose and put it at the service of reason. I lived on nothing but porridge for seven years in a camp, and my brainwork was done without sugar or phosphorus. If I were to tell you. . . ."

But you had to have gone through it to understand it.

The camp's interrogation cell was a hole scooped out of a hillside. The godfather, Lieutenant Kamyshan, had spent eleven months preparing Sologdin for his second sentence, a further tenner. He hit you on the lips with a stick, so that you spat blood and teeth. On days when he rode into the camp on horseback (he was an excellent rider), he would hit you with the handle of his riding crop.

The war was still on. Even the free population had nothing to eat. And those in the camps? Still less. What could you expect, then, in that cage in the mountain?

Sologdin's first interrogation had taught him his lesson, and this time he signed nothing. He got the scheduled tenner just the same. He was taken straight from the courtroom to the hospital. He was dying. His body was doomed to disintegration; it would accept neither bread nor gruel nor porridge.

There came a day when they tipped him onto a stretcher and carried him off to the morgue, where they would break his head open with a big wooden mallet before carting him to the burial ground. But he had suddenly stirred. . . .

"Tell me about it!"

"No, Larisa Nikolaevna! It's absolutely impossible to describe!" he assured her.

He could say it easily, cheerfully now.

And from there, from that terrible place, thenceforth . . . what remarkable powers of renewal he had! With all those years of captivity, all those years of work behind him, to what heights had he soared!

"Please tell me about it!"

The well-nourished woman looked up at him imploringly, her head on her folded arms.

There was one thing she might be able to understand: A woman had also been involved in the story. Kamyshan had picked on him all the sooner because he was jealous of Sologdin's relations with a female prisoner, a nurse. And not without reason. Sologdin's body still glowed with gratitude when he thought of her. It had almost been worth serving a second term for her sake. There was in fact some resemblance between the nurse and this copyist. Both were as ripe and plump as full ears of corn. Small, thin women were freaks as far as Sologdin was concerned. Nature's mistakes.

Yemina's index finger, with its neatly manicured, pink-polished nail, toyed idly with the crumpled corner of her tracing paper. Her head was almost resting on her folded arms, so that the towering crown of thick braids was turned toward Sologdin.

"I owe you a big apology, Dmitri Aleksandrovich. . . ."

"What for?"

"When I was standing by your desk once, I looked down and saw that you were writing a letter. It was quite accidental; you know how it can happen. Then there was another time—"

"When you, again quite by chance, took another squint. . . ?"

"And saw that you were writing a letter again, and it looked like the same one."

"What, you could even make out that it was the same one? What about the third time? Was there a third time?"

"Yes."

"So-o-o. . . . If this goes on, Larisa Nikolaevna, I will have to dispense with your services as a copyist. Which would be a pity, because your drawing is not at all bad."

"But it was a long time ago. You haven't written anything since."

"But I dare say you immediately informed Major Shikinidi?"

"Why do you call him Shikinidi?"

"Shikin, then. Did you?"

"How could you think such a thing?"

"It doesn't take much thought. Major Shikinidi must surely have given you the job of spying on my actions, words, and even thoughts." Sologdin took a pencil and made a mark on the white sheet. "Didn't he? Be honest!"

"Well . . . yes."

"And how many bad reports have you put in?"

"Dmitri Aleksandrovich! On the contrary. I always give you the very best reports!"

"Hmm . . . well, we'll believe it for the time being. But my warning remains in force. We obviously have here a harmless case of purely womanly curiosity. I will satisfy it. It was back in September. I spent not three but five days on end writing a letter to my wife."

"That's what I wanted to ask you, whether you have a wife. Is she waiting for you? Do you always write her such long letters?"

"Yes, I have a wife," Sologdin answered slowly and thoughtfully, "but I might just as well not have one. I can't even write to her now. When I did, they weren't long letters; it just took a long time getting them right. The art of letter writing, Larisa Nikolaevna, is a very difficult one. We often write our letters carelessly, and then we're surprised when we lose people dear to us. My wife hasn't seen me, hasn't felt the touch of my hand for many years now. Letters are the only tie by which I've held on to her for the past twelve years."

Yemina stirred. She slid her elbows to the edge of Sologdin's desk and propped herself up there, cupping her bold face in her hands.

"Are you sure you're still holding on to her? And if so, why, Dmitri Aleksandrovich? It's been twelve years already, and there are still another five left! Seventeen years! You're robbing her of her youth! Why? Let her live!"

Sologdin said gravely: "There are, Larisa Nikolaevna, women of a special kind. They are the consorts of Vikings, the bright-faced Isoldes with adamantine souls. You cannot have known them; your life has been one of comfortable stagnation."

"Let her live!" Larisa Nikolaevna urged him.

She was no longer the grande dame who sailed so majestically along hallways and up stairways in the sharashka. She sat clinging to Sologdin's desk. He heard her breathing loudly, saw her face flushed brightly with concern for his wife, whom she had never met, and thought that now she did indeed look almost like a peasant woman.

Sologdin looked at her quizzically. All women, he knew, were quick to spot the male in the ascendant, to catch the scent of success. Every single one of them craved the attention of the victor. Yemina could not possibly know about his conversation with Chelnov, about the results of his work, but she had somehow sensed it all. And she was beating her wings against the iron-meshed barrier of discipline between them.

Sologdin peeked into the depths of her open-necked blouse and made a mark on the pink sheet.

"Dmitri Aleksandrovich! That's another thing. I've been tortured by curiosity for several weeks now. What are those marks you keep making? And why do you cross them out after a few days? What does it mean?"

"I'm afraid you're showing your surveillance leanings again." He took up the white sheet. "But I don't mind telling you. I make a mark here every time I use a foreign word in Russian when it isn't unavoidable. The number of such marks is the measure of my imperfection. This one is for the word 'capitalism,' which I would have replaced with 'moneygrubbing' if I'd had my wits about me. 'Surveillance' in my slovenly haste I failed to replace with 'watchkeeping.' So I've given myself two bad marks."

"And those on the pink paper?"

"Ah, you've noticed that I make marks on the pink paper, too."

"Yes, and more frequently than on the white. Is that also a measure of your imperfection?"

"Yes," said Sologdin curtly. "On the pink paper, I fine myself, penalize myself, in your language, and afterward I punish myself accordingly. I work off my punishment by chopping wood."

"But what do you penalize yourself for?" she asked quietly.

It was bound to happen! No sooner had he reached the zenith than capricious fate had even sent him a woman, with apologies for the delay. Give everything or rob you of everything; that was fate's way.

"Why do you want to know?" he asked as sternly as before.

"Tell me, what are they for?" she repeated quietly, stubbornly.

This would be his revenge on them all, on the whole MVD clan!

"Haven't you noticed when I make those marks?"

"I have," she said faintly.

The door key, with its aluminum tag, lay on her tracing paper.

A big warm green woolen ball stood breathing hard before Sologdin.

Awaiting his orders.

Sologdin squinted and gave the command.

"Go and lock the door! Quick!"

Larisa sprang back from the desk, and her chair fell over with a crash as she stood up abruptly.

What had he done, impertinent slave? Was she on her way to complain?

She swept up the key, walked to the door, hips swaying, and locked it.

Sologdin made five hasty marks in a row on the pink paper.

All he had time for.

# 34

# Voiceprints

NOBODY WANTED TO WORK ON SUNDAY, free staff included. They drifted in listlessly, avoiding the normal weekday crush on the buses, and tried to arrange things so that they could get through to 6:00 p.m. undisturbed.

But that Sunday proved more hectic than any weekday. At about 10:00 a.m. three very long, very streamlined cars drove up to the main gates. The watch saluted. The cars drove through the gates, passed Spiridon, the red-headed yardman, who stood broom in hand peering at them, then rolled over snow-free gravel paths to the main entrance of the institute. High-ranking officers issued from all three cars, epaulets flashing, and without waiting for anyone to meet them, went right upstairs to Yakonov's office on the third floor. No one managed to get a good look at them. The rumor went around some of the laboratories that Minister Abakumov had arrived in person, accompanied by eight generals. In other laboratories people went on sitting quietly, unaware of the impending storm.

The rumor was half true: Deputy Minister Selivanovsky had arrived, accompanied by four generals.

But something unprecedented had happened: Engineer Colonel Yakonov was not yet at work. The frightened duty officer (swiftly pushing in the drawer in which he had been furtively reading a detective story) phoned Yakonov at home, then reported to the deputy minister that Colonel Yakonov had been in bed with a heart attack but was getting dressed and coming in. Meanwhile, Yakonov's deputy, Major Roitman, a lean man with a tailored tunic, struggling to straighten the sword belt that sat so awkwardly on him and stumbling over the strip of carpet (he was very nearsighted), hurried in from the Acoustics Laboratory and presented himself to his superiors. He had been in such a hurry not only because regulations demanded it but also to defend the interests of the opposition party in the institute, which he led; Yakonov always tried to squeeze him out of conversations with higher authority. Roitman already knew the full story of Pryanchikov's nocturnal outing and was eager to convince the high commission that the situation with the scrambler was not so hopeless as that, for instance, with the speech clipper. Although only thirty, Roitman had already won a Stalin Prize, and he fearlessly exposed his laboratory to visitations from on high.

He had perhaps ten listeners, of whom two more or less understood the technicalities. The others simply preserved a dignified silence. Oskolupov, however, had sent for Mamurin, who appeared shortly after Roitman, livid and stammering with rage in standing up for the clipper, which was, he said, nearly ready to be put into production. Shortly afterward Yakonov also turned up, with bags under his sunken eyes and a bluish tinge in his bloodless face, and sank onto a chair by the wall. The conversation became fragmentary and confused, and before long nobody had any idea how to salvage the doomed enterprise.

As bad luck would have it, the heart of the institute and the conscience of the institute, Operations Officer Comrade Shikin and Party Organizer Comrade Stepanov, had given way that Sunday morning to a perfectly natural temptation to stay away from work and leave the collective that they managed on weekdays to look after itself. (Behavior all the more pardonable because, as everybody knows, if the proper Party educational and organizational measures have been implemented, participation of managerial personnel in the work process is by no means essential.) Alarm and an acute awareness of his unexpected responsibility gripped the duty officer. At some risk to himself, he abandoned the telephones and hurried around the laboratories, informing their heads in a whisper that extraordinarily important guests had arrived, in order to make them redouble their vigilance. He was so flustered and in such a hurry to get back to his telephones that he ignored the locked door of the design office and had no time to look in at the Vacuum Laboratory, where Klara Makarygina was on duty and none of the other free workers had appeared.

The heads of laboratories in turn made no public announcements (you couldn't openly ask people to pretend to be working because the brass had arrived) but went around the workplaces warning everybody individually in an embarrassed whisper.

The whole institute, then, was at a standstill, waiting for the bosses. After a hurried conference some of the visitors remained in Yakonov's office, and others made for Number Seven, while only Selivanovsky accompanied Major Roitman down to the Acoustics Laboratory. To dodge this new chore, Yakonov had recommended "Acoustics" as a convenient base for the execution of Ryumin's commission.

"But how do you expect to identify the man?" Selivanovsky asked as they went along. Roitman had first heard of the commission five minutes ago and so had no thoughts on the matter. Oskolupov had done the thinking for him the night before, when he thoughtlessly undertook the task. All the same, Roitman's mind had been busy in the last five minutes.

He addressed the deputy minister informally and with no trace of servility. "Look," he said. "We have a visible speech device for recording speech visually. It prints off what we call voiceprints, and there's a man by the name of Rubin who can read them."

"A prisoner?"

"Yes. Senior lecturer in philology. Just lately I've had him working on the detection of individual speech peculiarities. And I hope that by voiceprinting this telephone message and comparing the results with the voiceprints of the suspects. . . ."

Selivanovsky looked doubtful.

"Hmm. . . . We will have to get Abakumov's approval for this philologist."

"You mean security clearance?"

"Yes."

Meanwhile, although they all knew in the Acoustics Laboratory that the brass had arrived, they simply could not overcome the numbing inertia of idleness. They made a show of activity, rummaging in drawers containing valves, scanning diagrams in magazines, gaping at the view from the window. Among the free employees the younger women huddled together gossiping in whispers, and Roitman's assistant tried to break it up. Simochka, luckily for her, was not at work; she was making up for the extra day she had put in and so was spared the torment of seeing Nerzhin all dressed up and radiant in anticipation of his meeting with the woman who had first claim on him.

Nerzhin felt as though it was his birthday. He looked in at the Acoustics Laboratory for the third time, not because he had any business there but because waiting for the long-overdue police truck made him restless and nervous. He did not sit on his own chair but on the window ledge, inhaling the smoke of a cigarette with enjoyment and listening to Rubin. Having failed to find in Professor Chelnov an appreciative audience for the ballad on Moses, Rubin was now reading it with quiet fervor to Nerzhin. Rubin was no poet, but the lines he dashed off were sometimes clever and full of feeling. Not long ago, Gleb had praised highly the breadth of vision he had shown in a study in verse of Alyosha Karamazov, who appeared simultaneously in the overcoat of a White officer defending Perekop and in the overcoat of a Red Army man storming Perekop. Now Rubin very much wanted Gleb to appreciate the Moses ballad and take to heart the message that waiting and believing for forty years is rational, necessary, and essential.

Rubin could not exist without friends; he suffocated without them. He found solitude so unbearable that he did not even allow his thoughts to ripen in his own head; as soon as he had so much as half a thought, he hastened to share it. He had been rich in friends all his life, but in prison it so happened that his friends did not share his views and those who did were not his friends.

No one in the Acoustics Laboratory was working, then, as yet, except for the ever blithe and busy Pryanchikov, who had gotten over the memory of Moscow by night and his crazy journey and was meditating a further improvement to his model, crooning,

*Bendzi-bendzi-bendzi-ba-ar*
*Bendzi-bendzi-bendzi-bar.*

At this point Selivanovsky and Roitman entered. Roitman went on with what he was saying: "In these voiceprints speech is visualized in three sets of measurements simultaneously; frequency is registered transversely across the tape, duration lengthwise along the tape, and volume by the depth of the impression. By this means every sound stands out as something so unique and original that it is easily identified, and you can even read back whatever has been said from the tape. Here we have"—he led Selivanovsky to the far end of the laboratory—"the VIR device, designed in our laboratory" (Roitman had forgotten himself that they had lifted it from an American journal), "and here" (cautiously steering the deputy minister in the direction of the window) "is Candidate in

Philological Sciences Rubin, the only man in the Soviet Union who can read visually recorded speech." (Rubin rose and bowed silently.)

As soon as Roitman had pronounced the word "voiceprint" at the doorway, Rubin and Nerzhin had pricked up their ears. Their work, treated as a joke by most people, was emerging at last into the light of day. It took Roitman forty-five seconds to lead Selivanovsky to them, but with the zeks' unique quick-wittedness, they had realized at once that Rubin would have to demonstrate his skill in reading from voiceprints. One of the regular speakers must read the text into the microphone, and Nerzhin was the only one present in the room. They also realized that, although Rubin really could read voiceprints, he might slip up in an examination, and this must not be allowed to happen; it could mean a backward somersault into the netherworld of the camps.

They understood each other at a glance.

"If you do it, and you can choose the sentence," Rubin whispered, "say, 'Voiceprints enable the deaf to use the telephone.'"

Nerzhin whispered in reply, "If he gives me a sentence, you'll have to decipher it from the tape. If I smooth my hair, you're getting it right; if I straighten my tie, you're wrong."

That was where Rubin rose and silently bowed.

Roitman went on in that hesitant, self-deprecating voice of his, which you would have known without looking at him must belong to an intellectual:

"Right, now Lev Grigorievich will demonstrate his skill. One of the speakers, say, Gleb Vikentich, will go into the soundproof box and read a sentence into the microphone, the machine will record it, and Lev Grigorievich will try to decipher it."

Standing one step away from the deputy minister, Nerzhin fixed him with an insolent Gulag stare.

"You want to think of a sentence?" he asked curtly.

"No, no," Selivanovsky answered politely, avoiding his eyes. "Make something up yourself."

Nerzhin obediently took a piece of paper, thought a moment, had an inspiration, and in the sudden hush handed what he had written to Selivanovsky in such a way that not even Roitman could read it.

"Voiceprints enable the deaf to use the telephone."

"Is that really so?" Selivanovsky asked in surprise.

"Yes."

"Go ahead and read."

The apparatus began humming. Nerzhin went into the soundproof booth (how disgraceful the sackcloth curtain looked at that moment! . . . that everlasting shortage of materials in the stores!) and shut himself off from the eyes and ears of the world. The apparatus chattered, and two meters of damp tape, marked with inky streaks and smudges, were deposited on Rubin's desk.

The whole lab stopped pretending to work and watched in suspense. Roitman was obviously nervous. Nerzhin left the booth and watched Rubin impassively from a distance. Everybody else was standing; Rubin alone remained seated, giving them glimpses of his bald spot. Taking pity on his impatient audience, he made no attempt to hide his hieratic ritual but quickly marked off sections of the still-damp tape with the usual blunt copying pencil.

"You see, certain sounds can be deciphered without the least difficulty, the accented or sonorous vowels, for example. In the second word the *r* sound is distinctly visible twice. In the first word the accented sound of *ee* and in front of it a soft *v*—for there can't be a hard sound there. Before that is the formant *a*, but we mustn't forget that in the first, the secondary accented syllable o is also pronounced like *a*. But the vowel *oo* or *u* retains its individuality even when it's far from the accent—right here it has the characteristic low-frequency streak. The third sound of the first word is unquestionably *u*. And after it follows a palatal explosive consonant, most likely *k*—and so we have *ukov'* or *ukavi*. And here is a hard *v*—it is clearly distinguished from the soft *v*, for it has no streak higher than 2,300 cycles. *Vukovi*—and then there is a resounding hard stop and at the very end an attenuated vowel, and these together I can interpret as *dy*. So we get *vukovidy*—and we have to guess at the first sound, which is smeared. I could take it for an *s* if it weren't that the sense tells me it's a *z*. And so the first word is"— and Rubin pronounced the word for "voiceprints"—"*zvukovidy*." He continued: "Now, in the second word, as I said, there are two *r* sounds and, apparently, the regular verb *ayet*, but since it is in the plural it is evidently *ayut*. Evidently *razryvayut* or *razreshayut*, and I'll find out which in a moment. Antonina Valeryanovna, was it you who took the magnifying glass? Could I please have it a moment?"

The magnifying glass was quite unnecessary, as the apparatus made bold, broad marks. It was an old con's spoof, and Nerzhin laughed quietly to himself, absently smoothing his already smoothed hair. Rubin gave him a fleeting glance and took the proffered magnifying glass. The general tension was growing, all the more so because nobody knew whether Rubin was guessing correctly so far. Selivanovsky was profoundly impressed.

"Amazing," he whispered. "Simply amazing."

Nobody noticed Lieutenant Shusterman tiptoeing into the room. He had no right to be there, so he kept his distance. He signaled to Nerzhin to hurry up, but instead of leaving the room with him stayed behind, waiting for a chance to summon Rubin. He wanted to send Rubin to make his bed again, this time properly. It was not the first time that he had bullied Rubin with such readjustments.

Meanwhile, Rubin had deciphered the word "deaf" and moved on. Roitman was radiant. Not merely because he had a share in Rubin's triumph but because he sincerely rejoiced in any practical success.

At that point Rubin happened to raise his eyes, encountered Shusterman's malignant scowl, realized why he was there, and bestowed on him a look of malicious glee, as if to say, "Straighten it yourself!"

"The final word, 'telephone,' we come across so frequently that I'm used to it and can recognize it immediately. And that's the whole thing."

"Astonishing!" Selivanovsky said yet again. "May I ask your name and patronymic?"

"Lev Grigorievich."

"Well, then, Lev Grigorievich, can you identify individual vocal peculiarities from voiceprints?"

"We call it 'individual speech type.' As a matter of fact, that is precisely what we're working on at present."

"That's very lucky! I think we can find a job that may interest you."

Shusterman left on tiptoe.

# 35

# Kissing Is Forbidden

THE TRUCK DETAILED to take the prisoners to their relatives broke down, and there was some delay while new arrangements were made by telephone. When Nerzhin was summoned from the Acoustics Laboratory at about 11:00 a.m., the other six were there already, half frisked or well and truly frisked, and waiting in a variety of postures, some slumped over the big table, some roaming around beyond the dividing line. Standing on the line, by the wall, was Lieutenant Colonel Klimentiev, erect, poised, and highly polished, a model officer about to inspect a parade. His black handlebar mustache and his black head gave off a powerful smell of eau de cologne.

He stood with his hands behind his back, apparently taking no interest in the proceedings, but by his very presence compelling the guards to search conscientiously.

At the dividing line Nerzhin walked into the outstretched arms of Krasnogubenky, one of the most spiteful and captious of the guards, who asked immediately: "What have you got in your pockets?"

Nerzhin had long ago stopped tumbling over himself to oblige, as newcomers do when they first encounter guards and escort troops. He did not trouble to answer and made no move to turn the pockets of his unfamiliar wool suit inside out. He looked at Krasnogubenky as though he felt sleep coming on and held his arms a few inches from his sides to let the guard dive into his pockets. After five years in prison and many such precautionary searches, Nerzhin no longer thought of it as an outrage, no longer felt as if dirty fingers were mauling his lacerated heart. Now nothing done to his body could cloud his happiness.

Krasnogubenky opened the cigarette case, Potapov's present, peered into the mouthpieces of the cigarettes to see whether anything was concealed there, poked a finger into the matchbox (there might be something under the matches), made sure that nothing was sewn into the hems of the handkerchief—and that was all he could find in Nerzhin's pockets. Next, he thrust his hand between Nerzhin's vest and his unbuttoned jacket, and patted him all over, feeling for anything that might have been tucked under the vest or between the vest and the dickey. Then he squatted on his heels, clasped one of Nerzhin's thighs in a tight two-handed grip, slid his hands from top to bottom, then did the same with the other leg. When Krasnogubenky squatted down, Nerzhin had a good view of the engraver, who was nervously pacing, and guessed why he was agitated. He had discovered in prison a talent for short-story writing. He wrote about life in a German POW camp, about his cellmates, about his appearances in court. With his wife's help he had smuggled out a few stories. But could they be shown to anyone outside? Even there they would have to be hidden. They couldn't be left inside either. And he would never be allowed to take the smallest scrap of paper away with him. But some old man, a friend of the family, had read them and let the author know through his wife that even in Chekhov such consummate and eloquent skill was rarely encountered. This appraisal had greatly encouraged the engraver.

He had, as usual, written a story in readiness for today's visit—a magnificent story, he believed. But at the very last moment, confronted by Krasnogubenky, he lost his nerve, turned away, wadded up the bit of tracing paper on which the story was written in microscopic script, and swallowed it. Now he was suffering agonies of regret that he had eaten the story. Perhaps he could have gotten away with it?

"Shoes off," Krasnogubenky said to Nerzhin.

Nerzhin lifted one foot onto a stool, unlaced his shoe, and kicked it off without looking where it landed, exposing a hole in his sock. Krasnogubenky picked up the shoe, groped inside it, and flexed the sole. Nerzhin kicked off the other shoe, with the same deadpan expression, and revealed another hole. Perhaps because there were such big holes in those socks, Krasnogubenky did not suspect that anything was hidden in them and did not ask Nerzhin to remove them.

Nerzhin put his shoes back on. Krasnogubenky lit a cigarette.

The lieutenant colonel had winced when Nerzhin kicked his shoes off. It was a deliberate show of disrespect to his guard. If he did not stand up for guards, prisoners would soon be thumbing their noses at senior prison staff. Klimentiev regretted his act of kindness yet again and almost decided to find some excuse for canceling Nerzhin's visit; the wretch was obviously unashamed of his criminal status and indeed seemed to revel in it.

"Pay attention!" he said sternly, and seven prisoners and seven guards turned to look at him. "You know the rules? You must give nothing to your relatives. You must receive nothing from them. Parcels may be handed over only through me. In your conversation you must not mention your jobs here, your working conditions, your living conditions, your daily routine, the layout of the plant. You are not to mention names. About yourselves you may say only that all is well with you and that there is nothing you need."

"So what are we supposed to talk about?" someone called out. "Politics?"

Klimentiev did not trouble to answer this blatant absurdity.

"About your crime," another prisoner grimly suggested. "And how sorry you are."

Klimentiev imperturbably rejected this.

"Talking about your case is also forbidden. Judicial proceedings are an official secret. Inquire about your family, your children. One more thing. Starting today, shaking hands and kissing are forbidden."

Nerzhin, who had been unmoved by the search and the stupid rules, which he knew how to circumvent, saw red when he heard that kissing was prohibited.

"We see each other just once a year. . . ," he croaked, and Klimentiev looked around, joyfully anticipating the continuation of his outburst.

Nerzhin could almost hear him barking, "Permission for visit withdrawn." He choked back his anger.

He had been given permission to receive a visit at the very last moment. It seemed somehow irregular and might easily be withdrawn.

Some such thought generally prevents people from blurting out the truth or demanding justice.

He was a veteran prisoner and should be able to control his anger.

Once the threat of mutiny had subsided, Klimentiev added dispassionately: "If there is any kissing or handshaking, the visit will be terminated immediately."

"But my wife doesn't know that!" the engraver said angrily.

Klimentiev was ready for this. "Your relatives will be warned," he said.

"It never used to be like this!"

"Well, this is how it's going to be now."

Idiots! And their indignation was idiotic. As if he personally, and not fresh instructions from above, were responsible for this procedure.

"How long will the visit last?"

"What if my mother comes? Will she be allowed in?"

"Each visit will last thirty minutes. I will admit only one person, the one previously notified."

"What about my five-year-old daughter?"

"Children under the age of fifteen are allowed in with adults."

"What about sixteen-year-olds?"

"They won't be admitted. Any questions? Time to get on the bus. This way out!"

Amazing! They were being taken not in a prison truck, as they always had been of late, but in a small-size, light blue city bus.

The bus was standing at the door of the staff building. Three guards, new ones apparently, in civilian dress and velour hats and keeping their hands in their pockets (on their revolvers), got on the bus first and occupied three of the corners. Two of them looked like retired prizefighters or perhaps gangsters. They were wearing very nice overcoats.

The morning frost was vanishing, but the thaw had not yet set in.

The seven prisoners stepped onto the bus by way of the only door, at the front, and took their seats.

Four uniformed guards followed.

The driver slammed the door and started the engine.

Lieutenant Colonel Klimentiev got into his car.

## 36

# Phonoscopy

At noon Yakonov himself was missing from the velvety hush and glossy comfort of his office. He was in Number Seven, officiating at the "wedding" of the clipper and the scrambler. The idea of uniting those two devices, born that morning in the mercenary mind of Markushev, had been snapped up by many others who saw some advantage to themselves. Only Bobynin, Pryanchikov, and Roitman were against it, and nobody listened to them.

Present in the office were Selivanovsky, General Bulbanyuk (representing Ryumin), Marfino's Lieutenant Smolosidov, and the prisoner Rubin.

Lieutenant Smolosidov was an unpleasant character. Perhaps you believe that there is some good in every living creature? Your search for it in Smolosidov would be rendered difficult by that unsmiling iron-hard stare and the sour twist of those thick lips. He occupied one of the lowliest positions in his laboratory; he was little more than a radio fitter, and he was paid no more than that of the lowliest female employee, less than two thousand a month. True, he stole another thousand from the institute in the form of the otherwise unobtainable radio parts he sold on the black market, but everyone knew that there was more than this to be said about Smolosidov's position and income.

The free employees in the sharashka—even the friends with whom he played volleyball—were afraid of him. They were frightened by his face, in which it was impossible to awaken a spontaneous reaction. And by the special trust that the highest authorities showed him. Where did he live? Did he in fact have a home? A family? He never accepted invitations from colleagues, never shared his leisure with them beyond the boundaries of the institute. He had three war medals on his chest and in an unguarded moment had boasted that all through the war Marshal Rokossovsky had not spoken a single word that he, Smolosidov, had not heard. When asked how this could be, he replied that he had been the marshal's personal radio operator. Nothing more was known about his past.

No sooner did the question arise as to which of the free workers could be trusted with the red-hot secret tape than the minister's inner office gave the order: Smolosidov.

Smolosidov was now installing a tape recorder on a little varnished table, and General Bulbanyuk, whose head was like a grotesquely overgrown potato with three bulges for ears and nose, was saying:

"You, Rubin, are a prisoner. But you were a Communist once, and you may be a Communist again some day."

Rubin would have retorted, "I'm a Communist right now!" but trying to convince Bulbanyuk of that was beneath his dignity.

"So the Soviet government and our Organs feel that they can trust you. The tape you are going to hear contains a state secret of world importance. We hope that you will help us to isolate this scoundrel who wants to see his native land menaced by the atomic bomb. It goes without saying that if you make the slightest attempt to divulge the secret, you will be annihilated. That clear?"

"Quite clear," snapped Rubin, whose greatest fear now was that he might not be allowed to hear the tape. Having lost all chance of private happiness long ago, Rubin had made mankind at large his family. The tape he had yet to hear was already of personal concern to him.

Smolosidov pressed the Playback button, and the quiet of the office was broken by the dialogue between a slow-witted American and a desperate Russian, with a faint rustling in the background. Rubin peered into the mottled diaphragm of the loudspeaker as though straining to discern the features of this enemy. Whenever he looked at anything so intently, his face became taut and harsh. It would be no good begging for mercy from a man with a face like that.

After the words (in bad Russian), "Who are you? Say your name," Rubin threw himself back in his chair. He was a different man. He had forgotten that others present were high-ranking officers, forgotten that it was a long time since major's stars had blazed on his shoulders. He relit his cigarette and rapped out, "All right. Just once more."

Smolosidov rewound the tape.

Everyone was silent. Everyone felt the touch of the fiery wheel.

Rubin chewed and mumbled the mouthpiece of his cigarette. He felt ready to burst. Suddenly he, of all people, the dishonorably discharged Rubin, was urgently needed! He, too, would have his chance to give Dame History a helping hand! He was back at his post! Once more defending the World Revolution!

Malignant Smolosidov hung over the tape recorder like a sullen dog. Pompous Bulbanyuk, elbows on Anton's spacious desk, supported his imposing potato head in hands half hidden by his loose-skinned neck. From what stock had this impenetrably complacent breed proliferated? From the weed of Commie-cockiness, maybe? How quick and clever his comrades had once been. Now the whole apparatus had fallen into the hands of these people. And they were bulldozing the whole country along the road to perdition. How could it have happened?

Rubin could not look at them. They disgusted him so much that he would have liked to toss a hand grenade at them then and there, in that office, and blow them to bits!

But, as things were, at this crossroads in history, they represented the positive forces, embodying as they did the dictatorship, and the fatherland, of the proletariat.

He must rise above his feelings! As hateful as they were, he must help them!

Hogs of this sort, from an Army-Group Political Department, had flung Rubin in jail because his cleverness and his honesty were more than they could bear. Hogs of the same sort, in the Chief Military Prosecutor's Department, had in the space of four years tossed a dozen anguished protestations of innocence from Rubin into the trash.

Yes, he must rise above his own unhappy lot! To save the idea! To rescue the banner! To serve the world's most advanced society!

The tape came to an end.

Rubin crushed his dead cigarette in an ashtray.

"All right. We'll give it a try," he said. "But if you haven't got a suspect, what are we looking for? We can't tape the voices of everybody in Moscow. Whose voice do we compare this with?"

Bulbanyuk reassured him: "We picked up four people on the spot, near the telephone booth. But our man is most probably not one of them. There are five people in the Ministry of Foreign Affairs who could have known. Not counting Gromyko and one or two others, obviously. I've jotted down those five names, without initials, titles, or the posts they occupy, so you needn't be afraid to accuse any one of them."

He held out a page torn from a notebook. The names written on it were:

1. Petrov
2. Syagovity
3. Volodin
4. Shevronok
5. Zavarzin.

Rubin read the names and made as if to copy the list, but Selivanovsky hastily prevented him.

"No, no! The list will be with Smolosidov."

Rubin handed it back. He was not offended but amused by all these precautions. As if the five names were not burned into his memory already! Petrov! Syagovity! Volodin! Shevronok! Zavarzin! Linguistic speculation had become a matter of habit with Rubin, and he had automatically registered the derivation of the names Syagovity ("bouncy") and Shevronok (= *zhavoronok*, "skylark").

"Please record other phone calls made by each of the five," he said curtly.

"You'll get them tomorrow."

"Another thing. Put the age of each by his name." Rubin thought a bit. "And a list of the foreign languages he knows."

Selivanovsky assented. "I've been wondering myself why he didn't switch to a foreign language. What sort of diplomat is he? Maybe he's just very crafty?"

"Maybe our man got some uneducated simpleton to do it for him," Bulbanyuk said, slapping the table with his flabby hand.

"Whom could you trust with a job like that?"

"What we need to find out as quickly as possible," Bulbanyuk explained, "is whether the culprit is in fact one of these five. If he isn't, we'll try another five, or another twenty-five for that matter!"

Rubin waited till he had finished and nodded at the tape recorder.

"I will need the tape the whole time, starting today."

"It will be with Lieutenant Smolosidov. You and he will be allocated a room to yourselves in the Top-Secret zone."

"They're clearing it now," Smolosidov said.

Rubin's service experience had taught him to avoid the dangerous word "when," in case he was asked the same question. He knew that there was only work for a week or two in this, but that if you spun it out, it could be good for months, whereas if you asked "When do you want it?" the bosses would say "By tomorrow morning." He asked a different question: "With whom can I discuss this work?"

Selivanovsky exchanged a glance with Bulbanyuk and answered. "Only with Major Roitman. With Foma Guryanovich. And with the minister himself."

"You remember my warning?" Bulbanyuk asked. "Want me to repeat it?"

Rubin rose without asking permission, looked at the general through half-closed eyes as though he was something very, very small, and said to no one in particular:

"I must go and think."

Nobody objected.

Rubin's face showed no emotion as he left the office. He walked unseeingly past the duty officer and down the strip of red stair-carpet.

He would have to draw Gleb into this new group. He would need to talk things over. The job would be a very difficult one. They had just barely begun working on voices. Preliminary classification. Provisional terminology.

He looked forward to his research with a true scientist's excitement.

This was, in effect, a new science: identifying a criminal by a voiceprint.

Till then, criminals had been identified by their fingerprints. That technique was called "dactyloscopy"—"finger scanning"—and it had evolved over the centuries.

The new science could be called "voice scanning" (that would be Sologdin's term), or "phonoscopy." And it had to be created in a matter of days.

Petrov. Syagovity. Volodin. Shevronok. Zavarzin.

# 37

## The Silent Alarm

NERZHIN FOUND A PLACE BY A WINDOW, leaned back comfortably on the soft seat, and yielded to the gentle swaying of the bus. He was sharing a double seat with Illarion Pavlovich Gerasimovich, the optics expert, a short, narrow-shouldered man with a markedly intellectual face and pince-nez, the typical spy portrayed in Soviet posters.

Nerzhin confided in him, keeping his voice down: "I ought to be used to it by now. I can sit quite happily on my bare backside in the snow; I can travel twenty-five to a truck on a freight train and watch the guards smash our suitcases—none of that upsets me; it never makes me blow my top. But there's only one live nerve that connects me with the world outside, my love for my wife; nothing can ever deaden it, and I can't bear anyone touching it. When we see each other once a year for half an hour, how can they forbid us to kiss? Those swine make us pay for this one visit by spitting on our finer feelings."

Gerasimovich's faint eyebrows came together in a frown. They made him look dejected even when he was only pondering his diagrams.

"There's probably only one way to make yourself invulnerable," he replied. "That's to kill all your affections and suppress all your desires."

Gerasimovich had been at the Marfino sharashka only a few months, and Nerzhin had not yet gotten to know him well. He liked the man, though he couldn't say why.

They said nothing more during the journey; traveling to see a relative is too great an event in a prisoner's life. It is time to awaken your forgotten soul from its slumber in the burial vault. Memories suppressed on other days now come to the surface. You rehearse the thoughts and feelings of a whole year, of many years, so that you can fuse them with those short minutes of union with someone dear to you.

The bus came to a stop outside the guardroom. The sergeant of the guard got up on the step and poked his head inside while his eyes counted the excursionists twice over. (The senior guard had already signed for seven head of prisoners inside the guardroom.) Then he crawled under the bus to make sure that no one was clinging to the springs (a disembodied devil couldn't have held on there for a minute) and went back inside. Only then did the inner and, after a short delay, the outer gate swing open. The bus crossed the enchanted boundary and with a cheerful swish of tires ran along the frosted Bishop's Road and past the Botanical Garden.

The zeks of Marfino could thank those who had made their establishment top secret for these outings. Relatives who came to see them were not allowed to know where the living dead were housed, whether they were transported from a hundred kilometers away or picked up at the Spassky Gate, whether they were driven in from the airport or from the next world; they were only allowed to see well-fed, neatly dressed people with white hands who had lost their old talkativeness and could only smile sadly and insist that they wanted for nothing.

These meetings were rather like those ancient Greek stelae, columns with bas-reliefs on which the deceased and their living relatives who had set up the monument were depicted together. But there was always a little space between this world and the world beyond the grave. The living gazed lovingly at the dead, while the dead looked toward Hades, with eyes neither cheerful nor sad, empty eyes, eyes that had seen too much.

As they went uphill, Nerzhin turned around to look at a view he had never seen properly before: the building in which they lived and worked, the dark redbrick seminary with its dull rusted hemispherical dome over their semicircular beauty of a room. Above it rose the "sixer," as hexagonal towers were called in Old Russia. From the south facade, behind which were the Acoustics Lab, Number Seven, the design office, and Anton's room, neat rows of unopenable windows gazed on the world with uniform blankness.

Suburban Muscovites or strollers in Ostankino Park could have no idea how many remarkable lives, thwarted ambitions, aborted passions . . . and secrets of state were crammed together in a red-hot, smoldering mass in that isolated old building on the edge of town. Even inside, the building was pervaded by an air of secrecy. One room knew nothing of the next. Neighbor knew nothing of neighbor. The operations officers knew nothing about the women—the twenty-two irrational, crazy, female free workers allowed into this austere building—just as these women did not know about one another what only heaven could know: that, with the sword hanging over them and the rules constantly dinned into their ears, every one of the twenty-two had either formed a clandestine attachment, found someone to love and kiss furtively, or taken pity on someone and kept him in touch with his family.

Gleb opened his dark red cigarette case and lit up with the special enjoyment that a cigarette can give at life's supreme moments.

Although the thought of Nadya dominated, monopolized his mind, his body was delighting in the unusual sensation of travel and wanted only to ride on and on. He wished that time could stand still and the bus drive on and on along the snow-covered road scarred with black tire tracks, past the park all white with hoarfrost, past briefly glimpsed children calling to each other in voices such as Nerzhin did not remember hearing since before the war—soldiers at the front and prisoners do not hear children's voices.

Nadya and Gleb had lived together for just a year. A year spent running around with briefcases. They were fifth-year students, working for their final exams.

Then, suddenly, the war was upon them.

Some people their age had funny little kids running around on short legs.

They did not.

A small child tried to run across the road. The driver swerved sharply to miss him. The child was frightened and stood stock-still, pressing a little hand in a blue mitten to his flushed face.

Nerzhin, who had not thought about children at all for years, suddenly saw clearly that Stalin had robbed him and Nadya of their children. Even if he was released after serving his sentence and they were together again, his wife would be thirty-six or perhaps forty years old. Too late to have a child.

Leaving Ostankino Palace to the left and the brightly dressed children skating on the lake to the right, the bus plunged into narrow side streets, shuddering over the cobblestones.

People describing prisons have always tried to lay the horror on thick. But perhaps prison is most horrible when there is no horror? When the horror consists in the gray routine never varying from week to week? When you forget that the one and only life given to you on this earth has been wrecked? When you are willing to forgive, have already forgiven the swine for all this? When your only thought is how to grab a crusty piece of bread, not one that is all crumb? Or how to get underwear with no holes in it, and not too small, next bath day?

You have to live it. You can't possibly imagine it. You can write, "A prisoner I in dungeon damp" or "Unbolt this dungeon dank and drear, / And bring me to my dark-eyed dear," without ever having been in jail; that's easily imagined. But it's primitive stuff. The reality of prison life can be fully appreciated only after years of confinement, without a break and with no end in prospect.

"When you come home," Nadya had written. That was the horror of it. For "you" there could be no homecoming. After fourteen years in the army and in jail, not a single cell of your body would be as it had been before. You could only be a newcomer. A new man, an unknown man bearing her husband's name would turn up, and his former wife would see that her first, her only love, for whom she had waited fourteen years, shutting herself off from the world, no longer existed, that he had evaporated, molecule by molecule.

All would be well if in this new, second life they came to love each other all over again.

But what if they did not?

And anyway, would you yourself want freedom after so many years; would you want to go outside into the frenzied whirl, so inimical to the human heart, so hostile to the peace of the soul? Would you not pause on the threshold of your prison and peer anxiously out: Should I or shouldn't I go there?

Suburban streets sped past the windows. The diffused glow in the night sky, seen from their confinement, made them think of Moscow as one great blaze of light, a dazzling sight. But here were rows of one-story and two-story houses, all in disrepair with peeling stucco and sagging wooden fences. Probably no one had touched them since the war. There had been other calls on people's energy. There were places between Ryazan and Ruzaevka, off the map for foreigners, where you could travel three hundred versts and see nothing but rotted thatch.

Resting his head against the vibrating, misted window, barely hearing himself above the noise of the engine, Gleb whispered very quietly: "Russia, my own. Russia, my life . . . how long must we suffer?"

The bus shot out onto the broad and busy square in front of the Riga Station. Trams, trolleys, cars, people, rushed about in the muddy light of that day of cloud and frost. The only splash of color was that of the violet uniforms that Nerzhin saw for the first time.

Gerasimovich between reveries had also noticed this parakeet finery and, eyebrows raised in surprise, said for the whole bus to hear: "Look at that! The boys in blue are back! Ol'-time cops, like before the Revolution!"

So that was what they were! Gleb remembered one of the Komsomol leaders saying in the early thirties, "You, comrades of the Young Pioneer movement, will never have the misfortune to see a real live tsarist policeman!"

"Well, now we have," said Gleb with a laugh.

Gerasimovich looked blank.

Gleb bent over to whisper in his ear:

"People are so stupefied that if you stood in the middle of the street right now shouting, 'Down with the tyrant! Hurrah for freedom!' they wouldn't know who the tyrant was and what you meant by freedom."

Gerasimovich sent the wrinkles rippling up his forehead:

"And are you sure you know?"

"I think I do," said Nerzhin, wryly.

"Don't be too sure too quickly. People have a very vague idea as to what kind of freedom a rationally ordered society needs."

"And have we any idea what a rationally ordered society would be like? Is such a thing possible?"

"I think it is."

"You couldn't give me even an approximate picture of it. Nobody has ever succeeded in doing so."

"But somebody will someday," Gerasimovich insisted with modest firmness.

They looked at each other quizzically.

"I would like to hear about it," Nerzhin said, but not as though it was urgent.

Gerasimovich nodded his small, narrow head. "I'll tell you sometime."

And again they sat shaking, their eyes absorbing the street, and let their minds wander.

It defied understanding that Nadya could have waited so many years for him. That she could have walked among this restless, feverishly questing crowd, knowing that men's eyes were upon her, and never feel her heart miss a beat. Gleb told himself that if it had been the other way around, if Nadya had been jailed and he had remained at liberty, he probably wouldn't have held out for as much as a year. He could never have imagined that his fragile sweetheart was capable of such rocklike steadfastness. In his first three years in prison, he had been sure that Nadya would change, rebound, find some distraction, get over her loss. But it had not happened. So that Gleb had now begun to take her waiting for granted and even to feel that waiting was no longer difficult for her.

Long ago, in the Krasnaya Presnya transit prison, when he was allowed to send his first letter after six months under interrogation, Gleb had written with a fragment of pencil lead on a scrap of crumpled wrapping paper, folded it into a cocked-hat shape, and mailed it without a stamp.

"My dearest! You waited for me through four years of war. Don't curse me, but it was all in vain. It's going to be another ten years. As long as I live, I could no more forget our brief time of happiness than I could forget the sun. But I want you to be free, from this day on. There is no need for your life also to be ruined. You must marry someone else."

But Nadya took this letter to mean just one thing: that "you no longer love me; if you did you would not give me up to anybody else."

In the army he had sent for her, and she had come all the way to the western front to join him, traveling with a forged army pass and bluffing her way through field checkpoints. What had been a bridgehead was by then a quiet, grass-grown spot out of the firing line, and there they snatched a few short days of stolen happiness. But when the opposed armies woke up again and went over to the offensive, Nadya had to go home, wearing the same ill-fitting soldier's tunic and carrying the same forged pass. A heavy truck carried her off along a forest track, waving to her husband until she was out of sight.

Disorderly lines thronged the bus stops. When a trolley bus came along, some people stayed in line, others elbowed their way to the front. At the turn into the Sadovaya ring road, the enticingly half-empty blue bus pulled up at a red light, just beyond an ordinary bus stop. One crazed Muscovite raced toward it, jumped onto the step, and banged on the door shouting, "Is this one going to the Kotelnicheskaya Embankment? Kotelnicheskaya?"

A guard yelled at him and waved him away.

"Yes, it is," Ivan the glassblower shouted, and burst out laughing. "Get in, pal, and we'll give you a lift." Ivan was a "nonpolitical" and so was allowed a monthly visit as a matter of course.

The other zeks all laughed with him. The Muscovite could not understand what sort of bus it was and why he wasn't allowed to board it. Still, he was used to the idea that many things in this life are not allowed, and he jumped off the step. Five other would-be passengers who had joined in the chase also gave up.

The blue bus turned left along the ring road. Which meant that they were not going to the Butyrki Prison, as usual. Obviously it would be the Taganka.

As he went westward with the advancing army, Nerzhin had picked up books in ruined houses, in the wreckage of public libraries, in sheds and cellars and attics, books that were banned, anathematized, and burned on sight in the Soviet Union. As you read those moldering pages, a mute, irrepressible tocsin sounded in your mind.

It was like in Hugo's '93. Lantenac is sitting on the dunes. He can see several belfries at once. There is commotion; all the bells are tolling the alarm, but a gale-force wind carries the sound away, and all he hears is . . . silence.

From his boyhood on, Nerzhin's inner ear had heard that muffled tocsin—the alarm bells, the groans, the calls for help, the shrieks of those who were perishing—all of them carried away from the ears of others by a relentless wind.

Nerzhin would have lived an untroubled life, devoted to the numerical integration of differential equations, if he had not been born in Russia and just when some murdered Great One's precious body had been consigned to the Beyond.

But the place where it had lain was still warm, and Nerzhin shouldered a burden which no one had laid on him: From those lingering particles he would resurrect the dead, show him to all as he really was, and dissuade them from seeing him as he was not.

Gleb had grown up without reading a single book by Maine Read, but at the age of twelve he had unfolded *Izvestia*, whose enormous pages could hide him from head to foot, and read carefully the stenographic report of the trial of the "engineer-saboteurs." The boy immediately disbelieved it all. He could not have said why. But if the reason eluded his conscious mind, he saw clearly that it was all lies, lies, and more lies. There were engineers in families he knew, and he could not imagine those people wrecking instead of building.

At thirteen or so, Gleb no longer went down to the street after finishing his homework. Instead, he sat reading the newspapers. He knew all the Soviet ambassadors in foreign countries, and all foreign ambassadors in the Soviet Union, by name. He read all the speeches made at congresses. Then at school they began expounding the rudiments of political economy in the fourth grade, and from the fifth grade on there was civics practically every day, plus a little Feuerbach. Then came Party history, in textbooks revised from year to year.

Gleb's antipathy to the falsification of history showed itself early and became acute while he was still a boy. He was still only in the ninth grade when one December morning he squeezed through to a newsstand and read that Kirov* had been assassinated. It was at once blindingly obvious to him that only Stalin

*Kirov: Sergei Kirov, an influential Bolshevik leader, was murdered in 1934. Rumors have persisted that Stalin masterminded the assassination.

could be Kirov's murderer. And he shuddered to think that he was alone in a crowd of grown men who could not understand such a simple thing.

Then the Old Bolsheviks themselves were put on trial, heaped on themselves the foulest abuse imaginable, and confessed to having worked for every foreign intelligence service under the sun. This was all so extravagant, so crude, so conspicuously over the top that it cried out to be disbelieved.

But the news anchor's histrionic voice boomed out from loudspeakers, and Gleb's fellow citizens huddled together on the pavement like trusting sheep.

Russian writers who dared claim descent from Pushkin and Tolstoy were sickeningly fulsome in their paeans to the tyrant. And Russian composers, trained in the street named after Herzen, fell over one another in the rush to lay sycophantic choral offerings at the foot of the throne.

While Gleb, throughout his youth, heard the mute clangor of the alarm bell! And an ineradicable resolve took root in him: to learn and to understand, to dig up the truth and exhibit it to others!

When Gleb went out for the evening onto the boulevards of his hometown, it was not to hanker after girls, which would have been more fitting at his age, but to dream of someday penetrating the Biggest, the Most Important Prison in the land—and there finding the traces of those who had died, and the key to the riddle.

A provincial, he did not yet know that this prison was called the Great Lubyanka.

And that if we want something badly enough, our wish will certainly be granted.

The years went by. All Gleb Nerzhin's expectations had been realized, though this had not made life easy or pleasant for him. He had been seized and carried to that very place, and he had met the survivors, people who were not a bit surprised by his conjectures but had a hundred times more to tell him.

Everything was indeed realized, but beyond this Nerzhin had nothing—neither scholarship, nor a life, nor even love for his wife. He felt that there was no better wife for him in all the world, yet he could hardly claim to love her. When one great passion fills the soul, it ruthlessly displaces all others.

The bus rattled over a bridge and wound its way through unlovely backstreets.

Nerzhin came to. "So it isn't the Taganka either? Where are we going then? I don't get it."

Gerasimovich, interrupting a train of thought no more cheerful, answered him. "We're approaching Lefortovo."

The gates opened to admit the bus. It drove into a service yard and pulled up in front of an annex to the tall prison building. Lieutenant Colonel Klimentiev was already at the door, a dashing figure without overcoat or cap.

It was not really very cold. Under the blanketing cloud the wintry gloom was windless.

At a sign from the lieutenant colonel, the guards alighted and lined up outside the bus, except for the two in the rear corner seats who stayed there with their hands on the revolvers in their pockets. Before they had time to take a look at the main prison block, the prisoners were trooping after the lieutenant colonel across the yard and into the annex.

There they found themselves in a long, narrow corridor, along which seven doors stood ajar. The lieutenant colonel walked ahead, issuing crisp orders, as though directing a battle. "Gerasimovich, over here! Lukashenko, you're in that one! Nerzhin, third door!"

Klimentiev next assigned a guard to each prisoner. Nerzhin got the gangster in disguise.

These little rooms were interrogation booths: bars at the window, which would have let in little enough light without them, the interrogator's armchair and desk under the window, a little table and a stool for the prisoner under interrogation.

Nerzhin moved the interrogator's chair nearer to the door for his wife and took the uncomfortable little stool, which had a crack in the seat that threatened to pinch him. He had once spent six months under interrogation, sitting on just such a stool at just such a wretched little table.

The door remained open. Nerzhin heard his wife's heels tap-tapping along the corridor, heard her dear voice: "Is this the one?"

She came into the room.

# 38

## Be Unfaithful to Me!

A BATTERED TRUCK BOUNCED over the bared roots of pine trees and snarled its way through the sand drifts, carrying Nadya home from the battle zone. Gleb watched the forest track grow longer, darker, narrower behind the truck and swallow it. Who could have told them that the end of the war would be not the end but the beginning of their separation?

Waiting for a husband to come home from the war is always hard, and hardest of all in its last few months: Shrapnel and stray bullets do not ask how much fighting a man has seen.

That was when Gleb stopped writing.

Nadya would run out to look for the mailman. She wrote to her husband, wrote to her friends, wrote to his commanding officers. There seemed to be a conspiracy of silence.

But she received no notification of burial.

In the spring of '45, triumphant salvos every evening hailed the capture of city after city: Königsberg, Breslau, Frankfurt, Berlin, Prague.

But no letter came. The world grew dark. She had no wish to do anything. But she could not let herself go. If he was alive and if he came back, he would reproach her for wasting her time. So she spent her days working for a higher degree in chemistry, studying foreign languages and dialectical materialism, and wept only at night.

Suddenly the Ministry of Defense stopped paying her allowance as an officer's wife.

That could only mean that he had been killed.

The four-year war ended immediately afterward! People crazed with joy ran through the delirious streets. Pistols were fired into the air. Every loudspeaker in the Soviet Union blared out victory marches over the battle-scarred and famished country.

Nadya was notified not that he was dead but that he was missing. Ever eager to arrest people, the state had always shied away from admitting it.

The human heart does not easily reconcile itself to the irremediable, and Nadya found herself indulging in comforting fantasies. Perhaps he had been sent to reconnoiter deep in enemy terrain? Could he be carrying out some "special mission"? A generation brought up to be suspicious and secretive could imagine mysteries where there were none.

There was a heat wave in southern Russia that summer, but the sun did not shine on the young widow. Still, she went on studying chemistry, languages, and dialectical materialism (*diamat*), for fear of disappointing him when he returned.

Four months after the war ended, it was surely time for her to accept that Gleb was no longer living. But that was when the crumpled triangle of paper arrived from Krasnaya Presnya: "My only love! It's going to be another ten years!"

Her family and friends could not understand her; she learns that her husband is in jail, and all at once she's bright and cheerful! How lucky that it wasn't twenty-five years, or even fifteen! It is only from the grave that people never return; from prison they do! There was even something romantic about their plight; a commonplace student marriage had become something noble, something sublime.

Nadya no longer needed to fear that he was dead or that his feelings had treacherously changed, and she felt a new uprush of strength. He was in Moscow, so she must go to Moscow to save him! (Her presence at his side would be enough to save him, or so she thought.)

But how could she get there? Posterity will never be able to imagine how difficult travel, and especially traveling to Moscow, was in those days. As in the thirties, a citizen had to produce documentary proof that official duties compelled him to become a burden on public transportation rather than sitting quietly at home. If he succeeded, he was given a docket entitling him to hang about in lines at railway stations, sleeping right there on a spittle-splashed floor, or else to slip someone a timid bribe at the back door of the booking office.

Nadya's excuse was that she intended to study for a higher degree in Moscow. She bought a ticket at three times face value and hurried to Moscow with a briefcase full of textbooks on her lap, together with a pair of felt boots for a husband whom the taiga awaited.

It was one of those supreme moments in life when good powers help us and we succeed in all we undertake. The country's finest graduate school accepted an unknown provincial girl with no money, or connections, or even a telephone number to her name. It was a miracle, but getting to see her husband in Krasnaya Presnya transit prison proved harder! No visits were allowed while the channels of the Gulag were choked by the incredible spate of prisoners from Europe.

But as she was standing by the timbered guardhouse, waiting for an answer to yet another futile application, Nadya saw a column of prisoners marched through the unpainted wooden gates of the prison to work on the docks of the Moscow River. One of those flashes of insight that prove so often accurate told Nadya that Gleb was among them.

Two hundred men were marched out. They were all at that transitional stage when a man is gradually shedding his "free" clothing and assuming the slovenly dark gray costume of the zek. Every one of them still had about him some memento of his past: a soldier's peaked cap with a colored band but without strap or star, or else calfskin boots not yet traded for bread or appropriated by the professional criminals, a silk shirt split down the back. . . . They were all close-cropped (some of them tried to shield their heads from the summer sun), all unshaved, all thin, some to the point of emaciation.

Nadya had no eyes for the rest of them. She sensed where Gleb was and spotted him immediately; he was walking along in his worsted tunic. Its collar was unbuttoned, the red piping was still there on his cuffs, and an unfaded strip on his chest showed where his medal ribbons had once been. He kept his hands behind his back, as they all did. He did not look, as they went downhill, at the sunlit spaces that you would expect to attract a prisoner, nor sideways at the women with parcels (no letters reached prisoners in transit, and he could not know that Nadya was in Moscow). He was just as yellow, just as emaciated as his comrades, but he was beaming as he listened with delighted approval to the dignified gray-bearded old man beside him.

Nadya ran alongside and called his name, but he could not hear her above the buzz of conversation and the frantic barking of the guard dogs. She ran on, gasping for breath, greedily drinking in the sight of him. How sorry she felt for him, rotting away month after month in dark, stinking cells! What happiness it was to see him, so near to her! How proud she was that his spirit was not broken! And how vexed that he was evidently not grieving, that he had forgotten his wife! And suddenly her pain was all for herself, as though he had robbed her of happiness, as though she, not he, were the victim!

But it was all over in a moment. A guard yelled at her, the dogs, red-eyed man-eaters, trained to terrify, strained at their leashes, barking and glaring. Nadya was driven away. The column filed down a narrow slope, and there was no room to squeeze in alongside. The last of the guards hung back to seal off the forbidden area, and Nadya, following behind, had no hope of overtaking the column, which disappeared from sight behind another blank fence.

In the evening and at night, when the inhabitants of Krasnaya Presnya, a district of Moscow famous for its fight for freedom, could not see them, special trains made up of cattle trucks pulled in at the transit prison; parties of convoy guards with unsteady lamps, raucously barking dogs, peremptory shouts, curses, and blows loaded prisoners forty to a truck and shipped them by the thousand to Pechora, Inta, Vorkuta, Sov-Gavan, Norilsk, to the camps of Irkutsk, Chita, Krasnoyarsk, Novosibirsk, Central Asia, Karaganda, Dzhezkazgan, Pribalkhash, the Irtysh, Tobolsk, the Urals, Saratov, Vyatka, Vologda, Perm, Solvychegodsk, Rybinsk, Potma, Sukhobezvodninsk, and many nameless smaller camps. Groups of a hundred or two were carried off by day in the backs of trucks to Serebryanny Bor, to Novy Yerusalim, to Pavshino, to Khovrino, to Beskudnikovo, to Khimki, to Dmitrov, to Solnechnogorsk, or by night to various places in Moscow itself, so that, hidden from view by blank billboards and safe behind barbed-wire entanglements, they could build a capital befitting an invincible great power.

Fate sent Nadya an unexpected but well-deserved reward: As luck would have it, Gleb was not packed off to the Arctic Circle but dumped in Moscow itself, in an elegant prison camp engaged in building accommodations for the senior staff of the Ministries of State Security and the Interior, a crescent-shaped building at the Kaluga Gate.

When Nadya hurried there to visit him for the first time, she felt as though he were halfway to freedom already.

Elegant cars, some with diplomatic license plates, drove up and down Great Kaluzhskaya Street. Buses and trolleys stopped where the railings around Neskuchny Park ended, and there was the guardhouse, looking like the shack at the entrance to any ordinary building site. The people swarming high up on the face of the new building wore torn and dirty clothes, but builders always look like that, and passersby never guessed that these were prisoners. Or if they did, they kept quiet about it.

Those were the days of cheap money and expensive bread. Things were sold at home, and Nadya handed in parcels for her husband. The parcels were always accepted, but permission to see him was rarely granted. Gleb was not fulfilling his quota of work. When she did see him, she hardly recognized him. Adversity always changes arrogant people for the better. Gleb was gentler; he kissed his wife's hands; he watched the changing light in her eyes. He felt as though he were no longer in prison. Camp life, which surpasses in savagery all that we know about the lives of cannibals or rats, had almost broken him. But he had by conscious effort risen above self-pity, and now he struggled to make her see reason.

"My dearest! You don't know what you are letting yourself in for. You will wait for a year, maybe three years, five years even; but the nearer the end, the harder waiting will become. The last few years will be the hardest. We have no children, so don't ruin your young life; give me up; marry somebody else!"

He did not altogether mean what he was saying, but he had to make the offer. And she protested without really meaning what she was saying: "Are you looking for an excuse to get rid of me?"

The prisoners lived in an unfinished wing of the house they were building. The women who brought them parcels could look over the fence as they got off the trolleys and see the faces of men crowding around two or three windows. Sometimes they could see "love-girls" among them. One "love-girl" standing at the window embraced her camp "husband" and shouted over the fence at his lawful wife: "Why don't you stop chasing him, you slut! Hand the parcel over, make it the last, and get lost! If I see you at the guardhouse again, I'll scratch your ugly mug to bits!"

The first postwar elections to the Supreme Soviet were approaching. Moscow prepared for them zealously, as if it were really possible for a voter to abstain or a candidate to fail. The authorities wanted to keep the "politicals" in Moscow (they were good workers) but had qualms; vigilance could be blunted. To give the rest a scare, some of them must be sent away. Alarming rumors of imminent transfer to the Far North went round the Moscow camps. Prisoners who had potatoes baked them to eat on the journey.

So that nothing could dampen the enthusiasm of the electorate, visits to prisoners in Moscow camps were prohibited pending the elections. Nadya took along a towel for Gleb with a note stitched onto it:

"My beloved! However many years go by, whatever storms may gather over our heads" (Nadya affected a high-flown style), "your little girl will be true to you as long as she lives. They say that your category is to be sent out of Moscow. You will be in distant places, cut off from any chance of a visit or even an exchange of stolen glances across the wires. If in that life of unrelieved gloom any distraction can lighten the burden on your heart, I shall resign myself. I authorize you, indeed I insist on it—be unfaithful to me; take up with other women. Do whatever you must to keep your spirits up! I am not afraid. I know that, whatever happens, you will come back to me, won't you?"

# 39

## Fine Words, Those, "To the Taiga!"

NINE-TENTHS OF THE CITY was still strange to her, but Nadya had mastered the geography lesson that so many Russian women have learned to their sorrow, the location of Moscow's prisons. They were, she found, numerous, and thoughtfully dotted about the capital at regular intervals, so that you need never be very far from one. Delivering parcels for Gleb, inquiring after him, visiting him, she had learned to distinguish the Big Lubyanka, which catered to the whole Soviet Union, from the Little Lubyanka, which served only the Moscow oblast. She learned, too, that every station had its detention cells; she had been in Butyrki and Taganka Prisons a time or two and knew which trams to take (the timetables were no help) for Lefortovo and Krasnaya Presnya. She herself lived hard by Matrusskaya Tishina, a prison abolished at the time of the Revolution, but reestablished and reinforced later on.

Since Gleb had been sent back from a distant prison camp to Moscow, and not to a camp this time but to a remarkable institution called a "special prison," where they were well fed and employed on scientific research, Nadya had started seeing her husband again from time to time. But wives were not supposed to know where exactly their husbands were kept—so husbands were brought in for these rare meetings to one or another of the Moscow prisons.

Visits to the Taganka were the cheeriest. This was a prison for common criminals, not political prisoners, and the regimen there was easygoing. Prisoners and visitors met in the guards' club. Prisoners were brought along the deserted Street of the Masons in an open bus, wives would be waiting for them on the pavement, and before the visit officially began, a man could embrace his wife, remain with her, tell her things not allowed by the rules, and even pass things to her. Arrangements during the visit were just as casual.

Husbands and wives sat side by side; there was only one pair of guard's ears for every four couples.

Butyrki was another cheerful, easygoing prison. It struck a chill into the wives, but prisoners who ended up there after the Lubyanka were delighted by the general laxity. The light in the "boxes" was not blinding; you could walk along hallways without keeping your hands behind your back, talk in a normal voice in your cell, look out under the "muzzles" on windows, lie on the plank bed in the daytime, or even sleep underneath it. Butyrki was soft in other ways, too; you could sleep with your hands under your overcoat, your glasses were not taken away for the night, matches were allowed in cells, they didn't gut every cigarette of its tobacco, and loaves sent in by your family were only cut in four, not into little pieces.

But wives knew nothing of these indulgences. They saw a fortress wall four times the height of a man, stretching a whole block along Novoslobodskaya Street. They saw iron gates between mighty concrete pillars, and no ordinary gates at that, opening automatically in a slow yawn to admit prison trucks and automatically closing behind them. Women visitors passed on admission through an opening in a stone wall two meters thick and were conducted around the grim Pugachev Tower between walls several times a man's height. Ordinary zeks saw their visitors through two sets of bars, with a guard pacing between them as though he himself were caged, while zeks of the higher category, "sharashka" people, and their visitors faced each other across a wide table with a solid partition underneath it so that feet could not touch and exchange signals, and with a guard standing like an unblinking effigy at the side of the table, listening to the conversation. But the most oppressive feature of Butyrki was that husbands seemed to materialize from the depths of the jail, exhaled by those thick, damp walls for half an hour to reassure their wives, like smiling ghosts, that they were comfortable and wanted for nothing, and then melting into those walls again.

This was the first time Nadya had visited Gleb in Lefortovo.

The senior guard checked off her name on his list and pointed toward an annex.

Several women were waiting already in a bare room with two long benches and a bare table. A wicker basket and shopping bags, evidently full of eatables, stood on the table. Although prisoners in the sharashka were adequately fed, Nadya, who had brought only some light pastry straws in a paper bag, felt resentful and ashamed that she couldn't treat her husband to something tasty even once a year. She had gotten up early, while the others in the dormitory were still asleep, to make these straws with all that was left of her flour, sugar, and butter rations. She hadn't had time to buy sweets or cakes and anyway had very little money until she could draw her grant. Visiting day coincided with her husband's birthday, and she had nothing to give him! A good book? She couldn't even do that after her last visit. She had brought him a little volume of Yesenin's poems, gotten hold of by a miracle. He had had an identical copy at the front, and it had disappeared when he was arrested. Alluding to this, Nadya had written on the title page, "So shall all else that you have lost return to you." But Lieutenant Colonel Klimentiev had ripped the inscribed page out in her presence and returned it to her, remarking that nothing in writing could be passed to prisoners; "texts" must go through the censor separately. When Gleb heard this, he ground his teeth and asked her not to bring any more books.

Four women sat around the table, one a young woman with a three-year-old girl. Nadya didn't know any of them. They acknowledged her greeting and continued their animated conversation. A woman of thirty-five or forty, in a fur coat that was far from new and a threadbare headscarf, sat on a short bench against the opposite wall with her legs crossed and arms folded. Her whole pose expressed her determination to avoid all contact and conversation. There was nothing resembling a parcel anywhere near her.

The company at the table would have made room for Nadya, but she did not feel like joining them. She, too, wanted to be alone with her thoughts that morning. She went over to the woman sitting by herself and said, "Do you mind?" There was barely room for two on the bench.

The woman raised her eyes. They were quite colorless. They showed no understanding of Nadya's question. They looked at Nadya and beyond her.

Nadya sat down, tucked her hands into her sleeves, inclined her head to one side so that her cheek sank into her imitation astrakhan collar, and sat as still as her neighbor. At that moment she didn't want to think about anything except Gleb, the conversation they would shortly be having, and something extending from the dim past into the invisible future, something that was not Gleb or Nadya but the two of them together, something usually called by the hackneyed word "love."

But she was unable to shut out the talk around the table. They were telling each other what their husbands were given to eat morning and evening, how often underwear was washed in prison. . . . How did they know? Surely they didn't waste the precious minutes of a visit on such things? They enumerated the foodstuffs they had brought—so many grams of this, so many kilos of that. All this was an example of that stubborn womanly solicitude that makes a family a family and keeps the human race going. But Nadya's thought was different—that it was an insult to reduce what should be great moments to the humdrum, the miserable small change of everyday. Did it never occur to these women to ask themselves who had dared to imprison their husbands? After all, their husbands need never have been behind bars, need never have been forced to eat prison food!

It was a long wait. They had been told to come at ten, but eleven o'clock came, and still no one had appeared.

A seventh visitor, a woman with gray hair, arrived late and out of breath. Nadya knew her from a previous visit; she was the engraver's wife, his third and also his first. She was very ready to tell her story; she had always adored her husband and thought him very talented. But one day he announced that he disliked her psychological profile, abandoned her and their child, and went off with another woman. He lived three years with this other, the redhead; then he was called up. He was taken prisoner almost immediately, but he had lived in Germany as a free man and, alas, had affairs there, too. On his way back home he was arrested at the frontier and sentenced to ten years. He let the redhead know that he was in Butyrki and asked her to send food parcels, but she had said, "If he'd betrayed me and not his motherland, I would find it easier to forgive him!" After that, he had pleaded with his first wife; she had started visiting and sending parcels, and now he kept begging her forgiveness and swearing eternal love.

A bitter remark made by the engraver's wife had echoed in Nadya's mind: "I dare say the best thing for us to do is to be unfaithful to our husbands while they're in jail; then they'll appreciate us when they come out. Otherwise they'll think nobody wanted us, nobody would have us while they were away." This had stayed with Nadya because she sometimes thought the same herself.

On this occasion, too, the new arrival gave a fresh twist to the conversation around the table. She started talking about the trouble she had had with the lawyers on Nikolskaya Street. They had long styled themselves the "Model" legal-aid bureau. But lawyers belonging to it charged thousands, spent a lot of time in Moscow restaurants, and left their clients' affairs to look after themselves. The day came when they got on the wrong side of somebody or other, were arrested, and were given ten years all around. The "Model" sign was taken down, but the bureau, though no longer "model," was replenished with new legal advisers, who, just like their predecessors, charged thousands and left their clients' affairs to look after themselves. They explained in confidence that big fees were necessary because they had to share them. They were charging not just for themselves; the business had to pass through many hands. The concrete wall of the law was like that of Butyrki, four times a man's height. Women could not take wing and flutter over it; they could only walk around it, humbly pleading with some little gate to open. The course of legal proceedings behind the wall of the law was like the mysterious workings of an awesome machine, which—though the guilt of the accused was evident, though the accused was pitted against the government—might at times miraculously spit out a winning lottery ticket. The women paid lawyers not for a win but for their dream of winning.

The engraver's wife believed implicitly that she would win in the end. It emerged from what she said that she had amassed forty thousand rubles by selling her room and from contributions made by relatives, and had used it to overpay four lawyers in succession; three petitions for clemency had been lodged, and five appeals on the substance of the case. She had followed the progress of all these appeals closely and had been given many assurances of a favorable review. She knew by name all the regular attorneys in the three main offices of the Public Prosecutor's Department and was acclimatized to the waiting rooms of the Supreme Court and the Supreme Soviet. As trustful people, and especially women, will, she attached exaggerated importance to every encouraging remark and every look that was not actually hostile.

"You have to write! Write to anybody and everybody!" she insisted, urging other women to dash off down the same path. "Our husbands are suffering. They won't be freed without an effort. You must write!"

This talk took Nadya out of herself but also touched a sore spot. The engraver's aging wife spoke with such passion that it was easy to believe her: She had stolen a march on them all, been cleverer than any of them; she would undoubtedly get her husband out of prison! Nadya began to reproach herself: What about me? Why couldn't I have done the same? Why haven't I been as loyal a wife?

She had only once had dealings with a "model" legal-aid office, drawn up only one appeal with a lawyer's help, and paid him only 2,500, which was probably too little. He had no doubt taken offense and done nothing.

"That's right," she said quietly, almost to herself. "Have we done all we can? Are our consciences clear?"

Those at the table did not hear her above the general conversation. But her neighbor looked around sharply, as though Nadya had elbowed her or insulted her.

"What can we do?" she said angrily, emphasizing every word. "That's all moonshine! Article 58 means—detain indefinitely! Article 58 means—you're not just a criminal; you're the enemy! You can't buy your way out of Article 58 for a million!"

The lines in her face were deeper. Her voice had the ring of incurable suffering.

Nadya's heart went out to the older woman. The tone of her voice seemed to apologize for what might sound like a pretentious reply.

"What I meant was that we do not sacrifice ourselves completely. The wives of the Decembrists spared themselves nothing; they gave up everything to follow their husbands. . . . If we can't hope to free them, perhaps we can get their sentences commuted to banishment? If he was sent to the very depths of the taiga, beyond the Arctic Circle, I would be content to follow him; I would give up everything. . . ."

The woman with the austere face of a nun under her shabby gray headscarf looked at Nadya with surprise and respect.

"You still feel strong enough to go to the taiga? How fortunate you are! I no longer have the strength for anything. The way I feel, if some well-off old man would have me, I would marry him. . . ."

"Could you abandon your husband? While he was behind bars?"

The woman took Nadya by the sleeve.

"My dear girl! Love was easy in the nineteenth century! Did any one of the Decembrists' wives really perform such a heroic feat? Did she have 'personnel departments' challenging her to answer questionnaires? Did she have to conceal her marriage like a plague sore or risk being sacked and deprived of the five hundred rubles a month which was her sole income? Was she ostracized in a communal apartment? Hissed at as an enemy of the people when she went to the pump in the yard? Did her own mother and sisters urge her to be sensible and divorce her husband? On the contrary! Wherever they went the Decembrist wives were accompanied by the admiring murmurs of the best people. Their heroic legend was a gift they graciously bestowed on poets. When they set off for Siberia in their own expensive carriages, they did not lose their Moscow residence permits, and with them the nine square meters of living space that was all that was left to them, nor did they have to worry about trivial problems ahead, like a black mark in a labor book, living in something the size of a cupboard, having no saucepan, not even a crust of black bread! Fine words, those, 'to the taiga!' Anyway, you may not have all that long to wait!"

Her voice seemed about to break. Her passionate eloquence brought tears into Nadya's eyes. She tried to excuse herself.

"My husband's been in prison nearly five years," she said. "And before that he was at the front. . . ."

"That doesn't count!" the woman retorted. "Being at the front isn't the same thing! Waiting is easy then! Everybody else is waiting, too. You can talk about it openly; you can read his letters to people. But when you have to wait and keep quiet about him, that's something else."

She said no more. She could see that Nadya didn't need to be told about it.

By now it was 11:30. Lieutenant Colonel Klimentiev came in at last, accompanied by the sour, fat sergeant major. The sergeant major began checking parcels, opening packages of factory biscuits, and breaking homemade cakes in two. He even broke Nadya's pastry straws, looking for the note, the money, or the poison that might have been baked inside them. Klimentiev meanwhile collected all the permits, entered the visitors' names in a big book, then drew himself up as though on parade and made an announcement in his precise way.

"Attention please! You know the rules? The visit lasts thirty minutes. Nothing must be passed directly to prisoners. Nothing must be accepted from prisoners. It is forbidden to question prisoners about their work, their living conditions, and their daily routine. Any infringement of these rules is punishable as a criminal offense. Furthermore, shaking hands and kissing are forbidden as of today. If this rule is broken, the visit is terminated immediately."

The women remained silent.

Klimentiev called the first name: "Gerasimovich, Natalia Pavlovna!"

Nadya's neighbor rose and went out into the hallway, walking clumsily in her prewar felt boots.

# 40

## A Rendezvous

THERE HAD BEEN TEARS while she was waiting, but Nadya went in to meet him joyfully.

When she appeared in the doorway, Gleb was already on his feet and smiling a greeting. His smile lasted while he took one step toward her and she one step toward him, but it filled her with exultant happiness; she saw that he was as close to her as ever! He had not changed toward her!

The bull-necked ex-gangster in the soft gray suit approached the little table and barred the way across the little room, preventing them from coming together.

"Let me at least touch her hand!" Nerzhin said indignantly.

"It's not allowed." The guard lowered his heavy jaw a fraction of an inch to emit the words.

Nadya's smile did not hide her dismay, but she signaled to her husband not to argue. She sank onto the chair placed ready for her. The stuffing was escaping from the leather upholstery in places. Generations of interrogators, who had sent hundreds of people to their graves and shortly followed them, had taken their turns on that chair.

"Happy birthday," said Nadya, trying to look cheerful.

"Thank you."

"What a coincidence. Us meeting today."

"Must be my lucky day."

Talking was proving difficult.

Nadya made an effort not to feel the guard's eyes upon her and his oppressive presence. Gleb was trying to sit so that the rickety stool would not cause him pain.

A small table across which prisoners faced their interrogators stood between husband and wife.

"In case I forget. I've brought you a bite to eat. Some of those straws like mother makes, remember? I'm sorry that's all it is."

"Silly girl, you shouldn't have bothered! We get everything we need."

"I don't suppose you get pastry straws? And you told me not to bring books. . . . Do you read your Yesenin?"

Nerzhin's face clouded over. It was more than a month since somebody had informed on him, and Shikin had taken the book away, saying that Yesenin was forbidden.

"Yes, I do."

(They had only half an hour; he really couldn't go into details.)

The room wasn't at all hot; in fact, it seemed to be unheated. But Nadya unbuttoned her collar and turned it down; she wanted her husband to see not only her new coat, made that year, which for some reason he hadn't mentioned, but her new blouse, too, and she thought that the blouse might lend a little color to her face, which must look sallow in that dim light.

With a single glance Gleb took in her face, her throat, her open-necked blouse. That look was the most important moment of the visit, and Nadya stirred as though offering herself to it eagerly.

"You've got a new blouse. Let's see a bit more of it."

She looked a little hurt. "What about the coat?"

"What about it?"

"The coat's new, too."

Gleb caught on at last.

"So it is. You've got a new coat." He ran his eyes over the black curls, not knowing that it was astrakhan, let alone whether it was real or artificial. No man on earth was less capable of distinguishing a five-hundred-ruble coat from one worth five thousand.

She threw the coat open, and he saw her neck, as smooth and girlish as ever, her weak slender shoulders, and, under the gathers of her blouse, her breasts, which had sagged miserably in all those years.

Mentally he reproached her for living a life in which new finery and new friends were a matter of course, but when he saw her pathetically sunken bosom, this fleeting thought gave way to pity. Her life, like his, had been crushed beneath the wheels of the gray prison truck.

"You're a bit thin," he said compassionately. "You must eat more. Can't you eat better?"

Am I so ugly then? her eyes asked.

You're as wonderful as ever, her husband's eyes answered.

(Although the lieutenant colonel had not prohibited these words, it was impossible to say them with a third person present.)

"I eat a lot," she said untruthfully, "but I'm always in a rush, and I've got a lot to worry about."

"Tell me about it."

"No, you first."

"Never mind me," Gleb said, smiling. "I'm all right."

"Well, then. . . ." She was embarrassed.

The guard was standing half a meter from the table, a solid bulldog of a man, staring down at husband and wife as fixedly and contemptuously as stone lions at the doors of great houses look upon passersby.

They had to find a safe tone, a language of eloquent hints that this man, obviously intellectually inferior, would not understand.

She changed the subject abruptly.

"Is that your own suit?"

"Mine? It's like a Potemkin village. Strictly temporary. For three hours only. Don't let the Sphinx put you off."

"I can't help it," she said plaintively, pouting like a little girl, sure now that her husband still found her attractive.

"We're used to seeing the funny side of it."

"Yes, but we aren't," Nadya said with a sigh, remembering her conversation with Gerasimovich's wife. Nerzhin tried to trap his wife's knees between his own, but even this contact was hindered by an awkward crossbar attached to the table at just the right height to prevent a prisoner under investigation from stretching his legs. The table wobbled. Supporting himself on his elbows and leaning closer to his wife, Gleb said with annoyance: "That's how it is—obstacles everywhere."

His look said, Are you mine? Truly mine?

Her gray eyes shone, telling him, I'm still the girl you loved. I'm just as I was. Please believe me!

"What about obstacles at work? Tell me about it. You say you aren't registered as a graduate student anymore?"

"No."

"Has your thesis been examined?"

"No again."

"Why ever not?"

"I'll tell you."

She began speaking very rapidly, afraid that they might not have much time left.

"Nobody presents a thesis in three years. They're given extensions. One girl spent two years writing a thesis on 'Problems of Public Catering'; then they made her change her subject."

(Why tell him this? It was of no importance at all.)

"My thesis is finished and typed, but I'm held up by the need to rework a few passages. . . ."

(Held up by the "struggle against subservience to the bourgeois West," but this wasn't the place to go into that!)

". . . and then there are photocopies to be made. And I don't know what to do about the binding. I've got plenty to worry about."

"But do they pay your grant?"

"No."

"So what are you living on?"

"My wages."

"Oh, you're working. Where?"

"Right there in the university."

"What sort of job?"

"It's just temporary. I'm an invisible helper, if you know what I mean. In general, I live from hand to mouth really. It's the same with the dormitory. I shouldn't really. . . ."

She glanced at the guard. She was going to say that the police should long ago have canceled her permit to live at Stromynka Street but quite by mistake had extended it for six months. She might be found out any day! All the more reason not to talk about it in the presence of an MGB sergeant.

"I only got this visit today because . . . it just so happened that. . . ." (Oh dear, half an hour wasn't long enough!)

"Wait a bit, you can tell me that later. What I wanted to ask was, are there any obstacles because of me?"

"Very serious ones, my dear. . . . They're giving me. . . . They want to give me a special topic. I'm doing my best to avoid it."

"What do you mean, a special topic?"

She sighed and glanced at the guard. His face, like that of a guard dog ready to bark or bite her head off at any moment, was suspended less than a meter from their faces.

Nadya made a helpless gesture. She would have had to explain that even in the university there were now practically no research topics without a security classification. The whole of science was being labeled secret from top to bottom. What this meant for Nadya was a new, more detailed questionnaire about her husband, her husband's relatives, and the relatives of those relatives. If she put down "husband convicted under Article 58," they would not let her present her thesis, let alone work at the university. If she lied—"husband reported missing on active service"—she would still have to give his name; they could look it up in the card index at the Ministry of the Interior, and she would be prosecuted for giving false information. Nadya had chosen a third solution, but she was reluctant to talk about it with Gleb's watchful eyes on her, and took refuge in animated chatter.

"Listen, I'm in an amateur concert party at the university. They send me to play in concerts all the time. Not long ago I even played in the Hall of Columns on the same evening as Yakov Zak."

Gleb smiled and shook his head as though he found it hard to believe.

"Well, it was a Trade Union evening, and it just happened that way . . . but still. And do you know, it was really funny they said my best dress was no good; I couldn't go on the platform in that. So they rang the theater and got another one sent, a lovely one, down to my heels."

"And when you'd played your piece, they took it off you?"

"Well. . . . Anyway, the girls say rude things about me because I'm mad about music, but I say it's better to be mad about something than somebody."

This wasn't just idle talk. She said it loud and clear. It was a clever way of letting him know the new rules she had made for herself. She leaned forward as though she expected a pat on the head.

Nerzhin looked at his wife, gratefully and anxiously. But for the moment he couldn't find the words of praise and approval she expected.

"But what about the special topic?"

Nadya lowered her eyes and hung her head.

"I was going to tell you. . . . But you won't take it to heart—*nicht wahr?* You once insisted that we should . . . get a divorce. . . ." Her last words were very quiet.

(This was the third possibility, the only one that promised her some chance of making a life for herself: Her dossier must contain not the word "divorced," because she would still have to give her ex-husband's name, his present address, the names of his parents, and even their birth dates, occupations, and address; no, it must say "unmarried." And for this she would have to get a divorce in another town and keep it quiet.)

Yes, he had once insisted on it. . . . But now he was of two minds. Only now did he notice that the wedding ring she had never been without was not on her finger.

"Yes, of course," he said very firmly.

Nadya rubbed the table with the palm of that same ringless hand, as though she was rolling stiff dough into a flat cake.

"Well then . . . would you object . . . if I have to do it?" She raised her head. Her eyes were wide. The pinpoints of her gray pupils implored him to understand and forgive. "It would be a sham," she added, in a single, almost inaudible breath.

"Good for you! It's about time!" Gleb agreed emphatically. In his heart he was far less positive, but he was putting off any attempt to make sense of it all until the visit was over.

"I may not have to do it!" she said, still pleading with him. She pulled her coat back over her shoulders, and at that moment she looked care-worn and exhausted.

"I wanted to know whether you agree, just in case. It may not be necessary."

"No, you're right, of course, it's a good idea," Gleb said mechanically. His mind was already on the main point he had written down on his list, and which it was now time to spring on her.

"It is important for you to be clear about things, my dear. You mustn't bank on my release when my sentence is over."

He himself was fully prepared for a second sentence and an indefinite term in jail. It had already happened to many of his comrades. This was something he couldn't put in a letter, and he had to speak out now.

Nadya looked apprehensive.

"The sentence you're given is nominal," Gleb said in a quick hard voice, misplacing the stresses on words so that the guard wouldn't keep up with him. "It can escalate in a spiral. History provides a wealth of examples. And if by some miracle my sentence does come to an end, you mustn't think that we can return to our own town and our old life. You must realize, get it firmly into your head; you can't buy a ticket to the land of the past. What I most regret, for instance, is that I'm not a shoemaker. How badly needed that sort of thing is in a settlement out in the taiga, in Krasnoyarsk, say, or on the lower reaches of the Angara! That's the sort of life we ought to prepare ourselves for!"

He had achieved his end. The retired gangster did not stir. He could only blink as the sentences sped past him.

But Gleb had forgotten, or rather failed to understand (as they all did), that those who are used to walking on warm gray earth cannot be expected to scale icy mountains at short notice. He did not realize that his wife went on, as she always had, methodically, meticulously counting the days and weeks of his sentence. For him his term was a bright, cold infinity; for her there remained 264 weeks, 61 months, a little over 5 years—a much shorter time than had passed since he went to the war from which he would not return.

As Gleb went on, the fear in Nadya's face turned to ashen terror.

Her words tumbled over one another. "No, no, no! Don't tell me that, my dearest!" (She had forgotten all about the guard and her inhibitions.) "Don't take away my hope! I refuse to believe it! I mustn't believe it! It simply can't be like that! You didn't think, surely, that I would really leave you?"

Her upper lip quivered; her face was contorted; her eyes expressed nothing but devotion, endless devotion.

"I do believe you, I do, my little Nadya!" Gleb said in a different voice. "That's what I thought."

She sank back in her chair and was silent.

The sprightly, dark-haired lieutenant colonel appeared in the doorway, cast a sharp eye on the three heads so confidentially close, and quietly called the guard aside.

The bull-necked gangster moved reluctantly, as though he were being dragged away from a delicious dessert, and went over to the lieutenant colonel. They were only four steps behind Nadya's back and exchanged only a sentence or two, but Gleb had time to ask in a muffled voice: "Do you know Sologdin's wife?"

Nadya had plenty of practice and was not left behind by this sudden switch.

"Yes."

"Know where she lives?"

"Yes."

"They won't allow him a visit. Tell her he—"

The gangster was back.

"Loves! Worships! Adores!" Gleb said, in his presence, speaking very distinctly. Precisely because the gangster was there, Sologdin's words somehow did not sound too extravagant.

"Loves—worships—adores," Nadya repeated with a sad sigh. She looked closely at her husband. She had scrutinized him in the past as closely as only a woman can, though because of her youth she might have missed something;

she had thought that she knew him, but she saw now a new man, a man she did not know.

She nodded her head sadly. "It . . . suits you."

"What does?"

"You know. This place. All this. Being here," she said, slightly varying her tone of voice to disguise her meaning—"being in prison suits him!"—from the guard.

But seeing him in a new light brought him no closer. It made him more of a stranger.

She, too, was saving up what she had learned until after the visit, when she could think it over and decide what it all meant. She did not know what her conclusions would be, but her heart went ahead of her mind, and she looked now for signs of weakness, weariness, illness, a plea for help—something to make a woman sacrifice the remainder of her life, wait another ten years if need be, and go to join him in the taiga.

But he was smiling! Smiling just as complacently as he had at Krasnaya Presnya! He was always so independent; he never needed sympathy from anyone. He even seemed to be comfortable on that small, bare stool; he seemed to be looking around with some enjoyment, collecting material for his history even in this place. He looked well, and his eyes sparkled with amusement at his jailers. Did he really need a woman's loyalty?

Nadya, however, had not yet thought all this.

And Gleb did not realize what she was close to thinking.

Klimentiev was at the door.

"Time's up!"

"Already?" said Nadya in surprise.

Gleb frowned in an effort to remember the most important items left on his list of "things to tell her," learned by heart before the visit.

"Oh yes! Don't be surprised if they move me to some place a long way from here and letters stop altogether."

"Might they? Where to?" Nadya cried.

Such frightening news. And he'd kept it to himself till now!

"God knows," he said with a shrug, but as if he meant it to be taken literally.

"Don't tell me you've started believing in God?"

(They hadn't managed to talk about anything!)

Gleb smiled. "Why not? Pascal, Newton, Einstein—"

"Weren't you told not to mention names?" the guard bawled.

"Time's up now!"

Husband and wife rose together, and now that there was no danger of the visit ending prematurely, Gleb reached over the table, put his arms around Nadya's slender neck, kissed it, and pressed his mouth to her lips. He had forgotten how soft they were. He had no hope of being in Moscow in a year's time to kiss them again. His voice shook with tenderness: "Do whatever is best for yourself. I shall always. . . ."

He didn't finish.

They looked into each other's eyes.

"What do you call this, then? I'm terminating the visit!" roared the guard, tugging at Nerzhin's shoulder.

Nerzhin broke away.

"So terminate it, damn you," he muttered barely audibly.

Nadya backed toward the door, waving good-bye to her husband with the fingers of one raised hand. A hand without a ring.

Still waving, she disappeared from the doorway.

# 41

## And Another One

GERASIMOVICH AND HIS WIFE KISSED.

He was short, but his wife was no taller.

They had been lucky with their guard, a decent, easygoing young fellow who didn't in the least mind their kissing. Indeed, it embarrassed him to have to intrude on them. Had it been possible, he would have turned away and looked at the wall for half an hour. But Lieutenant Colonel Klimentiev had given orders that the doors of all seven interrogation compartments should be left open so that he could keep watch on the guards from the hallway.

Not that he himself minded these people kissing. He knew that no state secret could leak as a result. But he was wary of his own guards and prisoners. There were informers among them who might "drip" on Klimentiev himself.

Husband and wife kissed. But it was not like the kisses that had thrilled them when they were young. This kiss, in defiance of fate and authority, was a kiss without color, taste, or odor, the pale kiss a ghost might bestow in a dream.

They sat down, separated by an interrogation table with a warped plywood top.

That clumsy little table had more of a history behind it than many a human life contains. Generations of prisoners, men and women, had sat there sobbing, numb with fear, fighting against murderous sleeplessness, some still proudly defiant, some signing trivial denunciations of family and friends. They were not usually allowed to handle pencils or pens, except for the few required to make depositions in their own handwriting. Those few had contrived to leave their marks, those peculiar absentminded scribbles and scratches that mysteriously preserve the tortuous workings of the unconscious.

Looking at his wife, Gerasimovich thought how unattractive she had become. There were deep hollows under her eyes, wrinkles around her eyes and mouth; her skin was slack—Natasha had obviously stopped caring about it. Her coat was prewar and should at least have been turned long ago; its fur collar had molted; that headscarf was from time immemorial, bought, he seemed to remember, with coupons in Komsomolsk-on-Amur, long ago, and worn by Natasha in Leningrad when she went to get water from the Neva.

But Gerasimovich suppressed the base thought that his wife was ugly. The woman before him was the only woman in the world for him, half of himself. He was looking at the woman with whom all his memories were entwined. However fresh and pretty a young girl might be, she could not overshadow Natasha; her memories would be too shallow, her experience too superficial.

When they first met at a house in Srednyaya Podyacheskaya Street, by the Lion Bridge, Natasha was not yet eighteen. It was a New Year's party, 1930. Twenty-five years ago, in six days' time. Looking back, you could see clearly what 1919, and 1930, had done to Russia. But every new year, as it arrives, is seen in rosy colors. You cannot know what associations that date will acquire in the people's memory. As always, they had believed in 1930.

But that was the year when Gerasimovich was arrested for the first time. As a "wrecker."

Illarion Pavlovich had begun work just as the word "engineer" was becoming synonymous with "enemy" and when proletarian pride demanded that every engineer be suspected as a wrecker. To make it worse, the young Gerasimovich's upbringing compelled him always to bow courteously and say "Excuse me, please" in a very gentle voice, to the right people and to the wrong people. At meetings he lost his voice and sat quiet as a mouse. He had no idea how irritating people found him.

But though the case against him was concocted with great skill, it would not stretch to more than five years. When he got to the Amur, he was immediately excused from close confinement, and his sweetheart joined him and became his wife.

There were not many nights when husband and wife did not dream of Leningrad. The day came when they were due to return. But it was 1935, and they were swept back by the tidal wave of arrests after Kirov's assassination.

Natalia Pavlovna was scrutinizing her husband just as closely. She had once watched the changes in his face, the hardening of his mouth, the cold and at times fierce glint through his pince-nez. Illarion had stopped bowing, stopped constantly apologizing. His past was always held against him, he was dismissed from job after job or employed on work below his qualifications, and they had traveled from place to place, always hard up; they had lost a daughter, lost a son. In the end, in desperation, they had risked going back to Leningrad. As it happened, in June 1941. In Leningrad they had even less chance of a tolerable existence. Her husband's record dogged him everywhere. But these experiences, instead of weakening the laboratory wraith, toughened him. He survived an autumn of trench digging. When the first snow fell, he became a gravedigger. In the besieged city, no profession was more essential or more remunerative. Survivors paid their last respects to the departed by giving away their beggarly cubic centimeter of bread.

Who could eat that bread without shuddering? Illarion's justification was that "our fellow citizens showed us no pity; we'll show them none!"

The couple came through their ordeal. Only for Illarion to be arrested again, before the siege ended. This time for "intending" to betray his homeland. Many arrests were made in Leningrad for treasonable intent—people who hadn't been in occupied territory could not be accused of actual collaboration. But if someone like Gerasimovich, a former convict, had come to Leningrad at the outbreak of war, it was obviously with the intention of joining the Germans. They would have arrested his wife as well, but she was dangerously ill at the time.

Natalia Pavlovna scrutinized her husband and, strangely, found that the years of suffering had left no deep mark on him. The gaze behind his gleaming pince-nez was as intelligent and steady as ever. His cheeks were not sunken; there were no wrinkles; he was wearing an expensive suit and a carefully knotted tie.

Anyone might think that she, not he, was the jailbird.

Her first, unkind thought was that he was having a fine old time in the special prison. He was obviously not bullied; he was working in his own field; his wife's suffering meant nothing to him.

But she stifled this spiteful thought and asked in a weak voice: "How are you getting on there?"

As if she had waited twelve months for this visit, spent 360 nights thinking of her husband on her chilly widow's couch, just to ask, "How are you getting on?"

And Gerasimovich, holding tight inside his narrow, constricted breast a whole life that had cramped and stunted his mental powers, a whole world as a prisoner in the taiga and the desert, in solitary confinement in between interrogations, and now in the comfort of a special prison, answered, "All right."

They had been given only half an hour. The sands were trickling away in an unstemmable stream down the glass throat of Time. Dozens of questions, wishes, complaints, struggled to be heard first, but all Natalia Pavlovna managed to ask was:

"When did you hear about the visit?"

"The day before yesterday. And you?"

"On Tuesday. The lieutenant colonel has just asked me whether I'm your sister."

"Because of your patronymic?"

"Yes."

When they were engaged and on the Amur, everyone had taken them for brother and sister. There was between them the sort of external and internal resemblance that makes husband and wife more than just a married couple.

"How are things at work?" Illarion Pavlovich asked.

She started. "Why do you ask? Have you heard?"

"Heard what?"

He knew something but didn't know if she had the same thing in mind.

He knew that prisoners' wives were always given a hard time outside.

But how could he know that she had been dismissed from her post the previous Wednesday because of her connection with him? She had already been told that she could visit him and had not immediately started looking for a new job. She was waiting until she saw him, as though a miracle might happen and their meeting might illuminate her life and show her what to do.

But how could he give her any practical advice, when he had spent so many years in prison and was unskilled in the ways of the world outside?

What she must decide was whether or not to renounce him.

Visiting time was running out in that drab, inadequately heated room, dimly lit through a barred window, and her hope of a miracle was ebbing with it.

Natalia Pavlovna realized that she could not convey her loneliness and her suffering to her husband in that miserly half hour, that he ran on rails of his own, lived a life as regular as clockwork, and would understand nothing. It would be better not to upset him.

The guard moved away to study the plaster on the wall.

"Tell me about yourself, please tell me." Illarion Pavlovich held his wife's hand across the table, and his eyes were warm with affection for her, as they always had been in the most grueling months of the siege.

"Larik! Are you likely to get any remission?"

She had in mind the system at the camp on the Amur where they credited you with two days served for every day worked, so that your sentence ended before the appointed date.

Illarion shook his head. "How could I? They've never given remission here; you know that. Invent something important, and they may let you out ahead of time. But the thing is"—he glanced at the guard, whose eyes were elsewhere—"the thing is that the inventions here are of a very dubious kind."

He dared not put it any more clearly.

He took his wife's hands and brushed his cheek against them.

Yes, in icebound Leningrad he had not scrupled to take as a burial fee the bread ration of someone who would need burying himself the day after.

But now—he couldn't bring himself. . . .

"Is it miserable for you by yourself? Are you very miserable?" he asked tenderly, rubbing his cheek against her hand.

Miserable? Right then she was horrified; the visit was slipping away; it would soon be broken off, and she would go out to the Lefortovo Rampart none the richer for it, go out into the joyless streets alone, alone, alone. . . . The stultifying aimlessness of every day she lived, everything she did. There was neither sweet nor hot nor bitter; her life was like dingy cotton wool.

He stroked her hand.

"Natalia, my love! If you reckon up my two terms and think how long it's been already, there's not much left now. Only three years. Only three."

"Only three?" She interrupted indignantly. She felt her voice trembling, felt that she was no longer in control if it. "Only three! For you it's 'only'! For you quick release would 'entail something objectionable.' You live among friends! You're doing the work you enjoy most! You don't have to be smuggled into somebody else's room! But I've been sacked! I've got nothing to live on! Nobody will take me on! I can't go on! I no longer have the strength! I can't stand another month of it! Not a single month! I will be better off dead! The neighbors shove me around just as they like; they've thrown my clothes chest out; they've pulled my shelf off the wall; they know I dare not say a word . . . that they could get me expelled from Moscow! I've stopped going to see my sisters and Aunt Zhenya; they all jeer at me and call me the biggest fool on earth. They keep at me to divorce you and marry somebody else! When will it end? Look what I've turned into! I'm thirty-seven! In three years I will be an old woman! I go home and I don't eat, don't tidy my room. I loathe it. I just collapse on the sofa and lie there exhausted. Larik, my dear, do whatever it takes to get out earlier! You're a genius! Invent something for them, so that they'll leave you in peace. I know you've got something for them right now! Save me! Sa-a-ave me-e-e!!"

She had not meant to say all this, grief-stricken as she was! Shaking with sobs and kissing her husband's small hand, she lowered her head onto the warped and splintery table that had seen many such tears.

"Pull yourself together, Citizeness, please," the guard said guiltily, glancing at the open door.

Gerasimovich's face was frozen in a grimace beneath his gleaming pince-nez.

The unseemly noise of her sobbing could be heard in the hallway. The lieutenant colonel loomed menacingly in the doorway, looked witheringly at the woman's back, and closed the door himself.

The regulations did not specifically forbid tears. They implicitly assumed that tears could not occur.

# 42

## And Among the Kids

"THERE'S REALLY NOTHING TO IT: You dissolve some chloride of lime and brush it over your passport—hey, presto! You just have to know how many minutes to leave it—and wipe it off."

"Then what?"

"When it dries, there won't be a trace. Nice and clean, good as new, you can sit down and scribble your new name in with India ink—Sidorov, Petyushin, whatever, born village of Kriushi."

"Didn't you ever get caught?"

"Doing that? Klara Petrovna. . . . Or would you mind if . . . if I just call you Klara when nobody's listening?"

"Please do."

"Well then, Klara, they got me the first time because I was a helpless, innocent kid. But the second time—not on your life! I held out from the end of '45 to the end of '47, with the police looking for me all over the country, and you know what those years were like; I had to fake not just my passport and residence permit but a work permit, ration coupons, registration with a food shop. On top of all that, I got extra bread cards with forged documents and lived by selling them."

"But that was . . . very wrong of you!"

"Who said it was right? I was forced into it; it wasn't my idea."

"You could just have worked."

"You don't get far 'just working.' What sort of job could I do anyway? I never had a chance to learn a trade. . . . No, I didn't get caught, but I made mistakes. Once, in the Crimea, there was a girl in the passport department . . . only don't think there was anything like that between us . . . she was just sympathetic . . . and let me into a secret—the serial number on my passport, you know, all those *zhshchas* and *lkhas*—indicated to those in the know that I'd been in occupied territory."

"But you hadn't!"

"Of course I hadn't, but it was somebody else's passport! And because of that I had to buy a new one."

"Where?"

"Klara! You've lived in Tashkent, you've been to the Tezik bazaar, and you ask me where? I was going to buy myself an Order of the Red Banner as well, but I was two thousand short. I only had eighteen thousand on me, and the fellow wouldn't budge . . . twenty thousand was his last offer."

"But what did you want it for?"

"Why did I need a medal? I just wanted to show off, like an idiot. If I had a cool head like you—"

"What makes you think mine's so cool?"

"Cool and sober. And you look so . . . intelligent."

"How you do talk!"

"Honestly. All my life I've dreamed of meeting a girl with a cool head."

"Why?"

"Because I'm so erratic myself, and she wouldn't let me do stupid things."

"I wish you'd get on with your story."

"Where was I, then? Oh yes! When I came out of the Lubyanka, I was dizzy with happiness. But somewhere inside me there was a little man on the watch, and he asks me what's so wonderful? What does it mean? They never let anybody go; the way the others in the cell explained it, guilty or not guilty, it's ten years jugged, five years muzzled, and off to the camp with you."

"What do you mean, muzzled?"

"Lord, how uneducated you are. And you a public prosecutor's daughter! You ought to take a bit of interest in your daddy's work! 'Muzzled' means you can't bite. You're deprived of civil rights. You can't vote or run for election."

"Hold on, there's somebody coming."

"Where? Don't worry, it's only Zemelya. Sit like you were before, please do! Don't move away. Open the file. That's it, pretend you're looking at it. . . . I realized right away that they'd let me out to put a tail on me, see which of the guys I would be meeting, whether I would visit the Americans at their country place again, and one way or another I would have no life at all; they'd put me back inside anyway. So I tricked them. I said good-bye to my mother, left the house in the night, and went to see a certain old fellow. He was the one who got me mixed up in all this forgery. For two years there was a nationwide search for Rostislav Doronin. I went under borrowed names to Central Asia, Issyk-kul, the Crimea, Moldavia, Armenia, the Far East. . . . Then I began to miss my mother very much. But I couldn't possibly show myself back home! I went to Zagorsk and got a job in a factory as a sort of general go-fer, and Mother used to come and see me on Sundays. When I'd been working there a few weeks, I overslept and was late for work. I was hauled up before the court!"

"Were you found out?"

"Not at all! I was sentenced to three months under my assumed name and sat in a detention center with my head shaved while police stations all over the country were on the alert for Rostislav Doronin, hair thick and red, eyes blue, nose regular, mole on left shoulder. It cost them a pretty penny, their nationwide search! I did my three months, got a passport from citizen commandant, and streaked off to the Caucasus."

"More travels?"

"Hm. I don't know whether I ought to tell you all of it. . . ."

"Go on!"

"You sound so sure. . . . But I can't really. You come from a different social background. You wouldn't understand."

"I will understand! Don't imagine my life has been all that easy!"

"It's just that you've looked at me so kindly these last two days. . . . I do really want to tell you about it. The thing is, I wanted to run for it. . . . Get right away from this crooked setup."

"What crooked setup?"

"Away from all this, you know, socialism! I can't stand it! It makes my gorge rise!"

"What does—socialism?"

"If there's no justice, what the hell do I want with socialism?"

"Yes, well, what happened to you is very hard. But where could you have gone? Outside, there's reaction, imperialism . . . how could you live there?"

"You're right, of course. Of course you're right! I wasn't serious about it. Anyway, you need the know-how."

"And how did you come to—"

"Land inside again? I wanted to get some schooling."

"There you are, you see. You hankered after an honest life. We all need to study. It's very important. It's a noble thing."

"Not always, Klara, I'm afraid. I got to thinking, later on in the prisons and camps. What can those professors teach anybody if they'd do anything to keep their jobs and never know what to say till they see today's paper? In an arts school, anyway? They don't teach; they fill your brains with fog. You studied in a technical school, of course."

"In an arts school as well."

"Did you drop out? You must tell me about it sometime. Anyway, I ought to have been a bit more patient, looked around for a school graduate's certificate; it isn't hard to buy one but . . . carelessness, that's what destroys us! I said to myself they won't still be looking for me; nobody's that stupid. I was just a kid; they must have forgotten about me long ago. So I took my old certificate, in my own name, and applied to the university, only to Leningrad this time, and to the Geography Department. . . ."

"Weren't you studying history at Moscow?"

"All those wanderings had given me a liking for geography. It's fascinating. Travel a lot and you'll see a lot. So what happened? I went to lectures for a week and . . . they bagged me! Back to the Lubyanka! And this time it was twenty-five years! And off to the tundra to do my fieldwork. I'd never been there before!"

"And you can make a joke of it?"

"What's the good of crying? There aren't enough tears to cry every time. I'm not the only one. They sent me to Vorkuta. You should see some of the bright guys there! Cutting coal. Vorkuta depends entirely on zeks. The whole north does! In fact, the whole country would be crippled without them. Thomas More's dream has come true, you might say."

"Whose? I'm so ignorant I'm ashamed."

"Old Thomas More, who wrote *Utopia*. He was honest enough to admit that there would inevitably still be some degrading jobs and some particularly onerous ones under socialism. Jobs nobody would want to do. To whom should they be assigned? More thought a bit and got the answer. Even under socialism there would be lawbreakers. Let's give *them* the dirty jobs! So you see today's Gulag was invented by Thomas More; it's a very old idea!"

"I can't get over it. What a way to live in our day and age: forging passports, moving from town to town, drifting with the wind. . . . I've never met anybody like you before."

"Klara, I'm not really like that either! Circumstances can turn anybody into a devil! Don't forget, being determines consciousness! I was a good boy; I did what my mother told me. I read Dobrolyubov's *Ray of Light in the Kingdom of Darkness*. If a militiaman crooked his finger at me, my heart would be in my boots. You change so gradually you don't notice. What was I supposed to do? Wait like a rabbit to be caught again?"

"I don't know what else you could do, but what a life! I can see how hard it must be for you! You are a permanent outlaw! A sort of superfluous man, an outcast."

"Well, sometimes it's hard. But other times, you know, it isn't. Because if you walk through the Tezik bazaar and take a look around . . . and they're selling shiny new medals, with citations you can fill in yourself. What crooked character is responsible? Where does he work? Which organization is he in, you wonder. Can you guess? I can tell you, Klara. I'm all for living honestly, as long as everybody's honest, every single person!"

"But if everybody waits for everybody else it will never get started. Everybody should—"

"Everybody should, but not everybody does! Listen, Klara, I'll put it more simply. What was the Revolution against? Against privilege! What were ordinary Russians sick of? Privilege. Some wore rags and some wore sables; some trudged around on foot, others rode in carriages; some went off to the factory when the horn blew, while others fed their fat faces in restaurants. Am I right?"

"Of course."

"Right. So why aren't people repelled by privilege now, but hungry for it? Why talk about the kid I used to be? Did I start it all? I look at older people. I've seen plenty in my time. I was living in a little town in Kazakhstan once. What did I see? Did the wives of the local bosses ever go to the shop? No, never! I was sent myself to deliver a crate of macaroni to the first secretary of the raikom.* A whole crate. The seal hadn't been broken. You can be sure there were other crates on other days."

"Yes, it's horrible! It's always sickened me. Do you believe me?"

"Of course I do. Why shouldn't I believe a real live person? I'd sooner believe you than a book sold in a million copies. . . . Well, then, these privileges get hold of people like an infection. If somebody can do his shopping in a different store from everybody else, he certainly will. If a man can get treatment in a special hospital, he will certainly do so. If he can ride around in a car of his own, he will ride in it. If there's a good time to be had somewhere and you need a pass to get there, he'll do whatever it takes to wangle himself one."

"You're right! It's horrible!"

"If he can build a fence to keep everybody out, he's bound to do it. Yet the

---

* Raikom: Soviet shorthand for a Raion Committee of the Communist Party. A raion is a district within an oblast, thus two steps below the national level.

son of a bitch was a boy himself once, climbing over some merchant's fence to steal apples. And thought he had a right to. But now he puts up a fence twice a man's height, a solid fence, so that nobody can peek in at him. He feels more comfortable that way. And again thinks he's in the right. In the market at Orenburg, war cripples living on scraps play heads and tails using a victory medal. They toss the medal and shout, 'Victory or Ugly Mug?' "

"Meaning what?"

"On one side it says 'Victory,' and on the other there's a . . . likeness. Ask your father to show you."

"Rostislav Vadimych. . . ."

"What the hell! Forget the 'Vadimych.' Just call me Rusya."

"I can't very well do that. . . ."

"If you don't, I will get up and leave. The bell's ringing for dinner. I'm Rusya to everybody, and you especially. I don't want you to call me anything else."

"Well, all right . . . Rusya. . . . I'm not entirely stupid myself. I've thought about it a lot. We have to fight it, yes! But not your way, of course!"

"My way? I haven't started fighting yet! I just thought to myself if equality's the thing, let everybody be equal; otherwise, they can shove it . . . oh dear, I'm sorry, I didn't mean to. . . . As it is, what do we see from childhood on? We hear all those fine words at school, but then we find you get nowhere without pulling strings and greasing palms, so we grow up crafty. The brazen ones have all the luck."

"No! No! Don't talk like that! In many ways ours is a just society! You're exaggerating! You've got it wrong! You've seen a lot, certainly, you've gone through a lot, but 'the brazen ones have all the luck' is a hopeless philosophy! It's just wrong!"

They heard Zemelya shout, "Ruska, the bell's rung for dinner, didn't you hear it?"

"All right, Zemelya. You go on, I'm coming. . . . Klara, let me tell you, seriously and solemnly, I wish with all my heart I could live differently. If only I had a friend with a cool head . . . or a sweetheart . . . so we could think things out together. Organize our life together properly. Yes, I'm a prisoner and in for twenty-five years. But . . . oh, if only I could tell you what a knife's-edge I'm balancing on! Any normal man would die of heart failure. But never mind that for now. Klara! What I mean is, I have volcanic reserves of energy! Twenty-five years at Veliky Ustyug, it means nothing to me! I can cut loose anytime."

"What?"

"You know—make a run for it. Only this morning I was thinking of a way to get out of Marfino. I swear to you that when my sweetheart—if ever I have one—says, 'Ruska! Run away! I'm waiting for you!' within three months from that day I'd escape, forge passports that nobody could pick holes in! Take her off to Chita! . . . To Odessa! . . . To—! And we'd start a new, honest, sensible, free life!"

"A fine life it would be!"

"You know how Chekhov's heroes are always saying 'in twenty years' time!' 'in thirty years' time!' 'in two hundred years' time!' Longing to do a good day's work in a brickyard and come home tired! The ridiculous dreams they had! But I'm not joking. I do quite seriously, absolutely seriously, want to study, to work! But not by myself! Klara, look how quiet it is, everybody's gone to dinner. Will you come to Veliky Ustyug? It's a monument to hoary antiquity. I haven't been there yet."

"What an extraordinary person you are."

"I was on the lookout for her at Leningrad University. I never imagined where I would find her."

"Who?"

"Klara, my dear! A woman's hands could mold me into any shape—make a great rogue of me, a cardsharp of genius, or the leading expert on Etruscan vases or cosmic rays. I'll be that if you want me to."

"What, forge your diploma?"

"No, I mean it! I'll become whatever you decide. All I need is you! All I need is that slow turn of your head when you come into the laboratory. . . ."

## 43

# A Woman Was Washing the Staircase

Major General Pyotr Afanasievich Makarygin, candidate in Juridical Sciences, had behind him a long career as prosecutor in "special cases," meaning those of which the public was for its own good best left in ignorance and which were therefore dealt with discreetly. (The millions of political cases were all of this kind.) Not every prosecutor was given access to such cases, in which the interrogation and the whole proceedings were conducted according to the rules and a verdict of guilty obtained.

But Makarygin was always welcome; apart from his long-standing connections in that world, he managed to combine very tactfully an unswerving devotion to the law with an understanding of the special character of the work done by the security services.

He had three daughters, all three by his first wife, his partner during the Civil War. She had died giving birth to Klara. The girls were brought up by a stepmother, who had, however, succeeded in being what is called a good mother to them.

The daughters' names were Dinera, Dotnara, and Klara. Dinera meant "Child of the New Era" (*Ditya Novoy Ery*), Dotnara "Daughter of the Working People" (*Doch Trudovogo Naroda*).

The daughters were born at two-year intervals. The middle one, Dotnara, had left high school in 1940 and gotten married, beating Dinera to it by a month. Her father thought it was too soon and was angry at first, but he was lucky in his son-in-law—a graduate of the Higher Diplomatic School, an able young man with good connections, son of a well-known father who had fallen in the Civil War. The son-in-law's name was Innokenty Volodin.

The oldest daughter, Dinera, would sit at home on the sofa swinging her legs and reading the whole of world literature from Homer to Farrère, while her stepmother visited her school to arrange a recalculation of her poor marks in mathematics. When she left school, she got into the Drama Department of the Institute of Cinematography (with some help from her father), married a quite-well-known director in her second year, was evacuated with him to Alma-Ata, took the leading role in one of his films, then divorced him and married a quartermaster general (also married before) and accompanied him to the front, or not exactly to the front but to that Third Echelon, the best of zones in wartime, beyond the range of enemy artillery but also exempt from the hardships of the home front. There, Dinera met a writer who was becoming fashionable, the war correspondent Galakhov, traveled around with him collecting copy on war heroes, and returned with him to Moscow after restoring the general to his previous wife.

So for the past eight years Klara had been the only daughter left in the family home.

The two older sisters had divided the good looks between them, leaving Klara neither beautiful nor even just nice-looking. She had hoped for some improvement in time, but there was none. Her face was frank and open but too mannish. There was a hardness about the temples and the angles of her chin. Klara had not been able to get rid of it, and in the end she reconciled herself to it and stopped noticing. The movements of her arms were ungraceful. Her laugh, too, was rather hard. For that reason she did not like laughing. She did not like dancing either.

When Klara was in the ninth grade, several things happened at once: Both her sisters got married, war broke out, and she was evacuated to Tashkent with her stepmother, sent there three days after the German invasion by her father, who himself left to serve as a divisional chief prosecutor.

They lived in Tashkent for three years, in the house of an old friend of her father's, who was deputy to one of the senior public prosecutors down there. The southern heat and the unhappiness of the town could not penetrate the closely drawn blinds of that quiet second-floor apartment near the officers' club. Many men had been called up from Tashkent, but ten times as many had moved into the city. And although every one of them had convincing documents to prove that Tashkent and not the front was where he belonged, Klara had an unverifiable feeling that the city around her was awash in sewage and that heroic purity and spiritual nobility had withdrawn to some place five thousand versts away. The age-old law of war was in operation: Although it was not of their own free will that people went to the front, the best and the most ardent found their way there; and on the same principle of selection, once there it was they who were most likely to perish.

Klara finished school in Tashkent. There was some argument as to where she should continue her education. She herself did not feel particularly drawn to anything; she had no definite ambitions. But the daughter of such a family had to enroll somewhere! It was Dinera who made up her mind for her; she insisted in her letters, and when she came to say good-bye before leaving for the front, that little Klara should study literature.

She did what she was told, although she knew from school what a bore this literature was: Gorky, so very right but so very unalluring; Mayakovsky, also very right but so stiff and awkward; Saltykov-Shchedrin, so very progressive, but you'd be yawning your head off as you read; Turgenev's blinkered gentry ideas; Goncharov's links with nascent Russian capitalism; Lev Tolstoy's conversion to the attitudes of the patriarchal peasantry (their teacher had advised them not to read Tolstoy's novels because they were very long and would only obscure the clear message of the critical articles that had been recommended); then they reviewed a whole bunch of writers nobody had ever heard of, such as Stepnyak-Kravchinsky, Dostoevsky, and Sukhovo-

Kobylin but didn't even have to memorize their names. This dreary procession filed past year after year, and Pushkin alone shone bright as the sun.

At school, literature had meant nothing but intensive study of "the message," the ideological standpoint adopted, the social class served by all these writers. They also read Soviet writers, both Russians and those of the fraternal nationalities. To Klara and her classmates, it remained incomprehensible to the end why so much attention was paid to them: They were not the cleverest of people (publicists and critics, and a fortiori Party leaders, were all cleverer); they were often mistaken, tying themselves up in contradictions when the truth was obvious to a schoolchild and falling under undesirable influences; yet they were the ones you had to write essays about, trembling for every misspelled word and every misplaced comma. These vampires who preyed on young souls could inspire nothing but hatred for themselves.

Somehow Dinera's experience of literature had been quite different, exciting and enjoyable. Dinera assured Klara that this was how it would be at the institute. But Klara found it no more enjoyable. At lectures, historical phonetics, monkish legends, the mythological school, and the comparative-historical school came and went, leaving no trace, while in study groups they discussed Louis Aragon and Howard Fast and the same old Gorky, with special reference to his influence on Uzbek literature. Klara sat through the lectures and, to begin with, went along to the study groups, always expecting to be told something very important about life—about life in wartime Tashkent, for instance.

When Klara was in tenth grade, a classmate's brother had tried, with his friends, to steal a basket of bread from a moving delivery tram and had been cut to pieces. At the university one day, she tossed a half-eaten sandwich into a trash can in the hallway. Immediately a student in her own year, and a member of the Aragon group, while clumsily trying to disguise his intentions, fished the sandwich out from amid the garbage and pocketed it. Another girl took Klara along to help her buy something in the Tezikov bazaar, the finest flea market in Central Asia, if not the whole Soviet Union. There were big crowds for two blocks around, and there was a particularly large number of men crippled in the war, hobbling on crutches, flourishing stumps of arms, scooting along, those without legs, on little carts, selling, telling fortunes, begging, demanding; Klara gave them some money, and her heart was nearly breaking. The most frightening of the war cripples was the "Samovar," as they called him: He had lost both arms and both legs; his boozy wife carried him on her back in a basket; people tossed money into it. When they had collected enough, they bought vodka and drank it, loudly abusing everybody and everything. Toward the center of the bazaar, the crowd was denser; you could hardly shoulder your way through the mob of black marketers, male and female. Prices were sky-high, up in the thousands, out of all proportion to local wages, but everybody took them for granted. The city's shops were empty, but here you could buy everything anyone could swallow, or wear above or beneath, or invent—down to American chewing gum, pistols, and manuals of both black and white magic.

But in the Literature Department, nobody ever talked of, and it was as if nobody even knew about, this side of life. In the literature they studied, the world was full of everything but what you saw with your own eyes all around you.

Miserably realizing that in five years it would end in her becoming a teacher herself, assigning little girls tiresome essays and pedantically looking for mistakes in spelling and punctuation, Klara began to spend most of her time playing tennis; there were good courts in the city, and she developed a powerful volley.

Tennis was a rewarding occupation. She enjoyed the physical exertion, and confidence in her game gave her greater assurance in other activities. Tennis took her mind off her disappointments at the university and the complications of civilian life in wartime. The clear-cut boundaries of the court, the sure flight of the ball. . . . More important still, tennis brought the joy of being noticed and praised by people around her, something very necessary to a young girl, and especially to a plain one. Suddenly she finds that she has skill! Quick reactions! A sharp eye! She thought she had nothing, and suddenly finds she has a great deal. She can hop around the court tirelessly, for hours on end, as long as there are a few spectators watching her movements. And the white tennis costume with the short skirt really suited Klara.

Deciding what to wear had in fact become a torment. She sometimes changed several times a day, and every time the agonizing problem was how to cover those thick legs. Which hat didn't look ridiculous on her? What colors suited her? What sort of collar would do something for that square chin? Klara had no insight into such things, and although she could afford to dress well, she was always dowdy.

She simply didn't know what made people "attractive." What did the word mean? Why wasn't she attractive? It could drive you crazy, and nobody could help you. Why weren't you what you should be? What was wrong with you? One, two, or even three mishaps you could put down to chance, incompatibility, inexperience; but she was always left with the same inexplicable bitter taste in her mouth. How could she overcome this injustice? It was not her fault that she was born like that!

In her second year Klara got so fed up with all that literary blather that she stopped going to classes.

The following spring the Soviet forces had advanced into Belorussia, and evacuees could begin to go home. Klara's family, too, returned to Moscow.

Even there, Klara had no real idea which higher educational institution would best suit her. She was looking for one where people didn't just talk but did something, so it had to be a technical school. But not one with heavy and dirty machinery. And so she landed in the Communications Engineering Institute.

She had made another mistake from lack of guidance but refused to admit it. She was stubbornly determined to finish her course and find a job, somewhere, anywhere. Besides, she was not the only girl in the course (there were few boys) who found herself there almost by chance. A new age was beginning; everybody was chasing the dream of higher education, and those who didn't get into the Institute of Aviation switched their applications to the Veterinary Institute, those rejected by Chemical Technology became paleontologists.

At the end of the war, Klara's father was very busy in Eastern Europe. He was demobilized in autumn 1945 and was immediately given an apartment in the new Ministry of the Interior building at the Kaluga Gate. Within a few days of his return, he took his wife and daughter to look at it.

The car glided to a stop just past the railings of the Pleasure Garden, short of the bridge over the Circle Line. It was late morning on a warm October day in a lingering Indian summer. Mother and daughter were both wearing light raincoats, and father his general's overcoat, unbuttoned to show his decorations.

The house under construction was crescent-shaped, with one wing fronting Great Kaluga Street and the other facing the Circle Line. It was going to be eight stories high, and the plan included a sixteen-story tower with a solarium and a statue of a twelve-meter-tall female collective farmer on the roof. There was still scaffolding around the building, and even the brickwork was incomplete on the side facing the street and square. The construction bureau had, however, given in to the impatience of its client (the Ministry of State Security) and was already leasing a finished section (the second), one stairway and all the apartments on it. The site was surrounded, as is always the case on busy streets, by a board fence; people in cars went by too quickly to notice, and people living across the road had stopped noticing the rows of barbed wire fixed to the top of the fence and the ugly guard towers looming over it. The procurator's family walked around the end of the fence to the finished section. They were met at the front entrance by a polite site manager. Klara paid no attention to the sentry who was also standing there. Nothing remained to be done. The paint on the banisters was dry, the door handles had been wiped clean, numbers had been screwed onto the front doors, the windows had been cleaned, but the stairs were still being scrubbed by a woman in dirty clothes crouched over her bucket so that her face could not be seen.

The site manager said, "Hey, you there!" and the woman stopped scrubbing and made room without looking up from her bucket and floor cloth for them to pass in single file. The procurator went past her. The site manager went past. The procurator's wife went past, almost brushing the charwoman's face with her heavily perfumed pleated skirt. Perhaps because the silk and the scents were too much for her, the woman, still bent over her bucket, raised her head to see whether there were many more of "them." To Klara that look of searing contempt was like the touch of red-hot metal. The expressive face smeared with dirty water was that of a sensitive and educated person. It wasn't just the shame you always feel when you step around a woman washing a floor, at the sight of that ragged skirt and that quilted jacket with the padding escaping. Klara felt deeply ashamed and also afraid. She stopped dead, opened her handbag, and was about to give its contents to the woman, but she did not dare.

"Move along there, can't you?" the woman said angrily. Holding in the skirt of her fashionable dress and the edge of her dark red coat and hugging the banisters, Klara fled upstairs.

In the apartment there were parquet floors, which would need no washing.

They liked it. Klara's stepmother told the site manager what still needed attention and was particularly unhappy that the parquet floor in one room creaked. The manager teetered on two or three wooden blocks and promised to replace them.

"Who does all this work? Who are the builders?" Klara asked abruptly.

The manager smiled but said nothing.

"Prisoners, of course," her father growled.

When they went back downstairs, the woman was no longer there. Nor was the soldier standing outside.

They moved in, a few days later.

Months went by, years went by, and Klara for some reason could still not forget that woman. She remembered the exact spot, on the next to last step of a long flight, and whenever she passed it, on days when she did not use the elevator, she remembered the crouching gray figure and the upturned face full of hatred.

Afterward, she always kept close to the banisters, fearing that she might step on the cleaning woman. She could neither explain this superstitious impulse nor repress it.

She did not, however, confide in her father or stepmother. She could not bring herself to mention it to them. Relations with her father had been strained ever since the war. He got angry with her and shouted that she had grown up with all sorts of crazy notions. She had a mind of her own; he called it wrongheadedness. Her memories of Tashkent and her reactions to Moscow life he found offbeat and unwholesome, and her way of generalizing from these episodes aroused his indignation.

She could not possibly tell him that the cleaning woman was still there on their stairs. Nor could she tell her stepmother. Was there anyone at all she could tell?

One day last year she had been going downstairs with her younger brother-in-law Innokenty, and before she realized what she was doing, she had taken him by the sleeve and pulled him aside at the spot where they had to step around the invisible woman. Innokenty asked what was wrong. Klara hesitated; he might think she was mad. Besides, she saw him only rarely. He was in Paris most of the time, he dressed like a dandy, and he always teased her and talked down to her as though she were a child.

But she made up her mind, stood still on the stairs, and told him with many gestures what had happened there.

He stopped playing the glamorous Westerner, stood still on the step where the conversation had come upon them, and listened, looking humble and rather lost, and for some reason hat in hand.

He understood perfectly!

From that moment on, they were friends.

# 44

## Out in the Open

To THE MAKARYGIN FAMILY Nara and her Innokenty had been far-off, disembodied relatives until a year ago. They had flitted through Moscow for one short week in a year and sent presents at holiday times. Klara, who had got used to calling Galakhov, her famous older brother-in-law, Kolya, was still shy and tongue-tied with Innokenty.

But last summer they had stayed longer, and Nara was often at her parents' apartment, usually complaining about her husband and the shadow over their marriage, which until recently had been so happy. She and Alevtina Nikanorovna discussed it at length, and if she happened to be at home, Klara listened, openly or surreptitiously. She could not have refrained even if she had wanted to. This was, after all, life's greatest mystery: What made people love each other or not love each other?

Her sister told them about all sorts of trivial incidents, disagreements, quarrels, suspicions, and also about Innokenty's professional misjudgments; he had changed so much, he showed no respect for the opinions of important people, and this affected their material position so that Nara had to go without things. As she told it, Nara was always right, her husband always wrong. Klara, privately, drew quite different conclusions. Nara did not know how lucky she was. She probably no longer loved Innokenty but only herself. What she cared about was not his work but the status it gave her, not his views and preferences, however they might have changed, but her possession of him, asserted for all to see. Klara was surprised to find that her sister resented her husband's suspected infidelities less than his failure to emphasize sufficiently in the presence of other women that she alone was supremely important to him.

The unmarried younger sister could not help comparing her own situation with Nara's and telling herself that, come what may, she would have behaved differently. How could Nara be satisfied with anything that left *him* unhappy? Their problem was aggravated by their childlessness.

Once Klara had opened her heart on the stairway, they were on such easy terms that she urgently needed to see more of him. She had such a backlog of questions that Innokenty was just the man to answer!

But the presence of Nara or any other member of the family would somehow make it awkward.

So when Innokenty suggested, shortly afterward, a day out in the country, her heart missed a beat and she agreed without thinking.

"No manor houses, museums, or famous ruins, though," Innokenty said with a faint smile.

"I don't like them either" was Klara's firm response.

Now that she knew some of his troubles, his halfhearted smile caused a twinge of sympathy.

"Switzerland and places like that can drive a man crazy," he said. "Wandering around ordinary Russian countryside is good enough for me. Think we can find any?"

Klara nodded vigorously. "We can if we try!"

It was left unclear whether this was to be an outing for two or for three. But Innokenty arranged to meet her on a weekday at the Kiev Station. He did not phone his home and would not call for Klara at Kaluga Gate, which made it obvious that there would be just the two of them and that Klara's parents were probably not supposed to know.

As far as her sister was concerned, Klara felt quite entitled to this outing. Even if his marriage had been perfect, Innokenty would have been just paying his family dues. As things were, Nara had only herself to blame.

Would there ever again be such a wonderful day in Klara's life? There would certainly be none for which preparations were so agonizing. What should she wear? If her women friends could be believed, no color suited her, but she had to choose one of them! She put on a brown dress and carried a blue coat. Her veil gave her more trouble than anything; the night before, she spent two hours trying it on, taking it off, trying it on again. Some lucky people can make their minds up at once! Klara was crazy about veils; especially in films, they made a woman enigmatic, raised her beyond the reach of critical scrutiny. Still, she decided against it. Innokenty had grown tired of French frippery, and, besides, it was going to be a sunny day. She did put on her black net gloves, though. Black net gloves were very pretty.

The Maloyaroslav train was waiting when they arrived. A small steam locomotive, it was splendid. They had no particular station in mind. They simply took tickets to the end of the line. The route was so new to them that they were both startled when fellow passengers mentioned a station called "Nara." If Innokenty had known about it, he might perhaps have chosen a different terminus. If Klara had ever known, she had completely forgotten.

"Nara, Nara, Nara. . . ." They heard the name over and over again in the course of the journey. It seemed to haunt them.

It was a cool morning for August. They were both cheerful and animated, and they were soon chatting freely about anything and everything. Occasional lapses into formality ended in laughter and made them feel even more at ease.

Innokenty was wearing some sort of Western sports outfit, unconcernedly creasing and rumpling what he evidently thought of as "casual clothes."

They had the whole day ahead of them, but Klara began eagerly interrogating him, switching erratically from questions about Europe to problematic aspects of Soviet life. She wasn't quite sure herself what she wanted to know! But she knew there was something! She longed to be cleverer! She had to get to the bottom of it!

Innokenty wagged his head comically.

"Do you really think . . . little Klara . . . that I understand any of it myself?"

"But you diplomats are there to show the rest of us the way, and now you tell me you don't understand."

"Ah, but all my colleagues do understand; it's only I who don't. And even I understood it all till some time last year or the year before last."

"Then what happened?"

"Do you know, that's another thing I don't understand," Innokenty said laughingly. "And anyway, my little Klara, who knows where the explanation should start? It goes back to the very beginning of things. Suppose a caveman suddenly popped out from under the seat here and asked us to explain in not more than five minutes how trains can run on electricity. What would we tell him? First of all, off you go and learn to read. Then get on with your arithmetic, algebra, draftsmanship, electrotechnology. . . . Have I forgotten anything?"

"I don't know . . . magnetics, perhaps?"

"There you are, you don't know either. And you're in your final year! Then I would say, 'Come back in fifteen years' time, and I'll explain it in five minutes, only by then you'll know it all yourself.' "

"Very well, I'm willing to learn. But how do I go about it? Where do I begin?"

"Well, our newspapers will do for a start."

A man with a leather satchel was passing through the train selling newspapers. Innokenty bought *Pravda* from him.

Klara had realized when they boarded the train that they would be having a rather special conversation, and she had sent Innokenty ahead to occupy an uncomfortable double seat by a door. Innokenty hadn't understood, but only there could they talk more or less freely.

"All right, now for our reading lesson," he said, unfolding the paper. "Take this headline: 'Women Filled with Labor Enthusiasm Overfulfill Norms.' Ask yourself why they have to think about norms at all. Don't they have anything to do at home? What it means is that the combined wages of husband and wife aren't enough to support a family. Whereas the husband's wage alone ought to be enough."

"Is it enough in France?"

"And everywhere else. Look, here's another bit: 'In all the capitalist countries together there are fewer day nurseries than in our country.' True? Probably. But one little detail is left out: In all other countries women are freer to bring up their children themselves, so they don't need all these nurseries."

The train shuddered. They were moving.

Innokenty found another text without difficulty, pointed to it, and spoke into her ear through the racket.

"Now take any apparently insignificant form of words: 'Member of the French parliament so-and-so made a statement' . . . about the hatred of the French people for the Americans. Did he, you ask? He probably did; we only print the truth! But something is left out. What party does he belong to? If he were not a Communist, they would certainly say so because it would make his utterance all the more valuable! So he is a Communist. But they don't say so! And that's the way it always is, Clairette. They'll write about record snowfall somewhere, with thousands of cars buried in drifts—a national disaster! But the artful implication is that where there are so many cars, it isn't worth building garages for them. These are all examples of freedom from information! The same sort of thing turns up in the sports pages: 'match ended in well-deserved victory'—no need to read on, obviously our side won. But if 'to the surprise of the spectators the jury declared so-and-so the winner,' so-and-so is obviously not one of ours."

Innokenty looked around for somewhere to throw away the newspaper. Obviously not realizing that this was another example of un-Soviet behavior! People had already begun looking around at them. Klara took the newspaper from him and held on to it.

"Anyway, sport is the opiate of the people," Innokenty concluded.

That surprised and offended her. And coming from such a slight person, it didn't ring at all true.

Klara shook her head indignantly.

"I play tennis a lot and I really love it."

Innokenty hurriedly corrected himself. "Playing games is fine. What is terrible is the passion for spectator sports. Sports for the mass spectator, football and hockey, make idiots of us."

The train rattled along. They looked through the window.

"So life is good there?" Klara asked. "Better than here?"

Innokenty nodded. "Better. But still not good. There's a difference."

"What is lacking there?"

Innokenty looked at her gravely. His earlier animation had given way to thoughtful calm.

"It's difficult to say. I find it surprising myself. There's something missing. In fact, there are many things missing."

Klara was by now completely at ease with him. She felt in his company an enjoyment that had nothing to do with flirtatious contacts and inflections—there were none—and she wanted to show her gratitude, to make him feel happier and more confident.

"You have . . . such an interesting job," she said soothingly.

"Who, me?" Innokenty sounded surprised. He had always been thin, and now he looked feeble and half starved. "To work in our diplomatic service, Klara my dear, you need a double wall in your chest. Two thicknesses of skull. And two separate memories."

He left it at that. Sighed and looked out the window.

Did his wife understand any of this? Did she do anything to encourage and comfort him?

Klara studied him carefully and noticed for the first time a distinctive feature: By itself, the upper part of his face looked quite hard, while the lower part, seen alone, was soft. From his broad and open forehead his features narrowed, slanting downward to a mouth so small and sensitive that it made him look helpless.

The day was getting hot. Woodlands sped merrily past. The route took them through heavily wooded country.

The farther the train went, the fewer city people there were left in the car, and the more conspicuous the two of them became. They looked like actors in costume. Klara took off her gloves.

They left the train at a stop in the forest. Peasant women with shopping bags full of groceries from town emerged from the next car. No one else was left behind with them on the platform.

The young people had meant to go into the forest. There was forest along both sides of the line, but it was dense, dark, and uninviting. As soon as the train moved its tail out of their way, the women walked over a timbered crossing together and made for a place past the trees to the right. Klara and Innokenty followed them.

Immediately beyond the track, grass and flowers grew shoulder high. Then the path plunged into a plantation of birch saplings. Beyond that was a mowed space with a single haycock and a goat tethered to a stake by a long rope, pensively browsing when it remembered to. The forest now closed in on their left, but the women stepped out briskly to the right, into the sunshine, and toward the open ground beyond a few more bushes.

The young people, too, decided that the forest could wait. Right now they were drawn irresistibly into that brilliant sunlight. The way there was by a firm, grassy field path. Between this and the railway line lay a field of some golden grain. Heavy ears on short, sturdy stalks. Whether it was wheat or some other crop they didn't know, but that made it no less beautiful. On the other side of the path, for almost as far as they could see, lay a bare, plowed field, waterlogged in places, drier elsewhere, with nothing growing on its great expanse. From where the train had stopped, the countryside into which they were now emerging had been invisible. So spacious was it that two eyes could not take it in without a turn of the head. They were shut in now by forest immediately beyond the railway line and in the distance ahead of them forest so dense that it looked like a wall with a serrated edge. Without knowing it, without setting out to find it, this was what they had longed for! Faces upturned to the sky, they stumbled slowly on, stopping now and then to gaze around. The railway line was now concealed by the plantation. Ahead of them, the upper half of a dark redbrick church with a bell tower came slowly into view from a dip in the ground. The peasant women were disappearing in that direction, and soon across the whole landscape there was no one and nothing else to be seen or heard: no human being, no farmstead, no trailer, no abandoned haymaker, nothing but the warm reveling of wind and sun, and birds lost in the void.

In two minutes their earnestness and their worries were forgotten.

"Is this Russia, then? Is this the real Russia?" Innokenty asked happily, squinting into the distance. He stopped and turned toward Klara. "I'm supposed to represent Russia, you know, but my own re-present-ation of Russia is nonexistent. I've never just walked around in Russia like this; it's always been airplanes, trains, big cities. . . ."

He intertwined his fingers with hers, at arm's length, as children or sweethearts do.

They wandered on like that, looking everywhere except where they were putting their feet. His free hand swung a hat, hers a handbag.

"Listen, Sister!" he said. "I'm so glad we came this way instead of going through the forest. If there's one thing missing in my life, it's that: a clear view all around. And a chance to breathe freely!"

"I can't believe that you don't see things clearly!" His plaintive tone had touched her. She would have offered him her own eyes if that would help.

"No," he said, swinging her hand. "I used to, but now everything is mixed up."

What did he mean? If it was all such a muddle, it couldn't be just his ideas; it must be his family life. If he had said just a little more, Klara would have found the courage to speak out, show him that she was on his side, that he was right, and that he must not despair!

"It might help to talk about it," she said tentatively.

But that was all. He had said all he meant to say.

It was getting hot. They took off their raincoats.

As far as the eye could see, there was now no one coming toward them and no one following them.

Occasionally a long train rolled slowly by beyond the screen of trees, almost noiselessly; only the smoke caught their attention.

The peasant women had long ago outdistanced them and turned off the main path. Now they were in the middle of the open field, blurred figures in the bright sunlight. Innokenty and Klara reached the point at which they had turned. A well-trodden path ran over the soft field, losing itself at times in tractor ruts. A path worn by little people tramping obliquely across the planner's great rectangular fields on their humdrum errands.

The path led toward the village around the church, but on the way it skirted a remarkable closely planted clump of trees, isolated out in the field, remote from the forest, and almost as far from the village, a strange, cheerful, flourishing copse of tall, straight trees. Small as it was, it dominated and beautified the landscape. Why was it there, out in the open field?

They made their way toward it.

Their hands parted. The path was wide enough only for one. Now Innokenty was walking behind Klara.

He is walking behind you, looking at your back. Looking you over. Your sister's husband. Your brother, then? Or. . .?

To talk to him, Klara had to stop and turn around.

"What are you going to call me? Just don't call me Clairette!"

"All right, I won't. That was before I knew you. In the West they like short pet names, just one or two syllables."

"So maybe I'll call you Ink?"

"Go ahead. That'll do nicely."

"Does anybody else call you that?"

The field was not as flat as they had thought. Ahead and to the left, there was a gentle downward slope; then the ground rose again to the clump of trees.

They could see now that these were mature birches. Rows of trees formed a rectangle, and others had been planted in the space inside it. There was something very surprising about this copse, so isolated and so detached from the landscape.

"When did it all start?" Klara asked.

"It?" That one little word could cover a number of things.

But he answered readily enough.

"Probably when I started going through my mother's cabinets. Or maybe even earlier, maybe a whole year earlier, but when I started going through the cabinets. . . ."

"After she died?"

"A long time after, a very long time. Not so long ago, in fact. You see, I . . . No, it's impossible to explain. . . . Dotty won't listen or doesn't understand."

(I would understand! Tell me all about Dotty! This is going to be a heart-to-heart talk! You'll feel so much better for it!)

"You see, young Klara, I was a very bad son. In her lifetime I never loved my mother as I should. I didn't come home from Syria all through the war, not even to her funeral. . . . Hey, d'you think it may be a cemetery?"

They stopped. And shivered, in spite of the heat. It was indeed a cemetery! Strange that it had taken them so long. . . . This place of inviolate shade standing among cultivated fields could have been nothing else.

Not that they could yet see crosses or graves. They were still at the bottom of the dip, picking their way over the soggy patches. (Innokenty was a clumsier jumper than Klara, and one of his shoes sank into the mud, but she did not want to offend him by offering a hand.) Now they were ascending the unexpectedly steep bank.

The boundaries of the graveyard were marked by no wall, no fence posts, no ditch, no embankment, only by the unbroken row of close-planted ancient birches. The soil of the field merged with a magnificent luxurious sward, free from weeds and not overgrown, though it was neither trampled nor mown. Just the sort of grass you would wish to find in a graveyard!

How shady and quiet it was! The purest and kindest refuge in that carefully landscaped locality.

Some of the graves were fenced. Others were simply nameless grass-grown hillocks. There were even quite recent ones.

Innokenty was surprised how much room there still was. "There are a hundred graves here at most, and there's easily room for fifty more. You probably don't need to ask anyone; you just come along and dig. Where my mother is buried in Moscow, there was all the bother of getting a permit from the Moscow Soviet, then greasing the cemetery superintendent's palm, and there isn't room to put your foot between graves, and to cap it all, they dig up old graves to make room for new ones."

Those old birches must have saved the spacious graveyard from tractors.

Their raincoats seemed to throw themselves on the ground, and they sat down without thinking, looking out over the rolling landscape. Now that they had left the sunlight for the shade, they had a clear view all around. The crossing keeper's hut at the stop was a distant white shape. Smoke crept over the tops of the trees lining the track.

They looked, breathed deeply, and were silent. It was comfortable sitting there. "Ink" rested his head on his raised knees and was still. Klara could see the back of his neck. It was scrawny, like that of a little boy, but it had received the unhurried attention of a skillful hairdresser.

"Such a tidy graveyard," Klara marveled. "No cattle dung, no spilled tractor fuel."

Innokenty sighed happily. "Yes. This is the place to be buried! I won't be so lucky! They'll shove me onto a plane in a lead coffin, then rush me off in a truck somewhere. . . ."

"It's a bit early to be thinking about that, Ink!"

"When everything is a lie, Klara dear, you get tired early. Very early, twice as quickly." His voice sounded weak and weary.

Was he thinking of his work? Of life in general? Or just of his wife?

Klara could not ask him to explain.

"What was in the cabinet, then?"

"In the cabinet?" Innokenty, always tense and preoccupied, frowned in concentration. "I'll tell you what was in the cabinet." But the very thought of explaining in detail seemed to tire him. "No, it's a long story. . . . Some other time perhaps."

If it was too long a story then, when wouldn't it be? Perhaps he was temperamentally capable of taking an interest only in what was new to him. If so, how could she ever catch up with his thoughts?

"You have no relatives left, then?"

"Just imagine, I have an uncle, my mother's brother. But I knew nothing about him either until last year."

"You've never met him?"

"Just once, when I was little. But I had no memory of him at all."

"Where does he live?"

"In Tver."

"Where?"

"In Kalinin, then. It's only two hours by train, but I can never get around to visiting him. Anyway, how could I when I'm never in Russia? I wrote to him, and the old man was overjoyed."

"Listen, Ink, you must go and see him! You'll be sorry later if you don't!"

"I intend to! I really do! I'll go someday soon. I promise."

Out of the punishing sun, Innokenty had recovered and was looking more cheerful.

Where to now? It was a long way to the forest, in any direction, and there were no paths. There was a field of sunflowers to one side of the graveyard and a beet field on the other. They could only return to their old path and follow the women toward the village. There would be more forest somewhere. They drifted on.

Innokenty had taken off his jacket. His shoulder blades stuck out sharply under his thin white shirt. He was wearing his hat again, for protection from the sun.

Klara was amused. "Know who you look like? Yesenin, coming home from Europe to his native village."

Innokenty grinned and made an effort to remember Yesenin's words. "My homeland . . . away from you what have I found . . . a stranger now to you, and to myself, knowing no longer how to plow or how to sow. . . ."

They were entering a deserted street. The facing rows of houses were ten meters apart, but the roadway was beyond repair, rutted and churned up by tractors and heavy trucks. There were knee-high ridges of baked mud in places, and in others pools of leaden sludge which no summer would ever be long enough to dry out. Communication between the two sides of the street would have been no more difficult if a river had flowed between them. There was firm footing only immediately in front of the houses, and once you had chosen one side of the street, you had to stick to it.

On their side a girl with a wicker basket walked quickly toward them.

"Little girl. . . ," Innokenty began, but quickly realized that she was older than he had thought. "Er . . . young lady. . . ." But by now she was almost upon him, and it turned out that she was a woman of nearly forty, remarkably small and with cataracts on both eyes. Afraid that she might suspect him of sarcasm, Innokenty no longer knew what to call her.

"What's the name of this village?" he asked.

"Rozhdestvo." Her clouded eyes barely glanced at them, and she walked quickly on.

The two young people exchanged a look of surprise. Rozhdestvo? What an unusual name. "Why Rozhdestvo?" they called after her.

"How should I know? It's just what they called it," she answered over her shoulder and went on.

Where had all those bustling women from the train trickled away to? There was no sign of life on the street or in the yards. Neither the ill-fitting, matchwood doors, which seemed to belong to chicken coops rather than houses, nor the unopenable double windows without ventilation panes looked as though human life could be concealed behind them. The traditional pigs and poultry were nowhere to be seen or heard. Only the wretched rags and blankets hung out on clotheslines in one of the yards showed that someone had been there that morning.

Hot sunlight flooded the silent air.

They caught sight of someone moving deep inside one of the yards. A stout old woman in galoshes was shuffling between puddles, examining something she held in her hand.

They called to her, but she did not hear.

They called again.

She looked up.

"I'm hard of hearing," she informed them in a cracked toneless voice. Her eyes showed no surprise at these sharply dressed passersby.

"Could we buy some milk from you?" Klara asked.

They didn't want milk, but she knew from her visits to collective farms that this was the best way to strike up a conversation.

"No cows," the old woman answered gravely. A yellow-white chick lay still in her hand, not struggling or twitching.

"Tell me, what was that church called?" Innokenty asked.

"What do you mean, *was* called?" She looked at him as though through a mist. There was a solemn self-assurance in her jowly face.

"Every church has a name, doesn't it?"

"That's about all it's got," she said. "They shut it down I don't know how long ago. . . . In the twenties. It's an hour by bus to the nearest church. There used to be a summer church near here, but the prisoners pulled it down."

"What prisoners?"

"The Germans."

"Why?"

"They sent the bricks to Nara. Look, my chicks keep dying. This is the fourth. Why d'you think that is?"

Klara and Innokenty shrugged sympathetically.

"Maybe she's crushing them?" The old woman said thoughtfully, shuffling toward the low door of her cottage. After that, they saw nothing at all moving, not a soul right to the end of the street. No dog showed itself or barked. There was nothing but two or three hens quietly grubbing away. Then a cat slunk out of the thistles, stalking something, no longer a domestic animal. It did not turn its head to look at the two human beings but sniffed the ground all around and went on, toward the no-less-dead main street, on which this one abutted.

Where the two streets broadened and intersected, they came upon the church, a squat, solid building of ornamental brickwork with inset brick crosses and, looming over it, a bell tower with rows of apertures at two levels. Moss and weeds grew there, and many swallows and still smaller birds hovered noiselessly around the tower, restlessly darting into the slits and out again. The dome of the bell tower was inaccessible and undamaged, but the metal sheeting had been stripped from the roof of the church and only its bare ribs remained. Both roof crosses had survived for two decades and still stood in their places. The door at the base of the bell tower was wide open, a paraffin lamp was burning in the darkness inside, and milk cans stood there, but there was no one to be seen. The door to the crypt of the church was also open, and sacks stood on the steps, but again there was no one around.

There must once have been a fence around the church, and a paved yard, but no trace of them remained. Heavy trucks and tractors had crisscrossed the ground on both sides of the church and between the church and the bell tower, leaving deep ruts in their convulsive eagerness to struggle through the mud without getting bogged down, reach the storehouse, and escape, perhaps for the last time. The sick, mutilated earth was covered with incrustations of mud like hideous gray scabs and putrescent puddles of leaden sludge.

There was the church. But the two young people took a long time finding a dry path across the street to it. They had to walk away to one side, then follow a tortuous route, jumping from spot to spot. Broken, mud-caked slabs of marble littered the road, and there were smaller pieces, and chips of clean marble, white, pink and yellow, by the walls of the church. Innokenty was feeling the heat but was not flushed. If anything, the sun had made him paler. The wisps of hair straying from under his hat were wet with sweat.

They went closer to the church. There was a foul smell in the hot still air—from stagnant water, dead cattle, or an open sewer somewhere? They began to regret coming and had no wish to inspect the church, even if there had been anything to see. Beyond the church the ground sloped down to a host of huge rounded willows, a whole kingdom of willows, and their only way of escape lay through that wall of green.

But someone was calling out to them. "Wouldn't have a smoke, would you, Citizens?"

A diminutive peasant with shoulders hunched up to his ears, as though he were permanently cold or frightened—but he looked crafty, too—had appeared from somewhere and was looking them over.

Innokenty looked apologetic but slapped his pocket as though he hoped against hope to find a pack.

"I don't smoke, Comrade."

"Too bad."

In spite of this disappointment, the neckless one did not go away but continued examining these exotic newcomers with his restless eyes. Although he couldn't see the car they must have come in, he obviously took them for a novel variety of the boss species.

"What was that church called?"

"Church of the Nativity," he said, no longer respectfully. He had made up his mind about them as soon as they spoke, and he vanished as suddenly as he had appeared.

But a little farther down the slope, they noticed another man, this one with an uncovered wooden leg. He was wearing a blue cotton shirt with white calico patches and resting on a stone under a lime tree.

"Where did all the marble come from?" Innokenty asked him.

"Eh?" was the patchwork peasant's reply.

"All those colored stones there."

"Oh, that. They smashed the altar." He thought a bit. "The iconostasis, I mean."

"What for?"

He thought again.

"To make the road."

"What's that smell around here?" Klara asked.

"Eh?" The one-legged man was surprised. He thought a bit. "Ah . . . must be from the cattle yard. . . . Our cattle yard's just over there."

He pointed, but they did not look. They were in a hurry to get away to the willow trees down below.

"What's down there?" they asked.

"Down there? Nothing." He thought. "Just a brook."

A path had been beaten down the slope. Klara felt like running downhill, but she looked anxiously at Innokenty's pale face and walked slowly at his side.

"A village like that really makes the graveyard attractive," she said, looking back. "Are you limping?"

"My shoe's chafing."

They stopped in the spreading shade of the first, huge willow and looked around. Away from the stench, all was moist and green and fresh, and they could see the church up on the hill, but not the dreadfully mutilated earth around it, only the dots that were birds darting and sailing around the belfry. The view was a pleasant one.

"You look very tired," Klara said anxiously. "You must have a rest. And take a look at your foot."

Throwing the coats down, he sat on the ground, leaning against a sloping trunk. He closed his eyes. Then lay back and gazed uphill at the church.

"You see, Klara dear, there are two Nativities. . . ."

"What do you mean, two?"

"Ours and the Western Christmas. Ours you've just seen. The Western Christmas is a sky lit up by neon signs, streets jammed with cars, people suffocating in shops, presents from everybody to everybody else. And in some wretched, dirty shopwindow—a crib and Joseph on a donkey."

"What do you mean, Joseph on a donkey?"

Before he could answer, they caught sight of something they had failed to notice before. A grave with an obelisk stood on the edge of the steep bank by the church, where a row of limes had somehow survived.

"A pity we missed that."

"I'll run over and take a look."

Klara darted across the hillside, ignoring the path. She ran as though she were enjoying it, but she didn't feel at all happy.

She stood for a while, reading the inscription, then came back just as nimbly, sure-footedly avoiding the potholes.

"Right then, whose do you think it is?"

"Some priest's?"

"It says, 'Eternal Glory to the Warriors of the Fourth Division of the People's Militia who died the death of the brave for the honor and independence' et cetera, from the Ministry of Finance."

"Ministry of Finance?"

His prominent ears twitched in surprise. "Would you believe it! Those poor clerks! How many of them fell here? I wonder. And how many men were there to a rifle? Fourth Militia Division, you say?"

"Yes."

"A division without weapons! And the fourth such. . . . What an absurd war it was. People's militia!"

"Why absurd?" Klara was puzzled.

Innokenty just sighed and looked downcast.

"Don't you feel well? Maybe we'd better be getting back, Ink? Let's not go any farther."

He sighed again.

"No, it's all right. Hot weather doesn't suit me. And I've got the wrong shoes on; I wasn't thinking."

"I wish I'd chosen a more comfortable pair myself. Where does it hurt? Let's put some newspaper under your heel; then it won't rub so much."

That did the trick.

Meanwhile, scudding clouds had appeared in the sky. From time to time, the sun was hidden, and it felt cooler.

"What do you say, Ink, shall we move on or not? We should have gone into the forest, shouldn't we? If you like, we can walk along the river; it'll be shady down there, too."

He was feeling better.

"What a weakling I am," he said. "Comes of spending my life in cars. You're a heroine! Come on, which bank do you prefer?"

Downstream there was a plank bridge. Cables attached to it were secured to the trunks of willows on either bank so that floods could not carry it away.

To cross or not to cross. Different banks, different paths, different conversation, a different outing.

They crossed. There was another symmetrically aligned plantation on the gently rising ground beyond the stream. The thirsty willows had chosen the water's edge, but behind them were rows and rows of birches and firs. There was a pond, too, with frogs and covered with fallen leaves. Its regular shape showed that it was man-made. Was this perhaps the derelict estate of some gentleman? There was no one to ask.

Seen from between the spreading willows, the church looked still more beautiful, high on the hill. This was the way that worshippers from another, nearby village would take, summoned by the bells.

But they had seen enough of villages and went on along the bank. It was very pleasant walking in this moist, shady, secluded world, where the stream gurgled and rippled in the shallows, while in deeper places the surface was still, except for occasional mysterious tremors, and everywhere dragonflies skimmed the water. There must surely be fish and crayfish. It would have been good to bare their legs up to the knees and wade like boys looking for crayfish, but there were impassable nettle beds and thickets of young aspens in their way.

A stout, weirdly twisted willow growing on their bank leaned out to span the stream, and its twisted branches were like the handrails of a bridge.

Klara clapped her hands. "A baobab! What a beauty! Let's go across it! It looks like better footing on the other bank."

Innokenty shook his head doubtfully, but Klara had already jumped boldly onto the slanting trunk. She extended a firm hand to him: "Come on!"

She felt sure that they were doing the right thing; surely on the other bank something would happen, something would be said, that would give meaning to this whole excursion.

Innokenty hesitantly held out his soft hand. The willow slanted gradually but rose high. Innokenty followed, taking short steps and apparently trying not to look down. But then a branch he took hold of barred his way, and he had to clamber over it. He did all this with a look of concentration and in complete silence. They landed without a scratch, but Ink had obviously not enjoyed the crossing.

Things were no better on this side. They had nothing much to say to each other. They heard the clatter of a tractor somewhere higher up. Very soon it became impossible to walk close to the water. They had to leave the shade and make for higher ground by the only possible path. Innokenty's limp was more and more pronounced.

They came out on a spacious yard with a single small building and a single open shed. The small building was probably an office; a pale pink flag with a ragged edge stirred feebly above it. The shed was just wide enough to accommodate in a single line the slogan "Forward to the Victory of Communism," exhorting a multitude of rusty red, blistery blue, and scabby green machines of unknown function, water wagons, a field kitchen, trailers with shafts erect, trailers with shafts earthward, all haphazardly abandoned over an expanse of land so scarred and rutted that it was almost impassable even on foot. There was no one in sight except a man in grubby overalls, wandering from one machine to another, bending down to look at something and straightening up again.

A single tractor was at work on a hillside.

There was no other path. Picking their way among the potholes as best they could, they crossed the yard. Innokenty was limping. It was hot again. They went back down to the stream.

At that point it flowed under a concrete bridge. A solid, prosaic bridge leaving nothing to choose between the two banks, the two destinies. They seemed to have arrived at a highway.

"Shall we try to get a ride?" Innokenty said. "We don't want to go back to the station again."

The day was only half over, but their outing was at an end.

Why was there always this hermetic screen between people? They could so nearly see, so nearly hear how to help each other.

But it was not to be. It could not be.

They found a little spring under the bridge, sat down, drank from it, and were about to wash their feet when they heard a heavy rumbling up above. They went out and looked up at the road from the bottom of the embankment.

A file of identical new-looking trucks with new-looking tarpaulin covers was rolling along the road. The end of the column was out of sight over the hill, and its head had reached the top of another hill.

There were trucks with aerials, breakdown trucks, trucks with barrels marked "Inflammable," and trucks with field-kitchen trailers. They carefully kept their distance, driving at intervals of precisely twenty meters, and the concrete bridge was not silent for a moment. In every cab an officer or sergeant sat beside an army driver. Soldiers, lots of them, huddled under tarpaulin covers; their faces could be seen through the window flaps and from the rear of each vehicle, looking indifferent, it seemed, to the place they had left, to the scene speeding past them, and to the place to which they were being driven, in suspended animation for the term of their service.

From the time they left their shelter, Klara and Innokenty counted one hundred trucks before the noise died away.

They walked back to where water gurgled around the sawed-off piles of a previous, wooden bridge.

Innokenty lowered himself onto a stone and said helplessly:

"My life is . . . in ruins."

"But why, Ink? Why is it in ruins?" Klara burst out in despair. "You keep promising to explain, but you don't tell me anything."

He looked at her with suffering eyes. Holding a broken stick like a pencil, he drew a circle on the damp ground.

"You see this circle? That's our country. That's the first circle. Now here's the second." A circle with a larger diameter. "That is mankind at large. You would think that the first forms part of the second, wouldn't you? Not in the least! There are barriers of prejudice. Not to mention barbed wire and machine guns. To break through, physically or spiritually, is well-nigh impossible. Which means that mankind, as such, does not exist. There are only fatherlands, everyone's fatherland alien to everyone else's. . . ."

• • •

It was about then that the Special Section sent Klara some forms to fill in. She had no difficulty with them: Her origins were impeccable; her life story was not long in the telling; it was lit by the even glow of prosperity; it was free from acts that might compromise a Soviet citizen.

The forms were in circulation for some months, and they gave complete satisfaction.

In the meantime, Klara had graduated from the institute and passed through the guarded gates of the mysterious Marfino complex.

# 45

# The Running Dogs of Imperialism

Klara and the other girls from the institute were subjected to a hair-raising briefing by the saturnine Major Shikin.

She learned that she would be working among most dangerous spies, running dogs of world imperialism and the American Intelligence Service, who had sold their motherland for a song.

Klara was assigned to the Vacuum Laboratory. This was the name given to the laboratory that made to order the numerous electronic tubes required by the other labs. The tubes were blown first in the little glassblowing shop next door, then emptied of air by three humming vacuum pumps in the Vacuum Laboratory proper, a large, dim room facing north. The pumps divided the room like a row of cabinets. Electric bulbs burned there even in the daytime. The floor was paved with flagstones, and the clatter of shoes and scraping of chair legs never ceased. Each pump had its own vacuum man (a prisoner) sitting or pacing beside it. Other prisoners sat at little desks in two or three places. The only free employees were a girl named Tamara and the captain in charge of the laboratory.

Klara had been introduced to this boss of hers in Yakonov's office. He was a plump, middle-aged Jew with an apathetic air. He made no attempt to frighten Klara further, just nodded to her to follow him.

"You, of course, know nothing and can do nothing?" he asked her, out on the stairway.

Klara mumbled something. As if being frightened was not enough, she would now be put to shame, exposed at any moment as an ignoramus and made a laughingstock.

She entered the lab inhabited by monsters in blue overalls as though it were a cage of wild animals. She was afraid even to raise her eyes.

The three vacuum men really did look like caged animals, pacing beside their pumps; they had an urgent order and had been denied sleep for two days running. But the prisoner by the second pump, a man in his forties with a bald spot and in need of a shave, stopped, beamed, and said:

"Hey! Reinforcements!"

Her fears vanished at once. There was so much simple good nature in this exclamation that Klara had to make an effort not to smile in return.

The youngest of the vacuum men, the one with the smallest pump, also stopped. He was hardly more than a boy, with a mischievous face and innocent eyes. The look he gave Klara was that of a man taken aback. No young man had ever looked at her like that before.

The oldest of the vacuum men was Dvoetyosov, whose pump, the huge one farther down the room, hummed loudest of all. He was tall, ungainly, lean except for his pendulous belly. He threw Klara a contemptuous glance from a distance and retreated behind his cabinet, as though to spare himself the sight of anything so disgusting.

Klara discovered later that there was no need to feel offended by this; he was the same with all the free staff, and when any of the bosses came in, he would deliberately switch on something noisy so that they would have to shout above the din. He was unashamedly careless of his appearance, could turn up with the last of his trouser buttons dangling loose at the end of a long thread or with a hole in the back of his overalls, and would thrust his hand inside his overalls to scratch with women present. He liked to say: "Look, this is my own country! Why should I worry what anybody else thinks?"

The prisoners, even the young ones, called the middle vacuum man simply Zemelya, which he didn't seem to mind in the least. His was a "sunny nature," and he never stopped grinning from ear to ear. Watching him closely in the weeks that followed, Klara noticed that he showed no regret for whatever was lost beyond recall, whether it was an irretrievable pencil or his blighted life. He was never angry about anything or with anyone; nor was he afraid of anyone. He was a really good engineer, but his expertise was airplane engines. He had been delivered to Marfino in error, had made himself at home, and was in no hurry to move on, rightly considering that the next place was unlikely to be better.

When the pumps were quieter in the evening, Zemelya liked to reminisce or listen to someone else's stories.

"You just took your five-kopeck piece and bought whatever you wanted," he said, smiling broadly. "Every step you took, there were people offering you something. It was all good stuff. Nobody tried to sell you crap. If you bought boots, they really were boots; they'd last ten years without a repair, or fifteen repaired. They didn't snip off the leather at the toecaps like they do now; they took it under the welt so that it went right around the foot. Then there were those fancy red boots—what did they call them?—with the crepe soles; it was a treat to wear them." He dissolved into smiles and screwed up his eyes, as though he were looking at a warm but not very bright sun. "Or take railway stations. . . . You never saw anybody lying on the floor, or sweltering all day and night outside the ticket office. . . . It took you just one minute to buy a ticket and get a seat; there was always room in the cars. They made the trains go fast; they weren't out to save coal. . . . That's how it was; living was simple, very simple in those days."

The oldest vacuum man would waddle out of the dark corner where his desk was safely hidden from the bosses, hands deep in pockets, to listen to these stories. He would take his stand in the middle of the room, his protuberant eyes looking quizzically at the speaker over his glasses.

"Zemelya, d'you mean to say you remember the tsar?"

"Just about," Zemelya said, with an apologetic smile.

Dvoetyosov shook his head. "Well, you shouldn't. We're supposed to be pumping for socialism."

Zemelya timidly demurred. "We've been told socialism's built already, Kostya."

"Eh?"

The senior vacuum man was popeyed with amazement.

"Yes, since 1933, or thereabouts."

"You mean when there was that famine in the Ukraine? Wait a bit, though, what are we slogging away for day and night now?"

"Building Communism, I suppose," said Zemelya, beaming.

"You don't say? So tha-at's what it is!" the senior vacuum man said in an idiotic nasal whine, and shuffled off back to his corner.

Klara wasn't sure whether they talked like this for their own amusement or for her benefit, but she didn't report them.

Her duties were uncomplicated; she and Tamara worked alternate shifts: from morning till 6:00 p.m. one day, and from after dinner until 11:00 p.m. the next. The captain was always there in the morning because the brass might want him in the course of the day; he never turned up in the evening, since he did not aspire to promotion. The girls' main task was to act as "duty officers," or, in other words, to keep an eye on the prisoners. By way of training, their boss also gave them little jobs about which there was no urgency. Klara and Tamara saw each other for only about two hours a day. Tamara had been working in the establishment for over a year and was at ease with the prisoners. Klara in fact suspected that Tamara was on quite intimate terms with one of them and brought him books, which, however, changed hands when no one was looking. Apart from this, Tamara went to an English class there in the institute, in which the pupils were free workers and the teachers (unpaid, of course, that was the great advantage) were prisoners. Tamara quickly dispelled Klara's fears that these people might do something awful.

In the end, Klara started talking to one of the prisoners herself. Not, to be sure, a political offender but a petty lawbreaker, one of the very few in Marfino. This was Ivan the glassblower, a superb craftsman, unfortunately for him. His old aunt used to say that he was a golden workman but a still more golden drunkard. He used to earn a lot, spend a lot on drink, and, when drunk, beat his wife and pitch into the neighbors. None of this would have mattered if his path hadn't crossed that of the MGB. An important comrade with no badges of rank summoned him in writing and offered him a job with a salary of three thousand rubles. Ivan, as it happened, worked in the sort of place where his basic wage was less but where he could bump it up by piecework. So he forgot who he was dealing with and asked for four thousand a month. His highly placed interlocutor offered an extra two hundred, but Ivan dug his heels in. He was sent packing. The next payday he got drunk and started making a row in the yard. In the past, the militia had turned a deaf ear to complaints, but this time they turned up in force and took Ivan in. He was tried the next day, given one year, and taken straight from the court to see the same important person without badges of rank, who explained that Ivan would be working in the place previously intended for him, only now they would not be paying him for it. If these terms did not suit him, he could go and mine coal in the Arctic Circle.

Now Ivan sat in Marfino blowing cathode-ray tubes of all shapes and sizes. His year was nearly over, but his conviction remained on his record; and to avoid being sent away from Moscow, he was begging the authorities to keep him on in the same job as a free worker, at fifteen hundred rubles if they liked.

Nobody else in the sharashka would have found such an artless tale with such a happy ending at all interesting; there were people in the sharashka who had spent fifty days in the death cell, and there were people who had known the pope and Albert Einstein personally. But Klara was shaken by it. It showed that, as Ivan said, "they can do just what they like."

She was distrustful of the political prisoners, and her cautiously official manner kept them at a distance. But even the glassblower's story was enough to awaken in her mind the suspicion that among these blue-overalled people others, too, might be completely innocent. If that was so, could her own father have condemned an innocent man in his time?

But once again there was no one to whom she could put this question, either in the family or at work. Her friendship with Innokenty, and that outing of theirs, had led to nothing, probably because he and Nara had gone abroad again soon afterward.

However, in the course of the year, Klara did at last make a friend, Ernst Golovanov. It wasn't at work that she met him. He was a literary critic, and Dinera brought him home one day. He wasn't much of a beau. Scarcely taller than Klara (and standing by himself he looked shorter), he had a rectangular forehead and a rectangular head on a rectangular trunk. He was only a little older than Klara, but he looked middle-aged; he had a paunch and had obviously never gone in for sports. (To tell the truth, the name in his passport was Saunkin, and Golovanov was a pseudonym.) But he was a well-read, intellectually mature, and interesting man and already a candidate member of the Writers Union.

They had gone to the Maly Theater together. The play was *Vassa Zheleznova*. It was a dismal affair. The theater was less than half full, which may have been why the actors seemed half dead. They came on looking bored, like clerks arriving at the office, and cheered up only when it was time to leave. It was almost humiliating to perform to such a poor house; the makeup and the characters became a silly joke unworthy of adults. At any moment somebody, speaking quietly as though in his own sitting room, might break the silence of the audience and say, "Why don't you good people stop this tomfoolery?" and the play would collapse in ruins. The humiliation of the actors was contagious. The whole audience felt as though they were taking part in some deed of shame and were too embarrassed to look at each other. It was just as quiet during the intermissions. Couples exchanged whispered remarks and walked noiselessly about the foyer.

Klara and Ernst were among those who trod this measure in the first intermission. Ernst stood up for Gorky, indignantly declaring that the performance was an insult to him, abusing People's Artist Zharov as—on this occasion at least—a shameless ham and, more daring still, condemning the bureaucratic inertia of the Ministry of Culture, which was sapping the vitality of the Soviet theater, with its marvelous tradition of realism and undermining the theatergoer's confidence in it. Ernst spoke as he wrote, in precise and well-rounded prose, never at a loss for words, and never leaving a sentence unfinished even when he was excited.

In the second intermission, Klara suggested that they should stay in their seats.

"I'll tell you why I'm sick of seeing both Ostrovsky and Gorky," she said. "It's because I'm sick of seeing the power of capital and parental oppression exposed, sick of seeing young girls forced to marry old men. I'm sick and tired of this war against phantoms. Fifty years, a hundred years on, we're still exorcising, still exposing things long vanished. You never see a play about things that do exist."

"There's some truth in what you say." Ernst looked at Klara curiously and with a kind smile. He had not been mistaken in her. This girl was nothing much to look at, but you'd never be bored with her. "What sort of thing do you mean?" There was nobody in the seats next to them or in the orchestra immediately below. Lowering her voice and trying not to betray any important state secret or the secret of her own sympathy for those people, she told Ernst that she worked with prisoners who had been represented as running dogs of imperialism, but that when she had got to know them better, they had turned out to be . . . such and such. The question that tormented her . . . maybe Ernst could tell her . . . could there, did he think, be innocent people among them?

Ernst heard her out and answered unhesitatingly, as though he had thought it over before. "There are, of course. That's inevitable, with any penal system."

Klara didn't want to think about systems. She was in a hurry to append the glassblower's conclusion. "But Ernst! That's as good as saying 'they can do what they want to.' That is horrible!"

Her strong tennis player's hand closed into a fist on the red velvet of the barrier in front of them. Golovanov laid his own short-fingered hand flat on the barrier nearby but did not cover Klara's hand; he did not take such liberties uninvited.

"No," he said, gently but firmly. "It isn't like that. Who is doing these things? Who is it who wants to do them? It is history. History does what it wants. You and I sometimes find it horrible, Klara, but it's time we were used to the fact that there exists a law of large numbers. The more material involved in a historical event, the greater the likelihood of individual incidental errors—judicial, tactical, ideological, economic, or whatever. We grasp the process only in its basic and determining outlines, and what matters most is the conviction that the process itself is necessary and inevitable. Yes, people sometimes suffer through no fault of their own. What about those killed in battle? Or those who perished quite senselessly in the Ashkhabad earthquake? Road victims? As traffic increases, the number of fatal accidents must grow. The wise philosophy of life is to accept that it is an evolutionary process and that there will be victims at every stage."

This explanation seemed to make sense. Klara became thoughtful.

The second bell had rung, and the audience reassembled.

In the third act, Roek, playing Vassa's younger daughter, suddenly rang true—rang loud and clear—and bade fair to drag the whole play out of the abyss.

Klara did not realize herself that what concerned her was not just any innocent man, wherever he might be, someone, say, who might already have rotted away beyond the Arctic Circle in accordance with the Law of Big Numbers, but this youngest vacuum man with the blue eyes and the dark golden complexion, hardly more than a boy in spite of his twenty-three years. Whenever he saw Klara and ever since their first meeting, the look of joyous adoration had never left his eyes, and it always excited and confused her. She could not know what allowances had to be made for Rostislav's two years in a camp, where he had never seen a woman. All she knew was that for the first time in her life she felt herself an object of enraptured admiration.

Admiration of Klara did not, however, dominate his thoughts exclusively.

Confined as he was, spending almost his whole day under electric light in a dim laboratory, the young man somehow lived a full, indeed, a hectic life; when he was not busy on some contrivance that was not for the bosses' eyes or surreptitiously studying English in working hours, he would be calling up friends in the other laboratories and dashing off to socialize in the hallways. His movements were always impetuous, and at any given moment he seemed to be in the grip of something passionately interesting. Admiring Klara was one of his passionately interesting occupations.

As busy as he was, he never neglected his appearance; there was always something immaculately white to be seen beneath the gaudy tie tucked into his overalls. (Klara did not know that this was the famous "dickey," Rostislav's invention, one-sixteenth of a prison-issue sheet.)

The young people whom Klara met outside (Ernst Golovanov in particular) were already on their way up in the world, and in everything they did or said—in their dress, their deportment, their conversation—they were careful not to let themselves down. In Rostislav's company Klara felt that a weight was lifted from her, that she, too, wanted to behave mischievously. She studied him discreetly, and her sympathy for him grew. She did not believe for a moment that he, of all people, and the good-natured Zemelya were among those running dogs of imperialism against whom Major Shikin had warned her. She was eager to discover what crime Rostislav in particular had been punished for and whether he had a long sentence to serve. (That he was unmarried she could see for herself.) She hesitated to ask him directly, imagining that such questions would be traumatic because they would resurrect his repugnant past, which he needed to shake off in order to rehabilitate himself.

Another two months or so went by. Klara was by now at home with them all, and they often discussed in her presence all sorts of idle topics that had nothing to do with their work. Rostislav made a habit of waiting until she was alone in the lab, when the prisoners on the evening shift went to dinner, and looking in to collect something left behind or to study a bit while it was quiet.

During these evening visits Klara forgot all the operations officer's warnings. . . .

The night before, impetuous words had burst from them, sweeping away the pathetic barriers that divide people, as floodwater breaks a dam.

The young man had no hideous past to live down. There was nothing to discover, except that he had been wantonly robbed of his youth and that he had an eager appetite to know and to experience all that he had missed.

She learned that he had lived with his mother in a village outside Moscow on a canal-side. He had just left school when some Americans from the embassy rented a country home in the village. Ruska and two of his friends were curious (and rash) enough to go fishing with the Americans twice. They thought that they had gotten away with it, and Ruska was admitted to Moscow University. But that September he was arrested on his way there, quietly, so that his mother did not know for some time where he had gone. (The Ministry of State Security, apparently, always tried to arrange things so that the person arrested would not have time to hide anything and his family and friends could not receive any cryptic message or signal.) They put him in the Lubyanka. (It was there, in Marfino, that Klara first heard of the prison with that name.) The interrogators tried to make Rostislav tell them what assignment American intelligence had given him and to what secret address he was supposed to report. He was, in his own words, still just a silly kid; he couldn't understand what they were getting at, and he cried all the time. Suddenly a miracle occurred; no one is ever released from the Lubyanka scot-free, but Ruska was.

That was in 1945. And that was as far as he had gotten last night.

The unfinished story had kept Klara in a state of suspense all night. This afternoon, ignoring all the rules of vigilance, not to mention the limits set by decorum, she had boldly sat down with Rostislav by his quietly humming pump, and they had resumed their conversation.

When the dinner break came, they were like children, taking alternate bites from the same big apple. It seemed strange to them that in all those months they had never really talked before. They had so much to say and so little time. When he impatiently interrupted her, he would touch her hands, and she did not object. But when the others had all left the room, sitting shoulder to shoulder with hands touching suddenly took on a new meaning. Klara saw those yearning blue eyes looking straight into her own, and Rostislav's voice faltered as he spoke.

"Klara! Who knows whether we will ever sit together like this again? For me this is a miracle. I adore you." (By now he was holding and caressing her hand.) "I may have to spend my whole ruined life in one prison or another. Make me happy; give me a moment that I can cherish even in solitary confinement! Let me kiss you!"

Klara felt like a goddess descending into a dungeon where a prisoner lay in chains. Rostislav drew her toward him and pressed his lips to hers in a violent kiss, the kiss of a prisoner for whom restraint had become torture. And she responded. . . .

After a time she freed herself and turned away. She was shaken, and her head was spinning.

"Please go away," she begged him.

Rostislav rose and stood before her uncertainly.

"Please leave me alone for now," Klara insisted.

He hesitated. Then he obeyed. He turned around in the doorway, looked at her piteously, imploringly, then almost lurched out of the room.

They all came back from the dinner break shortly afterward.

Klara dared not raise her eyes to look at Ruska or anyone else. That burning sensation. Was it shame? Not just shame. Happiness, then? If so, a troubled happiness.

She heard people saying that the prisoners were to be allowed a New Year's party.

She sat still for three hours, only her fingers moving as she braided a little basket for the tree from brightly colored plastic flexible cord.

By now Ivan the glassblower had returned from seeing his wife, and he blew two funny glass imps, armed with what might be rifles, then fashioned a cage from glass rods and hung inside it a bright moon, also of glass, which tinkled mournfully as it swung on its silver thread.

# 46

## The Castle of the Holy Grail

FOR HALF THE DAY a dull cloud hung low over Moscow, and it was not cold. But when the seven prisoners stepped out of the blue bus into the exercise yard, just in time for dinner, the first impatient snowflakes were making their lonely flight.

One of them, a regular hexagonal ministar, fell on the sleeve of Nerzhin's rusty old army coat. He stood still in the middle of the yard gulping fresh air.

Senior Lieutenant Shusterman happened to be there and warned him that since this was not an exercise period, he had better go indoors. Nerzhin was put out. He did not wish to, he simply could not, talk about his wife's visit, didn't want to confide in anybody or seek anybody's sympathy. Did not want to talk at all or to listen. All that he wanted was to be alone and to rerun through his mind all the impressions he had brought back with him before they blurred and became mere memories.

But solitude is the last thing you are likely to find in a sharashka or any other prison camp. Everywhere you went—in the cells, the "convicts' compartments" and cattle trucks on trains, huts in the camps, hospital wards—there were always people, people, people: people you knew and people you didn't want to know, thin people, fat people . . . but always people and more people.

On his way into the building (by the special entrance for prisoners, down wooden steps and along the basement hallway), Nerzhin paused to think where he should go next.

He had an idea.

He took the back stairs, which hardly anybody used, and went up past the broken chairs stacked there to the top landing on the third floor.

This landing had been converted to a studio for a prisoner named Kondrashov-Ivanov. He had no connection with the general work of the sharashka and was kept on as a sort of serf-artist. The vestibules and halls of the main building were spacious and needed pictorial adornment. Less spacious but more numerous were the private apartments of Deputy Minister Foma Guryanovich and his close colleagues, and these were still more urgently in need of large, beautiful, cost-free pictures.

Not that Kondrashov-Ivanov really satisfied these requirements: The pictures he painted were big, all right, and cost nothing, but beautiful they were not. The colonels and generals who came to view his gallery wasted their breath dinning into him how he ought to paint and what colors he should use, then accepted with a sigh what was on offer. Besides, his pictures improved greatly when mounted in gilt frames.

On his way up, Nerzhin passed a large canvas commissioned for the vestibule of the main building: *A. S. Popov Demonstrates the First Radio-Telegraph to Admiral Makarov.* As he turned onto the last flight and before he saw the artist, he caught sight of a painting high up on a blank wall: *The Blasted Oak.* A finished picture two meters high, which for some reason none of the artist's patrons had wanted.

Other canvases hung along the walls of the stairwell. There were some on easels. The light came from two windows, one on the north, the other on the west side. The Iron Mask's little window, with its grating and its little pink curtain, looked out on the landing itself, which was as near as it got to the light of day.

There was nothing else to be seen, not even a chair. Instead, there were two logs standing on end, one higher than the other.

The stairway was inadequately heated, the studio was always damp and cold, but Kondrashov-Ivanov's sleeveless jacket lay on the floor, and he himself stood motionless, tall and erect, with his arms and his legs sticking out of his skimpy overalls, not, apparently, freezing. The big glasses, which made his face large and stern, were pressed firmly down over his ears to allow for his abrupt twists and turns at a picture, brush in one hand, palette in the other, held at arm's length.

He looked around when he heard cautious steps.

Their eyes met, but their minds were still elsewhere.

The artist was not altogether pleased to see a visitor; just now he needed solitude and silence.

Yet he was more pleased than not, and there was no falsity in his hearty welcome. "Gleb Vikentich! Welcome!" Hospitable hands flourished brush and palette.

Good nature is a dubious asset for an artist; it enriches his imagination but wrecks his routine.

Nerzhin hesitated in embarrassment on the next-to-last step. He spoke almost in a whisper, as though there were some third person whom he feared to awaken.

"No, please, Ippolit Mikhalych! I've only come. . . . I hope you don't mind. . . . I wanted to be quiet for a bit."

"Yes, yes, of course!"

The artist nodded and said no more, perhaps remembering or reading in his eyes that Nerzhin had been to see a visitor. He retreated with a sort of bow, pointing with brush and palette to one of the stumps.

Nerzhin gathered up his coattails, which he had saved from shortening in the camp, and sank onto the stump, leaning back against the banisters. As much as he wanted to, he did not light a cigarette.

The artist's gaze was fixed again on the same spot in his picture.

They were silent.

Reawakened affection for his wife was a faint, pleasurable ache in Nerzhin's breast.

He felt as though his fingers, where they had touched her hands, her neck, her hair in farewell, were dusted with some precious pollen.

Year after year, you live deprived of what should be every man's right on this earth.

You are left with your mind (if any), your beliefs (if you are mature enough to have acquired any), and you are chock-full of concern for the general good. You might be a citizen of ancient Athens, a complete human being.

Only, the one thing needful is missing.

That one thing, the love of a woman, of which you are deprived, seems more momentous than all the world besides.

Those simple words—"Do you love me?" "Yes. Do you love me?"—unspoken except in looks or soundless movements of the lips, now fill your heart with quiet rejoicing.

At that moment Gleb could not remember or imagine any fault in his wife. She had all the virtues. And above all—loyalty.

A pity he had hesitated to kiss her at the beginning of the visit. Now that kiss was lost beyond recall.

Her lips were slack; she had forgotten how to kiss. She looked exhausted, like a hunted creature. How desperate she must be, to talk of divorce!

A legal divorce? Gleb had no objection. Tearing up a piece of officially stamped paper would mean nothing to him. The union of souls was no concern of the state. Nor, for that matter, was the union of bodies.

But he had been bruised and battered enough by life to know that events have their own inexorable logic. People never dream what the perverse consequences of their routine actions may be. Take Popov. When he invented radio, did he realize that he was letting loose pandemonium, inflicting torture by loudspeaker on solitary thinkers? Or take the Germans, who let Lenin through to bring down Russia and thirty years later found their own country split in two. Or take Alaska; they had been stupid enough to sell it for a song, and now Soviet tanks could not reach America over land! Such trivialities could determine the fate of the planet.

Or take Nadya. She wanted a divorce to escape from persecution. But once divorced, she would be married again before she knew it.

His heart had sunk when her ringless fingers had waved good-bye to him. That was how people said good-bye forever.

Nerzhin sat there in silence, and the excessive joy he had felt after the visit, the joy that had filled him to overflowing in the bus, gradually ebbed, banished by sober and gloomy thoughts. But this restored his mental equilibrium, and he was soon Nerzhin the old zek again.

"It suits you here," she had said.

Prison suited him!

It was true.

He did not really regret the five years he had spent inside. Even now, before he could see them in perspective, Nerzhin recognized that they were a uniquely necessary part of his life.

Where could you get a better view of the Russian Revolution than through the bars it had set in place?

What better place to get to know people?

And yourself.

Only the iron-hard path ordained for him could have spared him so many false steps, so much youthful vacillation.

This dreamer, Kondrashov-Ivanov, so impervious to the cruel jokes of the age, what had he lost by being imprisoned? He could not of course wander about the Moscow countryside with his paintbox. He had no table for still lifes. Exhibitions? He had never known how to "arrange" one for himself and in half a century had never shown a single picture in a reputable gallery. Money for his pictures? He had never been paid, even outside. Appreciative viewers? He probably attracted more of them here. A studio? Outside, he hadn't had anything as good as this. A single long, narrow room like a hallway had served him as studio and living quarters. To make room to work, he had to stack chair upon chair and roll up the mattress, so that callers asked whether he was moving. They had had only one table, so when a still life was set up on it, he and his wife ate off chairs until the picture was finished.

During the war there had been no oil for paints, and he had mixed his colors with rationed sunflower oil. He had to earn his ration cards, and they sent him to a chemical warfare division to paint portraits of women soldiers who obtained the best grades on military and political courses. Ten portraits were commissioned, but he chose just one of the ten best girls and wore her out with long sittings. Even so, his version of her was not at all what the top brass wanted to see, and *Moscow 1941*, as the picture was called, found no takers.

Yet the essence of 1941 was in that portrait. A girl in an anti-gas suit. Her head was thrown back, and she stared wildly at something hideous, something unforgivable before her. But this was no weak, girlish figure!

Hands trained for battle gripped the sling of her gas mask. The dark gray anti-gas suit, with its stiff creases and silvery glint where the light caught its folds, looked like a suit of armor. Nobility, cruelty, and vengefulness had come together and were engraved on the face of this determined Komsomol from Kaluga, this far-from-beautiful girl in whom Kondrashov-Ivanov had seen a Joan of Arc!

It was, you might think, very much in the spirit of the wartime slogan "We shall not forget! We shall not forgive!" but it went too far; it showed something savage, uncontrollable. It was rejected and never exhibited. It stood for years in the artist's little room, with its face to the wall, and went on standing there until he was arrested.

Leonid Andreev's son, Daniil, had written a novel and asked a couple of dozen friends to hear it. A Thursday salon, nineteenth-century style. That novel cost every member of the audience twenty-five years in a corrective labor camp. One of those who heard the seditious work was Kondrashov-Ivanov, great-grandson of the Decembrist Kondrashov, sentenced to twenty years for his part in the 1825 rising and remembered for the touching behavior of a French governess who loved him and followed him to Siberia.

True, Kondrashov-Ivanov did not end up in a camp. As soon as he had signed the receipt for his sentence, he was taken to Marfino and put to work, painting a picture a month on Foma Guryanovich's orders. In the past twelve months he had painted the pictures hanging there and others that had been removed. With fifty years behind him and twenty-five ahead, he had not lived but flitted effortlessly through that halcyon year, not knowing whether there would ever be such another. He did not notice what he was given to eat or to wear or how often his head was counted among all those others.

He was, of course, deprived of opportunities to meet and talk to other artists. Or to look at their pictures. Or to find out from albums of reproductions filtering through customs what direction painting was taking in the West.

Wherever it was going, it could have no influence on, no relevance to, the work of Kondrashov-Ivanov because, in the magic pentagram where all discoveries were made and all creation took place, all five angles were occupied once and for all: two by drawing and color, as only he could see them, two by universal good and universal evil, and the fifth by the artist himself.

He could not return on his own two legs to the landscapes he had once seen or with his own hands reproduce the same still lifes, but he had begun to see them more clearly and in their true colors in cells half darkened by "muzzles," and those he had never painted before he could paint now from memory.

One of these still lifes, based on the four-by-five ratio of the Egyptian square—Kondrashov attached very great importance to the proportions of the sides—was hanging right then next to Mamurin's window. Half of its surface was taken up by a brightly polished round copper tray standing up on edge. It was just an ordinary tray, but its effect was that of a hero's blazing shield. By it stood a jug of some dark metal, beaten and burnished, probably meant to hold water, not wine. And on the wall behind them was draped a piece of golden yellow brocade (Kondrashov was particularly attracted by all shades of yellow just now) that could be seen as the mantle of the invisible. There was something in the combination of these three objects that inspired courage and forbade retreat.

(The colonels had all refused this still life, insisting that the tray should be laid down flat and a cut melon or something of the sort placed on it.)

Kondrashov worked on several pictures at once, leaving them and coming back to them from time to time. He had never brought a picture to the stage at which his craftsman's eye could judge it perfect. He did not know for sure that there was such a stage. He always abandoned a picture when he no longer saw anything special in it, when his eye was so used to it that the changes he might make seemed more trivial at every return and he realized that he might be spoiling it rather than improving it.

He turned it to the wall, covered it up. The picture was rejected, estranged from him. But when he surrendered it gratis to hang amid pomp and luxury, he looked at it with a fresh eye, and the pang of parting was mingled with delight. If nobody saw it again, he had still painted it!

Nerzhin, all attention now, started inspecting Kondrashov's last picture. A wintry brook occupied the main place in it. It was almost impossible to tell which way the brook was flowing. In fact, it was hardly flowing at all; a film of ice was beginning to form on its surface. There were brownish tints in the shallows, reflected from fallen leaves covering the bottom. The first snow lay in patches on both banks, and the grass in between was brown and withered. Two willows grew by the brook, wraithlike and misty, wet from the powdery snow melting into them. But the most important part of the picture was the background: a dense rampart of olive-black firs with a single helpless birch gleaming in the front rank. Its gentle yellow glow made the host of sentinel conifers, with their sharp pikes raised skyward, look denser and darker still.

The sky was a motley scrabble, and the setting sun was muffled by ragged cloud, which it was too weak to pierce with a direct ray. The focal point of the picture was not this either. It was the chill water of the standing brook. It had fullness and depth. It was leaden yet translucent, and it looked very cold. It seemed to hold the balance between autumn and winter.

This was the picture on which the painter was now intent.

Artistic creation is subject to an inexorable law, which Kondrashov knew only too well. He had struggled against it but had ended by helplessly submitting. This law said that nothing he had done before had any value, none of it counted, none of it reflected credit on him. Only the picture on which he was working then and there was the summation of a lifetime's experience, the zenith of his powers, the one and only touchstone of his talent!

And he could see that it was not going to work!

But none of his previous pictures had been "going to work" until, briefly, it did. Now past despair was forgotten; this was the first time he had ever seemed to be learning to paint properly. And still it wasn't working; his whole life was a failure; he had never had any talent at all!

That water, now—it looked liquid and cold and deep and still, but none of that meant anything if it did not convey the wisdom, the completeness, the serenity that Kondrashov could never find in his passionate self but recognized and revered in nature. Did his water convey that sublime serenity, or didn't it? Miserably, hopelessly he struggled to decide. Did it, didn't it. . . ?

"Do you know, Ippolit Mikhailovich, you've more or less convinced me. These places of yours *are* Russia."

Kondrashov-Ivanov looked around sharply, "And not the Caucasus?"

His spectacles sat as firmly on his nose as if they were welded to it.

Though not the weightiest of his concerns, it had a certain importance. Many people were perplexed by Kondrashov's landscapes, finding them Caucasian rather than Russian. Perhaps because they were too majestic, too awesome.

"I feel sure such places can be found in Russia," Nerzhin said still more positively.

He rose from the stump and made the round of the landing inspecting *Morning of an Unusual Day* and other landscapes.

The artist nodded excitedly. "Of course, of course! Can be found and have been found! I could take you there if we didn't need an escort! The fact is that the public is under the spell of Levitan! We are used to seeing the

Russian landscape through Levitan's eyes, not unpleasant in its humble way but monotonous, featureless. But if there's nothing more to Russia, where did her self-burners come from? The mutinous streltsy? Peter the First? The Decembrists? The People's Will Party?"

"Uh-huh," Nerzhin said approvingly. "You're right there. But all the same, Ippolit Mikhailovich, I don't understand your passion for hyperbole. That crippled oak, for instance. Why does it have to be on the brink of a precipice? I feel sure there's an abyss down below—nothing less would satisfy you. And the sky isn't just stormy; it looks like a sky that has never known the sun. And all the hurricanes that ever blew anywhere in the last two hundred years have passed this way, twisting the tree's branches and struggling to claw it loose from the cliff. You're a Shakespearean, of course; anything evil must be inordinately evil. But that's ancient history. Statistically very few people find themselves in such situations. There's no need to spell 'good' and 'evil' with capital letters."

"I can't listen to such stuff!" The artist waved his long arms angrily. "Evil is ancient history, you say? Evil never really put in an appearance before our century. In Shakespeare's time what passed for evildoing was sport for callow youths! We ought to spell Good and Evil not just with capitals but with letters five stories high, letters that flash like lighthouses! Let's not split hairs! Statistically few! What about you and me and the rest of us here? And how many millions are there like us?"

"Well, yes . . ." Nerzhin said, shaking his head doubtfully. "If we're in a camp and we're invited to sell whatever conscience we have left for two hundred grams of black bread. . . . But that has no resonance, so to speak; it somehow doesn't show. . . ."

Kondrashov-Ivanov stood up still straighter, rose to his full not inconsiderable height. He gazed at something higher still ahead of him, like Egmont led to execution. "Prison camp should never break a man's spirit!"

Nerzhin laughed wryly.

"Shouldn't, perhaps, but it does. You haven't been in a camp yet, so you can't judge. You don't know how they crunch our fragile bones in the camps. It doesn't matter what you're like when you go in; you come out changed beyond recognition. As everybody knows, being determines consciousness."

"No, no, no!" Kondrashov-Ivanov spread his long arms, ready then and there to wrestle with the whole world. "No! No! No! That would be too degrading! If that were true, life wouldn't be worthwhile! If it is so, tell me, why do lovers remain faithful to each other when they're parted? 'Being' demands that they be unfaithful! And why do people in exactly the same circumstances, in the same camp even, behave so differently? Who can know for sure whether life molds man or the strong and noble human being molds life!"

Nerzhin was quietly confident that his experience of life was worth more than the fantasies of this ageless idealist. But he could not help admiring his sentiments.

"Every man is born with a sort of inner essence," Kondrashov said. "It is, so to speak, the innermost core of the man, his essential self. No 'being,' nothing extraneous, can determine him. Moreover, every man carries within himself an image of perfection, which is never dimmed and which sometimes stands out with remarkable clarity! And reminds him of his chivalrous duty!"

Nerzhin had by now returned to his seat on the log. He scratched the back of his head. "That's another thing," he said. "Why do you go in for all these knights and their knightly trappings? You seem to me to go too far, though Mitya Sologdin, of course, likes it. Your antiaircraft girl is a knight in armor; your copper tray is a shield. . . ."

"What?" Kondrashov was amazed. "You don't like it? I go too far, do I? Ha-ha-ha!" Operatic laughter echoed in the hollow stairwell like thunder in a mountain gorge. As though about to ride him down, he thrust out an arm toward Nerzhin, and his pointing finger was the head of his leveled lance.

"Who was it who expelled the knights from our lives? Lovers of money and trade. Lovers of orgies and feasting! What is it our age most lacks? Party members? No, sir, it lacks knights! In the days of chivalry, there were no concentration camps! No gas chambers!"

Suddenly he was silent. In a single movement he alighted softly from his steed and sank into a squatting position beside his visitor. His glasses flashed as he asked in a whisper: "Would you like me to show you something?"

Arguments with artists always end that way.

"Yes, of course."

Kondrashov, still stooping, shuffled off into a corner, pulled out a small canvas on a stretcher, and brought it over, keeping the gray obverse side toward Nerzhin.

"You know who Parsifal was?" he asked in a low voice.

"Wasn't he connected with Lohengrin?"

"His father. The guardian of the Holy Grail. I try to visualize that precise moment. The moment any man may experience, when he first catches sight of the image of perfection. . . ."

Kondrashov closed his eyes and drew in his lips. He had to prepare himself, too.

Nerzhin wondered why what he was about to see was so small.

The artist raised his eyelids.

"It's only a sketch. A sketch for the most important picture in my life. I will probably never paint it. It's the moment when Parsifal first caught sight of the . . . castle of the Holy . . . Grail!"

The picture was twice as high as it was wide. It showed a wedge-shaped crevice between two converging mountain precipices. On each of them, to the right and to the left, the trees on the fringe of a dense, primeval forest edged into the picture. Creeping bracken and ugly shrubs clung to the very edges and even the perpendicular walls of the two cliffs. High on the cliff to the left a light gray horse had emerged from the forest carrying a rider in a helmet and a scarlet cloak. The horse was not afraid of the abyss. Its hoof was raised ready, in obedience to the rider's will, either to back away or to cross the abyss; it had the strength to leap as though winged.

The rider himself had no eyes for the abyss before his horse. He was staring, in rapt amazement, into the depths of the picture, where an orange-gold radiance suffused the whole expanse of the sky above, emanating perhaps from the sun, perhaps from a still purer source concealed by the castle. Stepped and turreted, growing out of the stepped mountain and visible also from below through the cleft between the cliffs, between the trees and the ferns, rising to a needle point in mid-heaven at the top of the picture, hazy and indistinct, as if spun from shifting cloud, yet discernible in all the details of its unearthly perfection, ringed in a blue-gray aureole by the invisible supersun, stood the castle of the Holy Grail.

# 47

# Top-Secret Conversation

THE BELL FOR THE DINNER BREAK could be heard in every nook and cranny of the ex-seminary, and its ringing reached even Kondrashov's remote landing.

Nerzhin hurried out into the open.

The exercise yard was not spacious, but Nerzhin liked to make a path of his own, away from the others. As in his cell, it was three paces forward, three paces back, but if he was alone that was enough. In this way he derived from the exercise period a few blissful moments of solitude and readjustment.

Hiding his civilian suit under the long tails of his indestructible artillery overcoat (not taking your suit off in time was a serious breach of discipline, and he could be turned away from the exercise area, but it would be a pity to waste walking time by going to change), Nerzhin took brisk steps to get there and occupy the short path he had beaten between one lime tree and the next, on the very edge of the permitted zone, near the fence beyond which stood the bishop's shiplike house.

He did not want to dissipate his thoughts in idle conversation.

Snowflakes fluttered, so sparse and weightless that it could hardly be said to be snowing, though they did not melt on the ground. Nerzhin began walking, head in the air, looking up at the sky, not where he was going. His body was invigorated by deep drafts of air, and his soul fused with the peace of the sky, overcast and snow-laden though it was.

But somebody called his name. He looked around. Another shabby officer's overcoat and a winter cap (he, too, had been arrested at the front in winter): Rubin, half concealed by the trunk of a lime. Rubin felt embarrassed, felt that he was treating his friend and messmate badly; Nerzhin would be prolonging, in his own mind, the meeting with his wife, and Rubin had to interrupt him at that sacred moment. He showed his embarrassment by extending no more than half of his beard from behind the tree.

"Gleb, old friend! If I'm barging in at the wrong moment, just tell me and I'll disappear. But I do very much want a word with you."

Nerzhin looked at Rubin's gently imploring eyes, at the white branches of the lime trees, and at Rubin again. However long he went on pacing that lonely path, he could enjoy no more the mingled joy and sorrow in his heart. It was already cooling.

Life went on.

"That's okay, Lev. What is it?"

Rubin emerged and joined him on his path. Gleb gathered from his solemn unsmiling look that something important had happened. It would have been impossible to tempt Rubin more sorely than by burdening him with an earthshaking secret and forbidding him to share it with any of his closest friends! If the American imperialists kidnapped him from the sharashka that moment and started chopping him into little pieces, he would never reveal his top-secret assignment! But to be the only zek in the sharashka in possession of such a tremendous secret and not tell even Nerzhin, that called for a superhuman effort!

Telling Gleb was the same as telling no one. He would not pass it on. Anyway, it was only natural to confide in him, since he alone was au courant with the classification of voices and could understand how difficult and how important the task was. Besides, it was a matter of urgency to reach an understanding with him while there was time. Later on, there would be a frantic hurry; there would be no tearing yourself away from the tapes, things would become more and more complicated. . . . Lev had to have an assistant.

In short, ordinary professional prudence fully justified what might look like betrayal of a state secret.

Two shabby military caps and two threadbare overcoats . . . shoulders touching, feet muddying and widening the path, they slowly paced, side by side.

"My old friend! This conversation never took place—never, never! Even in the Council of Ministers, no more than a couple of people know what I'm going to tell you."

"I'm as silent as the grave, anyway. But if it's so desperately secret, maybe you shouldn't tell me. What you don't know can't keep you awake."

"Don't be silly! I wouldn't tell you if I didn't have to. They'll have my head if they find out. But I'm going to need your help."

"Spit it out, then."

Watching carefully to make sure that no one came too close to them, Rubin quietly explained about the recorded telephone call and the purpose of the work he had been asked to do.

Though Nerzhin had lost his natural curiosity since he had been in prison, he listened with intense interest and stopped in his tracks once or twice to ask questions.

"You see, old fellow," Rubin said in conclusion, "it's a new science, the science of phonoscopy, with its own methods and its own horizons. To embark on it alone would be both difficult and boring for me. How great it will be if we both put our shoulders to the wheel! To be the founders of a completely new science—there's something to be proud of!"

"And that's what he calls science!" Nerzhin muttered. "As far as I'm concerned, it stinks!"

"All right, Archesilaus of Antioch wouldn't have approved! But don't you want an early release? If we succeed, you'll get a hefty remission and a clean passport. And even if we don't, you'll make your position in the sharashka more secure; you'll become an indispensable expert! People like Anton won't dare lay a finger on you."

One of the limes bordering the path forked at chest height. This time, instead of turning around when he reached it, Nerzhin leaned back against it and rested his head in the fork. With his cap pulled down low on his forehead, he could almost have been one of the professional crooks, and the look he gave Rubin was in character.

This was the second time in twenty-four hours he had been offered a chance of salvation. And for the second time it gave him no joy.

"Listen, Lev. . . . All these atom bombs and rockets, and your newly hatched phonoscopy"—he spoke haltingly, as though he wasn't sure how to answer—"it's the jaws of the dragon. People who know too much have been walled up in dungeons since the dawn of time. If only two members of the Council of Ministers—obviously Stalin and Beria—know about phonoscopy, plus two idiots like you and me, we will get our remission via the muzzle of a gun at the back of the head. I wonder, incidentally, why the Cheka-MGB makes a point of shooting people in the back of the head. A low trick, I call it. I'd sooner take a volley in the chest, with my eyes open! They're afraid to look their victims in the eye, that's what it is! And with so much work to be done, they want to spare the executioners too much nervous strain!"

Rubin was at a loss for words. Nerzhin, too, fell silent, still lolling against the tree. You would have said that they had discussed everything under the sun, from every imaginable angle, that there were no surprises left for them, but the two pairs of eyes, the dark brown and the dark blue, looked questioningly into each other.

Rubin sighed. "But a telephone call like that is a crucial moment in world history. We have no moral right to ignore it."

Nerzhin roused himself. "So why don't you come straight out with it? Why all this flimflam stuff about new sciences and remission of sentences? Your object is to catch the rascal, I take it?"

Rubin's eyes narrowed and his features hardened.

"Yes! That's what I want! This rotten little Moscow fancy pants, this wretched little careerist, is obstructing the road to socialism and must be removed."

"What makes you think he's a fancy pants and a careerist?"

"I've heard his voice. And because he's so eager to curry favor with his foreign bosses."

"Aren't you just salving your conscience?"

"What do you mean?"

"He's evidently fairly high up in the service, so wouldn't it be simpler for him just to curry favor with Vyshinsky? It seems a funny way to curry favor—with people in another country, without even telling them your name."

"He's probably counting on turning up there. To go up the ladder, he'd have to keep on performing his boring old duties irreproachably, to earn some little decoration in twenty years' time, an extra palm leaf on his sleeve, or whatever. But in the West he could cause a world sensation and pocket a million!"

"Mmm, . . . well. . . . All the same, basing your judgment of somebody's motives on the sound of a voice in the 300- to 2400-hertz waveband. . . . What do you think—was he telling the truth?"

"You mean about the radio shop?"

"Yes."

"Up to a point he obviously was."

"You mean there's a rational kernel in it?" Nerzhin said, teasing him. "Oy, oy, oy, Levka! So now you're standing up for thieves?"

"They aren't thieves; they're intelligence agents."

"What's the difference? Another lot of fancy pants and careerists, in New York this time, may steal the secret of the atom bomb to line their pockets with three million rubles from the East! Only maybe you haven't heard their voices?"

"Idiot! The fumes from the night bucket have gone to your head! Prison has made you see everything in a false perspective! How can you compare people who are out to wreck socialism with those who serve it?"

Rubin's face expressed suffering.

Nerzhin shoved his cap farther back—he was feeling hot—and rested his head in the fork of the tree again.

"Listen, whose marvelous lines were those I heard a little while ago, about the two Alyoshas?"

"Things were different then, before I'd learned to discriminate, before my ideals were clearly defined. In those days . . . it was still possible. . . ."

"And now you see your ideal clearly in the shape of the Gulag?"

"No! In the shape of the ethical ideals of socialism! Capitalism has none, just greed for profit!"

"Listen!" By now Nerzhin was wedging his shoulders into the fork of the tree, preparing himself for a long discussion. "Could you kindly explain these socialist ideals you talk about? They're nowhere to be seen at present. All right, maybe somebody's botched the experiment, but when and where can we expect to see them; what do they amount to? Eh? Socialism, of whatever variety, is a sort of caricature of the Gospel message. Socialism promises only equality and a full belly, and that only by means of coercion."

"Isn't that enough? Has any society in history ever had as much?"

"You'll find equality and full bellies in any good pigsty! What a tremendous favor they've bestowed on us! Equality and plenty! Give us a moral society!"

"We will! Just don't make difficulties! Don't get in the way!"

"Don't make bomb stealing difficult?"

"What twisted minds some people have! How is it that all intelligent and straight-thinking people. . . ."

Nerzhin laughed. "Who? Yakov Ivanovich Mamurin? Grigory Borisovich Abramson?"

"All the really enlightened minds! All the greatest thinkers in the West! Sartre, for instance! They all support socialism! They're all against capitalism! That's almost a platitude by now! You're the only one who can't see it! *Pithecanthropus erectus*!"

Rubin loomed dangerously over Nerzhin and shook him with grappling fingers. Nerzhin planted his palms on Rubin's chest to push him away.

"Have it your way! Maybe I am an ape! But I refuse to use your terminology. I refuse to talk about what you call capitalism and socialism! I don't understand these words, and I won't use them!"

Rubin laughed and relaxed a little. "I suppose you prefer the Language of Utter Clarity?"

"Yes, if you like!"

"What do you understand?"

"I understand words like 'a family of one's own,' 'inviolability of the person.'"

"'Unlimited freedom,' perhaps?"

"No—moral self-limitation."

"Fetal philosopher! How far will you get with amorphous, protozoic concepts like that in the twentieth century? Those are all class-conditioned ideas! Dependent on—"

"Are they, hell!" Nerzhin freed himself and stood up out of his niche. "Justice is never relative. . . ."

"It's a class concept! Of course it is," said Rubin, brandishing an open hand over Nerzhin's head.

"Justice is the cornerstone, the foundation of the universe!" Nerzhin, too, waved an arm. Anyone watching from a distance might have thought that they were about to start fighting. "We were born with a sense of justice in our souls; we can't and don't want to live without it! Remember what Fyodor Ioanich says: 'I am not strong, I am easily deceived, but I can distinguish white from black. Give me your keys, Godunov!'"

"You've got nowhere to hide!" Rubin said threateningly. "You'll have to declare someday which side of the barricade you're on."

Nerzhin answered just as angrily. "That's another word you blasted fanatics have done to death! You've put up barricades all over the world! That's the horror of it! A man may want to be a citizen of the world, a little lower than the angels, but they grab him by the legs and pull him down! 'Whoever is not with us is against us!' Just leave me room to move in! Room to move in, I tell you!" Nerzhin pushed him away.

"We would leave you room—it's those on the other side who won't."

"You would, you say? When did you ever let anybody move freely? It's tanks and fixed bayonets every inch of the way. . . ."

"Look, my friend," said Rubin more gently, "look at it in historical perspective."

"To hell with your perspective! I want to live now, not 'in the long term'! I know what you're going to say! It's just a matter of bureaucratic distortions; this is a transitional period, a temporary state of affairs—but this transitional order of yours makes my life impossible; it tramples my soul underfoot; that's what your transitional system does, and I won't defend it, not being an imbecile!"

"I made a mistake disturbing you after your visit," Rubin said quite gently.

"Seeing my wife has nothing at all to do with it!" Nerzhin spoke as bitterly as ever. "I think just the same at any other time! We ridicule the Christians—silly so-and-sos, living in hopes of paradise and putting up with absolutely everything on this earth! But what have we got to look forward to? For whose sake do we suffer? For our mythical descendants? What difference does it make whether it's happiness for posterity or happiness in the next world? We can't see either."

"You never were a Marxist!"

"Alas, I was."

"You dog! You scoundrel! We learned how to classify voices together. What am I supposed to do now? Work by myself?"

"You'll find somebody."

"Who?" Rubin pouted. Incongruously, the expression on his bold, piratical features was that of a hurt child.

"No, pal. It's no good your taking offense. They drench me from head to foot with a certain yellowy brown liquid, and I'm supposed to get the atom bomb for them? No thanks!"

"For us, you idiot, not for them!"

"What do you mean, for us? Do you need the atom bomb? I don't. I'm like Zemelya; I have no ambition to rule the world."

Rubin thought of something else. "Joking apart, would you really let that little pimple make a present of the bomb to the West?"

"You're a bit mixed up, dear Lev." He touched the lapel of Rubin's overcoat affectionately. "The bomb is there, in the West. They invented it, and you're trying to steal it."

"They're the ones who've dropped it!" Rubin's brown eyes flashed. "And you're prepared to put up with that? You can connive at what the little pimple has done?"

Nerzhin answered in the same thoughtful tone.

"Lev, my friend, you want life and poetry to be the same thing. Why are you so angry with the man?"

Rubin looked sourer still.

"So you're ready to be on the receiving end? Ready for a second Hiroshima, this time on Russian soil?"

"And you think stealing the bomb is the way to prevent that? The bomb must be morally outlawed, not stolen!"

"Outlawed? How? Idealistic raving!"

"Very simply. You just have to believe in the United Nations. You were offered the Baruch plan—you should have signed on to it! But no, the Big Chief must have the bomb!"

Rubin was standing with his back to the exercise yard and the path, but Nerzhin, facing the other way, saw Doronin rapidly approaching and whispered a warning—"Careful, Ruska's coming. Don't turn around"—then went on hurriedly, with no apparent break in the conversation—"Tell me, did you come across the 689th artillery regiment out there?"

"Who did you know in it?" Rubin, not yet tuned in, reluctantly answered.

"Major Kandybu. A curious thing happened to him. . . ."

"Gentlemen!" said Ruska Doronin, in a cheerful, guileless voice.

Rubin turned round with a grunt and frowned at him.

"What do you want, Junior?"

Rostislav's candid gaze rested on Rubin. His face radiated honesty.

"Lev Grigorievich! It's very upsetting. I come to you with an open heart, and the very people I trust most look at me suspiciously. What can I expect from the rest? Gentlemen! I've come to make you an offer: If you like, I'll sell all the Judases during the dinner break tomorrow, at the very moment when they pick up their thirty pieces of silver!"

# 48

## The Double Agent

Not counting roly-poly Gustav with the pink ears, Doronin was the youngest zek in the sharashka. His good nature, his readiness to oblige, and his liveliness won all hearts. During the few minutes in which volleyball was allowed, Rostislav gave himself heart and soul to the game. If those nearest the net let a ball pass, he would dive forward from the baseline, dig out the ball, and fall to the ground, grazing knees and elbows till they bled. People liked his unusual first name, too, "Ruska"; it fully justified itself two months after his arrival, when his head, shaved in the camp, had grown a mop of red hair.

He had been brought from Vorkuta because the Gulag had him down in its card index as a milling-machine operator. The phony machinist was quickly replaced with a real one, but Ruska was spared the return journey to Vorkuta when Dvoetyosov undertook to teach him to operate the smallest of the vacuum pumps. Ruska soon got the hang of it. He clung to the sharashka as though it were a rest home; he had suffered all sorts of hardships in the camps and talked about them now with gleeful abandon. How he was nearly a "goner" working in a wet pit, how he had learned to skip work by pretending every day to have a high temperature, warming both armpits with heated stones of equal size so that there would never be more than a tenth of a degree difference (they tried to catch him by using two thermometers).

But though he laughingly recalled his past, which would certainly repeat itself sometime in the future since he was in for twenty-five years, Ruska revealed himself to very few, and only under oath of secrecy, in his major role, that of an absconder who had led the MGB sleuths by the nose for two years. A worthy godchild of that organization, he was no more desperate for publicity than it was.

He did not stand out from the rest of the motley crowd in the sharashka until that September day. The day on which Ruska approached in turn, with a mysterious look on his face, the twenty-five most influential prisoners, those who shaped public opinion in the sharashka, and excitedly told each of them tête-à-tête that Major Shikin had that morning sought to recruit him as an informer and that he, Ruska, had consented, with the intention of using his new position for the common good.

Rostislav Doronin's colorful dossier was adorned with five changes of name, and all sorts of black marks and cryptic symbols showing how dangerous he was, his predisposition to escape, and the need to keep him handcuffed in transit, but Major Shikin, eager to reinforce his team of informers, calculated that, being young, he was pliable, that he valued his place in the sharashka, and that he would therefore be loyal to his operations officer.

Secretly summoned to Shikin's office (you would be summoned perhaps to the secretariat and told, "Oh yes, just look in on Major Shikin"), Rostislav spent three hours with him. In that time, as he listened to the godfather's boring instructions and explanations, his sharp eyes had studied not only the major's large head, which had gone gray over his files of denunciations and spiteful tittle-tattle, his dark face, his tiny hands, his feet in boys' shoes, his marble desk set and his silk blinds; he had also read the headings on files and the pieces of paper under the glass desktop, mentally inverting the letters, although he was sitting a meter and a half from the edge of the desk, and had still found time to work out which documents Shikin seemed to keep in the safe and which he locked in his desk.

From time to time, Doronin's ingenuous blue eyes gazed into the major's, and he nodded in agreement. This blue-eyed naïveté concealed a seething mass of wild ideas, but the operations officer, who was accustomed to the gray uniformity of meek compliance, could not know that.

Ruska knew very well that Shikin could send him back to Vorkuta if he refused to become a stoolie.

Not only Ruska but Ruska's whole generation had been trained to think of "pity" as a degrading sentiment, of "kindness" as comic, and of "conscience" as priest's talk. On the other hand, it had been drilled into them that informing was at once a patriotic duty, the best way to help the subject of your denunciation, and good for the health of society. Ruska did not take all of this in, but it had a certain influence on him. The main question for him now was not whether becoming a stoolie was a bad thing or permissible but where it would get him. Young as he was, he was rich in experience; he had lived a turbulent life, met many interesting people in prison, listened to any number of fierce prison disputes, and never lost sight of the possibility that all these MGB archives might be exhumed someday and the secret collaborators face disgrace and prosecution.

So that agreeing to cooperate with the godfather was as dangerous in the long term as was refusal in the short term.

But quite apart from all these calculations, Ruska was a virtuoso adventurist. As he read the intriguing bits of paper upside down under Shikin's glass desktop, he shivered in pleasurable anticipation of an exciting game. He had wearied of inactivity in the claustrophobic comfort of the sharashka!

Inquiring exactly how much he would be paid, in order to make it look convincing, Ruska enthusiastically agreed.

When he had left, Shikin, well satisfied with his psychological acuteness, walked about his office rubbing tiny palm against tiny palm. Such an enthusiastic informant gave promise of a rich harvest of denunciations. Meanwhile, a no-less-complacent Ruska made the rounds of those zeks in whom he had confidence, confessing that he had agreed to become an informer for the sake of the sport, because he wanted to study MGB methods, and also to expose the real stoolies.

Even the older zeks could remember no similar confession. They asked Ruska doubtfully why he was risking his head by boasting. His answer was, "When there's a Nuremberg trial for this dog pack, you will give evidence in my defense."

Each of the twenty zeks who heard his news told one or two others, yet no one went and reported it to the godfather! This in itself put some fifty people safely beyond suspicion.

Ruska's adventure caused a stir in the sharashka. People trusted the boy. And went on trusting him. But, as always, the course of events had a logic of its own. Shikin demanded "material." Ruska would have to give him something. He made the rounds of his confidants and complained to them. "Gentlemen! You can imagine how much telling all the others are doing! I've only had the job a month, and Shikin is really putting the pressure on! Look at it from my point of view, and slip me a scrap of material!"

Some of them didn't want to know about it, but others slipped him something occasionally. It was unanimously decided to ruin a certain female who only worked out of greed, boosting the thousands her husband took home. She treated the zeks with contempt, frequently voiced her opinion that they should all be shot (she only talked like this among the female free employees, but the zeks soon got to know about it), and she herself had thrown two of them to the wolves, one for an affair with a female employee, the other for making a suitcase from material belonging to the state. Ruska told a pack of shameless lies about her; she posted letters for zeks, stole condensers from the store cabinet. . . . Although he could not offer Shikin a shred of proof and although the lady's husband, an MVD colonel, protested emphatically, nothing could prevail against such a secret denunciation. The lady was dismissed and left in tears.

Sometimes Ruska informed on prisoners, too, reporting innocuous trifles and with due warning. But then the warnings stopped. He kept his intentions to himself. No one questioned him, but they could not help knowing that he was still bearing tales of a sort he could not own up to.

So Ruska was overtaken by the fate of all double-dealers. As before, no one gave his game away, but everyone began to steer clear of him. The scraps of information he passed on about the timetable under Shikin's glass desktop, showing when each of his informers could pop into his office unsummoned and thus showing when they could be caught in the act, did not altogether compensate for his own membership in the stoolie fraternity.

Nerzhin was fond of Ruska in spite of his intrigues and did not suspect him of telling Shikin about the Yesenin volume. Losing the book had hurt Gleb in a way that Ruska could not foresee. He had assumed that it was Gleb's property and that, once this was made clear, it would not be taken from him. In the meantime, Shikin could be kept happy with a report that Nerzhin had a book hidden in his case, no doubt brought in by one of the girls.

WITH THE FRAGRANCE of Klara's kiss still on his lips, Ruska went out into the yard. The lime trees, white with snow, seemed to him to be in bloom, and the air seemed warm and spring-like. In his two-year game of hide-and-seek, he had been so preoccupied with boyish schemes to fool the sleuths that he had given no thought to the love of women. He had gone to prison a virgin, and now his evenings were a torment for which he found no solace.

Now, as he went out into the yard and saw the long, low headquarters building, he remembered that he meant to put on a show there at dinnertime next day. The time had come to advertise it. (To do so earlier might have ruined everything.) Still under Klara's spell and feeling three times as clever and sure of himself because of it, he looked around, spotted Rubin and Nerzhin at the far side of the exercise ground, and made straight for them. His cap was pushed back to one side, so that his whole brow, part of his crown, and a lock of hair were trustingly exposed to the not very cold air.

As Ruska approached, he could tell from Nerzhin's stern look and the frown that Rubin turned on him that he had interrupted a serious conversation. Obviously for his benefit, they switched to something unimportant.

Still, he swallowed his resentment and said his piece. "You are, I hope, familiar with the general rule in just societies that all labor must be remunerated? Well, tomorrow is the day when each of the Judases will receive his thirty pieces of silver for the third quarter of this year."

Nerzhin feigned indignation. "You mean to say those tightfisted so-and-sos are just paying them for the third quarter? They've worked four quarters, surely."

"The payroll needs a lot of signatures," Ruska explained apologetically. "I will be one of those collecting."

"You mean you get paid for the third quarter, too? You've only been on the job half a quarter."

"Ah, but I've distinguished myself!" Ruska treated them both to a disarming smile.

"Do you get paid in cash?"

"God forbid! You get a phony money order, and its face value is credited to you. They asked what name I wanted them to use for the sender? How about Ivan Ivanovich Ivanov? I was flabbergasted. How corny can you get? Can't you make it out as from Klava Kudryavtseva? I said. It's nice to think that some woman cares about you."

"So how much do you get a quarter?"

"That's the really clever bit. Officially an informer is allowed 150 rubles a month. But to make it look respectable, it's sent by mail, and the heartless post office takes three rubles in postal charges. The godfathers are too miserly to make it up from their own pockets and too lazy to suggest a three-ruble raise for stoolies. So the money orders will all be for 147 rubles. Since no normal person ever sends a money order for such a sum, those missing thirty ten-kopeck pieces are the mark of Judas. At dinnertime tomorrow you must crowd around headquarters and examine the money orders of those who've been to see the operations officer. The motherland should know who its stoolies are, don't you think, gentlemen?"

# 49

# Life Is Not a Novel

AT THAT SAME MOMENT, as a few sparse snowflakes reluctantly fell on the dark roadway of Matrosskaya Tishina Street, from which the wheels of cars had licked the last traces of recent snow, life for the girls in Room 318 of the Graduate Student Building on the Stromynka went on as it usually did on a late Sunday afternoon.

The big square window of Room 318 looked out on Matrosskaya Tishina. The long sides of the room went from window to door, and on each side three iron beds, head to foot, hugged the wall, with three rickety sets of wicker bookshelves between them. Two tables stood in line in the middle of the room, leaving only a narrow passage on each side between themselves and the beds. The one nearer to the window, heaped with books, exercise books, drawings, and reams of typescript, was the "dissertation" table; the other was for general purposes and at that moment was occupied by Olenka, who was ironing; Muza, who was writing a letter; and Lyuda, who was taking her curlers out with the aid of a mirror. All this left room for a washbasin, curtained off against the wall by the door (the girls were supposed to wash at the end of the hallway, but it was uncomfortable, cold, and too far away).

On the bed nearest the washbasin, Erzhika, the Hungarian girl, lay reading. She was wearing the robe known to her roommates as the "Brazilian flag." She had other exotic robes, which delighted the girls, but dressed very soberly when she went out, almost as though she were trying not to attract attention. She had got into the habit during her years in the Communist underground in Hungary.

The next bed in the row, Lyuda's, was a mess—Lyuda had just gotten up, and the blanket and sheet were trailing on the floor—but her blue silk dress, freshly ironed, and her stockings were carefully draped over the headboard and the pillows. A Persian mat hung above her bed. Lyuda herself, seated at the table, was loudly telling everybody how a certain Spanish poet, deported from his motherland in his boyhood, had paid court to her. She recalled in detail the decor of the restaurant, the orchestra, the menu, all the trimmings, what they had drunk. . . .

Olenka's iron was connected by a cord and "cheat" plug to the light fixture over the table. (To prevent waste of electricity, irons and electric hotplates were strictly forbidden in the Stromynka dormitory. There were no outlets, and the whole maintenance staff went around checking for "cheat" plugs.) Olenka listened to Lyuda, laughing occasionally, but paid close attention to her ironing. That jacket and the skirt that went with it meant everything to her. She would sooner have scorched her own flesh with the iron than that two-piece outfit. Olenka had only her grant to live on and never ate anything but potatoes and gruel; she saved the twenty kopecks of her trolley fare whenever she could get away with it and had nothing to decorate the wall above her bed except a map; but at least her evening finery was of good quality, and she had no need to be ashamed of any part of it.

Muza, who was far too plump and looked more than her thirty years with her rather coarse features and glasses, was having difficulty writing her letter on a table rocked by Olenka's ironing, and with Lyuda's tiresome story making her feel inferior. She would always have thought it rude to ask another person to stop talking. Trying to shut Lyuda up would simply have encouraged her to behave even more brazenly. Lyuda, a new arrival, was not studying for a higher degree. Having just graduated from the Institute of Finance, she was there ostensibly to attend a few classes in political economy but mainly to amuse herself. Her father, a retired general, sent her a lot of pocket money from Voronezh.

Lyuda had a primitive belief that only her encounters with men and her relations with them gave meaning to a woman's life. But the story she was now telling had a piquancy all its own. After three months of marriage at home in Voronezh and affairs with various other men, Lyuda had begun to regret that her virginity seemed to have passed in a twinkling. So, from the very first words exchanged with her Spanish poet, she had played the part of an ingénue, starting and prudishly shying away from the lightest touch on shoulder or elbow, and when the smitten poet's entreaties were at last rewarded with a kiss—"the first in her life"—she shuddered, oscillated between ecstasy and despair, and inspired twenty-four lines of verse, unfortunately not in Russian.

Muza was writing to aged parents in a remote provincial town. Papa and Mama were still just as much in love as newlyweds. Every morning as he left for work, Papa kept looking back and waving to Mama until he turned the corner, and Mama waved to him from the ventilation pane. Their daughter loved them just as dearly and had got into the habit of writing often and describing all her experiences in detail.

But now Muza was at a loss for words. Something had happened last Friday evening that for two days now had overshadowed her tireless labor, day in and day out, on Turgenev, the work that was her substitute for all else in life. What she felt was deep disgust, as though she had smeared herself with something obscene that could not be washed away or concealed or shown—something that made existence impossible.

What had happened was that on Friday evening, when she got back from the library and was getting ready for bed, she had been called into the dormitory's office and told to "step into the next room, please." In the next room sat two men in civilian clothes. They were very polite to begin with and introduced themselves as Nikolai Ivanovich and Sergei Ivanovich. Quite unconcerned that it was so late at night, they kept her there for an hour, two hours, three hours. They began by asking the names of her roommates and fellow students in the department (although of course they knew them as well as she did). Then followed a leisurely discourse on patriotism, which focused on the patriotic duty of all in the world of learning not to shut themselves up in their own particular subjects but rather to serve their people with all their resources and in every way possible. Muza saw no need to contradict; what they said was absolutely correct. But then the Ivanovich brothers invited her to "assist" them, meaning to meet one or the other of them at fixed intervals in this same office or at a site where political agitators gathered or in a club or perhaps in the university itself, the venue to be arranged, and there to answer specific questions or report in written form what she had observed.

That was the beginning of a long nightmare! They began talking more and more rudely, yelling at her, addressing her with insulting familiarity: "Why are you such a pigheaded fool? Anybody would think we were foreign spies trying to recruit you!" "She'd be as much use to a foreign spy as a fifth leg to a horse!" Then they told her straight out that they wouldn't let her present her thesis (she had only a month or two to go, and the thesis was nearly finished) and that they would ruin her academic career because sniveling ninnies like her were not the sort of scholars the country needed. This frightened her very much: It would be only too easy for them to get her expelled from graduate school. But then they took out a gun, "accidentally" pointing it at Muza as it was passed between them. The effect was the opposite of that intended. Her fear vanished. To be expelled from the university with a black mark against her would be worse than dying. The Ivanoviches released her at one in the morning, giving her until the following Tuesday, December 27, to think things over, and first making her sign a statement not to divulge any of this. They assured her that they got to know everything and that if she told anybody about their conversation or the document she had signed, she would be arrested and imprisoned immediately.

By what unlucky chance had the choice fallen on her? Now she was waiting hopelessly for Tuesday, incapable of working, remembering how so very recently she had no need to think about anything except Turgenev, when she had no oppressive weight on her mind but had stupidly failed to realize how lucky she was.

Olenka listened to Lyuda with a smile on her face. At one point she burst out laughing with her mouth full of water and nearly choked. Olenka had waited rather a long time because of the war, but now at twenty-eight she was as happy as could be and could forgive everybody everything—let them all find their happiness wherever they could; she had a lover, also a graduate student, and he would be coming to take her out that evening.

"I said to him, you Spaniards attach so much importance to honor, but now you have kissed me on the lips and I am dishonored!"

Fair-haired Lyuda's attractive if rather hard face expressed the despair of a girl dishonored.

All this time, skinny Erzhika lay reading Galakhov's *Selected Works*. This book was her introduction to a world of lofty, noble characters whose flawless integrity astounded Erzhika. Galakhov's personages were never shaken by doubt as to whether they should serve their country, whether or not they should sacrifice themselves. Erzhika still had a rather poor knowledge of the country's language and customs, which must be why she had yet to see such people for herself, but that only made it all the more important to learn about them from books.

All the same, she lowered her book, rolled on to her side, and joined Lyuda's audience. Here, in Room 318, she sometimes heard the most extraordinary and paradoxical things, such as that an engineer had refused to go work on a fascinating development site in Siberia and stayed on in Moscow selling beer instead, or that someone had presented a successful thesis and was now doing nothing at all. ("Can there really be unemployment in the Soviet Union?") Or that to obtain a Moscow residence permit, you had to bribe the militia heavily. "Surely that's just a momentary phenomenon?" asked Erzhika. (She meant "temporary.")

Lyuda continued the story of herself and the poet by saying that if she married him, there would be nothing for it but to put on a convincing show of being a virgin. And she went on to confide in them just how she intended to act the part on their first night.

Muza's brow was creased by suffering. It wouldn't be polite to put her hands over her ears with others looking. She made an excuse to turn away to her bed.

Olenka, though, sang out gaily, "You mean that the heroines of world literature had no need at all to confess their guilt to their bridegrooms and finish themselves off?"

"Of course the silly things didn't have to," Lyuda said with a laugh. "It's really very simple!"

However, Lyuda wasn't at all sure whether she should marry the poet.

"He isn't a member of the Writers Union, and he only writes in Spanish, so what sort of royalties will he be getting? He can't expect anything much!"

Erzhika was so shocked that she swung her feet to the floor. "You mean people in the Soviet Union marry for money, too?"

"When you've been around a bit, you'll know," Lyuda said, looking in the mirror. All her curlers were out now, and a mass of tight blond ringlets trembled as she tossed her head. Any one of them would be enough to ensnare a poetic youth.

"Listen, girls, I'm coming to the conclusion—" Erzhika began but broke off as she noticed the strange, downcast look on Muza's face. She seemed to be staring at something on the floor near Erzhika. Erzhika drew her legs up onto the bed and cried out, looking horrified, "Did one just go by?"

The girls burst out laughing. Nothing had gone by.

There, in Room 318, sometimes in broad daylight but more impudently still at night, fearsome Russian rats ran around squeaking, their paws beating a neat tattoo on the bare floor. Through all the years of struggle against Horthy, Erzhika had never dreaded anything as she now dreaded the thought that these rats might jump onto her bed and run over her body. In daylight the laughter of her friends helped to drive these fears away, but at night she tucked her blanket in tightly, covering herself from head to foot, and vowed that if she lived till morning she would leave Stromynka. Nadya, a chemistry student, occasionally brought poison and sprinkled it in the corners. The rats subsided for a while but were soon up to their old tricks again. Two weeks ago, Erzhika's vacillations came to an end. It had to be Erzhika, and not one of the other girls, who went one morning to draw water from the pail and brought up a drowned baby rat in the mug. She shuddered in disgust whenever she remembered the look of grave resignation on its little pointed face. Erzhika went that very day to the Hungarian Embassy and asked them to find her a home in a private apartment. The embassy addressed a request to the USSR Ministry of Foreign Affairs; the Ministry of Foreign Affairs passed it to the Ministry of Higher Education, which passed it on to the rector of the university, who referred it to his Student Accommodation Department. Its reply was that (a) there were no private lodgings available at present and (b) the complaint alleging that there were rats at Stromynka was the first of its kind. The correspondence went full circle and returned to the embassy, which nonetheless encouraged Erzhika to believe that she would be given a room.

Sitting there in her Brazilian flag, hugging her knees to her chest, Erzhika looked like an exotic bird.

"Girls, girls," she wailed. "I like you all so much, I wouldn't dream of leaving you if it weren't for the rats."

It was both true and false. She did like the other girls, but there was no one with whom she could share her acute anxieties about the destiny of Hungary. Isolated as it was in Europe, something incomprehensible had been happening in her country ever since the trial of László Rajk. Rumors reached her that Communists she had known in the underground had been arrested. Rajk's nephew, also at Moscow University, and other Hungarian students had been recalled, after which no letters had been received from any of them.

They heard the secret knock at the door ("Friends! No need to hide the iron!"). Muza rose and, limping slightly (young as she was, she suffered from rheumatism in her knee), went to lift the latch. Dasha, a tough girl with a large, crooked mouth, entered in a hurry.

"Girls, girls, girls!" She was laughing loudly but did not forget to fasten the door behind her. "I've got a suitor, and I nearly didn't escape his clutches! Which one, you ask? Go on, guess!"

"You mean to say you're so well provided?" Lyuda, rummaging in her suitcase, sounded surprised.

The university was in fact only slowly recovering from its wartime torpor. There were few male graduate students, and somehow none of them was the real thing.

"Hold on!" Olenka threw up her hands and fixed Dasha with a hypnotic stare. "Was it 'Jaws'?"

"Jaws" was a postgraduate student who had failed in dialectical and historical materialism three times running and been written off as a hopeless dunce.

"No, the Snackman!" crowed Dasha, pulling her earflapped hat from her neatly piled dark hair and hanging it on a peg. She stood just as she was by the door, in no hurry to remove the cheap coat with the lambskin collar made to look like beaver fur, which she had obtained with coupons from the university store three years ago.

"What, him?"

"I was on the trolley and he got on," Dasha said, laughing. "He recognized me right away. 'Where do you get off?' he asks. There was no escape; we got off together. 'Don't you work at the baths now?' he says. 'I've been I don't know how many times, and you weren't there.' "

"You should have told him. . . ." Dasha's laughter had enveloped Olenka like a spreading flame. "You should have . . . you should have told him. . . ," but she simply couldn't finish. Roaring with laughter, she sank onto the bed, taking care not to crease the two-piece outfit she had laid out there.

"What 'Snackman'? What baths?" Erzhika wanted to know.

"You should have said . . ." Olenka made a great effort, but another fit of laughter convulsed her. She stretched out her hands and tried to convey by twiddling her fingers the message that refused to pass her larynx.

Lyuda, too, burst into laughter, as did the uncomprehending Erzhika, and even Muza's somber and homely features softened in a smile. She took her glasses off to clean them.

" 'Where are you going?' he says. 'Who do you know on the campus?' " Dasha was choking with laughter. "I said I know one of the women janitors. She knits mittens."

"Mi . . . mi . . . mit . . . tens!"

"Kni . . . kni . . . knits . . . mittens!"

Olenka was patted on the back, and they suppressed their laughter. Dasha took her coat off. One look at her, so sturdy and lissome in her close-fitting sweater and her tight-waisted skirt, told you that she could do any job, bending and stretching all day long, without tiring. Turning back the flowery bedspread, she perched cautiously on the edge of her bed, which was as neat and pretty as any shrine, with its painstakingly plumped-up pillows, its lacy pillowcases, and the embroidered antimacassars on the wall above it. She told Erzhika the story.

"It was last autumn, while it was still warm, before you came. . . . I didn't know where to look for a boyfriend. There was nobody to introduce me to one. So Lyudka advised me to go for a walk at Sokolniki, only by myself. Girls only spoil their chances when they go around in pairs."

"It never fails!" Lyuda confirmed. She was carefully wiping a spot from the toe of her shoe.

"So off I went," Dasha continued. There was no trace of merriment in her voice now. "I walked about a bit, sat down, looked at the trees. And sure enough, after a bit somebody came and sat by me, not too bad to look at. What was he, I wondered. Turned out he worked in a snack bar. I didn't want to tell him I was a graduate student. Men are terrified of educated women as a rule."

"Don't say that!" Olenka protested. "That's enough to drive anybody to despair!"

When the iron monster of war was forced out, it left the world drastically denuded. Where there should have been men their own age, or ten to fifteen years older, moving and smiling, the war had left nothing but gaping black holes. Education was the one bright hope left for that ill-fated generation of women, and crude, senseless gibes could not be allowed to extinguish it.

"So I told him I was a cashier at a bathhouse. He wanted to know which one and what shift I worked. I thought I would never get away. . . ."

Dasha's cheerfulness had vanished. There was a wistful look in her dark eyes. She had worked all day in the Lenin Library, eaten a meager and unappetizing meal in the dining hall, and come home despondently anticipating a Sunday evening with nothing to do and nothing to look forward to.

In the wood-built schoolhouse of her native village, her intermediate schooling had been enjoyable. And going on to university had enabled her to detach herself from the kolkhoz and obtain a Moscow residence permit. But now she was a lot older; she had eighteen years of education behind her, without a break. She was sick of studying till her head throbbed painfully . . . and what was the point of it all? She wanted what any woman needs to make her happy, to bear a child. But there was no one to give her a child, no one for whom she could bear a child.

Pensively rocking herself, Dasha uttered her favorite saying in the now silent room: "No, girls, life isn't like in books."

There was an agronomist who worked in the Machine and Tractor Station back home. He wrote to Dasha, begging her to marry him. But any day now she would have a higher degree, and the whole village would say, Why did the silly girl need all that schooling? Just to marry an agronomist? Any work-team leader can do that. At the same time, Dasha felt that even with a higher degree she would be out of place, tied hand and foot: A teaching job in a university would be a dead end; she would never break into those higher circles where scholars enjoyed more freedom.

Women who entered the world of learning were praised to the skies, promised the earth—which made it all the more painful when they collided with hard reality.

Dasha had finished her zealous inspection of her lighthearted and fortunate neighbor. "Lyuda, dear," she said, "I would wash my feet if I were you!"

Lyuda looked round. "Should I?"

Unenthusiastically she retrieved a hotplate from its hiding place and attached it to the "cheat" plug instead of the iron.

Dasha was never still. She had to be doing something—anything—to shake off her misery. She remembered that she had bought a new article of underwear. Not her size, but you grabbed whatever was going. She found the thing and began taking it in.

Now that they had all quieted down, Muza could concentrate on her letter. Alas, it refused to be written! She reread her last few sentences, altered one word, and inked over a few illegible letters . . . but she was still getting nowhere. Her mother and father would sense at once that the letter was a lie. They would realize that their daughter was unhappy, that something nasty had happened, and wonder why she couldn't come straight out with it. Why was she lying for the first time ever?

If there had been no one else in the room, Muza would have groaned aloud. She would have simply howled, and perhaps that would have given her some slight relief. As it was, she threw down her pen and propped herself up on her elbows, hiding her face in her hands. So this was what it had come to! She had to make a choice that would affect her whole life, and there was no one to advise her, no one she could turn to for help now that she had signed that pledge of secrecy. And on Tuesday she would have to appear again before those two, so sure of themselves, with their well-rehearsed lines and their clever tricks. Life had been so good just the day before yesterday! And now all was lost. Because they would not give way. But neither could she. How could she discuss the "Hamlet and Don Quixote principles in man," remembering all the time that she was an informer, that she had a code name—Daisy, maybe, or Little Darling—and she had to collect information about the girls in the room here or about her professor?

Muza tried to wipe the tears from her tight-shut eyes without anyone noticing.

"Where's Nadya, then?" Dasha asked.

Nobody replied. Nobody knew.

But Dasha had thought of something to say about Nadya while she was sewing. "What do you think, girls, how long can she keep it up? 'Missing in action,' she says. The war's been over nearly five years now. Shouldn't she cut the cord?"

Muza threw up her arms and cried out in anguish. "How can you talk like that?" The wide sleeves of her gray checked dress slipped back to her elbows, baring her pudgy white forearms. "That's what real love means! True love doesn't stop short at the grave!"

Olenka pursed her ripe lips in a wry smile.

"Lasts beyond the grave? That's mystical nonsense, Muza. You don't forget, you have tender memories, but . . . love?"

"Of course," Dasha insisted, "how can you love a person who simply doesn't exist?"

"Honestly, if I could I'd send her a certificate of burial myself," Olenka said warmly. "Tell her he's dead, dead, dead and laid in the ground. Blasted war! It's five years ago now, and we still can't get away from it."

"During the war," Erzhika put in, "many, many people were driven far away, over the ocean. Maybe he's still alive, somewhere over there."

"It's just possible," Olga agreed. "Anyway, she can hope so. Still, Nadya has one tiresome characteristic. She's obsessed with her own sorrows and doesn't care about anybody else's. In fact, if she didn't have her sorrow, her life would be pretty empty."

Dasha waited until they had finished and then slowly drew the point of the needle along the hem, as though sharpening it. She knew, when she had started this conversation, how astonished they would shortly be.

"Listen, now, girls," she said weightily. "Nadya is just fooling us. What she says isn't true. She doesn't think her husband's dead at all. She isn't waiting for a missing man to return. She knows that her husband's alive. And she knows just where he is."

They all spoke at once: "What makes you think so?"

Dasha looked at them triumphantly. Her powers of observation had long ago earned her a nickname among her roommates: "the investigator."

"You have to know how to listen, darlings! Did she ever forget herself and speak as if he were dead? Ne-ever. She doesn't even like saying 'he was' this or that. She takes care not to say either 'he was' or 'he is.' If he really were missing, surely she would occasionally speak of him as though he were dead, wouldn't she?"

"What d'you think has become of him, then?"

"Can you really not guess?" cried Dasha, laying her sewing down altogether.

No, they couldn't.

"He's alive, but he's left her! And she's ashamed to admit it! So she's invented this 'missing' story."

"Now that I can believe!" said Lyuda, splashing away behind the curtain. "Yes, indeed!"

"So she's sacrificing herself for his sake," Muza exclaimed. "There's obviously some reason for her to keep quiet and not marry again!"

Olenka couldn't see that. "Why, what's she waiting for?"

"You're absolutely right, Dasha! You're so clever!" said Lyuda, popping out from behind the curtain in her slip, without her dressing gown, and barelegged, which made her look taller and more shapely than ever. "She feels humiliated, so she's pretending to be a goody-goody, faithful forever to her dead husband. She isn't sacrificing a damn thing; she's aching for somebody to be nice to her, but nobody wants her! You know how it is; you can walk down the street, and everybody looks around at you, but nobody would want *her* if she threw herself at them."

She disappeared behind the curtain.

"Shchagov comes to see her, though," said Erzhika. The "shch" gave her some difficulty.

"Comes to see her! That doesn't mean a thing," the invisible Lyuda retorted. "He hasn't taken the bait."

Erzhika was puzzled.

"What does that mean, the bait?" she asked.

They all laughed. Dasha stuck to her theme. "No, listen. Maybe she's still hoping to get her husband back from the other woman?"

They heard the secret knock again: "Friend—don't hide the iron."

They all stopped talking. Dasha took the hook off. Nadya came in, dragging her feet, looking old and drawn, as if she wanted to confirm Lyuda's sneers. Surprisingly, she didn't address a single word of casual politeness to the others, not so much as an "It's only me," or "What's new, girls?" She hung up her fur coat and went silently to her bed.

Erzhika resumed her reading. Muza hid her face in her hands again. Olenka was stitching the pink buttons to her new blouse more securely.

Nobody had anything to say. To ease the awkward silence, Dasha said weightily, as though summing up, "So you see, girls, life isn't like in books."

# 50

# The Old Maid

AFTER THE VISIT, Nadya wanted to see only others whom fate had treated badly and to talk only about those behind bars. So she had gone from Lefortovo right across Moscow to Krasnaya Presnya to see Sologdin's wife. She was not at home. (It would have been strange if she had been. Sunday was when she did the errands that she and her son had no time for during the week.) Nor could Nadya leave a note with the neighbors. She knew from Sologdin, and could easily imagine anyway, that the neighbors were hostile to his wife and spied on her.

She had climbed the steep stairs, dark even in daytime, excitedly anticipating the pleasure of talking to that sweet woman who shared her private sorrow.

She went down again. She was not just disappointed; she was shattered. And just as on a photographic film placed in colorless and innocent-looking developer the latent contours of a picture begin inexorably to appear, so all the dark forebodings lurking in the depths of Nadya's mind since the visit began to force themselves painfully upon her.

"Don't be surprised if I'm moved from here and my letters stop," he had said. If he went away, even these once-yearly meetings would come to an end. What would she do then?

He had said something about the upper reaches of the Angara. . . .

She remembered something else. Had he perhaps begun to believe in God? . . . Something he had let drop. . . . Prison would make a spiritual cripple of him, seduce him into mysticism, train him to be meek and submissive. His character would change. He would return a complete stranger.

Worst of all were those ominous words: "Don't bank on my release. The sentence they hand down is just a formality." Nadya had cried out, "I don't believe it! That can't be true!" But that was hours ago. Since then, she had retraced her steps across Moscow, deep in thought all the way from Krasnaya Presnya to Sokolniki. Now these thoughts stung like a swarm of wasps, and she had no defense against them. What was the good of waiting? Was it right to turn her own life into an appendage of her husband's? To sacrifice the precious gift of existence for a future that held nothing?

One good thing—there would be no women where he would be!

There was something about their meeting today, something that she could not quite define, something elusive but . . . irreparable.

And now she was too late for the students' dining hall. A minor misfortune, but enough to plunge her into deep despair. She immediately remembered that the day before yesterday she had been fined ten rubles for leaving a trolley at the wrong end. Ten new rubles was a tidy sum, the equivalent of a hundred old ones.

Light snow had begun to fall when she reached the Stromynka, and a little boy with a peaked cap pulled down over his eyes was selling Kazbek cigarettes loose. Nadya went up to him and bought two.

"Where can I get a match?" she asked herself out loud.

"Here you are, lady, help yourself!" the boy said obligingly, handing her a box of matches. "No extra charge!"

Without stopping to think how it would look to passersby, Nadya lit her cigarette on the second attempt, clumsily, so that only one side was burning, gave the boy his matchbox, and walked up and down the street instead of going into the dormitory. Smoking was not yet a habit, but this was not her first cigarette. The discomfort and disgust caused by the hot smoke somehow eased the ache in her heart.

Nadya threw the cigarette away half-smoked and went upstairs to Room 318.

Inside, she squeamishly avoided Lyuda's unmade bed and sank heavily onto her own, wanting more than anything in the world not to be asked anything by anybody just then.

When she sat down, her eyes were on the same level as the four typewritten copies of her thesis standing in four separate piles on the table. Nadya automatically remembered the endless fuss and bother she had had with it—arranging to have drawings photocopied, revising it, revising it again—and now it was back with her for a third attempt.

Remembering how hopelessly, impermissibly late the thesis was, Nadya remembered, too, the secret special assignment, her only hope of getting a little money and some peace. But the terrible eight-page application form stood in her way. It had to be handed in to the Personnel Department by Tuesday.

If she answered the questions honestly, it would mean expulsion before the week was out—from the university, from the dormitory, and from Moscow.

Or else—getting divorced immediately.

That was what she meant to do.

But it was a painful decision, and it would be tricky.

Erzhika had made her bed up as best she could. (She still wasn't very good at it. Bedmaking, washing, and ironing were all things she had learned to do only there, on Stromynka Street; there had always been servants to do these chores for her.) She reddened her cheeks but not her lips, before the mirror, and went off to work in the Lenin Library.

Muza was trying to read, but it was hard going. She noticed Nadya's morose inactivity and kept looking at her anxiously but could not quite bring herself to ask any questions.

"Ah, yes," Dasha remembered. "I heard people saying today that we will get twice as much book money this year."

Olenka looked up quickly.

"Are you serious?"

"Our dean told some of the girls."

"Let's see, how much will that be?" Olenka's face glowed with the excitement that money can inspire only in people who are not used to it or greedy for it. "Twice 300 is 600, twice 70 is 140, twice 5 is. . . . Hey!" she cried, and clapped her hands. "750! Now that's really something!"

She hummed a short tune. She had a pleasant little voice.

"Now you can buy yourself a complete Soloviev!"

"I don't think so!" Olenka chuckled. "I can have a dress made for that money, dark red, in crêpe georgette. Can't you see it?" She gathered the sides of her skirt between her fingertips. "With two ruffles!"

Olenka was still short of many things. It was only quite recently, in the last year, that she had begun to care again. Her mother had died the year before last after a very long illness. She was left without a single living relative. She and her mother had received notification of her father's and brother's deaths in the same week in 1942. Her mother had become seriously ill, and Olenka had had to leave university in her first year, miss a year, go out to work, and take a correspondence course.

But there was no sign of any of this in her sweet, chubby, twenty-eight-year-old face. She was, however, affected by Nadya's look of numb suffering as she sat on the bed opposite. It was beginning to depress them all.

Olenka asked the question. "What's wrong, Nadya dear? You were quite cheerful when you went out this morning."

Words of sympathy—but really an expression of irritation. It is strange how nuances in the tone of voice can betray our feelings.

Nadya recognized the note of irritability in her neighbor's voice. Besides, her eyes were on Olenka as she dressed, pinned a brooch (a flower in bloodred stones) to the lapel of her jacket, and perfumed herself.

The scent that surrounded Olenka with an invisible small cloud of happiness reached Nadya's nostrils like a pungent reminder of irreparable loss.

Nadya answered without relaxing her features, pronouncing each word as though it cost her a great effort. "Am I bothering you? Am I getting on your nerves?"

They stared at each other across the thesis-heaped table. Olenka drew herself up, and her rounded chin set in hard lines.

"Look, Nadya," she said distinctly. "I didn't mean to upset you. But as our mutual friend Aristotle said, man is a social animal. We can spread happiness around ourselves, but we have no right to spread gloom."

Nadya sat hunched up, looking much more than her age. Her voice was low and lifeless.

"Don't you know what it's like to be very unhappy?" she said.

"As it happens, I know only too well! You're unhappy, all right, but you mustn't be so obsessed with yourself! You mustn't get into that frame of mind when you think you're the only one in the world who knows what suffering is. It's possible that other people have gone through much more than you. Just think about it."

She said no more. But why should one missing person who could be replaced—because a husband is replaceable—mean more than a father and brother killed and a mother dead, three people in the nature of things irreplaceable?

She had nothing more to say, but she stood there motionless, staring unsmilingly at Nadya.

Nadya knew well enough that Olya was talking about her own bereavements. But she was unmoved. Yes, death meant an irreparable loss. But a person dies only once. After the initial shock your loss slips imperceptibly into the past. Grief gradually loses its hold on you. You perfume yourself, pin your ruby brooch on, and go to meet your boyfriend.

Whereas Nadya's sorrow was always with her, holding her in a grip that could not be unlocked. There in the past, in the present, and in the future. However she struggled, whatever she clutched at, she could never break loose from its cruel teeth.

But she could not defend herself without revealing everything. And her secret was too dangerous.

So Nadya backed down and told a lie.

"I'm sorry girls, I'm at the end of my tether. I haven't got the strength to keep on revising. How much of this am I supposed to take?"

Once she saw that Nadya was not belittling other people's sorrows, Olenka's resentment was allayed, and she quickly made peace.

"What's the problem? Got to weed the foreigners out? You're not the only one. Don't let it upset you!"

"Weeding the foreigners out" meant going through the text and replacing "Laue has shown" with "scholars have succeeded in showing," or "as Langmuir has conclusively demonstrated" with "as has been demonstrated." Whereas if any Russian, or for that matter any German or Dane in Russia's service, had distinguished himself in the slightest degree, it was essential to give his name in full and to emphasize his uncompromising patriotism and his immortal services to science.

"It isn't the foreigners; I chucked them out long ago. I've got to get rid of Academician Balandin now—"

"Isn't he one of ours. . .?"

"And his whole theory. Which is what my thesis is based on. It turns out that he's . . . that he's been. . . ."

Academician Balandin had suddenly sunk into the same abyss, the same subterranean world, where Nadya's husband languished in chains.

"Still, you mustn't take it so much to heart," Olenka insisted. "What about me and Azerbaijan?"

There had never been any good reason why this girl from Central Russia should want to study Iran. When she entered the History Department, she had no such thought in her head. But her young (and married) supervisor, for whom she wrote a term paper on Kievan Russia, had begun to press his attentions on her and was very insistent that she should specialize in medieval Russian history as a graduate student. Olenka had taken fright and defected to the Italian Renaissance, but the Italian Renaissance man wasn't old either and, when alone with her, behaved like a true Renaissance man. Whereupon Olenka, in despair, asked for a transfer to the decrepit professor of Iranian Studies and was now writing a thesis under his supervision. She would have brought it to a successful conclusion by now if the problem of Southern Azerbaijan had not surfaced in the newspapers. Olenka's leitmotif was not, as it should have been, that the province had since the beginning of time gravitated toward Azerbaijan and that Iran was completely alien to it. So the thesis was returned for rewriting.

"Just be thankful they're letting you correct it first. Worse things happen. Muza could tell you about . . ."

But Muza was no longer listening. She had been lucky enough to lose herself in a book, and the room around her no longer existed.

"A girl in the Literature Department defended her thesis on Zweig four years ago. She's been a senior lecturer for some time now. But they suddenly realized that she'd called Zweig a 'cosmopolitan' three times in her thesis and used the word approvingly. So the Higher Degrees Examination Board sent for her and took the diploma away. What a nightmare!"

Dasha chimed in. "Even chemists can get nervous breakdowns! So what are political economists like me supposed to do? Hang ourselves? Never mind; we survive somehow. Hurrah for Stuzhaila-Olyabyshkin, my savior!"

They all of course knew that Dasha was now on her third thesis subject. Her first had been "Problems of Communal Catering under Socialism." Straightforward enough twenty years earlier, when every Young Pioneer, Dasha included, knew for certain that family kitchens would very shortly be a thing of the past, that the home fires would go out, and that emancipated women would get lunch and dinner from "cooking factories." But as the years went by, the subject had become opaque and indeed dangerous. It was quite obvious that anybody—Dasha herself, for instance—who still ate in a dining commons did so out of dire necessity. Only two forms of communal feeding flourished: eating in restaurants—but there socialist principles were not conspicuously upheld—and in scruffy little snack bars selling nothing much except vodka. In theory the "cooking factory" continued to exist, inasmuch as the Leader of all Toilers had not found time in the past twenty years to address the subject. Which made it dangerous to express an opinion of your own. Dasha suffered endless torment until her supervisor gave her a different subject—thoughtlessly, however, taking it from the wrong list: "Retail Trade in Consumer Goods under Socialism." There proved to be a dearth of information on this subject, too. Speeches and directives invariably stated that consumer goods could and indeed must be produced and distributed, but, in practice, figures for the output of such items had begun to look rather pathetic in comparison with those for rolled steel and oil products. Would light industry grow and grow or gradually contract? The Academic Council itself did not know, and it turned the subject down in good time.

Well-meaning people put another idea into Dasha's head, and she obtained permission to work on "the nineteenth-century Russian political economist Stuzhaila-Olyabyshkin."

"I hope you've at least found a picture of your benefactor?" Olenka said, laughing.

"Do you know, I just can't find one!"

"That's most ungrateful of you!"

Olenka was trying to amuse Nadya, to share the elation she felt as her "date" drew nearer.

"I would find one and hang it over my bed. I can just see him: a handsome, elderly country gentleman with unsatisfied spiritual needs. After a hearty breakfast he sits in his dressing gown by the window, in the depths of the country—you know, like where Onegin met Tatyana, a place where history's storms are powerless, and as he watches a peasant wench feeding the piglets, he muses dreamily on

> *the wealth of nations,*
> *and what they live by. . . .*

"Then in the evening he enjoys a game of cards."

Olenka was overcome with laughter. She was flushed. She felt happier by the minute.

Lyuda, too, had now donned her sky blue dress and so deprived her bed of its fanlike covering. (Nadya winced painfully whenever her eyes strayed in that direction.) Before the mirror Lyuda first touched up her eyebrows and lashes, then with great precision painted herself a rosebud mouth.

"Make a note of this, girls." Muza often came out with unexpected remarks as naturally as though everybody was hanging on her words. "How do the heroes of Russian literature differ from the Western European variety? The favorite heroes of Western writers always aspire to a career, fame, money. But your Russian hero scorns meat and drink; all he seeks is justice and righteousness. Am I right?"

She immersed herself in her book again.

Dasha took pity on her and turned the light on.

Lyuda now had her boots on and reached for her fur coat. That was when Nadya nodded at Lyuda's bed and said in disgust: "Are you leaving us to clear up your mess again?" Lyuda flared up, and her eloquent eyes flashed. "Please do nothing of the sort! And don't dare touch my bed ever again!" Her voice rose to a shout. "And stop telling me how to behave!"

Nadya lost control of herself and began shouting all the things she had held back.

"Can't you understand that the way you behave is an insult to us! Maybe we have other things to think about besides your evening's entertainment!"

"Jealous, are you? Can't get a bite yourself?"

The faces of both girls were distorted. Women in a rage are always ugly.

Olenka opened her mouth to join in the attack on Lyuda, but she detected an unflattering innuendo in the words "evening's entertainment" and stopped short.

"There's nothing to be jealous of!" Nadya cried in a hollow, broken voice.

"So you lost your way to the nunnery"—Lyuda's voice rang out louder than ever as she smelled victory—"and now you're a graduate student. So sit up in a corner and stop playing mother-in-law. We're sick of it! Horrible old maid!"

"Lyudka! Cut it out!" Dasha yelled.

"Well, why doesn't she mind her own business? Old maid is what she is! Up on the shelf!"

Muza woke up at this and joined in the shouting, brandishing her book at Lyuda.

"How vulgar can you get?"

All five began shouting at once. Nobody heard or wanted to hear what anybody else said.

Nadya's throbbing head was no longer capable of thought, and she was ashamed of her outburst and her tears. Just as she was, in her best clothes, put on for the visit, she flung herself facedown on the bed and covered her head with the pillow.

Lyuda powdered her face yet again, arranged her curly blond tresses over the collar of her squirrel coat, let down a little veil that came just below her eyes, and without actually making the bed but throwing a blanket over it by way of compromise, left the room.

The others called to Nadya, but she did not stir. Dasha removed Nadya's shoes and turned the corners of her blanket up to cover her feet.

Then there was another knock, in response to which Olenka flitted out into the hallway, returned like the wind, tucked her curls under a little cap, dived into a fur jacket with a yellow collar, and advanced toward the door with something new in her walk. (Something that said, "I mean to be happy and expect to have to fight for it.")

So Room 318 had dispatched, one after the other, two charmingly dressed charmers to tempt the world beyond.

Room 318 had also lost with them its animation and laughter and had become quite dreary.

Moscow was an enormous city. And there was nowhere to go in it.

Muza stopped reading again, took off her glasses, and hid her face in her large hands.

"Silly Olenka!" Dasha said. "He'll have his fun with her and chuck her. I've heard he's got another woman somewhere. Let's hope there won't be a kid."

Muza looked out from between her hands. "She isn't tied to him in any way. If he turns out like you say, she can leave him."

"Not tied!" Dasha smiled a wry smile. "How could she be any more tied than she is?"

"You—you always know everything! What makes you so sure?" Muza asked indignantly.

"What more is there to know, when she spends the night there?"

Muza brushed this aside. "That doesn't prove a thing!"

"It's the only way nowadays. You won't keep a man any other way."

The girls fell silent, each busy with her own thoughts.

The snow outside was falling more heavily. It was getting dark already.

Water gurgled quietly in the radiator under the window.

The thought of the murderously dull Sunday evening ahead in this dog hole was unbearable.

Dasha thought of the snack-bar man she had rejected. A strong, healthy fellow. Why did she have to brush him off like that? He could have taken her after dark to some club away from the center, where nobody from the university ever went. And squeezed her up against a fence somewhere.

"Muza, love, let's go to the movies!" Dasha said.

"What's on?"

"*The Indian Tomb*."

"That's just rubbish! Commercial garbage!"

"Yes, but it's right here in the building."

Muza didn't even answer.

"Oh, come on! It's miserable here!"

"I'm not going. Find yourself something to do."

The lightbulb suddenly dimmed, and there was only the dull red glow of the filament.

"That's all we need. . . ." Dasha groaned. "Power cut. You could hang yourself in a place like this."

Muza sat like a statue.

Nadya was just as still on her bed.

"Muza, darling, let's go to the movies!"

There was a knock at the door.

Dasha looked out and came back saying, "Nadya! Shchagov's here. Are you getting up?"

# 51

## Fire and Hay

NADYA CRIED AND CRIED, gripping the blanket between her teeth to try and stop herself. Her head was damp under the pillow.

She would have liked to go out, to get away from that room till late night. But in the huge city of Moscow, she had nowhere to go.

It wasn't the first time her roommates had used such wounding words, called her "old hag," "misery guts," "the nun." What hurt most was the unfairness of it. She used to be so cheerful! But five years of lying leaves its mark. Five years of continually wearing a mask that cramps and pinches your face, hardens your voice, and numbs your thought. Maybe she really was by now an insufferable old maid? It was so difficult to see yourself clearly. It was only in a dormitory, where you couldn't stamp your foot at mother as you did at home, only there among your peers that you learned to recognize what was bad in yourself.

Apart from Gleb no one, no one at all, would ever understand her. . . .

But even Gleb did not really understand.

He had not told her what she ought to do, what she should be making of her life.

He had only said that he would not be released.

Her husband's swift and sure blows had shattered all the hopes that fortified her from day to day, bolstered her faith, gave her the strength to wait and preserve her independence.

He would never be released!

That meant that he had no need of her . . . that she was ruining her life . . . for nothing.

Nadya was lying face downward, staring fixedly through the gap between pillow and blanket at the patch of wall before her, and she could not, did not try to understand where all the light was coming from. She had thought that it was very dark, but suddenly she could make out the pimples in the crude whitewash on the familiar wall. Then suddenly Nadya heard, through her pillow, fingers beating a rhythm she recognized on the plywood panel of the door. When Dasha said, "Shchagov's here, are you getting up?" Nadya had already whipped the pillow from her head, jumped off the bed in her stockings, straightened her rumpled skirt, and tidied her hair while her feet felt for her shoes.

Muza, watching her in the wan half-light, was taken aback by her eagerness.

Dasha darted over to Lyuda's bed and quickly tucked in the bedclothes.

The visitor was then admitted.

Shchagov had draped an old army overcoat over his shoulders. He had not lost his soldierly bearing; he could bend, but he could not stoop. His movements were precise.

"Greetings, good people. I've come to see what you're up to with the light out so that I can try it myself. I'm bored stiff."

What a relief! In the yellowish gloom he could not see that her eyes were swollen and tearful.

Dasha answered him in the same tone. "So if the lights hadn't dimmed, you wouldn't have come?"

"Certainly not. Women's faces lose their charm when brightly lit. You see the spiteful looks, the envious glances"—he should have been there a little while ago!—"the wrinkles, the overdone makeup. If I were a woman, I'd get a law passed that lights should never be on full. That way they'd all be married in no time."

Dasha looked at him sternly. He always talked like that, and she didn't like his well-rehearsed facetiousness.

"May I sit down?"

"Please do," Nadya said, coolly hospitable. There was no trace of her recent tiredness, her anguish, her tears in her voice.

Unlike Dasha, she liked his self-assurance, his air of superiority, his low, steady voice. His presence was soothing. She even liked his jokes.

"I'd better sit down quickly. I may never get another invitation from these people. So then, what are you studious young ladies doing?"

Nadya was silent. She couldn't say much to him because they had quarreled the day before yesterday, and she had unthinkingly poked him in the back with her briefcase, which suggested a greater degree of intimacy than actually existed between them, then run away. It was stupid, childish; and she was glad that they were not alone now.

Dasha answered. "We're just going to the movies. We don't know who with."

"What's the picture?"

"*The Indian Tomb.*"

"Aha! Not to be missed! As a hospital nurse once said to me, 'There's lots of shooting, a lot of killing, and it's a simply marvelous picture.'"

Shchagov had made himself comfortable at the common table.

"But if you don't mind my saying so, good people, I expected to find singing and dancing here, and it's more like a funeral. Bumpy patch with parents? Latest ruling of Party Committee bothering you? I don't think it applies to graduate students."

"What ruling?" Nadya asked in a subdued voice.

"What ruling? That the social forces must check up on the social origins of students and make sure that they have indicated their parentage correctly. There's a wealth of possibilities here; somebody may have confided in somebody, or blurted out something in his or her sleep, or read somebody else's letter . . . things of that sort."

(More prodding and prying! How sick of it she was! How she longed to get away from it all!)

"What about you, Muza Georgievna? Have you been hiding something?"

"Despicable!" Muza exclaimed.

"You mean even that doesn't cheer you up? Maybe you'd like to hear a very funny story about a secret ballot at yesterday's meeting of the Mechanics and Mathematics Board?"

Shchagov was addressing them all, but his eyes were on Nadya. He had been wondering for some time what she wanted from him. Her interest was more obvious every time they met. If he was playing chess with someone, she would hover over the board and ask him to give her a game and teach her the openings. (It was just that chess is a marvelous way of killing time!)

Or she would invite him to hear her perform at a concert.

(Perfectly natural! You want to hear your playing praised by some not entirely indifferent listener!)

Then there was the day when she had a "spare" ticket for the cinema and invited him.

(She wanted to indulge in a fantasy . . . just for one evening . . . to be seen with an escort . . . have someone to take her arm.)

Then she had given him a little notebook for his birthday—but did it rather awkwardly, slipped it into his jacket pocket and almost ran away. What an odd way to behave—why run away?

(She was shy, that was all!)

He had caught up with her in the hallway and started wrestling with her, pretending that he was trying to return her present, and had even put his arms around her. She had been in no hurry to free herself but had let him hold her for a moment.

(It was so many years since she had experienced it that her arms and legs were paralyzed.)

And just now, that playful tap with the briefcase?

In his dealings with Nadya—as with everybody, absolutely everybody—Shchagov exercised iron self-control. He knew how easy it was to get involved with a woman and how difficult to extricate yourself. But when a lonely woman begs for help, simply begs for help, who could be so stiff-necked as to refuse?

When Shchagov left his room to walk over to 318, he knew for sure that he would find Nadya at home and felt a certain excitement.

His funny story about the secret ballot earned only a polite laugh or two.

"Are we or are we not going to get any light?"

Even Muza had lost patience.

"However, I note that you don't find my stories the least bit amusing. Especially Nadezhda Ilyinichna. From what little I can see of her, she looks as black as a thundercloud. And I know why. She was fined ten rubles the day before yesterday, and she misses them unbearably."

Nadya's immediate reaction to his jest was to seize her handbag, wrench it open, snatch the first thing she found, tear it up hysterically, and fling the pieces onto the common table in front of Shchagov.

"Muza! I won't ask you again!" Dasha wailed, grabbing her coat. "Are you coming or aren't you?"

"Oh, all right," Muza mumbled, and made for the coat hooks, limping slightly.

Shchagov and Nadya did not look around to see them go.

But when the door closed behind them, Nadya felt a little frightened.

Shchagov picked up the scraps of paper and looked at them closely. They were the crackling remnants of another ten-ruble note.

He rose, letting his overcoat fall onto the chair, and walked unhurriedly round the table to face Nadya, towering over her. He clasped her small hands in his large ones.

"Nadya!" It was the first time he had called her by her given name alone.

She stood stock-still, feeling helpless. The spurt of anger that had made her tear up the note was over as suddenly as it had begun. A strange thought flashed through her mind: There was no guard beside them bending his bovine head to listen. They could talk about anything they liked. And decide for themselves when to part.

She was close enough to his strong regular features to see that the left and right sides of his face were identical. She found the regularity of his features attractive.

He unclasped his hands and ran them along the sleeves of her silk blouse.

"Nadya!" he said coaxingly.

"Let me go!" she answered, but weakly, reluctantly.

"What am I to think?" he said, sliding his hands from her elbows to her shoulders.

"Think about what?" she asked faintly.

But she made no attempt to free herself.

He gripped her by her shoulders and drew her toward him.

The flame in her cheek could not be seen in the dim, yellowish light.

She put her hands on his chest and pushed him away.

"Whatever makes you think that—"

"I'm damned if I know what I'm supposed to think!"

He released her and walked past her to the window.

Water gurgled in the radiator.

Nadya straightened her hair with trembling hands.

Shchagov's hands trembled, too, as he lit a cigarette.

"You . . . know, don't you," he asked, pausing between words, "how dry hay burns?"

"Yes. The flame shoots up to the sky, and then there's just a heap of ash."

"Right up to the sky!" he said.

"And then—a heap of ash," she repeated.

"So why do you keep throwing fire onto dry hay?"

(Had she really been doing that? Could he really not understand? See that she wanted to feel attractive once in a while? Feel just for a minute that someone liked her better than other women, that she was still the best?)

"Let's go out somewhere! Anywhere!" she pleaded.

"We aren't going anywhere; we're staying here."

He was smoking in his usual calm fashion, gripping the holder between his strong lips, a little to one side. Nadya liked this habit of his, too.

"No, please, let's go out somewhere!"

"It's here or nowhere," he said peremptorily. "And I must warn you—I'm engaged."

## 52

# To the Resurrection of the Dead!

NADYA AND SHCHAGOV had felt drawn to each other because neither of them was from Moscow. The Muscovites whom Nadya met in graduate school and in laboratories carried within themselves the poison of their imagined superiority, or what they themselves called their "Moscow patriotism." However pleased her professor was with her work, in their eyes Nadya was an inferior being.

She could not remain indifferent to Shchagov, who was also a provincial but who cut his way through that milieu as an icebreaker cleaves clear water. She was in the reading room one day when a youngish senior research student, hoping to make Shchagov look small, asked him, with an arrogant toss of his snake's head: "Let me see . . . what locality do you come from exactly?"

Shchagov, who was taller than the questioner, stared at him with bored compassion, rocking slightly on his feet.

"You've never been there," he said. "It's a locality called the front line. I'm from a hamlet called Dugout."

No man's life proceeds at an even tenor through the years. There will always be a time when he realizes himself most fully, feels most deeply, makes the greatest impression on others—and on himself. All that happens afterward, however significant on the face of it, is most likely to be an abatement, the ebbing of that high tide. We never forget that time; we endlessly ring the changes on it. For some people it may even be their childhood, and they remain children all their lives. For others it is the time of first love, and it is they who have spread the myth that we love only once. There are those for whom the great time was when they were richest, most esteemed, most powerful; and they will still be mumbling without a tooth in their gums about their departed greatness. For Nerzhin the decisive period was prison. For Shchagov, life at the front.

Shchagov had experienced all the horrors of war. He was called up in its first month and returned to civilian life only in 1946. Through all four years of the war, there was hardly a morning when Shchagov could be sure he would live till evening. He never held an important staff job and was out of the front line only when in the hospital. He had retreated from Kiev in 1941 and on the Don in 1942. Even when the war was taking a turn for the better, Shchagov had to run for it in 1943 and again at Kovel in 1944. In roadside ditches, in flooded trenches, in burned-out buildings, he learned to appreciate a mess tin of soup, an hour of peace, the meaning of true friendship, and the meaning of life generally.

It would be decades before the marks left on Engineer Captain Shchagov healed completely. For the present he was incapable of dividing people into more than two categories: soldiers and the rest. Even on the streets of Moscow, where memory is short, he had kept his belief that the word "soldier" is the only guarantee of candor and goodwill. Experience had taught him not to trust anyone who had not undergone the ordeal by fire in battle.

When the war ended, Shchagov had no family left, and the little house they had lived in had been razed to the ground by a bomb. His possessions were what he had on and a suitcase packed with booty from Germany. True, to soften the impact of civilian life, newly demobilized officers received twelve months' pay "according to rank," which was a wage for doing nothing.

Like many soldiers returning from the front, Shchagov did not recognize the country he had spent four years defending. Young memories still preserved the mirage of equality, but at home its last pink wisps had disappeared. The country had become callous, utterly unscrupulous, and a great gulf had opened up between abject poverty and brazenly rapacious wealth. Soldiers returning from the front were, for a time at least, better men than they had been. They came back cleansed by the proximity of death, and they were hit all the harder by the changes at home, changes that had matured far from the battle zones.

These veterans were all back now, walking the streets, riding in the metro, but dressed any old way, so that they no longer recognized one another. And they had to accept the prevalence of the code they found here over their own, the code of the front line.

A man might clutch his head and wonder what he had been fighting for. Many in fact asked that question but quickly found themselves behind bars.

Shchagov did not ask. He was not one of those recalcitrants who never tire in the quest for universal justice. He knew that there was no changing the course of things; you could only choose whether to jump on board or not. It was clear that nowadays the daughter of a local officeholder was destined by birth never to dirty her hands, never to work in a factory. It was impossible to imagine the secretary of a district Party Committee, dismissed from his job, settling for one at a factory bench. The people who set norms in industry were not those who had to fulfill them; just as those who gave the order to attack were not those who had to carry it out.

None of this was new to our planet, only to a Revolutionary country. The galling thing was that years of service without ever removing his boots might seem to entitle Captain Shchagov to a share in the good life he personally had helped to win, but nobody recognized this right. He had to establish his right to it all over again; in bloodless battle this time, without gunfire, without grenades, he had to fight his way through the serried ranks of bureaucracy to get his claim stamped with the seal of official approval.

And through it all he had to keep smiling.

Shchagov had been in such a hurry to get to the front in 1941 that he had not troubled to complete his final year and graduate. Now, after the war, he had to catch up and struggle to obtain a higher degree. His subject was theoretical mechanics; he had thought of devoting himself entirely to it before the war. Things were easier then. He had returned to find that enthusiasm for learning—learning anything and everything—had become an epidemic since salary scales had been adjusted sharply upward.

So he had steeled himself for another long campaign. He had sold off the German booty bit by bit. He made no effort to keep up with the changing fashions in men's clothes and shoes but defiantly went on wearing the things he was discharged in—army boots, army breeches, a coarse tunic with four rows of medal ribbons and two wound stripes. But because of this, he had not lost the allure of the wartime soldier, and it gave him in Nadya's eyes an affinity with just such another, Captain Nerzhin.

Nadya, who was easily hurt by any little misfortune or affront, looked up to Shchagov, with his armor-plated worldly wisdom, like a little girl and regularly asked his advice. But even with him she stubbornly stuck to the lie that her Gleb had been reported missing in action.

Nadya had landed herself in all this—the "spare" cinema ticket, the playful tussle over the notebook—without realizing what was happening. This time she knew as soon as he entered the room and while he was bandying words with Dasha that he had only come to see her and that something was bound to happen.

And although she had just been weeping over the wreckage of her life, when she tore up the ten-ruble note she was suddenly renewed, eager to live life to the full, then and there.

In her heart she felt no contradiction.

Shchagov, once he had mastered the emotion that his brush with her had aroused, reverted to his usual deliberate manner.

He told the girl straight out that she should not count on marrying him.

When she heard that he was engaged, Nadya took a few halting steps about the room, then went to stand beside him at the window, silently tracing patterns on the glass with her finger.

He felt sorry for her. He would have liked to break the silence and say quite simply, with the frankness to which he had grown unused, "Poor little student, with no connections and no future, what do you have to offer me?" He had a perfect right to his piece of the cake (he would have taken it some other way if ours were not a country in which talented people are torn to pieces before they get anywhere). He felt an urge to confide in Nadya, tell her that though his fiancée lived a life of idleness, she was not hopelessly spoiled. She had a nice apartment in an expensive and exclusive building, where only top people were quartered. There was a doorman in the hall and carpet on the stairs—where did you ever see that in the Soviet Union nowadays? The main thing was that all his problems would be solved at once. What better way could there be?

He thought all this but said nothing.

Resting her temple against the glass and looking out into the night, Nadya spoke slowly. "That's fine. You have a fiancée. And I have a husband."

"A husband missing in action?"

"No, not missing," she whispered.

(How rash she was, giving away her secret!)

"You mean you hope he's alive?"

"I saw him. . . . Today. . . ."

(She had given herself away, but never mind; she didn't want him to think that she was a slut, throwing herself at him.)

It didn't take Shchagov long to work it out. He did not assume, as a woman might, that Nadya had been deserted. He knew that "missing, whereabouts unknown" nearly always referred to "displaced person," and that if such a person were "displaced" back to the Soviet Union, it would only be to disappear behind bars.

He moved closer to Nadya and took her elbow.

"You saw Gleb?"

"Yes," she said almost soundlessly, expressionlessly.

"Where is he? Inside?"

"Yes."

"So tha-a-at's it!" Shchagov said, as though relieved of a burden. He thought a moment. Then quickly left the room.

Nadya's senses were so numbed by shame and despair that she had not detected the new note in Shchagov's voice.

He had run away. So what? She was glad that she had told him. Now she was alone again with her honestly borne burden.

The filament in the bulb was still glowing feebly.

Dragging her feet as though they were too heavy for her, Nadya crossed the room, found the second cigarette in the pocket of her fur coat, reached for a box of matches, and lit up. She found some satisfaction in the nauseating harshness of the tobacco.

She wasn't used to it, and it made her cough.

In passing, she spotted Shchagov's overcoat lying on a chair in a shapeless heap.

Imagine his rushing out like that! She had given him such a fright that he had forgotten his coat.

It was very quiet, and she could hear the radio in the next room . . . could hear . . . yes, it was . . . Liszt's *Étude in F Minor.*

She used to play it herself at one time, when she was a girl; but had she really understood it? Her fingers had played the notes, but the word "disperato"— "despairing"—could have found no echo in her heart.

Leaning her brow against the window sash, Nadya pressed the palms of her hands against the cold panes.

She stood as though crucified on the black cross of the window frame.

There had been one little warm spot in her life, and now there was none.

But it took her only a few minutes to reconcile herself to the loss. She was her husband's wife again.

She stared into the darkness, trying to make out the chimney stack of the Matrosskaya Tishina prison.

Disperato! That helpless despair, when you struggle to rise from your knees and sink back again. That importunate high D flat, like a woman's hysterical shriek! Like a cry of inconsolable suffering!

The row of streetlamps outside carried her eyes into the pitch darkness of a future she would rather not live to see.

The étude ended, and 6:00 p.m., Moscow time, was announced.

Nadya had forgotten all about Shchagov, when he suddenly came in again without knocking.

He was carrying a bottle and two little glasses.

"All right, then, soldier's wife!" he said roughly, cheerfully. "Don't let it get you down. Take hold of this glass. Keep your head and all may be well. Let's drink to the resurrection of the dead!"

## 53

# The Ark

AT 6:00 P.M. ON SUNDAY, even in the sharashka, it was time to stop work till the next morning. There was no way of avoiding this tiresome interruption in the prisoners' work because the free workers would do only one shift on Sundays. It was an odious tradition, but even majors and lieutenant colonels were powerless against it, for they too had no wish to work on Sunday evenings. Only Mamurin, the Man in the Iron Mask, dreaded those empty evenings, when the free workers went away, and the zeks, who in spite of everything were in some sense people, were herded into their pens and locked in and he was left to wander alone through the deserted hallways, past sealed doors, to languish in his cell with washbasin, cabinet, and cot for company. Mamurin had tried hard to get permission for Number Seven to work on Sunday evenings, but he could not overcome the conservatism of the special prison authorities who did not want to double guards inside the prison.

And so it came about that 280 prisoners, flouting all conventional wisdom and regulations, spent Sunday evenings brazenly resting.

Their rest was of such a kind that anyone unused to it might have thought it a torment invented by the devil. The darkness outside and the need to be especially vigilant on Sundays made it impossible for the prison staff to arrange exercise periods in the yard or film shows in the big shed. After a year's correspondence with all the higher powers, it was also decided that musical instruments such as the accordion, guitar, balalaika, and harmonica—and a fortiori those of larger format—were forbidden in the sharashka, since their combined noise might be useful to prisoners trying to tunnel through the stone foundations. (Operations officers were continually trying to find out through informers whether any prisoner had a homemade panpipe or tin whistle, and anyone who played on comb and paper was called into the office and his offense specially recorded.) Obviously there could be no thought of allowing radios or the most pathetic little record player in the prisoners' quarters.

True, prisoners were allowed to make use of the prison library. But the special prison had no funds for buying books or a bookcase. They simply appointed Rubin prison librarian (he volunteered, hoping to get his hands on some good books), presented him with a hundred or so disheveled and collapsing volumes, among them Turgenev's *Mumu*, Stasov's *Letters*, and Mommsen's *History of Rome*, and told him to circulate them among the prisoners. The prisoners had long since read all these books or had no desire at all to read them and had to beg reading matter from the female free workers, which provided the operations officers with rewarding opportunities for searches.

For their leisure hours the prisoners had at their disposal ten rooms in two stories, two hallways, the upper and the lower, a narrow wooden stairway between the floors, and a bathroom under the stairway. Rest meant that prisoners could without restriction lie on their beds (and even sleep, if they could drop off in all that hubbub), sit on their beds, or walk around the room or from room to room (wearing nothing but their underclothes if they so wished), smoke as much as they liked in the hallways, argue about politics in the presence of stoolies, and use the bathroom without permission or hindrance. (Only those who have spent a long time in jail, relieving themselves twice daily on a word of command, can appreciate this last immortal freedom.) What their rest period amounted to was that their time was their own, not the state's. And that was enough to make them regard it as genuine.

For the prisoners a day off meant that the heavy iron doors were locked from the outside, after which no one came in to summon a prisoner or haul him out. For those few short hours not a sound, not a word, not an image could filter through from the outside world to trouble a man's mind. That was what their day of rest meant—the whole world outside, the universe with all its stars, the planet with its continents, capital cities with their blazing lights, the whole state with some at their banquets and others working voluntary extra shifts, sank into oblivion, turned into an ocean of darkness barely discernible through the barred windows by the dead yellow half-light from the lights in the prison grounds.

Flooded within by the MGB's inextinguishable electric light, the old seminary church was like an ark, with sides four bricks and a half thick, floating serenely and aimlessly through that black ocean of human destinies and human errors, leaving behind fading rivulets of light from its portholes.

During that Sunday night the moon might crack in two, new alps might rear up in the Ukraine, the ocean might swallow Japan, a universal deluge might begin, but the prisoners locked up in the ark would know nothing of it till the morning roll call. Nor could they be disturbed during those hours by telegrams from relatives, tiresome telephone calls, a child taken ill with diphtheria, or nocturnal arrest.

Those who sailed on in the ark were weightless and had only weightless thoughts. They were neither hungry nor full. They knew no happiness and so felt no anxiety about losing it. Their heads were not busy with trivial professional concerns, intrigues, the struggle for promotion; their shoulders were not burdened with worries about a place to live, fuel, bread, and clothing for their children. Love, which has brought man delight and torment from the beginning of time, could neither thrill nor distress them. Their sentences were so long that not one of them as yet gave any thought to the years after his release. Men of remarkable intelligence, education, and experience of life, they had nonetheless been too devoted to their families to leave much of themselves for their friends, but here they belonged only to their friends.

Light from glaring bulbs, reflected from white ceilings and whitewashed walls, pierced their enlightened heads with thousands of rays.

From here, from the ark forging confidently ahead through the darkness, the erratically meandering stream of accursed history was clearly visible—visible in its entirety, as though from an immense height, yet in detail, down to the last little pebble on the streambed, just as though they had plunged into its waves.

During those Sunday evening hours, matter and body could be forgotten. The spirit of masculine friendship and philosophy hovered beneath the canvas vault of the ceiling.

Perhaps this was the bliss all the philosophers of antiquity had striven in vain to identify.

## 54

# Leisure Amusements

Nowhere could thoughts move more freely and merrily than under the high vaulted ceiling over the altar in the semicircular room on the second floor.

All twenty-five inmates had assembled by six o'clock. Some hastily stripped to their underwear, eager to shed their irksome prison skins, and flopped heavily on their bunks or scrambled aloft like monkeys. Others flopped without removing their overalls; one or two stood up above waving their arms and shouting to friends across the room; yet others, in no hurry to do anything, shuffled around looking at nothing in particular, savoring in advance the pleasurable hours of freedom ahead, and uncertain what would be the pleasantest way to begin.

One such was Isaak Kagan, the short, black-haired "manager of the accumulator shop," as they called him. He was in a particularly good mood because he had come into a spacious well-lit room from the dark and badly ventilated battery-charging room in the cellar, where he lurked like a mole fourteen hours a day. He was nonetheless content to work in the cellar, saying that in a camp he would have folded up long ago. (He never behaved like those big-mouths who boast that they "lived better in the camp than outside.")

Outside, Isaak Kagan had begun by dropping out of an engineering course, then working in an engineering supply depot, doing his best to live a modest and inconspicuous life, negotiating the Epoch of Great Achievements unnoticed. He knew that it was both safer and more lucrative to remain inconspicuous. But his buttoned-up exterior concealed a burning passion for gain. Moneygrubbing was his full-time occupation. Political activity held no attraction for him. He did observe the Sabbath as best he could, even in the storeroom. But for some reason the MGB had chosen Kagan as one of its wheelhorses and began cornering him in locked rooms and innocent-looking meeting places, pressing him to become a stoolie. Kagan found this revolting. He lacked the candor and the courage (who did not?) to fling their loathsome proposal in their faces, but, inexhaustibly patient, he remained silent, mumbled incomprehensibly, played for time, evaded their questions, fidgeted on his chair, and somehow avoided signing any undertaking. Not that he was altogether incapable of informing. He would have informed without a qualm on anyone who had harmed or insulted him. But the idea of denouncing people who were kind to him, or neither kind nor unkind, nauseated him.

The MGB noted his obstinacy and bided its time. You can't guard against every eventuality. His fellow workers at the depot got talking one day. Somebody beefed about the tools; somebody else about the supply system; a third person about the planners. Isaak didn't so much as open his mouth but went on jotting down requisitions with a copying pencil. The bosses got to know about it (they'd probably masterminded it all anyway); every worker made a statement on what each of the others had said, and every one of them got ten years under Article 58, section 10. Kagan, too, went through five confrontations, but nobody could prove that he had said a single word. If Article 58 had been a little less elastic, they would have had to let Kagan go. But the investigator had one final weapon in reserve: point 12 of that article, on failure to inform. It was for his failure to inform that they had stitched Kagan up with an astronomical ten years of his own.

His remarkable mother wit had gotten Kagan out of a camp into the sharashka. At an awkward moment when he had been dismissed from the job of "deputy hut orderly" and was about to be banished to a lumber camp, he addressed a letter to the chairman of the Council of Ministers, Comrade Stalin, saying that if the government would provide him, Isaak Kagan, with the opportunity, he would undertake to devise a system of remote control for torpedo boats.

His reasoning was sound. No one in the government would have felt the slightest twinge of sympathy if Kagan had written as if to fellow human beings, telling them how very bad things were with him and begging them to save him. But for the sake of a major military invention, it was worth bringing the writer to Moscow immediately. Kagan was taken to Marfino, and a variety of bigwigs with light or dark blue epaulets came visiting and urged him to embody his audacious technical concept in a finished product. Kagan, however, was now in receipt of white bread with butter and in no hurry. He replied with impressive sangfroid that he was not a torpedo artificer and naturally required the help of such a person. After another two months, they produced a torpedo expert (also a zek). Whereupon Kagan patiently explained that he was not a marine engineer and would naturally need help from someone of that sort. After another two months, they delivered a marine engineer (yet another zek). Kagan said with a sigh that radio was not his specialty. There were lots of radio engineers in Marfino, and one of them was immediately attached to Kagan. Kagan assembled his team and in a quiet, level voice, so that no one could suspect him of mockery, made this announcement: "Well, friends, now that you have all been brought together, you can, by pooling your efforts, easily invent a system of radio control for torpedo boats. I would not presume to advise you, the experts, as to the best way of doing it." All three were in fact dispatched to a naval sharashka. As for Kagan, he had made a niche for himself in the battery-charging room while he had been playing for time, and everybody had gotten used to him.

Kagan was now badgering Rubin, who was lying on his bunk, but from a distance so that Rubin could not reach him with a kick.

"Lev Grigorievich," he said. His speech was thick and rather indistinct but unhurried. "Your sense of duty to society has clearly declined. The masses thirst for entertainment. Only you can supply it, yet you have buried your nose in a book."

Rubin waved him away. "Isaak, you can go to . . ." He had settled down to read, lying on his belly, with his camp vest draped over the shoulders of his overalls (the window between him and Sologdin was open "one Mayakovsky," and there was an agreeable breeze with a hint of fresh snow).

Kagan doggedly persisted. "No, seriously, Lev Grigorievich. We would all very much like to hear your talented 'Crow and Fox' again."

"And who told tales to the godfather about it?" Rubin snapped. "Was it you?"

To amuse his public the previous Sunday evening, Rubin had improvised a skit on Krylov's fable "The Crow and the Fox," replete with camp slang and expressions unsuitable for women's ears, which had earned him five encores and a hoisting, but on Monday Major Myshin had sent for him and interrogated him on a charge of corrupting morals, in connection with which depositions had been extracted from several witnesses, and the original of the fable, together with a written explanation, from Rubin.

After lunch this Saturday, Rubin had put in two hours' work in the new room allotted to him, identified the wanted criminal's typical "speech tune" and "bands of resonance," run them through the "visible speech" apparatus, hung the wet tapes up to dry, and formed some preliminary conjectures and suspicions, but was still not particularly excited about his new line of work when he watched Smolosidov sealing the room for the night. After this, Rubin had joined the stream of zeks on their way to the prison building like cattle returning to the village at night.

As always, he had under his pillow, under his mattress, under his bed, and in his locker, higgledy-piggledy with his food, a dozen or so extremely interesting books—interesting, that is, to him alone, which is why they were not stolen. There were Chinese-French, Latvian-Hungarian, and Russian-Sanskrit dictionaries. Rubin had been busy for two years with a grandiose work in the spirit of Marx and Engels, tracing all words in all languages to the concepts "hand" and "manual labor." (He had no inkling that the Coryphaeus of Linguistic Science had the night before raised the headman's ax over Academician Marr.) He also had Čapek's *War with the Newts*, a collection of stories by very progressive (i.e., pro-Communist) Japanese writers, Hemingway's *For Whom the Bell Tolls* in English (he had ceased to be progressive, so Russian translation was lagging), a novel by Upton Sinclair that had never been translated into Russian, and Colonel Lawrence's memoirs in German, acquired as part of the confiscated property of the Lorenz company.

There was an enormous number of books, indispensable books, books of the first importance in the world, and his greed for them had made it impossible for Rubin to produce one of his own. Right now he was ready to go on and on reading long after midnight, with never a thought of the working day ahead. But Rubin was also at his wittiest and his appetite for argument and oratory keenest in the evening, so that it didn't take much to mobilize these talents in the service of the public. There were people in the sharashka who did not trust Rubin, taking him for a stoolie (because of his ultra-Marxist views, which he did not conceal), but there was no one in the place who did not delight in his powers of invention.

The memory of "The Crow and the Fox," embellished with clever borrowings from criminal slang, was so vivid that many of those in the room loudly seconded Kagan's plea for some new gag. And when Rubin, morose and bearded, raised himself and emerged as if from a cave from the cover afforded by the bunk above him, they all abandoned whatever they were doing and prepared to listen. All except Dvoetyosov on his top bunk, who went on cutting his toenails so savagely that clippings flew into the distance, and Abramson under his blanket, who did not look up from his book. Curious people from other rooms blocked the doorways, and one of them, the Tatar Bulatov in his horn-rimmed spectacles, rapped out: "Come on, Lyova! Let's have it!"

Rubin had no wish at all to gratify people most of whom hated or despised all that was dear to him; he knew, too, that another jape would inevitably mean more unpleasantness no later than Monday, more nervous strain, further interrogation by "Shishkin-Myshkin." But Rubin was the proverbial hero who would sacrifice his own father for the sake of a funny remark, so he pretended to frown, cast an expert eye over his audience, and said in the sudden hush: "Comrades! I am amazed by your frivolity. How can you think of fun when brazen criminals are at large among us, as yet undetected? No society can flourish without a just legal system. I consider it necessary to begin our evening with a modest trial. As a warm-up."

"Good idea!"

"Whom shall we try?"

There was a chorus of "Doesn't matter who!" "Comes to the same thing!"

"Amusing! Most amusing!" Sologdin said encouragingly, making himself comfortable. He had earned his evening's rest as never before and needed entertainment.

Cautious Kagan, sensing that the game he had started might overstep the boundaries of discretion, faded from the foreground and sat on his bed.

"The identity of the defendant you will learn as the trial proceeds," Rubin announced. (He hadn't yet decided himself.) "I may as well be public prosecutor, since that office has always aroused very special emotions in me." (Everybody in the sharashka knew that certain prosecutors were among Rubin's pet hates and that he had for five years been engaged in single combat with the All-Union and with the Main Military Prosecution Services.)

"Gleb! You'll be presiding judge. Choose yourself two colleagues quickly. They must be impartial, objective, and, in a word, completely subservient to your will."

Nerzhin had slipped off his shoes down below and was sitting on his top bunk. As Sunday went by and the familiar prison world closed in around him, his meeting with Nadya seemed more and more remote. In response to Rubin's call, he drew himself up to the rails at the end of the bed and let his feet dangle between them, so that he appeared to be seated on a judicial bench looking down on the room.

"All right—where are my assessors? Get up here!"

A lot of prisoners had gathered in the room, and they all wanted to listen to the trial, but nobody wanted to be an assessor, whether out of caution or from fear of looking ridiculous. To one side of Nerzhin, on another top bunk, lay Zemelya the vacuum man, reading his morning paper again.

"Ulyba!" Nerzhin said, tugging at the paper. "You've educated yourself enough. The way you're going, you'll be wanting to rule the world soon. Tuck your legs under and be a jury man!"

Applause was heard from below. "Come on, Zemelya!"

Zemelya thawed easily and could not resist for long. All smiles, he hung his balding head over the bedrail and said: "To be the people's choice is a great honor! Just think what you're doing, friends! I have no education; I don't know how. . . ."

General laughter ("None of us know how; we're all only learners!") greeted his objection, and he was duly elected.

To the other side of Nerzhin lay Ruska Doronin. He had undressed, covered himself from head to foot with his blanket, and hidden his ecstatically happy face under a pillow. He didn't want to hear or see anything or to be seen. Only his body was there; his thoughts and his feelings were following Klara on her way home. She had finished braiding the basket for the tree and presented it discreetly to Ruska just before she left. He was holding it under the blanket and kissing it.

Realizing that it would be pointless to try to stir Ruska, Nerzhin looked around for someone else.

He called to Bulatov. "Amantai! Amantai! Come and join the jury!"

Bulatov's eyes flashed mischievously. "I would, only there's nowhere to sit! I'll stay here by the door and be bailiff."

Khorobrov (by this time he had given Abramson and two others their haircuts and set to work on a new client, who was sitting in the middle of the room stripped to the waist to save him the trouble of removing hairs from his underclothes later) shouted out, "Who needs two jury men? You've got the verdict up your sleeve anyway. One's enough! Get the show on the road!"

"He's right, you know," Nerzhin said. "Why pay a man for nothing? So where's the defendant? Bailliff, bring in the defendant! Silence in court!"

He rapped on the bed frame with his large cigarette holder. The talking died down.

There were calls of "Get on with the trial!"

Some of the public remained standing; others were seated.

"Yea, though I ascend into the heavens, Thou art there; though I descend into hell, Thou art there," Potapov intoned in a lugubrious voice from below the presiding judge's seat. "Though I make my abode in the depths of the sea, even there Thy right hand will discover me!" (Potapov had picked up a little scripture in his pre-Revolutionary secondary school, and his precise engineer's mind had preserved the words of the prayer book.)

Also down below, under the jury man, the rattle of a spoon stirring tea was distinctly heard.

"Valentulya!" Nerzhin shouted threateningly. "How many times have you been told not to rattle your spoon?"

"Put him on trial," Bulatov yelled, and several obliging hands dragged Pryanchikov from the twilight of his lower bunk into the middle of the room.

"Cut it out!" Pryanchikov struggled furiously to free himself. "I've had enough of public prosecutors! I'm sick and tired of courts and courtrooms! What right does any man have to sit in judgment on another? Ha-ha! It's ridiculous! I despise you, you pipsqueak!" he yelled at the presiding judge. I don't give a . . . for you!"

While Nerzhin had been putting his makeshift court together, Rubin had thought it all out. His dark brown eyes shone with the light of inspiration. He absolved Pryanchikov with a magnanimous gesture.

"Release that fledgling! Valentulya, with his passion for universal justice, will do very well as official defense counsel! Give him a chair!"

There is in every joke an elusive moment at which it either becomes crude and offensive or is transmuted by inspiration. Rubin draped a blanket round his shoulders like a robe, climbed onto a locker in his stockinged feet, and addressed the presiding judge. "State Counselor of Justice! The defendant has failed to present himself and will be tried in absentia. Let us begin!"

Spiridon, the yardman with the ginger mustache, was one of the crowd in the doorway. His pendulous cheeks were scored with harsh wrinkles; but, strangely, merriment was always about to break out of the net. He scowled at the officers of the court.

Behind Spiridon the long, fine-drawn, waxy face and woolen ski cap of Professor Chelnov could be seen.

Nerzhin called the court to order in a rasping voice: "Your attention, Comrades! The military tribunal of the Marfino sharashka is now in session. The case before us is that of—"

The prosecutor supplied a name: "Olgovich, Igor Svyatoslavich."

Nerzhin caught on and continued in a nasal drawl, as if reading: "The case before us is that of Olgovich, Igor Svyatoslavich, prince of Novgorod-Seversk and Putivl, approximate date of birth . . . Clerk of the Court, why the devil is it only approximate? . . . Attention! In view of the fact that the court has nothing in writing before it, the prosecutor will read the indictment."

# 55

## Prince Igor

RUBIN BEGAN SPEAKING as easily and fluently as if his eyes really were skimming a written document (he had been tried or retried four times over, and the procedural formulas were imprinted on his memory).

"Act of indictment on completion of investigation of case number five million slash three million six hundred and fifty-one thousand, nine hundred and seventy-four, the accused being Olgovich, Igor Svyatoslavich.

"The prosecution in the present case is brought against Olgovich, I. S., by the Organs of State Security. Investigation has established that Olgovich, being at the time leader of the valiant Russian army in the field, holding the title of prince and the post of commander of a warrior band, proved to be a dastardly traitor to his motherland. His treasonable activity took the form of surrendering of his own free will to Khan Konchak, now unmasked as a sworn enemy of our people, and furthermore surrendering into captivity his son Vladimir Igorevich, as also his brother, his nephew, and the full complement of his warrior band with all their arms and all supplies and equipment for which he was responsible.

"His treasonable conduct manifested itself further in the fact that he from the very beginning allowed himself to be taken in by a trick, to wit, an eclipse of the sun, contrived by the reactionary clergy, and in consequence did not take the lead in mass political briefing of his warrior band as it set out to 'quaff the Don from its helmets.' I make no mention here of the unhygienic condition of the Don River in those years, before the introduction of double chlorination. Instead of all this, the accused confined himself to a completely irresponsible exhortation to his army, when already in sight of the Polovtsians.

*Brothers, this we sought, let us now stiffen our sinews!*

INVESTIGATOR'S REPORT, VOL. 1, SHEET 36

"The disastrous significance for our motherland of the defeat of the combined warrior bands of Novgorod-Seversk, Kursk, and Putivl is best characterized in the words of Svyatoslav, grand prince of Kiev:

*God gave the heathen into my hand to chasten them*
*But thy youth was hasty.*

IBID., VOL. 1, SHEET 88

"It is, however, a naive mistake on the part of Svyatoslav, resulting from his class blindness, to ascribe the poor organization of the whole campaign and the fragmentation of Russia's military effort to the youth of the accused, failing to understand that what we are concerned with here is a treasonable act planned long in advance.

"The criminal himself has succeeded in eluding interrogation and trial, but we have from the witness Borodin, Aleksandr Porphirievich, and also a witness who has expressed a wish to remain unknown and will henceforth be known as the Author of the Lay, irrefutable depositions not only exposing the abominable role of Prince I. S. Olgovich during his conduct of the battle itself, which was joined in meteorological conditions unfavorable to the Russian command:

*The winds blow, bearing now the arrows,*
*Raining them upon Igor's ranks*

and in equally unfavorable tactical conditions:

*From all sides the enemies advance,*
*Hemming our men in all ways.*

IBID., VOL. 1, SHEETS 123, 124;
DEPOSITION OF THE AUTHOR OF THE LAY

but also revealing the still more revolting behavior of Olgovich and his princely offspring in captivity. The living conditions of both of them in so-called captivity show that they stood high in the favor of Khan Konchak and objectively were being rewarded by the Polovtsian high command for the treasonable surrender of their warrior band.

"Thus, for instance, it is established by the testimony of the witness Borodin that, while in captivity, Prince Igor had a horse of his own, and indeed more than one:

*Take any horse, choose where thou wilt!*

IBID., VOL. 1, SHEET 233

"Khan Konchak, on this occasion, said to Prince Igor:

*Dost thou yet think thyself a prisoner?*
*Is it a prisoner's life thou leadest?*
*Art thou not rather my dear guest?*

IBID., VOL. 1, SHEET 281

and further

*Say truly—is this the way a prisoner lives?*

IBID., VOL. 1, SHEET 300

"The Polovtsian khan here reveals the full cynicism of his relations with the traitor prince:

*For your valor, for your great daring*
*I have come to love you, prince.*

INVESTIGATOR'S REPORT, VOL. 2, SHEET 5

"More thorough investigation has revealed that these cynical relations existed long before the battle on the Kayala River:

*For thou wert always dear to me.*

IBID., SHEET 14; TESTIMONY OF THE WITNESS BORODIN

and even

*Thy faithful ally, trusty friend and brother*
*And not thy foe I'd be. . . .*

IBID.

"All this puts the accused in focus as an active aider and abettor of Khan Konchak and a Polovtsian agent and spy of long standing.

"On the basis of the facts here set out, Olgovich, Igor Svyatoslavich, born 1151, native of the city of Kiev, Russian, not a Party member, no previous convictions, citizen of the USSR, warlord by trade, having served as commander of a warrior band with the rank of prince, and having been awarded the Varangian Order, First Class, the Order of the Little Red Sun, and the Golden Shield medal, is charged as follows: that he committed a vile act of treachery to his motherland, accompanied by sabotage, espionage, and collaboration over many years with the Polovtsian khanate, that is to say, that he committed the crimes envisaged in Article 58, subsections 1b, 6, 9, and 11 of the Criminal Code of the Russian Socialist Federation of Soviet Republics.

"Olgovich is by his own admission guilty of the charges brought against him and stands convicted by the testimony of witnesses in the form of a poem and an opera.*

"In accordance with article 208 of the Criminal Procedural Code of the RSFSR, the present case has been referred to the prosecutor so that he may bring the accused to trial."

Rubin paused to take a deep breath and triumphantly surveyed the assembled zeks. Swept along on the flood tide of his fantasy, he could no longer stop. Peals of laughter from the bunks and the doorway spurred him on. He had already said more and spoken more caustically than he would normally wish to with a sprinkling of stoolies among his audience or to people bitterly hostile to the regime.

Spiridon, under the graying ginger mop straggling over his brow and ears and down his neck, had not laughed once. He surveyed the scene with a frown. Fifty years old and a Russian, he had never heard of this prince of long ago who had been taken prisoner, but faced with the familiar surroundings of the courtroom and the impregnable self-assurance of the prosecutor, he relived his own experiences, and instinctively understood the gross unfairness of the prosecutor's arguments and the woes of the hapless prince.

Nerzhin spoke again, in the same nasal drawl.

"In view of the absence of the accused, and there being no need to cross-examine witnesses, we will proceed to counsel's arguments. I call upon the prosecutor again."

He glanced at Zemelya, his jury man, who nodded agreement to this and whatever was to come.

"Comrade Judges!" Rubin cried sternly. "I have only a little to add to the concatenation of terrible accusations, the foul tangle of crimes that has been unraveled before your eyes. I should like first to reject emphatically the decadent view so widely held that a wounded man has a moral right to surrender. That is radically opposed to our way of thinking, Comrades. Especially where Prince Igor is concerned. We are told that he was wounded on the field of battle. But what proof is there of that 765 years later? Has any record of his

* Poem and opera: The poem is *The Lay of Igor's Campaign*, the anonymous Russian epic composed near the end of the twelfth century. The opera is Alexander Borodin's *Prince Igor*, composed in the nineteenth century. In 1185, Igor Svyatoslavich, Prince of Novgorod-Seversk, led an undermanned raid against the invading Polovtsians, a nomadic Turkic tribe; he lost and was captured but later escaped. The famous work inspired other renditions of the story, including the opera by Borodin. In the present version, told as travesty, the joke is that Igor is being tried according to the ideological standards of the Soviet system of justice.

wound, signed by the divisional medical officer, been preserved? One thing is sure, that no such document is on the investigator's file, Comrade Judges!"

Amantai Bulatov took off his glasses, and without their bold, mischievous twinkle, his eyes were quite sad.

He, Pryanchikov, Potapov, and several others among the prisoners crowding around had been imprisoned for "betraying their country" in precisely the same way: surrendering "voluntarily."

"Furthermore," the prosecutor thundered, "I wish to draw special attention to the disgusting behavior of the accused in the Polovtsian camp. Prince Igor has no thought at all for his motherland, only for his wife:

*Thou art alone, my dove, my pretty one,*
*Thou art alone. . . .*

"Analytically this is entirely understandable, since his Yaroslavna is a young wife, and his second, and obviously such a female is not greatly to be relied on, but the fact is that Prince Igor stands revealed as an utterly selfish man. Anyway, for whom, I ask you, were the Polovtsian dances danced? For him, of course! And his odious offspring promptly enters into a sexual liaison with Konchak's daughter, although Soviet subjects are categorically forbidden by the relevant competent organs to marry foreign women! And this at a time when Soviet-Polovtsian relations were strained to the utmost—"

Kagan piped up from his bunk: "Just a moment! How does the prosecutor know that the Soviet regime already existed in Russia at that time?"

Nerzhin hammered for order: "Bailiff! Remove that venal agent of a foreign power!" But before Bulatov could move, Rubin deftly parried the thrust.

"Allow me to reply! Dialectical analysis of the text gives convincing proof. Read what the Author of the Lay says: 'Red banners flap in the breeze at Putivl.' That seems clear enough. The noble prince Vladimir Galitsky, head of the Putivl district office of the Commissariat of War, is recruiting a people's militia, consisting of Skula and Yeroshka, to defend their native city at the very time when Prince Igor is ogling the naked limbs of Polovtsian women. I readily concede that we can sympathize with him here, but then Konchak invites him to choose 'whichever beauty pleases thee.' Why, then, does the wretch not avail himself? Who among you here present can believe that a man would voluntarily deny himself a woman? We find hidden here the ultimate cynicism; expose it, and the accused has not a leg to stand on. I mean his so-called escape from captivity and his 'voluntary' return to the motherland! Who can believe that a man who has been offered 'whichever horse thou wouldst, and gold' would voluntarily abandon all that and return to his motherland? How could it possibly be so?"

That very question had been put to returning ex–prisoners of war, Spiridon among them, by their interrogators: Why would you be returning, unless they've recruited you?

"There can be only one explanation: Prince Igor had been enrolled by the Polovtsian intelligence service and planted to disrupt the Kievan state! Comrade Judges! I, like you, am seething with noble indignation. I humanely demand that you sentence the son of a bitch to be hanged! Or rather, since capital punishment has been abolished, that you clobber him with twenty-five years inside, followed by five years' deprivation of civil rights. In addition, I ask for a special recommendation of the court that the opera *Prince Igor* be banned as completely amoral and tending to popularize treasonable attitudes among Soviet youth! Borodin, A. P., a witness in this case, should face criminal charges and be put under arrest to curb his activities. Others who should be called to account are the aristocrats (a) Rimsky and (b) Korsakov,* since if they had not put the finishing touches to this misbegotten opera, it would never have been staged. I have no more to say!"

Rubin jumped heavily down from the locker. Speech had become a painful effort to him.

No one was laughing now.

Without waiting to be called, Pryanchikov rose from his chair and spoke to the hushed room in a low, faltering voice: "*Tant pis*, gentlemen! *Tant pis*! Is this the twentieth century or the Stone Age? What do we mean by treason? In the age of nuclear fallout! semiconductors! the electronic brain! Who has the right to judge a fellow man, gentlemen? Who has the right to deprive him of freedom?"

"Excuse me, have we got to defense counsel's plea already?" Professor Chelnov intervened politely, and everybody turned toward him. "I should like first as supervisory prosecutor to adduce certain facts omitted by my esteemed colleague, and—"

Nerzhin encouraged him. "Of course, of course, Vladimir Erastovich! We are always in favor of the prosecution and against the defense, and always prepared to countenance any breach of judicial procedure. Please go on!"

* Rimsky and Korsakov: Nikolai Rimsky-Korsakov, a famous nineteenth-century Russian composer, joined with Alexander Glazunov to complete Alexander Borodin's opera *Prince Igor*. The joke here is that the speaker thinks Rimky-Korsakov is two persons.

A restrained smile hovered on Professor Chelnov's lips. He spoke very quietly, and if he could be heard easily, it was only because he was listened to respectfully. His faded eyes seemed to stare at something beyond his audience, as though the pages of a chronicle were being turned for him. The pom-pom on his woolen cap made his face seem still sharper and more dubious.

"I wish to point out," said the professor of mathematics, "that Prince Igor should have been unmasked before he was appointed commander in the field and when he first filled in our personal data form. His mother was a Polovtsian, the daughter of a Polovtsian prince. Himself half Polovtsian by blood, Prince Igor was allied with the Polovtsians for many years. He had been 'an ally true, a trusty friend' to Konchak before the expedition! In 1180 when he was routed by the sons of Monomakh, he and Khan Konchak fled from them in the same boat! Later on, Svyatoslav and Ryurik Rostislavich summoned Igor to join in the great all-Russian expeditions against the Polovtsians, but Igor declined, making the 'black ice' his excuse: 'Thick was the rime.'

"Perhaps this was because Konchak's daughter Svoboda was already betrothed to Igor's son Vladimir? Finally, who helped Igor to escape in the year with which we are concerned, 1185? Another Polovtsian.

"The Polovtsian Ovlur, whom Igor then 'made mighty.' And Konchak's daughter afterward brought Igor his grandson. . . . For suppressing these facts, I propose that the Author of the Lay also be called to account, together with the music critic Stasov, who overlooked the treasonable tendencies in Borodin's opera, and finally Count Musin-Pushkin, who must surely have had a hand in the burning of the only manuscript of the lay? It is obvious that someone who stood to gain by doing so has tried to cover the tracks."

Chelnov then gave way, indicating that he had concluded.

The same faint smile hovered on his lips.

There was silence.

"Is nobody going to speak for the accused?" Isaak Kagan sounded indignant. "The man needs a defender!"

"There's nothing to be said for the rat," Dvoetyosov shouted. "Put him up against the wall!"

Sologdin frowned. What Rubin had said was very amusing, and he had still more respect for Chelnov's knowledge, but Prince Igor was a representative of ancient Russian chivalry, of the most glorious period in Russian history, and should therefore not be made even indirectly a figure of fun. It had left a bad taste in Sologdin's mouth.

"No, no, say what you like, I shall speak for the defense." Isaak, growing bolder by the minute, craftily surveyed his audience. "Comrade Judges! As an honorable member of the bar, I fully associate myself with all the arguments of the state prosecutor." He spoke with a drawl and slurred his words. "My conscience tells me that Prince Igor should not only be hanged but quartered as well. True, capital punishment has not been on our humane statute book for nearly three years, so we are compelled to find a substitute for it. Nonetheless, I fail to understand why the prosecutor is so suspiciously softhearted. (It suggests that he, too, should be looked into!) Why does he miss one gradation on the penal scale and arrive at twenty-five years' hard labor? There is, as you know, a punishment in our Criminal Code only slightly less severe than the death sentence, a penalty much more fearful than twenty-five years at hard labor."

Isaak paused to heighten the effect.

There were cries of "What penalty, Isaak?" The more impatient they were, the slower he spoke, the more innocent he looked.

"Article 20, subsection A."

Many of those present were rich in experience of prison, but no one had ever heard of such an article.

There were shouts of "What's it say?" and indecent suggestions from around the room. "Cut his . . . off?"

"Very nearly," Isaak assented, with a straight face. "To be precise, spiritual castration. Article 20, subsection A, prescribes as punishment that the criminal be declared an enemy of the toiling masses and expelled from the USSR! Let him die like a dog out there in the West! I have no more to say."

Modestly averting his head, looking smaller and shaggier than ever, he went back to his bed.

An explosion of laughter shook the room.

"What! What!" Khorobrov roared, choking with laughter, and making his customer flinch, as the clippers jumped in his hand. "Expulsion? Is there really such an article?"

There were cries of "Why don't you ask for a stiffer sentence, then?"

Spiridon smiled a crafty peasant smile.

They all started talking at once and wandering around the room.

By now Rubin was lying on his belly again, trying to make headway with his Mongolian-Finnish dictionary. He cursed his idiotic habit of showing off. He was ashamed of the act he had just put on.

His sarcasm was aimed only at unjust judges, but people did not know where to stop and made fun of the most precious of all things, the idea of socialism itself.

# 56

## Winding Up the Twentieth

ABRAMSON, MEANWHILE, lay as before, shoulder and cheek snug against a plump pillow, greedily devouring *The Count of Monte Cristo.* He had turned his back on the proceedings. Courtroom comedy did not appeal to him. He did look around briefly when Chelnov spoke, because the details were new to him. At one time Abramson was easily aroused to a frenzy of eloquence and could hold forth endlessly without getting hoarse. But twenty years of exile, transit prisons, investigation centers, solitary confinement, labor camps, and sharashkas had left him insensitive and indifferent to suffering—his own and that of those around him.

The mock trial that had just taken place was dedicated to the fate of the 1945–46 "stream." Abramson could acknowledge theoretically that the fate of former POWs was tragic, but they were only one stream, one of many, and not the most remarkable. Insofar as the ex–prisoners of war were interesting, it was because they had seen many foreign lands ("real live false witnesses," Potapov jokingly called them); but, all in all, their "stream" was an undistinguished one; they were merely helpless victims of war, not people who had voluntarily chosen political struggle as their way of life.

Every stream of zeks into the NKVD pool, like each new generation of people on earth, has its own history and its own heroes.

And it is difficult for one generation to understand another.

As Abramson saw it, these people could not possibly be compared with titans like himself who, at the end of the twenties, voluntarily chose banishment to the Yenisei when they could have retracted what they had said at Party meetings and gone on living comfortably. They were all given the choice. But these were people who could not bear the distortion and degradation of the Revolution and were ready to sacrifice themselves to sanitize it. This "youthful tribe unknown" had entered the cells thirty years after the October Revolution and simply repeated, with a sprinkling of peasant obscenities, the very things for which the Cheka's execution squads had shot, burned, and drowned people in the Civil War.

So Abramson, although he felt no personal hostility to particular ex-

POWs and never argued with them individually, did not like the breed as a whole.

In any case he had (or so he assured himself) long since ceased to react to arguments, confessions, and eyewitness accounts from fellow prisoners. He had long lost the curiosity he may have felt in his youth about what was being said in another corner of the cell. Once he had lived for his work, but his enthusiasm had long ago burned itself out. He could not live for his family because he was not from Moscow, he was never allowed visitors, and letters that came to the sharashka had been unwittingly drained of the juices of real life by their writers before the censor ever saw them. Nor did he let the newspapers hold his attention: A glance at the headlines made it obvious what the paper would be saying. He could listen to music on the radio for not more than one hour a day, and his nerves could simply not stand programs consisting of words or lying books. So that although somewhere deep inside himself, beyond seven defensive barriers, he had preserved not just a lively but a painfully acute interest in what was happening in the world, and to the creed to which he had dedicated his life, externally he affected total indifference to everything around him. The Trotskyist who had survived his turn to be shot, starved to death, or harried into the grave now preferred not books red-hot with truth but those that diverted him and helped to while away his interminable sentence.

Ah, but in 1929, out in the taiga, on the Yenisei, they had not been reading *Monte Cristo.* Pretending that it was to celebrate the New Year, they flocked to the distant village of Doshchany on the Angara, which was reached by a three-hundred-verst sledge track through the taiga, from places a hundred versts deeper into the forest for a conference of exiles on their country's situation, international and domestic. It was more than fifty-eight degrees below zero. The slow-but-sure iron stove in the corner was quite inadequate to warm the exaggeratedly spacious Siberian hut; the built-in Russian stove was in ruins (which was why the hut had been given to the exiles). The walls of the hut were frozen through. At intervals in the dead of night, the timbers would emit a sharp sound like a rifle shot.

The conference opened with a report by Satanevich on the policy of the Party in the countryside. He took off his cap, releasing an unruly black forelock, but kept on his short fur coat with the eternal English phrase book ("We must know our enemy") sticking out of one pocket. Satanevich always assumed the role of leader. He was, so it was said, subsequently shot during a strike at Vorkuta.

In his report, Satanevich recognized the rational kernel of the Party's policy. The conservative peasantry had to be curbed by draconian Stalinist methods, or else the tide of reaction would inundate the cities and drown the Revolution. (It was time now to admit that the peasantry had overwhelmed the cities anyway, drowned them in a petit-bourgeois flood, drowned even the Party apparatus that had been sapped by purges, and so destroyed the Revolution.)

Alas, the more passionate the debates were, the more they damaged the unity of the puny group of exiles. It became clear that there were not just two opinions, not just three, but as many as there were people. Toward morning, too tired to go on, they would wind up the official part of the conference without agreeing on a resolution.

Then they ate and drank from the state's crockery, decoratively nestling among fir twigs that hid the ruts and ragged splinters of the table. The thawing twigs smelled of snow and resin and pricked people's hands. They drank moonshine liquor. They proposed toasts and swore that none of those present would ever capitulate and sign a recantation. A political storm would break in the Soviet Union any month now!

Then they sang famous Revolutionary songs: "La Varsovienne," "Our Banner Flutters Over the Whole World," "The Black Baron." . . .

And they went on arguing about anything and everything.

Roza, who had worked in a Kharkov tobacco factory, had sat on her feather mattress (she had brought it with her from the Ukraine to Siberia and was very proud of the fact), smoking one cigarette after another and scornfully tossing her short curly hair: "I can't stand intellectuals! They revolt me with their 'fine distinctions' and 'complications.' Human psychology is much simpler than pre-Revolutionary writers chose to portray it. Our task is to free humanity from its superfluous spiritual burdens!"

Somehow or other they got around to women's jewelry. One exile, Patrushev, formerly a public prosecutor in the Crimea, whose fiancée had in fact recently come from Russia to see him, exclaimed defiantly, "Why do you want to make the society of the future poorer than it need be? Why shouldn't I dream of a time when every girl will be able to wear pearls? When every man will be able to crown the bride of his choice with a diadem?"

What an uproar this had created! How furiously they had pelted him with quotations from Marx and Plekhanov, from Campanella and Feuerbach.

The society of the future! How confidently they talked about it!

The sun rose on the new year, the one thousand nine hundred and thirtieth, and they all went outside to admire it. It was a bracing, frosty morning with columns of pink smoke rising straight toward the pink sky. Women were driving cattle along the broad, white Angara to their watering place, a hole in the ice with fir logs around it. The men of the village and their horses were nowhere to be seen. They had been packed off to fell and haul timber.

Two decades went by. The causes they had toasted lost their bloom and their relevance. Those who remained firm to the end were shot. And those who capitulated were shot just the same. Abramson was left behind with his memories—and an understanding of those years that matured unseen in one sharashka after another, like a sapling under a bell jar.

Abramson's eyes were on his book but not reading, when Nerzhin came and sat on the edge of his bed.

They had met first in a cell in Butyrki Prison three years before. Potapov was in the same cell. Abramson was nearing the end of his first ten-year jail sentence at the time, and his cellmates were impressed by this experienced prisoner's air of ice-cold authority, his deep-rooted skepticism about prison matters; but secretly he cherished the insane hope that he would shortly return to his family.

They had gone their different ways. Abramson was in fact shortly released, by some oversight, and was free just long enough for his family to pull up stakes and move to Sterlitamak, where the militia was willing to give him a residence permit. But no sooner had his family moved than they pulled him in, subjected him to a single interrogation, in which he was asked whether he was indeed the Abramson who had been in exile from 1929 to 1934 and since then in jail. Having established that he had in fact served and completed and even somewhat exceeded the term to which he had been sentenced, the Special Tribunal rewarded him for it with a further ten years. Those in charge of the special prisons (sharashkas) discovered from the main All-Union card index that their former employee was inside again and promptly yanked him out to work for them. Abramson was transported to Marfino, where, as you always do in the convict world, he met old acquaintances, Nerzhin and Potapov among them. When they stood together on the stairway smoking, Abramson felt as though he had not spent a year as a free man, at home with his family, had not rewarded his wife with an additional daughter, felt that it had all been the sort of cruel dream that breaks a prisoner's heart and that prison was the only concrete reality in this world.

Nerzhin had sat down by Abramson to invite him to his birthday party. Abramson belatedly wished him many happy returns and, squinting from under his glasses, asked who would be there. The realization that he would have to struggle into his overalls, ruining the Sunday hours that would have been so pleasantly and profitably spent in his underwear, and that he would have to abandon an entertaining book for what they called a birthday party gave Abramson no pleasure at all. The worst of it was that he did not expect to have a good time but was more or less certain that a political argument would flare up, as futile and as unrewarding as ever, and that it would be impossible not to get involved and equally impossible to let himself be involved, because revealing his most private thoughts to "junior" prisoners would be like exhibiting his wife in the nude.

Nerzhin went through the guest list. Rubin was the only one in the sharashka who was on close terms with Abramson, though he would have to be told off for today's farce, which was unworthy of a true Communist. Sologdin and Pryanchikov Abramson did not like. Though, strangely enough, Rubin and Sologdin were supposed to be friends, perhaps because they had been neighbors on the bedboards at Butyrki. The prison administration made little distinction between them and, when the November anniversary celebrations came around, whisked them off to Lefortovo for a holiday away from it all.

Still, Abramson could not refuse the invitation. He was informed that the merrymaking would begin in half an hour's time. Between Potapov's and Pryanchikov's beds. Just as soon as Andreich had made the artificial cream.

While they were talking, Nerzhin noticed what Abramson was reading and said: "As it happens, I once started rereading *Monte Cristo* in prison but didn't finish it. I couldn't help noticing that although Dumas tries to make the reader's flesh creep, the Château d'If as he portrays it is a thoroughly patriarchal prison. Never mind his disregard of such nice little details as the daily carrying out of the night bucket—Dumas doesn't mention it because, being a free man, he never thinks of it—just ask yourself why Dantes succeeded in escaping? Because, of course, there were no cell searches for years on end, although they are supposed to be carried out weekly. Consequently their tunneling went undiscovered. Then again, the screws in charge of them were not relieved regularly, though, as we know from experience of the Lubyanka, they should be changed every two hours, so that the next guard can look for signs that the one before has been negligent. Furthermore, nobody entered or peeped into the cells at the Château d'If from one morning to the next.

There weren't even any spy holes in the doors. In short, it wasn't a prison but a seaside holiday resort! They thought nothing of leaving a metal saucepan in a cell, and Dantes used it to scoop a hole in the floor. To cap it all, they trustingly sewed the dead man up in a sack, without first branding his body with a red-hot iron in the morgue, then failed to pierce it with a bayonet in the guardhouse. Dumas should have worried less about atmosphere and more about elementary procedure."

Nerzhin never read just for amusement. What he looked for in a book were allies and enemies. He reached a precisely formulated verdict on every book he read and liked to force it on others.

Abramson, who knew this tiresome habit of his, listened without raising his head from the pillow, observing him calmly through his square glasses.

"All right, I'll be there," he said, then made himself more comfortable and went on with his reading.

# 57

## Prisoners' Petty Matters

NERZHIN WENT TO HELP Potapov make the cream. His hungry years in German prison camps and Soviet prisons had convinced Potapov that the process of mastication was not something to be ashamed of or treated lightly but one of the most delectable things in life and one in which its true meaning is revealed.

*I count the hours to dinner, I count the hours to tea,*
*But perhaps the hour of supper is dearer still to me*

was a favorite quotation of this outstanding Russian power-station engineer, who had devoted his whole life to transformers with a capacity of thousands and thousands and thousands of kilowatts.

Potapov was one of those engineers whose hands are as nimble as their brains, so he quickly became an uncommonly good cook. In the *Kriegsgefangenenlager* he used to bake an orange cake using nothing but potato peelings, and in the sharashkas he had specialized in desserts and become an expert.

At that moment he was at work over two lockers placed together in the dimly lit passage between his own bed and Pryanchikov's; a pleasant twilight was created by the mattresses on the upper bunks, which obstructed the light from the bulbs in the ceiling. Since the room was a semicircle and the beds stood along its radii, the passage was narrow at its entrance and broadened out toward the window. Potapov was also making full use of the enormous windowsill (its width was four and a half thicknesses of brick); tin cans, plastic containers, and basins stood there in close array. Potapov was performing his rite, trying to whip condensed milk, cocoa concentrate, and two eggs (Rubin had slipped some of these gifts to him; he regularly received parcels from home and always shared their contents) into something with no name in human speech. He chided Nerzhin for meandering around and ordered him to improvise some extra glasses (one was the cap of a Thermos bottle, two were small chemical beakers from the labs, and Potapov had molded two from greaseproof paper). Nerzhin suggested converting two shaving mugs into additional glasses and undertook to rinse them conscientiously with hot water.

A restful Sunday atmosphere descended on the semicircular room. Men perched on the beds of recumbent friends for a chat. Men read and exchanged casual remarks with neighbors. Yet others lay doing nothing, with their hands behind their heads and their eyes fixed unblinkingly on the white ceiling.

Conversations merged in a general hubbub.

Zemelya, the vacuum man, was taking his ease. He lay on his upper bunk, wearing only his underpants (it was rather hot up there), stroking his shaggy chest, smiling his invariable benevolent smile, and telling Mishka the Mordvin, two yards away by air, the following story:

"If you really want to know, it all began with that half kopeck."

"What half kopeck?"

"In those days—1926, 1928, you were only a boy—there was a sign over every cash desk saying, 'Ask for your half kopeck change.' There was such a coin, a half kopeck. The girl at the desk handed it over without a word. Anyway, we had the NEP then; it was just like peacetime."

"You mean there wasn't a war?"

"I'm not talking about war, you dope! When I say peacetime, I mean before Soviet power. Oh yes. . . . Under the NEP, people in government offices worked six hours, not like now. And they managed all right. And if they kept you behind as much as fifteen minutes, they paid you overtime. Now what do you think was the first thing to vanish? The half kopecks. And that's when it all started. After that the copper coins vanished. Then in '30 the silver, and there wasn't any small change at all. You could ask till you were blue in the face; you wouldn't get any change. Since then things have never been right. There was no small change, so they started counting in rubles. Take a beggar—he doesn't ask nicely for 'a kopeck for the love of Christ' anymore; it's more of a demand: 'Citizens, give me a ruble!' When you pick up your pay at the office, the kopecks are shown on the stub, and that's it. If you ask for them, they only laugh—what a cheapskate! But they're the idiots! When you give a man his half kopecks, you're showing respect for him; if they don't change your ruble at sixty kopecks, they're shitting on you. People didn't hold out for their half kopecks, so they lost half their lives."

On the other side, another prisoner, also on a top bunk, looked up from his book and said to his neighbor, "Absolutely useless, the tsarist government! Listen to this, Sasha my friend: A woman Revolutionary went on hunger strike for eight days to make the prison governor apologize to her, and the clown did just that. Try making the big chief at Krasnaya Presnya apologize!"

"Our lot would have been feeding the stupid woman through a pipe on the third day and slapping a fresh sentence on her for provocation. Where did you get that from?"

"Gorky."

Dvoetyosov, who was lying not far away, shot up.

"Who's reading Gorky?" he asked in a menacing bass.

"I am!"

"What the hell for?"

"What else is there to read?"

"You'd be better off in the shithouse, communing with your soul. World's full of damned readers, damned humanists—dirty bums, the lot of you."

Below them a debate was in progress on that age-old prison theme: When's the best time to get thrown in? The wording of the question fatalistically assumed that imprisonment was unavoidable. (There is a general tendency among prisoners to exaggerate their own numbers. When there were only twelve to fifteen million of them, they were convinced that there were twenty or thirty million. Zeks felt sure that their rulers and the MVD were almost the only male persons at liberty.) When's the best time to go inside? means Is it better when you're young? Or in your declining years? Some (usually younger men) cheerfully argued that it was better early in life: It gave you time to learn what life was all about, what was precious and what was shit, so that at the age of thirty-five or so, a man with a "tenner" under his belt could build his life on sound principles. Whereas, they argued, a man who went inside later in life would be tearing his hair because he had not lived as he should, because the life he had led was one long chain of mistakes and it was now too late to put them right. Others (usually older men) on such occasions no less cheerfully argued that, on the contrary, if a man goes inside later in life, it is very much like retiring on a pension or withdrawing to a monastery, after taking from life all that it has to offer (this "all" in the reminiscences of zeks narrows down to enjoyment of the female body, smart clothes, rich food and drink), and there isn't much they can do to an old man in a camp. Whereas they can knock the stuffing out of a young man and leave him such a wreck that he'll never want to "have a go at a woman" again.

This was how they argued in the semicircular room that day, and how prisoners always argue, some to console themselves, some rubbing salt in their own wounds, but their arguments and anecdotes were husks that held no kernel of truth. On Sunday evening it turned out that the right time to go inside is . . . anytime, but when they got up on Monday morning, it was obvious that there is never a good time.

Yet that isn't quite true either.

The "best time to go inside" argument was one of those that do not exasperate the debaters but pacify them, soothe their souls with philosophic melancholy. These debates never ended in explosions.

Thomas Hobbes says somewhere that if the truth that "the sum of the angles of a triangle is equal to 180 degrees" threatened anyone's interests, blood would be shed for it.

But Hobbes did not know the convict mentality.

The argument in progress on the end bunk by the door was in fact one of those that can lead to blows or bloodshed, although it affected nobody's interests. A turner had come to spend the evening with his friend, an electrician. They began by talking for some reason about Sestroretsk and then went on to talk about the stoves in houses at Sestroretsk. The turner had spent a winter there and remembered clearly what the stoves were like. The electrician had never been there himself, but his brother-in-law was a stove installer, a first-class workman, and had built stoves right there in Sestroretsk, and what he used to say about them was just the opposite of what the turner remembered.

They began by simply contradicting each other, but the quarrel reached the stage of quivering voices and personal insults, and the noise began to drown out all other conversations in the room. Each man felt humiliated by his inability to prove beyond doubt that he was right. They looked in vain for an arbitrator among those around them until they suddenly remembered that Spiridon, the yardman, knew about stoves, enough at any rate to tell one of them that the crazy sort of stove he was talking about didn't exist in Sestroretsk or for that matter anywhere on earth. To the great relief of everybody in the room, they hurried off to find him.

But in the heat of the moment, they forgot to close the door, and another, no less excruciating, argument overflowed from the hallway: Should the beginning of the second half of the twentieth century correctly be celebrated on January 1, 1950, or January 1, 1951? The debate had evidently started some time ago and was bogged down in arguments about the year in which Christ was born on December 25. Somebody slammed the door. The head-splitting noise ceased, and in the sudden silence Khorobrov could be heard talking to the bald-headed designer above him.

"When we begin the first flight to the moon, a meeting will of course be held around the rocket before blastoff. The crew will make a solemn commitment to economize fuel, to exceed the cosmic speed record in flight, not to stop the spaceship for repairs en route, and to pass their landing test on the moon with top marks. One of the three crew members will be the political officer. On the way, he will conduct uninterrupted mass-indoctrination work with the pilot and the navigator, explaining the importance of space travel and soliciting comments for the wall newspaper."

This was overheard by Pryanchikov as he darted across the room with towel and soap. A balletic leap brought him to Khorobrov's bed, and he assumed an awesome frown.

"Ilya Terentich!" he said. "I can put your mind at rest. It will not be like that."

"How will it be then?"

Pryanchikov put his finger to his lips like someone in a detective film.

"The first to reach the moon . . . will be the Americans."

He burst into ringing, childish laughter and ran off.

The engraver was sitting on Sologdin's bed. They were engrossed in a conversation about women. He was forty and, although his face was young, quite gray. This made him very good-looking.

He was on top of the world today. True, he had made a mistake that morning; he had scrunched his latest story up into a ball and swallowed it, although, as it turned out, he could have got through the body search with it and passed it to his wife. But to make up for this, she had told him that she had shown his previous stories to a few trusted friends, and they were all thrilled with them. Praise from friends and relations might of course be exaggerated and not altogether deserved, but damn it, where could he get a fair assessment? Whether it was done well or badly, the engraver was preserving the truth for all time, the cries of tortured souls, what Stalin had done to millions of Russian POWs. And now he was proud, happy, fulfilled, and determined to go on with his writing. Today's visit had been satisfactory in other ways, too; he had a devoted wife waiting for him, working to obtain his release, and her efforts would soon prove successful. He was seeking an outlet for his elation in the long story he was telling to this unremarkable, though not exactly stupid, man Sologdin, whose past and future were drab and colorless in comparison to his own.

Sologdin was lying stretched out on his back with an open book facedown on his chest, bestowing on the speaker an occasional flashing glance. With his little blond beard, his bright eyes, his high forehead, and his regular features, Sologdin was like an Old Russian knight—and unnaturally, indecently handsome.

He, too, was on top of the world. He heard within himself a sort of triumphant chant celebrating a cosmic victory—his own victory over the whole world, his omnipotence. His release could not be more than a year away. After which a dizzy career perhaps awaited him. Moreover, his body was not aching for a woman, as it usually did; it was appeased and purged of its turbid longings.

So seeking an outlet for his elation and for amusement, he let his attention glide lazily along the meanderings of a story that meant nothing to him, a story told by this not-at-all stupid but perfectly ordinary man, to whom nothing so wonderful could possibly happen.

He often listened to people, as if patronizing them, trying not to let it show only out of politeness.

The engraver began by telling him about his two wives in Russia, then went on to reminisce about Germany and the charms of the German women with whom he had been intimate. He drew a comparison between Russian and German women that was new to Sologdin. He said that having lived with both, he preferred the Germans. Russian women were too sure of themselves, too independent, too demanding in love. They loved with eyes wide open, studying the loved one's failings, discovering that he was not as noble, not as courageous, as they could wish. If you loved a Russian woman, you always had the uncomfortable feeling that she was your equal, whereas a German woman was as pliant as a rush in her lover's hands, for he was her god, the greatest and best man on earth; she surrendered herself unreservedly to his tender mercy. She dreamed only of how best to please him, and because of this, the engraver had felt more of a man, felt that he was "lord and master" with German women.

Rubin had rashly gone out into the hallway for a smoke, but not one of his fellow prisoners walked past without an irritating remark. Sick of the pointless argument out there, he crossed the room, hurrying back to his books, but someone on a lower bunk clutched his trouser leg and asked, "Is it true, Lev Grigorievich, that in China stoolies' letters don't need stamps? If so, would you call that progressive?" Rubin freed himself abruptly and went on his way. But an electrical engineer, hanging down from a top bunk, caught him by the collar of his overalls and began ramming home his last words on a subject they had argued about before.

"Lev Grigorievich! We have to adjust the conscience of mankind in such a way that people take pride only in the work of their own hands and feel ashamed to be overseers, managers, or party leaders. We must make it so that a minister conceals his rank just like a sewer man conceals his occupation. The minister's job is no less necessary but is shameful. If a girl marries a state official, let it be a disgrace to her whole family! That's the sort of socialism I would be content to live under!"

Rubin freed his collar, broke through to his bed, lay on his belly, and went back to his dictionaries.

## 58

# A Banquet of Friends

Seven men were seated around a festive table made by pushing three lockers of different heights together and covering them with a piece of bright green paper, another prize of war from Lorenz AG. Sologdin and Rubin had joined Potapov on his bed. Abramson and Kondrashov sat by

Pryanchikov, and the birthday boy had made himself comfortable on the broad windowsill at the head of the table. Zemelya was already dozing up above, and the other neighbors were missing. The two double bunks and the space between them, cut off from the rest of the room, were like a compartment in a train.

Nadya's pastry straws, a confection never before seen in the sharashka, were displayed on a plastic dish in the middle of the table, looking comically inadequate for seven male mouths. Then there was ordinary cake, and cake smeared with "crème," dubbed accordingly "patisserie." There was also creamy toffee, made by heating an unopened can of condensed milk. Behind Nerzhin's back lurked a dark liter jar containing the delectable something or other for which the wineglasses were intended. It was made from a few drops of spirits, obtained from the zeks in the chemical laboratory in return for a piece of "quality" insulating material. This was diluted (four parts water to one part spirits) and then colored with cocoa concentrate. The result was a brown liquid of low alcohol content, which was nonetheless impatiently awaited.

"What do you say, gentlemen?" Sologdin, reclining picturesquely, his eyes shining even in the half darkness of the closed compartment, had a suggestion: "Let's each try and remember when he last sat at a festive board."

"Yesterday, with the Germans," Rubin growled. He couldn't stand sentimentality.

Sologdin's occasional use of the word "gentlemen" in company was, Rubin thought, a sign that twelve years of imprisonment had addled his brain. It was impossible to believe that any man could pronounce the word seriously thirty-two years after the Revolution. Sologdin had many other freakish notions, which could all be explained in the same way. Rubin tried to keep this in mind and not to flare up even when he found himself listening to something preposterous.

(Abramson, incidentally, thought Rubin's partying with the Germans no less weird. Internationalism was all very well, but there were limits!)

"No, no," Sologdin persisted, "I mean a real banquet, gentlemen." He was glad for any opportunity to use that proud form of address. Since so much more of the earth's surface was reserved to the "comrades," it was Sologdin's view that on the cramped islets where prisons stood, those who did not like the word "gentlemen" must lump it. "The marks of a real banquet are a rich, pale-complexioned tablecloth, wine in cut-glass decanters, and, needless to say, elegant women."

He wanted to go on savoring the feast in anticipation, but Potapov inspected table and guests with a critical housewife's eye and interrupted in his grumpy way. "Listen, boys, before 'Midnight strikes and the unsleeping watch descends' to catch us with this poison, we'd better move on to the official part of the proceedings."

He gave Nerzhin the signal to pour.

They were silent, but while the glasses were being filled, memories, welcome and otherwise, crowded in.

"It's a long time ago," Nerzhin sighed.

Potapov came out of his trance: "So long I just can't remember."

He had some vague recollection of somebody's wedding in the midst of a mad whirl of work before the war, but he could not be sure whether it was his own or one to which he had been invited.

Pryanchikov woke up. "Well, if you can't, I can. *Avec plaisir.* Let me tell you about it. In Paris in 1945, I was—"

Potapov stopped him.

"Wait a bit, Valentulya. Let's just—"

"To the friend in whose honor we are gathered here!" Kondrashov-Ivanov pronounced the toast more loudly than was necessary, drawing himself up still straighter. "May he be—"

But before the guests could reach for their glasses, Nerzhin raised himself slightly from the sill—there was barely room for him by the window—and said quietly, "My friends! Forgive this departure from tradition, but. . . ."

He took a deep breath; he was agitated. The warmth beamed on him from seven pairs of eyes had forged some purpose within him.

"Let us be fair! Not everything in our lives is black! We have, for instance, this form of happiness, the ease and freedom of high school conviviality; we can exchange thoughts freely, without fear or concealment. Were we so fortunate when we were free?"

"Well, we weren't free all that often," Abramson said with a laugh. Childhood apart, he had spent less than half his life at liberty.

"Friends!" Nerzhin warmed to his theme. "I'm thirty-one years old. Life has pampered me at times and plunged me into the depths at others. In accordance with the law of sinusoidal motion, there may yet be sudden surges of hollow success and false greatness ahead of me. But I swear to you that I shall never forget that true human greatness that I have come to know in prison! I am proud that my modest anniversary today has brought together such a select company. Let's not embarrass ourselves with pompous speeches. Let's drink to the friendship that flourishes in prison vaults!"

Paper cups soundlessly bumped glass and plastic. Potapov smiled apologetically, straightened his primitive spectacles, and, carefully spacing his words, recited:

*The sons of this illustrious clan,*
*Keen rhetoricians to a man*
*In anxious Nikita's house assembled,*
*Or where discreet Ilya dissembled.*

They drank the brown beverage slowly, trying to define its bouquet.

"It's got a bit of a kick, anyway," Rubin said approvingly. "Bravo, Andreich."

"It certainly has," Sologdin agreed. He was in a mood to praise anything today.

Nerzhin laughed. "A very rare occurrence! Lev and Mitya actually agree about something! I don't remember it happening before!"

"Oh yes you do."

"No, Gleb my friend. Don't you remember Lev and me agreeing around New Year's sometime that an unfaithful wife can't be forgiven but an unfaithful husband can?"

Abramson laughed wearily: "Good heavens, what male wouldn't say yes to that?"

"Well, that specimen over there"—Rubin pointed at Nerzhin—"maintained at the time that a woman could also be forgiven, that there was no difference."

"You really said that?" Kondrashov asked quickly.

Pryanchikov's laugh rang out. "What a nut! There's an enormous difference!"

"The very structure of the body and the means of coupling show that there is an immense difference!" Sologdin exclaimed.

"No, it goes deeper than that," Rubin protested. "It's part of nature's grand design. A man is more or less indifferent to quality in women but has an instinctive appetite for quantity. Thanks to that, few women are completely overlooked."

Sologdin raised his hand in a graceful gesture of acknowledgment. "Hence," he said, "the charitable character of Don Juanism."

"Well, then, women hanker after quality, if you want to put it that way."

Kondrashov wagged a long finger. "Their unfaithfulness is a quest for quality! That way their progeny is improved!"

Nerzhin defended himself. "Don't blame me, friends! Look, when I was growing up there were red banners flapping overhead, with 'Equality' in golden letters! 'Equality.' Since when, of course—"

"Oh no, not equality again!" Sologdin growled.

"What have you got against equality?" Abramson looked indignant.

"Nothing, except that it doesn't exist in the natural world! People are not 'born equal'; that's a myth invented by those idiots . . . those . . . those know-it-alls" (you had to guess that he meant the Encyclopedists). "They had not the least understanding of heredity. People are born unequal spiritually, unequal in willpower, unequal in ability."

"Unequal in possessions, unequal in social status." Abramson took up the tale, mimicking Sologdin.

"Well, where did you ever see equality of possessions? Where did you ever manage to create it?" Sologdin was getting heated. "There never was such a thing, and there never will be! It's unattainable except by beggars and saints!"

Nerzhin interrupted before the argument could become a quarrel.

"Since then, life has hammered a bit more sense into my stupid head, of course, but in those days I thought if nations are equal and human beings are equal, surely men and women must also be equal. In all respects."

"Nobody's blaming you!" Kondrashov's eyes were as emphatic as his words. "Don't give in too soon!"

"These delusions of yours are pardonable only on account of your youth," Sologdin ruled. (He was six years older.)

"Theoretically Gleb is right," Rubin said hesitantly. "I'm ready to break a hundred thousand lances myself for the equality of men and women. But embrace my wife after somebody else has embraced her? *Br-r-r!* It's a biological impossibility!"

"If you ask me, gentlemen, it's ridiculous even talking about it," Pryanchikov piped, but as usual he wasn't allowed to have his say.

"There's a simple solution, Lev Grigorievich," Potapov said firmly. "You yourself mustn't embrace anyone except your wife!"

"Well, you know how it is. . . ." Rubin made a gesture of helplessness, and a broad smile lost itself in his piratical beard.

The door opened noisily, and somebody came in. Potapov and Abramson looked around. No, it wasn't the guard.

"What about it—*delenda est Carthago?*" Abramson nodded toward the liter jar.

"The sooner the better. Who needs a spell in solitary? Come on Vikentich, pour!"

Nerzhin poured out what was left, scrupulously ensuring that the shares were equal.

"Maybe you'll allow us to drink a birthday toast now?" Abramson asked.

"No, brothers. As it's my birthday, I shall claim one privilege—to break with tradition. . . . I saw my wife today. And in her I saw all our tormented, terrorized, and persecuted wives. We put up with our lot because there's no escape. But what about them? Let's drink to those who have voluntarily shackled themselves—"

"Yes! To those heroines!" Kondrashov-Ivanov exclaimed.

They drank.

And were silent for a while.

"Look at the snow!" Potapov remarked.

They all looked round. Behind Nerzhin, beyond the misted windows, the snow itself could not be seen, but they glimpsed a flurry of black shadows of snowflakes cast on the prison windows by the lamps and searchlights in the grounds.

Somewhere beyond the curtain of that copious snowfall, there were people, and Nadya Nerzhina was one of them.

"We're even fated to see the snow as black, not white," Kondrashov exclaimed.

"We've drunk to friendship. We've drunk to love! These are fine things, timeless things," Rubin said.

"As far as love is concerned, I never had any doubt about it. But to tell the truth, before I served at the front and then landed in prison, I didn't believe in friendship, especially the sort that . . . you know, that makes you 'lay down your life for a friend.' In the normal course of things, a man has his family, and that leaves him no room for friendship. Am I right?"

"That's a view widely held," Abramson replied. "There's a song you often hear played by request on the radio: 'I tread the valley's even path.' Just pay attention to the words! It's one long nauseating whine, the self-pitying moan of a mean spirit:

*Friends are friends, and comrades faithful*
*Only till the dark days come.*"

The artist was outraged. "It wouldn't be worth living a single day longer if you thought like that. Might as well hang yourself!"

"It's just the opposite, really. Friendship begins when the dark days come."

"Who wrote it anyway?"

"Merzlyakov."

"What a name! Who's Merzlyakov, Lev, old man?"

"Poet. Born twenty years before Pushkin."

"You know his biography, of course?"

"Professor at Moscow University. Translated Tasso."

"Is there anything Lev doesn't know? Except higher mathematics?"

"Yes, elementary mathematics."

"He keeps on saying, 'Let's open the brackets,' and he thinks the square of a negative number is negative."

Pryanchikov butted in, sputtering in his eagerness to be heard, like a child at table with adults. "Gentlemen. I feel bound to show you that Merzlyakov was sometimes right!"

He was in no way inferior to his companions; he had a quick mind, was witty and engagingly frank. But he lacked the self-control and composure of a grown man, so that he seemed fifteen years younger than they were, and they treated him like an adolescent.

"It's a proven fact: The man who eats out of the same dish is the one who betrays you! I had a close friend; he and I escaped from a Nazi concentration camp and hid from search parties together. Later on, I got into the family of a big businessman, and he was introduced to a French countess. . . ."

"Really?" said Sologdin, impressed. Titles like "count" and "prince" still held an irresistible charm for him.

"There's nothing surprising in that. Some Russian prisoners of war even married marchionesses!"

"You don't say!"

"Well, when Colonel General Golikov began his repatriation swindle, I wouldn't go, of course; in fact, I did my best to talk the other Russian idiots out of it, and suddenly I met this best friend of mine. And just imagine, he was the one who betrayed me! gave me up to the Geebees!"*

---

* Geebees: A version of *gebisty*, a slang term for the MGB, the Ministry of State Security.

"What a wicked thing!" the artist exclaimed.

"Let me tell you how it was."

They were nearly all listening to Pryanchikov's story now. But Sologdin wanted to know how POWs came to marry countesses.

To Rubin it was quite clear that the jolly and amiable Valentulya, with whom it was perfectly possible to be friendly in the sharashka, had, looked at objectively, been a reactionary figure in Western Europe in 1945, and that what he called treachery on the part of a friend (meaning that the friend had assisted Pryanchikov to return involuntarily to his native land) was not treachery but the friend's patriotic duty.

One story led to another. Potapov remembered the booklet that was handed to every repatriate, "The Motherland Forgives, The Motherland Calls." It said in black and white that the Presidium of the Supreme Soviet had ruled against the prosecution even of repatriates who had served in the German police. These elegantly produced, profusely illustrated booklets, with their nebulous hints at unspecified adjustments to the collective farm system and the social order in the Soviet Union, were confiscated during the search at the frontier, while the repatriates themselves were put into prison trucks and dispatched to counterespionage headquarters. Potapov had read one of these booklets with his own eyes, and although it had nothing to do with his own decision to return, he found this dirty little trick on the part of an enormous state peculiarly distressing.

Abramson was dozing behind his staring glasses. He had known that there would be all this silly talk. How else could the regime have rounded up that mob?

Rubin and Nerzhin had both spent the first year after the war in counterespionage depots and jails immersed in the stream of POWs flowing in from Europe. They felt as if they had themselves endured four excruciating years in captivity, and they were no longer particularly interested in the stories of repatriates. Instead, they joined in persuading Kondrashov to talk about art. Rubin regarded Kondrashov as a mediocre artist and not very serious person whose views were divorced from economic and historical reality. Yet whenever they conversed, without realizing it himself, Rubin drank in the artist's words like living water.

Art, to Kondrashov, was not just an occupation or a branch of knowledge. It was the only possible way of life. All that he saw around him—landscapes, objects, people, colors—evoked one of the twenty-four tonalities. (Rubin was labeled "C minor.") All that he heard or felt—a human voice, the mood of a moment, a novel, a tonality—had a color, and Kondrashov could tell you without hesitation what it was (the key of F-sharp major was dark blue and gold).

There was one state of mind Kondrashov had never experienced—indifference. He made no secret of his immoderate likes and dislikes. He was famous for his uncompromising judgments. He was a devotee of Rembrandt and a debunker of Raphael. An admirer of Valentin Serov and fiercely hostile to the Itinerant School. He was incapable of qualified approval; for him there was no midpoint between boundless enthusiasm and boundless indignation. He could not stand Chekhov. He was repelled by Tchaikovsky ("He suffocates me! He robs me of hope and the will to live!") but felt such an affinity with Bach's chorales and Beethoven's concertos that he might have composed them himself.

"Must pictures be true to nature?" was the subject for discussion this time.

"Well, suppose you want to depict a window opening onto a garden on a summer morning," Kondrashov said. His voice was youthful, with an occasional shrill note when he was excited. If you closed your eyes, you might think you were listening to an adolescent arguing.

"If you faithfully copy nature, if you depict it all just as you see it, will it really be all? What about the singing of the birds? The freshness of the morning? The purity of the scene? While you are painting, you are aware of these things; they enter into your experience of the summer morning. But how are you to preserve them in the picture? How can you avoid denying them to the viewer? Obviously you have to find some substitute for them, using the only resources you have, color and composition."

"So you can't just copy?"

"Of course not! And anyway"—Kondrashov was beginning to get carried away—"you begin every landscape, and every portrait, by admiring nature and thinking, how marvelous! how fine! if only I could show it just like that, just as it is! But you get deeper into your work, and suddenly you realize. . . . Just a minute! Hang on! So much for nature! This is simply absurd, just nonsense, completely incongruous! Look here, for instance! And here! It ought to be like this! And like that! That's how you paint!" Kondrashov looked triumphantly and challengingly at his companions.

"Yes, but 'ought to be' takes you down a very dangerous road, old man!"

Rubin protested. "You'll find yourself making angels and devils out of flesh-and-blood people, which, in fact, is just what you do. Say what you like, if you paint a portrait of Andrei Andreich Potapov, it ought to be Potapov."

"But what does portraying him as he really is mean?" Kondrashov protested. "There must of course be an external resemblance—same facial proportions, same shape eyes, same color hair. But isn't it rather rash to suppose that we can see reality just as it is? Especially spiritual reality? Who can see that or know it? And if I look at a sitter and discern in him qualities finer than those he has so far revealed, why shouldn't I make so bold as to depict them? Help the man find himself and rise to higher things?"

Nerzhin clapped his hands. "Why, you're a one hundred percent socialist realist. The deputy minister doesn't know what a treasure he has in you!"

"Why should I undervalue his soul?" Kondrashov's glasses, immovably fixed to his nose, flashed angrily in the half darkness. "Let me tell you, the most important thing about portrait painting, and indeed about all relationships, is that whatever one person sees and identifies in another is evoked and activated in that other person! Understand?"

"In short," Rubin said dismissively, "objectivity means nothing to you, in this as in other things."

"Yes, indeed! I'm unobjective and proud of it!" Kondrashov thundered.

Rubin was taken aback. "Eh? eh? What's that you say?"

"You heard! I'm proud of being unobjective!" Kondrashov's words were like the blows he might have struck if the upper bunk had not cramped his swing.

"What about you, Lev Grigorievich? What about you? You are unobjective, too, but consider yourself objective, and that's much worse! That's where I'm superior; I'm unobjective, and I know it! I take credit for it! That's the essential me!"

"Not objective? Me?" Rubin seemed astonished. "If I'm not objective, who on earth is?"

"Nobody!" the artist cried exultantly. "Nobody at all! Nobody ever was, and nobody ever will be! In fact, every cognitive act has an emotional coloring, has it not? The truth that is destined to be the end result of long inquiries is surely dimly present in our minds before our inquiries even begin! We pick up a book feeling a vague antipathy for the author, we foresee before we have read the first page that we will pretty certainly not like it, and of course we don't! You've embarked on a comparison of a hundred of the world's languages, you've only just finished lining up your dictionaries, there's forty years of work ahead of you, but you're already sure that you'll succeed in proving that all words derive from a word for 'hand'! Do you call that objectivity?"

Nerzhin, highly gratified, roared with laughter at Rubin. Rubin laughed, too—how could anyone be angry with this holy innocent!

Kondrashov had not mentioned politics, but Nerzhin was quick to do so.

"Go one step further, Ippolit Mikhalych! Just one, I beg you! What about Marx? I feel sure that before he had begun his economic analyses or compiled any statistical tables, he knew in advance that under capitalism the working class faces absolute impoverishment, that it is the best part of mankind, and hence that the future belongs to it. Hand on heart, Lev, isn't that the truth?"

Rubin sighed. "My dear friend . . . if we could never foresee what we were going to find. . . ."

"You see, Ippolit Mikhalych! And that is what they base this 'progress' of theirs on! How I hate that meaningless word 'progress'!"

"Well, in art there is no 'progress'! There can be none!"

Nerzhin was delighted. "No, indeed! Indeed there isn't! That's what's so good about it! The seventeenth century had Rembrandt, and Rembrandt's still here—just try and go one better today! Whereas seventeenth-century technology seems primitive to us now. Or think of the great inventions of the eighteen seventies. To us they look like children's toys. Yet those were the years in which *Anna Karenina* was written. If you know of anything finer, I would like to hear about it!"

Rubin seized his opening.

"Hold on, there, maestro. You do at least leave us with some progress in engineering? You don't call that meaningless."

"Anyway, Gleb Vikentich," Abramson put in, "your argument can be turned inside out. It can be taken to mean that scientists and engineers have done great things over the centuries and made progress, while the art snobs have obviously just been playing the fool. Parasites. . . ."

"In it for the money!" Sologdin exclaimed. He seemed pleased about it.

He and Abramson, poles apart, were allies for the space of a single thought.

Pryanchikov applauded.

"Bravo! Bravo! Well done, boys! That's just what I was trying to tell you yesterday in the Acoustics Lab!" (He had been talking about the superior merits of jazz, but it seemed to him now that Abramson was expressing his own thoughts for him.)

"I think I can make peace between you!" Potapov laughed knowingly. "There has been in the course of this century one historically well-attested occasion on which a certain electrical engineer and a certain mathematician, painfully aware of a lacuna in the belles-lettres of their fatherland, jointly composed a short piece of fine writing. Alas, it was never written down; they had no pencil."

"Andreich!" cried Nerzhin. "Couldn't you reconstruct it?"

"With a bit of a struggle and your help. It was my one and only opus. So I ought to be able to remember it."

"Gentlemen, this is going to be fun!"

Sologdin brightened and settled himself more comfortably. Jeux d'esprit of this sort were the thing he really enjoyed in prison.

"But you surely realize that, as Lev Grigorievich teaches us, no work of art can be understood unless we know the history of its creation and the social requirement it meets."

"You're improving, Andreich."

"So, dear guests, eat up the cake that was made for you. The story of its creation is as follows: In the summer of the year one thousand nine hundred and forty-six, in a hideously overcrowded cell in the nursing home called Bu-Tyur—the administration had stamped that inscription, meaning Butyrskaya Tyurma, Butyrki Prison, on the crockery— Gleb and I were lying side by side under the bed planks to begin with, then on the bed planks, gasping for air, groaning from hunger, and we had nothing to occupy ourselves with except light conversation and observation of behavior. . . . I'm not sure which of us said it first. What if. . . ?"

"You did, Andreich. You said, 'What if. . . ?' In any case, the key image from which the piece takes its title certainly belongs to you. . . ."

"Well, Gleb and I asked ourselves . . . what if . . . what if suddenly into our cell. . . ."

"Don't tease! What did you call it?"

"All right, all right, let's try and remember that ancient tale between us, shall we?" Potapov's voice, cracked and muffled, was like that of an inveterate devourer of dusty folios. "Its title was 'The Buddha's Smile.'"

# 59

## The Buddha's Smile

"THE EVENTS RECORDED in our remarkable narrative relate to that famous summer of blazing heat in 194– when prisoners outnumbering the proverbial cartload of monkeys languished, clad only in loincloths, in stifling air behind the fishy-eyed opacity of the world-renowned Butyrki Prison's muzzled windows.

"What can one say of that useful and smoothly functioning establishment? It traced its ancestry to the barracks of Catherine the Great. In the cruel age of that empress, bricks were not grudged for those fortresslike walls and vaulted arches.

*The stately castle was constructed*
*As castles should constructed be.*

"After the death of Voltaire's enlightened pen pal, those hollow halls where once the clumsy tramp of carabineers' jackboots reechoed were derelict for many long years. But as progress, universally longed for, advanced upon our fatherland, the royal descendants of the aforesaid imperial lady thought fit to accommodate there both heretics, who sought to rock the Orthodox throne, and obscurantists, who stood in the way of progress.

"The mason's trowel and the plasterer's spatula helped divide those enfilades into hundreds of commodious yet cozy cells, while the unsurpassed skill of our fatherland's blacksmiths forged unbendable bars for the windows and tubular bed frames to be lowered for the night and raised by day. The finest craftsmen among our talented serf population made their precious contribution to the immortal fame of Butyrki Castle; weavers wove sackcloth covers for the bed frames, plumbers laid an ingenious sewage system, tinsmiths riveted together capacious four- and six-gallon night buckets with handles and even lids, carpenters cut feeding flaps in the doors, glaziers installed spy holes, locksmiths fitted locks, and in the ultramodern times of People's Commissar Yezhov a special breed of craftsmen in reinforced glass poured opaque, molten glass over wire netting and erected those 'muzzles,' unique of their kind, which shut off from the heinous prisoners the last visible corner of the prison yard, the prison chapel, and a patch of blue sky.

"For the convenience of guards with, as a rule, only rudimentary education, the curators of the Butyrki rest home had exactly twenty-five bed frames fixed to the walls of each cell, making possible simple arithmetical calculations: Four cells equals a hundred head of prisoners; one corridor, two hundred.

"And so for decades on end, this therapeutic establishment flourished, without ever incurring the censure of society and without complaint from prisoners. (Witness the infrequency of censure and complaints in *Stock Exchange Gazette* and, subsequently, their total absence from *Workers' and Peasants' Deputies' News—Izvestia*, for short.

"But time was not on the side of the major general in charge of Butyrki Prison. Even in the early days of the Second World War, it proved necessary to exceed the statutory norm of twenty-five to a cell and to install additional inmates, who were left without bunks. When the surplus assumed menacing proportions, bed frames were left permanently lowered, the sacking covers were replaced by boards, and the triumphant major general and his colleagues started wedging fifty men into each cell. Then, after the historic victory over Hitlerism, as many as seventy-five. This, again, posed no problem for the guards: They knew that there were now six hundred head to a corridor and were paid a bonus.

"In this congestion it no longer made sense to give out books, chess sets, and dominoes; there weren't enough to go around anyway. As time went by, the enemies of the people received a smaller and smaller bread ration, fish was replaced by the flesh of amphibians and hymenoptera, and cabbage and nettles by cattle fodder. The dreaded Pugachev Tower, where the empress had kept that hero of the people on a chain, was now made to serve a pacific purpose as a silo.

"People poured in; new prisoners arrived all the time; oral traditions faded and were garbled; people forgot, if they had ever known, that their predecessors had reclined on canvas sacking and read banned books (it was only from prison libraries that the authorities forgot to remove them). When ichthyosaurus broth and silage soup were borne into the cell in steaming pails, the prisoners drew their feet up onto the bedboards, drew their knees up tightly to their chests in the confined space, and braced themselves on all four paws, and in this canine posture, baring their teeth like so many yard dogs, kept a sharp eye on how much swill was ladled into each bowl. The pails made their round, 'from the night bucket to the window' and 'from the window to the radiator,' after which the inhabitants of the bedboards and of the kennels underneath them, fell to, threatening each other's bowls with tails and paws, and the only sound to disturb the philosophical silence of the cell was that of seventy-five mouths slurping life-giving porridge.

"And everyone was content. Neither in the trade union newspaper *Trud* nor in the *Bulletin of the Moscow Patriarchate* was a single complaint to be found.

"Cell 72 was a cell among other cells with nothing to distinguish it from the rest. It was already doomed, but the prisoners peacefully dozing under its bedboards or cursing on top of them knew nothing of the horrors in store. On the eve of the fatal day, they were as usual making leisurely preparations for bed on the cement floor near the night bucket or lying in their drawers on the bedboards, fanning themselves (the air was hot and stagnant, because the cell was not ventilated from one winter to the next), killing flies, and telling each other how nice it had been in Norway or in Iceland or in Greenland during the war. The time sense that all zeks perfect by long practice told them that there were only five minutes left before the screw on duty bellowed through the feeding flap, 'Come on, get to bed, it's after time!'

"But suddenly the prisoners' hearts missed a beat as they heard keys turning in the locks! The door flew open, and there stood a dapper captain with white gloves, looking ex-treme-ly agitated. A retinue of lieutenants and sergeants buzzed behind him. In funereal silence the zeks were led out into the corridor 'with belongings.' (A whisper went around that they were on their way to be shot.) In the corridor five times ten men were counted off and bundled into neighboring cells just in time to grab a bit of sleeping space. These fortunate ones had escaped the fearful fate of the other twenty-five. The last thing those left outside their well-loved Cell No. 72 saw was some sort of infernal machine with a sprayer attached to it driving in through their door. Then they were made to do a right turn and marched, to the rattling of guards' keys against belt buckles and the snapping of fingers (recognized signals in Butyrki meaning 'prisoner under escort approaching'), through several internal steel doors and down several flights of stairs to a hall, which was not the execution cellar, not an underground torture chamber, but the changing room, well known to the zek tribe, of the celebrated Butyrki baths. The dressing room had a suspiciously innocent, everyday look—the walls, benches, and floor covered with chocolate brown, red, and green tiles, the carts noisily trundling on rails from the heat sterilization room with diabolical hooks to hang prisoners' lousy clothes on. Playfully slapping and punching (for the prisoner's Third Commandment is 'grab what's offered'), the zeks scrambled for the red-hot hooks and hung on them their long-suffering clothes, already discolored, singed, and in places burned through by fumigation at ten-day intervals, while two old crones, hell's sweltering handmaidens, long since indifferent to the sight of naked prisoners, rolled the clattering carts into Tartarus, slamming the iron doors behind them.

"The twenty-five prisoners were left in the changing room, locked in on all sides. They had nothing in their hands except handkerchiefs or strips torn from shirts, which served the same purpose.

"Those of them whose skinny frames retained a thin layer of leathery flesh on that modest part of the body by means of which nature has blessed us with the gift of sitting—those happy souls seated themselves on warm stone benches, inlaid with emerald and reddish brown tiles. (The Butyrki bathhouse is far superior in the luxury of its fittings to the Sandunovski baths, and the story goes that curious foreigners sometimes gave themselves up to the Cheka just to enjoy a bath there.)

"Other prisoners, so emaciated that they could only sit on something soft, paced the antechamber from end to end, making no attempt to cover their shame and seeking to penetrate the veil of mystery in heated arguments.

> *Their starved imaginations*
> *Hungered for fatal sustenance. . . .*

"They were, however, kept in the antechamber for hours on end, so that speculation flagged, their bodies were covered with heat spots, and their stomachs, accustomed as they were to sleep from 10:00 p.m. on, pleaded piteously to be filled. The dominant party was now that of the pessimists, who held that poison gas was already seeping in through the gratings in the walls and floor and that they would all shortly die.

"But a door burst open, and everything changed. The usual two guards in dirty dustcoats with hair-choked clippers to shear the sheep did not appear, nor were two or three pairs of the bluntest scissors on earth thrown in for the prisoners to break bits off their nails, oh no! Instead, four apprentice barbers wheeled in four stands with brilliantine, hair cream, nail varnish, and even theatrical wigs. Four ample and imposing master barbers, two of them Armenians, followed. And right there in the barber's shop, by the door, they . . . no, they didn't shave the prisoners' pubic regions pressing on the blunt clippers with all their might in sensitive spots; instead, they dusted the area with pink powder. The prisoners' withered cheeks felt the feather-light touch of a razor, and their ears were tickled with a whispered 'Is that uncomfortable?' Their heads were not close-cropped; indeed, they were offered wigs. Their chins were not scalped; customers who so wished were left with the beginnings of beards and sideburns-to-be. Meanwhile the apprentice barbers were prostrate, trimming toenails. In conclusion, as they went through the door to the baths, they were not asked to hold out their hands for a twenty-gram splash of evil-smelling goo; instead, a sergeant stood there handing each man, against a signed receipt, one sponge, daughter of the coral reefs, and one whole bar of Lilac Fairy toilet soap.

"After this they were locked in the bathhouse, as usual, to wash to their heart's content. But the prisoners were not interested in washing. Their arguments were hotter than the Butyrki's hot water. The dominant party now was that of the optimists, who held that Stalin and Beria had fled to China, that Molotov and Kaganovich had embraced Catholicism, that Russia now had a provisional government of Social Democrats, and that elections to the Constituent Assembly were already under way.

"At this point the familiar exit door was opened with the ritual clatter, and in the mauve vestibule a series of most extraordinary happenings awaited them; each man was given a fleecy towel . . . and a full bowl of oatmeal porridge, the equivalent of six daily portions for a convict at hard labor. The prisoners threw their towels on the floor and, without spoons or other aids, bolted the porridge down at astonishing speed. Even the major there present, who had grown old in the prison service, was surprised and ordered another bowl all around. They ate another bowl each. What came next none of you will ever guess. They brought in . . . not frostbitten, not rotten, not black, but what may be called normal, edible potatoes."

"Now you've gone too far," Potapov's hearers protested. "That simply can't be true!"

"But that's just how it was! True, they were of the pig potato variety, small and unpeeled, and after they'd already filled their stomachs, the zeks might have refused to eat them, but the diabolical cunning of the thing was that the potatoes were brought not in individual portions but in one common bucket.

The prisoners rushed at it with savage howls, inflicting painful knocks upon one another and scrambling over one another's bare backs, and within a minute the empty bucket was rolling over the stone floor with a clatter.

"By that time their naked bodies had dried. The old major ordered the zeks to pick their towels up from the floor and addressed them as follows: 'Dear brothers! You are all honest Soviet citizens, only temporarily isolated from society, some for ten, some for twenty-five years, for your not-too-serious misdemeanors. In spite of the lofty humanism of the Marxist-Leninist creed, in spite of the clearly expressed will of the Party and government, in spite of the repeated instructions of Comrade Stalin in person, those in charge of Butyrki Prison have many errors and irregularities to account for. These are now being corrected.'

"They're sending us home! the zeks brazenly decided.

" 'Henceforth we shall treat you as though you were at a holiday resort.'

"Their spirits sank: We're not getting out!

" 'In addition to all that was previously allowed, you are now allowed

(a) to worship your own gods;
(b) to lie on your bunks, whether by day or by night;
(c) to leave the cell and go to the bathroom without let or hindrance;
(d) to write your memoirs.

" 'In addition to things previously prohibited, you are now forbidden

(a) to blow your noses on sheets and curtains, the property of the state;
(b) to ask for second helpings;
(c) to contradict the authorities or complain about them when important visitors enter your cell;
(d) to take Kazbek cigarettes from the table without asking.

" 'Anyone who breaks one of these rules will be punished with fifteen days in an unheated punishment cell and consigned to one of the remoter camps without the right to correspondence. Is that clear?'

"Scarcely had the major concluded than . . . what? Did the carts rattle out of the heat-disinfection chamber bearing the prisoners' underwear and their tattered jackets? No, the hell that had swallowed their rags did not return them, but in came four nice young linen keepers, demurely blushing and smiling sweetly at the prisoners, as if to reassure them that they still had some hopes as men, and began distributing sky blue silk underwear. Then the zeks were given fine cotton shirts, discreet ties, bright yellow American shoes, received under Lend-Lease,* and synthetic worsted suits.

"Speechless with dread and delight, the prisoners were marched back in columns of two to their own Cell No. 72. But heavens, what a transformation!

"Out in the hallway their feet stepped on to a strip of rich carpet leading enticingly to the bathroom. Then, as they entered the cell, currents of fresh air played around them, and the immortal sun shone right into their eyes. (The night had gone by while they were busy, and it was now bright morning.) They found that during the night the bars had been painted pale blue, the 'muzzles' taken down from the windows, and on the former Butyrki chapel, within the prison yard, a swiveling mirror had been fixed and a guard stationed there to adjust it so that a steady stream of reflected sunlight played upon the windows of Cell No. 72. The walls of the cell, a dark olive green only yesterday, had been sprayed with bright gloss paint, on which artists had depicted doves with streamers in their beaks, inscribed 'We are for Peace!' and 'Peace to all the World!'

"The bug-ridden bedboards might never have existed. Canvas underlays had been stretched onto the bed frames, with mattresses and feather pillows tucked into them, and sparkling white blankets and sheets peeped from under coquettishly turned-down spreads. By each of the twenty-five bunks stood a locker, long shelves on the walls held books by Marx, Engels, Saint Augustine, and Thomas Aquinas, and in the middle of the cell stood a table with a starched tablecloth and on it flowers in a vase, an ashtray, and an unopened pack of Kazbeks. (All the other extravagances of this magical night were regularized by clever bookkeepers, but Kazbek cigarettes were too much of a luxury to be concealed under any heading on an expense account. The prison commandant had decided to spring for a pack of Kazbeks himself, which was why the penalty for misuse of them was so stiff.)

* Lend-Lease: The large-scale program of United States aid supplying the Allies with military equipment during World War II.

"But the greatest transformation was in the corner where the night bucket used to stand. The wall had been washed spotlessly clean and painted. A big lamp flickered before an icon of the Virgin and Child; nearby was the miracle worker Saint Nicholas of Mirlikia, in gleaming vestments, and a tall statue of a Catholic Madonna on a stand, while in a shallow recess, left for some reason by the original builders, there were copies of the Bible, the Koran, and the Talmud, and a small, dark bust of the Buddha. The Buddha's eyes were half closed and the corners of his lips drawn back so that a smile seemed to play on his dark bronze face.

"Replete with porridge and potatoes and staggering under the unmanageable abundance of new impressions, the zeks undressed and fell asleep at once. A gentle zephyr stirred the lace curtains at the windows, which gave no admittance to flies. A guard stood at the half-open door to see that nobody swiped the Kazbeks.

"They luxuriated undisturbed till noon, when the white-gloved captain hurried in extra-ord-in-arily flustered and announced that it was time to rise. The zeks quickly dressed and straightened their beds. A small round table with a white dustcover was then pushed into the room, copies of *Bonfire*, *The USSR Builds*, and *America* were placed upon it, two antique armchairs on casters and also dust-sheeted were wheeled in, and an unbearable silence, full of foreboding, followed. The captain tiptoed between the beds, carrying a handsome white stick to rap the fingers of those who reached for *America*.

"In the agonizing silence the prisoners listened. As you very well know from your own experience, hearing is the most important of the prisoner's senses. His vision is usually limited by walls and 'muzzles'; his sense of smell is overwhelmed by ignoble odors; there are no new objects for him to touch. But his hearing develops to an extraordinary degree. He identifies sounds immediately, even those from the far end of a corridor; he can tell the time by them and interpret what is going on, whether they're bringing the hot water around, taking somebody outside for exercise, or passing on a parcel.

"Hearing brought the beginnings of a solution to the riddle; the steel grating near Cell No. 75 clanged, and a large number of people entered the corridor. The prisoners heard hushed exchanges and footsteps muffled by carpets; then they could distinguish women's voices and the rustle of skirts, after which the governor of Butyrki Prison appeared right at the door of Cell No. 72 and said cordially, 'And now Mrs. Roosevelt might be interested in visiting one of our cells. Which shall it be? Let's pick one at random. No. 72 here, for instance. Open up, Sergeant.'

"And into the cell came Mrs. Roosevelt, accompanied by a secretary, an interpreter, two respectable matrons of the Quaker persuasion, the prison commandant, and several persons in civilian clothes or MVD uniforms. The white-gloved captain withdrew into the background. Mrs. Roosevelt, widow of the president and as progressive and penetrating as her late husband, had done much in defense of human rights and had now made it her business to visit America's valiant ally and see for herself how UNRRA aid was distributed (noxious rumors had reached America that UNRRA's groceries did not reach the common people) and also whether in the Soviet Union freedom of conscience was in any way restricted. She had already been shown simple Soviet citizens (Party officials and MGB officers in disguise), who in their rough workmen's overalls thanked the United States for its disinterested aid. Now Mrs. Roosevelt had insisted on visiting a prison. Her wish had been granted. She sat down on one of the armchairs, her retinue arranged itself around her, and exchanges through the interpreter began.

"Sunlight reflected from the swiveling mirror still flooded the cell. The breath of Aeolus gently stirred the curtains.

"Mrs. Roosevelt was very pleased to find that in a cell chosen at random and taken unawares, everything was so amazingly white, there was a complete absence of flies, and, although it was a working day, the lamp before the icon was aglow.

"At first the prisoners were too shy to stir, but when the interpreter translated the distinguished visitor's first question—'was it to keep the air clean that not one of the prisoners was smoking?'—one of them rose casually, unsealed the box of Kazbeks, lit one, and offered a cigarette to a friend.

"The major general looked black.

"'We are fighting against smoking,' he said with heavy emphasis, 'because tobacco is poisonous.'

"Another prisoner sat down at the table and began scanning *America*, for some reason very rapidly.

"'What are these people being punished for? That gentleman reading the magazine, for instance?' the distinguished visitor asked.

"'That gentleman' had been given ten years for rashly making the acquaintance of an American tourist.

"'That man,' the major general answered, 'was an active Hitlerite; he served in the Gestapo, personally burned a Russian village down, and raped, if you'll excuse the word, three Russian peasant women. The number of infants killed by him is incalculable.'

"'Has he been sentenced to death by hanging?' Mrs. Roosevelt cried.

"'No, we have hopes of reforming him. He has been sentenced to ten years of honest labor.'

"The prisoner's face expressed suffering, but instead of intervening, he continued reading the magazine with fevered haste.

"At that moment a Russian Orthodox priest with a big mother-of-pearl pectoral cross just happened to walk into the cell, evidently making his normal round, and was flummoxed to find senior officers and foreign guests there.

"He made as if to withdraw, but his modest demeanor pleased Mrs. Roosevelt, and she asked him to carry on doing his duty. The priest promptly thrust a pocket Testament on one of the bewildered prisoners, sat down on another prisoner's bed, and addressed the man, who was petrified with surprise. 'Well then, my son, you asked me last time to tell you about the sufferings of Our Lord Jesus Christ.'

"Mrs. Roosevelt requested the major general to ask the prisoners in her presence whether any of them wished to address a complaint to the United Nations.

"'Attention, prisoners!' the major general said menacingly. 'What were you told about the Kazbeks? D'you want a spell in the cooler?'

"The prisoners had been as silent as if they were under a spell, but now a babble of indignant voices arose:

"'Citizen governor, we've got nothing to smoke!'

"'We're going out of our minds.'

"'We left the stash in our other trousers!'

"'We just didn't know.'

"The illustrious lady saw the unfeigned indignation of the prisoners, heard their heartfelt protests, and listened to the translation all the more attentively: 'They unanimously protest against the distressing situation of the blacks in America and ask the UN to look into the matter.'

"Some fifteen minutes passed in agreeable dialogue of this sort. The moment came when the duty officer for the hallway reported to the commandant that dinner had arrived. The guest asked them not to mind her and to go ahead with serving the meal. The door was opened wide, and pretty young waitresses (probably the linen keepers in different uniforms) brought in tureens containing a simple chicken soup with noodles and ladled it into bowls. Instantly it was as though a primitive reflex had transformed the well-behaved prisoners: They jumped up on their beds in their shoes, pressed their knees to their chests, placed their hands palm down beside their feet, and in this canine posture watched with jealous eyes how much soup went into each bowl. The philanthropic ladies were shocked, but the interpreter explained to them that such was the Russian national custom.

"The prisoners could not be persuaded to sit at the table and eat with the electroplated nickel spoons. They had already fished out their own worn wooden spoons, and no sooner had the priest said grace and the waitresses carried the plates around to the beds, informing them that there was a dish on the table for the disposal of bones, than a terrible suctional *tutti* was heard, followed by a concerted crunching, and all that had been put on the plates vanished forever. The dish for disposal of bones was not required.

"'Maybe they're hungry?' the anxious visitor absurdly suggested. 'Maybe they want some more?'

"'Nobody want more?' the general asked hoarsely.

"Nobody did. They all knew the wise camp saying, 'Ask for more, and you'll get it from the law.'

"However, the zeks swallowed meatballs and rice with the same indescribable rapidity.

"Compote was not on the menu, as it was a weekday.

"Fully assured that the stories spread by ill-wishers abroad were malicious lies, Mrs. Roosevelt left the cell with her retinue and said outside in the corridor: 'How uncouth, how primitive these unfortunates are! We can hope, however, that after ten years here they will have acquired some culture. This is a magnificent prison you have!'

"The priest left with the retinue, skipping out before the cell door was slammed.

"When the guests had left the corridor, the white-gloved captain darted back into the room.

"'On your feet!' he yelled. 'Line up in pairs! Out in the corridor!'

"And observing that not everyone had understood his words correctly, he clarified them for the benefit of laggards with the sole of his boot.

"Only then was it discovered that one ingenious zek had taken permission to write memoirs literally and, while the others were all asleep in the morning, had racked up two chapters: 'How I Was Tortured' and 'Encounters in Lefortovo.'

"The memoirs were promptly impounded and the overeager writer booked for further investigation on a charge of 'foully libeling the Organs of State Security.'

"Once again with snapping of fingers and jingling of keys—'prisoner and escort'—they were led through numerous steel doors to the changing room, iridescent as ever with its malachite green and ruby red tiles. There they were relieved of everything they had been given, right down to the sky blue silk underwear, and an especially thorough body search was carried out, in the course of which one zek was found concealing in his cheek the Sermon on the Mount, torn out of a Testament. For this he was slapped on his right cheek, then made to turn his left. The coral-reef sponges and the Lilac Fairy were also taken from them, and once again every zek was made to sign his name in confirmation.

"Two guards in dirty overall coats came in and set about shearing the prisoners' pubic areas with blunt and clogged clippers, then denuded cheeks and skulls with the same instruments. In conclusion, twenty grams of evil-smelling liquid soap substitute were poured into each palm, and they were all locked in the bathhouse. There was nothing for it—the prisoners washed yet again.

"Then the exit door was opened with the ritual clatter, and they went out into the violet vestibule. Two aged women, handmaidens of hell, thunderously trundled their carts out of the heat-disinfection chamber, and there on the red-hot hooks hung the rags that our heroes knew so well.

"Dejectedly they returned to Cell No. 72, where they found their fifty comrades lying once more on the bug-ridden bedboards, burning with curiosity to learn what had happened. The windows were again blocked with 'muzzles,' the doves painted over with dark olive paint, and a four-gallon night bucket stood in the corner.

"Nothing had been forgotten, except the little bronze Buddha enigmatically smiling in his niche."

# 60

# But We Are Given Only One Conscience, Too

WHILE THIS STORY WAS BEING TOLD, Shchagov had put a high gloss on his well-worn but still respectable calfskin boots, donned what had been his dress uniform, after cleaning and pinning on his medals and sewing the wound stripes on his sleeve (army uniform, alas, was becoming fatally unfashionable in Moscow, and Shchagov would soon have to join in the desperate scramble for suits and shoes), and set out for the Kaluga Gate on the other side of Moscow. He had been invited, through his army friend Erik Saunkin-Golovanov, to a party at the home of Public Prosecutor Makarygin.

The party was mainly for the young, but it was also a family occasion to celebrate the award of the Red Banner of Labor to the public prosecutor. Some of the young people present were not, in fact, very close connections, but Daddy was footing the bill. The girl whom Shchagov had described to Nadya as his fiancée was sure to be there. There was, in fact, nothing definite between them, and it was time for him to press harder. That was why he had called Erik and asked him to arrange an invitation.

With a few opening remarks in readiness, he climbed the stairs (where Klara was always reminded of the woman she had seen cleaning them) and entered the apartment in which four years earlier the man whose wife he had just nearly stolen had crawled on his knees in ragged quilted trousers laying the parquet floor.

Apart from tightening his hold on his intended, what Shchagov most devoutly hoped to get from that evening was his fill of appetizing food. He knew that the best of everything would be provided in unsinkable quantities. He also knew that guests at such feasts were doomed to behave as though they were there simply to amuse one another, feigning indifference to food and barring the way to it. Shchagov must continue to entertain his opposite number, exchanging jokes and smiling politely, while appeasing his stomach, which was shriveling, thanks to the student refectory.

He did not expect to see a single genuine soldier at the party, anyone who like himself had threaded his way through mine lanes and stumbled wearily over plowed fields in what was grandiosely called an attack. His comrades were scattered, lost forever, killed in the hemp fields outside some village or against the wall of a barn or on an assault craft . . . and he was entering this warm and comfortable world alone, not to ask, "Where were *you*, you bastards?" but to become one of them and to eat his fill.

Perhaps his habit of dividing people into soldiers and nonsoldiers no longer made sense? Some people found it embarrassing to wear even the combat medals that had once cost them so dearly and shone so brightly. You couldn't accost everybody and ask "Where were you then?" It made less and less difference whether a man had fought or dodged the draft. There is a time to remember and a time to forget. Life is for the living. The dead have their glory.

Shchagov pressed the bell. The girl who opened the door was presumably Klara.

There were already quite a few coats, men's and women's, hanging in the little lobby. The warm party atmosphere reached him there—the cheerful buzz of voices, music from a record player, the clatter of crockery, a medley of joyous smells from the kitchen.

The telephone rang out there in the lobby, and Klara lifted the receiver, urging Shchagov with her left hand to take his coat off.

"Ink? Hello. What? You haven't left yet? . . . This very minute! . . . Ink, you know Daddy will be offended. Even your voice sounds feeble. . . . Oh well, if all you can say is 'I just can't!' Hang on, then, I'll call Nara."

"Nara!" she shouted into the next room. "Your ever-loving is on the line. Come and speak to him." (To Shchagov.) "Take your coat off." (He already had.) "And your galoshes." (He wasn't wearing them.) (To Nara.) "Know what? He doesn't want to come."

Wafting perfume from some exotic clime, Klara's sister Dotnara came into the lobby. Shchagov knew from Golovanov that she was married to a diplomat. She was strikingly handsome rather than beautiful, and she moved with the graceful ease that is the glory of Russian womanhood.

She took the receiver and began talking affectionately to her husband. She was in Shchagov's way, but he felt no need to hurry past this fragrant obstacle. He stood looking at her. Padded shoulders were very much in fashion, but Dotnara looked all the more feminine for refusing to hide the delicate curve of her upper arm. There was something else unusual about her dress. She was wearing a sleeveless dress but over it a fur-trimmed jacket with slit sleeves gathered at the wrist.

Not one of the three standing so awkwardly close together in the cozily carpeted lobby could have imagined that disaster lurked in that innocent, shiny black tube and that trivial discussion about coming or not coming to a party.

That afternoon Rubin had ordered additional recordings of calls made by each of the suspects. This was the first time Volodin had answered his telephone since then. As he raised the receiver, a tape in the central exchange of the Ministry of State Security began rustling and recording—the voice of Innokenty Volodin.

As a precaution he had decided not to use the phone for the present. But his wife had gone out, leaving a note; he was to be at his father-in-law's that evening without fail.

He was calling now to beg off.

After yesterday's call to the embassy—was it really only yesterday? it seemed ages ago—the suspense had become harder and harder to bear. He had not expected to be so agitated, never imagined that he could be so afraid for himself. He was seized by dread in the night, certain that he was about to be arrested. He longed for morning to come, so that he could leave the house. He had spent the whole day in a state of restless anxiety, understanding nothing of what was said to him and not even listening. Regret for his impulse was compounded by craven terror, but by evening those feelings had degenerated into apathy; he no longer cared what happened.

It would probably have been easier for Innokenty if that interminable day had not been a Sunday. He would have been in the office, looking for clues as to whether his posting to the UN in New York was going ahead or had been canceled. But on Sunday there was no way of guessing whether the holiday lull held peace or menace.

Throughout the last twenty-four hours, his call to the embassy had seemed to him suicidally rash. Nor could it possibly do any good. And anyway, to judge by that dithering idiot of an attaché, they were not worth defending.

There was nothing to show that he had been found out, but his heart ached with an inexplicable presentiment, and the anticipation of disaster grew stronger and stronger. The last thing he wanted was to go where people were enjoying themselves. He was trying to persuade his wife, speaking hesitantly, as people do when they have something unpleasant to say. His wife persisted, and the peculiarities of his "individual speech pattern" were recorded on a narrow strip of magnetic tape, to be turned into the "sound pictures" on wet film that would be laid out before Rubin the next morning.

Dotty was not talking in the peremptory tone she had adopted in recent months. Softened, perhaps, by the weariness in her husband's voice, she begged him to come, if only for an hour.

Innokenty gave in.

But when he put down the receiver, his hand remained on it, and he stood motionless, as though letting his fingerprints be taken. He felt that he had left something unsaid.

He suddenly felt sorry not for the wife with whom he had lived and lived no longer, and whom he meant to leave forever in a few days' time, but for the fair-haired tenth-grade schoolgirl, with curls down to her shoulders, whom he used to take dancing between the tables at the Metropole, the girl with whom long ago he had begun to discover what life was about. Their passion was fierce, impervious to reason, and they refused to hear about waiting a year before they married. Innokenty's mother, already seriously ill, was against it, but what mother does not oppose her son's choice? So was the public prosecutor, but what father lightheartedly surrenders a charming eighteen-year-old daughter? But against all opposition, the young people got married, and their unclouded happiness was a byword among their common acquaintances.

Their married life began with the very best auguries. People in their social circle did not know what it meant to go anywhere on foot or to use the metro. Even before the war they preferred flying to a sleeper on an express train. They never had to worry about furnishing an apartment; wherever the young couple went—in the countryside around Moscow, in Tehran, on the Syrian coast, in Switzerland—a fully equipped dacha, villa, or flat would be waiting for them. Their outlook on life was identical. No inhibitions, no obstacles must come between wish and fulfillment. "We are people who behave naturally," Dotnara used to say. "We don't pretend; we wear no disguise. Whatever we want we go all out for!" As they saw it, "We are given only one life"—and so must take from life all that it has to offer. But not, perhaps, a child, because a child is an idol that sucks the vital juices out of you and repays you with no sacrifice of its own, not even with gratitude.

With views such as these, they were well suited to their milieu, and it was well suited to them. They were eager to sample every new, exotic fruit. To learn the taste of every rare brandy and what distinguished the wines of the Rhone from those of Corsica and of all the earth's vineyards besides. To wear every kind of clothing. Dance every dance. Swim at every resort. Sit through two acts of every unusual theatrical occasion. Page through every book that made a stir.

For six of the best years in a man's or a woman's life, each gave all that the other could ask. Six years that largely coincided with those in which much of mankind were saying heartbreaking farewells, dying on the battlefield or under the rubble of shattered cities, years when crazed adults were stealing crusts of bread from children. The world's grief did not pale the cheeks of Innokenty and Dotnara.

We are given only one life, remember! . . .

But in the sixth year of their married life, when the bombers were grounded and the guns fell silent, when tremulous green shoots were struggling through the black cinders and people everywhere had begun to remember that we only live once, all the fruits of the earth, all that it is good to smell, to feel, to eat, to drink, to handle, palled on Innokenty and began to disgust him.

Alarmed by these feelings, he fought against them as though they were an illness. He hoped in vain that they would pass. The worst of it was that he could not explain them. It might seem that everything he could wish for was within his grasp, but something important was lacking. At twenty-eight and in perfect health, Innokenty felt that his own life and the life of all around him had reached a dead end.

He stopped enjoying the company of close friends who had once amused him. This one suddenly seemed unintelligent; that other was coarse; yet another too full of himself.

But it wasn't just his friends. He began to detach and distance himself from the flaxen-haired Dotty (he had long ago started using this Europeanized version of Dotnara's name), from the wife to whom he used to feel indissolubly joined.

There was a time when the thought of her was a piercing joy. When he could never tire of her lips, even when he felt lifeless and despondent. He had known no other lips like hers. Of all the beautiful and clever women he met, Dotty alone existed for him, and suddenly he could not help seeing in her a lack of refinement and began to find her opinions intolerable.

Her remarks about literature, art, and the theater in particular now seemed to him invariably wide of the mark, jarringly crude and imperceptive, and she delivered herself of them so categorically. Sharing silence with her was as good as ever, talking to her more and more difficult.

Innokenty began to feel cramped by their monotonously glamorous lifestyle, but Dotty would not hear of any change. To make matters worse, instead of ruthlessly abandoning things in favor of something new and better, she had developed a habit of greedily treating as permanent possessions all the things she found in each of their apartments. Dotty had used her two years in Paris to send home big cardboard boxes full of lengths of fabric, shoes, dresses, and hats. Innokenty disliked this, but the more glaringly their wishes diverged, the more emphatically she insisted that she was right. Had she only recently acquired or had she always had, unnoticed by Innokenty, that unpleasant way of chewing, or rather chomping, especially when she ate fruit?

The trouble, of course, lay not in his friends, not in his wife, but in Innokenty himself. There was something lacking in his life, and he did not know what it was.

His friends had long ago decided that he was an "Epicurean," and he readily accepted the label, without really knowing what it meant. Then one day, at home in Moscow with nothing to do, he had had the amusing idea of reading what his "master" had in fact taught. He started searching the cabinets left by his late mother for a book about Epicurus that he remembered seeing in his childhood.

Going through the old cabinets was a task Innokenty began with an unpleasant sensation of stiffness, a reluctance to bend, to move heavy objects around, to breathe dust. Even this was unusually hard work for him, and he soon tired. But he forced himself to go on, and a refreshing breeze seemed to play on him from the depths of those old cabinets, which had a ripe smell all their own. He found the book on Epicurus, among other things, and read it later, but more important was what he discovered, from her letters, about his late mother, whom he had never understood and to whom he had felt close only as a child. Even her death had left him almost unmoved. In early childhood a vision of silvered bugles raised toward an ornate ceiling and the song "Let Leaping Flames Light Up the Blue Night" had fused with Innokenty's idea of his father. A father whom he did not really remember at all; he had been killed in 1921, suppressing the peasant rebellion in Tambov province. But he was surrounded by people who never tired of telling him about the heroic naval officer's glorious role in the Civil War. Hearing those praises sung everywhere and by everybody, Innokenty began to feel very proud of his father and his fight for the common folk against rich people wallowing in luxury. Whereas he rather looked down on his anxious mother, nursing her unspoken grief in the midst of her books and hot-water bottles. Like most sons, he did not stop to think that, besides himself and his upbringing, his mother had some sort of life of her own. That she could be ill and suffer. And now she had died at the age of forty-seven.

His parents had spent hardly any time together. But this, too, was something the boy had no occasion to think about, and it never occurred to him to question his mother.

Now the whole story unfolded in her letters and diaries. Their marriage was not a marriage but a whirlwind event, like everything in those years. Circumstances had flung them roughly and briefly together, circumstances allowed them to see very little of each other, and circumstances parted them. But in these diaries his mother was revealed as not just an appendage to his father, as their son had been accustomed to thinking, but as someone with a world of her own. Innokenty now learned that his mother had loved another man all her life and had never been able to marry him. That it was perhaps only for the sake of her son's career that she had borne till the day she died a name that was alien to her.

Stored in the cabinets were bundles of letters tied with colored ribbons of fine fabric. Letters from girlhood friends and from friends and acquaintances of later years, actors, artists, and poets long forgotten or mentioned nowadays only disparagingly. Old-fashioned exercise notebooks with blue morocco covers held his mother's diaries, written in Russian and French in her strange hand; it was as though a wounded bird had skimmed the page and scratched an erratic trail with its faltering claw. Recollections of literary soirées and theatrical events took up many pages. He was deeply moved by her description of herself, an enraptured girl, standing on the station in Petersburg one white June night among a crowd of admirers all weeping for joy as they welcomed the Moscow Arts Theater company. Pure love of art reigned triumphant in these pages. Innokenty could think of no such company nowadays; nor could he imagine anyone missing a night's sleep to welcome it, except those dragooned by the Department of Culture, carrying bouquets funded from the public purse. And obviously, no one would ever dream of shedding tears on such an occasion.

The diaries led him on and on. There were pages headed "Ethical Notes"; "Goodness shows itself first in pity," said one of them.

Innokenty wrinkled his brow. Pity? A shameful feeling, degrading to the one who pities and the one who is pitied—so he had learned at school and in life.

"Never think yourself more right than other people. Respect other people's opinions even when they are inimical to yours."

That was pretty old-fashioned, too. If I have a correct worldview, can I really respect those who disagree with me?

He almost forgot that he was reading and seemed to hear clearly his mother's frail voice.

"What is the most precious thing in the world? I see now that it is the knowledge that you have no part in injustice. Injustice is stronger than you, it always was and always will be, but let it not be done through you."

If Innokenty had opened the diary six years earlier, he would not even have noticed those lines. But now he read them slowly and with surprise. There was nothing esoteric in them and much that was simply untrue, but still he was surprised. Even the words in which his mother and her women friends expressed themselves were outdated. In all seriousness, they began certain words with capital letters—Truth, Goodness, Beauty, Good and Evil, the Ethical Imperative. In the language used by Innokenty and those around him, words were more concrete and easier to understand—progressiveness, humanity, dedication, purposefulness.

But although Innokenty was progressive and humane and dedicated and purposeful (purposefulness was what all his contemporaries most prized and cultivated in themselves), sitting there on a low stool by the cabinets he felt that something he had lacked was stealing into his heart.

There were also albums of old photographs, clear and sharply defined. Several separate bundles consisted of Moscow and Petersburg theater programs. There was the theatrical daily *Spectator*. And the *Cinema Herald*. (He hadn't realized that they went back so far.) And piles and piles of magazines, all sorts of magazines—their names alone were enough to make a man dizzy: *Apollo*, *Golden Fleece*, *The Hyperborean*, *Pegasus*, *World of Art*. There were reproductions of unknown paintings and sculptures (not a trace of any of them in the Tretyakov Gallery) and of stage sets. Poems by unknown poets. Innumerable magazine supplements, with dozens of European writers of whom Innokenty had never heard. But it wasn't just individual writers; there were whole publishing houses long forgotten, as if the earth had swallowed them: Gryphon, Dogrose, Scorpion, Musagetes, Halcyon, Northern Lights, Logos.

He sat there for days on end, on the little stool by the wide-open cabinets, breathing their air, intoxicated with it and with his mother's little world, which his father had once entered, wearing a black raincoat, girded with hand grenades, and bearing a Cheka search warrant. Early twentieth-century Russia, with its ideological battles, its dizzy proliferation of trends and movements, its unbridled imagination, and its anxious forebodings, looked out at Innokenty from these yellowing pages—Russia of the last pre-Revolutionary decade, which he had been taught at school and in the institute to regard as the most shameful and most barren in Russia's history, a decade so hopeless that if the Bolsheviks had not come to the rescue, Russia left to itself would have rotted and collapsed.

It had, indeed, been a garrulous decade, too sure of itself at times, yet somehow impotent. But what a proliferation of new growth! What a burgeoning of new ideas!

Innokenty realized what he had been robbed of till now.

Dotnara had arrived to carry her husband off to some official reception. Innokenty had stared at her uncomprehendingly, then frowned, picturing that pompous assembly where everybody would unreservedly agree with everybody else, where all would spring to their feet with alacrity to drink the first toast—"To Comrade Stalin!"—then eat and drink a great deal with no further thought of Comrade Stalin and then play cards like idiots.

His eyes returned from an unfathomable distance to his wife, and he begged her to go alone. That anyone should prefer poking about in old albums to real life at a reception seemed crazy to Dotnara. Innokenty's finds in the cabinets were bound up with vague but never-dying recollections of his childhood, and they meant a great deal to him but nothing to his wife.

His mother had triumphed; she had risen from the grave and taken her son from his bride.

Once launched, Innokenty could not stop. If he had been misled about one thing, perhaps there were others.

For some years now, he had lacked both the wish and the energy to study. (His fluent French, which had been such a help in his career, he had acquired in childhood from his mother.) But now he began reading avidly. His blunted and jaded appetites gave way to this new passion for reading.

He found, though, that even reading was a special skill, not just a matter of running your eyes along the lines. He discovered that he was a savage, reared in the caves of social science, clad in the skins of class warfare. His whole education had trained him to take certain books on trust and reject others unread. From boyhood he had been sheltered from erroneous books and had read only those that were warranted sound, so that he had got into the habit of believing every word, of submitting without question to the author's will. When he began to read authors who contradicted one another, his resistance was low, and he could not help surrendering to whichever of them he had read last. What he found most difficult of all was to lay down his book and think for himself.

Why, he wondered, had the February Revolution disappeared from Soviet calendars, as though it was an insignificant detail in the chronology of 1917? Why, indeed, were they so reluctant to call it a revolution? Perhaps only because it made no work for the guillotine? But the tsar had been overthrown, and with him a regime six centuries old, at a single push; and nobody rushed to pick up the crown, everybody sang and laughed and exchanged congratulations, yet there was no place for this day in a calendar that meticulously noted the birthdays of greasy swine like Zhdanov and Shcherbakov.

Whereas October 1917, which all Soviet books in the twenties called a coup, was magnified as the greatest Revolution in the history of mankind. What were Zinoviev and Kamenev accused of in October 1917? Of betraying the "Secret of the Revolution" to the bourgeoisie. But can you prevent a volcano from erupting by looking into the crater? Can you block the path of a hurricane when you receive a weather report? Could they have "betrayed the secret"? Only the secret of a narrow conspiracy! And that tells us everything. There was no elemental, nationwide flare-up in October; all that happened was that the conspirators assembled at a given signal.

Shortly afterward, Innokenty was posted to Paris. There he had access to all shades of world opinion and to all Russian émigré literature (though, of course, he had to look over his shoulder at bookstores). He could read and read and read! Though his duties, of course, got in the way.

Until then he had thought that his job was the best and his lot the luckiest he could possibly have hoped for. But now he began to feel that there was something sordid about it. Being a Soviet diplomat meant not only delivering, day in and day out, statements at which people with their heads screwed on right were bound to laugh. The other part of the job was more important, the secret part: meeting characters with code names, collecting information, passing on instructions and money.

In his carefree youth, before his crisis, Innokenty had seen nothing reprehensible about this backdoor business; he had thought it fun and made light work of it. Now it was distasteful, repellent.

The great truth for Innokenty used to be that we are given only one life.

Now, with the new feeling that had ripened in him, he became aware of another law: that we are given only one conscience, too.

A life laid down cannot be reclaimed, nor can a ruined conscience.

But there was no one, no one at all in Innokenty's circle, not even his wife, to whom he could tell all these new thoughts. She had not understood or sympathized with the belated affection he had felt for his dead mother; nor did she understand why anyone would take an interest in events that were over and done with, never to return. If she had known that he had begun to despise his job, she would have been horrified; this job of his was the foundation of their glittering prosperity.

The gap between them had widened so far in the past year that he could no longer risk revealing himself.

But even on leave in the USSR, Innokenty had no intimates. Touched by Klara's naive story about the cleaner on the stairway, he had hoped for an instant that here at last was someone he could talk to freely. But from the first steps they took, the first words they exchanged on their walk, he saw that he was mistaken. Impassable thickets lay between them, too dense to disentangle and tear asunder. And although it would have been quite natural for him to complain about his wife to his wife's sister and although that would have brought them closer together, he was disinclined to do it.

Why? For one thing, a strange law decrees that it is futile trying to develop an understanding with a woman if she is not physically attractive to you; somehow your lips are sealed; you are paralyzed by the hopelessness of trying to say all you need to say; frank and simple words elude you.

Then again, he had not gone to see his uncle, had made no effort to go when he should have. What was the good? A complete waste of time. There would be nothing but tedious, pointless interrogation and exclamations of wonder about "abroad."

Another year went by, in Paris and in Rome. He arranged to go to Rome without his wife. Only to learn on his return that he had shared her with an officer on the General Staff. She was unrepentant, indeed stubbornly self-righteous about it, and shifted all the blame onto Innokenty; he should not have left her by herself.

Yet he felt no pain, no sense of loss, but rather relief. Since then he had been at a desk in the ministry for four months, in Moscow the whole time, but they lived like strangers. Divorce was out of the question, however; it would ruin a diplomat's career. And Innokenty was marked out for posting to the UN Secretariat in New York.

This latest posting pleased him but also frightened him. He liked the United Nations as an idea, not its charter but what it could be, given a general willingness to compromise and to avoid malicious point scoring. He was very much in favor of world government. What else could save the planet? But that was the spirit in which Swedes or Burmese or Ethiopians could go to the UN. He was propelled by an iron fist at his back. Once again he was packed off with a secret mission, an undeclared purpose, a double memory, and a poisonous hidden brief.

During those months in Moscow, he did at last find time to visit his uncle at Tver.

# 61

## The Uncle at Tver

INNOKENTY HAD NOTED with surprise that his uncle's address included no apartment number. It proved unnecessary. He did not take long looking for it: a sagging, one-story wooden house among others like it on a paved side street without trees or fences. Innokenty was not sure at first whether to knock at the lopsided front door with patterned panels or the wicket in the yard gate. He tried both, but no one opened up or called out. He shook the wicket. It was nailed shut. He pushed the front door. It wouldn't budge.

The poverty-stricken look of the house made him surer than ever that he should not have come.

He looked up and down the lane for someone to ask, but the whole place was deserted under the noonday sun. Until an old man came round the corner carrying two full buckets. He carried them with stiff caution, caught his foot once, but did not stop. One of his shoulders was slightly higher than the other.

He was heading that way, diagonally, following his own shadow, and he was aware of the visitor, although his eyes never left the ground. Innokenty took one step away from his suitcase, then another.

"Uncle Avenir?"

Bending his knees more than his back, Uncle Avenir set the buckets down neatly, without spilling a drop. He straightened up, removed the dirty yellow pancake of a cap from his close-cropped gray head, and wiped away the sweat with the same clenched hand. He struggled to say something but opened his arms instead, and before he knew it, Innokenty was bending down (his uncle was half a head shorter) and pricking his smooth cheek on his uncle's unshaved face. His hand had somehow found the jutting shoulder blade that made his uncle's shoulder crooked.

Uncle Avenir raised both hands to Innokenty's shoulders and held him at arm's length for inspection.

He meant to say something suitably solemn, but what came out was "You're rather thin."

"So are you."

His uncle wasn't just thin, he obviously had all sorts of ailments and disabilities, but as far as Innokenty could see in the bright sunlight, Uncle Avenir's were not the dim and apathetic eyes of an old man.

He grinned lopsidedly.

"Me! I don't go in for banquets. What are you here for?"

Innokenty was glad that he had taken Klara's advice and bought sausage and smoked fish, which could probably not be had in Tver for love or money. He sighed.

"I've got worries, Uncle."

His uncle looked him over with lively eyes that had kept their power.

"Maybe you have. Maybe you only think so."

"Do you have to go far for your water?"

"One block, two blocks, and another half block. But they aren't very big blocks."

Innokenty bent down and lifted the buckets to carry them inside. They were heavier than he had expected. They might have had iron bottoms.

His uncle walked behind, laughing.

"What a worker you'd make! I can see you aren't used to it."

He took the lead and unlocked the door. In the narrow passageway he put his hands on the yoke and steadied the buckets onto a bench. The natty blue suitcase was put down on a crooked floor of wobbly, ill-fitting boards. The door was bolted immediately, as though Uncle expected intruders.

The hallway had a low ceiling, a small window looking onto the yard gate, two closet doors, and two for people. Innokenty began to feel ill at ease. He had never before let himself in for anything like this. He regretted coming and tried to think of an excuse to rush off toward evening, not to stay the night.

The doors to the rooms and between rooms were all crooked; some were lined with felt; others were double doors with old-fashioned ornamentation. You had to bend your head at every doorway and take care not to bump it on the ceiling lamps. The air in the three small rooms was stale because the second window frames were a permanent fixture, wedged in with cotton and colored paper. Only the ventilation panes opened, but strips of shredded newspaper hung fluttering before them to scare the flies away.

The dispiriting poverty of it all—this squat and crooked shack, ill-lit and airless, with not a stick of furniture standing squarely on the floor—was something Innokenty had read about but never seen for himself. Not all of the walls were even whitewashed; in places the timbers were daubed with dark paint. Dusty, yellowing newspapers hung everywhere, serving as "wall carpets." Several thicknesses of newspaper hid the glass doors of cabinets, the niche in the sideboard, the tops of windows, and the wall behind the stove. Innokenty felt trapped. He must get away before the day was over!

His uncle, though, seemed proud rather than ashamed as he showed Innokenty various desirable features: the homely earth closet for summer and winter use, the washstand, the arrangements for catching rainwater. Needless to say, vegetable peelings did not go to waste.

Innokenty could imagine what sort of wife would shortly appear! And what the bed linen would be like!

But still, this was his mother's brother; he knew about her life from childhood on and was in fact Innokenty's only blood relation. Bolt now, and he would never learn all he needed to know, never even be able to think his own problem through.

And anyway his uncle's directness and his one-sided grin pleased Innokenty. In those first few words he sensed that there was more to the man than had appeared in the two short letters.

In times of general mistrust and treachery, kinship gives at least an initial hope that the man you are dealing with has not been thrown in your way for some underhanded purpose, that his route to you was a natural one. You can tell a kinsman, even a dim one, things that you could not discuss with the most luminous of sages.

Uncle Avenir was not just thin; he had withered away till there was only the indispensable minimum left on his bones. But such people are long-lived.

"How old are you, exactly, Uncle?"

(Innokenty hadn't even a rough idea.)

His uncle looked at him hard and answered enigmatically: "I'm his contemporary."

"Whose?"

"The Man himself."

His gaze was unwavering.

Innokenty smiled readily. This was familiar ground. Even in the years when he had cheered in unison with everybody else, the Man's vulgar manner, his crass speeches, his glaring stupidity had left a bad taste.

When his remark was met neither with polite incomprehension nor with lofty disapproval, Uncle Avenir brightened and risked a little joke.

"Ahem! You must admit that it would be presumptuous of me to die first. If I can squeeze into second place in the line, I will."

They both laughed. The first spark had leaped between them. After that it was easier.

Uncle Avenir's clothes were dreadful. The shirt under his jacket didn't bear looking at. The ragged collar, lapels, and cuffs of his jacket had been mended and were fraying again. His trousers had been patched so often that there was little of the original material to be seen, and the patches were of different colors, some plain gray, some checkered, some striped. His shoes had been repaired and restitched so often that they looked like a convict's clogs. Uncle Avenir, however, explained that these were his working clothes and that he never went farther than the pump and the bread shop in them. He was, however, in no hurry to change.

He did not waste much time on the rooms but took Innokenty to see the yard. The day was now very warm, cloudless, and windless.

The yard was only thirty meters by ten, but it belonged entirely to Uncle Avenir. He was separated from his neighbors by ramshackle sheds and gappy fences, but they served their purpose. There was room for a paved area and a paved path, a tank for rainwater, a feeding trough, a woodpile, a summer stove, and there was still room left for a garden. Uncle Avenir took him around and introduced him to every tree and plant; just from their leaves, without flowers or fruit, Innokenty would have recognized none of them. There was a Chinese rosebush, a jasmine, a lilac, a flower bed with nasturtiums, poppies, and asters. There were two luxuriantly leafy black-currant bushes; Uncle Avenir complained that although they had blossomed abundantly, they had produced hardly any berries because there had been a sudden frost at pollination time. There was one cherry tree and one apple tree, with props to bear the weight of the latter's branches. The weeds had all been pulled up, and only the plants that should have been there were there.

There must have been a lot more crawling on the knees and work with fingers than Innokenty could appreciate. But he understood sufficiently to say, "It must be very hard for you, Uncle! How do you manage all that bending and digging and carrying?"

"I'm not afraid of that, Innokenty. Carrying water, chopping wood, digging, as long as you don't overdo it—that's the normal way for a person to live. You're more likely to suffocate in one of those five-story egg boxes, sharing a flat with the leading class."

"Which class is that?"

"The proletariat."

The old man eyed him speculatively again. "The domino bashers, the ones who keep the radio on from early morning till late at night. They only leave themselves five hours and fifty minutes to sleep. They break bottles where passersby can tread on the glass; they dump their trash out there in the middle of the street. Have you ever wondered why they're supposed to be the leading class?"

Innokenty shook his head. "Hmm . . . well . . . that's something I've never understood."

"They're the most barbarous class!" his uncle said angrily. "Peasants commune with the soil, with nature, and learn their morality from it. Intellectuals are engaged in the noble work of thinking. But these people spend all their lives within dead walls making dead things with dead machines. How can they ever learn anything?"

They walked on and sat down for a while, looking around them.

"No, I don't find it hard work. Everything I do here I do with a clear conscience. When I empty the slops, it's with a clear conscience. I scrape the floor with a clear conscience. If I rake out the ashes and light the stove, there's nothing bad in that. But if you've got a position to hold down, you can't live like that. You have to truckle . . . and you have to be dishonest. I beat a retreat every time. I couldn't even stand being a librarian, let alone a teacher."

"What's so hard about a librarian's job?"

"Just go and try it. You have to trash good books and praise bad ones. You have to mislead undeveloped minds. What job would you say can be done with a clear conscience?"

Innokenty knew too little about other jobs to say anything. The only job he had held was against his conscience,

The house, it seemed, was Raisa Timofeevna's and had been for a long time. She was the one who had a job, as a hospital nurse. She had grown-up children who had set up house elsewhere. She had taken Uncle Avenir under her wing when he was physically and mentally in a poor way and destitute. She had set him on his feet again, and he was eternally grateful to her. She worked double shifts. Uncle Avenir didn't mind a bit preparing their meals, washing dishes, and doing all the housework.

Behind the bushes up against the fence there was, as there should be in every real garden, a secluded bench, its legs set in the ground. Uncle and nephew sat down.

No, it was no hardship, Uncle Avenir insisted, developing his theme with the stubbornness of old age. His was the natural way to live, not on asphalt but on a piece of land that would let a spade in. Never mind that the whole plot was only three spades long and two spades wide. He had been living that way for ten years and was glad of it; he could ask for no better lot. However rickety and full of gaps, those fences were his protection, his fortifications. Only bad things came from outside—the din of radios, tax demands, orders to carry out community service. Every unexpected knock at the door meant something unpleasant. So far nobody had come bearing good news.

No, it was no hardship. There were much greater hardships.

Such as?

The old man in the patched clothes and the flat cap was less and less mistrustful, but he gave Innokenty a cautious sideways look. There were things you shouldn't venture into with strangers after two years, let alone two hours. Still, this boy seemed to have some idea, he was kin, so . . . keep it up, boy, keep it up!

"The hardest thing of the lot," Uncle Avenir said, burning with indignation, "is having to hang the flag out on public holidays. Householders have to hang out flags." (Say it now or never!) "Compulsory show of loyalty to a government that perhaps you don't respect."

Look out! Is he madman or sage, this emaciated and bedraggled creature blurting out his thoughts to you? Sleek from good living, draped in an academic gown and speaking unhurriedly, he would by general consent be a sage.

Innokenty did not recoil, did not instantly protest. But his uncle took refuge behind a reliably broad back.

"Have you read anything by Herzen? Read him properly?"

"Yes . . . I think so."

His uncle bore down on him, thrust the crooked shoulder at him (he had acquired a spinal curvature poring over books in his youth).

"Herzen asks what are the limits of patriotism. Must love for your native land extend to any and every government it may have? Must you go on abetting it in destroying its own people?"

Simple and cogent. Innokenty repeated it, to see if he had got it right.

"Must love for your native land extend to. . . ?"

But by now they were at the opposite fence, and Uncle Avenir's eyes scanned the cracks at which neighbors might be eavesdropping.

Their conversation had gotten off to a good start. Back inside the house, Innokenty no longer felt that he was suffocating and no longer thought of leaving. Strangely, he did not notice the hours go by; it was all so interesting. Uncle Avenir bustled about to the kitchen and back. They reminisced about Innokenty's mother. They looked at old snapshots, and Uncle made him a present of some of them. He had, however, been a lot older than his sister, and they had not been children together.

Raisa Timofeevna came home from work. She was a severe woman of fifty, and she returned Innokenty's greeting grudgingly. He shared his uncle's embarrassment and also felt a strange fear that she would ruin everything for them. They sat down at a table covered with dark oilcloth to what might have been either dinner or supper. It was difficult to see what sort of meal they would have had if Innokenty had not brought half a suitcase full of food with him and sent his uncle out to get vodka. The hosts did pick a few of their tomatoes. And supplied the potatoes.

Still, their kinsman's generosity and the fine fare put a sparkle in Raisa Timofeevna's eyes and relieved Innokenty of any feeling of guilt—for all the times when he had not come in the past and for coming now. They drank a shot, then another, and Raisa Timofeevna began airing her grievances against the good-for-nothing Avenir: He'd made a mess of his life; he couldn't get on with people in any place of work because of his awkward character, but that wouldn't matter so much if he would just stay quietly at home! But oh no, he couldn't resist spending his last few kopecks on newspapers. He even bought *New Times* now and then; that was expensive, and he didn't buy them to enjoy them; in fact, he got furious with them, and sat up night after night dashing off answers to articles, then never sent them in but rather burned them after a day or two because even keeping them in the house was unthinkable. This pointless scribbling occupied half of his time. He also went to hear visiting lecturers talk about the international situation, and she was always terrified that he would get up and ask a question and never come home. He didn't ask questions, though, and always got home safe and sound.

Uncle Avenir made little effort to defend himself. He laughed apologetically, but his lopsided grin gave no hope of amendment! And anyway, Raisa Timofeevna's complaints were halfhearted; she seemed to have given up hope long ago. And she obviously didn't begrudge him those "last few kopecks."

Their dark house with its unpainted walls and its bare rooms became cozier as soon as they closed the shutters. That soothing seclusion from the world outside is something our age has forgotten. Each shutter was held to by a strip of iron, from which a flange protruded through an opening into the house, where a peg was inserted in its eyehole. They didn't need this to keep thieves out; they could have left the windows wide open; there was no loot to be had. But once the bolts were shot, the soul could relax its vigilance. They could not have managed any other way; the footpath ran under their windows, and passersby seemed to be barging into the room with their heavy tread, their loud voices, and their foul language.

Raisa Timofeevna went to bed early, and Uncle Avenir, moving and speaking quietly in the middle room (his hearing too was unimpaired), revealed yet another of his secrets: the swatches of yellowed newspaper hung up out of the sun and dust were just a noncriminal way of preserving the most interesting news from times past. ("Why are you keeping that particular newspaper, Citizen?" "I'm not keeping it; it just happens to be there.") He couldn't mark them, but he knew by heart what he could find in any one of them. They were hung up in such a way that the interesting bits could be got at without undoing a whole bundle every time.

They stood side by side on two chairs, Uncle Avenir wearing his glasses, and read what Stalin had to say in 1939: "I know how the German people loves its Führer, and I therefore drink to his health!" In a 1924 newspaper over the window, Stalin was defending "the loyal Leninists Kamenev and Zinoviev" against the accusation that they had tried to sabotage the October coup.

Innokenty was carried away by the excitement of the chase, and even in the feeble light of a forty-watt bulb, they would have gone on scrambling about the walls and rustling paper, trying to decipher the smudged and faded lines; but his wife's reproachful cough on the other side of the wall worried Uncle Avenir, and he said: "Let's call it a day. You aren't leaving tomorrow, are you? We'd better put the light out; it uses a lot of juice. Why, I ask you, do they charge so much for electricity? However many power stations we build, it doesn't get any cheaper."

They put the light out. But they didn't feel like sleeping. In the small third room, a bed had been made up for Innokenty; his uncle perched on the edge of it, and they went on whispering for an hour or two like enraptured lovers who need no light for their billing and cooing.

"It was all done by fraud," Uncle Avenir insisted. In the dark you would never have taken his firm voice for that of an old man. "Instead of a government true to its word—'Peace to the people! Bayonets into the ground!'—a year later deserter squads were hunting peasants in the woods and shooting them as a lesson to the rest! The tsar never did that. 'Workers' Control of Production'? Nowhere did it last a single month. The central government got a stranglehold on everything. If they'd said in 1917 that production norms would be raised year in and year out, who would ever have followed them? 'An end to secret diplomacy and secret appointments,' and in no time they were stamping everything 'Secret' or 'Top Secret.' Was there ever a country in which the people knew less about their government than we do?"

Skipping from decade to decade and subject to subject was somehow easier in the dark, and Uncle Avenir was soon telling Innokenty that throughout the war large contingents of NKVD troops were garrisoned in all big provincial towns and never moved up to the front. Whereas the tsar had put all his guard regiments through the grinder and was left with no internal troops to put down Revolution. As for the muddleheaded provisional government, it had no troops at all at its disposal.

"Another thing, about this last war between the Soviet Union and Germany. How do you see it?"

Talking to him was so easy! Innokenty unhesitatingly found words that would never have occurred to him but for this dialogue.

"I see it as a tragic war. We defended our country, and we lost it. It became the private estate of the Man with the Big Mustache and nothing more."

"We lost a lot more than the seven million they talk about," his uncle said. "Of course we did. And for what? Just to draw the noose tighter around our necks. It's the most unfortunate war in Russian history."

Then he went backward again, to the Second Congress of Soviets. Only three hundred out of the nine hundred deputies were present, there was no quorum, and so the congress had no power to confirm the Council of People's Commissars.

"I never knew that!"

They had said good night twice, and Uncle Avenir had asked whether he should leave the door open because it was a bit stuffy; but then for some reason the atomic bomb surfaced, and he came back to whisper fiercely, "They'll never make it themselves!"

"They may. In fact, I've heard that the first bomb will be tested very shortly."

"Nonsense!" Uncle Avenir said confidently. "They'll announce it, but who can check? They haven't got the industrial base for it. It would take them twenty years."

He turned to leave the room and came back yet again.

"But if they do succeed in making it, we're done for, Inok. We will lose all hope of freedom."

Innokenty lay on his back, his eyes drinking in the thick darkness.

"Yes, it will be dreadful. . . . They won't let it lie idle. . . . And without the bomb they'll never dare go to war."

"War is never the way out." (Uncle Avenir was back again.) "It isn't the advancing armies, the fires, and the bombing that make war terrible; it's terrible mainly because it gives stupidity legitimate power over intelligence. Still, that's the way it is with us even without war. . . . Now, go to sleep."

Household chores will not stand neglect. All that Uncle Avenir had skimped on that day awaited him the next morning, in addition to his usual routine. Before he left for the market, he took down two wads of newspaper, and Innokenty, knowing by now that it would be impossible to read them in the evening, hastened to look at them by daylight. The dried-out and dust-laden pages were unpleasant to the touch and left nasty smudges on the tips of his fingers. At first he kept washing or wiping the dirt off, but after a while he stopped noticing it, as he had stopped noticing all the house's defects—the uneven floors, the poor light from the windows—and his uncle's shabbiness. The earlier the year, the stranger it was to read about. He knew now that he would not be leaving that day either.

In the evening they all dined together again. Uncle Avenir was lively and cheerful, reminiscing about his student years, the Philosophy Department, noisy and jovial student Revolutionary circles in the days when there was no more interesting place than prison. He had never joined a political party, because all party programs, as he saw it, did violence to man's free will, and he did not acknowledge the prophetic superiority of party leaders to the rest of mankind.

Raisa Timofeevna interrupted his reminiscences from time to time to talk about her hospital and all the snapping and snarling that was part of her (and everybody else's) life.

Once more they closed the shutters and bolted them. Then Uncle Avenir opened a chest in one of the storerooms and with the aid of an oil lamp (there was no wiring there) pulled out some warm clothes smelling of mothballs, some of them just rags. Then he held the lamp high and showed his nephew his treasure: the smooth, painted bottom of the chest was lined with a copy of *Pravda* from the second day of the October Revolution. The banner headline read: COMRADES! WITH YOUR BLOOD YOU HAVE INSURED THAT THE CONSTITUENT ASSEMBLY, THE RIGHTFUL MASTER OF OUR LAND, WILL BE DULY CONVENED.

"That was before there had been any elections, of course. They didn't know yet how few would vote for them."

He repacked the chest slowly and neatly.

It was in the Constituent Assembly that the paths of Innokenty's father and uncle had crossed. Artem, his father, was one of the leaders of the land-based sailors who had dispersed the unspeakable Constituent Assembly, while Uncle Avenir had demonstrated in support of that long-promised and eagerly awaited body.

The demonstration with which Uncle Avenir had marched had gathered at the Troitsky Bridge. It was a mild, overcast winter day without wind or snow, and many of them wore open-necked shirts under their sheepskin coats. There were many students, high school pupils, and young ladies. Post office workers, telegraphers, civil servants. And miscellaneous individuals like Uncle Avenir. There were red flags carried by socialists and Revolutionaries and one or two green and white Kadet flags. A second demonstration, starting from the factories over the Neva, was entirely Social Democratic but also carried red flags.

This story was told last thing at night, and in the dark again, so as not to annoy Raisa Timofeevna. The house was shut up tight and in uneasy darkness, as all houses in Russia used to be in the far-off and forgotten time of feuds and murders, when people listened anxiously to the menacing sound of footsteps in the street and, if there was a moon, peered out through cracks in the shutters. There was no moon that night, and the streetlight was some way from the house. There were no gaps in these shutters, but a faint light struggling through the unshuttered window in the hallway and the wide-open door of their room occasionally allowed Innokenty to distinguish the movements rather than the contours of his uncle's head against the surrounding blackness. Unsupported by the shine of his eyes and the tormented lines of his face, his voice asserted itself all the more youthfully and assuredly.

"We marched grimly, in silence, not singing. We understood the importance of the occasion, but perhaps we didn't fully understand. This was the one and only day of a free Russian parliament, something that had not existed in the preceding five hundred years and would not exist in the one hundred years ahead. Who wanted this parliament anyway? How many of us had gathered, from all over Russia? Five thousand. . . . They opened fire on us from gateways, from rooftops, and then from the sidewalks, and they weren't shooting in the air but aiming point-blank at the demonstrators, chest high. Two or three fell out with each volley; the rest marched on. . . . None of us returned their fire; we didn't have a single revolver between us. They wouldn't let us get as far as the Tauride Palace. It was densely surrounded by sailors and Latvian sharpshooters. The Latvians decided our fate, little knowing what was in store for Latvia. On the Liteiny the Red Guards barred the way: 'Break it up! Get on the pavement!' They opened fire in short bursts. Red Guards tore one of the red flags out of our hands; I could tell you a thing or two about those Red Guards. . . . They broke the pole and trampled the flag underfoot. . . . Some of the demonstrators scattered; some ran back the way they'd come. The Red Guards fired on them from behind and killed some. They found it so easy, those Red Guards, shooting peaceful demonstrators in the back. Just imagine it, and remember that the Civil War hadn't begun yet! But their code of behavior was already worked out."

Uncle Avenir took a deep breath. "Nowadays January ninth is a red-letter day in the calendar, but January fifth you can't even mention in a whisper."

He heaved another sigh.

"And then there was the low trick they played pretending that they opened fire on us because the demonstration was organized by supporters of Kaledin. What did we have to do with Kaledin? I ask you. Some people can't understand the idea of opposition within their own ranks. Who are these people who walk among us, speak our language, and demand what they call freedom? We must at all costs disown them, connect them with the enemy outside, and then we can comfortably open fire on them."

The silence in the darkness was more tense and meaningful than ever.

The old wire mattress creaked as Innokenty pulled himself up against the bedboard.

"What happened inside the Tauride?"

"On the eve of the Epiphany?" Uncle Avenir took a deep breath. "The mob, the okhlos,* was in full cry. . . . Deafening three-fingered whistles. . . . Filthy language drowned the speeches. They banged their rifle butts on the floor, with or without reason. They were on guard duty, you see. Guarding whom, against what? So-called soldiers and sailors, half of them drunk, spewing in the refreshment room, snoring on sofas, spitting out the husks of their sunflower seeds all over the foyer. Put yourself in the place of a deputy, an educated man, and tell me what you would do with that filthy rabble. A tap on the shoulder or a quiet telling-off would be blatant counterrevolution! An insult to sacred mob rule! Besides, they were wearing crossed machine-gun belts over their tunics. They had grenades and Mausers at their belts. In the hall where the Constituent Assembly met, they sat with rifles even among the general public, stood in the passageways rifles in hand, leveled them at speakers as though they were targets on the range. Somebody would be talking about some sort of democratic peace and the nationalization of the land, and twenty muzzles would be trained on him, foresights and backsights in alignment. If they killed him, it wouldn't even cost them an apology! Bring on the next one! Sitting there with their rifles aimed at the speaker's mouth! That's all you need to know about them. That's what they were like when they took over Russia, that's what they always had been, and that's what they'll be as long as they live. They may change in some respects but not in essentials. Then there was Sverdlov, snatching the bell from the senior deputy's hand, shoving him aside, refusing to let him declare the assembly open. Lewin sat in the government box laughing up his sleeve, reveling in it all. As for People's Commissar Karelin, one of the Left SRs, he was roaring his head off! He didn't have the wit to realize what he was letting himself in for! In six months' time his own gang would be snuffed out! You know the rest . . . you've seen it at the cinema. The cloth-headed commissar with the cudgel, Drubber Dubenko, sent his boys to declare the superfluous assembly closed. The dry-land sailors with their cartridge belts and pistols rose to catch the chairman's eye. . . ."

"Including my father?"

"Yes, including your father. The great Civil War hero. Almost at the very

* Okhlos: Greek word for *mob*.

time when your mother . . . gave in to him. They loved smacking their lips over delicately nurtured young ladies from good homes. That was the most mouthwatering prize the Revolution had to offer them."

Innokenty's brow, ears, cheeks, and neck were burning. He was on fire, as though he himself had taken part in some vile act.

His uncle pressed a hand on his knee, leaned closer and asked, "Have you never felt the truth of the saying that the sins of the parents are visited on the children? And that you must cleanse yourself of them?"

# 62

## Two Sons-in-Law

THE PUBLIC PROSECUTOR'S FIRST WIFE had gone through the Civil War with him. She was a proficient machine-gunner; her life was regulated by the latest instructions from her Party cell. She could never have raised the house of Makarygin to its present level of prosperity. Indeed, it is difficult to imagine how, if she had not died giving birth to Klara, she could have adjusted to the intricate twists and turns of the times.

Alevtina Nikanorovna, Makarygin's present wife, on the other hand, had transformed the family's life, enriching and filling with new sap what had been a stunted and parched existence. She had no very clear conception of class distinctions, and political instruction had taken up very little of her time. What she knew for certain was that a respectable family cannot thrive without good cooking and an abundance of good quality bed and table linen. And that as the family consolidates its position, such important outward signs of prosperity as silver, cut glass, and fine carpets must make their appearance. Alevtina Nikanorovna's great talent was for acquiring these things without great expense, never missing a good buy—at closed auctions, in the private shops for employees in the procuratorial and judicial system, in commission shops, or in the flea markets of "newly incorporated territories." She made special journeys to Lvov and Riga when no one could get there without a pass and when old ladies were only too glad to sell their heavy tablecloths and their dinner services for a song. She became a great expert on glassware. She did not collect the glass now produced by the state Glass Combine, warped in its passage through relays of indifferent hands, but old-fashioned crystal that somehow preserved the character of its creator and sparkled with his craftsmanship. A great deal of it had been confiscated by court order in the twenties and thirties and sold later to a privileged few.

That evening, as always, the table was beautifully laid and the food so plentiful that the two very young Bashkir maids, the Makarygins' own and another borrowed from the neighbors for the party, could hardly keep up with the rapid succession of dishes. Both girls were from the same village, Chekmagush, and had left school together the summer before. Their faces, tense and flushed from the heat of the kitchen, showed awareness of the importance of the occasion and eagerness to please. They were satisfied with their position and hoped that not by next spring but by the one after they would have earned enough and bought the right clothes to find husbands in the city instead of going back to the kolkhoz. Alevtina Nikanorovna, a fine figure of a woman whom no one would call old, watched the servants with approval.

What particularly preoccupied the hostess was the last-minute change of plan. It was to have been a party for the youngsters. The only older people present were to be members of the family. Makarygin had given a banquet for his colleagues two days earlier and this time had invited only the Serb Dushan Radovich, an old friend of his from the Civil War and subsequently a professor in the long-abolished Institute of Red Professors. Apart from him, a humble girlhood friend of the prosecutor's wife, in Moscow on a shopping expedition from the rural district where her husband was a minor Party official, had been allowed to attend. But then, quite unexpectedly, Major General Slovuta, also a prosecutor and a very important man in the service, had arrived back from the Far East (where he was involved in the sensational trial of the Japanese officers accused of planning bacteriological warfare), and it was impossible not to invite him. But now, in Slovuta's presence, they felt ashamed of those semilegal guests, the prosecutor's old friend and the friend of his wife's youth, both hardly friends anymore. Slovuta might think that the Makarygins entertained riffraff. This thought was complicating and poisoning Alevtina Nikanorovna's evening. She seated her old friend, who was miserable because she was married to a nitwit, as far from Slovuta as possible, and made her talk quietly and attack her food less greedily. At the same time, the hostess was gratified that her friend tried every dish, asked for recipes, and was enchanted in turn by the tableware and the guests.

It was for Slovuta's sake that they had invited Innokenty so pressingly, insisting that he should come in his diplomatic uniform, with the gold braid, and so, together with their other son-in-law, the celebrated writer Nikolai Galakhov, make the occasion no ordinary one. But to his father-in-law's annoyance, the diplomat had arrived late, when supper was over and the young people had drifted away to dance.

Innokenty had reluctantly given in and put on that accursed uniform. On the way there, he had felt like a lost soul. But staying at home was just as impossible. There was nowhere he could bear to be. And yet, when he entered, sour faced, an apartment full of people, of animated chatter, laughter, and color, he felt that this was the one place in which he could not possibly be arrested and quickly recovered his equilibrium, indeed felt more relaxed than usual. He eagerly drank what was poured out for him, eagerly helped himself from one dish and another; for twenty-four hours he had scarcely been able to swallow, but now his appetite was happily roused.

His high spirits mollified his father-in-law and made conversation easier at the "distinguished" end of the table, where Makarygin had been desperately maneuvering to prevent Radovich from firing off some provocative remark, to keep Slovuta happy, and to make sure Galakhov was not bored. Now, lowering his rich bass voice, he began jokingly reproving Innokenty for not gladdening his old age with grandchildren.

"What do you think of him and his wife?" he grumbled. "Here they are, a well-matched couple, a ram and a ewe—and what do they do, they just live for themselves, get fat, not a care in the world. They've got it made! And they burn the candle at both ends! Ask this young dog, and he'll tell you he's an Epicurean. Am I right, Innokenty? Own up, now, you're a follower of Epicurus, aren't you?

It was impossible, even as a joke, to call a member of the All-Union Communist Party a Young Hegelian, a Neo-Kantian, a subjectivist, an agnostic, or—God forbid—a revisionist. But "Epicurean" sounded so inoffensive that it couldn't possibly affect a man's claim to be an orthodox Marxist.

Radovich, who knew and cherished every detail in the biographies of the Founding Fathers, seized his opportunity to contribute.

"Well, Epicurus was a good man, a materialist. Karl Marx himself wrote a dissertation on Epicurus."

Radovich was wearing a threadbare semimilitary tunic, and his skin was dark parchment stretched over a blocky head. (He had never left the house without his Budenny helmet until just recently, when the militia started pulling him over.)

Innokenty warmed to the theme and looked challengingly at these unsuspecting people. What a bold step it was, to intervene in a struggle between Titans! At that moment he saw himself as the darling of the gods. For Makarygin, and even for Slovuta, both of whom might have aroused his contempt at any other time, he felt a sort of affection, because they were fellow men and also contributors to his present safety.

"Epicurus?" He accepted the challenge, eyes twinkling. "Yes, I'm his follower; I don't deny it. But it may surprise you to learn that 'epicurean' is one of those words which are wrongly understood in common usage. When people want to say that someone has an inordinate appetite for life, is sensual, lustful, or even just a hog, they say, 'He's an epicurean.' No, wait a minute, I'm serious about this!" He cut short their protests, excitedly waving the empty tall-stemmed wineglass he held in his thin, sensitive fingers. "In fact, Epicurus is just the opposite of our general conception of him. He most certainly does not incite us to take part in orgies. Among the three main evils that prevent men from being happy, Epicurus includes insatiable desires! You didn't know that, did you? He says that in reality man needs very little, and for that very reason his happiness is not at fate's mercy! He frees man from fear of fate's blows, and that makes Epicurus a great optimist!"

"You do surprise me!" Galakhov said, and took out a leather-bound notebook complete with white ivory pencil. In spite of his resounding fame, Galakhov behaved like one of the boys and went in for winking and backslapping. His graying blond hair made a picturesque contrast to his swarthy, rather fleshy features.

"Quick, give him another drink," Slovuta said to Makarygin, pointing to Innokenty's empty glass, "or he'll talk our heads off."

His father-in-law filled his glass, and once more Innokenty drank with enjoyment. At that moment he almost felt himself that Epicurus's philosophy was worth adopting.

Slovuta, whose face was puffy but not that of an old man, treated Makarygin with a certain condescension (his promotion to colonel general had already been approved) but was delighted to make Galakhov's acquaintance. He pictured himself later that evening making another visit he had in mind and casually announcing that an hour ago he had been having a few drinks with Kolya Galakhov, who had told him. . . . But Galakhov, too, had arrived late and, for once, said nothing at all; no doubt his mind was on his next novel. Concluding that there was nothing to be gotten from the celebrity, Slovuta was ready to leave.

Makarygin, however, urged him to stay a bit longer and persuaded him that they "must worship at the altar of tobacco," by which he meant the collection he kept in his study. He himself smoked Bulgarian pipe tobacco, which he got through a friend, and made do with cigars in the evening. But he liked to impress his guests by regaling them with different blends in turn.

The door to his study was right behind them. Their host opened it and invited Slovuta and his sons-in-law to step inside. The sons-in-law, however, made excuses and left the older men to their own company. Makarygin, more afraid than ever that Dushan would let his tongue run away with him, stood aside to let Slovuta enter and wagged a warning finger at the Serb in the doorway.

The brothers-in-law were left by themselves at the deserted end of the table. They were at that happy age (Galakhov was the older by a few years) at which, though still considered young, they were no longer dragged off to dance, and they could indulge in men's talk among the half-empty bottles to the accompaniment of music somewhere in the background.

A week ago, in fact, Galakhov had conceived the idea of writing about the imperialist conspiracy and the struggle of Soviet diplomats for peace, not a novel this time but a play, which would make it easier for him to avoid all the unfamiliar details of locale and dress. This was an excellent opportunity to interview his brother-in-law, simultaneously noting the characteristics of a typical Soviet diplomat and extracting detailed information about life in the West, where the whole action of the play was to take place but where Galakhov himself had been only very briefly, at one of the "progressive" congresses. Galakhov realized that it wasn't quite the thing to be writing about a way of life of which you knew nothing, but in recent years he had found that life abroad or some hoary historical theme or even fantasy about the inhabitants of the moon yielded more easily to his pen than the real life all around him, where every path lay through a minefield of taboos.

The servants were rattling tea things. The hostess looked about her and, with Slovuta out of the way, no longer tried to keep her old friend's voice down as she insisted that even in the Zarechensky raion there were good medical facilities, good doctors, and that the children of Party activists were separated from the rest in early infancy and assured of an uninterrupted supply of milk and unstinted penicillin injections.

Music reached them from a record player in the next room and the metallic boom of a television set from the room beyond.

Bright-eyed and confident after his triumphant defense of Epicurus, Innokenty assented.

"It's the privilege of writers to interrogate. Like investigating officers, endlessly questioning people about their crimes."

"What we look for in a man is not his crimes but his virtues, his positive characteristics."

"Then the demands of your work are at odds with those of your conscience. You say you want to write a book about diplomats?"

Galakhov smiled.

"Say what you like, Ink, these things need more thought than a New Year interview. You need to stock up with material in advance. And you can't start questioning just any diplomat. It's my good luck we're related."

"And your choice shows how perceptive you are. A diplomat who wasn't a relative would tell you a load of nonsense. There are things we need to hide, you know."

They looked into each other's eyes.

"I realize that. But I won't be trying to show that side of your work. I'm not—"

"Aha! What mainly interests you, then, is embassy life, our daily routine, what goes on at receptions, the presentation of credentials, and all that. . . ."

"No, I want to go deeper than that. I want to show how certain things are refracted in the minds of Soviet diplomats."

"Refracted, eh. . . . Right, I've got it. And I'll tell you all about it before the evening's out. But you tell me something first. What about the war? Have you given up writing about it? Have you exhausted the subject?"

Galakhov shook his head. "It can never be exhausted."

"Yes, that war was your good luck. Where else would you have found your conflicts and tragedies?"

Innokenty was still smiling.

The writer's brow clouded over.

"The war theme," he said, "is engraved on my heart."

"And you've created masterpieces in that genre!"

"And I daresay it will be with me forever. I will keep returning to it as long as I live."

"Perhaps it would be better not to?"

"I must! Because the war stirs noble emotions in men's souls. . . ."

"It does, I agree. But what does all this war literature come down to? How to take up battle stations, how to carry out a saturation bombardment, 'we'll never forget, never forgive,' an officer's command is law to his subordinates. But all that is much better put in army regulations. Oh, yes, and you also show what difficulty the wretched officers have in locating anything on a map."

Galakhov frowned. Commanding officers were his favorite military characters.

"Are you talking about my last novel?"

"Of course not, Nikolai! But do works of imagination really have to reproduce army regulations? or newspaper articles? or slogans? Mayakovsky, for one, took pride in using an excerpt from a newspaper as the epigraph to a poem. In other words, he prided himself on not rising above the level of a newspaper. If that's how you think, what's the point of literature? After all, a writer exists to teach other people. Isn't that what was always expected of him?"

The brothers-in-law met infrequently and did not know each other well.

"What you say is true only under bourgeois regimes," Galakhov replied cautiously.

Innokenty wasn't going to argue with that.

"Of course, of course. Our laws are quite different. . . . I didn't mean to. . . ." He made a circular movement with his hand. "Please believe me, Kolya. I really like you. . . . And that's why I particularly want to ask you . . . while I'm in the mood . . . as one of the family. . . . Have you ever asked yourself . . . How do you see your place in Russian literature? I mean, you've written enough for a six-volume collected works. You're thirty-seven . . . they'd already bumped Pushkin off at your age. You're not in danger of that. Still, you can't evade the question: Who are you? Is this tormented age any the richer for your ideas? Apart, of course, from the incontrovertible ideas you yourself owe to socialist realism." Innokenty abandoned sarcasm and asked his next question as though it hurt.

"Tell me, Kolya, don't you sometimes feel ashamed of our generation?"

Small furrows came and went on Galakhov's brow, and he sucked his cheeks in.

"You're touching me on a sensitive spot," he answered, staring at the tablecloth. "What Russian writer hasn't secretly tried on Pushkin's frock coat? Or

Tolstoy's blouse?" He turned his pencil this way and that on the tablecloth and looked at Innokenty with eyes that had nothing to hide. He, too, felt an urge to speak out, to say things that couldn't be said with other writers present. "When I was a kid, at the beginning of the Five-Year Plans, I thought I would die happy if I could just see my name in print over a poem. I imagined that would be the beginning of immortality. But then. . . ."

Dotnara advanced on them, avoiding empty chairs or pushing them out of her way.

"Ini! Kolya! You won't shoo me off, will you? Are you talking about something too clever for me?"

She couldn't have chosen a worse moment.

As she came toward them, the very sight of her, the thought that she was an inescapable part of his life, suddenly brought home to Innokenty the dreadful truth. He remembered what awaited him. The party and the humorous exchanges at table ceased to exist. His heart sank. His throat was hot and dry.

Meanwhile, Dotty stood waiting for an answer, toying with the edges of her raglan blouse. Her fair hair fell loosely over her narrow fur collar. She knew how to make the best of herself and had ignored nine years of changing hairstyles. She was flushed—or was it the cherry red blouse that made her look like that? And there was that doelike tremor of the upper lip that he knew and loved. It happened when someone paid her a compliment or obviously found her attractive. But why just now?

She had been trying for so long to emphasize how independent of him she was, how different her view of life was from his. Why this sudden change? A presentiment that they were to part? Why was she suddenly so meek and affectionate? Why that doelike twitch of the lip?

Innokenty could never forgive her and had not even asked himself whether he could forgive her for the long spell of incomprehension, estrangement, and unfaithfulness. He knew that she, too, could not change all at once. But this meekness of hers warmed his cramped heart. He took her hand and drew her onto a chair beside him, something that would have been impossible between them all through the autumn.

Dotty submitted gracefully, sat down beside her husband, and clung to him, not indecorously close but close enough for all to see how much she loved him and how happy she was to be with him. It occurred to Innokenty briefly, with Dotty's future in mind, that it would be better for her not to make this show of an intimacy that did not really exist. But he gently stroked her arm in the cherry red sleeve.

The writer's white ivory pencil lay idle.

Leaning on the table, Galakhov stared past husband and wife at the big window, which was lit by the streetlights at the Kaluga Gate. He could not talk frankly about himself with women around. Nor, perhaps, without them.

But . . . nowadays his poems, however long, appeared in print. Hundreds of theaters throughout the country put on his plays after their run in Moscow. Girls copied out his verses and learned them by heart. The central press had happily put its pages at his disposal during the war. He had tried his hand at the feuilleton, the long short story, criticism. And finally his novel had appeared. He had won one Stalin Prize, then another and yet another. And where had it gotten him? Strangely, he had won fame but not immortality.

He himself had not noticed when and how he had overburdened the bird of immortality and crippled its flight. Perhaps it had taken wing only in those few lines that schoolgirls memorized. As for the plays, the stories, the novel, they had died on him before he had reached the age of thirty-seven.

But why should anyone strive for immortality? Most of Galakhov's fellow writers had no thought of immortality. What mattered to them was their position in their own lifetime. To hell with immortality, they said; surely it's more important to influence the course of events here and now? And influence it they did. Their books served the people, they were published in print runs of hundreds of thousands, government subsidies assured their dissemination to libraries everywhere, and special book-promotion months were organized for them. Of course, much that was true could not be written about. But they consoled themselves with the thought that circumstances would change someday, and they would return to the same events, show them in a different and truer light, publish amended versions of their old books. Meanwhile, the thing to do was to write at least that quarter, that eighth, that sixteenth, or—yes, damn it!—that one thirty-second part of the truth which was permitted. Write about love and kisses and the beauties of nature if you like; any little thing was better than nothing.

But Galakhov was oppressed by a feeling that every decent page was harder to write than the last one. He forced himself to work to a timetable, struggled against his yawning fits, his mental sluggishness, his wandering thoughts, his habit of listening for the mailman and breaking off to look at the newspapers. He saw to it that his study was aired, that the room temperature was 18°C, that his desk was clean and polished; otherwise, he could not write.

Whenever he started on a new, large work, he was full of fire and swore to himself and his friends that this time he would make no concessions, that he would write a real book. He sat down enthusiastically to write the first pages. But he soon began to notice that he was not alone, that an image floated up and hovered ever more distinctly before him, the image of the one for whom he was writing and with whose eyes he willy-nilly reread each newly written paragraph. And this one was not the reader, his brother, friend, and contemporary, nor was he a generalized critic, but for some reason always the illustrious critic in chief, Yermilov.

Galakhov could not help imagining Yermilov reading this new work with his chin flattened against his chest, preparing to open fire on it with an enormous (it had happened before) full-page article in *Literary Gazette*. He would give it some such title as "Unwholesome Trends" or "Another Look at Certain Fashionable Tendencies on Our Tried and Tested Path." He would not get straight to the point but would begin with some sacrosanct statement by Belinsky or Nekrasov with which only a villain could fail to agree. Then he would carefully twist these words, turn them around till they meant something quite different, and Belinsky or Herzen would be seen passionately attesting that Galakhov's new book showed him to be an antisocial, antihuman figure with shaky philosophical foundations.

Trying paragraph after paragraph to anticipate Yermilov's objections and adjust himself to them, Galakhov soon weakened in his efforts to express himself fully. Of its own accord the book spinelessly curled up and collapsed. When he was already halfway through, Galakhov saw that a different book had been foisted on him, and he had another failure on his hands.

"Oh, yes, you were asking what Soviet diplomats are like." Innokenty resumed where he had left off. But his voice was hollow, and he wore a wry smile. "You can easily imagine them for yourself. Firm ideological convictions. High principles. Total dedication to the cause. Profound personal devotion to Comrade Stalin. Unswerving adherence to instructions from Moscow. Some have a very good, others a poor knowledge of foreign languages. And then of course their great enthusiasm for the pleasures of the flesh. Because, as the saying goes, we only live once."

# 63

## The Diehard

RADOVICH WAS A LONGTIME LOSER, an all-around loser. It had started back in the thirties—lectures canceled, books rejected, and to cap it all he was plagued by ill health. He had a splinter from one of Kolchak's shells in his chest, he had suffered from a duodenal ulcer for fifteen years, and every morning for many years past he had carried out the excruciating procedure of irrigating his stomach through the esophagus, without which he could not eat and go on living.

But Radovich's misfortunes were also his salvation. A conspicuous figure in Comintern circles, he had survived in the critical years only because he had never set foot outside a hospital. Illness had been his refuge again in the past year, when all the Serbs left in the Soviet Union had either been dragooned into the anti-Tito movement or thrown into jail.

Realizing how equivocal his position was, Radovich made a superhuman effort to restrain himself to say nothing, to avoid being drawn into fanatical disputes, to live the subdued life of an invalid.

Now, too, he was holding himself in check, helped by the "smoker's table." This was a small, oval table of dark wood, placed conveniently in the study to hold cigarette papers and a roller for filling them, a selection of pipes in a rack, and a mother-of-pearl ashtray. Near the table stood a tobacco cabinet of Karelian birchwood with numerous drawers containing a variety of cigarettes with cardboard mouthpieces, cigarettes without mouthpieces, cigars, pipe tobaccos, and even snuff.

Listening in silence to Slovuta's account of preparations for biological warfare and the hideous crimes of Japanese officers against humanity, Radovich eagerly sniffed the contents of the drawers, trying to decide what to settle for. Smoking was suicide, strictly forbidden by all his doctors. But since he was also forbidden to drink or to eat (he had eaten practically nothing that evening), his sense of smell and his tastebuds were particularly sensitive to shades of difference between tobaccos. Life without smoking seemed flat. In his straitened circumstances he preferred to buy "homegrown" tobacco in peasant markets and roll his own cigarettes in newspaper. As an evacuee in

Sterlitamak, he used to buy a leaf of homegrown from some old man with a private plot and dry it and cut it himself. Preparing his tobacco helped him to think in the empty hours of bachelorhood.

If Radovich had put his oar in, he would not in fact have said anything very terrible. His own views were not so far away from what the state required people to think. But Stalin's Party, which was even less tolerant of fine shades of difference than of clashing colors, would have beheaded him in a trice for the smidgen of difference between them.

Luckily he managed to contain himself, and the conversation moved on from the Japanese to the relative merits of particular cigars, of which Slovuta knew so little that he almost choked on an incautious puff, to the fact that although the number of prosecutors grew from year to year, their work steadily increased.

"What do the crime statistics have to say?" Radovich asked. An apparently casual question—his parchmentlike features were expressionless.

The crime statistics had nothing to say. They were dumb, they were invisible, and nobody knew whether they still existed.

Which did not prevent Slovuta from saying, "The statistics tell us that the number of crimes is going down."

He had not seen the actual figures, but he had read what the papers had to say about them.

He added just as sincerely, "But there's still plenty of crime. It's a legacy from the old regime. The people are very corrupt. Corrupted by bourgeois ideology."

Three-quarters of those who went through the courts were born after 1917, but this did not enter Slovuta's head. It was not something he had read.

Makarygin tossed his head. He didn't need to be told this!

"When Vladimir Ilyich told us that the cultural Revolution would be much more difficult than the October Revolution, we couldn't take it in. We realize now how farsighted he was."

Makarygin had a backless head and prominent ears.

They puffed away companionably, filling the study with smoke.

Half of Makarygin's small, highly polished desk was occupied by a big inkstand with a representation almost half a meter high of the Spassky Tower, complete with clock and star. The two massive inkwells (made to look like turrets on the Kremlin Wall) were dry. It was a long time since Makarygin had done any writing at home. He had plenty of time during office hours, and he wrote his letters with a fountain pen. Behind the glass doors of the Riga bookcases stood legal codes, collections of laws, sets of *Soviet State and Law*, the *Great Soviet Encyclopedia* (the old erroneous edition, complete with "enemies of the people"), the new *Great Soviet Encyclopedia* (still with "enemies of the people"), and the *Small Encyclopedia* (also with mistakes and also containing "enemies of the people").

It was a long time since Makarygin had opened any of these volumes because all of them, including the still officially operative but in fact hopelessly out-of-date Criminal Code of 1926, had been felicitously replaced by a bundle of supremely important and for the most part secret instructions, each of which he knew by its number—083 or 005/2742. These instructions, encapsulating all the wisdom of the judicial system, he kept in a single small file in his office. Here, in his study, books were kept not to be read but to inspire respect. The books Makarygin did read—in bed, on trains, at health resorts—were detective stories, which he kept hidden in a windowless cabinet.

A big portrait of Stalin in his generalissimo's uniform hung over the desk, and there was a small bust of Lenin on a shelf.

Slovuta was a big-bellied man bursting out of his uniform, and the folds of his neck hung over his stiff collar. He looked around the study and gave it his approval.

"This is what I call living, Makarygin."

"I don't know. . . . I'm thinking of getting a transfer to oblast level."

"Oblast level?" Slovuta turned it over quickly in his mind. His was not the face of a thinker—the heavy jaw and fat cheeks were its strong features—but he was quick to grasp essentials.

"Well, there might be some sense in it."

They both knew what the point would be, and Radovich didn't need to know. Oblast prosecutors got "packets" in addition to their basic salary. In the central military procuracy, you had to reach high rank before you could expect that.

"Your older son-in-law is a triple laureate?"

"He is," the prosecutor answered proudly.

"And the younger one hasn't made counselor first class yet?"

"Only second class at present."

"He's damned smart, though; he'll make ambassador someday! Who do you think of marrying your youngest to?"

"She's an obstinate wench, Slovuta. I've tried to marry her off, but she won't have it."

"An educated girl like her. What's she looking for? An engineer?"

When Slovuta laughed, not only his belly but the whole upper part of his body heaved convulsively. "With eight hundred rubles a month? Take my advice, and marry her to a Chekist*; that's the best bet."

As if Makarygin didn't know it! In fact, he regarded his own life as a failure because he hadn't managed to break into that charmed circle. The dimmest little operations officer in the most out-of-the-way hole had more power and got a bigger salary than an important law officer in the capital. The whole procuracy was regarded as a pointless farce, not worth its keep. Makarygin's failure to become a Chekist was an inwardly bleeding wound.

"Right, then. Thank you for not forgetting me, Makarygin. Don't press me to stay; I'm expected elsewhere. And you, Professor, look after yourself; don't go getting ill again."

"All the best, Comrade General."

Radovich got up to say good-bye to the departing guest, but Slovuta didn't hold out his hand. Radovich's hurt look followed his fellow guest's broad, round-shouldered figure as Makarygin escorted him to his car. Left alone with the books, he turned his attention to them. He drew his hand along a shelf and, after some hesitation, pulled out a book and was making for a chair when suddenly he noticed another small volume in a motley red-and-black binding on the table. He picked that up, too.

This other book burned his lifeless parchment-skinned hands. It was *Tito:Traitor in Chief*, by a certain Renaud de Jouvenel, just published in a first edition of one million copies.

Countless thousands of base, vicious, lying books had come Radovich's way in the last dozen years, but it seemed a long time since he had held in his hands anything so obscene. He skimmed the new book's pages with an old bookworm's practiced eye, and it took him two minutes to work out who had thought such a book necessary and why, what sort of reptile its author was, and how much additional animus it would stir up against innocent Yugoslavia. His eye was caught by this sentence:

---

* Chekist: A Chekist belongs to the Cheka, a shorthand term for the original name of the Soviet secret police (1917-1922), the full name being the All-Russian Extraordinary Commission for Combating Counterrevolution and Sabotage and Speculation.

"There is no need to dwell in detail on László Rajk's motives for confessing: *He did confess—so obviously he was guilty*." Radovich, disgusted, put the book back where it had been. Of course there was no need to dwell in detail on his motives! No need to dwell in detail on the way interrogators and torturers beat Rajk, tormented him with hunger and sleeplessness, spread him out on the floor, perhaps, so that they could pinch his genitals with the toe of a boot. (Abramson, a prisoner of long standing with whom Radovich had felt a close affinity from the moment they met at Sterlitamak, had told him all about the NKVD's little ways.) He had confessed—so obviously he was guilty! The *summa summarum* of Stalinist justice!

But Yugoslavia was too sore a point to touch on in conversation with Pyotr, then and there. So when his host returned, automatically casting a loving glance at the new decoration lying beside the tarnished older ones, Dushan was sitting quietly in his chair and reading a volume of the *Encyclopedia*.

"They don't lavish honors on public prosecutors," Makarygin said with a sigh. "They gave some away for the thirtieth anniversary, but only a few people got them."

He very much wanted to talk about decorations and why he had been one of those honored on that occasion, but Radovich lowered his head and went on reading.

Makarygin took another cigar from the drawer and plopped down on the sofa.

"Thank you, Dushan, for not sounding off. I was afraid you might."

"What could I have said to embarrass you?" Radovich asked in surprise.

"Lots of things!" Makarygin clipped his cigar. "You're always sticking your neck out." He lit his cigar. "Like when he was telling us about the Japanese . . . it was on the tip of your tongue."

Radovich shot upright. "Because a filthy police provocation stinks ten thousand kilometers off!"

"Dushan! You must be out of your mind! Don't dare talk like that in my presence! How can you talk like that about our Party?"

Radovich hedged.

"I'm not talking about the Party. I'm talking about Slovuta and his ilk. Why have we suddenly discovered in 1949 what the Japanese were up to in 1943? After all, we've had Japanese prisoners here for four years. And what's this about the Americans dropping Colorado beetles on us from the air? Is that true as well?"

Makarygin's bat ears reddened.

"Why shouldn't it be? And if it doesn't quite add up, it's still politically necessary."

The parchment-colored Radovich began turning pages irritably.

Makarygin smoked in silence. Should never have invited the man. Only let myself down in Slovuta's eyes. Old friendships aren't worth bothering about. Best to let them remain memories. The man can't even behave with normal politeness, show some awareness of what gives his host pleasure and what worries him, as any guest should.

He smoked on. Unpleasant scenes with his youngest daughter came into his mind. Whenever they dined without guests, just the three of them, in recent months, what should have been a relaxed and cozy family meal had become a dogfight at the table. The other day she had been pounding a nail down in her shoe, singing some meaningless rigmarole as she did so, but to a tune her father knew only too well. Trying to keep cool, he remarked, "You might have chosen a different song to go with that job, Klara. 'The Wide, Wide World's Aflood with Tears' is a song people died or went to Siberia singing."

Out of sheer willfulness or for whatever reason, she bridled and said, "Did they, now, noble souls! Went to Siberia, did they? Well, they're still going!"

The prosecutor was taken aback by the impertinence and impropriety of the analogy. How could anybody so completely lose all sense of historical perspective? Barely restraining himself from striking his daughter, he tore the shoe from her hands and hurled it to the floor.

"How can you make such comparisons! Between the party of the working class and that fascist scum!"

She was so hardened that she wouldn't cry even if you punched her in the head. She stood there with one shoe on and one stockinged foot on the parquet floor.

"Spare me the rhetoric, Daddy! What do you have to do with the working class? You were a worker for two years once, but you've been a prosecutor for thirty now! Call yourself a worker—there isn't so much as a hammer in the house! Being determines consciousness—you're the one who taught us that!"

"Social being, you idiot! And social consciousness!"

"Take your choice, then. Some live in palaces and some in pigsties; some ride in cars and others have holes in their shoes. Which society are you talking about?"

Her father was left gasping. The age-old impossibility of briefly and clearly explaining to foolish young minds the wisdom of their elders. . . .

"You're just stupid! You understand nothing, and you refuse to learn!"

"So teach me! Teach me! Whose money do you live on? Why do they pay you thousands when you produce nothing?"

The prosecutor had no answer to that; or, rather, the answer was obvious, but you couldn't come straight out with it. He could only say heatedly, "Well, what do you do to earn eighteen hundred in your institute?"

His hard feelings toward his old friend were suddenly forgotten.

"Tell me, Dushan," he said, "what am I going to do with this daughter of mine?"

Makarygin's ears stuck out from his head like the wings of a sphinx. A look of bewilderment was strangely out of place on that face.

"How could it come to this, Dushan? When we had Konchak on the run, could we ever have imagined what sort of gratitude we would get from our children? If they have to take the platform and swear allegiance to the Party, the wretches rattle it off inaudibly as if they were ashamed."

He told Radovich the story of the shoe.

"What ought I to have answered?" he asked.

Radovich took a grubby scrap of chamois leather out of his pocket and cleaned his glasses. There was a time when Makarygin had known all the answers, but his mind seemed to have gone to sleep.

"What should you have said? You should have told her about cumulative labor. Education, special qualifications, are a form of accumulated labor and are more highly paid." He put his glasses on again and looked hard at the prosecutor.

"Still, the girl is basically right. We were warned often enough."

The prosecutor was taken aback. "Warned? By whom?"

"We must know how to learn from our enemies." Dushan raised a bony finger. '"The Wide, Wide World Is Drowned in Tears.' How many thousands do you get? While a cleaner gets 250 rubles?"

One of Makarygin's cheeks twitched. Dushan had become spiteful. Envied others because he had nothing himself.

"You've gone crazy in your hermit's cave! You're out of touch with real life! You'll come to a bad end! What am I supposed to do, go along tomorrow and ask to be paid 250 a month? How could I live on that? Anyway, they'd take me for a madman and kick me out! Nobody else is going to refuse the money!"

Dushan pointed at the bust of Lenin. "Remember how Ilyich refused to eat butter during the Civil War? Or white bread? Did people think *he* was mad?"

Dushan sounded almost tearful.

Makarygin warded off his attack with splayed fingers.

"Bah! You mean you believed it? Lenin didn't go without butter, never fear. In fact, there was a pretty good staff dining room in the Kremlin even in those days."

Radovich rose. His foot had gone to sleep, and he limped over to the shelf and picked up a framed photograph of a young woman in a leather jacket holding a Mauser.

"Didn't Lena side with Shlyapnikov? Do you remember what the Workers' Opposition said?"

"Put it down!" Makarygin had turned pale. "Don't disturb her memory! You're just a diehard! A diehard!"

"No, I'm no diehard! I just want Leninist purity."

Radovich lowered his voice.

"Nobody writes about it here. In Yugoslavia there's workers' control in industry. . . ."

Makarygin gave an unfriendly laugh. "Of course, you're a Serb, and it isn't easy for a Serb to be objective. I understand and I forgive you. But. . . ."

But . . . they had reached the brink.

Radovich fell silent and shrank into himself, became a desiccated little man again.

"Finish what you were saying, you diehard, you!" Makarygin angrily demanded. "According to you, the semifascist regime in Yugoslavia is real socialism? And what we have here is a degenerate form? That's all old stuff. We heard it long ago. Only, those who said it are in kingdom come now. You'll be saying next that we're doomed to perish in the struggle with the capitalist world. Am I right?"

"No! No!" Radovich shot up again, his face radiant with prophetic certainty. "That will never happen! The capitalist world is consumed by much worse contradictions. Great Lenin foretold, and I firmly believe, that we shall soon witness armed conflict over markets between the United States and Britain!"

# 64

## Entered Cities First

IN THE BIG ROOM they were dancing to a record player, one of the new, console type. The Makarygins had a cabinet full of records. There were the speeches of their Father and Friend, mumbling and droning with his Georgian accent. (No home could be called well supplied without them, though normal people, the Makarygins included, never listened to them.) There were songs about "Our Own, Our Beloved Leader" and songs in which airplanes "came first," while girls took second place (though listening to them here would have been as improper as speaking seriously of biblical miracles in a pre-Revolutionary drawing room). The records in fashion now were imported but not to be found in the shops and never broadcast by Soviet radio. They even included songs sung by the émigré Leshchenko.

The furniture took up too much room for all the couples to dance at once, so they took turns. The young people present included girls who had been Klara's classmates; a man from their class whose job now was jamming foreign broadcasts; the girl, a relative of the prosecutor, who was responsible for Shchagov's presence; a nephew of the prosecutor's wife, a lieutenant in the Internal Security Troops whom everybody called a "frontier guard" because of his green piping (his company was in fact attached to the Belorussian Station in Moscow to inspect passengers' documents on trains and carry out arrests that proved necessary en route). One young man, a statesmanlike figure with smooth, already thinning hair, stood out from all the rest; he already had the Order of Lenin but wore just the ribbon, without the medal itself, carelessly (or carefully?) pinned slantwise.

This young man was twenty-four or so, but his comportment—the restrained movements of his hands, the gravely pursed lips—was intended to make him look at least thirty. He was one of the highly valued consultants employed by the Presidium of the Supreme Soviet, and his main job was drafting speeches to be delivered by deputies at future sessions. The young man found this work extremely boring, but his prospects were of the brightest. Getting him to attend her party was in itself a triumph for Alevtina Nikanorovna, and marrying him to Klara was her wildest dream.

To the young man himself, the only interesting thing about the party was the presence of Galakhov and his wife. He had danced three times with Dinera. In her long black dress of imported silk she seemed to be sheathed in shiny black leather, with only her smooth, white forearms showing. Flattered by the responsiveness of such a famous woman, the young man grew bolder and tried to detain her after they had danced.

She, however, had spotted Saunkin-Golovanov, who did not dance and was at ease nowhere outside his editorial office, sitting in the corner of a sofa. She made straight for this square head mounted on a square body. The young consultant glided after her.

"E-rik!" she cried. "Why didn't I see you at the premiere of *1919*?"

Golovanov brightened.

"Went last night," he said and moved up to make more room on the sofa, although he was at the very end already.

Dinera sat. The consultant sat down beside her.

If Dinera felt like an argument, it was hopeless trying to avoid it. Indeed, you'd be lucky if she let you get a word in edgewise. She was the subject of an epigram of sorts current in Moscow literary circles: "Oh how I enjoy my silent hours with you—I have to, for you never let me speak." With no literary position and no Party office to inhibit her, Dinera boldly (but never overstepping the mark) attacked playwrights, scriptwriters, and producers, not sparing even her own husband. Her daring judgments, together with the daring way she dressed and her daring past, which everybody knew about, made her very attractive and agreeably enlivened the vapid judgments of timid literary officeholders. She attacked literary critics in general and the articles of Ernst Golovanov in particular. Golovanov showed forbearance and tirelessly alerted Dinera to her anarchistic errors and petit bourgeois backslidings. He was happy to keep up this humorous pretense of friendly enmity; his literary future depended on Galakhov.

"Do you remember," said Dinera, striking a dreamy pose for which the hard back of the sofa proved too uncomfortable—"do you remember in another of Vishnevsky's plays, *An Optimistic Tragedy*, that chorus of two sailors? One says, 'Isn't there too much blood in this tragedy,' and the other says, 'No more than in Shakespeare.' Now that's what I call clever! So you go to this new Vishnevsky play all agog. And what do you get? It's realistic enough, of course, and the portrayal of the Leader is impressive, but, but . . . what else can you say?"

"What more do you want?" the consultant protested. "I don't remember ever seeing such a moving representation of Iosif Vissarionovich. Many people in the audience shed tears."

"I had tears in my eyes, too," Dinera retorted. "That's not what I'm talking about." She turned to Golovanov again. "Hardly anybody in the play has a name. The dramatis personae are all faceless—three Party secretaries, seven senior officers, four commissars. It's like the minutes of a meeting. And yet again, brief glimpses of the 'little brothers,' those sailors forever on the move from Belotserkovsky to Lavrenev, from Lavrenev to Vishnevsky, from Vishnevsky to Sobolev"—Dinera emphasized each name with a blink and a toss of the head—"you know from the start which are the goodies and which are the baddies, and how it will all end. . . ."

"Well, what's wrong with that?" Golovanov asked in amazement. He livened up when he was talking shop. He looked like a hound following a good scent. "Why do you always want the unreal but superficially entertaining? Is life really like that? In real life did our fathers ever doubt how the Civil War would end? Did we ourselves ever doubt how the Fatherland War would end, even when the enemy was on the outskirts of Moscow?"

"And is a playwright ever in doubt how his play will be received? Explain to me, Erik, why first nights in Moscow are never a flop? Why don't playwrights live in dread of a first-night flop? Honestly, I won't be able to stop myself one of these days; I will put my fingers in my mouth and give such a whistle!"

She mimed it prettily, though it was obvious that no whistle would result.

"Certainly I'll explain!" Golovanov said, unperturbed. "Plays in our country do not and cannot fail because playwright and public are in harmony both on the artistic and ideological level."

This was too boring. The consultant straightened his yellow-and-blue tie once, straightened it again, and rose to leave them. One of Klara's classmates, a thin, amiable girl, had been quite openly eyeing him all evening, and he decided to dance with her. A two-step. Then one of the Bashkir maids started carrying ice cream around. Two chairs had been pushed into the narrow space in front of the balcony door. The consultant steered his partner toward them, sat her down, and complimented her on her dancing.

She smiled encouragement and began chattering.

The budding statesman had come across willing females often enough but had not yet tired of them. This girl, now—all he need do was tell her where and when to turn up. He eyed her slender neck, her still-unripe breasts, and, taking advantage of the fact that curtains partly concealed them from the room, graciously captured the hand that lay on her knee.

She began talking excitedly. "Such luck meeting you here like this, Vitaly Yevgenievich! Don't be angry with me for troubling you off duty. Only, I could never get past Reception at the Supreme Soviet" (Vitaly removed his hand from hers). "Your Secretariat has had papers from the camp about my father for six months now, he's had a stroke, and he's still there, paralyzed, and I'm petitioning for a pardon." (Vitaly leaned back helplessly in his chair and dug his spoon into the ball of ice cream. The girl had forgotten hers. Her hand clumsily brushed against the spoon, which somersaulted, left a spot on her dress, and fell by the balcony door. She let it lie.) "His right side is completely paralyzed! If he has another stroke, he'll die, and he hasn't got long to live anyway. Why keep him in prison any longer?"

The consultant looked sour.

"It's . . . it isn't very tactful of you to approach me here, you know. Our office number isn't secret. Call me there, and I'll make an appointment. What is your father in for, anyway? Article 58?"

"No, no, certainly not!" the girl exclaimed with relief. "You surely don't think I'd dare ask you if he were a political offender? He was sentenced under the law of August seventh!"

"It comes to the same thing. Remission has also been abolished for people sentenced under the law of August seventh."

"But that's horrible! He'll die in that camp! Why keep a terminally sick man in prison?"

The consultant looked her straight in the eye.

"If we take that line, what will be left of the whole legal code?" He grinned. "After all, he was duly tried and found guilty! Just think! What if he does die in the camp? People die in camps just like anywhere else. When the time comes, what does it matter where anybody dies?"

He got up in annoyance and walked away.

The glass door to the balcony looked out on the restlessness of the Kaluga Road. Headlights, car horns sounding warnings, traffic lights flashing red, yellow, green under the steadily falling snow.

The girl without tact picked up her spoon, put down her cup, crossed the room quietly, unnoticed both by Klara and by the hostess, went through the dining room where tea and cakes were being gotten ready, put her street things on in the hallway, and made for the door.

Galakhov, Innokenty, and Dotnara stood aside as the despondent girl passed through the dining room. Golovanov, in high spirits after his talk with Dinera, greeted his patron with his old playfulness.

"Nikolai Arkadievich! Stop! Confess, now! In the bottommost depths of your soul you are not a writer, but . . . what?" (This sounded like a repetition of Innokenty's question, and Galakhov looked embarrassed). "A soldier, that's what!"

Galakhov smiled bravely. "Yes, of course, I'm a soldier!"

He screwed up his eyes like a man staring into the distance. Not even the most triumphant day in his career as a writer had left such proud memories or, more important, such a feeling of purity as the day when he had impulsively taken off in a reckless endeavor to reach the headquarters of a half-surrounded battalion, landed in a raging storm of heavy-artillery and mortar fire, and later that evening eaten out of the same mess tin as the three officers of the battalion staff, in a dugout shaken by gunfire, and felt himself the equal of those hard-baked warriors.

"So allow me to present my army friend Captain Shchagov."

Shchagov stood erect, refusing to lower himself by a show of respect for a superior. He was pleasantly tipsy; he had drunk just enough not to feel the pressure of his feet on the floor. And as he had become more relaxed, his present surroundings had become more manageable, more welcoming—the bright, warm room, the luxurious carpeting and solid furniture that spoke of assured affluence, a milieu he had entered with his nagging wounds and unslaked hunger merely to reconnoiter but that promised to become his future.

Shchagov had been feeling ashamed of his modest decorations in this company, where a beardless boy wore the ribbon of the Order of Lenin pinned casually askew. But as soon as the famous writer saw those campaign medals and the two wound stripes, he swung his hand at Shchagov's and shook it heartily.

"Major Galakhov!" he said, smiling. "Which front were you on? Come and sit down and tell me about it."

They moved to the settee, making Innokenty and Dotty move up. They invited Ernst to join them, but he made a sign and disappeared, rightly assuming that this meeting of old warriors should not be a dry occasion. Shchagov told them how he and Golovanov had become friends in Poland, one mad day in 1944 (September 5), when Soviet troops had broken through to the Narev and their impetus had carried them over the river, fording it on planks almost, because they knew that it was easy enough on the first day but that on the second they wouldn't have a dog's chance. They had cheekily pushed their way through the Germans along a corridor no more than a kilometer wide, and the Germans had tried to cut them off, throwing in three hundred tanks from the north and two hundred from the south.

As soon as they began exchanging wartime memories, Shchagov forgot the language he used every day in the university, and Galakhov forgot not only the language of publishing houses and writers' committees but even more completely the carefully calculated and controlled idiom in which books are written. It was impossible to convey the full-blooded drama, the smoky tang of life at the front in those well-worn, smoothly polished literary locutions. Before they had spoken a dozen words, they felt a desperate need for oaths that were quite unthinkable in that place.

Golovanov reappeared with three glasses and a half-empty bottle of cognac. He moved a chair up so that he could see both of them and filled the three glasses.

"To soldiers' friendship!" Galakhov said, screwing up his eyes.

"To those who didn't come back!" was Shchagov's toast.

They drank. The empty bottle went behind the settee.

Golovanov steered the conversation his own way. He told them how on that memorable day he, a newly fledged war correspondent two months out of the university, had traveled to a forward position for the first time, got a ride on a truck (carrying antitank mines to Shchagov), and sped from Dlugosiedlo to Kabat along a corridor so narrow that the "Northern Germans" were lobbing mortar bombs onto the "Southern German" positions, and how on that same day one Soviet general returning to the front from home leave drove straight into the German lines in his Jeep. That was the end of him.

Innokenty had been listening, and he asked them what the fear of death felt like. Golovanov, in full flow, answered promptly that at such desperate moments you don't fear death; you simply don't think about it. Shchagov raised his eyebrows and demurred.

"You aren't afraid of death until you get really shaken up. I was never afraid of anything until I experienced that. I got in the way of a heavy air raid, and for some time after, I was afraid of bombs and nothing else. Then I got shell-shocked and became afraid of artillery. People say you needn't be afraid of the whistling bullet; of course not, the one you hear isn't meant for you. You won't hear the one that kills you. Death needn't really concern you; while you exist, death doesn't; when death comes, you're no more."

They had put "Baby Come Back to Me" on the record player.

Shchagov's and Golovanov's reminiscences did not interest Galakhov. He had not witnessed the operation they were talking about; he did not know Dlugosiedlo and Kabat; and, what was more, he had not been a small-time correspondent like Golovanov but a strategic commentator. Battles, in his mind, did not take place around a rotten plank bridge or a shattered water tower; his was the wider vision, the field marshal's view of the overall logic of events.

So Galakhov gave the conversation a new twist.

"War, war, war. We go into it ridiculous civilians and come back with hearts of bronze. Erik, did they sing 'The Song of the Front-Line Correspondents' in your sector?"

"Didn't they, though!"

"Nera!" Galakhov called out. "Come over here, Nera. Come and help us sing the 'Front-Line Correspondents' song."

Dinera came closer, nodding eagerly. "Whatever you say, my friends. I was a front-line girl myself!"

They turned the record player off and began singing, the three of them. What they lacked as musicians they made up for in sincerity.

*From Moscow to the border*
*We advance in battle order. . . .*

An audience gathered around them. The younger guests stared curiously at Galakhov. You didn't meet a celebrity like him every day.

*From vodka and rough weather*
*Our throats are like cracked leather*
*But we'll thank you kindly not to say a word. . . .*

The moment they began singing, Shchagov went cold inside. He kept on smiling, but he felt guilty toward those who could not be present, those who had swallowed the waters of the Dnieper back in 1941 or taken a mouthful of Novgorod pine needles in 1942. These wordsmiths didn't really know the front line, which they had now turned into a holy place. There was an unbridgeable gulf between even the most daring of war correspondents and the front-line soldier, a gulf as wide as that between an aristocrat who cultivated his land and a peasant plowman. War correspondents were not tied by service regulations and officers' orders to the immediate business of fighting, so nobody could call it treason if they showed fright, refused to lay down their lives, and fled from the battle zone. Hence the psychological gulf that yawned between the front-line soldier, whose legs had taken root in some outpost, who had no escape and might die right there, and the war correspondent who had wings and who could be back in his Moscow apartment the day after tomorrow. And anyway, where did they get all that vodka that made them so hoarse? From the C in C's ration? A soldier got 200, or as little as 150, grams before going into an attack.

*In the places where they sent us*
*No tanks were ever lent us.*
*If a newsman should get killed, then never mind.*
*In a worn-out Moskvich roadster*
*Armed with an empty holster*
*We entered cities first—and the rest behind.*

This "entered first" referred to two or three anecdotal occasions when war correspondents who couldn't read a relief map properly rushed along a good road (a Moskvich couldn't manage a bad one), landed in some town in no-man's-land, and tore out again like scalded cats back the way they had come.

Innokenty listened, head down, and found a meaning of his own in the song. He knew nothing at all about war, but he did know about Soviet newspapermen. Your Soviet reporter was not the hard-done-by character celebrated in these verses. He did not lose his job for missing a scoop. He had only to show his press card and he was treated like a person in authority, someone entitled to issue "directives." The information he obtained might be correct or incorrect; he might send it to his paper in good time or with some delay; his career did not depend on that but on ideological correctness. A correspondent with the correct worldview had no real need to rush off to some hellhole in the battle zone. He could write his dispatches just as well behind the lines.

Dotty's hand had closed around her husband's wrist, and she sat quietly beside him, content neither to speak nor to understand the clever talk. This was her most delightful habit. She wanted just to sit there like a dutiful wife and let everybody see how happy they were together.

Little did she know how, very soon now, she would be bullied and terrorized, whether Innokenty was picked up here or got clean away and remained over there.

When she had thought of nothing but herself, when she had been insensitive and domineering, eager to crush him, to force her own shoddy values on him, Innokenty had thought—Very well, let her suffer, let her learn her lesson, it will do her good.

But this was the old, the gentle Dotty, and he was acutely sorry for her. He had been unfair.

He felt more painfully ill at ease, unhappier from one moment to the next. It was high time for him to leave this stupid party—if only he could be sure that worse did not await him at home!

Klara emerged from the half-darkened smaller room after a perfunctory attempt to adjust an erratic television set for the benefit of would-be viewers. She stood in the doorway, amazed to see Innokenty and Dotnara sitting so close and contentedly together, and realized, not for the first time, that every marriage has unfathomable secrets best not disturbed.

The party had really been arranged for her, but she had not enjoyed it one little bit. Indeed, she had found it painful and depressing. She had rushed around making people welcome and trying to keep them happy, but her heart was not in it. Nothing amused her; none of the guests interested her. And the new dress, green crêpe satin with brighter insets in the collar and the bodice and at the wrists, probably did no more for her than all her others.

She had allowed a new acquaintance, the square-headed critic, to be wished on her, but their exchanges had been cool, artificial, and somehow unnatural. He had sat on the sofa for half an hour, argued about nothing with Dinera for another half hour, then started drinking with the other old soldiers. Klara felt no urge to latch onto him and lure him or drag him away.

But she would not have many more chances. She would not be in bloom much longer. If she missed her chance now, she could expect something older and worse, or nothing at all.

Had it been only that morning? Right there in Moscow? That thrilling conversation, the blue-eyed boy's ecstatic look, the soul-shaking kiss, and . . . her solemn promise to wait. Was it only today that she had spent three hours braiding a basket for a New Year's tree?

It could not have been on planet Earth. It could not have been in the flesh. Nothing like it had happened in a quarter of a century. She must have dreamed it.

## 65

# A Duel Not by the Rules

ALONE ON HIS UPPER BUNK, staring at a ceiling vaulted like the dome of heaven or burying his head in a feverish pillow as though it were Klara's bosom, Rostislav felt faint with happiness. Half a day had passed since her kiss had left him dizzy, and he was still reluctant to defile his happy lips with idle speech or gross food.

"You couldn't wait for me," he had said. "You couldn't possibly. . . ."

"Why not?" she had replied. "Of course I could."

From below, a rich, youthful voice, muted so that it would not carry too far, broke into his thoughts.

"Blind faith—nothing else—keeps antediluvians like you going. Your beliefs are false, though. Your whole life long, science and you have always been strangers."

"Look, this argument is becoming pointless. If Marxism isn't science, what is? The Revelations of Saint John the Divine? Khomyakov on the Slav soul?"

"You've never caught as much as a whiff of real science! You people aren't . . . *creators*. So you haven't the least idea what science really is! The subjects of all your philosophizing are figments, not realities! Whereas in true science all propositions derive directly from a strictly defined starting point."

"Listen, old pal! It's just the same with us. Our whole economic doctrine is deduced from the nuclear concept of commodity. And our whole philosophy stems from the three laws of the dialectic."

"Concrete knowledge is validated by the ability to apply its findings in practice."

"My friend! What's this I hear? You base your epistemology on the empirical principle? So you're one of nature's materialists." (Rubin pursed his lips to slur the sibilants). "A rather primitive one, at that."

"You always wriggle out of an honest man-to-man argument! You prefer to overwhelm your interlocutor with gobbledygook!"

"While you as usual don't just talk, you pontificate! Like the Delphic oracle! The oracle of Marfino! What makes you think I'm so desperately keen on arguing with you? For all you know, it may bore me as much as trying to drill it into some old troglodyte that the sun doesn't go round the earth. Good luck to him, I say—if ignorance is bliss."

"You don't want to argue with me because you don't know how to. None of you do, because you avoid people who think differently, and you won't risk denting your nice, tidy ideology! So you get together, with no outsiders present, to flaunt your understanding of the Founding Fathers. Each of you borrows ideas from the others, and after a little wear they fit in nicely with his own. Anyway, outside"—lowering his voice—"with the Cheka around, who dares argue with you? But when you land in jail, here in Marfino, say"—speaking normally again—"you meet people who really can argue! And you're like fish out of water! All you can do is yell at people and abuse them!"

"It seems to me you've done most of the yelling so far."

Sologdin and Rubin, absorbed in their eternal disagreement, were still sitting at the empty birthday table, oblivious of all else. Abramson had long since retired to read *The Count of Monte Cristo*, and Kondrashov-Ivanov to meditate on the greatness of Shakespeare. Pryanchikov had hurried off to page through a borrowed issue of last year's *Ogonyok*; Nerzhin had left to see Spiridon the yardman; Potapov, carrying out his housewifely duties in full, had washed the pots, put back the lockers where they belonged, and was now lying with a pillow over his head to shut out light and noise. Many of those in the room were asleep already, others quietly reading or talking, and the hour had come when you begin to wonder whether the duty officer has forgotten to switch the main lights off and the blue light on. And Sologdin and Rubin were still sitting on Pryanchikov's empty bed, hidden by the remaining locker.

Only Sologdin really felt like arguing. The day had been a day of victories for him, and they had left him seething with excitement. In any case, Sunday evening, in his timetable, was always set aside for entertainment. And what better fun could there possibly be than shaming and confounding this champion of the prevailing cretinism?

On this occasion Rubin found their debate irksome and absurd. He had unfinished work on his hands, and on top of that a new, extremely difficult task had devolved upon him, the creation of a whole new science! He had to make a start single-handedly early next morning, and he should really be conserving his strength. And then there were two letters demanding his attention, one from his wife and one from his mistress. There would never be a better time to answer them, giving his wife important advice on bringing up the children, and his mistress tender reassurances. Other things, too, had claims on him—the Mongolian-Finnish, Spanish-Arabic, and other dictionaries, Čapek, Hemingway, Lawrence. . . . And on top of all that—something he hadn't been able to get around to all evening, what with the mock trial, the teasing remarks from his neighbors, and the birthday ritual—the finalization of a major project of great public importance.

But the prison's debating rules had him in their grip. Rubin must never let himself be defeated in argument, because in the sharashka he represented the ideology of progress. So he was forced to sit there with Sologdin, as though tied hand and foot, trying to ram into him rudimentary ideas that ought to be within the grasp of children in nursery school.

Sologdin was now quietly and gently laying down the law.

"I can tell you from my experience in the camps that a proper debate must be conducted like a duel. We agree on an umpire; we can call on Gleb, for instance. We take a sheet of paper and draw a vertical line down the middle. Across the top of the page, we write the subject of the discussion. Then each of us, on his own half, expresses as clearly and succinctly as possible his views on the question. To prevent thoughtless slips in the choice of words, there is no time limit."

"You must take me for a fool," Rubin said sleepily, his puckered eyelids half closed. His bearded face looked infinitely weary. "Are we supposed to go on arguing all night?"

"Certainly not," Sologdin said, eyes twinkling merrily. "That's the marvelous thing about a proper man-to-man argument. Some people can go on idly bandying words and disturbing the air to no purpose for weeks on end. But an argument on paper can be over in ten minutes; it is immediately obvious if the opponents are talking about completely different things or if there is no real disagreement between them. When there is a clear case for continuing, the two sides start writing their views down alternately, each on his own half of the paper. Just like a duel—parry and thrust, or shot for shot. And just think—evasiveness and substituting different words for what was said before are impossible, and the result is that after two or three exchanges one side emerges clearly victorious and the other a clear loser."

"And there's no time limit?"

"To ensure that truth prevails? Certainly not."

"And do we then go on to fight with broadswords?"

Sologdin's flushed face darkened.

"I knew it! You pitch into me—"

"No, you started it. . . ."

"Call me all sorts of names—you've got bags of them. Caveman, backslider" (avoiding the "incomprehensible" foreign word "reactionary"), "king of lickspittles" (his rendering of "certified lackey"). You have a larger stock of insults than of scientific terms. And when I stand up to you and propose an honest debate, you have neither time nor appetite for it; you're too tired. Yet you found both the time and the will to rip the guts out of our whole country!"

"Out of half the world!" Rubin politely corrected him. "We always have time and strength for action. But for pointless jawing? What have you and I got to talk about? We've said all we have to say to each other."

"What have we got to talk about? I leave it to you to choose," Sologdin said with a gallant gesture. "Choose your weapons! Name the place!"

"Right, then. My choice of subject is . . . nothing!"

"That's against the rules!"

"What rules? Where do you get all these rules from? What sort of inquisition is this? Why can't you understand that fruitful argument is impossible without some sort of common ground; there obviously has to be some sort of agreement on fundamentals."

"There you go! Just as I said! You want us both to accept the theory of added value and workers' rule"—the term for "dictatorship of the proletariat" in the Language of Utter Clarity. "And there'd be nothing left to argue about except whether certain flourishes were added by Marx on an empty stomach or Engels after a good dinner."

There was no escape from this scoffer! Rubin boiled over.

"Why, oh why, can't you see that this is just stupid! You and I have nothing to say to each other! However you look at it, we are from different planets. You still think, for instance, that the duel is the best way to seek redress for a grievance!"

"Disprove it if you can!"

Sologdin leaned back, beaming.

"If we had duels, who would dare slander another person? Who would dare jostle weaker people?"

"Why, those swaggering blades of yours would! Your knights erroneous! The darkness of the Middle Ages, those stupid, arrogant knights, the crusades—all that is the high point of history as far as you are concerned!"

Sologdin sat to attention and brandished one finger over his head.

"Yes, the highest point in the history of the human spirit!"

"And all those great cargoes of crusaders' loot? What a sickening hidalgo you are!"

"And you're an Old Testament fanatic! A man possessed!" Sologdin retorted.

"I suppose you regard Belinsky, say, and Chernyshevsky and all our greatest educators as half-educated sons of village priests?"

"Long-skirted seminarians!" Sologdin added joyfully.

"And I suppose you regard Revolution—let's leave ours out of it—the French Revolution, say, a century and a half after the event, as the work of a mindless mob in thrall to its diabolical instincts—and the destruction of a nation? Am I right?"

"Yes, of course! Just try proving the opposite. The greatness of France ends with the eighteenth century. What came after the revolt? A handful of great men, yes, but in the wrong place and at the wrong time. A nation in terminal decline! Continual changes of regime have made France the laughingstock of the world. France is impotent! Will-less! Null! A handful of dust!"

Sologdin burst into demonic laughter.

"Savage! Troglodyte!" Rubin said indignantly.

"And France will never get on its feet again! Unless it's with the help of the Church of Rome!"

"That's another thing! The Reformation, to you, means not the inevitable liberation of the human mind from ecclesiastical shackles but—"

"But madness and blindness! Lutheran devil worship! The disruption of Europe! The self-destruction of the European peoples! Worse than the two world wars!"

"There you are, then! You're a fossil! An ichthyosaurus! What is there for us to discuss? Look what a tangle you've got yourself into! Let's just part friends."

Sologdin saw that Rubin was about to get up and go away. That simply couldn't be allowed! His bit of fun was walking out on him! Before it had even got started. He reined himself in and became unrecognizably mild.

"Forgive me, Lev, my friend, I got carried away. It's late, of course, and I don't insist on our tackling one of the major questions. Let's just try out the 'duel' procedure on some neat little topic. I'll give you some headings"—meaning "themes"—"to choose from. Would you like something literary? That's your field, not mine."

"Give it a rest, can't you."

This was his chance to leave without damage to his reputation. Rubin started getting up, but Sologdin hurriedly forestalled him.

"All right. A moral heading: the role of pride in the life of a human being."

Rubin yawned with boredom.

"What are we, schoolgirls?"

He rose and stood between the beds.

"What about this one, then?" Sologdin said, seizing his hand.

"Get lost." Rubin waved him away, laughing. "Everything's topsy-turvy in that head of yours. You're the one man on the face of the earth who still doesn't recognize the three laws of the dialectic. From which all else follows!"

Sologdin's pink palm dismissed this charge.

"What d'you mean, don't recognize? I do in fact recognize them."

"Wha-at? You've recognized the dialectic?" Rubin spluttered, lips protruding. "Darling boy! Let me give you a kiss! Have you really, though?"

"I haven't just recognized the dialectic; I've thought about it. Every morning for two months! Which is more than you've done!"

"Even thought about it, have you? You're getting more intelligent every day! But in that case what is there for us to argue about?"

"What d'you mean?" Sologdin was indignant. "First there's no common ground, so there's nothing to argue about; then when there is common ground, there's nothing to argue about! That won't do! Kindly get on with it!"

"Why are you such a bully? What is it you want to argue about?

Sologdin was also on his feet now and waving his arms.

"All right, then! I'm ready to fight on the most unfavorable conditions. I will defeat you with a weapon wrested from your own dirty paws! What we will discuss is whether you yourself really understand your three laws! You people are like cannibals dancing around a fire without the least idea what fire is. I can trip you up on those laws as often as I like."

"Go ahead, then!"

Rubin could not help raising his voice. He was annoyed with himself but bogged down again.

"All right." Sologdin sat down. "Take a seat."

Rubin stayed on his feet.

"Now, where's the best place to begin?" Sologdin mentally savored some possibilities. "These laws now—they show us the *direction* of development, am I right?"

"Direction?"

"Yes. Which way a . . . a . . . process"—the word stuck in his throat—"is going."

"Of course."

"And where do you see that happening? Where, precisely?" Sologdin asked coldly.

"In the laws themselves. They exemplify movement."

Rubin sat down himself. They began talking in a quiet, matter-of-fact way.

"Which law precisely tells us the direction of that movement?"

"Not the first, obviously. . . . The second. Or maybe the third."

"Hm. The third, you say. And how do we determine it?"

"Determine what?"

"The direction of movement, what else?"

Rubin frowned. "Listen, what exactly is the point of all this scholasticism?"

"You call this scholasticism? That shows how unfamiliar you are with the exact sciences. If a law gives us no numerical coordinates and we don't know the direction of development either, we don't know a damn thing. Right. Look at it from another angle. You frequently and glibly trot out the term 'negation of the negation.' But what do you understand by those words? Can you, for instance, answer this question: Does negation of the negation always take place in the course of development, or doesn't it?"

Rubin thought for a moment. An unexpected question. Not usually put that way. But never let the other man see that you're stuck for an answer!

"Generally speaking," he said. "As a rule."

"There you go!" Sologdin roared triumphantly. "All those cant words!

You've devised thousands of these little phrases—'generally speaking,' 'as a rule,' and so on—to avoid straight talk. Somebody says 'negation of the negation' and your brain prints out, 'single grain, produces stalk, stalk produces ten grains.' It sets my teeth on edge! It makes me sick! Give me a straight answer: *When* does negation of the negation occur, and when does it not occur? When should we expect it, and when is it impossible?"

All trace of Rubin's apathy had disappeared. He collected his wandering thoughts and concentrated on this uncalled-for but nonetheless important debate.

"When does it occur, and when doesn't it—what practical difference does that make?"

"I like that! This is one of the three laws by which you explain absolutely everything, and you ask whether it has any practical importance. It's pointless talking to you!"

"You're putting the cart before the horse," Rubin said indignantly.

"More verbiage! More claptrap!"

"Cart before horse," Rubin insisted. "We Marxists would be ashamed to proceed from the laws of the dialectic themselves to concrete analysis of phenomena. So we have no need whatsoever to know 'when it occurs' and 'when it doesn't.'"

"Well, let me give you the answer! Only, you'll say right away that you knew it all along, that it's obvious, that it goes without saying. . . . Listen, though; if it is possible to reverse a process so that a thing is restored to its previous condition, negation of the negation has not taken place. Suppose, for instance, a nut is tightened to the limit, and you want to loosen it; you just turn it the opposite way. There we have a process in reverse, a transition from quantitative to qualitative change, but no 'negation of the negation'! But if the former qualitative state cannot be reproduced by movement in the reverse direction, then development may proceed through negation, but even so only if repetitions are allowed. In other words, irreversible changes will be negations only where the negation of the negations themselves is possible."

"Ivan is a man, so what is not Ivan is not a man," muttered Rubin. "You're like somebody on parallel bars."

"Back to our example. If while tightening the nut, you were to break the thread, then unscrewing it will not restore its previous quality, its unbroken thread. You can only reproduce that quality now by melting down the nut, rolling a hexagonal bar, shaping it on a lathe, and finally cutting a new nut."

"Wait a bit, Mitya," Rubin said mildly. "You can't seriously use the tightening and loosening of a nut to exemplify the laws of the dialectic."

"Why not? Why shouldn't a nut do as well as a grain of corn? No machine can hold together without nuts. Well, then, each of the states I've enumerated is irreversible; it negates the previous state, but the new nut in relation to the old, damaged one is the negation of the negation. Simple, eh?" Pointing his neatly trimmed goatee at Rubin.

"Wait a bit! What makes you think you've beaten me? It follows from what you've said yourself that the third law gives us the direction of development."

Sologdin bowed, hand on heart.

"If you weren't such a quick thinker, my dear Lev, I would hardly do myself the honor of talking to you. You're right; the third does just that. But we must learn how to take what the law gives us. Do you know how? How to use the law, instead of worshipping it? You have deduced that it tells us the direction of development. To which we say, does it always do so? In the physical world? In animate nature as well? In society? Well?"

"Hm, well," Rubin said thoughtfully, "maybe there's a rational kernel in all this. But most of what you say, my dear fellow, is mere twaddle."

Sologdin flared up again and cut him short with a gesture.

"You are the twaddlers!"

He could have been brandishing a sword, hemmed in by Saracens. "You don't understand a single one of your laws, although you deduce everything from them."

"I keep telling you, we do not."

"Don't deduce everything from them?"

Sologdin was so astonished that his sword arm froze.

"No, we don't."

"So they're just a tail to pin on the donkey? In that case, how did you decide in which direction society was going to develop?"

"Listen, can't you!" Rubin intoned his answer for extra emphasis. "What are you, a block of oak or a human being? We resolve all questions by concrete analysis of the material facts. Got it? All questions having to do with society are answered by analysis of the class situation."

"So why the dialectic?" Sologdin roared, heedless of the silence around them. "The three laws aren't really needed at all."

"Oh, yes they are. Very much so."

"What for? If nothing can be deduced from them? If you don't need them to find out the direction of change—why all that twaddle? If all you can do is keep parroting negation of the negation, why in hell's name do you need them at all?"

Potapov, who had been trying in vain to shelter himself from the growing storm, angrily whipped the pillow from his ear and raised himself on one elbow.

"Listen, friends!" he said. "If you can't sleep yourself, show some respect for those who can"—pointing obliquely upward at Ruska's bunk—"or find a more suitable place."

The wrath of Potapov, that lover of order and moderation, the hush which had settled on the whole semicircular room, and their awareness that they were surrounded by stool pigeons (though Rubin of course could fearlessly shout his beliefs on this subject) would have brought any sober person to his senses.

But these two sobered up only slightly. Their long dispute, the latest of many, was just beginning. They realized that they had to leave the room, but they were incapable by now of lowering their voices or of relaxing their grip on each other. They were still bandying insults as the door to the hallway closed behind them.

The white light went out almost as they left, and the blue nightlight was turned on.

Ruska Doronin's wakeful ear had been closer than any other to the debate, but no one could have been less interested in collecting "material" for use against them. He had heard Potapov's hint and understood it, without seeing the finger aimed at himself. He felt the helpless resentment we all experience when we are reproached by those whose opinions matter to us.

When he began his dangerous double game with the operations officers, he had allowed for everything, he had cheated the vigilance of his enemies, and now he was on the verge of a spectacular triumph with the "147 rubles" affair. But he had no protection against the suspicions of his friends. His solitary scheme, simply because it was so out of the ordinary and so secret, had earned him disgrace and contempt. It surprised him that these mature, sensible, experienced people lacked the generosity of mind to understand him and believe that he was not a traitor.

Whenever we lose the sympathy of others, the one who goes on loving us becomes triply dear.

And if that one is a woman. . . .

Klara! She would understand! He would tell her all about this risky scheme tomorrow, and she would understand.

With no hope of going to sleep, or indeed any wish to, he tossed and turned in his sweaty bed, remembering Klara's questioning eyes, searching for the flaws in his plan to escape under the wire and along the gulley to the high road, where he would just take a bus straight to the city center.

Once he was there, Klara would help him.

He would be harder to find in a city of seven million people than in the bare expanses of Vorkuta. Moscow was the place for an escape!

# 66

## Going to the People

RUBIN AND SOLOGDIN indulgently referred to Nerzhin's friendship with the yardman, Spiridon, as his "going to the people," in quest of that great homespun truth Gogol, Nekrasov, Herzen, the Slavophiles, Lev Tolstoy, and finally the much-maligned Vasisuali Lokhankin had sought in vain before him.

Whereas Rubin and Sologdin themselves had never sought that homespun truth, because each of them possessed the ultimate truth, crystal clear and his very own.

Rubin knew for certain that "the people" is an artificial generalization, that every people is divided into classes, and that even they change as time goes by. Seeking a superior understanding of life in the peasant class was unimaginative and futile. The proletariat was the only consistently and thoroughly Revolutionary class, the future belonged to the proletariat, and only the collectivism and selflessness of the proletariat gave life a higher meaning.

Sologdin was no less certain that "the people" is the formless raw material of history, from which the sturdy, crude, but indispensable legs of that Colossus—the Spirit of Man—are molded. "The people" was a collective term for the totality of crude and faceless creatures hopelessly straining in the harness to which they were born and from which death alone would release them. Only rare individuals scattered like brilliant stars around the dark sky of existence were endowed with superior insight.

They both knew that Nerzhin would get over it, grow up a bit, come to his senses.

Nerzhin had indeed already outgrown many of his wilder ideas.

Nineteenth-century Russian literature, so full of heartache for "our suffering brothers," had left him, as it leaves all who read it for the first time, with an image of "the People"—personified as a gray-haired saintly figure with a halo, in a silver frame, uniting in itself wisdom, moral purity, and spiritual greatness.

But the place for that image was the bookshelf—or that long-lost world, the fields and byways of the nineteenth century.

Russia in fact no longer existed—only the Soviet Union, and in it the big city in which Gleb had grown up. Success upon success had rained on young Gleb from the cornucopia of learning. He had discovered that he was a quick thinker, but there were others who thought even quicker and who overwhelmed him with their knowledge. "The People" stayed on his bookshelf, but in his mind the only people who mattered were those who carried in their heads the cultural treasures of the world—encyclopedic connoisseurs of antiquity and the fine arts, people of wide and varied erudition. He had to belong to this elite. Failure to win acceptance meant a life of misery.

Then the war came, and Nerzhin found himself serving in a horse-drawn transport unit. Choking with the indignity of it, he clumsily chased horses around the pasture, trying to throw a halter around their necks or jump on their backs. He had never learned to ride, he couldn't handle a harness, he couldn't fork hay, and a nail would bend double under his hammer, as though deriding this unskillful workman! The worse things went for Nerzhin, the more raucously those around him—the unshaved, foulmouthed, pitiless, utterly unlikable people—guffawed.

In time, Nerzhin made his way up from the ranks and became an artillery officer. Youthful and nimble again, he walked around smartly belted, elegantly flourishing a pliant twig broken off for the purpose—he carried nothing else.

He rode daringly on the footboards of trucks, swore roundly at river crossings, was ever ready to move out at midnight and in foul weather, and had behind him—obedient, devoted, eager to serve, and therefore decidedly likable—the People. And his own small sample of the people listened readily, or so it seemed, to his pep talks about the great People that had risen as one man to defend its country.

Then Nerzhin was arrested. In his first prisons, under investigation or awaiting transfer, and in the first camps, which had stunned and numbed him, he was horrified to discover that some of the elite had another side to them: In circumstances in which only firmness, willpower, and loyalty to friends showed the true worth of a prisoner and determined the fate of his comrades, these refined and sensitive and highly educated connoisseurs of the exquisite rather often turned out to be cowards, quick to surrender, and, thanks to their education, disgustingly ingenious in justifying their dirty tricks. Such people quickly degenerated into traitors and toadies. Nerzhin came to see himself as not so very different from them. He recoiled from those with whom he had once proudly identified. He began to loathe and to ridicule things he had revered. His aim now was to become ordinary, to shed the affectations—the exaggerated politeness, the preciosity—of the intellectuals. In the years of unrelieved disaster, in the worst moments of his shattered life, Nerzhin decided that the only valuable, the only important people were those who worked with their hands, planing timber, shaping metal, tilling the soil, smelting iron. He tried now to learn from simple laboring people the wisdom of their infinitely skillful hands and their philosophy of life. So Nerzhin had come full circle and arrived at the idea so fashionable in the nineteenth century, that of "going to"—going down to—"the people."

But the circle was not quite a closed one; it ended in a spiraling tail unimaginable to our grandfathers. Unlike the educated gentlefolk of the nineteenth century, the zek Nerzhin could descend without dressing up in strange clothes and feeling with his foot for the ladder; he was simply slung bodily into the mass of the people, in ragged padded trousers and a patched tunic, and given a daily work quota. Nerzhin shared the lot of simple people not as a condescending gentleman, always conscious of the difference and so always alien, but as one of themselves, indistinguishable from them, an equal among equals.

It was not to ingratiate himself with the muzhik but to earn a soggy hunk of bread for the day that Nerzhin had to learn to pound nails in straight and plane planks so that they fitted perfectly. After his cruel training in the camps, another of Nerzhin's misconceptions fell away. He realized that he could lower himself no further. There was nothing, and no one, down there.

He was cured, too, of his illusion that the People, with their age-old homespun wisdom, were superior to himself. Squatting with them in the snow at their escort's command, hiding with them from the foreman in the dark corners of a building site, heaving handbarrows over freezing ground, and drying his foot rags in the huts with them, Nerzhin saw clearly that these people were in no way his betters. Their endurance of hunger and thirst was no greater than his. They were no more stouthearted than he was, faced with the stone wall of a ten-year sentence. No more farsighted and no more resourceful at critical moments, in transit from prison to camp or during body searches. They were, though, more gullible and more easily deceived by stool pigeons. They fell more readily for the crude deceptions of the authorities. They looked forward to an amnesty, though Stalin would sooner turn up his toes than grant it. If some thug of a guard happened to be in a good mood and smiled at them, they hastened to smile back. They were also much greedier for trivial favors: a "supplementary," a hundred grams of rancid lard cake, a pair of hideous prison trousers, just as long as they were newish or a bit flashy.

Most of them lacked a "point of view" of the sort that a man treasures more than life itself.

All that was left to him, Nerzhin decided, was to be himself.

Once he had recovered—perhaps finally, perhaps not—from this last of many infatuations, Nerzhin saw the People differently. None of his books had prepared him for his new insight. "The People" did not mean all those who speak your language, nor yet the chosen few branded with the fiery mark of genius. Neither birth nor the labor of your hands nor the privileges of education admit you to membership of the People.

Only your soul can do that.

And each of us fashions his soul himself, year in and year out.

You must strive to temper and to cut and polish your soul so as to become a human being. And hence a humble component of your people.

A man with such a soul cannot as a rule expect to prosper, to go far in his career, to get rich. Which is why for the most part "the People" is not to be found at the higher levels of society.

# 67

## Spiridon

ROUNDHEADED SPIRIDON, on whose face only a practiced eye could distinguish respect from mockery, had aroused Nerzhin's interest as soon as he arrived in the sharashka. There had been carpenters and mechanics and turners there before him, but Spiridon's unspoiled naturalness made him different. Here, without a doubt, was a representative of the People on whose wisdom Nerzhin could draw.

He felt, however, a certain awkwardness. He could find no excuse for getting to know Spiridon more closely. He had at first nothing to talk to him about, they did not meet at work, and they lived in different parts of the prison. The small group of manual laborers lived in a separate room and spent their leisure hours apart from other prisoners, so that, when Nerzhin started visiting Spiridon, they all, Spiridon among them, decided that he was a wolf on the prowl, seeking prey for the godfather.

Spiridon considered himself the least important person in the sharashka and could not imagine why operations officers should be targeting him, but since they turned up their noses at no carrion, he had to be on his guard. When Nerzhin came into the room, Spiridon would light up with pretended joy, make room for him on the bunk, and with a stupid look on his face start talking about something a million miles from politics: how to catch a spawning fish with a spike or catch it by the gills with a forked stick in still water or lure it into a net; how he had hunted "elk and brown bears" (but better steer clear of "the black bear with a white tie"!); how lungwort is used to get rid of snakes, while the "woodpecker herb" is "mighty good for mowing." Then there was the long story of his courtship of Marfa Ustinovna in the twenties, when she belonged to the drama group at the village club; her parents wanted to marry her off to a rich miller, but she loved Spiridon and eloped with him, and they were secretly married on St. Peter's day.

While Spiridon was telling him all this, those sore eyes hardly moved. They seemed to say from under his bushy ginger eyebrows, "Why do you keep coming here, wolf? You can see for yourself you'll get slim pickings."

In fact, any stoolie would have despaired long ago and abandoned this uncooperative victim. Nobody could have been so curious about Spiridon's hunting career as to come along and listen patiently to his revelations every Sunday evening.

But Nerzhin, who, to begin with, felt shy when he looked in on Spiridon, was also the Nerzhin with an insatiable longing to solve here in prison problems he had not thought through as a free man. He kept it up month after month and, far from wearying of Spiridon's stories, felt refreshed by them; they were like the breath of a river at dawn, like the breeze that freshens a field in the afternoon, and they took him back to that unique seven years in the life of Russia, the seven years of the New Economic Policy, the equal and the like of which Russia had never known from the time of the first clearings in the primeval forest, long before the coming of Rurik's men, to the most recent "dis-amalgamation" of collective farms. Nerzhin had caught a glimpse of that time while he was still too young to understand, and he greatly regretted not having been born a bit earlier.

Abandoning himself to Spiridon's warm, husky voice, Nerzhin never once tried to trick him into talking about politics. So Spiridon gradually began to trust him and plunged into the past without being forced to it. He was no longer inhibited by constant wariness, the deep furrows in his brow disappeared, and a quiet smile played on his ruddy face.

Only his impaired eyesight prevented Spiridon from reading in the sharashka. Occasionally, in an attempt to adapt his own speech to Nerzhin's, he would work in words such as "principle," "period," and "analogously," usually in the wrong place. In the days when Marfa Ustinovna had performed with the village drama circle, he had heard the name "Yesenin" from the stage, and it had remained in his memory.

"Yesenin?" Nerzhin said in surprise. "Great stuff! I've got his poems here in the sharashka. They're hard to come by nowadays." And he took along the little book in a jacket carpeted with embossed autumn maple leaves. Could it be that a miracle was about to happen? he wondered. Would the semiliterate Spiridon understand Yesenin?

No miracle took place. Spiridon didn't remember a line of what he had heard. But he greatly enjoyed "Tanyusha Was Oh, So Pretty" and "Threshing."

Two days later Major Shikin called Nerzhin in and ordered him to hand over Yesenin for censorial inspection. Nerzhin never discovered who had informed on him. But now that he had clearly been victimized by the godfather and lost his Yesenin, more or less because of Spiridon, Gleb was finally seen to be trustworthy. Spiridon began to talk to him as an equal and a friend, and their conversations no longer took place in the room but under the stairs inside the main prison building, where nobody could hear them.

On the last five or six Sunday evenings, Spiridon's stories had given Nerzhin glimpses of the profundity for which he had longed. The life of a Russian peasant, indistinguishable from millions of others, who had been seventeen in the year of the Revolution and just over forty when the war with Hitler began, unfolded before Nerzhin's eyes.

Hurricanes had raged around him. He had become head of the family at fourteen (his father was called up for the war with Germany and killed in action) and had gone out to mow with the old men. ("I learned to use a scythe in half a day.") At sixteen he was employed in a glassworks and marching to open-air meetings under red banners when it was announced that the land now belonged to the peasants. Spiridon rushed back to his village and took a plot. That year he and his mother, younger brother, and sisters strained every sinew, and by the Feast of the Protectress, they had corn for the winter. But after Christmas the authorities started forcibly exacting all the grain they could for the towns: Come on, hand it over, more, more, more. Then after Easter, Spiridon's year was called up—the eighteens, and he'd just turned nineteen. The Red Army was about to grab him. But Spiridon saw no advantage in leaving his land for the army, so he and some of the other village lads took off into the woods and became "Greens" ("Leave us alone and we'll leave you alone"). Later on, though, it wasn't safe even out in the woods. So they went over to the Whites, who had popped up briefly in their district. The Whites interrogated them, wanted to know if there was a commissar among them. There was no commissar, so the Whites knocked the ringleader on the head to encourage the others, made them wear tricolor cockades, and gave them rifles. The Whites generally did things in the old way, as under the tsar. After they'd fought for the Whites a bit, Spiridon and his comrades were taken prisoner by the Reds. (They didn't put up much resistance; in fact, they gave themselves up.)

The Reds shot the officers and ordered the rankers to remove the cockades from their caps and put on armbands. Spiridon remained with the Reds till the end of the Civil War. He had fought in Poland, too, and after that his unit had become part of the Labor Army. He had thought he would never get home. Then at Shrovetide they were taken to Petersburg and in the first week of Lent marched across the sea over the ice to capture some fortress. Only then did Spiridon manage to get home.

He returned to his village in the spring and eagerly set to work on the patch of land he had fought to make his own. Others came back from the war work-shy and all talk, but not Spiridon. He quickly put his holding on a firm footing ("A good husbandman can walk down the yard and pick up a ruble"), married, and got himself some horses.

The government itself was of two minds at the time. It looked to the poorer peasants for support, but nobody wanted to join the ranks of the poor. Those peasants who liked work were eager to better themselves. A new word was borne in on the breeze: "intensifier." It meant anyone who wanted to get the best out of his farm without hired labor, relying on science and native wit. With his wife's help, Spiridon Yegorov became an "intensifier."

"A good wife makes all the difference in life," Spiridon always said. Marfa Ustinovna was the joy of his life; marrying her was the luckiest thing he ever did. Because of her he did not drink and hang around with idlers. She had borne him three children in successive years, two sons and then a daughter, but still pulled her weight, side by side with her husband, and their holding had flourished. She was literate; she read a magazine called *Be Your Own Agronomist*, and that was how Spiridon became an "intensifier."

Intensifiers were made a fuss over; Spiridon and Marfa were given subsidies and seed. They went from strength to strength, from well-off to better-off, and began to think of building themselves a brick house, not knowing that their good fortune was about to run out. Spiridon was generally respected; he sat on the platform at meetings as a Civil War hero and by now a Party member.

At that point, their home was completely destroyed by fire; they barely managed to rescue the children. They were left with nothing.

But they were given little time to grieve. They had scarcely begun to struggle to their feet after the fire when a thunderclap came from distant Moscow. The "intensifiers," unthinkingly fostered by Moscow, were now just as unthinkingly rechristened "kulaks" and weeded out. Marfa and Spiridon were glad that they had not got around to building their brick house.

Fate had played one of its favorite tricks, and their misfortune proved to be a blessing.

Spiridon Yegorov might easily have been marched off by the GPU to die in the tundra, but instead he was appointed commissar for collectivization to herd the people into collective farms. He took to wearing a minatory revolver on his hip, personally evicted people from their houses, and sent them off under police escort, empty-handed, without belongings, kulaks and nonkulaks alike.

Spiridon's behavior at this and at other critical moments in his career defied easy explanation or class analysis. Nerzhin did not reproach him, not wanting to reopen old wounds, and anyway it was easy to see that all this had left Spiridon troubled at heart. He had started drinking—and drank as though the whole village had once been his—and now he was messing up everything. He had accepted the rank of commissar but neglected his duties. He turned a blind eye to the peasants who killed off their beasts and entered the kolkhoz without hoof or horn to their name.

For all this, Spiridon was dismissed, and they did not stop at that; he was ordered to put his hands behind his back, and two militiamen, one behind and one in front, revolvers drawn, marched him off to jail. He was tried quickly ("In our whole pe-ri-od they've never wasted time trying people"), given ten years for "economic counterevolution," and sent off to the White Sea Canal and, after that was finished, to the Moscow-Volga Canal. There Spiridon worked at times as a manual laborer and at times as a carpenter. He got good rations, and it was only for Marfa, left behind with their three children, that his heart ached.

But then Spiridon's case was reopened. The charge of "economic counterrevolution" was changed to "dereliction of duty," and as a result he became a "class ally" instead of a "class enemy." He was called in and informed that he would now be entrusted with a rifle to stand guard over his fellow prisoners. Only yesterday Spiridon, like any decent zek, had abused the escort troops with the vilest of language and the convicts among them with words even stronger, but he now took the proffered rifle and marched out his comrades of yesterday under escort, because this shortened the term of his imprisonment and gave him forty rubles a month to send home.

Before long, the camp commandant was congratulating him on his release. Spiridon got his documents made out, not for a kolkhoz but for a factory at Pochep. He collected Marfa and the children and was soon appearing on the factory honors board as one of the best glassblowers. He did all the overtime he could to recoup his losses from the fire. Husband and wife began to think about a little cottage with a garden and further schooling for their children. The children were fifteen, fourteen, and thirteen when the war broke out. The front moved quickly toward the settlement in which they lived. The authorities evacuated everybody they could to the East, the whole population of Pochep included.

At every turning point in Spiridon's life story, Nerzhin awaited the next surprise with bated breath. He half expected to hear that Spiridon, resenting as he must his years in camp, had stayed behind to await the Germans. Not at all. Spiridon had behaved at first as people do in the best patriotic novels: He buried his belongings, and as soon as the factory equipment was evacuated by rail and the workers given carts, he put his wife and three children on one of them and—"It isn't my horse and it isn't my whip, so off we go and I'll never say 'whoa' "—retreated from Pochep all the way to Kaluga, with thousands of others.

But near Kaluga something went wrong, and their column broke up. There were now only hundreds of them rather than thousands. Moreover, the men were to be enlisted at the first recruiting office along the route and their families sent on without them.

As soon as it became clear that he faced separation from his family, sure as ever that he was doing the right thing, Spiridon took to the woods, waited till the front had rolled past, put his family on the same old cart, pulled by the same horse, except that it was no longer state property but his very own to keep, and took them all the way back to Pochep and from there to his native village, where he settled in a deserted hut. He was told to take as much of the former kolkhoz land as he could work—and to work it. Spiridon plowed and sowed with no qualms of conscience, ignoring the war bulletins, working steadily and confidently, as though he was back in the far-off years when there was no kolkhoz and no war.

Partisans came to him and said, "Pull yourself together, Spiridon; you should be fighting, not plowing." "Somebody has to plow," Spiridon answered and refused to leave the land. They tried to force people to join the Partisans. As he explained it now, it wasn't enough that young and old would just as soon be creeping up on the Germans, knife between teeth, as sit at home chewing their crusts; no, what happened was that instructors from Moscow were parachuted in to drive the peasants out with threats or fatally compromise them.

The Partisans managed to kill a German dispatch rider right in the middle of the village. They knew the German rules. The Germans drove in immediately, turned the people out of their houses, and burned the whole village to the ground.

Once again Spiridon did not hesitate. The time had come to settle accounts with the Germans. He took Marfa and the children to her mother and hurried off to join the same group of Partisans in the forest. He was given an automatic rifle and, working just as conscientiously and methodically as he had in the factory and on the land, he picked off Germans patrolling the railway line, attacked convoys, helped to blow up bridges, and visited his family at holiday times. In spite of everything, he still had his family.

But the front was rolling back their way. They flattered themselves that Spiridon would get a Partisan medal when Soviet troops arrived. It was even announced that Partisans would be incorporated into the regular army and that their days in the forest would soon be over.

Then a lad came running with the news that the Germans had moved all the inhabitants from the village where Marfa was living.

Spiridon was not waiting for the Red Army or for anything else. Without a word to anyone, he abandoned his gun and his two drums of ammunition and rushed off to find his family. He merged with the flood of displaced people, pretending to be a civilian, walking beside the same old cart, flicking the same little horse with his whip. Sure as always that he was doing what was right and proper, he trudged along the congested road from Pochep to Slutsk.

Nerzhin clutched his head and rocked from side to side.

"Dear oh dear oh dear! What extraordinary things you tell me, Spiridon Danilych! I can't take it all in. You went over the ice to Kronstadt; you were one of those who set up this Soviet regime of ours; you forced people into the collective farms. . . ."

"Well, didn't you help to set it up?"

Nerzhin was at a loss for an answer. The conventional view was that his father's generation had established the regime and that in 1917, at that solemn moment, every one of those heroes clearly realized what he was doing.

The smile on Spiridon's lips grew broader.

"You helped set it up, all right. Didn't you realize?"

"No, I didn't," Nerzhin whispered, going over in his mind his three years as an officer at the front.

"Well, it's like that sometimes; we plant rye, and what comes up is goosegrass."

But Nerzhin wanted to get on with his sociological investigation.

"What happened next, Spiridon Danilych?"

What happened next?!

He could, of course, have made a break for the forest yet again. He tried it once, but there was a hair-raising encounter with bandits, and he narrowly saved his daughter from them. So he stayed with the column. Besides, he had begun to realize that the Soviet authorities would not believe him, would remember that he hadn't joined the Partisans right away and that he had deserted. He decided that he might as well be hanged for a sheep as for a lamb and went all the way to Slutsk. There they were put on trains and given food coupons to last them as far as the Rhineland. At first, the whisper went around that children could not be taken, and Spiridon started looking for a chance to turn back. But everyone was accepted, so he abandoned his horse and cart without a second thought and joined the train. He and the two boys were assigned to a factory near Mainz, and his wife and daughter were sent to work for farmers.

One day at the factory a German foreman struck Spiridon's younger son. Without stopping to think, Spiridon jumped up and threatened the foreman with an ax. Under German law Spiridon could have been shot. But the foreman calmed down, went up to the mutineer, and, as Spiridon now told the story, said: "I myself—*Vater*, I you—*verstehe*."

He did not report the matter, and Spiridon learned soon afterward that the foreman had that very morning received notification of his son's death in Russia.

Remembering that foreman in the Rhineland, the case-hardened Spiridon was not ashamed to wipe a tear away with his sleeve.

"Since then I've never been angry with the Germans. They burned my house down and did all those other bad things, but that *Vater* wiped the slate clean. He had a heart, that man! There's another sort of German for you!"

That was one of the rare, the very rare, events to shake the redheaded peasant's dogged certainty that he was always right. Otherwise, through all the difficult years, through all the cruel vicissitudes, self-doubt had never unmanned Spiridon at the decisive moment. Spiridon Yegorov was horrifyingly ignorant, his mind was closed to the highest creations of the human spirit and human society, but his actions and decisions were marked by a steady and unwavering common sense. For instance, knowing that the Germans would have shot all the village dogs, he calmly buried the severed head of a cow in light snow, something he would never have done ordinarily. Needless to say, he had never studied geography or German, but when they were digging trenches in Alsace and things started getting rough (to top it all, the Americans were raining down bombs on them), he took his older son and ran away. He couldn't read German signs or ask anyone the way. He lay low in the daytime and traveled only by night, over unknown country, as the crow flies, avoiding roads, covered ninety kilometers, and crept from house to house till he found the farm near Mainz where his wife was working. There he and his son holed up in a bunker in the orchard until the Americans arrived.

Spiridon had never been teased by any of the eternally unanswerable questions—whether sensory perception supplies true knowledge, whether we are capable of knowing "things in themselves." He was sure that he saw, smelled, and understood things without possibility of error.

Spiridon's moral code was just as uncomplicated and quietly confident. He spoke ill of no one. He never bore false witness. He used foul language only when necessary. He killed only when at war. He had got into fights only for his bride. He wouldn't steal a crumb or a rag from any other person, but he robbed the state whenever opportunity offered, with a cool conviction that it was right. He had, as he said, "sampled a few women" before his marriage—but didn't the great Aleksandr Pushkin confess that he found the commandment "Thou shalt not covet thy neighbor's wife" a particularly hard one to keep?

And now, fifty years old, a prisoner, almost blind, and obviously doomed to die right here in prison, Spiridon showed no inclination to play the saint, to despond, to repent, or—least of all—to "reform." He simply took his busy broom in his hands and swept the yard from dawn to dusk, day in and day out, in a life-and-death struggle against the commandant and the operations officers.

Whoever the power holders were, Spiridon was always at odds with them.

What Spiridon loved was the land.

What Spiridon possessed was his family.

Concepts such as homeland, religion, and socialism, little used in ordinary everyday conversation, might have been completely unknown to Spiridon. His ears were deaf to them; he could not get his tongue around them.

To him, homeland meant family.

Religion meant family.

Even socialism meant family.

To all the disseminators of the rational and good and eternal, all the writers who had called Spiridon and his like "God bearers" (though he was unaware of it), the priests, the Social Democrats, the volunteer agitators and professional propagandists, White landowners and Red kolkhoz chairmen who had themselves dealt with Spiridon in the course of his life, he had just one angry, but of necessity silent, message: "Why don't you all go . . . !"

# 68

## Spiridon's Criterion

THE TREADS OF the wooden staircase creaked and groaned as feet tramped and shuffled overhead. Now and then, fine dust and scraps of rubbish rained down on them, but Spiridon and Nerzhin hardly noticed.

They sat, clasping their knees, on the unswept floor, in greasy, worn-out blue overalls, their seats stiff with dirt. It was rather uncomfortable sitting like that, leaning back on the sloping boards lining the underside of the stairs. They looked straight ahead, their eyes fixed on the peeling side wall of the bathroom.

Nerzhin chain-smoked, as he always did when he was trying to work something out, placing his crushed cigarette ends in a row by the rotting baseboard underlining the triangle of dirty whitewashed wall beneath the stairs. Spiridon, like everybody else, received his allowance of White Sea Canal cigarettes—with a picture on the pack to remind him of the murderous work he had done in that murderous part of the world which had almost been his grave—but he was a strict nonsmoker, obeying the orders of the German doctors who had given him back three-tenths' vision in one eye, given him back light.

Spiridon had kept his grateful respect for German doctors. When he was blind beyond hope of recovery, they had driven a long needle into his spine, put ointment in his eyes, kept them bandaged for a long time, then removed the bandages in a half-darkened room and said, "Look!" And the world was lit up again! The dim nightlight seemed to Spiridon like bright sunshine. Spiridon could make out with his one eye the silhouette of his savior's head, and he bent to kiss his hand.

Nerzhin imagined the Rhenish doctor's tense, preoccupied face softening at that moment. Looking at the redheaded savage from the eastern steppes, liberated from his bandages, hearing that warm voice choked with gratitude, perhaps he would be thinking that the savage was meant for better things and was not to blame for being what he was.

From the German point of view, his behavior had been worse than that of a savage.

Immediately after the war, Spiridon and his family were living in an American camp for displaced persons. He met a man from his own village, a relative by marriage and a "dirty dog," said Spiridon, because of something he had done when they were cobbling together the kolkhoz. Spiridon and he had traveled as far as Slutsk together but had been separated in Germany. So of course they had to celebrate their reunion, and all they had was a bottle of raw alcohol brought along by the in-law. The spirits weren't proofed, and they couldn't read the German label; but it was costing them nothing. Evidently, even the wary Spiridon, whose circumspection had saved him from a thousand dangers, still had his share of his fellow countrymen's reckless fatalism. So . . . pull the cork, brother! Spiridon knocked back a tumblerful, and his pal downed the rest in one swig. Luckily, Spiridon's sons weren't there, or they would have been given a shot apiece. When he woke up shortly after midday, Spiridon was alarmed to find the room in darkness so early. He put his head out the window, but there was no more light outside, and he couldn't for the life of him understand why the American staff building across the street and the sentry outside it had no upper halves. He hoped to conceal this disaster from Marfa, but by evening he was completely blind.

His drinking companion died.

After the first operation the eye doctors told him to take it easy for a year, then they'd operate again, and he'd recover the sight in his left eye in full and his right eye in part. This was a firm promise. All he had to do was wait.

"But our lot—the dirty bums—filled our ears with lying tales, told us there were no collective farms anymore, that all was forgiven, our brothers and sisters were expecting us, all the bells were ringing. . . . Enough to make you slip out of your American shoes and run home barefoot."

This was too much for Nerzhin. "Danilych!" he said urgently, as if it were not too late for Spiridon to reconsider. "You knew things were never like they said! It was you who talked about planting corn and goosegrass coming up! What on earth possessed you? Surely you didn't believe them?"

Spiridon laughed, fine wrinkles around his eyes.

"Who, me? I knew for sure they'd slip the hard collar on me, Gleb, my boy. I was in the lap of luxury with the Americans; I'd never have come back willingly."

"We know the bait they generally used. Men came back because their families were here. But yours was right there under your wing. Who enticed you back to the Soviet Union?"

Spiridon sighed. "I said to Marfa Ustinovna right away, 'They'll promise us a lake, old girl, but who knows whether they'll let us lap from a stinking puddle?' She just ruffled my hair a bit and said, 'Let's just wait till you've got your eyes back; then we'll see. Let's wait for the other operation.' But the three kids were so excited, they just couldn't wait; they kept on at us: 'Daddy! Mama! let's go home! Back where we belong! Anybody would think there aren't any eye doctors in Russia. We smashed the Germans, didn't we? Somebody must have looked after the wounded. Our doctors are better than theirs!' They said they had to finish school in Russia; my older boy only had two more classes to take when we left. My little girl, Vera, never stopped sniveling and blubbering. 'D'you want me to marry a German?' she kept saying. As if there weren't plenty of Russians for her on the Rhine; but no, the silly girl thought she'd miss her number-one suitor if she didn't come back here. . . . They had me scratching my head. 'Children, children,' I told them, 'there are doctors in Russia, all right, but life there is murder; your father's already had one narrow escape; why are you so desperate to get there?' But no, it's only the burned child that fears the fire."

So Spiridon had joined the ranks of those destroyed by their children.

His mustache, ginger bristles touched with gray, quivered as he remembered. "I didn't believe their leaflets for one second: I knew I would go straight to jail. Still, I thought they'd heap all the blame on me and leave the children out of it. It wasn't their fault. I'd be locked up, but the kids could lead their own lives. Only, those scoundrels had their own ideas; they laid hands on the family as well."

Men and women had been separated at the frontier and sent on in different trains. Spiridon's family had held together all through the war, but now it fell apart. Nobody asked whether you were from Bryansk or Saratov. His wife and daughter were deported, without trial, to the Perm oblast, where his daughter now worked on a power saw in a lumber camp. Spiridon and his sons were whisked behind the wires; the boys, as well as their father, were tried for treason and given ten years each. Spiridon landed in the camp at

Solikamsk with his younger son and was at least able to mother him a bit for the next two years. The other son was thrown into one of the remote Kolyma camps.

This, then, was home. So much for his daughter's dream suitor and his sons' education.

What with the ordeal of interrogation and malnutrition in camp (he gave half his daily ration to his son), Spiridon's eyesight did not improve; indeed, he began to lose the sight of his good, left eye. Out there in the depths of the forest, with all around him snarling and snapping like wolves, asking the doctors to restore his sight would have been almost like asking to be taken alive up to heaven. What passed for a hospital in camp could not have told him whether there was treatment for his eyes to be had in Moscow, still less, set about treating them itself.

With his head in his hands, Nerzhin puzzled over his enigmatic friend. He could neither look up to this peasant, this victim of events, nor look down on him. He could only sit shoulder to shoulder with him, and eye to eye. Their conversations seemed to be compelling Nerzhin, more and more insistently, to ask one question. The whole pattern of Spiridon's life demanded an answer to that question. The time to ask it seemed to have come.

Was the complexity of Spiridon's life, his repeated abandonment of one warring side for the other, simply a matter of self-preservation? Or was it somehow an illustration of Tolstoy's belief that in this world no one is ever right and no one is ever to blame? That the Gordian knots of history cannot be cut with a presumptuous sword? Perhaps the more or less instinctive actions of this redheaded peasant exemplified the universal philosophical system known as skepticism?

The social experiment that Nerzhin had mounted seemed to be yielding, that very day, there under the staircase, surprising and brilliant results.

"I'm worried to death, Gleb," Spiridon was saying, rubbing his unshaved cheek hard with a gnarled and work-worn hand as though he were trying to skin it. "It's four months since I had a letter from home."

"I thought you said the Snake had a letter for you?"

Spiridon looked at him reproachfully. (His eyes might be dim, but they were fixed in a meaningless stare like those of a man born blind.)

"What good is a letter four months late?"

"If you get it tomorrow, bring it along, and I'll read it to you."

"There's no hurry now."

"Maybe a letter got lost in the mail? Maybe the godfathers have kept you waiting deliberately? Don't worry yourself for nothing, Danilych!"

"What do you mean, for nothing? My heart's aching for Vera. The poor girl's only twenty-one, and she's there without her father and brother, and her mother's nowhere near."

Nerzhin had seen a photograph of this Vera, taken the previous spring. A big, buxom girl with large, trusting eyes. Her father had brought her safely through a world war. When she was fifteen, thugs had tried to rape her in the forests around Minsk, and he had saved her with a hand grenade. But what could he do now, from prison?

Nerzhin imagined the dense Perm forest, the power saw chattering away like a machine gun, the hideous roar of tractors hauling logs, the trucks with their rear wheels bogged down and their radiators raised to heaven as if in prayer, the grimy, foul-tempered tractor drivers who had forgotten the difference between obscene words and others—and among them a girl in overall jacket and trousers provocatively emphasizing her womanly shape. She would be sleeping around the campfire with them. Nobody would pass by without pawing her. No wonder Spiridon's heart ached for her.

Words of comfort would be worse than useless. Try to take his mind off it, and seek in him a counterbalance to your intellectual friends! Perhaps, Gleb thought, this is when I will learn the fundamentals of homespun peasant skepticism, so that I can base myself on it in the future.

He laid his hand on Spiridon's shoulder, still leaning back against the sloping underside of the stairs, and began hesitantly framing his question: "There's something I've been wanting to ask you for a long time, Spiridon Danilych. Don't misunderstand me. . . . I've heard so much about your ups and downs. . . . You've had a hell of a life . . . like many others, I suppose . . . very many . . . you've been shoved around from pillar to post always looking for something that may not exist . . . but there must have been some point in it. What I mean is . . . I would like to hear what you think . . . when we try to understand life, what"—he nearly said "criterion"—"what yardstick should we use? For example, are there really people on this earth who deliberately set out to do evil things? Who say to themselves, I want to hurt people, to inflict all the pain I can, to make their lives impossible? I don't really think so, do you? That saying of yours about sowing rye and goosegrass coming up. . . . At least it was rye they sowed, or so they thought. It may be that all human beings want to do good or think they're acting for the best, but nobody is infallible, we all make mistakes, and some people are quite brazen about it, which is why they do each other so much harm. They can convince themselves that they're doing good, but the results are bad."

Perhaps he hadn't expressed himself very clearly. Spiridon was looking askance, frowning as though he suspected a trap.

"Suppose you make a glaring mistake, and I want to correct you. I speak to you about it, but you ignore me, gag me, try to shove me in jail. What am I to do? Hit you over the head with a stick? It's all very well if I am right, but suppose I just imagine I am, suppose it's just a stubborn idea I've gotten into my head. What if I push you off your perch and take your place, and then if things don't go the way I want, it's my turn to pile up corpses? What I mean is, if you can't be sure that you're always right, should you or shouldn't you intervene at all? When we're at war, we always think we're in the right, and the other side thinks they are. Can anybody on this earth possibly make out who's right and who's wrong? Who can tell us that?"

Spiridon's frown had disappeared, and he answered as readily as if he'd been asked which guard would be on duty next morning. "I can tell you: Killing wolves is right; eating people is wrong."

"What? What's that you say?"

The simplicity and certainty of Spiridon's answer took Nerzhin's breath away.

"Just that," Spiridon said. "The wolf killer is in the right; the man-eater is not."

Gleb's face felt warm breath from under that mustache as Spiridon leaned close to whisper: "Gleb, if somebody told me right now there's a plane on the way with an atom bomb on board—d'you want it to bury you like a dog here under the stairs, wipe out your family and a million other people, only old Daddy Whiskers and their whole setup will be pulled up by the roots so that our people won't have to suffer anymore in prison camps and collective farms and logging teams"—Spiridon braced himself, pressing his tensed shoulders against the stairs as though they threatened to collapse on him, with the roof itself and all Moscow to follow—"believe me, Gleb, I'd say, 'I can't take it anymore, I've run out of patience,' and I'd say"—he looked up at the imaginary bomber—"I'd say, 'Come on, then! Get on with it! Drop the thing!'"

Spiridon's face was contorted with fatigue and suffering. A single tear ran over the reddened rim of each unseeing eye.

# 69

## Behind a Closed Visor

THE OFFICER WHO CAME ON DUTY LATE that Sunday evening was a trim young lieutenant with two token squares of mustache under his nostrils. After lights out, he paraded in person along the upper and lower hallways of the special prison, chasing the prisoners, always reluctant to turn in on Sundays, to bed. He would have made a second sally if he could have torn himself away from the buxom little nurse in the sickbay. She had a husband in Moscow, but he could not reach her in the restricted area during the twenty-four hours she would be on duty. The lieutenant had high hopes that this was his night to get somewhere with her, though so far she had eluded his grasp, laughingly telling him over and over again to "stop playing the fool."

So instead of chasing the prisoners a second time, he sent his aide, the sergeant major. Knowing that the lieutenant would not check up on him, indeed would not set foot outside the sickbay before morning, the sergeant major made no great effort to put them all to bed. For one thing, after many years of service he had finally tired of being a police dog, and for another, he knew that grown men who had to go to work the next day would not forget that they needed sleep.

Extinguishing the lights in the hallways and on the stairs of the special prison was not allowed because it might help escapers or rioters.

So Rubin and Sologdin had twice avoided dismissal and still stood hugging the wall in the main hallway. It was after midnight, but they had no thought of sleep.

It was one of those furious, unresolvable arguments with which Russians, unless they come to blows instead, like to conclude a convivial evening.

But it was also the sort of ferocious argument that can take place only in jail; outside, a single view, that of the regime, reigns unchallenged.

The duel on paper had proved a failure. In the past hour or so, Rubin and Sologdin had taken the other two laws of the hapless dialectic apart, but the arguments they bounced off each other, finding no snag, no salutary ledge to slow their descent, rolled rapidly into the mouth of the volcano.

"If there are no contradictions, then there is no unity either?"

"So?"

"What do you mean, So? You're afraid of your own shadow! Am I right or am I wrong?"

"Right, of course."

Sologdin beamed. Fired by this glimpse of a weak spot in Rubin's defenses, he crouched, sharp-featured, ready to pounce.

"Well, then, whatever is free of contradictions doesn't exist? So why did you promise a classless society?"

"'Class' is a foreign word."

"Don't try to wriggle out of it. You know that a society free of contradictions is an impossibility, yet you shamelessly promised it. You. . . ."

In 1917 they had both been five-year-olds, but each of them, in his argument with the other, was ready to answer for the whole history of mankind.

"You crucified yourselves to do away with oppression, but you inflicted worse, far worse, oppressors on us. Was it worth killing so many millions of people for that?"

"You're too jaundiced to see clearly," Rubin shouted, forgetting the need to lower his voice for fear of compromising the opponent who was so eager to throttle him. (His own arguments, however loud, could not damage him, since he was on the side of the regime.)

"When you enter the classless society, your hatred will still prevent you from recognizing it."

"But right now—is it classless now? Give me a straight answer just this once! Just for once, don't dodge the question. Is there or is there not a new class, a ruling class?"

How difficult Rubin found it to answer that very question! He could see for himself that there was such a class. And that if it entrenched itself, it would deprive the Revolution of all sense and meaning.

But no shadow of weakness, no hint of uncertainty, troubled the lofty brow of this true believer.

"Do you mean it's detached from the rest of society?" he asked loudly. "Can you really distinguish precisely between the rulers and the ruled?"

Sologdin's voice rang out boldly in reply: "I can indeed! Foma, Anton, and Shishkin-Myshkin are the rulers, and we—"

"No, but are there really any fixed lines of demarcation? Class divisions resulting from inheritance of property? No, everything has to be earned by service. Prince today, in the gutter tomorrow. Isn't that the way of it?"

"If it is, so much the worse! If every member of society can be brought down, there's only one way he can make sure of survival—by doing whatever he's ordered to do. A gentleman in the old days could be as impertinent as he liked; the powers that be couldn't take his noble birth away from him."

"You and your precious little gentlemen! People like Siromakha!" (Siromakha was the sharashka's number-one stool pigeon.)

"Or take the merchant class. The market forced them to use their heads and react to changed circumstances quickly. Not like those friends of yours! Just think what a hopeless bunch they are—no concept of honor, no breeding, no education, no imagination, they hate freedom. The only way they can hang on to their positions is by debasing themselves."

"It doesn't take much intelligence to realize that this is a transitional bureaucratic group, and that as the state withers away—"

"Wither away?" Sologdin yelled. "Those people? Voluntarily? They won't go away till they're slung out by the scruffs of their necks! Your state wasn't created because of the 'moneybags'—meaning 'capitalist'—encirclement. It was created to cement by cruelty an unnatural way of life! If you people were alone on this earth, you'd go on forever making your state stronger and stronger!"

With so many years of repression and forced silence behind him, it was an immense relief to fling his views in the face of a companion who would listen and who was at the same time a confirmed Bolshevik and so of course responsible for all that had happened.

For his part, Rubin had outraged all those he had encountered from his first days in the counterespionage unit's cell at the front and through a long succession of cells elsewhere by proudly proclaiming that he was a Marxist and had no intention of renouncing his views, even in prison. He had grown used to being a sheepdog in a pack of wolves, defending himself single-handedly against forty or fifty at a time. His lips were raw and cracked from futile arguments, but it was his duty, his absolute duty, to explain to the blind their blindness, to wrestle with enemies among his cellmates in order to save them, since most of them were not really enemies but ordinary Soviet people, victims of Progress and the imperfections of the penal system. Personal grievances had clouded their consciousness, but if war with America should break out tomorrow, and these people were given weapons, they would almost to a man forget how their lives had been shattered, forgive their tormentors, think no more of the grief their sundered families had suffered, and rush to sacrifice themselves in defense of socialism, as Rubin himself would.

At the critical moment, Sologdin would obviously do the same; it could not be otherwise! Only dogs and traitors would behave differently!

Their argument bounded over sharp, lacerating stones until it reached this very point.

"Where, I ask you, is the difference? According to you, a former zek who's done ten years for squat and turns his weapons against his jailers is a traitor to his country! Whereas the German whom you have processed and sent back to his own lines to break his oath of loyalty and betray his fatherland you call a 'progressive'!"

"How can you compare the two?" Rubin sounded astonished. "Objectively, my German is for socialism, and your zek is against it. Can you really say there's any comparison?"

If the hot fury expressed in them could melt the substance eyes are made of, Sologdin's eyes would have gushed out in blue streams.

"It's no good talking to you! For thirty years you've lived by this device"—in the heat of the moment, he let slip the foreign word, but it was a good one, from the age of chivalry—" 'the end justifies the means.' But if you were asked point-blank whether that's what you believe, I'm sure you'd deny it! Oh yes you would!"

"What makes you think so?" Rubin asked, cool and conciliatory. "In my personal affairs I don't acknowledge it, but if we're talking about society as a whole, that's another matter. For the first time in human history, our aim is so lofty that we can say just that: The end justifies the means employed for its attainment."

"So you're prepared to go that far!" Sologdin's rapier sang as he lunged at a vulnerable spot. "Just remember this, then—that the loftier your aim, the nobler must be your means. Treacherous means destroy the end itself!"

"What do you call treacherous means? Are you perhaps denying the legitimacy of Revolutionary means?"

"When did you ever have a Revolution? Mayhem isn't Revolution; axes dripping blood aren't Revolution! Who could even begin counting those massacred or executed? The world would be horror-struck!

Like an express train rushing through the night, stopping nowhere, past rural stops, past wayside signal lights, across empty steppes, and through brightly lit towns, their argument sped over light and dark places in their memories, and everything that briefly loomed threw an uncertain light on, elicited a muffled echo from, their uncontrollably swaying, coupled thoughts.

"To pass judgment on a country, you must first know at least a little about it," Rubin said angrily. "You've been moldering in camps for twelve years. And how much did you see before that? The Patriarch's Ponds? Did you go on Sunday outings to Kolomenskoye?"

"What gives you the right to judge?" Sologdin kept his voice down to a muffled cry, as though he were being strangled. "Shame on you! You should be ashamed! Remember all those who went through Butyrki Prison when you were there—Gromov, Ivantyev, Yashin, Blokhin—they told you the sober truth, told you their life stories; don't tell me you weren't listening. And what about this place? What about Vartapyetov? Or that other man, what's his name, now. . . ?"

"Who? Who? Why should I listen to them? Blind men, all of them! All they do is howl like beasts with their paws caught in a trap. As they see it, their own failure in life means that socialism is a flop. Their observatory is the slop bucket; the aromas of the slop bucket are the breath of life to them."

"Is there anybody, then, anybody at all you're capable of listening to? If so, who?"

"The young! The young are on our side! And they are the future!"

"The young? You're imagining things! They couldn't care less about your shining lights!" (meaning "ideals").

"What gives you the right to speak for the young? I fought in the front line with them, went on reconnaissance with them, and all you know is what you've heard from some wretched émigré in a transit prison. How can you say the young have no ideology when there are ten million Komsomols in the country?"

"Komsomols! Kom-somols! Are you a halfwit or something? What you call the League of Communist Youth is just a device for the conversion of wrapping paper into membership books."

"Watch your mouth! I was a member myself. The Komsomol was our banner! Our conscience! Our selfless, romantic dream! The Komsomol movement was all that to us!"

"Gone, and best forgotten!"

"Anyway, who's talking? After all, you were a Komsomol yourself in those days."

"Yes, and I've paid in full for it! Been punished for it! You make a deal with Mephistopheles . . . Margarita! Her honor lost! Her brother dead! Her child dead! Madness! Perdition—"

"Never mind Margarita! It can't be true that your Komsomol days have left nothing in your soul."

"Soul, did you say? How your language has changed in the last twenty years! Nowadays you talk about 'the soul' and 'conscience' and 'sacrilege.' . . . I would have loved to hear you utter such words in your pious Communist days in 1927! . . . You corrupted a whole generation of young Russians. . . ."

"Looking at you, you could be right."

"And then you set to work on the Germans, the Poles. . . ."

On and on they charged, incapable now of matching argument and response, their thoughts no longer following each other in logical sequence, with no eyes for, no awareness of, the hallway, in which the only others left were two fanatical chess players and the old blacksmith with his hacking smoker's cough, and where their agitated arm-waving, their inflamed faces, and their aggressively poised beards, one black and bristly, one neat and fair, were so conspicuous.

"Gleb!"

"Gleb!"

Seeing Nerzhin and Spiridon coming upstairs from the bathroom, they both called out at once, each of them hoping to double his forces. Gleb was walking toward them anyway, alarmed by their shouting and gesticulation. Any passing idiot would have realized without hearing a word that they had gotten on to dangerous political matters. Nerzhin went up to them quickly, and before they could, both at once, fire contradictory questions at him, prodded each of them in the ribs.

"Sense! Sense!"

This was the code word they had all three agreed on. If two of them were involved in a heated argument, the third would put a stop to it by reminding them in this way of the danger of informers.

"Have you gone mad? You've already earned yourselves another tenner each. Aren't you satisfied? Dmitri! Think of your family!"

There was no hope of parting them peacefully—or, for that matter, with a jet from a hose.

"Just listen to him!" Sologdin said, shaking Gleb by the shoulder. "He sets all our sufferings at nought. They're warranted as far as he's concerned. The only sufferings he cares about are those of Negroes on plantations!"

"Well, I've told Lev before, charity begins at home."

"What narrowness! You're no internationalist!" Rubin exclaimed, glaring at Nerzhin as though he were a pickpocket caught in the act. "You should have heard the rot he's been talking. He thinks the autocracy was a blessing for Russia! All our conquests, all our dirty tricks, the Straits, Poland, Central Asia. . . ."

Nerzhin's verdict was swift and firm. "In my view, it's high time we set all our colonies free, for the salvation of Russia, and concentrated our people's efforts on the internal development of the country."

"That's childish!" Sologdin retorted peevishly. "If you had a free hand, you'd shake the land of your fathers to pieces. . . . You tell him—is all that Komsomol romanticism of theirs worth a bent kopeck? Remember how they taught peasant children to denounce their parents? How they wouldn't leave those who'd grown the grain so much as husks to choke on? And he has the nerve to mouth the word 'virtue'!"

"Oh, a noble soul you are! Call yourself a Christian? You're nothing of the sort!"

"Don't blaspheme. Don't talk about things you don't understand."

"You think that just because you aren't a thief or an informer, that's enough to make you a Christian? Where's your love for your neighbor? There's a saying that just fits you: The hand that makes the sign of the cross also sharpens the knife. No wonder you're such a fan of medieval bandits! You're a typical conquistador!"

"Flatterer!" Sologdin struck a picturesque pose.

"You're flattered? Horrible, horrible!"

Rubin ran the fingers of both hands through his thinning hair. "Do you hear him, Gleb? Tell him what a poseur he is! I'm fed up with his posturing! He's forever pretending to be Alexander Nevsky!"

"Now, that I don't find a bit flattering!"

"What do you mean?"

"Alexander Nevsky is no sort of hero as far as I'm concerned. And no saint. So I don't take what you said as a compliment."

Rubin was silenced. He and Nerzhin exchanged a baffled look.

"So what has Alexander Nevsky done to upset you?" Nerzhin asked.

"Kept chivalry out of Asia and Catholicism out of Russia. He was against Europe," Sologdin said, still breathless with indignation.

Rubin returned to the attack, hoping to land a blow.

"Now this is something new! Something quite new! . . ."

"Why would Catholicism have been good for Russia?" Nerzhin inquired, looking judicial.

"I'll tell you why!" The answer came like a flash of lightning. "Because all the people who had the misfortune to be Orthodox Christians paid for it with centuries of slavery! Because the Orthodox Church never could stand up to the state! A godless people was defenseless! The result was this cockeyed country of ours! A country of slaves!"

Nerzhin's eyes were popping out.

"I just don't understand. Wasn't it you who blamed me for not being patriotic enough? Now you're giving the land of your fathers a drubbing."

But Rubin had seen a break in his enemy's defenses. He leaped in quickly.

"What's become of Holy Russia? And the Language of Utter Clarity? And the campaign against 'birds' words'?"

"Yes, indeed!" added Nerzhin. "What's the point of the Language of Utter Clarity if ours is a cockeyed country?"

Sologdin beamed. He stretched out his arms and made circular movements with his hands.

"A game, gentlemen! A game! A joust with lowered visor! We all need exercise! We must strive at all times to overcome resistance. We are imprisoned for good, and we must pretend to hold views as remote as possible from our real ones. As I've told you, one of the nine spheres. . . ."

"Roundnesses, you mean."

"No, spheres!"

Rubin flared up again. "So that was humbug, too! This country isn't good enough for you. But who if not you reckless God botherers was responsible for Khodynka and Tsushima and the debacle of 1915?"

Sologdin gasped.

"So the murderers' hearts bleed for Russia now, do they? Wasn't it you who butchered Russia in 1917?"

"Sense! Sense!" Gleb punched both of them in the ribs again. But the debaters were oblivious. They could no longer see him through the red mist before their eyes.

"What makes you think you'll ever be forgiven for collectivization?"

"Remember what you told us in Butyrki? That your only object in life was to grab yourself a million? Why do you need a million to get to the Kingdom of Heaven?"

They had known each other for two years. And now they were distorting all that they had learned about each other in heart-to-heart conversations, insulting each other as hurtfully as they could. Every little thing either of them could recall was flung in the other's face as an accusation.

"Don't you understand ordinary human language?" Nerzhin croaked. "Wrap it up! Wrap it up!"

He made a helpless gesture and left them to it. At least there was nobody else in the hallway, and all those in the rooms were asleep.

"Shame on you! You corrupter of men's souls! Those creatures who preside over East Germany are your nurslings!"

"You puffed-up pygmy! How pathetically proud you are of your drop of gentry blood!"

"If the Shishkin-Myshkins are furthering the good cause, why don't you help them? Why not squeal for them? Shikin, too, will give you a good report. And they'll review your case."

"Talking like that could get you a bloody nose!"

"I don't see why. Look at it this way. Since all the rest of us are rightly here, and only you are not, our jailers must be in the right. That's only logical."

By now they were exchanging random insults, scarcely listening to each other, each of them intent on one thing only—landing his blows where they would hurt most.

"You're an inveterate liar! Everything you do and say rests on a lie! Yet you pontificate as though you never let go of your crucifix."

"You didn't want to discuss the importance of pride in a man's life, but you really should try to borrow a bit of pride from somewhere. Twice a year you humbly petition them for a pardon—"

"Lies! For a review of my case, not a pardon."

"The answer's always no, but you go on humbly begging. You're like a little dog on a chain; whoever holds the chain has you in his power."

"Wouldn't you humbly beg if you could? In your case, release is ruled out. Otherwise you'd crawl on your belly for it!"

Sologdin shook with indignation. "Never!"

"I tell you, you would! You just lack the means of attracting attention!"

They had tormented each other to the point of exhaustion. Innokenty Volodin could not have imagined that his fate would be influenced by a tedious nocturnal argument between two prisoners in a sealed and secluded building on the outskirts of Moscow.

Each of them wanted to be executioner, but both were victims in this quarrel. They had long ago lost the thread, and the quarrel was not really theirs, but between two radically opposed and equally destructive forces.

Each was well aware of the other's destructive potential. Each knew for certain that whether yesterday's or tomorrow's blind and mindless conquerors prevailed, both were as impervious to reason as those prison walls.

Rubin was almost tearing his hair.

"Tell me this, then: If you always thought as you do now, how could you join the Komsomol?"

For the second time in half an hour, Sologdin was so exasperated that he betrayed himself unnecessarily.

"What else could I do? Did you leave us the option of not joining? If I hadn't been in the Komsomol, I wouldn't have gotten into the institute in a thousand years. I'd have been digging ditches!"

"So you pretended? You put on a disgusting little act."

"No! I simply went into the attack with visor lowered!"

What Rubin inferred from this was agonizing, heartstopping.

"So if there's a war, and you get your hands on a weapon. . . ."

Sologdin raised himself to his full height, folded his arms, and backed away from Rubin as though he had leprosy.

"You don't think I'd defend you, do you?"

"Your words reek of blood!" Rubin clenched his hairy fists.

Whatever they said or did next—take each other by the throat, fly at each other with fists flailing—would have been a feeble expression of their feelings. All that was left to them was to seize machine guns and fire a burst. That was the only language the loser would have understood.

But there were no machine guns.

They parted, breathing heavily, Rubin hanging his head, Sologdin head in the air.

Sologdin might have hesitated earlier, but now he savored in advance the joy of hitting those dirty dogs where it hurt! Don't give them their encoder! Don't let them have it! You don't have to be one of those pulling their triumphal chariot! If you do, you'll never show them up for the mediocrities they are! They shout themselves hoarse; they deafen us with their laws of historical inevitability: "It cannot be otherwise!" is their constant cry. They write history the way they want it, twist the hidden causes to suit themselves.

Rubin went away to his corner and clasped his painfully throbbing head in his hands. He saw clearly now that there was one, only one, crushing blow he could inflict on Sologdin and the whole pack of Sologdins. The only way to ram anything into those thick heads. No factual arguments, no historical justification, would ever convince them that you were right! The atomic bomb—that was the one thing they would understand! He must overcome his illness, his weakness, his reluctance, and—first thing tomorrow morning—get his nose down and pick up the trail of that anonymous miscreant. He must save the atomic bomb for the Revolution!

Petrov! Syagovity! Volodin! Shchevronok! Zavarzin!

## 70

# Dotty

IT WAS AFTER MIDNIGHT, and Innokenty and Dotty were on their way home by taxi. A heavy snowfall was emptying the streets, half hiding buildings behind its white veil. It seemed to promise peace and oblivion.

The warm feeling for his wife stirred by her unexpected docility at his father-in-law's home remained with him now that there was no one to see them. Dotty prattled uninhibitedly, about everyone and everything—the party, the guests, whether Klara would ever get married and to whom. . . . Innokenty listened indulgently.

He was relaxing, resting after the intolerable strain of the last twenty-four hours. And somehow there was no one he would have found more restful at that moment than this dear, degraded, unfaithful rejected woman—in spite of everything, his indispensable fellow traveler along the road of life.

Absentmindedly he put an arm around her shoulders. They stayed like that for the rest of the journey. His body throbbed once more for the contact with this woman that he had renounced forever.

He looked sideways at her. Glanced at her lips. Lips unlike any others, lips that you could press to your own in a long, long kiss and never feel sated.

Innokenty knew from experience that there were few other women, if any, of whom this was true. He knew that no woman combined all the characteristics you might hope to find in her. You would have to select piecemeal and combine one woman's lips with another's hair, another's complexion, and various features from yet others to produce what nature refused to provide. And, of course, you would need to select the preferred temperament, character, mentality, habits.

It wasn't Dotty's fault that she wasn't perfect. Nobody was. And she had many good points.

What, he wondered, if this woman had never been his wife or mistress, what if he knew that she belonged to another but was sitting there submissively with his arm around her on the way to his apartment? What would his feelings toward her be then? Surely he would not hold it against her that she had been in the arms of other men? Many other men? Why, then, did he find the thought humiliating just because she was his wife?

Yet, however absurd, however despicable he felt it to be, this woman, defiled as she was, was all the more fatally attractive to him.

He took his arm away.

Better, of course, to think of anything rather than his pursuers. Of the ambush perhaps awaiting him at home. On the stairs? Or actually inside his apartment? They could get in easily enough.

That, in fact—he could see it clearly!—was just what was about to happen. They would be there already, in his own apartment, lying in wait. And the moment he unlocked the door, they would rush into the hallway and pounce on him.

Perhaps these peaceful minutes in the back of a cab with his arm around the unsuspecting Dotty were in fact his last minutes of freedom.

Perhaps, though, it was time he told her something?

He looked at her compassionately, tenderly even. Dotty was immediately conscious of that look, and her upper lip quivered endearingly.

What, though, could he tell her in a few words, even after he had paid and dismissed the cabbie? That country and government were not the same thing? . . . That it would be criminal to let a crazy regime get its hands on such a superhuman weapon? That their country did not need military might and that only when they were rid of it would they really begin to live?

These were things hardly any of those in power would understand, not to mention the scientists who were feverishly laboring to produce some sort of bomb. So how could the overdressed, luxury-loving wife of a diplomat be expected to understand?

Then again, he remembered how often Dotty had clumsily interrupted a heart-to-heart conversation with some crass, irrelevant remark. She was tactless, always had been, and no one could feel the want of something never possessed.

He avoided looking at her and remained silent on the landing. He turned the first key in the lock, inserted the Yale key, and stood aside as usual to let her go first. Was he letting her walk into a trap? Perhaps it would be better that way. She had nothing to lose, and he would see them and . . . No, he wouldn't run for it, but he'd have five more seconds to think of something!

Dotty walked in and switched on the light.

Nobody jumped them. There were no strange coats on the hooks. No footprints left by careless intruders.

This meant nothing. He would still need to inspect every room.

But deep down he was convinced that no one was lurking! Bolt the door at once! Double bolt it! Open it to no one! We're fast asleep! Nobody home!

His body was suffused with a warm feeling of security.

And Dotty was there to share his safety and happiness.

He felt grateful to her as he helped her take off her coat.

She bowed her head so that he could see the nape of her neck and her unusual hairline and said penitently, softly, but clearly, "Beat me! Thrash me like a peasant thrashes his woman!"

She looked up at him, wide-eyed. She meant it! There was no hint of tears. She never broke down and wept as most women do. Her eyes would be moist for just a moment, then so dry that they looked dull and vacant.

But Innokenty was no peasant. He could not bring himself to beat his wife. It would never have occurred to him that such a thing was possible.

He laid his hands on her shoulders.

"Why are you so crude sometimes?"

"I'm crude when I'm hurting badly. Beat me!"

They stood there awkwardly, at a loss.

"I've been so unhappy this last day or two. So terribly unhappy," Innokenty said plaintively.

Dotty, no longer penitent, said what it was right for her to say, and those luscious lips whispered, "I know! But I can make you feel better!"

"I don't think so," he said with a miserable laugh. "Even you can't do that."

"There's nothing I can't do," she insisted in a low voice. "What good would it be loving you if I couldn't make you forget your troubles?"

And Innokenty found himself pressing his lips to hers, as in the time he liked best to remember.

The relentless dread in his soul was overwhelmed by a feeling of bliss.

They went through the flat, still entwined, and with no thought of a trap.

Innokenty was lost in a universe of warm maternal love.

No longer shivering.

Dotty was his universe.

## 71

# Let's Agree That This Didn't Happen

THE SHARASHKA WAS ASLEEP AT LAST. Zeks, 280 of them, slept in the bluish lamplight, hugging their pillows or flat on their backs, some breathing soundlessly, some snoring horribly, some crying out incoherently from time to time, curled up to keep warm or sprawling to seek relief from the stifling heat. They slept on two stories of the building and on two-tiered bunks, and they dreamed: old men of their families, young men of women. They dreamed of lost possessions, a train, a church, their judges. . . . Their dreams were all different, but whatever they dreamed, the sleepers were miserably aware that they were prisoners. If in their dreams they roamed over green grass or through city streets, it could mean only that they had tricked their jailers and escaped or had been released in error and were now wanted men. That total, blissful forgetfulness of their shackles imagined by Longfellow in "The Prisoner's Dream" was denied them. The shock of wrongful arrest, followed by a ten- or twenty-year sentence, the baying of guard dogs, the sound of escort troops priming their rifles, the nerve-racking jangle of reveille in the camps, seep through all the strata of ordinary experience, through all their secondary and even primary instincts, into a prisoner's very bones so that, sleeping, he remembers that he is in jail before he becomes aware of smoke or the smell of burning and gets up to find the place on fire.

Mamurin the has-been was asleep in his solitary cell. The off-duty shift of guards was sleeping. So was the shift now supposedly on watch. The female medical orderly on duty, after resisting the lieutenant with the two tabs of mustache all evening, had yielded some little time ago, and they, too, were now both asleep on the narrow couch in the sickbay. And, finally, the dim little guard posted on the main stairway by the chained iron door to the prison, once he saw that no one was coming to check up on him, cranked his field telephone a time or two without result and fell asleep in his chair, resting his head on a locker and forgetting that he was supposed to peek from time to time through the little window into the hallway of the special prison.

The 281st prisoner had lain low till the hour when the Marfino prison routine ceased to operate. He then quietly left the semicircular room, screwing up his eyes at the bright light outside and treading on the cigarette ends littering the hallway. He had put his boots on without foot rags and draped his threadbare army overcoat over his underwear. His grim black beard was disheveled, his thinning hair had strayed in all directions, and there was a look of suffering on his face.

He had tried in vain to fall asleep and had gotten up to pace the hallway. He had tried this remedy before. It always calmed him down and brought relief from the burning pain at the back of his head and the tearing pain near his liver.

He had left the room to stretch his legs but, insatiable reader that he was, had brought a few books with him and inserted the first draft of his "Project for Civic Temples" in one of them, together with a blunt pencil. All these things, together with a pack of light tobacco and his pipe, he laid out on the dirty table and began walking down the hallway and back, clasping his overcoat.

He was aware that all prisoners suffered, enemies of the state jailed by their enemies no less than those who were jailed for nothing. But he regarded his own position (and Abramson's, too) as tragic in the Aristotelian sense. The blow had been struck by the hands of those he loved most. Soulless bureaucrats had jailed him for loving the common cause with indecent ardor. The prison guards and their superiors gave expression in their activities to the infallible law of progress, but because of a tragic misunderstanding Rubin was at loggerheads with them day in and day out. Whereas his fellow prisoners were no comrades of his. In every cell he had been in, they had reproached him, abused him, been ready almost to bite him, because they saw only their own misery and were blind to the great design. They persecuted him not for truth's sake but to take out on him what they could not take out on their jailers. They baited him, little caring that every such attack tied his insides in knots. And in every cell, at each new encounter, in every discussion, it was his duty to try to convince them, with unflagging enthusiasm and in disdain of their insults, that, overall and in the main, things were going as they should: industry flourishing, agriculture highly productive, science abubble with new ideas, the world of the arts dazzling in its rainbow brilliance.

Every such cell, every such argument, was a sector of the front, on which Rubin stood alone in defense of socialism.

His opponents often took advantage of their superior number to pass themselves off as "the people" and represent Rubin and his like as a handful of oddities. But he knew that this was a lie! The people was out there, beyond those prison walls, beyond the barbed wire. The people had taken Berlin, met the Americans on the Elbe; trainloads of discharged soldiers had poured eastward to reconstruct the Dnieper Hydroelectric Station, set the Donbass to work again, rebuild Stalingrad. It was his feeling of oneness with those millions that sustained Rubin in his claustrophobic struggle single-handed against dozens of fellow prisoners at a time.

Rubin rapped on the pane set in the iron doors—once, twice, and the third time loudly. At the third knock the dim screw, still half asleep, rose and put his face to the window.

"I feel unwell," Rubin said. "I need medicine. Take me to the medical orderly."

The guard thought a bit, then said, "All right. I'll give them a call."

Rubin resumed his pacing.

He was altogether a tragic figure.

He had passed through prison gates before any of those now locked up here.

A grown-up cousin, whom sixteen-year-old Lev idolized, had given him some type to hide. Young Lev jumped at the chance. But he had not been on his guard against the boy next door, who had spied on him and denounced him. Lev had not given his cousin away; he had spun a yarn about finding the type under the stairs.

That solitary confinement cell in the Kharkov "investigation prison" twenty years earlier came back to him as he tramped with measured tread back and forth along the hallway.

The prison had been built on the American model. It was like an open well, several stories deep, with iron landings connected by iron stairs. At the bottom of the well sat a traffic controller with little flags. Every sound echoed loudly through the prison. Young Lev heard someone being dragged noisily up a flight of stairs, and suddenly an earsplitting yell shook the prison: "Comrades! Greetings from the icebox! Down with Stalin's torturers!"

They beat him (that unmistakable sound of blows on soft flesh!), held his mouth shut, stifling his shouts until they stopped altogether, but then three hundred prisoners in three hundred solitary cells rushed to their doors to bang on them and scream:

"Down with the murdering dogs!"

"Drinking the workers' blood!"

"We've got another tsar on our backs!"

"Long live Leninism!"

And suddenly from some of the cells passionate voices struck up the "Internationale": "Arise, ye starvelings of oppression!"

The whole invisible throng of prisoners, oblivious of all else, roared out, "And the last fight let us face. . . ."

Lev could not see them, but he felt sure that many of the singers had tears of exaltation in their eyes, as he did.

The prison had buzzed like a disturbed hive. A bunch of guards with keys cowered terror-stricken on the stairs, silenced by the immortal proletarian hymn. . . .

The pain in the back of his head came in waves. The ache in the small of his back was excruciating.

Rubin rapped on the window again. At his second knock the sleep-sodden face of the same guard swam into view. He opened the hinged pane and muttered, "I called, but they aren't answering."

He made as if to close the window, but Rubin gripped the frame to prevent it. Suffering agonies, he raised his voice in exasperation.

"So why not use your legs! Can't you understand? I'm sick! I can't sleep! Call the medical orderly."

"Oh, all right," the screw said.

And shut the window.

Rubin resumed his desperate pacing, along a hallway fouled with spittle, littered with cigarette butts, getting nowhere, and feeling that he was making just as little progress through the hours of night.

His vision of the Kharkov jail, which he always recalled with pride—though those two weeks of solitary confinement had blackened his record, complicated his life ever since, and aggravated his present sentence—was followed by other memories, galling memories always kept to himself.

One day he was called to the Party office at the tractor plant. Lev thought of himself as one of the founders of the factory; he was on the editorial staff of its newsletter. He ran around the workshops encouraging the young, bucking up the older workers, pinning up "news flashes" about the achievements of shock brigades, about delays, and about slovenly work.

A lad of twenty in a Russian shirt, he went into the Party office as confidently as he had once entered the office of the secretary of the Ukrainian Central Committee. On that occasion he had said, quite simply, "Good day, Comrade Postyshev," and the First Secretary had held out his hand. So now he behaved in just the same way to a forty-year-old woman with close-cropped hair tied up in a red headscarf.

"Good day, Comrade Pakhtina! You sent for me?"

"Good day, Rubin." She shook his hand. "Sit down."

He sat.

There was a third person in the room, not a worker by the look of him, wearing a tie, a suit, and low yellow shoes. He sat on one side, looking through some papers and ignoring the new arrival.

The Party office was as austere as a confessional, decorated and furnished throughout in flame red and workaday black.

The woman talked halfheartedly to Lev about factory business, which they ordinarily discussed enthusiastically. Then suddenly she sat back in her chair and said firmly, "Comrade Rubin! You must not hold things back from the Party!"

Lev was astounded. What could she mean? Didn't he work with all his might, damage his health, turn night into day for the Party?

No! That wasn't enough!

So what more was expected of him?

At this point the outsider politely intervened. He addressed Lev with an old-fashioned formality that grated on a proletarian ear. He said that Lev must, honestly and without reservation, tell all he knew about his married cousin: Was it true that he had been an active member of an underground Trotskyist organization and now tried to conceal this from the Party?

Both pairs of eyes were fastened on him, and he had to say something immediately.

Lev had learned to look at the Revolution through that very cousin's eyes and knew from him that it was not always as neat and festive as a May Day parade. Yes, the Revolution was springtime, and that was why there was so much mud for the Party to flounder in until it found a firm footing.

But that, after all, was four years ago. The controversies within the Party had petered out. People hardly remembered the Bukharinites, let alone the Trotskyists. Stalin was slavishly, unimaginatively copying all the proposals for which the great heresiarch had been banished from the Soviet Union. Like a thousand coracles cobbled together to make an ocean liner, a thousand peasant holdings were amalgamated and called a collective farm. The furnaces of Magnitogorsk were already smoking, and tractors from the four pioneer factories were tilling the kolkhoz soil. The ambitious slogans of the First Five-Year Plan would soon be out of date. Objectively, all this had been accomplished to the greater glory of World Revolution, so was it worth fighting now over the name to be attached to these great deeds? (Lev had forced himself to love the new name, too. Yes, Lev had come to love HIM!) So why arrest now, why take vengeance on those who had dissented earlier?

"I don't know; he was never a Trotskyist," Lev heard himself saying, but that was the young Lev. His reason told him that he must speak like an adult, without puerile romanticism; refusal to cooperate was now pointless.

The Party secretary spoke, chopping the air for emphasis. "The Party! Is it not the most important thing in our lives? How can we withhold anything from the Party? Refuse to open our hearts? To the Party? The Party does not punish! The Party is our conscience! Remember what Lenin said. . . ."

Ten pistol barrels staring him in the face would not have intimidated young Lev Rubin. Threats of the icebox or banishment to Solovki would not have wrested the truth from him. But the Party! He was incapable of lying or prevaricating in that red-and-black confessional.

Rubin revealed what group his cousin had belonged to, and when, and what he had done.

The woman preacher was silent. It was the polite stranger in the yellow shoes who spoke: "Let me see if I've understood you correctly." He read out what he had written. "Now sign. Right here."

Lev recoiled. "Who are you? You're not the Party!"

"Why do you say that?" The visitor was offended. "I, too, am a member of the Party. I'm an investigating officer of the GPU."

• • •

Rubin rapped on the window again. The guard appeared, obviously torn from his sleep and breathing heavily.

"What are you knocking for now? However many times I call, there's no answer."

Rubin's eyes were hot with indignation. "I asked you to go down there, not to call. My heart is bothering me! I may die!"

"Now don't you go and die on me." The screw's drawling voice sounded conciliatory, almost sympathetic. "You'll last till morning. You know I can't go away and leave my post."

"What sort of idiot d'you think would run off with your post?" Rubin shouted.

"It isn't that; it's against regulations."

Rubin himself almost believed that he was about to die, his head was throbbing so violently. The guard looked at his agonized face and made up his mind.

"Oh all right, get away from the peephole and don't knock anymore. I'll pop down. "

Rubin assumed that he had gone, and the pain abated slightly.

He began pacing the hall again. Memories that he had no wish at all to awaken drifted through his mind. Things that he must forget if he wished to be made whole again.

Rubin had been anxious shortly after his first spell in jail to atone for his sin against the Komsomol and he was in a hurry to prove to himself and to the only Revolutionary class how useful he could be. So he set off with a Mauser over his shoulder to help collectivize a village.

He had run three versts barefoot, firing as he went, to escape from a crowd of infuriated peasants—and what had it meant to him at the time? "Now I've had a taste of civil war." That was all.

Blow up the pits in which grain is hidden. Stop peasants grinding corn and baking bread. Don't let them draw water from the well. If a peasant child is dying—go ahead and die, you villains, you and your children with you; you're not going to bake bread! That solitary cart pulled by a drooping horse through the deathly hush of the village at dawn caused no twinge of pity. It was a sight as unremarkable as a tram-car in town. The handle of a whip knocks on a shutter: "Any dead in there? Out with them."

On to the next shutter.

"Any dead? Out with them."

And before long it's "Hey! Is there anybody alive in there?"

Now all this was imprinted on his brain in red-hot letters. It burned. And sometimes he imagined that he had been wounded—for that! Imprisoned—for that! His illnesses were for that!

That was only fair. But now that he knew how horrible it had been, knew that he could never do it again, now that he had paid for it all, how could he cleanse himself of it? Who was there to say it never happened? We will now assume that it never happened! Behave as though it never happened!

What excruciating torment a sleepless night can be for a soul grieving over past mistakes.

THIS TIME THE GUARD SLID BACK the windowpane unasked. He had finally steeled himself to leave his post and go down to the staff room. He found them all asleep. There was nobody to answer the phone. He had roused the sergeant major, who listened to his report, gave him a dressing-down for leaving his post, and, knowing that the medical assistant was sleeping with the lieutenant, did not take the liberty of awakening them.

"Nothing doing," the guard said through the gap in the window. "I went myself and reported. They said they couldn't do anything. Said leave it till morning."

"But I'm dying! I'm dying," Rubin said hoarsely. "I'll break the pane! Call the duty officer right away! I'm going on hunger strike!"

"How can you go on hunger strike? Nobody's offering you anything to eat," the screw very reasonably retorted. "Breakfast time tomorrow, that's the time to go on hunger strike. . . . Oh, well . . . keep waiting a bit, and I'll give the sergeant major another call."

Rankers, sergeants, lieutenants, colonels, generals—with their fat jobs and their fat pay envelopes—none of them cared one little bit what became of the atom bomb . . . or a prisoner at his last gasp.

Last gasp or not, he must try to rise above it all!

Struggling against pain and nausea, Rubin tried to keep up his measured pacing. Suddenly he remembered Krylov's fable "The Damascene Blade." It had meant nothing to him as a free man, but in jail. . . .

A sharp saber was thrown onto a scrap heap, taken with the rest of the old iron to market, and sold to a peasant for a song. The peasant used the blade to strip bark and to chip tapers from logs. The blade became jagged and rusty. One day, under a bench in the peasant's hut, a hedgehog asked the blade if it wasn't ashamed. The blade's answer was that which in his thoughts Rubin had often given himself: "The shame is not mine; the shame is his who lacked the wit to understand the feats I can perform."

# 72

# Civic Temples

RUBIN FELT WEAK in his legs and sat down, resting his chest against the edge of the table.

However vehemently he had contradicted Sologdin, listening to him had been all the more painful because there was a grain of truth in what he had said. Yes, some of those in the Communist Youth Movement were not worth the cardboard used to make their membership cards. Yes, the foundations of morality had been sapped, and people, especially the younger generation, were losing their feel for what was right and noble. Societies, like fish, go rotten from the head. Who was there to set an example for the young?

In older societies, people knew that a moral code needs safeguards: a church and a priest with authority. What Polish peasant woman even now takes any serious step in life without consulting her parish priest?

As things were, the preservation of moral standards was perhaps much more important to the land of the Soviets than the Volga-Don Canal or the Angara Hydroelectric Station.

What could be done about it? His "Proposal for the Establishment of Civic Places of Worship," already completed in first draft, was Rubin's contribution. He must use this sleepless night to finalize it and try to smuggle it out with his next visitor. Once outside, it would be typed and submitted to the Central Committee. He could not send it under his own name; the Central Committee would reject advice of this sort from a political prisoner. Nor could it be sent anonymously. One of his old army friends would have to sign it. Rubin would gladly sacrifice authorial fame in a good cause.

Fighting down the waves of pain in his head, out of habit he packed his pipe with Golden Fleece, though he had no wish to smoke right then—indeed, felt an aversion to it—took a puff, and began looking through his project.

Wearing an overcoat over his underwear, sitting at a bare, roughly planed table littered with crumbs and tobacco, breathing the stale air of the unswept corridor, along which sleepy zeks hurried from time to time on their nocturnal errands, the anonymous author examined the disinterested project that he had roughed out in his hasty scrawl on several sheets of paper.

The preamble spoke of the need to raise the moral level of the population, high though it already was, and to enhance the significance of anniversaries and family occasions by introducing solemn ceremonies. For this purpose Civic Temples should be established everywhere, each of them a majestic building dominating its locality.

The organizational details were set out in several sections, each broken up into paragraphs, so as not to overtax the brains of authority. Civic Temples should be built in centers of population of a certain size, in order to serve a particular territorial unit; the dates to be commemorated should be specified for each of them; likewise the duration of the ceremonies. Young people, as they came of age, should attend in groups and, in the presence of a great concourse, take a special oath of loyalty to the Party, their fatherland, and their parents.

The project was particularly insistent that temple servants should wear special garments symbolizing their snow white purity. That the ritual form of words should be rhythmically phrased. That no means of having an impact on the sense organs of those who visited the temples should be overlooked. A special fragrance in the air, melodious music and singing, colored glass and floodlights, murals by skilled artists, and the architectural design of the temple as a whole should serve to develop the aesthetic taste of the population.

Every word of the project had to be selected with painstaking discrimination from an array of synonyms. Otherwise, unperceptive and superficial people might conclude from a carelessly used word that the author was simply proposing to revive Christian temples without Christ. But this was profoundly untrue! Someone who liked to draw historical analogies might also accuse the author of copying Robespierre's cult of the Supreme Being. But of course that, too, was not the same thing at all—not at all!!

The author considered the most original part of the project to be the section on the new—no, not priests but temple attendants, as he called them. He considered that the key to the success of the whole project lay in establishing throughout the nation a corps of authoritative attendants who enjoyed the love and trust of the people because of their own irreproachable and selfless way of life. The Party authorities were to select candidates for training as temple attendants, transferring them from their present employment, whatever it might be. Once the initial acute shortage was overcome, training courses would get longer and more thorough year by year, giving the attendants a broad general education with special emphasis on elocution. (The project daringly asserted that the art of public speaking had declined in the Soviet Union, possibly because no one was in need of persuasion, since the whole population unconditionally supported its very own state.)

Meanwhile, Rubin was not in the least surprised that nobody came to look at a sick prisoner who had chosen the wrong time to die. He had seen the same thing only too often in counterespionage units and transit prisons.

So when the key grated in the lock, his instinctive reaction was one of terror; he had been caught at dead of night doing something he shouldn't be doing, and the consequence would be some excruciatingly tedious punishment. He swept up his papers, his book, his tobacco, and would have fled to his room, but he was too late; the stocky, plug-ugly sergeant major had spotted him and was calling to him from the open door.

His mind cleared, and he was painfully aware again that he was alone, abandoned, insulted, humiliated.

"Sergeant Major," he said, walking slowly toward the duty officer's deputy. "I've been trying to get the medical assistant for more than two hours now. I will make a complaint about the medical assistant and about you to the Prison Administration of the Ministry of State Security."

The sergeant major was conciliatory. "I couldn't get here any sooner, Rubin; there was nothing I could do about it. Let's go."

In fact, all he could do when he learned that a prisoner, one of the most noxious prisoners at that, was making a disturbance was to knock on the lieutenant's door. There was no answer for some time; then the female medical assistant looked out and disappeared again. In the end, the lieutenant emerged looking disgruntled and gave the sergeant major permission to bring Rubin along.

Rubin put his arms into the sleeves of his coat and buttoned it to conceal his underwear. The sergeant major took him along the basement hallway of the sharashka, and they went up into the prison yard by a flight of wooden steps on which a thick covering of snow had settled. In the picturesquely quiet night, with white flakes falling copiously, dim and dark places as far as the horizon seemed to be punctuated by a multitude of slender white columns.

Rubin and the sergeant major crossed the yard, leaving deep tracks in the fluffy snow. Under this pleasant overcast sky, which the lights of the sleeping city made smoky brown, feeling the touch of the cool hexahedral flakes like the fingers of innocent children on his uplifted head and feverish face, Rubin stood stock-still and closed his eyes. A blissful calm filled his whole being, all the sweeter for being so brief. From this he could draw the strength to live. This was happiness. To go nowhere, ask for nothing, want nothing, just to stand there the whole night through, blissfully, blessedly, as trees stand, catching the snowflakes on his upturned face.

At that very moment, from the railway line less than a kilometer away from Marfino, came a long, warbling hoot, the strangely moving, lonely cry of a train that reminds us in ripe years of childhood because in our childhood it promised us so much for our prime.

If only he could stand there just half an hour, he would be himself again, in body and spirit, and he would compose a moving little poem about train whistles in the night.

If only he didn't have to follow his escort!

But his escort was already looking back suspiciously, wondering whether Rubin had thoughts of escaping into the night.

Rubin's legs went where they were meant to go.

The medical assistant was rosy from the sleep of youth, and a flush played on her cheeks. She had white overalls on but was obviously not wearing tunic and shirt, or anything much, underneath. Most prisoners would have taken note of this, and so at any other time would Rubin, but in his present frame of mind he could not demean himself by thinking of this vulgar creature who had made him suffer torments all night.

"Please give me a triple dose and something to help me sleep—only not Luminal; I want to get off right away."

"We've got nothing for insomnia," she answered automatically.

"Please do what I ask," Rubin insisted. "I've got a job to do for the minister first thing in the morning, and I can't get to sleep."

This mention of the minister, together with the likelihood that Rubin would go on standing there stubbornly begging for his powder (as well as her expectation from certain indications that the lieutenant would shortly rejoin her), made the medical assistant depart from her usual practice and provide medicine.

She got powders from a cabinet and made Rubin take the lot, with water. (In prison regulations a powder is regarded as a weapon and must be put into a prisoner's mouth, never into his hands.) Rubin asked what the time was and learned that it was 3:30. As he walked back across the yard and looked back at the limes lit up by reflected light from the five-hundred- and two-hundred-watt lamps in the camp grounds, he took deep breaths of snow-scented air, bent down to grab handfuls of sparkling fluffy snow, and rubbed his face, rubbed his neck, filled his mouth with the weightless, incorporeal ice-cold stuff.

His soul was in communion with the freshness of the world.

## 73

# A Circle of Wrongs

THE DOOR FROM THE BEDROOM to the dining room was ajar, and he heard the wall clock's single loud stroke and the lingering echoes that followed.

Half-past something. Adam Roitman would have looked at his wristwatch, which was ticking away sociably on the bedside table, but he was afraid that switching the light on suddenly would awaken his wife, who slept sometimes on her side and sometimes prone, with her face pressed against her husband's shoulder.

They had been married nearly five years, but feeling her close to him, sleeping in her funny way, warming her chilly little feet between his legs, made him feel tenderly protective even when he was only half awake.

Adam had woken from an uneasy sleep. He would have liked to go to sleep again, but last night's news and the unpleasantness at work came back to him, anxious thoughts chased one another, his eyes refused to close, and he was in that middle-of-the-night wide-awake state in which it is useless trying to sleep.

The buzz of voices, the shuffling of feet, and the noise of furniture moved around in the Makarygins' apartment overhead had gone on late into the night but had long since ceased.

A faint grayish light seeped in through the gap where the curtains did not quite meet.

In his night attire, flat on his back, and sleepless, Adam Veniaminovich Roitman no longer felt that his position was secure and himself a cut above other people, as he did in the daytime, thanks to his epaulets (major, Ministry of State Security) and his medal (Stalin Prize winner). He lay there supine and felt, like any ordinary mortal, that the world was overpopulated and unkind and that living in it was not easy.

Last night, when the merrymaking at the Makarygins' was in full swing, an old friend of Roitman's, also Jewish, had called on him. He had arrived without his wife, very worried, full of stories about fresh harassments, discriminatory regulations, dismissals, and even banishment.

None of this was news. It had begun last spring, with the apparently innocent mention in brackets of the Jewish names that certain theater critics had dropped. Then it had crept into literature. In one scandal sheet, a pink newspaper that dabbled in everything except what was supposed to be its concern—literature—someone had whispered the poisonous word "cosmopolitan." The word they had all been waiting for! A beautiful word, a proud word, a word that made the whole world one. At one time, it had been bestowed on the noblest of geniuses—Dante, Goethe, Byron—but in this gutter newspaper it became a pallid, wizened, hissing thing and now meant only . . . "Jew."

After which it crept away, shamefacedly hiding in files behind closed doors.

Now the cold draft had reached the scientists. In the past month Roitman, who had been steadily, brilliantly advancing toward glory, had suddenly felt the ground giving way under his feet.

Did his memory deceive him? During the Revolution and for a long time afterward, "Jew" had meant "more reliable than Russians." Russians were checked further back. Who were your parents? What was their source of income before 1917? Jews were all in favor of the Revolution. Then, suddenly, lurking behind the backs of a bunch of nobodies, who should take on the role of scourge of the Israelites but Joseph Stalin?

If a group of people are persecuted because they were once oppressors, or members of a privileged caste, or because of their political views, or their circle of acquaintance, there is always a rational (or pseudorational?) explanation for it. You are always aware that you yourself have chosen your lot, that you need not have stayed in that particular group. But . . . nationality? (Here Roitman's nocturnal interlocutor lodged an objection: People surely did not choose their social origins either but were punished for them.)

But what hurt Roitman most was that you may want with all your heart to belong, to be like everybody else, yet you are snubbed, rejected, told that you are an outsider, a lost soul. A Jew.

The wall clock in the dining room began striking with unhurried dignity. Roitman had listened for the fifth stroke but was glad that there were only four. Still time to get some sleep.

He changed position. His wife cleared her throat without waking and instinctively snuggled up again to her husband.

There was not the slightest sound from his son, asleep in the dining room. He never cried out or called them.

The clever three-year-old was the pride of his young parents. Adam Veniaminovich delighted in telling even the prisoners in the Acoustics Lab about his son's funny little ways and mischievous pranks. With the insensitivity common in happy people, he failed to realize that this could be painful to men deprived of fatherhood. (He thought it a convenient topic of conversation; it brought him closer to the prisoners without in any way compromising him.) The child prattled away fluently, but his pronunciation was shaky. He imitated his mother in the daytime and his father in the evening. (His mother's brogue was from somewhere along the Volga. Adam's speech was thick, and there were regrettable faults in his pronunciation.)

Happiness, if it comes at all, often knows no bounds. This was the case with Adam. Love, marriage, and the birth of his son had come at the end of the war, together with his Stalin Prize. Not that the war had been hard on him. Roitman and some who were now his friends in the Marfino Institute had spent the war in peaceful Bashkiria earning good money from the Commissariat of the Interior for their work on the first coded telephone system. That system looked primitive now, but it had brought them their Stalin Prize. What enthusiasm, what passion they had put into it! Where had it all gone, that enthusiasm, that eagerness to learn, those flights of fancy?

With the keen-sightedness of a man lying awake in the dark with nothing to divert his inward gaze, Roitman suddenly realized what had been lacking in the last few years. Once, he had done it all himself. Now he did not.

He had slipped—when? how?—from the role of creator to that of a supervisor of creators. . . .

Like a man scalded, he took his arms from around his wife and hitched his pillow higher.

Yes, yes, yes! It was so easy, so irresistibly pleasant, when you were leaving for home on Saturday evening, enjoying in anticipation the two nights and a day of domestic comfort ahead and preoccupied with your plans for Sunday, to say, "Valentin Martynych! Don't forget now, you'll have to come up with some way of eliminating those nonlinear distortions tomorrow! Lev Grigorievich! You will take a look at that article in *Proceedings* tomorrow, won't you? And make a brief list of the main points?" When he returned to work refreshed on Monday morning, it was like a fairy tale; an abstract in Russian of the article in *Proceedings* would be on his desk, and Pryanchikov would report on ways to eliminate nonlinear distortions, if he hadn't done the job himself on Sunday.

A very comfortable setup!

Nor did the prisoners feel any resentment toward Roitman. Indeed, they liked him. Because he behaved toward them like a normal decent human being, not a jailer.

But the creative experience, the joyous lightning flash of inspiration, the mortification of unexpected setbacks—all that was a thing of the past.

He freed himself from the bedspread and sat up in bed, clasping his knees and resting his chin on them.

What had he been doing all these years? Intriguing. Fighting for the top place in the institute. He and some of his friends had done everything they could to blacken and topple Yakonov, believing that his eminence and savoir faire would put them in the shade and that he would monopolize the Stalin Prize. His younger colleagues took advantage of the fact that Yakonov, with his tarnished past, would never be admitted to the Party, and they made Party meetings the arena for their attacks on him. They would call on him to make a report, then either ask him to withdraw or discuss it in his presence and adopt a resolution (on which only Party members were allowed to vote). According to these Party resolutions, Yakonov was always in the wrong. Roitman sometimes felt sorry for him—momentarily.

But there was no other way.

What a menacing turn things had now taken! The "youngsters" did not stop to think, when they were harrying Yakonov, that four out of the five of them were Jews. And now Yakonov never wearied of proclaiming from every possible platform that cosmopolitanism was the socialist fatherland's most vicious enemy.

Yesterday had been a fateful day in the history of the Marfino Institute. After the minister's outburst, the prisoner Markushev had come up with the idea of combining the clipper and the "vocoder." It probably made no sense, but it could be presented to the higher-ups as a radical improvement, and Yakonov had given instructions for the immediate transfer of the vocoder unit, Pryanchikov with it, to Number Seven. Roitman was quick to object, in Selivanovsky's presence, but Yakonov patted him on the shoulder, as though he were a hotheaded friend who had to be humored, and said: "Adam Veniaminovich! Don't make the deputy minister think that you put your special interests above those of the Department of Special Technology."

That was what made the present situation so tragic. They punch you in the kisser, and you mustn't cry! They try to wring your neck in broad daylight, and you're expected to stand up and applaud!

The clock struck five. He had missed the half hour.

He wasn't at all sleepy and was beginning to feel uncomfortable in bed.

Very carefully, one foot at a time, Adam slipped out of bed and into his slippers. Noiselessly, avoiding a chair in his way, he went to the window and drew the silk curtains a little farther apart.

What a lot of snow had fallen!

Directly across the yard was the neglected far end of Neskuchny Sad. Its steep slopes were blanketed with snow and overgrown with stately white-decked pines. White fluff outlined the window frame.

But the snowfall was almost over.

The radiator under the window was rather hot to his touch.

There was another reason why he had achieved so little as a scientist in recent years: He had been driven to distraction by meetings and paperwork. Politics class every Monday, technical class every Friday, Party meetings twice monthly, Party bureau meetings also twice monthly; he was summoned to the ministry in the evening two or three times a month; there was a special discussion on security once a month; a monthly research plan had to be drawn up, a monthly progress report written; personal reports on every prisoner had to be sent in for some reason every three months (a whole day's work, that). And then some subordinate would come along every half hour to get his signature; every wretched little condenser the size of a bonbon, every meter of wire, every radio valve, needed a signed authorization from the head of the laboratory, without which the stockrooms would release nothing.

If only he could get rid of all that red tape, give up the battle for supremacy, pore undisturbed over his diagrams, handle a soldering iron, locate his miraculous curve through the greenish eye of an electronic oscillograph, he would sing "boogie-woogie" as lightheartedly as Pryanchikov. What bliss it would be not to feel those epaulets pressing on his shoulders, forget the need to keep up appearances, to be himself, like a small boy—and make something, use his imagination.

"Like a schoolboy!" A random memory of himself as a boy, an episode he had not remembered for many years, surfaced in his night thoughts with pitiless clarity.

Twelve-year-old Adam, wearing his Young Pioneer's scarf, stood before an assembly of all the Young Pioneers in his school, a look of noble outrage on his face, denouncing an agent of the class as an enemy in a trembling voice and demanding his expulsion both from the Young Pioneers and from their Soviet school. The previous speakers, Mitka Shtitelman and Mishka Luksemburg, had also joined in exposing Oleg Rozhdestvensky as an anti-Semite, a churchgoer, a person of alien social origin, annihilating the trembling culprit with their hostile gaze.

It was the end of the twenties, when for boys like Adam life meant politics, wall newspapers, classroom democracy, earnest debate. In that southern town about half of the group was Jewish. Some of the boys were the sons of lawyers, dentists, or small traders, but they were all fantastically insistent on their proletarian origin. Whereas this classmate of theirs tried not to talk about politics, moved his lips soundlessly when they sang the "Internationale" in chorus, and had joined the Pioneers with obvious reluctance. The enthusiasts among the boys had long suspected him of being a counterrevolutionary. They had watched him closely, hoping to catch him. They had not been able to prove that he was of suspect origin. But Oleg gave himself away one day by saying that "everyone has the right to say whatever he thinks." Shtitelman pounced on him: "Whatever he thinks? Nikola once called me an ugly Yid. Is that allowed, too?"

That was the origin of the case against Oleg. Friends of his came forward to denounce him. Shurik Burikov and Shurik Vorozhbit had seen the culprit going into the church with his mother and coming to school with a little cross around his neck. A round of meetings followed—pupils' committee, group committee, Pioneer assemblies, playground huddles—and at all of them twelve-year-old Robespierres came forward and in the presence of the studying masses stigmatized the abettor of anti-Semites and peddlers of religious opium, who had been too frightened to eat for a fortnight and had told no one at home that he had been expelled from the Pioneers and would shortly be expelled from school.

Adam Roitman had not been the ringleader—he had been drawn into it by others—but even now his cheeks burned with shame and self-disgust when he thought of it.

Insult and injury had come full circle! And there was no way out, just as there was no escape from his contest with Yakonov.

Where should you start reforming the world? With other people? Or with yourself?

By now his head was heavy enough, and his heart empty enough, for him to sleep.

He went back and crawled quietly under the blanket. He simply must go to sleep before it struck six.

In the morning he would step up the work on phonoscopy! That could be his trump card! If he succeeded with that, the project might expand into a separate Research Inst. . . .

## 74

# Monday Dawn

Reveille in the sharashka was at 7:00 a.m.

But on Monday morning a guard entered the room where the laborers lived long before reveille and shook the yardman by his shoulder. Spiridon gave one loud snore, recovered consciousness, and looked at the guard in the dim light from the blue bulb.

"Get dressed, Yegorov, the lieutenant wants you," the guard said quietly.

Yegorov lay there open-eyed but did not stir.

"Didn't you hear? I said the lieutenant wants you."

"What's up? Have you gone crazy or something?" Spiridon asked, still without moving.

The guard shook him. "Get up now. Get up. Don't ask me what it's about."

"Lord, oh Lord!" Spiridon stretched, put his ginger-haired hands behind his head, and yawned lengthily. "Bring on the day when I don't have to get up anymore! What time is it?"

"Soon be six."

"Not six yet?! . . . All right, you go. Needn't wait."

He went on lying there.

The guard hesitated, then left.

The blue lamp lit a corner of Spiridon's pillow as far as the oblique shadow of the upper bunk. Partly in the light, partly in shade, Spiridon lay with his hands behind his head, motionless.

He was regretting that he had not seen the end of his dream.

He had been riding on a cart loaded with dry brushwood (and, under it, some logs he had concealed from the forester). He seemed to be riding from the forest back home to his house in the village but by an unfamiliar road. Though he didn't recognize the road, he saw clearly, with both eyes (they were both good in his dream!), where bulging roots were breaking the surface, where lightning had splintered a tree, where there were small pine needles or sand in which wheels might sink and get stuck. Spiridon could also smell in his dream the varied scents of early autumn, and he breathed them in greedily. Even in his sleep he was acutely aware that he was a zek, that he was serving a sentence of ten years with a five-year "collar," that he seemed to have absented himself from the sharashka, that they must have missed him by now but hadn't yet sent the dogs after him, so he must hurry up and get the firewood to his wife and daughter.

But what most of all made it a happy dream was his horse—not any old horse, but the best that Spiridon had ever owned, his roan mare Grivna, bought as a three-year-old to work the little farm he had after the Civil War. Her coat would have been all gray but for the bay underhair; gray and bay merged in a color that could best be called pink. With this horse he had begun to prosper, and he had put her between the shafts when he eloped with Marfa Ustinovna. As he rode along now, Spiridon was surprised and delighted to find Grivna still alive and as young as ever, hauling her load uphill with never a stumble and struggling spiritedly through the sandy patches. Grivna's thoughts always showed in her sensitively pricked-up ears. She never looked back. A twitch of her ears told her master that she knew what was wanted of her and could cope. Even a distant glimpse of a whip would have been an insult to Grivna. Spiridon left the whip behind when he was out with her.

In his dream he felt like getting down from the cart and kissing Grivna on her muzzle, so overjoyed was he that she was still young and would obviously still be alive and waiting when his sentence ended. But as they went down the slope toward the stream, he realized that his cart was tilting to one side, that branches were slipping off, and that the whole load threatened to collapse at the ford.

A sudden jolt flung Spiridon to the ground, and it turned out to be the guard shaking him.

He lay in bed remembering not only Grivna but dozens of horses he had driven and worked with in his life (every one of them was etched on his memory like a living person, as well as thousands he had seen elsewhere, and it galled him to think how wantonly, against all reason, those best of helpers had been exterminated, some starved to death for want of hay and oats, some flogged to death while they worked, some sold to Tatars as meat). Anything at all reasonable Spiridon could understand. But he could not understand why they had done away with horses. They had tried to kid everybody that the tractor would do the horse's work. Instead, the whole burden had fallen on the women.

It wasn't just the horses, though. Hadn't Spiridon himself chopped down fruit trees on peasant farms so that the people there would have nothing to lose? That way they'd give in more easily and join the collective.

"Yegorov!" This time the guard yelled at him from the doorway, waking two other prisoners.

"I'm coming, blast you!" Spiridon yelled back, lowering his feet to the ground. He wandered over to the radiator to retrieve his dry socks.

"Where are you off to, Spiridon?" his neighbor the blacksmith asked.

"Our masters are calling me. To earn my rations," the yardman said angrily.

Spiridon was no slugabed at home, but in prison he didn't like having to get himself together in the dark. To be forced out of bed before it's light is about the worst thing that can happen to a prisoner.

But in the North Urals Camp they got you up at five. So it was best to grin and bear it in the sharashka.

Spiridon adjusted his long army foot rags to cover the space between his wadded trousers and army boots. Dressed and shod, he slipped into loose blue overalls, shrugged on his black overcoat, donned his fur hat, buckled a frayed canvas belt around his waist, and set off. He was let out through the steel door of the prison and walked on unescorted. The steel tips on his shoes grated on the concrete floor of the underground hallway. He climbed the narrow steps into the yard.

Spiridon could see nothing in the snowy gloom, but his feet told him beyond all doubt that something like eighteen inches of snow had fallen. So it must have been snowing heavily all night. Kicking the snow as he went, Spiridon made for the light over the staff room door.

At that moment, the duty officer—the lieutenant with the miserable little mustache—appeared on the threshold of the administrative building. He had left the medical assistant a little while ago to find the world untidy; snow had fallen. So he had sent for the yardman. The lieutenant tucked both hands into his belt and said, "All right, Yegorov, get on with it. Clear a path from the main entrance to the guardhouse and from here to the kitchen. And another over there, across the exercise yard. Get on with it."

"If everybody has a bit, there'll be nothing left for the husband," Spiridon muttered as he set off across the virgin snow with his shovel.

"What's that you said?" the lieutenant asked angrily.

Spiridon looked around. "I said *Jawohl*, Boss, *Jawohl*." (Which was what he used to say when the Germans gave him orders.) "Tell them in the kitchen to slip me a few potatoes."

"All right. Get sweeping."

Spiridon always behaved sensibly and avoided clashes with his bosses, but on this occasion he felt particularly sore—because it was Monday morning, because he was forced to slave away again before his eyes were really open, because there was a letter from home waiting for him and he had a premonition that it brought bad news. He felt a burning pain in his chest as the miseries of fifty years on this earth crowded in on him.

The snow had stopped falling. The limes were breathlessly still, white not with yesterday's frost, which had vanished by suppertime, but with snow that had fallen overnight. Spiridon judged by the darkness of the sky and the stillness of the air that the snow would not hold.

He started sullenly, but once he had warmed up, after the first hundred shovelfuls, the work went steadily and even enjoyably. Spiridon was like that, and so was his wife; however heavy the troubles that weighed on them, Spiridon and Marfa sought relief in work. And found it.

Disobeying orders, Spiridon did not begin by clearing a path from the guardroom for the bosses. He used his own judgment and started with the path to the kitchen, then made a circular track, three broad wooden shovelfuls wide, around the exercise yard for his fellow zeks.

But his mind was on his daughter. His wife and he himself had lived their lives. His sons were behind barbed wire, but they were men. "Young men should get tough for when life becomes rough." But his daughter. . . !

Although he had no sight in one eye and three-tenths vision in the other, Spiridon had made an absolutely regular oval track around the exercise yard by 7:00 a.m., when the first enthusiasts, Potapov and Khorobrov, had climbed the steps from the basement, having risen and washed before reveille, to take their morning exercise.

Fresh air was rationed and precious.

"What's all this, Spiridon?" Khorobrov asked, turning up the collar of the threadbare civilian overcoat in which he had been arrested all those years ago. "Didn't you get to bed last night?"

"D'you think those reptiles let a man sleep?" Spiridon replied. But he no longer felt so angry. That hour of silent work had dispelled his dark thoughts about his jailers. Without putting it into words, Spiridon knew in his heart that if his daughter was in trouble through some fault of her own, that made things no easier for her, and he must respond with kindness, not curse her.

Even this weighty thought about his daughter, which had come down to him from the lime trees waiting rigidly for the dawn, was gradually pushed to the back of his mind by the trivial concerns of the day: the two planks buried somewhere under a snowdrift, the need to mount his brush on a sturdier broomstick. . . .

First, though, he had to clear a path from the guardroom for cars and for the free workers. Spiridon shouldered his shovel and disappeared around the corner of the sharashka.

Sologdin, lithe and trim, with a padded jacket draped loosely round his shoulders, which never felt the cold, went by, toward the woodpile. (When he walked along like this, he often heard in his imagination a voice saying, "There goes Count Sologdin.")

After yesterday's ludicrous wrangle with Rubin and Rubin's exasperating accusations, he had slept badly for the first time in the two years he had been in the sharashka, and now he needed air and solitude and space to think it all over. He had sawed wood ready; all he had to do was chop it.

Potapov was strolling around slowly with Khorobrov, lifting his wounded leg stiffly. He was wearing the ordinary soldier's overcoat he had worn as a member of a tank crew in the assault on Berlin. (He had been an officer before he was taken prisoner. Ex-POWs did not retain officer rank.)

Khorobrov had barely had time to shake off his drowsiness and wash, but his mind was already alert for opportunities to vent the hatred that never slept in him. The words bursting from his lips seemed to trace a futile loop in the dark air and return like a boomerang to wound the speaker.

"Not so long ago, we used to read that the Ford conveyor belt turns the worker into a machine and is the most inhuman form of capitalist exploitation. But fifteen years later, the conveyor belt, under the novel name of the 'continuous production line' is extolled as the best and most modern mode of production. Chiang Kai-shek was our ally in 1945, but his enemies succeeded in overthrowing him in 1949, and now he is a reptile and his followers the 'Chiang Kai-shek clique.' Now they're out to topple Nehru, and his regime is described as 'the rule of the big stick.' If they succeed in bringing him down, we will read about the 'Nehru clique fleeing to the island of Ceylon.' If they don't succeed, it will be 'our noble friend Nehru.' The Bolsheviks are such shameless opportunists that if it suddenly proved necessary to convert all Russia to Christianity again, they would unearth the appropriate passage from Marx to show that it was compatible with atheism and internationalism."

Potapov was always melancholy in the mornings. That was when he had time to think about his ruined life, about a son growing up without a father and a wife pining for her absent husband. Later on, his work would take his mind off everything else.

Potapov thought that Khorobrov was probably right but that he was too peevish and too ready to let the West sit in judgment of the Soviet Union. Potapov himself believed that the Soviet people and the Soviet regime must somehow—just how he did not know—settle their family quarrel themselves. So, awkwardly dragging along his damaged leg, he walked on in silence, breathing as deeply and evenly as he could.

Shattered by his meeting with his wife the day before, Gerasimovich had stayed in bed all day on Sunday, as if sick. Her cry as she left had shaken him badly.

He could no longer just wait quietly for his sentence to run its course. Those last three years would be too much for Natasha. He had to do something about it. "You could do something right now if you wanted to!" she had said reproachfully, knowing how clever he was.

Yes, there was something he could use, but it was too precious to put into those hands in return for crumbs from their table.

If only he could come up with something . . . something trivial, but enough to earn him remission. But things don't happen like that. Neither science nor life gives us anything gratis.

He felt no better the next morning. It had cost him an effort to come out for exercise. He was well wrapped up but chilled to the bone, and he wanted to go back inside immediately. But he had run into Kondrashov-Ivanov, walked once around the circuit with him, and was his captive for the rest of the exercise period.

"What? You mean to say you don't know about Pavel Dmitrievich Korin?" Kondrashov sounded surprised, as if this was something every schoolboy knew. "Well, well, well! They say he's got this remarkable picture—only nobody's seen it—*Vanishing Russia*, it's called. Some say it's six meters, some twelve. He's kept on a tight rein, his work is never exhibited, he's painted this picture in secret, and when he dies, they'll probably impound it."

"Why, what does it show?"

"I only know what I've been told; I can't vouch for it. It's said to show an ordinary road in central Russia, in a hilly place, with clumps of trees. People are streaming along the road, looking preoccupied. Each individual is painted in painstaking detail. The sort of faces we find in old family photographs but don't see around us anymore. Radiant Old Russian faces—peasants, plowmen, craftsmen—with high foreheads and full beards, people whose complexions, eyes, and thoughts were still clear and youthful in their seventies. The faces of girls whose ears are protected from foul language by invisible golden pendants, girls you couldn't imagine in the Gadarene mob around the dance floor. Dignified old women. Silver-haired priests walking along in their vestments. Monks. Duma deputies. Overripe students in double-breasted jackets. Schoolboys in quest of universal truths. Haughty beauties in early-twentieththth-century town clothes. Somebody greatly resembling Korolenko. Then more peasants, and more, and more. . . . The most terrible thing is that these people are not in separate groups! Chronological order no longer exists. They are not talking to one another! They don't look at one another; perhaps they can't even see one another. They carry no travelers' bundles on their backs. They simply . . . go on and on. And they're not just walking along that particular highway; they are walking away altogether. Departing. . . . We are seeing the last of them. . . ."

Gerasimovich halted abruptly.

"I'm sorry, I must be alone for a while!"

He turned sharply on his heel, left the artist in mid-gesture, and walked off in the opposite direction.

He felt feverish. Not only could he see the picture as vividly as if he had painted it himself; he couldn't help thinking that. . . .

Morning had set in.

A guard went around the yard shouting that the exercise period was over. As they went in through the underground hallway, the other prisoners found themselves jostling a morose Rubin, his grim beard emphasizing the sickly pallor of his face. He was trying to push through in the opposite direction. He had overslept and was too late not only for woodchopping (that was unthinkable anyway after his quarrel with Sologdin) but for his morning walkabout. After his brief, artificial sleep Rubin's body was limp and numb. He felt that hunger for oxygen that is unknown to those who can breathe freely whenever they want. He was trying to fight his way out to the yard for a single gulp of fresh air and a handful of snow to rub himself with.

But the guard standing at the head of the steps would not let him pass.

Rubin stood in the concrete pit down below. A little snow had found its way down there, and there was a refreshing draft. He performed three slow, circular movements with his arms, taking deep breaths, then collected some snow from the floor of the pit, rubbed his face with it, and wandered back into the prison.

Spiridon, now wide awake and very hungry after clearing a path for cars all the way to the guardhouse, went the same way.

In the prison HQ the two lieutenants—the one with the two little squares of mustache, who was going off duty, and the new arrival, Lieutenant Zhvakun—opened a large envelope and studied the orders left for them by Major Myshin.

Lieutenant Zhvakun, a dense, fat-faced ruffian, had risen to the rank of sergeant major during the war, serving as a divisional executioner (or, in the official terminology, "executive officer attached to the military tribunal"), and he had earned further promotion as a result. He greatly valued his position in Special Prison No. 1, and since literacy was not his strong suit, he perused Myshin's instructions twice to be sure of getting them right.

At 8:50 the two of them went around the prisoners' rooms to inspect and to announce, as instructed: "All prisoners are to submit to Major Myshin in the course of the next three days a list of their immediate relatives set out as follows: number of relatives in list, name of relative (surname, given name, patronymic), degree of affinity, place of work, home address. 'Immediate relatives' means mother, father, legal wife, sons and daughters of a legal registered marriage. Other relatives—brothers, sisters, aunts, nieces, grandchildren, and grandmothers—do not count as immediate relatives. As of January first, prisoners will be allowed to correspond with or receive visits from immediate relatives as defined in this list and no one else.

"Furthermore, as of January first, the size of a prisoner's monthly letter must not exceed one double page of an exercise notebook."

This order, so mean and inexorable, defied understanding. No exclamations of despair or indignation sped Zhvakun on his way, only sarcastic cries of "Happy New Year!" and "Cuckoo!"

"Denounce our relatives?"

"You mean the sleuths can't find them?"

"Why doesn't it say whether we should write in small letters or capitals?"

Zhvakun, counting heads, tried simultaneously to memorize who had shouted, so that he could report them to the major.

Treat them well or treat them badly, prisoners are never satisfied.

# 75

# Four Nails

THE ZEKS DISPERSED to their workplaces in a daze.

Even the old hands were stunned by the savagery of these new regulations. They were doubly cruel. To begin with, it would be impossible in the future to preserve the tenuous lifeline to their loved ones without betraying them to the police. And many of those outside had thus far managed to conceal the fact that they had relatives behind bars. Otherwise, their jobs and their homes would not be safe. Just as cruel was the exclusion of unregistered wives and children, as well as brothers and sisters. (And of course cousins. After the war—the air raids, the evacuations, the famine—many zeks had no closer surviving relatives.) When you're about to be arrested, you aren't given time to go to confession and Holy Communion and to put your affairs in order. So many men had left behind loyal partners whose passports were not smudged with a registry office stamp. Such a partner was now officially "no relation."

An Iron Curtain encircled the whole, vast country, and within it another one—of steel, tight and impenetrable—was being lowered around Marfino.

Even the most incorrigible enthusiasts for the daily grind were demoralized. When the bell went, they took their time moving out, blocking the hallways, smoking, talking. Seated at their workplaces, they went on talking and smoking. One question exercised them above all others: Surely it could not be true that the Ministry of State Security had so far failed to collect and systematize in its central card-index information about all relatives of prisoners? Newcomers and simple souls considered the ministry omnipotent and omniscient; it could not possibly need this "census by denunciation." Longtimers shook their heads knowingly, explaining that the security services, like the rest of the state machine, were grossly overstaffed and muddleheaded, that the register of relatives in the ministry was chaotic, that personnel departments and security officers sat tight behind their black-leather-upholstered doors, not attempting to "catch mice" (their official rations sufficed), and failing to analyze the answers to innumerable questionnaires. Nor did prison administrators forward promptly the required excerpts from their records of visitors and parcels received. All of this meant that if you now gave Klimentiev and Myshin the list they were asking for, you could inflict a fatal blow on your relatives.

The more they talked like this, the less they felt like work.

As it happened, this was the first morning of the last week of the year, and the bosses had decreed that the institute must put on a heroic spurt to fulfill the monthly plan for December and the plan for 1949. It would also draft and formally adopt its annual plan for 1950, its quarterly plan for January–March, an interim plan for January, and finally a plan for the first ten days of January. The paperwork involved would be done by the bosses themselves. The real work was left to the prisoners. Today, of all days, it was important that they should show enthusiasm.

The officers in charge of the institute knew nothing at all about the destructive announcement made that morning by the prison command in accordance with its own annual plan.

Nobody could accuse the Ministry of State Security of living according to holy writ! But biblical language aptly described one of its characteristics: Its right hand did not know what the left was doing.

Major Roitman, with no trace of his overnight anxieties on his freshly shaved face, had assembled all the prisoners and free workers in the Acoustics Laboratory to exchange ideas on the new plans. Roitman had a long, intelligent face and protruding negroid lips. He was wearing an incongruous and quite unnecessary shoulder belt over a rather baggy tunic.

He wanted to put a brave face on it himself and encourage the zeks, but the odor of failure already hovered under the vaulted ceiling. The middle of the room looked bare and forlorn now that the vocoder bench had been taken out. Pryanchikov, that pearl in the Acoustics Lab's crown, was missing. So was Rubin, now behind a locked door with Smolosidov on the third floor. Roitman himself was in a hurry to get it over with and go upstairs to join them.

Of the free workers Simochka was missing. She had replaced a colleague on the after-dinner shift. That was something to be thankful for! Some slight relief to Nerzhin in his present mood. He would not have to exchange notes and signals with her.

He sat in the discussion group lolling against the comfortably pliant back of his chair with his feet on the lower stave of another chair. Most of the time he was looking through the window. Outside, a westerly and obviously wet wind had sprung up. It had given a leaden look to the cloudy sky, and the snow on the ground would soon be loose and crunchy. Yet another senseless sloppy thaw was on the way.

After a poor night's sleep, the skin of Nerzhin's face was slack, and in the gray morning light it looked deeply furrowed. He was experiencing that Monday-morning feeling familiar to many prisoners. It was as if he lacked the strength to move or even to live.

One visit a year! And he had been allowed his one visit only yesterday. He had thought that all that was most urgently necessary had been said, that it sufficed for a long time ahead! But now . . . ?

When will I be able to tell her? Will I write? But how can I mention it in a letter? How can I mention your place of work? After yesterday it's obviously impossible anyway.

Will I say, Since I don't want to give information about you, we must stop corresponding? The address on the envelope would amount to a denunciation!

What if I don't write at all? What would she think? Only yesterday I was smiling at her. Can I stop talking to her forever the very next day?

He felt as if a vise, not the vise of poetic metaphor but a huge, metalworker's vise with notched lips and gaping maw, was closing around his trunk and squeezing the breath out of him.

There was no way out of it! Whatever he did would be wrong.

Roitman, soft-spoken and shortsighted, peered mildly through his pebble glasses and spoke of plans, plans, and still more plans, but not in the voice of authority. There was a hint of fatigue in his voice, and he seemed to be pleading with them.

His words, however, were falling on stony ground.

Nerzhin sat hemmed in by chairs and workbenches, clamped in the metal jaws so that he could neither breathe nor move. His despondency showed in the downturned corners of his lips. His eyes were fixed unseeingly on the dark fence and the guard tower with a screw up top, exactly in line with his window.

Angry thoughts raced behind that meekly passive face.

The years would go by, and all those who had listened with him to that morning's announcement, all those who were now morose or indignant or despondent or seething with fury would . . . well, some of them would be in their graves, some would become feebly complacent, some would forget the whole thing, disavow their experience, ease their minds by suppressing their prison memories, while yet a fourth group would stand the truth on its head and say that what had been done was not ruthless but merely sensible. He doubted whether a single one of them would want to make today's torturers regret what they had done to the human heart!

People had an astounding capacity to forget! Forget the solemn vows made in 1917. Forget what was promised in 1928. Year after year, they had descended, dazed and docile, step by step, losing their pride and freedom, accepting ever lower standards in dress and nutrition, and as a result their memories had become shorter, and the longing to creep meekly into some hole, to live out their lives as best they could in some hole, some crevice, some crack in the floor, had grown on them.

This only reinforced Nerzhin's feeling that he had a duty to discharge, a mission to carry out, for all of them. He knew that it was not in his own obstinate nature to be deflected, to cool off, to forget.

For all the cruel things they had done—interrogations under torture, prisoners dying of starvation in the camps, this morning's announcement—let four nails crucify their memory! Nail them, through palms and shins, to the cross, and let them hang there with their lies and stink until the sun grows cold and life on planet Earth is extinct.

If nobody else could be found to do it, Nerzhin would drive in those four nails himself.

A man in the grip of a metalworker's vise could not wear the skeptical smile of a Pyrrho.

His ears heard, though they were not listening to what Roitman was saying. It was only when the lieutenant began to use the words "socialist obligations" over and over again that Nerzhin shuddered in disgust. He had more or less reconciled himself to "plans." He was an ingenious drafter of plans himself. He could contrive to slip into the annual plan a dozen imposing items involving little work; the work would have been partly done already, or it would demand no great effort, or it might be an optical illusion. Every time he submitted a beautifully crafted plan, it was approved and accepted as the limit of what could be expected of him, but then his superiors immediately contradicted themselves and showed their contempt for the feelings of a political prisoner by suggesting from month to month that Nerzhin should go one better with a supplementary "scientific socialist obligation" of his own.

Roitman was followed by other speakers, first a free worker, then a zek, after which he asked, "What do you have to say, Gleb Vikentich?"

Nerzhin did not turn a hair.

In the dark recesses of his mind, he gripped those four iron nails.

These people were as ruthless as wild beasts, and he must show animal cunning in his dealings with them.

As though he had only been waiting for Roitman's challenge, Nerzhin rose with alacrity, his face a picture of ingenuous interest.

"The articulation group's plan for 1949 has been fulfilled in all particulars ahead of time. At present, I am engaged on working out the application of probability theory to the articulation of interrogative sentences, and I plan to finish this by March, which will make it possible to analyze interrogative sentences scientifically. In addition to this, even if Lev Grigorievich is busy elsewhere, I will carry on with the classification of human voices both by the subjective-descriptive method and by objective measurement with apparatus."

"Yes, yes, yes! The voices! That's very important," Roitman interrupted, thinking of his plans for phonoscopy.

The austere pallor of Nerzhin's face and his tousled hair spoke of a life as a martyr to science, the science of articulation.

"We must also step up socialist competition; that will be a big help," he concluded confidently. "We, too, will announce our socialist obligations by January 1. Our duty, as I see it, is to work harder and better in the coming year than we did last year." (When he had done nothing at all.)

Two other zeks spoke up. The most natural thing for them to do would have been to confess to Roitman and the whole assembly that they could not turn their minds to plans or their hands to work because they had just been finally robbed of the illusion that they still had families, but that was not what their boss expected of them, keyed up as he was for a great burst of productive effort. Even if someone had said such things, Roitman would merely have blinked in hurt dismay, and the meeting would have continued along predetermined lines.

It ended. Roitman sprinted up to the third floor, taking the stairs two at a time, and knocked on the door of Rubin's top-secret room.

Conjecture was already raging there. The magnetic tapes were being compared.

# 76

## Favorite Profession

SECURITY OPERATIONS at the Marfino establishment were subdivided between Major Myshin, godfather of the prison, and Major Shikin, godfather on the production side. Belonging as they did to different government departments and drawing their salaries from different paymasters, they were not rivals. But indolence prevented them from collaborating; their offices were in different buildings and on different floors, security operations are never discussed on the telephone, and since they were equal in rank, each of them thought it would demean him to take the initiative and pay his respects to the other. So they continued to work on men's minds as they always had, one of them by night, the other by day, without meeting for months on end, although they both spoke in their quarterly reports and plans of the need for close coordination of security operations at Marfino.

Reading *Pravda* one day, Major Shikin lingered over the headline of an article: "The Profession He Loves." (The article was about an agitator who loved nothing in the world so much as explaining things to people: explaining to workers the importance of raising productivity, to soldiers the need to sacrifice their lives, to electors the correctness of the policies of the Communist and Non-Party Bloc.) Shikin liked the phrase. He, too, he decided, had made the right career choice; he had never in his life felt drawn to any other profession, he loved the one he had chosen, and it loved him.

Shikin had gone through the GPU training school, then the diploma courses for investigators, but he had done very little investigation in the strict sense and could not really call himself an investigator. He had worked as a security officer in the transport network. He had been used by the People's Commissariat of Internal Affairs as a special scrutineer of hostile votes cast in "secret" elections to the Supreme Soviet. During the war he had been in charge of military censorship on one of the fronts, had served on a repatriation commission, then in a camp for returning prisoners of war, after which he had helped to organize the deportation of the Greeks from the Kuban to Kazakhstan, and finally he had become senior security officer in the Marfino Research Institute.

This was the profession that Shikin dearly loved. And which of his comrades-in-arms did not?

It was not a dangerous profession. In every security operation superior force was ensured: two or three armed officers to a single enemy, neither armed nor forewarned, and often half awake.

It was, however, well paid. Officers had access to the best special shops. They lived in the best apartments (confiscated from convicts). They drew higher pensions than army officers. They took their vacations in first-class resorts.

It was not exhausting work. There were no production norms. True, friends had told Shikin that in 1937 and again in 1945 investigating officers had worked like cart horses, but he had never been rushed off his feet and couldn't quite believe it. There were good spells when you could doze at your desk for months on end. The style of work in the Ministries of the Interior and State Security was nothing if not leisurely. The natural leisureliness of all comfortable people was supplemented by the leisureliness officially prescribed as the best means of psychological pressure on a prisoner to get a statement out of him: the unhurried sharpening of pencils, the careful selection of pens and paper, the patient recording of all sorts of superfluous details and officially required data. The leisureliness of the work had a most beneficial effect on the nerves of the Chekists and accounted for their longevity.

The routine of operational work was no less precious to Shikin. It was essentially a form of stocktaking, pure and simple (making it a manifestation of one of socialism's most fundamental characteristics). An interview was never just that; it had to be rounded off with a written denunciation, a signed protocol, an undertaking not to make false depositions, not to divulge confidential matters, not to leave the district, an acknowledgment of notification. . . . What this work required was precisely the patient attention to detail and methodical habits that were such a distinctive feature of Shikin's character. Without them you could only create chaos with all those bits of paper, instead of classifying them and filing them so that you could put your hand on any item at any time. (Shikin, being an officer, could not perform manual tasks such as filing official papers, so this was done by a special confidential secretary, a lanky, weak-sighted woman borrowed from the main prison office.)

But what Shikin liked most of all about his work was the power it gave him over other people, the feeling of omnipotence, and the aura of mystery.

Shikin was flattered by the respect, indeed the awe, which he inspired in colleagues who, although themselves Cheka men, were not security operations officers. They were all, Engineer Colonel Yakonov included, bound to give Shikin an account of their activities on demand, whereas he was accountable to none of them. As he went up the broad, carpeted main stairway—dark-featured, with close-cropped graying hair, carrying a large briefcase under his arm—girl lieutenants in the Ministry of State Security shrank bashfully from him, though there was plenty of room, and hastened to greet him first, and Shikin was proudly conscious of his importance and uniqueness.

If anybody had told him—but nobody ever did—that he had earned the hatred of others, that he was a tormentor of other people, he would have been genuinely indignant. He had never been one to inflict pain for pleasure or for the sake of it. He knew, of course, that such people existed. He had seen them on stage and in films, sadists with a passion for torturing people, inhuman monsters, but they were always either White Guardists or fascists.

Shikin was only doing his duty. His only aim was to ensure that nobody did or thought anything harmful.

One day a bundle containing 150 rubles was found on the main staircase of the sharashka, which was used by both free employees and zeks. The two lieutenants, both technicians, who found it could neither conceal it nor surreptitiously try to find the owner, precisely because there were two of them. So they handed their find over to Major Shikin.

Money dumped on a staircase used by zeks, who were most strictly forbidden to have money—this was an event of the highest political significance! Shikin, however, did not make a big thing of it. He simply put up a notice on the stairway: "Whoever has lost 150 on the stairs can reclaim them from Major Shikin at any time."

It was not a small sum. Yet such was the respect and awe felt by all for Shikin that days and weeks went by, and nobody came forward to claim this tiresome item of lost property. The notice faded and gathered dust, one corner came unstuck, and in the end somebody's blue pencil added a postscript in block letters: "Choke on it, you dog."

The duty officer tore the notice down and took it to Shikin. For a long time afterward he took walks around the laboratories looking for a pencil with the right shade of blue. Shikin did not deserve the crude insult. He had absolutely no intention of pocketing the money. What he really wanted was for the person concerned to come forward so that an example could be made of him and the case discussed in detail at conferences on vigilance.

But of course the money could not simply be thrown away! So two months later, the major presented it to the lanky maiden with the walleye who filed his papers once a week.

Shikin had been a model family man until the devil tripped him up and shackled him to this secretary. Her thirty-eight wasted years showed in her face, her legs were thick and ugly, she stood head and shoulders above him, . . . but he had discovered in her something he had never experienced before: He could hardly wait for her weekly visit. When he was moved to temporary quarters while his office was under repair, he couldn't help himself and so far forgot the need for caution that two prisoners, a carpenter and a plasterer, overheard them and even saw them through a crack. It got around, and the zeks chuckled among themselves over their spiritual director. They even thought of writing to Shikin's wife; only they didn't know the address. Instead, they denounced him to his superiors.

They did not succeed, though, in toppling the senior operations officer.

Major General Oskolupov gave Shikin a dressing-down, not because of his liaison with the secretary (that was between her and her principles), nor yet because this liaison was conducted in office hours (since Major Shikin had no fixed office hours), but only for letting prisoners find out about it.

ON MONDAY, DECEMBER 26, Major Shikin arrived at work a little after 9:00 a.m., although nobody would have said anything if he had not turned up till lunchtime.

Opposite Yakonov's office on the third floor, there was a niche, or lobby, with no electric lighting, in which two doors faced each other, one to Shikin's office, one to that of the Party Committee. Both doors were upholstered with black leather, and neither bore any inscription. The proximity of these two doors facing each other in the dark lobby was very convenient for Shikin: Curious eyes could not be sure which door people were sneaking through.

As he approached his office on this occasion, Shikin met Stepanov, the secretary of the Party Committee, a thin, unhealthy man with opaquely glittering glasses. They shook hands, and Stepanov quietly asked him in. "Comrade Shikin!" (He never called anyone by his name and patronymic.) "Step inside, and we'll knock the balls about a bit!"

This was an invitation to play on the miniature billiards table in the Party Committee's office. Shikin did sometimes go in and bang the balls about, but a lot of important business awaited him, and he declined with a dignified shake of his silvering head.

Stepanov sighed and went off to chase the balls around by himself.

Shikin entered his office and placed his briefcase tidily on his desk. (His papers, all secret or top secret, had to be kept in a safe and never left the room, but he would not have made much of an impression walking around without a briefcase. He used it to carry home copies of *Bonfire*, *Crocodile*, and *Around the World*. (Subscribing to them himself could have cost him a kopeck or two.) Then he took a stroll along the carpet, paused at the window, and turned back toward the door. It was as if his thoughts had been waiting there in his office for him, lurking behind the safe, the cabinet, the sofa; and now they crowded around all at once, demanding attention.

So much to be done! So much to be done.

He rubbed his graying crewcut with both hands.

For a start, he had to review an innovation to which he had given many months of thought. Yakonov had sanctioned it, and the laboratories had been instructed accordingly, but it was not yet operating smoothly. The new rule required staff to keep secret logbooks. Thorough examination of security precautions in the Marfino Institute had convinced Shikin—and he was very proud of his discovery—that as yet there was no real secrecy in the place. Yes, there were man-high steel safes in every room (the loot from Lorenz AG had included fifty of them). Yes, all secret and semisecret documents were locked up in these safes for the lunch break, the supper break, and the night. But there was a fatal oversight: Only finished and half-finished work was locked up. The flashes of inspiration, the preliminary hypotheses, the tentative conjectures that held most promise for the future and could be seen as next year's work in embryo were as yet not locked away. An adroit spy with some technical knowledge would only have to get through the barbed-wire fences into the prison precinct, find a bit of blotting paper with one of those drawings or diagrams in a trash can somewhere, then make his way out of the precinct again, and American intelligence would be looking over the shoulders of the researchers. Nothing if not conscientious, Major Shikin had once made Yegorov the yardman examine the whole contents of the trash can in the yard. They had found two soggy scraps of paper stuck together by snow and ash on which nonetheless traces of diagrams were clearly visible. At the risk of dirtying his hands, Shikin held this bit of trash by its corners and carried it to Colonel Yakonov's desk. Yakonov had no escape! So Shikin's project for the introduction of personal secret logbooks was adopted. Suitable ledgers were promptly obtained from the ministry's stockrooms. Each had two hundred pages, numbered, perforated, and bearing wax seals. These logbooks were to be distributed to everyone except the fitters, the turners, and the yardman. Nothing was to be written down except on the pages of a personal logbook. There was another important innovation here besides the elimination of dangerous rough drafts: The thought processes of personnel were open to inspection! Since dates had to be entered daily, Major Shikin could check whether this or that prisoner had done much thinking on Wednesday and how many new ideas he had had on Friday.

Two hundred fifty such logbooks would be an additional 250 Shikins, one of whom would hover importunately over each prisoner. Prisoners are always cunning and lazy; they always try to avoid work if they possibly can. You can check up on a manual worker by looking at his output. Checking up on an engineer or scientist is not so easy, but that was where Shikin's innovation came in! (Such a pity that there are no Stalin Prizes for security operations officers.) This was the day chosen to verify that a logbook had been handed to each prisoner and that entries were being made.

Another of Shikin's chores for the day was to complete the list of prisoners to be transferred in the near future and to find out exactly when the transport would be available.

Shikin was also preoccupied with an ambitious affair he had initiated but that had made little progress so far—"the Case of the Broken Lathe." The mounting of a lathe had been cracked while a dozen prisoners were lugging it from Laboratory No. 3 to the workshops. The investigation had been going on for a week, and something like eighty pages of evidence had been recorded, but the truth of the matter was as elusive as ever; none of the prisoners concerned was new to the game.

It was also necessary to investigate the origin of the book by Dickens, as Doronin had reported, prisoners in the semicircular room were reading, especially Abramson. Summoning Abramson, an old lag, for questioning, would be a waste of time. The thing to do was to call in the free personnel he worked with and throw a scare into them by pretending that Abramson had confessed.

Shikin had so much to do today. (And of course he didn't know yet what news his informers would have for him! Didn't know that he was going to have to look into that insulting parody of Soviet judicial procedure, "The Trial of Prince Igor.") A despairing Shikin rubbed his temples and brow vigorously, calling this unruly throng of thought to order.

Uncertain where to begin, he decided to go among the masses, or, in other words, to patrol the hallway in the hope of meeting an informant, who would by a twitch of the eyebrows indicate that he had something urgent to report, something that couldn't wait for his scheduled visit.

But the moment he reached the duty officer's desk, he heard him talking on the telephone about some new group.

He couldn't believe it! Such indecent haste! Setting up a new group on Sunday, in his absence?

The duty officer told him all about it. It was a nasty blow! The vice minister had turned up, various generals had turned up, and Shikin had not been there! He had never felt so aggrieved. The vice minister might think that Shikin did not worry himself sick about security! Besides, he should have been there to warn them in time not to include that accursed Rubin in such an important group—that double-dealer, that utter fraud, who swore that he believed in the victory of Communism, yet refused to become an informant! And then, that beard he wore, the scoundrel! A symbol of defiance! He should be forcibly shaved!

Making haste slowly, taking careful little steps in his little boy's shoes, ox-headed Shikin made for Room 21.

There were, however, ways of dealing with Rubin. Just the other day he had put in another of his applications to the Supreme Court for a judicial review. It was in Shikin's power to accompany the petition with a laudatory report on Rubin or a nasty, negative one, as on previous occasions.

The door of Room 21 was blank, without glass panes. The major pushed the door, but it was locked. He knocked. He heard no footsteps, but the door opened slightly, and Smolosidov's forbidding black forelock filled the aperture. Seeing Shikin, he did not budge; nor did he open the door any wider.

"Morning," Shikin mumbled.

Smolosidov took half a step back but continued to bar the way. He crooked a finger at Shikin, who squeezed into the narrow opening and looked where he was pointing. A small piece of paper was pinned to the other panel of the door, inside.

LIST OF PERSONS WITH ACCESS TO ROOM 21

1. Deputy Minister of State Security Selivanovsky.
2. Head of Department Major General Bulbanyak.
3. Head of Department Major General Oskolupov.
4. Head of Group Engineer Major Roitman.
5. Lieutenant Smolosidov.
6. Prisoner Rubin.

*By order of the Minister of State Security Abakumov*

Shikin, overawed, stepped back into the hallway.

"I would . . . er . . . just like a word with Rubin," he whispered.

"Can't be done," Smolosidov whispered back.

And closed the door.

# 77

# The Decision Taken

CHOPPING WOOD IN THE FRESH MORNING AIR, Sologdin reviewed his decision of the night before. Ideas unchallenged by a sleepy mind cannot always stand the light of day.

He had lost count of the logs he had chopped, forgotten that he was swinging an ax. He was thinking.

But the inconclusive debate with Rubin prevented him from thinking clearly. Arguments that would have floored Lev last night crowded his mind now that it was too late.

But what vexed him, what galled him most, was the absurd turn the debate had taken; it was as if Rubin had won the right to judge Sologdin's behavior and in particular the step he must take today. He could delete Lyovka Rubin's name from the scroll of friendship but could not strike out the challenge he had delivered. It lingered . . . and it rankled. It threatened to rob Sologdin of credit for his invention.

Yet, on the whole, the debate had been well worthwhile, as debate always is. Praise opens a safety valve, reduces internal tension, and so is always harmful to us. Whereas abuse, however unfair, serves as much-needed fuel for a man's boiler.

All things in their prime have, of course, a hunger for life. Dmitri Sologdin, with his exceptional abilities, physical and mental, had a right to his harvest, his share of life's blessings. But he himself had said only yesterday that noble ends are attainable only by noble means.

Sologdin had greeted that morning's announcement from the prison administration with a broad smile. It was yet another proof of his foresight. He himself had decided to break off his correspondence with his wife, and in good time. She would not be plagued by uncertainty.

The hardening of the prison regime was simply the latest of many warnings that the whole situation would become grimmer and grimmer and that no one would ever walk free just because he had "done his time."

The only way out was to earn remission.

When the prisoners thronged the stairs at 9:00 a.m., Sologdin was among the first. He went up to the design office, bold and bursting with health, fingering his blond beard ("Here comes Count Sologdin").

His triumphantly shining eyes met Larisa's eager gaze.

She had been yearning for him all night! What joy it was to have the right to sit by him and admire him. Perhaps exchange a note with him.

It was not the moment for that. Sologdin averted his eyes as he bowed politely and immediately gave Yemina some work to do; she had to run down to the engineering shops and find out how many of the bolts specified in order 114 had been run off so far. And would she please be quick about it.

Larisa looked at him, puzzled and anxious. She left the room.

The gray morning gave so little light that overhead lamps were burning and drawing-board lamps lit up one after another.

Solodgin unpinned the dirty sheet of paper covering his drawing board, and the main circuit of his encoder met his eyes.

Two years of his life had gone into this work. Two years of strict intellectual discipline. Two years of the most productive morning hours; nothing great is created later in the day.

Had it all been for nothing?

But should a man love such a bad country? This people estranged from God, a people that had committed so many crimes and shown no sign of remorse—was this nation of slaves worthy of sacrificial victims, geniuses who had laid their heads on the block unknown and unsung? For a hundred, for two hundred years to come, this people would be content with its trough. Should the torchbearers of human thought be sacrificed for them?

Was it not more important to preserve and hand on the torch? You could deal a still heavier blow later.

He stood poring over his creation.

He had only a few hours, perhaps only a few minutes, to solve the greatest problem he would ever face.

He unpinned the main sheet. It flapped down like the sail of a frigate.

One of the office girls was, as usual on Mondays, making the rounds of the designers collecting unwanted drawings for destruction. Discarded sheets were not to be torn up and thrown in refuse bins but burned out in the yard after official authorization.

(Was it lax of Major Shikin to put his trust in fire? Surely, a Design Office Security Operations Office should have been set up alongside the design office to monitor all drawings sent by the latter for destruction?)

Sologdin picked up a soft copying pencil, drew several bold lines through his sketch, and scribbled over it.

Then he unpinned it, tore a strip off it, laid the dirty cover sheet over it, slipped another piece of wastepaper underneath, screwed the whole lot up, and handed it to the girl.

"Here you are, three sheets."

Then he sat down and pretended to be consulting a reference book while he kept half an eye on what became of his drawing. He wanted to see whether one of the other designers would come to look through the discarded sheets.

But suddenly it was conference time. They all gathered around and sat down.

The lieutenant colonel in charge of the design office remained seated and spoke perfunctorily about plan fulfillment, new plans, and reciprocal socialist obligations. He had included in the plan, without believing it for a minute, a promise to produce a technically sound design for an encoding machine by the end of the year and was now qualifying this so as to allow his designers loopholes for a possible retreat.

Sologdin sat in the back row serenely gazing past all those heads at the wall beyond. His face was smooth and unclouded, and no one would have supposed that he had something on his mind. He seemed simply to be using the meeting as an opportunity to take a rest.

In reality, he was thinking furiously.

Suddenly he was stunned by the most obvious of misgivings: Maybe they'd been watching him closely since yesterday, when Anton had set eyes on that piece of paper? Perhaps the girls would be relieved of his encoder as soon as they got through the door with it?

He writhed like a man impaled. He sat impatiently through the meeting and hurried over to the girls. They were already drawing up the list for signature.

"I gave you one sheet by mistake," he said. "Sorry. Here it is. This one."

He carried it to his workplace and laid it facedown on his desk. Larisa was not there; nobody could see him. He took a large pair of scissors and quickly cut the drawing into two uneven pieces, then into four, then cut each of the quarters into four again.

That would be safest. Another oversight on the part of Major Shikin. He should have made them do their drawings in books with numbered and stamped pages. Facing the corner with his back to the room, Sologdin stuffed all sixteen scraps of paper into the bosom of his baggy overalls.

He always kept a box of matches in his desk.

He left the design office, looking preoccupied, and turned from the main hallway into a side passage that led to the bathroom.

The zek washing his hands under the tap in the first room was Tyunyukin, a notorious stoolie. To the rear were the urinals and four stalls. The first was locked (Sologdin tried the door), the two middle ones half-open and unoccupied. The fourth door was closed, but it yielded to his hand. It had a good bolt.

Sologdin stepped inside, locked the door, and stood stock-still.

He took two pieces of paper from under his overalls, got his box of Victory matches out, and waited. He could not strike a match yet, in case someone saw the flame reflected by the ceiling or smelled fumes spreading through the bathroom.

Somebody else came in. Then both he and the occupant of the first stall went out. Sologdin struck his match. The phosphorus flared up and shot onto his chest. At his second try the flame was too weak to get a hold on the twisted brown body of the match. It sputtered and went out in a miserable wisp of smoke.

Sologdin silently mouthed a few popular prison-camp oaths. Nonflammable, incombustible matches! What other country could produce them? If you set out to make them, you couldn't! "Victory"! What victory could they ever have won?

The third match snapped between his fingers. The fourth was already broken when he took it from the box. The fifth had no phosphorus on the sides of the head.

Sologdin frantically pried out several matches and struck the whole bunch at once. They lit. He held the paper to the flame. The thick drawing paper did not burn readily. Sologdin turned it so that the flame was at the bottom. It flared up and began to burn his fingers. He carefully placed the burning sheets in the toilet bowl, away from the water. Then took out a second batch and lit it from the first, adjusting those so that they would burn completely. The black ash curled up and floated on the water like a little boat.

The second batch was ablaze by now. Sologdin let go of it and put more sheets, then yet more, on top of it. The new bits smothered the flame, and pungent smoke rose from the smoldering mass.

At that moment somebody came in and shut himself up in the stall two over. While the smoke was still rising!

It could be a friend.

It could equally well be an enemy.

Perhaps the smoke would not get that far. But perhaps the other man had already noticed the smell of burning and was about to give the alarm.

There was a tickling in Sologdin's throat, but he suppressed his cough.

Then suddenly the whole mass of paper flared up and a shaft of yellow light struck the ceiling. The heat of the flame was intense. It dried the sides of the toilet bowl and seemed likely to crack them.

There were still two small pieces left, but Sologdin did not put them into the bowl. The fire was burning out. He flushed the toilet noisily. The water compressed the heap of black ash and carried it away.

Sologdin waited, motionless.

Two other people came in just for a chat.

"All he thinks of is getting to heaven on somebody else's back."

"Just check it on the oscillograph, and never mind the rest."

They left, but someone else immediately arrived and locked himself in.

Sologdin stood there, humiliated by having to hide. He suddenly realized what was on the last scraps of paper. One was a corner piece, showing just the very edge of his drawing. Tearing off the bit that mattered, Sologdin threw the rest into the wastebasket. But the other piece contained the very heart of his design. He began very patiently tearing it into pieces so small that he could scarcely hold them between his fingernails.

He flushed the toilet again and dashed out to the hallway under cover of the noise.

Nobody had noticed him.

Once in the main hallway, he slowed down. A wry thought occurred to him; you set fire to the ship of hope, and all you feel is fear that a toilet bowl may crack or that somebody may notice a smell of burning.

He went back into the design office, listened absently to Yemina's news from the engineering shop, and asked her to hurry up with the copying.

She didn't understand.

How could she?

He himself didn't understand yet. There was so much that was still unclear to him. Oblivious to the need to "look busy," Sologdin did not touch his instrument case, his books, or his drawings. He sat with his head in his hands, eyes open but unseeing.

Any minute now someone would come and summon him to the engineer colonel's office.

He was in fact summoned, but to the lieutenant colonel.

A complaint had arrived from the filter laboratory that they still hadn't received the drawing (of two brackets) they had ordered. The lieutenant colonel was not a harsh man. He only frowned and said, "Dmitri Aleksandrovich, surely it can't be as complicated as all that? It was ordered on Thursday!"

Sologdin pulled himself together. "I'm sorry. I've nearly finished them. They'll be ready in an hour."

He hadn't even begun, but it wouldn't do to admit that there had never been more than an hour's work in it.

# 78

# The Professional Party Secretary

In the early days of Marfino, their trade union had great moral significance in the lives of the institute's free employees.

Everyone knows that a trade union could be a key factor in socialist production. It alone could selflessly request the government to make the working day and the working week longer, to raise production norms and lower wages.

If people in towns had nothing to eat or nowhere to live (or, as so often, neither of those things), the trade union—who else?—would come to the rescue, authorizing its members to cultivate collective holdings on their days off and build houses for the state in their leisure hours. The trade unions were the foundation on which all the conquests of the Revolution, and the ever-firmer position of the boss class, rested.

A general meeting of trade-union members was the best place to demand the dismissal of a fellow worker guilty of complaining or demanding his rights, if the management dared not dismiss him otherwise. When work property was written off as of no further use to the state but was still usable by the director on the domestic level, no signature could look so spotlessly pure on the necessary document as that of the local TU secretary. Moreover, the trade unions paid for themselves, with the thirtieth percentage point that the state could not very well withhold from the worker's wage in addition to the 29 percent deducted to cover tax and a "voluntary" contribution to the State Loan.

In matters great and small, the trade unions became, day in and day out, a veritable school of Communism.

In spite of which the Marfino Institute's trade union was suppressed. A highly placed comrade in the Moscow City Party Committee had gotten wind of its existence and been horrified: "What are you thinking of?!" he had gasped, without even adding the word "comrades." "This smacks of Trotskyism! Marfino is a military establishment; what's it doing with a trade union?"

The union was abolished the very same day.

Life at Marfino was not, however, shaken to its foundations. The only result was that the importance of the Party organization, not inconsiderable before, grew and grew. The Oblast Committee of the Party recognized Marfino's need for a full-time Party secretary. After scrutinizing a number of dossiers submitted by the Personnel Department, the bureau decided to recommend

> *Stepanov, Boris Sergeevich, born 1900, native of the village of Lupachi, rural district of Bobrovsk. Social origin—family of farm laborers, after the Revolution village policeman, no professional qualifications. Present social position—office worker. Education—four years elementary school plus two-year training school. Party member from 1921, engaged in Party work from 1923, no deviations from the Party line, took no part in opposition groups, has not served in armed forces or institutions of White government, has not lived under enemy occupation, has not been abroad, knows no languages, does not know the languages of any non-Russian peoples of the USSR, suffers from shell-shock, has Order of Red Banner and medal "For Victory over Germany in the Fatherland War."*

When the Obkom made its recommendation, Stepanov was away in the Volokolamsk district, engaged as an agitator in the harvest campaign. If the collective farmers sat down to eat or simply for a smoke, he took advantage of every leisure minute to make them gather around, or in the evenings summoned them to the kolkhoz office, so that he could tirelessly explain, in the light of the world-conquering doctrine of Marx-Engels-Lenin-Stalin, how important it was that the land should be sown every year with good-quality seed, that the yield should be as much in excess of the seed sown as possible, and that the crop should be harvested without wastage or pilfering and handed over with all possible speed to the state. Forgoing rest, he moved on to the tractor drivers and explained to them, in the light of the same immortal doctrine, the importance of economizing on fuel, the need to take good care of equipment, the utter inadmissibility of standstills. He also, reluctantly, answered questions about poor maintenance work and the unavailability of overalls.

Meanwhile, a general meeting of the Marfino Party organization had enthusiastically accepted the recommendation of the Obkom and elected Stepanov, sight unseen, full-time secretary. A co-op official in the Yegorov district, relieved of his post for embezzlement, was sent to agitate in Volokolamsk, while in Marfino an office next to that of the secret operations officer was fitted out for Stepanov, and he assumed control.

He began by formally taking over from his part-time predecessor, Lieutenant Klykachev. Klykachev was as lean as a wolfhound, quick on his feet, and tireless. He ran the code-cracking lab, supervised the cryptographic and statistical groups, presided over the Komsomol seminar, was the moving spirit of the "youth group," and had still found time to act as secretary to the Party Committee. And although his superiors considered Klykachev rigorous, while his subordinates called him a nitpicker, the new secretary at once suspected that Party business in the Marfino Institute had been neglected. For Party work demands the whole man, with nothing left over for other activities.

It was as he had expected. The takeover occupied a whole week, during which Stepanov did not once leave his office.

He perused every document in the place and got to know every Party member, from his or her dossier first and only then in the flesh. The new secretary's hand weighed heavily on Klykachev.

One dereliction after another came to light: unanswered questionnaires, defective personal files, failure to provide detailed assessments of the character and performance of each member and candidate member. The same fatal flaw vitiated all of the previous secretary's initiatives: Nothing that he undertook was adequately documented, and so those activities themselves appeared spectral.

"Who's going to believe it? Who's going to take your word for it that these measures really were implemented?" Stepanov exclaimed, holding a smoking cigarette above his bald head.

He explained patiently that Klykachev's activities existed only on paper (since his word was the only evidence for them!) and not in reality (meaning not on paper, not in the form of official reports!).

Who cares, for instance, whether or not the institute's physiculturists (he was talking about prisoners, of course) play enthusiastic volleyball in the lunch hour (and even make a habit of running over into working time)? Maybe they do. Neither you nor I nor anybody else will be going down to the yard to see whether the ball really is in the air. But if they've played so often and accumulated so much experience, shouldn't they share it with others in a special physical-culture wall newspaper called, say, *Red Ball*? If Klykachev then took the paper down regularly and filed it in Party records, no inspection team could doubt for a moment that "Operation Volleyball" was a reality carried out under Party supervision. As things were, who would take Klykachev's word for it?

And so it went on and on. "You can't file the spoken word" was the profound dictum with which Stepanov took up his duties.

A Catholic priest would not believe that anyone could lie in the confessional, and it would never enter Stepanov's head that lies can be told even in written records.

Skinny Klykachev, with his chronic wheeze, did not argue with Stepanov but feigned grateful agreement and followed his example. While Stepanov soon softened toward Klykachev, thus demonstrating that there was no malice in him, he listened intently to Klykachev's misgivings about Engineer Colonel Yakonov: Should an important research institute have at its head someone with such a dubious record, someone who was quite simply "not one of us"? Stepanov was already very much on his guard. He now made Klykachev his right-hand man, told him to drop in at the Party office whenever he felt like it, and good-naturedly shared with him the treasures of his own Party experience.

So Klykachev got to know the new Party organizer sooner and better than anyone. "The young" adopted his sarcastic nickname for Stepanov: "the Shepherd." But it was thanks to Klykachev that relations between Stepanov and "the young" were not as bad as they might have been. "The young" were quick to realize that it made life much easier if the Party organizer was obviously not their man but an impartial stickler for rules and regulations.

And what a stickler Stepanov was! Tell him that someone was to be pitied, that someone should be spared the full rigor of the law and shown clemency, and his brow, loftier since his hair had receded, would crease in pain and his shoulders slump as if an additional burden had been laid on them. Until, fired by the ardor of his faith, he found the strength to rise to his full height and turn on interlocutors right and left so sharply that little white squares, reflections of the windows, flashed in the leaden lenses of his spectacles.

"Comrades! Comrades! What is this I hear? How can you talk that way? Remember! You must uphold the law at all times! Uphold the law, however hard you find it! Uphold the law with all your might! Only thus, only in this way, can you really help the person for whose sake you came close to breaking the law! Because the law is devised to serve society and mankind, though we often fail to realize this and in our own blindness seek to circumvent the law!"

Stepanov, for his part, was pleased with "the young," who showed a taste for Party meetings and Party criticism. He saw in them the nucleus of a sound collective, such as he always tried to create at each new place of work. The collective that failed to expose lawbreakers in its midst, the collective that sat mum through meetings, was a collective that Stepanov rightly considered unsound. Whereas if a collective, to a man, fell upon one of its members, the very one at whom the Party Committee had pointed a finger, that collective was in the eyes of Stepanov, and those above him, a sound one.

Stepanov had many similar ideas, so firmly fixed in his mind that any departure from them was impossible. He could not, for instance, imagine a meeting that did not end with a tumultuous resolution castigating individual members and mobilizing the collective as a whole to break production records. He was particularly fond of "open" Party meetings, which non-Party people also attended on a "voluntary-compulsory" basis, only to be torn to shreds with no right to defend themselves or to vote. If before the vote was taken, pained or even indignant voices were heard asking, "What is this? A Party meeting? Or a criminal court?" Stepanov would peremptorily interrupt whoever was speaking, even the chairman; sprinkling a sedative powder on his tongue with a shaky hand (since his shell-shock, excitement made his head ache, and he always got agitated when the Party's infallibility was under attack), he would walk into the middle of the room, directly under the ceiling lights, so that the large beads of sweat on his bald brow stood out, and say, "Are we to take it, then, that you are against criticism and self-criticism?" Then, emphatically flourishing his clenched fist as if hammering his thoughts into the heads of his listeners, he would explain that "self-criticism is the supreme dynamic law of Soviet society, the main engine of its progress! It is time you understood that when we criticize members of our collective, it is not with a view to putting them on trial, but to keep every member of staff in a state of creative tension every minute of the day! About this there cannot be two opinions, Comrades! Of course, not every kind of criticism is needed! What we need is businesslike criticism, meaning criticism that is not directed at tried and tested leading cadres! We must not confuse freedom to criticize with the freedom of petit bourgeois anarchism!"

With which he withdrew to the carafe and washed down another powder with a swig of water.

Thus was the triumph of the Party's general line ensured. And the result was always that a sound collective, including members scourged and crushed by the resolution (condemning their "criminally slack attitude to their work" and their "failure to meet completion dates, bordering on sabotage"), unanimously voted for it.

It sometimes happened that Stepanov, though so fond of extended and closely argued resolutions and though happily aware in advance of the line that speakers could be expected to take and the final verdict of the meeting, was short of time to draft a resolution in full beforehand. On such occasions, when the chairman called on Comrade Stepanov to present the draft resolution, he would mop his brow and bald patch and speak as follows:

"Comrades! I have been very busy and have not had time to check certain circumstances, names, and facts. . . ."

Or: "Comrades! The directorate sent for me today, and I have not yet been able to draft a resolution."

In either case, he would add: " I ask you therefore to vote on a resolution in general terms, and I will attend to the details tomorrow, when I have time."

And the Marfino collective proved its soundness by raising its hands without a murmur, although it did not know (and did not ask) who exactly was to be lashed and who lauded in that resolution.

The new Party organizer's position was further reinforced by his avoidance of intimate relationships. Everyone addressed him respectfully as "Boris Sergeich." He accepted this as his due but did not himself call anyone at the site by his first name and patronymic. Even in the heat of a desktop billiards match (the green baize was always in evidence in the Party Committee's room), he would exclaim, "Put the balls up, Comrade Shikin!" or "Off the rail, Comrade Klykachev!"

Stepanov did not much like people appealing to his better nature. He himself never appealed to anyone's finer feelings. So that the moment he sensed dissatisfaction in the collective or resistance to his initiatives, instead of loud remonstrances or quiet permission, he took a large sheet of blank paper, wrote at the top in bold letters, "The below-mentioned comrades are required by such and such a date to . . ." do this, that, and the other, then ruled columns for "recipient's name," "serial number," and "acknowledgment of receipt" and handed it to his secretary to take around. The comrades indicated read it, sputtered their fury over an impervious sheet of paper, and had no choice but to sign and, having signed, to do as they were bidden.

Stepanov's "release" from other duties was also release from wandering in the dark. The radio had only to announce that heroic Yugoslavia no longer existed, only the Tito clique, and within five minutes Stepanov would be explaining the Comintern resolution as cogently and confidently as if he personally had been pondering it for years. If anyone timidly called Stepanov's attention to a contradiction between yesterday's and today's instructions, to gaps in the institute's equipment, to the inferiority of Soviet apparatus, to difficulties with living accommodations, the "liberated" Stepanov simply smiled and his glasses gleamed because whoever it was must surely know what he was about to say: "Well, what can we do about it, Comrades? It's a departmental muddle. But progress is undoubtedly being made, with this problem as with others. You won't deny that, I'm sure!"

Stepanov did have certain human weaknesses, though not very important ones. He liked being praised by his superiors, for instance, and being admired by ordinary Party members as an experienced leader. He enjoyed these tributes because they were no more than his due.

He was also fond of vodka, but only if someone treated him or if it were served at a banquet, and he invariably complained, as he drank, that vodka was murder to one in his state of health. Which was why he never bought it himself or treated anyone else.

These were perhaps his only faults.

"The young" sometimes argued among themselves as to how "the Shepherd" should best be described. "My friends!" Roitman said, "he is the prophet of the bottomless inkwell. He is the soul of the rubber-stamped document. Such people are an inevitable feature of the transition period."

But Klykachev bared his teeth in a grin and said, "Simpletons! If we get within biting distance, he'll gobble us up, shit and all. Don't think he's stupid. He's learned what it's all about in his fifty years. Why d'you think every meeting adopts a motion tearing someone to pieces? He's waiting for the history of Marfino, that's why! He's storing up scraps of evidence just in case. Whatever turn things take, any inspection team will be convinced that the full-time secretary gave repeated warnings and did his best to alert the public." The treacherous Klykachev depicted Stepanov as a devious intriguer, who would stop at nothing to give his three sons a good start in life.

Stepanov did indeed have three sons, who were forever asking their father for money. He had steered all three toward the History Department, knowing that for Marxists history is not a difficult discipline. His calculation looked sound enough, but he (like the state's general education plan) had failed to allow for a sudden glut of Marxist historians: Supply greatly exceeded demand from schools, colleges, crash courses; exceeded demand in Moscow itself; then throughout the Moscow oblast; and finally everywhere this side of the Urals. When the first son graduated, instead of staying at home to support his parents, he left for far-off Khanty-Mansiisk. The second son was offered a post in Mongolia, and it seemed doubtful whether when the third son finished his studies, he would find anything nearer than the island of Borneo.

Their father clung all the more tenaciously to his job and his little house on the outskirts of Moscow with his 0.12 hectares of garden, his barrels of sauerkraut, and his two or three porkers. For Stepanov's wife, a stolid person, perhaps a little out of step with the times, fattening those pigs was her main interest in life, as well as a prop for the family budget. Sunday was the day she had chosen for a trip to town with her husband in order to buy a piglet. This operation (successfully accomplished) was why Stepanov had not come to work that day, although Saturday's interview had left him ill at ease and impatient to be back at Marfino.

That Saturday, in the Political Department, Stepanov had been given a shock. An official person, a very important one, round and rosy—there were roughly 280 pounds of him—in spite of the cares of office, had glanced at the spectacles mounted on Stepanov's narrow nose and asked in a baritone drawl, "Ah, Stepanov, what are you doing about the Hebrews?"

Stepanov pricked up his ears, unsure that he had heard correctly.

"The Jews!" And (seeing that the other man still did not understand)—"the Yids, then."

Caught off balance and not daring to repeat that double-edged word, which not so long ago could earn you twenty years for anti-Soviet agitation and at one time get you put against a wall, Stepanov mumbled, ". . . Er . . . well. . . ."

"Well, what are you thinking of doing about them?"

But then the telephone rang, the important senior comrade lifted the receiver, and their conversation was at an end.

Stepanov anxiously read through a whole bundle of directives, instructions, and guidelines there in the department, but the black letters on white paper carefully skirted the Jewish problem.

All that Sunday, as they went to buy the pig, he thought and thought and clawed his chest in despair. Age had evidently dulled his wits. What a disgrace! An experienced Party worker like Stepanov fails to spot a major campaign in the making and even finds himself indirectly implicated in the intrigues of the enemy because that whole Roitman-Klykachev group. . . .

Stepanov arrived at work on Monday morning not knowing what to think. After Shikin had said no to a game of billiards (Stepanov had planned to pump him), the full-time secretary, suffocating for want of instructions, locked himself in the Party Committee quarters and banged the balls around for two hours on end, occasionally jumping one of them off the table. The enormous bronze bas-relief on the wall—the heads of the Four Founding Fathers superimposed in profile—witnessed several brilliant shots with two or all three balls pocketed at once. But the silhouettes in bas-relief maintained their bronze impassivity. Three of the four each studied the nape of the genius in front, and not one of them suggested how Stepanov could avoid destroying a healthy collective and even reinforce it in the new situation.

Exhausted, he heard the telephone ring at last and pounced on the receiver.

The message was, first, that instead of the usual Party and Komsomol instruction classes that evening, he should assemble everybody for a lecture on "Dialectical Materialism: The Progressive Worldview," to be given by a lecturer from the Oblast Committee. And, second, that a car was even then on its way to Marfino, with two comrades who would provide the appropriate guidelines for the campaign against kowtowing to foreign countries.

The full-time secretary took heart, cheered up, doubled a ball into a pocket, and hid the billiards table behind the room divider.

His spirits were further raised by the thought that the pink-eared piglet bought yesterday had eaten its swill eagerly, turning up its nose at nothing, both the night before and again that morning. There was reason to hope that it would fatten up quickly and cheaply.

# 79

## The Decision Explained

ENGINEER COLONEL YAKONOV was in his office with Major Shikin.

They sat conversing man-to-man, though they despised and detested each other.

Yakonov liked using the words "We in the Cheka" at meetings. But to Shikin he was what he had always been, an enemy of the people who had traveled abroad, served a sentence, been pardoned, and even taken to the bosom of the Security Service, but was nonetheless *not* not guilty. The day must inevitably come when the Organs would unmask Yakonov and arrest him again. Shikin would be delighted to rip off those epaulets with his own hands! The diligent major with the head too big for his body was irked by the engineer colonel's extravagant condescension and the lordly self-assurance with which he bore the burden of authority. Shikin, accordingly, always did his best to emphasize his own importance and that of the operations which the engineer colonel undervalued.

On this occasion, he was suggesting that at the next general conference on "vigilance" Yakonov should report on security arrangements in the institute, severely criticizing their laxity. The conference could advantageously coincide with the relegation of unconscientious zeks to the camps and the introduction of the new secret logbooks.

Engineer Colonel Yakonov felt exhausted after yesterday's attack. There were dark pouches under his eyes, but his features had not lost their pleasing fullness. He nodded agreement as the other man spoke, but deep inside, behind all the barriers that no eye, except perhaps that of his wife, ever penetrated, he was thinking that this hoary-headed major, who had gone gray poring over reports by stoolies, was an obscene bug, that his activities were idiotically futile and his proposals invariably cretinous.

Yakonov had been given a single month. In a month's time his head might be on the block. He had to struggle out of the armor of command, break out of the shell of seniority, settle down in a quiet place with the plans before him, and think for himself.

But the outsize leather chair in which he sat was negation enough; the engineer colonel must answer for everything but could take a hand in nothing. All he could do was pick up the receiver and sign papers.

Then again, all that petty squabbling with Roitman's group was taking too much out of him. It was a war he waged because he was forced to. It was not in his power to squeeze them out of the institute. He just wanted to enforce unquestioning obedience. Whereas they wanted to drive him out and were indeed capable of destroying him.

Shikin was speaking. Yakonov's gaze narrowly avoided him. His eyes were open, but mentally he had left behind the pudgy body in a tunic and made his way home.

Home! My home is my castle! How wise the English are, the first to realize that truth. On your own little territory, only your own laws apply. Four walls and a roof reliably separate you from your beloved fatherland. Your wife's gently smiling eyes greet you on your threshold. The merry chatter of little girls (alas, already fodder for a school that was itself like a stultifying government department) soothes and amuses you, wearied and badgered and harassed as you are. Your wife has already taught them both to prattle in English. She sits down at the piano and plays a tuneful Waldteufel waltz. Dinnertime and the after-dinner hours soon pass, you are on the threshold of night, but your house is free from pompous high-ranking idiots and spitefully captious young men.

His working day comprised so much that was painful, so many humiliations, such desperate feats of self-control, so much administrative hustle that Yakonov had begun to feel his age, and if only he could, he would gladly have sacrificed his job and stayed at home, in his own cozy little world.

Not that he was no longer interested in the world outside. He took a very lively interest in it. It would, he thought, be difficult to find in the history of the world a time more fascinating than our own. World politics was to him a game of chess played on a hundred boards simultaneously. But he had no wish to be a player, still less a pawn, the head of a pawn, the base of a pawn. . . . His ambition was to be a mere spectator, to savor the game at ease in his pajamas and old-fashioned rocking chair in a book-lined room.

Yakonov was fully equipped for such a pastime. He knew two languages, and foreign radio stations vied with one another in supplying him with information. The Ministry of State Security received foreign journals before anyone else in the Soviet Union and distributed technical and military publications to its own institutes uncensored. And these publications all liked to slip in a little item on politics, on the coming global conflict, on the future political organization of the planet. . . . Rubbing shoulders with senior security officers, Yakonov couldn't help hearing details unavailable to the press. Nor did he draw the line at translated books on diplomacy and espionage. And then, of course, he had a logical mind and well-honed ideas of his own. That was Yakonov's game of chess: sitting in his rocking chair watching the East-West match and trying to divine the future from the moves they made.

But whose side was he on? His heart was with the West. But he had no doubt which side would win. He would not stake a single chip against it. The Soviet Union would be victorious. Yakonov had known it ever since his Western European trip in 1927. The West was doomed just because it lived so well—and lacked the will to risk its life in defense of the good life. Eminent Western thinkers and statesmen rationalized their irresolution, their eagerness to put off the battle, told themselves that the East was mending its ways, that it had noble ideals. . . . Whatever did not fit in with this way of thinking was summarily dismissed as slander or as a temporary phenomenon.

It was a universal law, with no exceptions: Ruthlessness always wins. All history, alas, and all the prophets bore witness to it.

In early youth, Anton had taken to heart a saying often heard at the time: "People are all swine." The longer he lived, the more frequently he saw this truth confirmed. And the surer he became of it, the easier life became for him. Because if people were all swine, there was no need to do anything for anyone but yourself. Let no one ask us to sacrifice on the "altar of society"; there's no such thing! The folk had expressed this truth very simply long ago: "Your own shirt is closest to your body."

That was why the custodians of dossiers and souls had no need to worry about Yakonov's past. When he looked back on his life, he realized that only those who did not think quickly enough at some critical moment landed in jail. Really clever people would foresee the danger. Take evasive action and survive as free men. You exist only as long as there is breath in your body; why spend your life behind bars? No! Yakonov's renunciation of the convict world was genuine, heartfelt, not mere pretense. No one else would have given him four spacious rooms, a balcony, and seven thousand a month, or at least not in a hurry. The regime had wronged him; it was wrongheaded, inept, cruel, but its cruelty was the surest manifestation of its strength!

Since it was impossible for him to give up work altogether, Yakonov was preparing to join the Communist Party, as soon as, and if, it was ready to accept him.

Shikin was now handing him a list of zeks doomed to set out for the camps the next day. Sixteen candidates had previously been agreed on, and Shikin now approvingly added two names from Yakonov's desk notepad. Their contract with the prison authorities was for twenty. They had to "rustle up" the missing from somewhere and inform Lieutenant Colonel Klimentiev not later than 5:00 p.m.

But no candidates came to mind immediately. It seemed always to be the case that the best of the experts and technical staff were unreliable in the operations officer's eyes, whereas the useless loafers were favorites of his. This made it difficult to agree on relegation lists.

Yakonov spread his fingers. "Leave the list with me. I'll give it a bit more thought. You do the same. We'll talk on the phone."

Shikin rose without haste and (he should have restrained himself but couldn't) complained to this inappropriate person about the minister's behavior: The prisoner Rubin had been admitted to Room 21, Roitman had been admitted, while he, Shikin, and, yes, even Colonel Yakonov were not to be admitted to what was part of their own establishment. Unthinkable!

Yakonov raised his eyebrows and lowered his eyelids, so that for one moment his face was that of a blind man.

"Yes, major," he mumbled. "Yes, my friend, it is hurtful, but I dare not look directly at the sun."

In fact, Yakonov's attitude to Room 21 was complicated. When, late on Saturday night, in Abakumov's office, he had heard from Ryumin about that telephone call, Yakonov was thrilled by these exciting new moves in the world chess game. Afterward, his own crisis had made him forget it all. Yesterday morning, recovering after his heart attack, he had readily supported Selivanovsky's proposal to leave it all to Roitman. (It was a slippery business; the fellow was a hothead; maybe he would break his neck.) But Yakonov had not lost his curiosity about that rash telephone call, and he was still annoyed that they would not let him into Room 21.

Shikin left, and Yakonov remembered that the most enjoyable of tasks awaited him. There had been no time yesterday. If he could speed up the absolute encoder significantly, it would be his salvation with Abakumov in a month's time.

He rang the design office and ordered Sologdin to bring his new design along.

Two minutes later, Sologdin knocked and entered. Well built, with a curly beard, in dirty overalls—and empty-handed.

Yakonov and Sologdin had hardly ever spoken to each other. Yakonov had never had occasion to summon Sologdin to his office, and the engineer colonel had no use for such an insignificant person in the design office or when they passed each other in the hallway. But now, glancing at the new arrival's name and patronymic under the glass plate on his desk, Yakonov smiled approval and warmly welcomed him.

"Take a seat, Dmitri Aleksandrovich. I'm very glad to see you."

With his arms tight against his sides, Sologdin came closer, bowed silently, and remained upright, motionless.

"I hear you've prepared a little surprise for us on the quiet," Yakonov rumbled. "The other day, it may have been on Saturday, I saw your design for the main sequence of the absolute encoder. . . . But why don't you sit down? I got only a cursory look at it, and I'm dying to discuss it in detail."

Sologdin, half facing Yakonov, stiff as a duelist awaiting his opponent's shot, did not lower his eyes before that friendly gaze. He spoke as if dictating his answer.

"You are mistaken, Anton Nikolaevich. I have indeed done my best with the encoder. But what I have managed to produce and what you saw is horribly imperfect and all that my modest abilities permit."

Yakonov leaned back in his chair and good-naturedly demurred.

"Come, come, my dear fellow, no false modesty, please! I only glanced at your solution, but I formed a very favorable impression of it. Vladimir Erastovich, whose opinion matters more than yours or mine, was most complimentary. Now I'm going to give orders that I can't see anybody else at present, and you can bring along your drawing and your calculations, and we'll think about it. Shall we send for Vladimir Erastovich?"

Yakonov was not the philistine managerial type, interested only in end product and output. He was an engineer, he had once been an ardently enthusiastic engineer, and now he was feeling in anticipation the pleasure that the product of long and successful mental effort can afford. This was the only pleasure that his work still had to offer. He smiled sweetly at Sologdin, almost as though he were begging a favor.

Sologdin was also an engineer, of fourteen years standing. And a convict for twelve of them.

He felt a pleasurable chill as he lowered his visor and said deliberately, "I repeat, Anton Nikolaevich, you are mistaken. It was a rough draft, unworthy of your attention."

Yakonov, now just a little annoyed, frowned and said, "Well, now, let's just take a look. Go and get your draft."

His epaulets were golden with a light blue border and three stars. Three big stars, arranged in a triangle. Just like those that had suddenly replaced the pips on Lieutenant Kamyshan, senior operations officer at Gornaya Zakrytka, in the months when he was beating Sologdin to a pulp, only a bit smaller.

"That rough sketch no longer exists," Sologdin said hesitantly. "I spotted some serious, ineradicable errors in it, and I . . . I burned it."

(He had driven the sword home and twisted it twice.)

The colonel turned pale. In the menacing silence, only his labored breathing could be heard. Sologdin tried to breathe noiselessly.

"What? . . . How? . . . With your own hands?"

"Of course not. I handed it over for burning. Following the correct procedure. They were burning our waste today."

His voice was dull, subdued. There was no trace of his usual ringing self-assurance.

"Today? So maybe it's still intact?" Yakonov said hopefully.

"It was burned. I was watching through the window," Sologdin answered deliberately.

Clutching the arm of his chair with one hand and seizing his marble paperweight with the other, as if he meant to brain Sologdin, the colonel raised his big body and with an effort leaned forward over the desk.

Sologdin stood like a dark blue statue, head tilted backward.

The two engineers had no further need of questions and answers. Their eyes locked, and a glare charged with insane tension passed between them.

I'll annihilate you! the colonel's bulging eyes said.

Hang a third sentence around my neck! the prisoner's eyes shouted back.

A deafening storm seemed about to break.

But Yakonov, clasping his eyes and his brow as though the light was hurting them, turned away and went over to the window.

Sologdin gripped the back of the nearest chair and wearily lowered his eyes.

A month! Just one month! Am I really done for? The message stood out stark and clear in the colonel's mind.

A third spell inside! I will never survive it, Sologdin told himself. His heart was in his boots.

Yakonov turned around to face Sologdin again.

An engineer is an engineer! his eyes seemed to say. How could you?

But Sologdin's eyes were blindingly bright; and their answer was, A prisoner's a prisoner! You've forgotten what it's like!

They stared at each other with hypnotic hatred, each seeing himself as he might have been, and could not unlock their gaze.

Yakonov could yell, thump the desk, ring for someone, lock him up; Sologdin was prepared even for that.

Instead, Yakonov took out a clean, soft white handkerchief. Wiped his eyes. And looked mildly at the prisoner.

It cost Sologdin an effort to stand firm for those extra minutes.

The engineer colonel rested one hand on the windowsill and beckoned to the prisoner with the other.

Sologdin took three steps toward him.

Hunched like an old man, Yakonov asked, "Are you a Muscovite, Sologdin?"

"Yes."

"Look out there, then. See the bus stop on the main road?"

It was clearly visible from the window.

Sologdin looked toward it.

"The center of Moscow is a half hour's ride from here," Yakonov informed him quietly. "You could be getting on that bus in June or July this year. But you've decided not to. I dare say you'd have been given your first vacation in August. You could have gone to the Black Sea. Could have been swimming. How long is it since you got in the water, Sologdin? Of course, prisoners aren't allowed to."

"Not when they're timber rafting?"

"I wouldn't call that swimming! Anyway, you'll end up so far north that the rivers never thaw!"

You sacrifice your future, sacrifice your reputation; that's not enough for them. You must lose your livelihood, abandon your home, skin yourself alive, land yourself in a labor camp.

"Sologdi-in!" Yakonov almost wailed, placing his two hands on the prisoner's shoulders as if to prevent himself from falling. "Surely you can reproduce it! I don't believe there's anyone in the world who doesn't want the best out of life. Why destroy yourself? Explain it to me: Why did you burn the drawing?"

The untroubled, incorruptible, innocent blue gaze of Dmitri Sologdin did not waver. And Yakonov could see his own large head reflected in one dark pupil. A light blue circle with a black pinpoint in the middle—and beyond them the whole unexpected world of one unique person.

How fortunate the man who keeps his head, controls the course of events to the last, ensures that what happens next is for him to decide! Why destroy myself? Sologdin was thinking. For that lost, that debauched, that godless people?

He answered Yakonov with a question: "Why do you think I did it?"

The rosy lips between mustache and beard curved slightly in what might have been a mocking smile.

"I don't understand," Yakonov said. He removed his hands from the other man's shoulders and walked away. "Suicides I do not understand."

And from behind his back, he heard that clear, confident voice: "Citizen Colonel! I'm a complete nonentity; no one has ever heard of me! I didn't want to forfeit my freedom for nothing—"

Yakonov turned around abruptly.

"If I hadn't burned the drawing but laid it before you ready for use, our lieutenant colonel or you, Foma Guryanovich or anybody you like, could have packed me off to a camp and put any name he liked on the drawing. And lodging complaints from transit prisons is a very tricky business, believe you me. They take pencils away; they won't give you paper; your applications go astray. . . . A prisoner in transit can never be in the right."

Listening to all this, Yakonov felt something like admiration for the man. (He had taken a liking to him the moment he walked in.)

"Well, then . . . can you undertake to reproduce the drawing?" The question came not from an engineer colonel but from a helpless human being at the end of his tether.

"All that I had on paper . . . in three days." Sologdin's eyes flashed. "And in five weeks I can produce a full outline sketch with detailed specifications. Will that do?"

"A month! One month! We must have it in a month!" Hands pressed against the desk, he swung around to confront this diabolical engineer.

"Very well, you will have it in a month," Sologdin assented coolly.

But Yakonov was suddenly suspicious again.

"Hold on . . . you said a moment ago that it was a worthless rough draft, that you'd found fundamental and irreparable errors in it."

Sologdin laughed out loud. "Lack of phosphorus, oxygen, and fresh impressions sometimes plays strange tricks on me. I suffer a sort of blackout. But now I will side with Professor Chelnov and say all is as it should be."

Yakonov smiled back at him, smiled with relief, and sat down. He was full of admiration for Sologdin's aplomb and the skill with which he had steered their conversation.

"You've been playing a risky game, my friend. It might easily have ended differently."

"Not really, Anton Nikolaevich. I think I have a pretty clear idea of the institute's position . . . and your own. You understand French, of course? '*Le hasard est roi.*' Long live the main chance! When we catch a rare glimpse of it, we must jump and land squarely on its back!"

Sologdin could not have been more at ease if he had been chatting with Nerzhin at the woodpile.

He sat down at last, still gazing cheerfully at Yakonov.

"So what do we do?" the engineer colonel asked amicably.

Sologdin answered as if reading from a printed text a decision made long ago.

"I would like to bypass Foma Guryanovich at the first stage. He's just the sort of person who likes to be coauthor. I don't anticipate any little trick of that sort from you. Don't tell me I'm wrong."

Yakonov happily shook his head. He was too relieved to want coauthorship.

"Next, let me remind you that as things stand, the draft has been burned. If you think well of my project, find some way to mention me directly to the minister. Or, at the very least, to the deputy minister. And let him, personally, be the one to sign the order appointing me designer in chief. That will be my insurance, and then I can get to work. We'll form a special group—"

The door was suddenly flung open wide, and skinny, bald-headed Stepanov, opaquely gleaming, entered without knocking.

"Right, Anton Nikolaevich," he said sternly. "We have something important to discuss."

Stepanov addressing someone by his given name and patronymic! Unbelievable.

Sologdin stood up. "So I can expect the order?" he said.

The engineer colonel nodded, and Sologdin went out. With a light but firm step.

Yakonov did not immediately fathom what the Party organizer was talking about with such animation.

"Comrade Yakonov! I've been visited by comrades from the Political Administration and given a thorough dressing-down. I have made serious mistakes. I have permitted a group of . . . let's call them homeless cosmopolitans to move in on our Party organization. And I have been guilty of political shortsightedness in failing to make your life a misery. But we must fearlessly acknowledge our mistakes! So let the two of us draft a resolution immediately, then convene an open Party meeting and strike a powerful blow against the slavish worship of all things foreign!"

Yakonov's situation, which had looked so desperate early yesterday, had taken a sharp turn for the better.

# 80

# One Hundred Forty-Seven Rubles

BEFORE LUNCH, the duty officer, Zhvakun, pinned up in the hallway of the special prison a list of those who were to report to Major Myshin during the break. Officially, a prisoner was summoned in this way to receive letters or to be informed of a remittance credited to his account.

The delivery of a letter to the inmate of a special prison was a secretive procedure. In the world outside, you would simply entrust it to a peripatetic mailman, but nothing so crude was possible here. The prisoner's spiritual father—or godfather—having read the letter himself to make sure that it contained no treasonable thoughts, handed it to the prisoner behind closed doors, with a few edifying remarks. No attempt was made to disguise the fact that the letter had been opened, so that any illusion of intimate contact between the prisoner and his nearest and dearest was destroyed. A letter that had passed through many hands, been minutely examined for useful additions to a man's dossier, and received internally the censor's smudgy black stamp lost all personal significance. It had become a state document. In some special prisons this was so well understood that a prisoner's letter was not handed over at all: He was merely allowed to read it, twice if he was lucky, in the godfather's office, and sign it to confirm that he had done so. If a prisoner reading a letter from his wife or mother made notes to aid his memory, he aroused as much suspicion as if he had been caught copying General Staff documents. A prisoner in such a place also had to sign photographs sent from home to confirm that he had seen them, after which they were added to his prison dossier.

So, then, the list was posted, and prisoners stood in line for their letters. With them stood others who wished to dispatch the one letter each of them was allowed for December. This, too, had to be handed to the godfather. Under cover of these operations Major Myshin could summon his stoolies for unscheduled meetings and talk to them without fear of interruption. So that it would not be obvious which interviews were most important to him, he sometimes detained an honest zek or two and kept the others guessing.

This meant that everyone in the line was suspected by someone. Sometimes, however, they knew exactly who was putting their lives "in pawn" and smiled at him ingratiatingly.

Soviet penal practice, though not based directly on the experience of Cato the Elder, faithfully followed his injunction not to let slaves be too friendly with one another.

As the lunch bell rang, zeks rushed up from the basement and across the yard without coats and caps—the wind was damp but not cold—and darted through the door of the prison HQ. Because new regulations governing correspondence had been announced that morning, the line was unusually long—some forty men—and there was no room for all of them in the hallway. The duty officer's assistant, a martinet sergeant major, brought all the resources of a ripe physique into play, counted off twenty-five men, and told the rest to take a walk and come back during the supper break. Those allowed in he lined up against the wall, well away from the bosses' offices, and he paced the hallway continually to keep order. Each zek in turn walked past several doors, knocked at Major Myshin's office, and awaited permission to enter. When he emerged, the next man was admitted. The sergeant major directed the traffic throughout the lunch break.

Spiridon had begged to be given his letter early in the morning, but Myshin had been adamant. He would get it, like all the others, in the lunch break. But half an hour before lunch Major Shikin had summoned him for questioning. If Spiridon had made the required statement and admitted everything, who knows, he might have been in time to get his letter. But he had dug his heels in. Major Shikin could not let him leave unchastened. So he had sacrificed his lunch break (and anyway, he preferred to avoid the crush in the free workers' dining room) to continue his interrogation.

First in the line for letters was Dyrsin, an engineer from Number Seven, a key member of its staff, and a wreck of a man. It was more than three months since he had received a letter. He kept asking Myshin, but "Nothing for you" and "Nobody's writing" were all the answers he got. He asked Mamurin to send somebody to look. Waste of breath. Nobody was sent. But today his name was on the list, and fighting against the pain in his chest, he had rushed to be first in line. He had no family left except for a wife as worn-out by ten years of waiting as he was.

The sergeant major waved Dyrsin in, and Ruska Doronin was now next. Ruska, with his devil-may-care grin and floppy blond forelock. Seeing the Latvian, Hugo, one of his confidants, behind him in line, tossed his hair back, winked, and said in a whisper, "I'm here to collect my money. Money I've earned."

"Move up," the sergeant major ordered.

Doronin shot forward, passing Dyrsin as he returned dejected.

"Well?" Amantai Bulatov, his workmate, asked Dyrsin, once they were out in the yard.

Dyrsin's face, always unshaved, always doleful, looked even longer.

"I don't know. He says there is a letter, but come back after the break and we'll talk."

"Bastards!" Bulatov said, with a flash of anger through his horn-rimmed glasses. "I keep telling you they hold our letters back. Refuse to work!"

"They'd pin a second sentence on me," Dyrsin said with a sigh. He was always hunched, his head drawn down into his shoulders, as though he had been struck sharply from behind with something heavy.

Bulatov sighed with him. If he was so militant, it was because he still had so much time to do. A zek becomes less and less sure of himself as the day of release draws nearer. Dyrsin was into his last year.

The sky was an unrelieved gray, with no darker clouds and no gleam of light. It had no depth; it was not vaulted; it was like a dirty tarpaulin stretched above the earth. The snow had settled into a porous mass under the keen wet wind, and its morning whiteness was beginning to look rusty. It hardened into slippery brownish hillocks under the feet of men taking exercise.

But the constitutional went on as usual. The weather would never be foul enough to make prisoners wilting for lack of air in the sharashka forgo their walk. After long confinement they enjoyed being buffeted by gusts of damp wind that blew the stale air and stale thoughts out of a man.

The engraver darted to and fro among the strollers, took one zek after another by the arm, and asked his advice. His plight, as he saw it, was singularly dreadful. He had been unable to formalize his marriage in prison, and now his partner (his first) was not regarded as his legal wife. He had no right to correspond with her and, since he had used up his allowance of letters for December, no means of letting her know that he would not be writing. People sympathized with him. His position was indeed absurd. But each of them felt his own pain more keenly than the next man's.

Kondrashov-Ivanov, tall, stiff as a ramrod, and hypersensitive, moved slowly along, gazing over the heads of the walkers, and informed Professor Chelnov in an ecstasy of pessimism that when your dignity was trampled underfoot, to go on living was to debase yourself. Any man with courage had a simple way to escape this chain of humiliations.

Professor Chelnov, wearing his eternal woolen hat and his plaid shawl around his shoulders, contented himself with a quotation from Boethius's *De Consolatione Philosophiae*.

A group of volunteer stoolie hunters had gathered near the entrance to HQ: Bulatov, whose voice carried right across the yard; Khorobrov; Zemelya, the amiable fellow from the Vacuum Lab; Dvoetyosov, sporting his Gulag jacket on principle; quick-witted Pryanchikov, who had a finger in every pie; Max, the leader of the Germans; and one of the Latvians.

"The country needs to know who its stoolies are!" Bulatov repeated, encouraging them in their determination not to disperse.

"We've got a pretty good idea already," Khorobrov answered, standing in the doorway and running his eyes over the men standing in line. He could be fairly sure of some of those lining up for their thirty pieces of silver. But of course it was only the least clever among them who aroused suspicion.

Ruska rejoined the company. It cost him an effort not to flourish his money order. Heads together, they all hurriedly inspected it. It was from a mythical Klavdia Kudryavtseva, addressed to Rostislav Doronin, and for 147 rubles!

Returning from lunch, Artur Siromakha, supersquealer and stoolie supreme, took his place at the end of the line and ran his lackluster eyes over the stoolie hunters. He looked the group over because he made a habit of noting everything, but for the moment he attached no importance to it.

Ruska retrieved his money order and left the group, according to plan.

The third man to enter the godfather's office was the forty-year-old electrical engineer who, in the privacy of the old sanctuary the night before, had opined that ministers and sewers were more or less the same thing, then had become a child again and started a pillow fight on the upper bunks.

The fourth to enter, with his quick, light step, was Viktor Lyubimichev. Always hail-fellow-well-met, he would bare his teeth in a winning smile and address young and old alike as "Old pal." This easy cordiality hinted at a guileless nature.

The electrical engineer reappeared in the doorway with an open letter. He was so absorbed in his reading that he almost missed the step. Still unseeing, he descended sideways, and no one in the group of hunters bothered him. He was lightly dressed and bareheaded, with the wind ruffling his hair, which was still that of a young man in spite of all he had been through. He was reading his first letter, after eight years of separation, from his daughter Ariadne, a fair-haired six-year-old clinging around his neck when he had left for the front en route to POW camp and then a Soviet jail. When he had heard prisoners of war crunching layers of typhus-carrying bugs underfoot in their huts and stood in line for four hours or more for a ladleful of foul-smelling dishwater soup, the memory of that precious little bundle of brightness drew him on, as Ariadne's thread had drawn Theseus, to survive and return. But back in his native land, he had gone straight to jail without seeing his daughter. She had been evacuated with her mother to Chelyabinsk. They had remained there. Ariadne's mother had found another partner, and it was a long time before she told the girl that her father still existed. In a painstaking, slanting schoolgirl hand, Ariadne had written, without blots:

*Dear Papa, hello!*

*I didn't answer before because I didn't know where to start and what to write. I can be forgiven for that because I had gotten used to thinking that my father had died. It seems quite strange that I suddenly have a father.*

*You want to know what sort of life I have. It's the same as everybody else's. You can congratulate me on joining the Komsomol. You ask me to tell you if there's anything I need. I need lots of things, of course. Right now I'm saving up for some boots, and to get a light overcoat made. Papa! You say come and visit you. But is it really urgent? To travel some place a long way off looking for you wouldn't be very nice, would it? You'll come here when you're able. I wish you success in your work. So long for now.*

*I kiss you.*
*Ariadne*

*Papa, have you seen the movie* First Glove*? It's marvelous. I never miss a single movie.*

"Shall we check up on Lyubimichev?" Khorobrov asked.

"Forget it, Terentich," they protested. "Lyubimichev's one of us."

But, deep down, Khorobrov sensed that there was something wrong with the man. And right now he had been closeted too long with the godfather.

Viktor Lyubimichev had big, wide-open eyes. Nature had endowed him with the supple body of an athlete, a soldier, and a lover. Life had plucked him from the running tracks of the Young Athletes' Stadium and planted him in a Bavarian concentration camp. In that deathtrap, into which their enemies herded Russian soldiers whose own Soviet government denied the Red Cross access to them—in that small, jam-packed hellhole—only those who most decisively renounced narrow, class-conditioned notions of virtue and conscience survived: the man who acted as interpreter and betrayed his comrades, the man who became a camp orderly capable of striking fellow countrymen in the face with his stick, the man who worked as a bread cutter or a cook and ate the bread of the starving. There were two other possible routes to survival: working as a gravedigger or as a sanitary orderly. For digging graves and for cleaning out latrines, the Nazis allowed an extra ladleful of porridge. Two men could manage the latrines, while fifty or so went gravedigging every day. Day in and day out, a dozen hearses carted the dead away to be dumped. Summer 1942 was approaching, and with it the turn of the gravediggers themselves. Viktor Lyubimichev, with the ardor of an organism that had lived too little, longed to go on living. He resolved that if he was to die, he would die last, and showed himself willing to become a camp orderly. But by a lucky chance a shady character who appeared to have once been a Soviet political officer turned up in the camp, urging them to go and fight the Communists. Men signed on, Komsomols among them. There was a German army cookhouse outside the camp gate where volunteers were allowed to "eat their bellyful" of gruel. Afterward, Lyubimichev had fought in France, hunting down Resistance fighters in the Vosges, then defending the Atlantic Wall against the Western Allies. During the great trawl of '45, he somehow slipped through the net, went home, married a girl as bright-eyed and lissome as himself, and left her behind in their first month when his past caught up with him. The prison population at the time included Russians who had served with the very same Resistance movement that Lyubimichev had hunted in the Vosges. In Butyrki, prisoners played dominoes furiously, reminisced about life and battles in France, and hoped for parcels from their families. Then they were all given a level ten years. So Viktor Lyubimichev's whole life had conditioned him to believe that nobody, from the man in the street to the man in the Politburo, ever had, or ever could have, principles; nor could those who presumed to judge them.

Clear-eyed and suspecting nothing, he made no attempt to avoid the hunters but walked straight up to them, holding what looked very much like a postal money order.

"Brothers, who's eaten? What's the main course? Is it worth going?"

Khorobrov nodded at the piece of paper in Viktor's lowered hand.

"Get much?" he asked. "Enough to go without lunch?"

Lyubimichev shrugged it off.

"No, not a lot," he said, trying to stuff the receipt into his pocket. He hadn't bothered to hide it sooner because they all feared his strength, and he thought that no one would dare to challenge him. But while he was talking to Khorobrov, Bulatov, as if in fun, bent down, craned his neck, and pretended to read: "Hey! One thousand four hundred and seventy rubles! You can tell Klimentiadis where to stick his grub now!"

If it had been any other zek, Viktor would have made a joke of it, shoved his face away, and hidden the money order. But Amantai could not be left thinking that his subordinate was rolling in money. Gulag rules forbade it. So Lyubimichev pleaded not guilty. "Where's the thousand? Look for yourself!"

They all saw that the order was in fact for 147 rubles.

"Funny they couldn't send a level 150," Amantai said coolly. "Off you go then, schnitzel for seconds."

But before he had finished speaking and before Lyubimichev could move on, Khorobrov was up in arms. He had forgotten that he was supposed to contain himself, smile, and ride on with the hunt. Forgotten that what mattered was identifying stoolies; destroying them was impossible. He had suffered too much from them, seen so many others come to grief because of them. He hated those snakes in the grass more than honest hangmen. Now somebody young enough to be his son and handsome enough to be a sculptor's model had turned out to be one of those volunteer reptiles.

"Scumbag!" Khorobrov blurted out. "Buying remission with our blood!"

Lyubimichev, a fighter and always ready for a fight, flinched and drew his fist back for a short-arm jab.

"Bog-trotting half-wit," he said menacingly.

But Bulatov forestalled him. "Cut it out, Terentich," he said, restraining Khorobrov.

While Dvoetyosov, a clumsy giant in a Gulag donkey jacket, seized Lyubimichev's raised right fist with his own left hand and held it tight.

"Buddy, buddy," he said, with a contemptuous smile. His voice was so tense that it might have been a lover's whisper. "No politics here!"

Lyubimichev turned abruptly, and his clear, wide eyes were very close to Dvoetyosov's myopic stare.

He did not raise his other fist. Those owl-like eyes and the grip of a peasant hand told him that if a blow was struck, one or the other of them would not just fall over but would drop dead.

"Buddy, buddy," Dvoetyosov said again. "The main course is schnitzel. Go eat your schnitzel."

Lyubimichev wrenched himself free and made for the basement steps with his head in the air. His satin-smooth cheeks were aflame. He was wondering how to get even with Khorobrov. He still didn't realize how seriously the accusation had damaged him. He would allow no one to question his worldly wisdom. But he evidently had a lot to learn.

How could they have guessed? Where had they gotten it from?

Bulatov watched him go and held his head in his hands.

"Mother, oh Mother!" he said. "Who can you trust after that?"

This whole scene had involved little movement, so that neither the promenading zeks nor the two guards stationed on the boundaries of the exercise yard had noticed anything. Only Siromakha, standing in line and looking back through the doorway, had seen it all through half-closed, tired eyes—and understood!

"Listen, boys," he said to those ahead of him, "I've left a circuit switched on. Could you let me go first? I'll be quick."

They laughed. "Everybody's left something switched on! We've all got babies to mind!"

They wouldn't let him pass.

"I just want to go and switch it off!"

Siromakha sounded worried.

He rounded the hunting party, vanished into the main building, and ran up to the third floor without pausing to get his breath. But Major Shikin's office door was locked from inside; the key was in the lock. An interrogation? A tryst with the gawky secretary? Siromakha withdrew, defeated.

He should have rejoined the line, but the instinct of a hunted animal was stronger than his need to earn his keep. The thought of walking back past that group of infuriated men terrified him. They could lay hands on him without provocation. He was only too well known in the sharashka.

Meanwhile, Doctor of Chemical Sciences Orobintsev, a small bespectacled person wearing the expensive fur coat and hat he had worn when free (he had arrived at Marfino without seeing the inside of a transit prison and had not yet been "unloaded"), had emerged from his interview with Myshin and assembled a group of simple souls like himself, including the bald-headed designer. He had an announcement to make. A man, of course, believes mainly what he chooses to believe. Those who wanted to believe that submitting a list of relatives was not the same as denouncing them but rather a sensible regulatory procedure formed Orobintsev's present audience. He had already presented his own list of names, arranged in neat columns, and spoken to Myshin. Now he was authoritatively relaying the major's clarification of certain points: where to enter the names of minors and what to do if you were not their natural father. Myshin had offended the professor's sense of propriety only once. When Orobintsev had said regretfully that he could not remember exactly where his wife was born, Myshin had bared his fangs and said, "Pick her up in a whorehouse, did you?"

Now the gullible innocents were listening to Orobintsev instead of joining the group sheltering under three lime trees with Abramson at its center.

Abramson, lazily smoking after an ample lunch, was telling his audience that there was nothing new about these restrictions on correspondence, that it used to be even worse, that the ban would not last forever but only until some minister or general was replaced, so there was no need to be downhearted, but meanwhile they should, if possible, refrain from submitting a list until it all blew over. Abramson was naturally slit-eyed, and when he removed his glasses, his gaze seemed to show more plainly than ever his boredom with the prison world. He had seen it all before; the Gulag Archipelago could hold no new shocks for him. He had been in prison so long that he seemed to have lost all feeling, and what to other people was a tragedy he accepted as merely a modification of routine.

Meanwhile, the hunters, reinforced in numbers, had caught another stoolie; there were jokes all around as they extracted a pay stub for 147 rubles from Isaak Kagan's pocket. When asked how much he had been given, he said "nothing": He had been sent for by mistake; he had no idea why. When they forcibly extracted the pay stub and cried shame on him, Kagan not only did not blush, not only did not hurry away, but clung to one of his accusers after another, swearing over and over again that it was a pure misunderstanding, that he would show them all the letter from his wife saying that she had been three rubles short at the post office and so could only send 147. He even tried to drag them off to the battery-charging room to show them this letter. Shaking his shaggy head and oblivious of the scarf slipping from around his neck and almost trailing on the ground, he gave a very plausible explanation of his failure to reveal in the first place that he had received a money order. Kagan was by nature the most tenacious of bores. Once start talking to him, and your only hope of escape was to acknowledge that he was absolutely right and let him have the last word. Khorobrov, who occupied the next bunk, knew that Kagan had been arrested for "failure to report" (failing to denounce someone) and so could not get duly angry. He merely said: "What a shit you are, Isaak! Outside, thousands wouldn't buy you. Here you sell yourself for hundreds!"

But maybe they'd threatened to send him to a camp?

Isaak, unabashed, kept pleading innocence and might have ended by convincing them all. But in the meantime they had caught another informer, a Latvian this time. Their attention was diverted, and Kagan walked away.

The second shift was summoned to lunch, and the first emerged to take exercise. Nerzhin, wearing his overcoat, came up the steps. He spotted Ruska Doronin immediately, standing on the boundary of the exercise yard. Ruska, eyes triumphantly shining, gazed upon the hunt he had organized but glanced from time to time at the free workers' yard and the approach from the main road. Klara would shortly arrive by bus for the evening shift and pass that way.

He grinned at Nerzhin. "See that?" he said, nodding toward the hunt. "Heard about Lyubichimev?"

Nerzhin stopped and gave him a hug.

"Congratulations! But I'm afraid for you."

"Pah! You haven't seen anything yet. This is just the start."

Nerzhin shook his head, laughed, and walked on. He met Pryanchikov, all smiles as he hurried off to lunch, hoarse from shouting at the stoolies in his light voice.

He greeted Nerzhin with a laugh.

"You've missed the whole show, pal! Where's Lev?"

"He has an urgent job to do. He can't come out for the break."

"What, more urgent than Number Seven? Ha-ha! No job's that urgent."

He hurried away.

Mixing with no one, avoiding conversation, Bobynin, a big man with a shaved head that was uncovered whatever the weather, and little Gerasimovich, with his crumpled cloth cap pulled down over his eyes and the collar of his short overcoat turned up, strode in circles of their own. Bobynin looked as if he could have comfortably swallowed Gerasimovich.

Gerasimovich shivered in the wind and kept his hands in his coat pockets. A puny sparrow of a man.

The sparrow in the proverb, with a heart as big as a cat.

# 81

# The Scientific Elite

BOBYNIN WAS MARCHING along in the outer circle of strollers, keeping to himself and oblivious to the commotion around the stoolies, when little Gerasimovich tacked toward him like a fast launch intercepting a big ship.

"Aleksandr Yevdokimovich!"

Accosting and obstructing others in the exercise yard was considered bad form among the prisoners, and anyway these two hardly knew each other. But Bobynin came to a stop.

"I'm listening."

"I have a very important question for you. It has to do with scientific research."

"Ask away."

They walked on, side by side, not too slowly, not too quickly.

Gerasimovich, however, went halfway around while he framed his question.

"Don't you feel ashamed of yourself sometimes?"

Bobynin, taken aback, swiveled his great cannonball of a head to look at his companion. (But they kept walking.) His eyes returned to the view ahead: lime trees, the big shed, people, the main building.

He thought it over for a good three-quarters of a circuit, then said, "Indeed I do."

Another quarter circle.

"So . . . why?"

A half circle.

"I want to go on living, damn it. . . ."

A quarter circle.

". . . I don't really know what to think."

Another quarter circle.

"It varies from one minute to the next. . . . Yesterday I told the minister that there's nothing left for me. But it wasn't true. I have my health, haven't I? I have hope. I'm quite possibly number-one candidate for. . . . I could be released before I'm too old, meet the one and only woman . . . have children. . . . Then again, it can be interesting, damn it. Right now it is interesting. . . . I despise myself, of course, for feeling that way. . . . There are moments when. . . . The minister tried leaning on me. . . . I wasn't having any. . . . You get drawn in, willy-nilly. . . . Ashamed? Yes, of course."

They were silent for a while.

"So don't blame the system. It's our own fault."

A full circle.

"Aleksandr Yevdokimovich, what if you were offered early release as a reward for making an atom bomb?"

Bobynin glanced curiously at his companion. "Well, would you do it?"

"Never."

"Sure?"

"Never."

A full circle. But a slightly different one.

"You find yourself wondering sometimes what they're like—the people who make the atom bomb for *them*. Then you take a closer look at us, and you think they're probably no different. Maybe they even attend politics classes."

"Oh, come on!"

"Why not? It would be good for morale."

An eighth of a circle.

"As I see it," the little fellow went on, "a scientist ought to know all about politics, including the politicians' secret plans; in fact, he ought to feel sure that someday he'll take control of policy himself. Either that or he should treat it as an impenetrable fog, a black hole, and make no political judgments, take a purely ethical view instead and ask himself, 'Can I entrust such undeserving, indeed such utterly worthless, people with control over the forces of nature?' Those who say 'America is a threat to us' have one foot in the quagmire already; that's a childish misconception, not a scientific judgment."

"Yes, but what will they be thinking on the other side of the ocean?" the giant asked doubtfully. "And what are we to make of the new American president?"

"I don't know; maybe it's the same over there. Maybe there's nobody to. . . . We scientists can't get together in an international forum and reach an understanding. But our intellectual superiority to all the politicians in the world makes it possible for every one of us, even in jail, even in solitary, to find a correct common solution and act accordingly."

Full circle.

"Yes."

Another circle.

"You may be right."

Quarter circle.

"Let's continue this colloquium in the lunch break tomorrow. Let's see, your name is Illarion. . . ."

"Pavlovich."

Another incomplete circle—a horseshoe.

"Another thing . . . concerning Russia. Somebody told me today about a painting called *Vanishing Russia*. Do you know about it?"

"No."

"Well, it hasn't been painted yet. And maybe I've got it wrong. Perhaps it's just a title, an idea. In Old Russia there were conservatives, reformers, statesmen; now there are none. In Old Russia there were priests, preachers, bogus holy men in rich households, heretics, schismatics; now there are none. In Old Russia there were writers, philosophers, historians, sociologists, economists; now there are none. And of course there were Revolutionaries, conspirators, bomb throwers, rebels; they, too, are no more. There were artisans wearing headbands, and there were tillers of the soil with beards down to their waists, peasants in troikas, daredevil Cossack horsemen, hoboes roaming free . . . none of them left, none at all! The shaggy black paw raked them all in during the first dozen years. . . . But while the plague raged, living water still filtered through . . . and its source was ourselves, the scientific elite. Yes, engineers and scientists were arrested and shot, but fewer of us than of other groups. Because any mountebank can churn out ideological drivel for them, but physics obeys only the voice of its master. We studied nature, whereas our brothers studied society. We're still around; our brothers are no more. So who inherits the unfulfilled destiny of the elite in the humanities? Perhaps we do? If we don't take a hand, who will? And who says we can't manage it? Though we've never laid hands on them, we've weighed Sirius B and measured the kinetic energy of electrons; surely we can't go wrong with society? But what are we doing instead? Making them a gift of jet engines! Rockets! Scrambler telephones! Maybe even the atomic bomb! Anything, just so long as we live comfortably. And—*interestingly*! What sort of elite are we if we can be bought so cheaply?"

Bobynin sighed like a blacksmith's bellows.

"It's a very serious problem," he said. "Let's carry on tomorrow, all right?"

The bell was ringing for work.

Gerasimovich caught sight of Nerzhin and arranged to meet him after nine that evening in the artist's studio on the back stairs.

He had already promised to tell him about the rationally constructed society.

# 82

# Indoctrination in Optimism

MAJOR MYSHIN'S WORK DIFFERED in scope and character from that of Major Shikin. It had its own pluses and minuses. Its main privilege was that he read prisoners' letters and decided whether to send them on. Its disadvantages were that the relegation of prisoners to camps, withholding their wages, allocating them to nutritional categories, determining the frequency of their relatives' visits, and a variety of other routine harassments were not in Myshin's hands. He found much to envy in the rival organization of Major Shikin, who was always the first to hear news even from inside the prison. And so he attached all the more importance to proctoring the prison yard through his net curtains. (Shikin was denied this resource: His window, unfortunately, was on the third floor.) Observation of prisoners' habitual behavior also supplied Myshin with additional material. From his lookout he supplemented reports received from informants, saw who walked with whom and whether their conversation was animated or casual. Later on, when handing over or accepting a letter, he liked to catch a man off guard with a sudden question: "Incidentally, what were you talking to Petrov about during the lunch break yesterday?"

In this way he sometimes obtained quite useful information from a flummoxed prisoner.

During today's lunch break, Myshin ordered the next zek on his list to wait a few minutes and cast an eye over the courtyard. (He did not, however, see the stoolie hunt in progress at the far end of the building.)

At 3:00 p.m. the lunch break was over. The officious sergeant major dismissed those who had not been interviewed and was ordered to admit Dyrsin.

Ivan Feofanovich Dyrsin was endowed by nature with high cheekbones, sunken cheeks, thick speech, and a comic surname. He had been recruited by the institute via a night school for workers, where he had been a diligent and modestly successful pupil. He had talent but no skill in advertising it, so that he had been underrated and sold short all his life. Nowadays, everybody who felt like it in Number Seven took advantage of him. As his "tenner" neared its end, he was more afraid than ever of the powers that be. He dreaded, above all, being resentenced. He had seen many cases of that in the war years.

His original conviction was itself an absurdity. He had been jailed early in the war for "anti-Soviet agitation," denounced by neighbors who coveted his apartment (and subsequently obtained it). It became clear that he had engaged in no such agitation—ah, but he *might* have done so, since he listened to German radio. He had in fact never listened to German radio—but he *might* have done so, since he had an illegal German radio in the house. In fact, he had no such radio—but he *might* very well have had one, since he was a radio engineer, and information received led to the discovery of a box containing two valves in his apartment.

Dyrsin had had more than his fill of wartime prison camps, the sort in which people ate unripe grain stolen from the horses and the sort in which they mixed flour with snow under a sign reading "Camp Site" nailed to a pine tree on the fringe of the taiga. During Dyrsin's eight years in the land of the Gulag, his wife became a haggard old woman and their two children died. Then somebody suddenly remembered that he was an engineer. They brought him to Marfino, fed him the best butter, and gave him a hundred rubles a month to send home to his wife.

Now, for some unknown reason, he was no longer getting letters. Perhaps his wife was dead.

Major Myshin sat with his clasped hands resting on the desk. There were no papers on the desk, the inkwell was closed, his pen was dry, and his overripe, mauve-complexioned face was, as ever, expressionless. His brow was so fleshy that no wrinkle, whether of age or thought, could ever disturb its smoothness. His cheeks, too, were fleshy. Myshin's face was that of a terra cotta idol. Pink and purple dyes had been mixed into the clay before it was baked. His eyes were professionally lifeless, expressionless, with that special arrogant blankness that remains with such people even in retirement.

Something unprecedented happened: Myshin told Dyrsin to take a seat! (Dyrsin started wondering what calamity was in store for him, and what would be on the charge sheet.) After the brief silence prescribed by the manual, Myshin said, "You're forever complaining. That's all you ever do—complain. Telling people you've had no letters for two months."

"It's more than three, Citizen Major," Dyrsin timidly reminded him.

"Three, then; what's the difference? But have you ever asked yourself what sort of person your wife is?"

Myshin spoke unhurriedly, pronouncing each word distinctly and pausing between sentences.

". . . What sort of person your wife is. Eh?"

"I don't understand," Dyrsin stammered.

"What d'you mean, don't understand? What's her political profile like?"

Dyrsin turned pale. He had thought that he was prepared for anything, inured to everything. He wasn't.

He said a silent prayer for his wife. (He had learned to pray in the camp.)

"She's a whiner, and we don't need whiners," the major explained firmly. "And she suffers from a peculiar form of blindness: She doesn't see the good things in our life, and she emphasizes only what is bad."

"For God's sake! Tell me what's happened to her!" Dyrsin implored him, shaking his head violently.

"To her?" Myshin said, with a still-longer pause for emphasis. "To her? Nothing." (Dyrsin breathed again). "As yet."

In no hurry at all, he took a letter from a drawer and passed it to Dyrsin.

"Thank you!" Dyrsin gasped. "Can I go now?"

"No. Read it here. I can't let you take it to your quarters. What idea of life outside would prisoners get from letters like that? Read it."

He froze. A mauve idol. Fit to bear all the burdens of his office.

Dyrsin drew the letter from its envelope. He noticed nothing special about it, but it might have made an unfavorable impression on anyone else, seeming to mirror the woman who had written it. It was on coarse paper, like wrapping paper, and every line she had written buckled and drooped toward the right-hand edge of the page.

The letter, dated September 18, read as follows:

*Dear Vanya,*

*I'm sitting here writing, but I really want to sleep, and I can't. I come home from work and go straight into the garden to dig potatoes with Manyushka. They've turned out small. I didn't go anywhere on vacation; I didn't have anything to go in; everything is in rags. I wanted to save a bit of money to come and see you, but it never works out. Nika came to see you that time, and they told her there's no such person here, and her mother and father told her off, they said why did you go; now they'll have you on the list and be watching you. Altogether, relations with them are pretty strained, and they aren't talking to L.V. at all.*

*Things are bad with us. Granny has been in bed over two years now; she doesn't get up; she's just skin and bones; she doesn't look like she's dying; but she doesn't get any better; she's worn us all out. There's a horrible smell because of Granny, and there are quarrels all the time. I'm not on speaking terms with L.V.; Manyushka has broken up with her husband; her health is poor; her children won't do what she tells them; when we get home from work, it's terrible, everybody cursing everybody else. Where can I escape to? When will it all end?*

*Anyway, a big kiss*
*from me. Keep well.*

She hadn't even signed it or written "Yours."

Waiting patiently until Dyrsin had read and reread the letter, Major Myshin set his white eyebrows and mauve lips in motion and said, "I didn't give you that letter when it arrived. I realized that it was just the mood of a moment, and you need to be in good spirits for your work. I was waiting for her to send a good letter. But look what she sent last month."

Dyrsin looked up sharply but said nothing. Pain, not reproach, showed on his unprepossessing face. He took the second opened envelope with trembling fingers and drew out a letter written in the same broken-backed, erratic lines, but this time on a page from an exercise notebook.

*October 30*
*Dear Vanya!*

*You are offended because I don't write more often, but I get home from work late and go nearly every day into the forest for sticks, and by then it's evening. I'm so tired I'm ready to drop; I sleep badly at night; Granny keeps me awake. I get up early, five in the morning, and I have to be at work by eight. It's a warm autumn still, thank God, but winter will soon be upon us! You can't get coal at the depot; you have to be important or know somebody. Not long ago my bundle fell off my back, and I just dragged it along the ground after me, I hadn't the strength to pick it up, and I thought, "I'm an old woman, and here I am hauling a load of brushwood!" I've got a rupture in my groin from the weight. Nika came home for the holidays; she's gotten quite nice looking, but she didn't even call on us. I can't think of you without hurting. I have nobody to turn to. I shall go on working as long as I have the strength, but I'm afraid I may get bedridden like Granny. Granny has lost the use of her legs; she's all swollen; she can't lie down or get up without help. And they don't take people that ill in the hospital; it doesn't pay them. L.V. and I have to lift her up every time. She does it under herself; the place stinks horribly; this is no life; it's forced labor. She can't help it, of course, but I can't stand any more of it. In spite of your advice not to swear at each other, we do it every day; all you ever hear from L.V. is "bastard" and "shitbag." And Manyushka swears at her children. You don't think ours would have grown up like that, do you? You know, I often feel glad they aren't here anymore. Little Valery started school this year; he needs lots of things, but there's no money. Except that Mania gets maintenance from Pavel, through the court. Well, there's nothing more to write for now. Look after yourself. I kiss you.*

*It wouldn't be so bad if I could get a good sleep on holidays. But you have to drag yourself to the demonstration.*

Dyrsin was stunned by this letter. He put his hand to his cheek as though he was trying to wash it and could not.

"Well? Have you read it, or haven't you? You don't seem to be reading. Come on, you're a grown man. Literate. You've done time. You know what to think of that letter. During the war they locked people up for letters like that. A demonstration is an occasion everybody enjoys, and she talks about dragging herself there. Coal? Coal isn't just for important people; it's for all citizens; you just have to take your turn, of course. Well, I was of two minds whether or not to give you letter number two, but now we've got number three, and it's just like the others. I've given it a lot of thought and decided it's got to stop. You've got to stop it yourself. Write her something . . . you know, optimistic sounding, positive, something to keep the woman's spirits up. Make her see that she mustn't complain, that it'll all come right in the end. Anyway, they're a lot better off than they were; they've inherited some money. Read this."

The letters were coming in chronological order. Number three was dated December 8.

*Dear Vanya,*

*I've got sad news for you. Granny died on November 26, 1949, at 12:05 p.m. When she died, we didn't have a single kopeck, but Misha, bless him, gave us two hundred rubles; it didn't cost a lot, but of course it was a pauper's funeral, no priest and no music; they simply took the coffin to the cemetery on a cart and tipped it in the hole. It's a bit quieter in the house now, but it seems sort of empty. I'm poorly myself; I get in a terrible sweat at night; pillow and sheet are wet through. A gypsy woman has prophesied that I will die this winter, and it will be a happy release from a life like this. L.V. probably has TB; she coughs and even spits blood; as soon as she gets home from work she starts cursing and swearing; she's as bad-tempered as an old witch. She and Manyushka are getting me down. I seem to have all the bad luck; I've got another four bad teeth, and two have fallen out already, I need dentures, but there's no money for that either, and anyway there's a waiting list.*

*The three hundred rubles you were paid for three months' work came just in time; we were freezing. Our turn at the depot came up (No. 4576), but they only give you coal dust; it isn't worth bringing back. Manyushka added two hundred of her own to your three hundred, and we paid a driver to bring us lump coal. Our potatoes won't last till spring—just imagine, two gardens, and nothing to dig up; there was no rain and the crop failed.*

*The children are nothing but trouble. Valery gets bad marks and hangs out somewhere after school. The headmaster sent for Manyushka and said what sort of mother are you that you can't manage your children. And Zhenka, he's only six, but they both use filthy language; they're just low-lifes, the pair of them. I spend all my money on them, and the other day Valery called me a bitch; if that's what you get from a nasty little kid, what will they be like when they grow up? We can pick up our inheritance next May, they say, but it will cost us two thousand, and where can we get that from? Elena and Misha are bringing a court case; they want to take L.V.'s room away from her. When Granny was alive, she just wouldn't say who should get what, however many times we told her. Misha and Elena are also poorly.*

*I wrote to you last autumn, twice in fact, if I remember rightly; aren't you getting my letters? Where do they go astray?*

*I'm sending you a forty-kopeck stamp. What's the news there? Are they going to release you, or aren't they?*

*There's some very beautiful kitchenware on sale in the shop, aluminum saucepans and bowls.*

*A big kiss from me.*
*Keep well.*

A spot of moisture had run across the paper, blurring the ink.

Once again it was difficult to tell whether Dyrsin was still reading or had finished.

"Well, do you see what I mean?"

Dyrsin did not stir.

"Write a reply. A cheerful reply. I'll allow you four pages or a bit more. You once wrote to her that she should trust in God. Well, that's better than nothing, I suppose. Reassure her; tell her you'll soon be back. Tell her you'll be getting a big wage."

"But will I really be allowed to go home? Not banished?"

"That's for higher authority to decide. But keeping your wife's spirits up is your duty. She's your life companion, after all."

The major was silent for a while.

"Or maybe you'd like somebody a bit younger now?" he suggested understandingly.

He would not have been sitting there so calmly if he had known that his favorite informer, Siromakha, was cooling his heels in the hallway, consumed with impatience to see him.

# 83

# The King of Stool Pigeons

IN THE RARE MOMENTS when he was not preoccupied with the struggle for existence, truckling to his masters, or trying to work, Artur Siromakha, no longer as tense and wary as a leopard, was seen to be a rather languid young man. He had the build of an athlete, but his face was that of an actor jaded by too many performances, and his vague blue-gray eyes seemed clouded by sadness.

Two quick-tempered men had called Siromakha a stoolie to his face, and both were speedily transported. Since then, nobody had repeated the word in his hearing. People were afraid of him. A prisoner was never confronted with the stoolie who had denounced him. He would never know whether he was accused of planning to escape, to commit a terrorist act, or to join a mutiny.

He would simply be told to collect his belongings. And whisked off to . . . a camp? Or perhaps to a high-security jail for interrogation?

Tyrants and jailers use their knowledge of human nature skillfully. As long as a man is capable of unmasking traitors, inciting a crowd to revolt, or sacrificing his life to save others, hope is not yet dead in him; he still believes that all may yet be well, still clings to the pathetic shreds of happiness left to him, and so is silent and submissive. But once he is shackled and prostrate, has nothing left to lose, and so is capable of heroism, only the stone box of an isolation cell will feel the force of his belated fury. Unless the chill breath of a death sentence renders him indifferent to all earthly things.

Siromakha had not been publicly unmasked or caught in the act, but no one doubted that he was a stoolie. Some avoided him; others thought it safer to be friendly, to join with him in a game of volleyball and smutty talk. That was how they got along with other stoolies, too. So life in the sharashka looked peaceful enough, but beneath the surface, war to the death was raging.

Artur could talk about other things besides women. *The Forsyte Saga* was one of his favorite books, and he discussed it quite intelligently. (Though Galsworthy shared his favors with a bunch of well-thumbed detective stories.) Artur also had an ear for music. He was fond of Spanish and Italian airs, he could whistle snatches of Verdi and Rossini in tune, and he had gone once a year to a concert in the Conservatoire, feeling that life would be incomplete without it.

The Siromakhas were gentry, impoverished gentry. At the beginning of the century, one Siromakha had been a composer, another sentenced to forced labor for a serious crime, while yet another had declared enthusiastically for the Revolution and served in the Cheka.

When Artur came of age, he had felt that an assured independent income was essential to someone of his tastes and needs. An uneventful, stick-in-the-mud existence, a daily grind from *x* a.m. to *y* p.m., and a twice-monthly pay envelope subject to hefty deductions for tax and State Loan subscriptions did not appeal to him at all. When he went to the movies, he quite seriously sized up all the famous female stars as potential partners. He could easily imagine himself making a dash for Argentina with Deanna Durbin.

A university education was obviously not the route to such a life. Artur put out feelers for a job in which he could flit lightly from flower to flower. And a job of the right kind was looking for him. They met. The job did not pay as well as he could have wished, but it exempted him from the draft during the war and so saved his life. While fools out there were moldering in clay trenches, Artur—smooth-cheeked, creamy-complexioned, grave-faced Artur—was strolling nonchalantly into the Savoy Restaurant. (Ah, that moment when you cross the threshold of a restaurant and the cooking smells and the music lap around you while you select your table.)

Artur's whole being sang that he was on the way up. People who regarded his employment as ignoble aroused his indignation. He put it down to ignorance or envy. His was a job for the talented. It demanded powers of observation, a good memory, quick wits, and the ability to dissemble, to act a part. It was work for an artist. It had to be hush-hush, of course. Without secrecy it would cease to exist. But secrecy was essential for purely technical reasons. Like, say, the protective visor needed by an electric welder. Otherwise, Artur would not have dreamed of keeping his work secret. There was nothing morally reprehensible about it!

One day, finding that he was living beyond his means, Artur had joined a coterie with designs on state property. He was jailed. Artur was not the man to take it amiss: He blamed himself for getting caught. From his very first days there, Artur naturally felt that his sojourn behind barbed wire was merely a continuation of his old occupation in a different form.

The security services did not let him down. He was not sent logging or down a mine but given a job in the Cultural and Educational Section. This was the only place in the camp with a little light, the one cozy corner where you could look in for half an hour before lights out and feel human again: scan a newspaper, hold a guitar, remind yourself of verses you once knew or the incredible life you once led. The camp's "Dilly Tomatoviches" (the hardened criminals' name for incorrigible intellectuals) frequented the place, and Artur, with his artist's soul, his sympathetic eyes, his Moscow memories, and his talent for skimming the surface of any subject whatsoever, was very much at home there.

He lost no time in reporting a number of individual "agitators," a "group" with anti-Soviet attitudes, two escape attempts not yet at the planning stage but (he said) contemplated, and the camp's very own version of the "Doctors' Plot"*: Medical saboteurs were deliberately prolonging the treatment of patients—in other words, letting them rest up in the hospital. All these

* Doctors' Plot: Stalin's paranoid fantasy in the early 1950s that Jewish doctors were conspiring to kill off the Soviet leaders by poisoning them.

sitting ducks had their sentences prolonged, whereas Artur's was reduced by two years.

In Marfino, Artur did not neglect the profession that had served him so well. He became the pet, the soul mate, of both godfather-majors, and the most dangerous informer in the institute.

But while taking advantage of his denunciations, the majors did not share their own secrets with him. So Siromakha did not know which of the two had used Doronin as an informer and was most in need of up-to-date news of him.

Much has been written about the astounding ingratitude and disloyalty of humanity at large. But there are exceptions. With reckless prodigality, Ruska Doronin had confided his "double agent" scheme not just to one zek, not just to three, but to twenty or more. Each of them had told several others. Doronin's "secret" became the property of nearly half the institute's inhabitants, and people talked about it almost openly in their living quarters. Yet not a single stoolie—and there was one to every five or six men in the sharashka—had heard anything, or at any rate no one had reported it. The most observant, the keenest scented of them, archstoolie Artur Siromakha, had himself heard nothing until today!

He felt now that his honor as an informant was at stake. The godfathers, sitting in their offices, might miss a trick, but that he should. . . . He was in imminent danger of inclusion in the transfer list, just like the others. Doronin had proved to be a nimble foe. Siromakha must hit back just as swiftly. (He had not yet realized the scale of the disaster. He thought that Doronin had shown his hand only that day or the day before.)

But Siromakha could not go bursting into people's offices. He must not lose his head and pound Shikin's door or even hurry up to it too frequently. Those lining up to see Myshin were turned away when the three o'clock bell rang. The most importunate zeks argued with the man on duty in the staff hallway, and Siromakha, clutching his belly as if in pain, approached the medical orderly and stood waiting for the group to disperse. Dyrsin was called into Myshin's office. Siromakha assumed that there was nothing to keep him there, but the interview seemed never-ending. Risking Mamurin's displeasure—he had missed an hour's work in Number Seven, where the air was thick with the fumes of soldering irons, rosin, and plan talk—Siromakha waited for Myshin to dismiss Dyrsin. Waited in vain.

He must not give the game away, even to the rank-and-file guards gawking at him in the hallway. Losing patience, he went upstairs to Shikin's office, returned to Myshin's hallway, then back upstairs again. At his last attempt he was luckier. From the dark lobby outside Shikin's office, he heard the unmistakable rasping voice of the yardman through the door; no one else in the sharashka spoke like that.

He immediately gave the secret knock. The door opened slightly, and Shikin appeared in the aperture.

"It's very urgent," Siromakha whispered.

"Just a minute," Shikin answered.

Siromakha walked briskly toward the far end of the hallway, in order to avoid the yardman when he emerged, then hurried back and barged into Shikin's room without knocking.

# 84

# As for Shooting . . .

MAJOR SHIKIN HAD BEEN INVESTIGATING "the Case of the Broken Lathe" for a week and was still baffled; all he knew for sure was that this lathe—with its open graduated sheave, its manually operated rear spindle, and its dual transmission (manual or belt drive), manufactured in Russia in 1916 in the heat of the First World War—had been, on orders from Yakonov, disconnected from its motor in No. 3 Laboratory for delivery to the engineering workshops. Since the two sides could not agree on how to transport it, the laboratory staff was ordered to get the lathe down to the basement corridor, where the engineers would take over, wrestle it upstairs to the yard, and across the yard to the workshops. (There was a shorter way, which did not involve lowering the lathe into the basement, but this would have meant allowing zeks onto the front yard, in full view of the main road and park, which for security reasons could not be allowed.)

Of course, now that something irreparable had happened, Shikin privately recognized that he was as much to blame as anyone; he had attached no importance to this major industrial operation and had failed to keep a close eye on it. The mistakes of men of action are obvious enough in historical perspective; nobody is infallible!

In the event, the staff of No. 3 Laboratory, comprising one supervisor, one man, one disabled man, and one girl, could not move the lathe unaided. So, without authorization, ten prisoners were recruited at random from various rooms. No one had even thought of noting their names, and it cost Major Shikin two weeks of hard work to collate different accounts and reconstitute the full list of suspects. These ten prisoners had actually lowered the heavy lathe from the first floor to the basement. The engineers, however, had not provided a working party (their boss, for technical reasons of his own, was in no hurry to get his hands on the lathe) or even sent someone to check and confirm delivery. The ten conscripted zeks, having dragged the lathe down to the basement without supervision, dispersed. The lathe stood for several more days blocking the hallway in the basement (Shikin himself had bumped into it). When, at last, people from the engineering workshops came for it, they spotted a crack in the plate, made a fuss, and left the lathe where it was until they were compelled to remove it three days later.

Shikin's "case" was based on that fatal crack. It might not be the reason why the lathe was still not working (Shikin had heard doubts expressed), but the implications of the crack were much wider than the crack itself. The crack signified that hostile forces, as yet unmasked, were at work in the institute. It signified also that those in charge of the institute were blindly trusting and criminally slack.

If the investigation was successful, and the criminal and real motives of his crime exposed, it would be possible not only to punish one man and deter others but to make the crack the occasion of a major political-educational campaign in the collective. And, finally, Major Shikin's professional honor demanded that he unravel this sinister tangle!

But it was not easy. So much time had been lost. The prisoners who had moved the lathe would by now have made a criminal compact and agreed to vouch for one another. Not a single free worker (a horrifying oversight, this!) had been present, and there was only one informer among the ten carriers, a worm-eaten character whose greatest feat to date had been to report a bedsheet cut up for dickeys. He had helped to complete the list of ten men but had nothing else to offer. For the rest, all ten zeks, brazenly confident that they would escape punishment, maintained that they had carried the lathe to the basement undamaged, had not slid it downstairs on its mounting, and had not bumped it from step to step. Moreover, according to their evidence, no one had been holding that part of the lathe under the rear mandrel where the crack had developed; they were all gripping it beneath the sheave and the spindle. In pursuit of the truth, the major had drawn several diagrams of the lathe, showing where each of the carriers stood. But as the interrogations proceeded, Shikin seemed more likely to master the turner's trade than to discover who was responsible for the crack. The only person who could be accused, if not of sabotage, of intent to carry out sabotage, was the engineer Potapov. Losing his temper after three hours of questioning, he had blurted out, "Look, if I'd wanted to wreck that old washtub, I'd simply have sprinkled a handful of sand in the bearings, and that would have done the trick! Why bother to smash the mounting?"

This statement from a hardened saboteur Shikin promptly recorded, but Potapov refused to sign it.

What made this investigation so difficult was that Shikin could not resort to the usual means of getting at the truth: solitary confinement, the punishment cell, a smack or two in the kisser, short rations, nighttime interrogations. . . . He could not even take the elementary precaution of holding those under investigation in separate cells. They had to put in a full day's work and so must be allowed to eat and sleep normally.

Still, as early as Saturday, Shikin managed to wring out of one prisoner the admission that when they were descending the last steps and blocking the narrow doorway, Spiridon the yardman appeared, shouted, "Hold on, boys, let me give a hand!" took hold of it—so becoming the eleventh man—and helped to carry it to its destination. The only conclusion to be drawn from the diagram was that he had gripped the base beneath the rear mandrel.

It was this valuable new thread that Shikin proposed to unravel that Monday, neglecting reports on "The Trial of Prince Igor" received from stoolies early in the morning. Immediately before lunch, he summoned the ginger-haired yardman, who came from work just as he was, in a donkey jacket held together by a frayed canvas belt, took off his big-eared cap and fumbled with it guiltily, the very picture of a peasant waiting on his lord to beg a patch of arable land. He was careful, too, not to step off the little rubber mat and leave footmarks on the floor. Shikin glanced disapprovingly at his wet boots and sternly at the man himself, then let him stand there while he sat in his easy chair silently scanning various documents. From time to time, as if shocked by the evidence of Yegorov's criminality, he shot a startled glance at this bloodthirsty beast, caged at long last. (Procedures prescribed by the science of interrogation for denting a prisoner's morale.) A half hour of unbroken silence went by behind Shikin's locked door, the lunch bell rang loud and clear, reminding Spiridon of the letter he expected from home, but Shikin paid no attention to bells. He went on silently shuffling thick folders and transferring things from one drawer to another, frowning over document after document, and glancing briefly at dejected, hangdog, shamefaced Spiridon, as though astounded by what he read.

The last drop of water from Spiridon's boots had finally trickled onto the mat and left them quite dry when Shikin said, "All right, then: Come closer!" (Spiridon moved toward him.) "Stop there! This here—what is it?"

He held out a photograph of a youngster in German uniform, bareheaded.

Spiridon bent over, screwed up his eyes, glanced at it, and said apologetically: "I'm a little bit blind, see, Major. Let me get a close look."

Shikin gave permission. Still holding his shaggy cap in one hand, Spiridon framed the photograph with all five fingers of the other, turned it to catch the light from the window at different angles, moved it past his left eye, and scrutinized it minutely.

"No," he said with a sigh of relief. "Never seen him."

Shikin took the photograph back.

"Yegorov," he said sadly, "denial will only make it worse for you. All right, then, sit down"—he indicated a distant chair—"we're in for a long talk, too long for you to stay on your feet."

After which he fell silent and buried himself in his papers again.

Spiridon backed over to the chair and sat down. At first he laid his cap on the chair next to him, but after a sideways look at its spotless soft leather, he changed his mind. Resting his cap on his knees, he sat hunched up, drooping, a picture of abject contrition.

He was, in fact, thinking, What a snake you are! What a dirty dog! When am I going to get my letter? Maybe you've got it here?

To Spiridon, who had undergone investigation twice in his time, been "reinvestigated" once, and seen thousands of prisoners under investigation, Shikin's little game was crystal clear. But he knew that he must pretend to take it seriously.

"The fact is we've received further information about you," Shikin said, with a deep sigh. "It seems you got up to all sorts of mischief in Germany."

"It might not have been me, though," Spiridon said reassuringly. "Believe me, Citizen Major, us Yegorovs were like flies in Germany. I've even heard say there was a General Yegorov."

"What do you mean, not you? Of course it's you! Look here"—he jabbed the file with his finger—"Spiridon Danilovich! And your date of birth."

"My date of birth? So it isn't me," Spiridon said confidently. "I always kidded the Germans I was three years older."

"All right, then." Shikin's face brightened, and he spoke more briskly, as if he saw no need to continue this tedious interrogation. He pushed all the documents away.

"Before I forget. You helped to carry a lathe down to the basement ten days ago. Remember, Yegorov?"

"Er, yes."

"So where did you run into a bit of trouble? On the stairs or down in the hallway?"

"Bit of trouble?" Spiridon sounded surprised. "There wasn't any fighting."

"Where did you bash the lathe?"

"God bless you, Citizen Major, why would we be bashing a lathe? How could a lathe upset anybody?"

"Yes, well, that's just what I'm wondering. Why did it get broken? Maybe you just dropped it?"

"Dropped it? We held its little hands and went ever so carefully, like it was a child."

"And you yourself, where were you holding it?"

"Me? On this side, of course."

"Which side?"

"My side."

"Did you grip it under the rear mandrel or under the spindle?"

"I wouldn't know anything about mandrels, Citizen Major. Let me just show you."

He rose, slapped his cap down on the next chair, and turned around as if lugging the lathe through the office door.

"I was bent over like this, see. Backing. And those two got stuck in the door, see."

"Which two?"

"I don't know them from Adam. We haven't stood godfathers to each others' kids. I shouted, 'Stop! Let me get a better grip!' And that great big what-do-you-call-it goes. . . ."

"What what-do-you-call it?"

"You know what I mean!" said Spiridon, over his shoulder. He was beginning to get angry. "The thing we were carrying, of course."

"The lathe, you mean?"

"The lathe, then! I shifted my grip." He bent his knees and tensed his body to show how. "One fellow squeezed in at the side, another shoved his way through, and between the three of us, we managed to keep hold of it easy enough."

He straightened up.

"In my time on the kolkhoz, we shifted heavier things than that. Six of our women could have managed that lathe, easy as pie, and carried it a verst. 'Where's that lathe?' they'd say. 'Let's go and lift it just for fun!'"

"Do you mean it wasn't dropped?" the major asked menacingly.

"I'm telling you it wasn't!"

"So who broke it?"

"It really did get busted?" Spiridon sounded surprised.

"Hmmm, well. . . ."

He had finished showing how the lathe was carried, so he sat down again and was all ears.

"Was it undamaged? When they collected it?"

"I didn't see, so I can't say. Maybe it was broken before."

"And when you set it down, how was it?"

"It wasn't damaged then, I keep telling you!"

"Except for the crack in the mandrel?"

"There wasn't any crack," Spiridon answered confidently.

"How could you see there wasn't, you walleyed devil? You're as good as blind, aren't you?"

"I'm blind, Citizen Major, when it comes to paper. When I'm doing my job, I can see everything. You and the other citizen officers keep dropping your cigarette butts when you walk across the yard, and I have to rake it clean; even when there's white snow on the ground, I rake it all up. You can ask the commandant."

"So what are you saying? You put the lathe down and looked it over carefully?"

"What do you think? We'd done the job, so we stopped for a smoke, as usual. We all gave the lathe a friendly slap."

"Friendly slap? What with?"

"The flat of the hand, of course, like this, on its side, like you might a horse in a sweat. One of the engineers said, 'A nice little lathe, this. My granddad was a turner; he worked on one like this.'"

Shikin sighed and reached for a clean sheet of paper.

"It looks very bad, Yegorov, your refusal to confess even now. We will have to bring charges. It's obviously you who broke the lathe. If it wasn't, you'd point to the culprit."

He spoke confidently, but inside he was no longer so sure of himself. He had been master of the situation, he had been the interrogator, the yardman had answered readily and in great detail, but the first hours of the investigation—the prolonged silence, the photographs, the raising and lowering of the voice, the lively discussion of the lathe—had been a complete waste of time. That this ginger-headed prisoner, with the permanent obliging smile and the deferentially bowed shoulders, had not yielded immediately meant he never would.

When Spiridon had mentioned General Yegorov, he had already firmly concluded that this confrontation had nothing at all to do with Germany, that the photograph was a fake, that the godfather was bluffing and had summoned him precisely because of the lathe. It would have been a miracle if he had not been sent for. The other ten had been shaken like pear trees in autumn for a whole week. After a lifetime of hoodwinking authority, Spiridon had easily held his own in this tiresome game. But so much pointless talk grated. What vexed him most was the further delay in handing over his letter. And although Shikin's office was a nice, warm, dry place to sit in, nobody else would be doing Spiridon's work out in the yard, and it would just mount up for tomorrow.

Time was going by, and the bell for the end of the break had rung long ago, when Shikin ordered Spiridon to sign an admission of responsibility under Article 95 for making false depositions, recorded his own questions, and twisted Spiridon's answers to the best of his ability.

At this point, there was a sharp tap on the door.

As he showed out Yegorov, whose muddleheadedness had gotten on his nerves, Shikin encountered the businesslike reptile Siromakha, who could always give you the gist in a few words.

Siromakha glided in noiselessly. The startling news he had brought and his special position among the informers put Siromakha on the same footing as the major. He closed the door behind him and, before Shikin could take hold of the key, raised his hand in a melodramatic gesture. He was playacting.

Speaking clearly but quietly, so that no one could overhear him through the door, he reported that "Doronin is going around showing people his money order for 147 rubles. He's fingered Lyubimichev, Kagan, and five others. Doronin's lot ganged up in the yard and trapped them. Is he one of yours?"

Shikin grabbed his collar and tugged at it to ease his neck. His eyes looked as though they had been squeezed out of deep holes. His thick neck was a dull red. He rushed to the telephone. His face, usually supremely complacent, was that of a madman.

Siromakha arrived not at walking pace but in a series of catlike jumps to prevent the major from lifting the receiver.

"Comrade Major!"—as a prisoner he ought not to say "Comrade" but as a friend he was obliged to—"not right away! Catch him unawares."

Elementary prison wisdom! But even this he had to be reminded of!

Zigzagging as though he saw a bear behind him, Siromakha backed toward the door. He did not take his eyes off the major.

Shikin took a drink of water.

"Can I go, Comrade Major?"

It was hardly a question.

"If I learn anything more, I'll come back this evening or tomorrow morning."

Sense slowly returned to Shikin's goggling eyes.

"Nine grams of lead, that's what the swine can expect" were his first hoarse words. "I'll fix him!"

Siromakha left noiselessly, as though from a sickroom. He had only done his duty as he saw it and was in no hurry for his reward.

He was not altogether sure that Shikin had a future as a major in the Ministry of State Security.

This was an exceptional event not just at the Marfino Institute but in the whole history of the security services. Rabbits had every right to die. They had no right to fight back.

THE CALL TO THE HEAD of the Vacuum Laboratory came not from Shikin directly but through the man on duty at a desk in the hallway of the institute: Doronin was to report to Engineer Colonel Yakonov immediately.

The overhead lights had been on for some time in the Vacuum Lab, although it was only four in the afternoon. It was always dark there. The head of the laboratory was absent, so it was Klara who took the call. She had just arrived for the evening shift, later than usual, had been chatting with Tamara, and had not once looked at Ruska, though Ruska's burning gaze never left her. The hand that held the receiver was still wearing a scarlet glove. She spoke with downcast eyes, while Ruska stood at his pump three steps away devouring her with his gaze, imagining how that evening, when everybody else had gone to supper, he would take that head in his hands and kiss it. With Klara so close, he lost all awareness of his surroundings.

She raised her eyes (no need to look for him, she sensed his presence) and said: "Rostislav Vadimovich! Anton Nikolaevich wants to see you at once, urgently!"

She could not have spoken differently with people watching and listening—but her eyes! Her eyes were different! Substitutes! As though a dull, lifeless film had formed over them.

Ruska obeyed mechanically, without wondering what this unexpected summons to the engineer colonel might mean. He could think of nothing but Klara's expression. He looked back at her from the doorway: Her eyes were following him, but she averted her gaze immediately.

Unfaithful eyes. She had looked away because she was afraid.

What could have happened to her?

With his mind on her alone, he went up the stairs to the duty officer, his normal wariness in abeyance, unmindful of the need to prepare himself for surprise questions, for a head-on attack, as a nimble-witted prisoner should—and the orderly officer barred the way to Yakonov's office and pointed to Major Shikin's door in the depths of the dark lobby.

Except for Siromakha's advice, Shikin would have called himself, and Ruska would immediately have expected the worst, alerted a dozen friends, and above all contrived to speak to Klara, find out what was wrong, and either carry away ecstatic belief in her or be released from his commitment. There, at the godfather's door, realization came too late. Under the eyes of the institute's orderly officer, he ought not to hesitate; he could not turn back; he must not arouse suspicion (if he was not already suspect). Ruska did nevertheless turn around to hurry back downstairs, but the prison duty officer, Lieutenant Zhvakun, the former executioner, summoned by telephone, was already on his way up.

So Ruska went in to Shikin and took a few steps forward, bracing himself and trying to look unconcerned. Drilled by two years under investigation and a gambler of genius by nature, he stilled the storm within him and rapidly switched his mind to new dangers. Looking boyishly guileless and eager to please, he went in, saying, "May I? I'm at your service, Citizen Major."

Shikin was sitting awkwardly, slumped forward against his desk, dangling one arm and swinging it like a whip. He rose to meet Doronin, and the whip arm swept upward to strike him in the face.

As the other arm swung back to strike, Doronin retreated toward the door and prepared to defend himself. Blood was trickling from his mouth, and an unruly lock of fair hair had fallen over one eye.

Too short to reach his face now, Shikin stood before him baring his teeth and sputtering threats. "You dirty, rotten swine! Betray me, would you? Say good-bye to life, you Judas! We'll shoot you like a dog! Shoot you in a cellar!"

It was two and a half years since capital punishment had been abolished in that most humane of countries. But neither the major nor his unmasked informer cherished any illusions: What can you do with one who falls from favor . . . except shoot him?

Ruska looked absurd, with his tousled hair and blood running down his chin from a lip swelling as you watched.

Nevertheless, he straightened up and brazenly replied, "Shooting, now that will need thinking about, Citizen Major. I'll see you behind the wire as well. You've been a general laughingstock for four months now, and you're still drawing your pay? They'll tear those epaulets off you! But as for shooting, we will have to wait and see."

## 85

# Prince Kurbsky

THE CAPACITY FOR HEROIC DEEDS—for actions that make extreme demands on a person's strength—depends to a greater or lesser extent on willpower. Some people are born heroes; others are not. The heroic acts that cost the greatest effort are those performed spontaneously by sheer willpower. Such actions are easier if they are the culmination of years of purposeful effort. And for the man born a hero, great deeds are blessedly easy, as easy as breathing.

Ruska Doronin, for instance, had lived as an outlaw, a wanted man, sought all over the Soviet Union, with the carefree smile of an innocent child. The thrill of risk, the fever of adventure, must have been injected into his bloodstream at birth.

Respectable Innokenty, fortunate Innokenty, could never have brought himself to vanish and flit around the country under a false name. Arrest might be imminent, but it would never enter his head that he could do anything to prevent it.

He had made his telephone call to the embassy on impulse, without stopping to think. His discovery had come as a surprise—and too late for him to wait those few days until he arrived in New York. He had called like a man possessed, although he knew that all telephones were bugged and that he was one of the very few people in the ministry who knew Georgy Koval's secret.

He had simply flung himself into the abyss because the thought that they could brazenly steal the bomb and in a year's time start brandishing it was intolerable. But he had not been prepared for the shattering impact of the stony bottom. He had cherished a wild hope that he could flutter out of it, escape responsibility, fly across the ocean, get his breath back, and tell his story to the press.

But even before he reached the bottom, he had relapsed into impotent despair, spiritual exhaustion. His short-lived resolve had snapped, and terror was consuming him like a flame.

He had felt it most acutely that Monday morning, when he had to force himself to begin living again, to go to work, anxiously trying to detect menacing changes in the looks and voices of those around him.

Still outwardly self-possessed, Innokenty was internally a wreck, incapable of fighting back, of seeking a way out, of trying to escape.

It was not quite 11:00 a.m. when his boss's secretary, denying him access, informed Innokenty that his appointment—so she had heard—had been held up by the vice minister.

This news, though not definite, came as such a shock that Innokenty did not insist on being seen and seeking confirmation. But nothing else could explain the delay, once his departure had been approved. The document accrediting him to the United Nations already bore Vyshinsky's stamp. He had obviously been found out.

The world seemed to have become a darker place. His shoulders felt as if he were carrying a yoke with two full pails. Back in his room, it was as much as he could do to lock the door and remove the key so that they would think he had left. He could do this only because the usual occupant of the other desk had not returned from an official trip.

Innokenty's insides had turned into a nauseous jelly. He waited for the knock. He was terror-stricken. Any minute now they would come and arrest him. A fleeting thought—Don't open the door. Make them break it down.

Or hang yourself before they come in.

Or jump out of the window. From the third floor. Right into the street. Two seconds in flight—and smash. Consciousness extinguished.

A thick stack of papers lay on the desk, the auditors' estimate of Innokenty's debts. He had to check the account and return it before leaving for abroad. But even the sight of it made him feel sick.

The heating was on, but he felt cold, shivery.

His feebleness disgusted him! He was passively awaiting his doom.

Innokenty lay flat, facedown, on the sofa. With the whole length of his body pressed against the sofa, he got from it some support, a kind of reassurance.

His thoughts grew confused.

Was it really him? Could he really have had the nerve to telephone the embassy? And if so, why? At the other end, someone speaking Russian with an accent. "Call the Canadians. . . . Just who are you? How do I know you're telling the truth?" Those arrogant Americans! They'll live to see their farmers collectivized to a man. Serve them right.

Should never have called . . . sorry for myself . . . ending my life at thirty . . . perhaps under torture. . . .

But no, he didn't regret calling. It had to be done. It was as though someone had been leading him, and he had felt no fear.

No, it wasn't that he had no regrets; he no longer had the will to regret or not to regret. As his sense of imminent danger faded, he lay still: hardly breathing, hugging the sofa, wishing only that it would all end, that they would soon take him away . . . or something.

But luckily no one knocked; no one tried the door. And the telephone did not ring once.

He lost consciousness. Oppressive dreams, absurd dreams, pursued one another, until his head was bursting and he awoke. Unrefreshed, indeed more fatigued, feebler than before he had fallen asleep, exhausted by all the arrests or attempted arrests he had undergone in his dreams. He was too weak to rise from the sofa and shake off his nightmares or indeed to stir at all. Too weak to resist the sickening drowsiness sucking him back into sleep.

He slept again at last, dead to the world. Slept with his mouth open, drooling onto the sofa. The damp patch and the midmorning bustle in the hallway woke him up.

He rose, unlocked the door, and went for a wash. They were bringing tea and sandwiches around.

No one was about to arrest him. The colleagues he met in the hallway and the main office behaved toward him as they always did.

This proved nothing. How could anyone else know?

But their unchanged looks and voices raised his spirits.

He asked the girl to bring him really hot, really strong tea and drank two glasses of it with enjoyment. He felt his confidence growing.

But he still could not bring himself to insist on seeing the chief. To try to find out. . . .

The sensible solution was obviously to do away with himself. He would simply be obeying his instinct of self-preservation, sparing himself suffering.

But only if he knew for sure that they were going to arrest him.

Perhaps they weren't?

The telephone rang. Innokenty jumped. His heart stood still, then began beating quite audibly.

It was only Dotty. Dotty's marvelously musical telephone voice. Dotty talking like a wife reinstated in her conjugal rights. She asked how things were and suggested going out somewhere that evening.

Once again Innokenty felt a glow of gratitude and affection. Bad wife or not, she was closer to him than anyone.

He did not tell her that his posting might have been canceled. Instead, he imagined himself in a theater that evening, perfectly safe; people weren't arrested in the theater in full view of the audience!

"All right, get tickets for something cheerful," he said.

"The operetta, maybe? It's something called *Akulina*. There's nothing much on otherwise. It's *The Law of Lycurgus* at the little Red Army Theater and *Voice of America* at the big one. The Arts is doing *The Unforgettable*."

"*Law of Lycurgus* sounds too good to be true. The worst plays always get great titles. Book for *Akulina*. And we'll take in a restaurant after."

"Okay! Okay!" Dotty laughed happily into the telephone.

(And stay there all night so they won't find me at home! They always came in the night, of course.)

Innokenty was gradually recovering his self-possession. What if he was suspected? Shchevronok and Zavarzin were more familiar with the details than he was; they must surely be the prime suspects. And, anyway, suspicion was one thing, proof another.

Suppose I am in danger of arrest; there's nothing I can do about it. Should I be hiding things? There's nothing to hide. So why worry?

By now he felt strong enough to pace the floor as he thought it over. Suppose they are going to arrest me. It may not be today or even this week. So should I stop living? Or should I spend my last few days enjoying myself like crazy?

Why had he panicked like that? Only last night, damn it, he had—oh, so wittily—defended Epicurus. Why not follow his advice? His ideas seemed sensible enough.

Thinking that he ought to look through his notebooks for entries best suppressed, he remembered that he had once jotted down excerpts from Epicurus. He found the place. "Our private feelings of satisfaction and dissatisfaction are the ultimate criteria of good and evil," he read.

That meant nothing to Innokenty in his present state of mind. He read on.

"Know that there is no such thing as immortality. Therefore, death is not an evil; it is simply irrelevant to us. As long as we exist, there is no death, and when death comes upon us, we do not exist."

Well said! Innokenty leaned back in his chair. Who was it I recently heard saying just that? Yes, of course, that young war veteran at the party last night.

Innokenty pictured to himself the garden in Athens. Epicurus, a swarthy septuagenarian in a tunic, was holding forth from marble steps, while he, Innokenty, in modern dress, perched on a pedestal, in a casual sort of American pose, listened.

"Belief in immortality was born of the greed of insatiable people who squander the time that nature has allotted us. But the wise man will find that time sufficient to make the round of attainable delights and, when the time to die arrives, leave the table of life replete, making way for other guests. For the wise man one human span suffices, while the foolish man would not know what to do even with eternity."

Brilliant! But here's the rub: What if you are dragged from the table not by nature, in your seventies, but at thirty, by the Ministry of State Security?

"One should not fear physical suffering. He who knows the limits of suffering is proof against fear. Prolonged suffering is always insignificant, while acute suffering is never for long. The wise man will not lose his spiritual calm even under torture. His memory will bring back to him his former sensual and spiritual gratifications and, in spite of his present bodily suffering, will restore his spiritual equilibrium."

Innokenty began gloomily pacing the office floor.

That was what he dreaded, not actually dying but being arrested and physically tortured.

Epicurus says you can rise above torture, does he? If only I had such strength of character.

Innokenty knew only too well that he did not.

He would die without regret if he knew that people would someday learn that there had been such a citizen of the world and that he had tried to save them from nuclear war.

If the Communists got the atom bomb, the planet was doomed.

But they would shoot him like a dog in the dungeon and hide his case file where it could never be found.

He threw back his head as a bird does to let water trickle down its taut throat.

But no, the idea that they might tell the world about him was more painful still. We are so befogged, he thought, that we cannot distinguish traitors from friends. What was Prince Kurbsky?* A traitor. And what was Ivan the Terrible? The beloved father of his people.

But *that* Kurbsky had escaped his terrible ruler. Innokenty had not been so lucky.

If he was exposed, his fellow countrymen would enthusiastically stone him! How many would understand him? A thousand out of two hundred million if he was lucky. How many remembered the rejection of the sensible Baruch plan: Deny yourselves the atom bomb, and the American bombs will be put under international lock and key? Above all, how did he have the

---

* Prince Kurbsky: Andrei Kurbsky (1528-1583), an outstanding military leader who came into prominence as a close friend of Tsar Ivan IV ("the Terrible"). Kurbsky later denounced Ivan's cruelties in a series of letters addressed to Ivan, who responded with letters branding Kurbsky a traitor.

audacity to decide what his country should do when that right belonged to the Supreme Power alone?

You prevented the Transformer of the World, the Forger of Happiness from stealing the bomb? That means you denied the bomb to your motherland!

But what did the motherland want with it? What did the village of Rozhdestvo want with it? That half-blind female dwarf? The old woman with the dead chicken? The one-legged peasant in rags and tatters?

Who, of all the people in the village, would condemn him for that telephone call? Individually, none of them would even understand the problem. But should they be herded into a village meeting, they would vote unanimously to condemn him.

They were short of roads, textiles, planks, glass. . . . Give them back their milk, their bread, maybe even their church bells—but what good was the atom bomb to them?

What vexed Innokenty most was that his telephone call might not have prevented the theft after all.

The filigreed hands of the bronze clock pointed to 4:45.

It was getting dark.

# 86

# No Fisher of Men

IN THE TWILIGHT a long black Zim passed through the wide-open guardhouse gates, accelerated around the asphalted bends of the Marfino Institute's yard, cleared of snow by Spiridon's broad shovel and black again after the thaw, rounded Yakonov's Pobeda, and pulled up sharply before the institute's stone portals.

The major general's adjutant bounded out of the front seat and briskly opened the rear door. Pudgy Foma Oskolupov, in a blue-gray overcoat too tight for him and a general's astrakhan hat, braced himself, waited for the adjutant to fling wide the outer and inner doors of the institute, and made his way upstairs. He looked preoccupied. Behind the antique standard lamps on the first landing, a space had been partitioned off to serve as a cloakroom. The woman in charge hurried out, as if to take the general's overcoat, though she knew very well that he would not surrender it. He did not, nor did he remove his hat, but went on up one flight of the divided stairway. Prisoners and female free workers using the stairs vanished in a hurry. The general in the astrakhan hat did his best to preserve his dignity while ascending with the haste that the circumstances demanded. The adjutant left his own coat in the cloakroom and caught up.

"Find Roitman," the general said over his shoulder. "Warn him that I will be with the new group in half an hour, expecting results."

On the third floor he did not head for Yakonov's office but went in the opposite direction, toward Number Seven. The duty officer caught sight of his back and glued himself to the phone, trying to locate Yakonov and warn him.

Number Seven was in a state of collapse. It didn't take an expert (which Oskolupov certainly was not) to realize that nothing was working, that all the systems rigged up after months and months of trial and error had been torn down, wrenched apart, wrecked. The wedding of the clipper to the scrambler had begun with the dismantling of the bridal pair—panel by panel, block by block, almost condenser by condenser. There was smoke in the air from soldering irons and cigarettes. A hand drill buzzed. Men were arguing over their work. Mamurin was yelling hysterically into his telephone.

In spite of the smoke and din, two men noticed the major general's arrival. Lyubimichev and Siromakha always kept half a wary eye on the entrance. They were not separate persons but indefatigable, self-immolating mates, unswervingly loyal, eager to serve, ready to work twenty-four hours a day and give ear to all the weighty thoughts of authority. When Number Seven's engineers conferred, Lyubimichev and Siromakha joined in as equals. (They had, in fact, learned a good deal in the hustle and bustle of Number Seven.)

When they spotted Oskolupov, they put their soldering irons down in a hurry; Siromakha rushed to warn Mamurin, who was on his feet shouting into the telephone, while Lyubimichev, out of the goodness of his heart, seized his boss's easy chair and hurried on tiptoes toward the general, looking for instructions where to put it. In another man this might have seemed like toadying, but in lofty, broad-shouldered Lyubimichev, with his amiably ingenuous look, it was the homage of youth to an esteemed elderly person. Setting the chair down and shielding it from everyone except Oskolupov,

Lyubimichev flicked imaginary dust from the seat, observed only by the major general, and stepped briskly to one side. There he and Siromakha stood stock-still, in eager anticipation of questions and instructions.

Oskolupov sat down. He kept his tall fur hat on but undid one button of his overcoat.

The laboratory was suddenly silent. The drill stopped whirring; cigarettes went out; voices were hushed. All that could be heard was Bobynin, still in his den, booming instructions to the electricians, and Pryanchikov, lost to reason, still wandering around the wreckage of his scrambler with a hot soldering iron in his hand. The others looked on and waited for their superior to speak.

Mopping his brow after his difficult telephone conversation (arguing with the head of the engineering workshops—they had bashed the prefab panels too hard), Mamurin approached and exhaustedly greeted his former workmate, now elevated to heights that he himself would never reach. Oskolupov extended three fingers. Mamurin had become so pale and wan that it seemed a crime to allow a man in such a state out of bed. The blows of the last twenty-four hours—the minister's anger and the shattered clipper—had hit him harder than his high-ranking colleagues. The muscles under his skin were wire-drawn. If a man's bones can lose weight, Mamurin's had. For more than a year he had lived for the clipper, believed that the clipper, like the Little Humpbacked Horse in the fable, would carry him to safety. No attempt to gloss over the disaster, not even Pryanchikov's arrival under Number Seven's roof with his scrambler, could conceal the catastrophe from him.

Oskolupov knew how to direct an operation without understanding it. He had learned long ago that all you need do is provoke an argument between knowledgeable subordinates. That was what he did now. He frowned at them and said, "Well, then, how's it going?" compelling his subordinates to speak out.

It was the beginning of a pointless, boring discussion that merely interrupted their work. They spoke reluctantly, sighing, and whenever two of them started speaking at once, both gave way.

The two keynotes of this discussion were "we must" and "it's difficult." The "must" theme was developed by the frenzied Markushev, supported by Lyubimichev and Siromakha. Short, pimply, energetic Markushev spent day and night feverishly devising ways of distinguishing himself and earning remission of sentence. He had suggested combining the clipper and the scrambler, not because as an engineer he was sure that it would work but because Bobynin and Pryanchikov would become less and he himself more important. Much as he disliked working "for love," with no hope of enjoying the fruits of his work, he now felt indignant with his despondent colleagues. For Oskolupov's benefit he hinted that the engineers were not pulling their weight.

He was "only human"—one of that widely disseminated breed that creates oppressors in its own likeness.

Grief for the past and faith in the future were written all over Lyubimichev's and Siromakha's faces.

Mamurin lowered his translucent yellowish face into his fleshless hands and, for the first time since he had been in command of Number Seven, remained silent.

Khorobrov could scarcely conceal the malicious glint in his eyes. He was overjoyed to be witnessing the burial of two years of endeavor by the Ministry of State Security. He had always been readier than any of them to contradict Markushev and exaggerate difficulties.

Oskolupov, for some reason, was particularly critical of Dyrsin, accusing him of lack of enthusiasm. When Dyrsin was agitated or hurt by unfairness, his voice almost failed him. Because of this handicap, he was always found guilty.

Yakonov came in while they were talking and out of politeness contributed to a discussion that made no sense in Oskolupov's presence. Then he called Markushev over and balanced a scrap of paper on his knee, so that they could hastily sketch an alternative scheme.

Oskolupov would have liked more than anything to tear into them and bawl them out: He had perfected his technique to the finest nuances of intonation during his years in authority. This was what he was best at. But he saw that right now it would not be helpful.

Oskolupov may have felt that his conference was getting nowhere, or he may have suddenly felt like a change of air before his fateful month of grace ended. Whatever the reason, he rose while Bulatov was still talking, made for the exit, looking grim, and left the whole staff of Number Seven to agonize over the predicament in which their slackness had landed the head of the Department of Special Technology.

Protocol compelled Yakonov to rise with his superior and carry his fleshy bulk after the astrakhan hat, which just reached to Yakonov's shoulder. They walked along the hallway in silence, but now side by side. The departmental director did not like his chief engineer walking beside him. Yakonov was taller by a head—and a towering head at that.

It was now Yakonov's duty—and it could even be to his advantage—to tell the major general about the amazing, unexpected success with the encoder. Ever since Abakumov's late-night reception, Oskolupov had glared at him like a maddened bull. This good news would clear the air.

Only . . . the drawing was not in his hands. Sologdin's remarkable self-possession, his convincing show of readiness to go to his death rather than surrender the drawing gratis, had persuaded Yakonov to keep his word; he would bypass Oskolupov and report to Selivanovsky that night. Oskolupov would be furious, but he would have to calm down quickly.

Moreover, seeing Oskolupov so downcast, so fearful for his future, Yakonov enjoyed leaving him to agonize for a few days longer. The engineer in Yakonov felt a sort of painful concern for the project, as though he had devised it himself; and just as Sologdin had foreseen, Oskolupov would inevitably muscle in and claim coauthorship. The moment he heard the news, without so much as a glance at the drawing, he would move Sologdin to a separate room and try to keep out those who should be helping him. He would send for Sologdin, browbeat him, set impossible completion duties, call up every other hour from the ministry to hurry Yakonov along. And he would end with the vainglorious conviction that only his close supervision had set the encoder on the right lines.

All this was so sickeningly obvious that Yakonov was happy to say nothing for the moment.

Once in his office, he did, however, help Oskolupov off with his overcoat, something he would never have done with others present.

"What's your Gerasimovich doing?" Oskolupov asked, sitting down on Yakonov's armchair without even removing his hat.

Yakonov sank onto a visitor's chair.

"Gerasimovich? You mean when did he get back from Spiridonovka? In October, I think it was. Since then, he's been working on a television set for Comrade Stalin."

(The one with a bronze plate reading "To Great Stalin from the Chekists.")

"Call him in."

Yakonov made the call.

"Spiridonovka" was another of the Moscow special prisons. Just recently, a very clever and useful gadget had been produced there under engineer Bobyor's supervision—an attachment to an ordinary local telephone. What was particularly clever about the device was that it worked precisely when the telephone was not working; as long as the receiver was reposing in its cradle, everything said in the room could be monitored by the security services' control point. The device found favor and was put into production. When a suitable subscriber was identified, his line was cut, and the victim himself called in a repairman who pretended to be mending the phone and bugged it.

The forward thinking of the authorities (the authorities must always be thinking ahead) was now focused on other gadgets.

An orderly looked in at the door: "The prisoner Gerasimovich."

"Send him in," said Yakonov. He was sitting on a small chair, exiled from his desk, numb, and in danger of toppling over to right or left.

Gerasimovich came in, catching his foot on the strip of carpet as he adjusted his pince-nez. Confronted with these two heavyweights, he looked smaller and narrower in the shoulders than ever.

"You sent for me," he said, moving forward and looking between Oskolupov and Yakonov at the wall beyond.

"Uh-huh," Oskolupov replied. "Sit down."

Gerasimovich sat. He took up only half a chair.

"You're . . . let's see"—Oskolupov searched his memory—"You're . . . an optician, aren't you, Gerasimovich? More of an eye man than an ear man, right?"

"Yes."

"And you . . . er"—he rolled his tongue as if licking his teeth clean—"seem to be well thought of."

He paused. Screwing up one eye, he looked hard at Gerasimovich with the other.

"Do you know Bobyor's work?"

"I've heard about it."

"Uh-huh. And you've heard that we've recommended Bobyor for early release?"

"I didn't know that."

"Well, now you do. How long have you got left?"

"Three years."

"Tha-at long!" Oskolupov sounded surprised, as if all his prisoners were in for just a month or two. "Dear me, that *is* a long time." (He had recently cheered up one newcomer by telling him that ten years was . . . "a flea bite. Some men are inside for twenty-five.")

"I daresay you wouldn't mind earning remission yourself?"

A strange coincidence, Gerasimovich thought, so soon after Natasha's plea yesterday.

He steeled himself. He never allowed himself to smile or make any concession when talking to the bosses.

"How would I get it? You don't find it lying around in the hallway."

Oskolupov rocked back in his chair.

"Television sets won't get you remission, of course. But what if I transfer you to Spiridonovka in a day or two and put you in charge of a project? You can get it done in six months and be home this autumn."

"What sort of work, if I may ask?"

"We've got lots of work lined up there; you can take your pick. Here's one idea: planting microphones in park benches. People jabber away regardless in those places; it's amazing what you hear. But maybe that's not in your line?"

"No, that isn't in my line."

"But we've got something for you, too, I'm sure. Two jobs—both important, both urgent. And both right up your alley, am I right, Anton Nikolaich?" (Yakonov nodded confirmation.)

"One is a night camera using those . . . what d'you call them . . . ultrared rays. So you can photograph a man at night in the street, see who he's with, and he'll never know till his dying day. They've produced rough drafts abroad; all that's needed is . . . creative copying. And making the apparatus simpler to handle. Our agents aren't as clever as you. The second thing is small potatoes, but we need it urgently. A simple camera, but so tiny it can be fitted into a doorpost. So that as soon as the door opens, it will photograph whoever goes in or out. In the daytime or with electric lights on. Never mind in the dark, that doesn't matter. This is another little gadget we would like to put into production. What do you say? Will you take it on?"

Gerasimovich's pinched face was turned toward the window. He did not look at the major general.

The word "doleful" was not in Oskolupov's vocabulary, so he could not have defined the fixed expression on the prisoner's face.

He had no wish to. He was waiting for a reply.

Natasha's prayer had been heard! In his mind's eye, Illarion saw her bloodless face, her eyes glassy with unshed tears.

For the first time in all those years, going home was a possibility within his grasp. His heart was aglow.

All he had to do was what Bobyor had done: Make room behind the wire for a couple of unsuspecting mugs from outside.

"Couldn't I . . . couldn't I just stay on television?" Gerasimovich stammered.

"Are you refusing?"

Oskolupov frowned in surprise. That angry look was never long absent from his features.

"For what reason?"

All the laws of the cruel prison world told Gerasimovich that taking pity on comfortable know-nothings, enjoying their freedom without a care in the world, was as eccentric as not killing pigs for fatback. The mugs outside did not have immortal souls. Zeks earned them the hard way, serving their never-ending sentences. Outside, men used the liberty allowed them selfishly and stupidly, mired in their petty schemes and futile endeavors.

But Natasha was his helpmate for life. She had been waiting while he served his second term. She was a feeble little thing, fading fast, and his own life would flicker out with hers.

"Do I need reasons?" he answered in a faint voice. "I just can't do it. I couldn't cope."

Yakonov, whose mind had been wandering, now looked closely at Gerasimovich. Another one determined to defy common sense, he thought. But the universal rule—"look out for number one"—would surely operate here, too.

Oskolupov tried persuasion.

"You just aren't used to serious assignments anymore, so you're a bit afraid of them. But if you can't manage it, who can? All right, I'll let you think it over."

Gerasimovich rested his brow on his small hand and said nothing.

After all, it wasn't the atom bomb. In the scale of world events, it was an imperceptibly minute detail.

"But what is there to think about? This is just the sort of thing you've been trained to do."

Why not just keep quiet! Fool them! Take the job on, spin it out, get nothing done. But Gerasimovich rose, looked contemptuously at the barrel-bellied, flabby-cheeked, pig-faced degenerate wearing a general's hat, and said in a ringing voice: "No! It isn't what I was trained to do! Putting people in prison isn't my trade! I am no fisher of men! It's enough that we've been imprisoned ourselves. . . ."

# 87

## At the Fount of Science

THE DISPUTE WITH SOLOGDIN was still weighing on Rubin's mind the next morning. Arguments left half developed kept occurring to him. But the day that followed was a lucky one, and he was able to put their inconclusive squabble behind him.

He was in the quiet little top-secret den on the third floor. It had heavy curtains at door and window, a shabby sofa, and a threadbare rug. The soft furnishings muffled sound, but there was hardly any noise anyway; Rubin was wearing earphones, listening to his tapes, and Smolosidov, looking haggard and scowling at Rubin as if he were an enemy rather than a workmate, said not a word all day. As far as Rubin was concerned, Smolosidov could have been an automaton, there simply to substitute one reel for another.

Donning his earphones, Rubin listened over and over again to the fateful call to the embassy and then to the taped conversations of the five suspects supplied to him. Sometimes he believed his ears; sometimes he could not bring himself to believe them and resorted to the serpentine audiovisual printouts made of all the conversations. Ribbons of white paper many meters long festooned the broad table and trailed on the floor. Every now and then, Rubin seized the album, in which specimen sound pictures were classified sometimes by phonemes, sometimes according to the basic tone of particular male voices. With a copying pencil blunt at both ends (for Rubin, sharpening a pencil was a task requiring lengthy preparation), he marked places on the tapes that particularly interested him.

Rubin was carried away. His dark brown eyes were ablaze. He smoked—pipe or cigarettes—incessantly, and there was ash everywhere: on his unkempt, matted beard, the sleeves of his greasy overalls (a button was missing from one cuff), the table, the tapes, the armchair, and the album containing the audiovisual specimens. He had forgotten his liver and his painful hypertonia, forgotten that he had eaten nothing since the cake at yesterday's birthday party. He was by now in that state of heightened awareness when vision is sharp enough to single out a grain of sand and memory readily supplies all that it has stored over the years.

He had not once asked what time it was. He had made just one attempt, on arrival, to open a ventilation pane, in order to make up for the fresh air he had missed, but Smolosidov said sullenly, "Don't do that! I've got a cold." After that, he did not leave his seat all day, did not once go to the window to see the snow turning gray and crumbly under the damp west wind. He did not hear Shikin knocking and Smolosidov refusing to let him in. He saw Roitman come and go, as if through a fog, and muttered something to him without looking around. He was oblivious of the bell for the lunchtime break and the back-to-work bell. Eating is a sacred ritual for the zek, but Rubin's instinctive hunger was only aroused when someone—Roitman once more—shook him by the shoulder and pointed to fried eggs, dumplings in sour cream, and stewed fruit on a side table. Rubin's nostrils twitched, his jaw dropped in surprise, but his thoughts still seemed to be elsewhere. Surveying this food of the gods in bewilderment, as though wondering what it was meant for, he moved to the little table and began swallowing without tasting, in a hurry to get back to his work.

Rubin did not appreciate his meal, but it had cost Roitman more than if he had provided it as his own expense; he had "sat on the phone" for two hours getting first the Special Technology Department, then General Bulbanyuk, then the Prison Administration, then the Supply Department, and finally Lieutenant Colonel Klimentiev to authorize the issue of so much food. Those at the other end of the phone had in turn to square bookkeepers and other persons. The difficulty was that Rubin was only entitled to the rations of a category 3 prisoner, and Roitman was trying to get him into "category 1" (the "dietetic variant," at that) for a few days while he worked on a job of special importance to the state. After all the others had agreed, the prison itself raised practical objections: ingredients requested unavailable in prison stores, cook paid at appropriate rate for preparing individual menus likewise unavailable. . . .

Roitman now sat facing Rubin across the table, not looking at him like a taskmaster awaiting the fruits of a slave's labor but smiling affectionately at this overgrown child, enchanted with him, envying his inspiration, choosing the right moment to discover where that half day's work was leading and to join in himself.

Rubin finished off the food, and his features relaxed as he returned to his senses. For the first time since early morning, he smiled.

"You shouldn't have fed me so well, Adam Veniaminovich. *Satur venter non studet libenter.* A traveler always breaks the back of his journey before he stops to eat."

"Just look at the clock, Lev Grigorievich! It's a quarter past three!"

"Eh? I thought it wasn't twelve yet."

"Lev Grigorievich! I'm consumed with curiosity; what have you come up with?"

This was not an order from a superior. Roitman seemed to be pleading with Rubin, afraid that he would refuse. When his better feelings were allowed to show, Roitman was very likable, in spite of his ungainly appearance and thick lips, which were always parted because of the polyps in his nose.

"It's just a beginning! Just preliminary conclusions, Adam Veniaminovich."

"And what are they?"

"Some of them may be disputable, but one is incontrovertible: The science of phonoscopy, born today, has a rational core."

"You aren't letting yourself get carried away, are you, Lev Grigorievich?"

Roitman was as eager to believe as Rubin, but his own training told him that in an "arts man" like Rubin enthusiasm might prevail over scientific rigor.

"When did you ever see me carried away?" Rubin asked rather huffily, smoothing his untidy beard. "All the work we've been doing as a team for nearly two years now, all these phonetic and stylistic analyses of Russian speech, our study of sound pictures, classification of voices, examination of national, group, and individual intonations, all that Anton Nikolaich regarded as an idle pastime—and, let's admit it, we ourselves felt doubt creeping in at times!—all that is now yielding its cumulative results. Maybe we should get Nerzhin over here; what do you think?"

"If the business expands, by all means. But for the present we have to show that we deserve to survive by completing our first assignment."

"First assignment! That first assignment is half of an entire science! It can't be done in a hurry."

"But . . . Lev Grigorievich . . . you mean, . . . Surely, you realize how urgently necessary it all is?"

He understood all right. Lyovka Rubin, member of the League of Communist Youth, had grown up with those words ringing in his ears. They were written large in the slogans of the thirties. There was no steel, no electricity, no bread, no textiles. There were needs, and there was urgency—and blast furnaces were erected, steel mills set rolling. Then, before the war, Rubin the scholar, blissfully engrossed in the study of the leisurely eighteenth century, had become soft. But the old rallying cry—"urgently needed!"—of course still awakened a response and compelled him to follow through to the end any task he undertook.

"Urgently needed!" Who could doubt it when there was a risk that this greatest of traitors might slip through the net?

The light from outside was fading. They lit the overhead lamp, sat down at the worktable, and examined the sample passages marked on the audiovisual tapes with blue or red pencil: characteristic sounds, consonant combinations, lines showing intonations. They did this together, just the two of them, ignoring Smolosidov. He had not left the room for a single minute all day long. He sat now over a magnetic tape, guarding it like a sullen black dog, looking at the backs of their heads, and this unwavering hard stare pressed on their skulls and brains. Smolosidov deprived them of something very small but supremely important—unconstraint; he witnessed their vacillations, and he would witness their confident report to higher authority.

They took turns to affirm and deny. Roitman was inhibited by his mathematical training but spurred on by hope of promotion. Rubin's disinterested desire to establish the new science on solid foundations was sobering, but he risked being carried away by his Five-Year Plan training and his duty to the Party. In the end, they settled for a short list of five suspects, agreeing without much discussion that there was no need to tape the voices of the four detained at Sokolniki underground station—they had been arrested too late anyway—nor those of the handful of Ministry of State Security personnel offered by Bulbanyuk as a last resort. They also ruled out, as psychologically implausible, the supposition that the caller was not the person who knew the facts but someone acting for him.

Even with just five, they had their work cut out. They listened to all five voices live and compared them with that of the culprit. Then they repeated the process, using audiovisual tapes.

"Look what a great help audiovisual analysis is!" Rubin declared enthusiastically. "You can tell that the criminal begins by trying to disguise his voice. But how does the change show on the audiovisual tape? All that happens is that the frequencies are lower, but the characteristic vocal tune hasn't changed! That is our main discovery—the vocal tune. Even if the criminal had tried to disguise his voice throughout, he could not have concealed its most distinctive features."

"But we still don't know enough about the limits within which voices can be changed," Roitman insisted. "It may be that the range of variability in microintonations is very wide."

Just listening to them, you might be unsure whether these were two different voices or the same one, but on the audiovisual tapes differences in volume and frequency seemed to show up more clearly. (Unfortunately, their audiovisual recording apparatus was still crude; it distinguished too few frequency bands and tended to indicate volume in unreadable smears. Their excuse must be that it had not been intended for such crucial work.)

Of the five suspects, Zavarzin and Syagovity could quite confidently be excluded (if indeed the nascent science allowed conclusions to be drawn from a single conversation). Petrov, too, could be tentatively excluded (Rubin, flushed with enthusiasm, rejected him outright). The voices of Volodin and Shchevronok, however, resembled that of the criminal in the frequency of their basic tone and shared with it certain phonemes (*o*, *r*, *l*, and *sh*) and were similar in their specific speech tunes.

The similarity of these voices should provide a starting point for the development of their new science—phonoscopy—and the elaboration of its methods. Study of the fine distinctions between them should enable them to devise and perfect the sensitive apparatus of the future. Rubin and Roitman leaned back in their chairs with the triumphant air of creators. They could foresee an organization similar to that which existed for fingerprints: an All-Union Voice Library, where the voice patterns of all who had ever come under suspicion would be on record. Any criminal conversation could be recorded, referred to the audiovisual archive—and the criminal would instantly be identified as surely as the thief who leaves his fingerprints on the door of a safe.

At this point, Oskolupov's adjutant looked around the door to warn them that his boss would be along shortly.

This brought them to their senses. Science was all very well, but right now they must formulate their conclusions and defend them with a single voice before the head of the department.

Roitman believed, in fact, that what they had achieved was important enough in itself. But knowing that his masters liked certainties not hypotheses, he gave in to Rubin, agreed to consider Petrov's voice above suspicion and to report to the major general that Shchevronok and Volodin were the only suspects remaining. These two must be further examined in the next few days.

There was one complicating factor; according to information received, two of the three rejected, Syagovity and Petrov, didn't know a word of any foreign language, whereas Shchevronok spoke English and Dutch, and Volodin spoke French like a native, fluent English, and a little Italian. It seemed improbable that at the critical moment when mutual incomprehension threatened to terminate the conversation, a man who knew his listener's language would have uttered not so much as an impatient exclamation in it.

"In addition to everything else, Lev Grigorievich," Roitman mused, "we must not overlook the psychological aspect. We must try to imagine what sort of man could bring himself to make such a telephone call. What was his motive? Then compare our imaginary picture of him with the concrete images we have of the suspects. We must ensure that in future we phonoscopists are supplied not only with a suspect's voice and name but with a brief account of his position, his activities, his lifestyle, perhaps even a curriculum vitae. I think I could construct some sort of psychological sketch of our criminal right now. . . ."

But Rubin, who only the night before, arguing with the artist, had said that objective knowledge is uncolored by emotional preconceptions, had already decided in favor of one of the two suspects.

"I have, of course, already given some thought to the psychological aspects, Adam Veniaminovich, and they seem to tip the balance in favor of Volodin. In his conversation with his wife . . ." (Volodin's conversation with his wife had influenced Lev more than he realized. Her musical telephone voice had troubled his senses. If anything was to be appended to the tape, Lev would have opted for a photograph of Volodin's wife) ". . . in his conversation with his wife, Volodin seems notably listless, subdued, apathetic even, and this is very characteristic of a criminal afraid that he is under observation. There's nothing of the sort in Shchevronok's cheerful Sunday chatter, I quite agree. But a pretty pair we will look if we start relying from the word 'go' on extraneous considerations rather than the objective data of our science. I've got quite a lot of experience of work with audiovisual records by now, and you must believe me: A number of subtle indications convince me beyond doubt that the criminal is Shchevronok. Only shortage of time has prevented me from measuring these clues on the tape and translating them into the language of numbers." (Something for which this "arts man" never had time!) "But if somebody took me by the throat here and now and told me to mention just one name and swear that he's the criminal, I would almost without hesitation name Shchevronok!"

"But that's not what we're going to do, Lev Grigorievich. Let's get to work with the gauge and do our translation into the language of numbers; then we can talk."

"Think how long it will take! It's supposed to be urgent!"

"But if the truth demands it?"

"Look for yourself, then; just look for yourself!"

Rubin fingered the tapes again, showering ash on them, heatedly insisting on Shchevronok's guilt.

Oskolupov found them engaged in this when he stomped in authoritatively on his short legs. They all knew him well, and the hat pulled down over his brow and the curl of his upper lip told them that he was acutely dissatisfied.

They jumped up, and he sat in a corner of the sofa, thrust his hands into his pockets, and growled at them.

"Well?"

It was an order.

Rubin behaved correctly and left it to Roitman.

As Roitman made his report, Oskolupov's flabby face was expressive of deep thought, his eyelids were sleepily lowered, and he didn't even rise to look at the specimens of tape presented to him.

Rubin listened to Roitman, and his heart sank. Even in the carefully chosen words of this clever man, the essence, the inspiration of his research had been missed. Roitman summed up by saying that Shchevronok and Volodin were the suspects, but further recorded conversations were needed to make a final judgment possible. After which, he looked at Rubin and said, "But perhaps Lev Grigorievich wants to add something or make a correction?"

Rubin regarded Oskolupov as a blockhead, pure and simple. But then and there he was also the eye of the state, the representative of Soviet power, and the unwitting representative of all those forces of progress to which Rubin had surrendered himself. So Rubin spoke passionately, flourishing tapes and albums of audiovisual recordings. He begged the general to understand that although their present conclusion left two possibilities, there was nothing uncertain about the science of phonoscopy itself; it was just that the time allowed was too short for a definitive conclusion, and more recordings were needed; but his personal tentative conclusion was that. . . .

The boss, no longer half asleep, listened for a while with a contemptuous frown before interrupting Rubin's explanation.

"I don't need all this if-ing and but-ing. I don't give a damn for your so-called science. I want to catch the criminal. Give it to me straight. You've got the criminal here, on this table, right? He isn't walking around scot-free? Somebody else—not one of these five?"

He glowered at them while they stood before him with nothing to support them. The paper tapes Rubin was holding trailed on the floor. Behind their backs, Smolosidov crouched over the tape recorder like a black dragon.

Rubin felt deflated. He had expected the conversation to go quite differently.

Roitman, who was more accustomed to the manners of the boss class, plucked up courage and said, "Yes, Foma Guryanovich. I really am . . . we really are. . . . We're sure that . . . it's between these five."

(What else could he say?)

Oskolupov screwed up his eyes more tightly.

"You take full responsibility for what you're saying?"

"Yes, we . . . yes . . . we take responsibility. . . ."

Oskolupov struggled up from the sofa.

"I didn't force you to say it, mind. I'm going straight to the minister to make my report. We'll arrest both the sons of bitches!"

(From the way he said it and the hostile look he gave them, Rubin and Roitman might as well be the two to be arrested).

Rubin protested.

"Wait a bit longer. Just another twenty-four hours. Give us a chance to prove it conclusively."

"Well, when the interrogation begins, we'll put a microphone on the interrogator's desk and you can record them for three hours at a time if you like."

"But one of them has to be innocent!" Rubin exclaimed.

"What's that mean—innocent?" Oskolupov's green eyes opened wide in surprise. "Not guilty of anything at all? Security will know how to deal with it; they'll find something."

He left with never a kind word for the adepts of the new science.

That was Oskolupov's managerial style: Never praise your subordinates if you want them to work harder. It was not a style he himself had invented. It had been handed down from on high, by the Man himself.

They sat down on the very chairs on which not so long ago they had dreamed of a great future for their embryonic science. And were silent.

It was as though what they had constructed with such precision and delicacy of touch had been trampled underfoot. As though phonoscopy were not wanted at all.

If two could be arrested instead of one, why not all five to make absolutely sure?

Roitman felt keenly how precarious the new group was, remembered that half of the Acoustics Lab had been disbanded, remembered yet again his uneasy feeling in the small hours that the world was a bleak place and he was alone in it.

As for Rubin, the enthusiasm that had kept him working, hour after hour, lost to the world, had burned itself out. He remembered his aching liver, his aching head, remembered that his hair was falling out, that his wife was getting older, that he still had five years to serve, that with every year the apparatchiks, damn them, were driving the Revolution deeper and deeper into the morass—and now they'd made a pariah of Yugoslavia.

Both Roitman and Rubin kept their thoughts to themselves and sat there in silence.

Smolosidov, with his eyes on the backs of their heads, was also silent.

Rubin had been quick to pin up a map of China on the wall, with the territory held by the Communists colored with a red pencil.

This map, at least, was heartwarming. In spite of everything, in spite of everything—we are winning!

A KNOCK AT THE DOOR SUMMONED ROITMAN. The joint Party and Komsomol political education session was just beginning.

He had to round up his subordinates and put in an appearance himself.

# 88

## The Leading Ideology

MONDAY WAS THE DAY APPOINTED by the Central Committee of the Party for political study, not just in the Marfino special prison but throughout the Soviet Union. Every Monday schoolchildren in the top classes, housewives in housing cooperatives, veterans of the Revolution, and gray-haired academicians sat at desks from six to eight in the evening and unfolded the notes they had made on Sunday. (It was the Leader's adamant wish that citizens be required not only to answer questions from memory but also to produce their own written synopses of each lesson.)

Year after year, beginning on October 1, they studied in depth the errors of the Populists, the errors of Plekhanov, and the struggle of Lenin and Stalin against Economism, Legal Marxism, Opportunism, Tailism, Revisionism, Anarchism, Recallism, Liquidationism, God-seeking, and Spineless Intellectualism. They lavished time on the elucidation of Party statutes half a century old (and long since superseded), on the difference between the old *Iskra* and the new *Iskra*,* on "One Step Forward, Two Steps Back," on Bloody Sunday, and arrived at last at the famous chapter of the *Short Course in the History of the Communist Party* that expounds the philosophical foundations of Communist ideology—and that was where for some reason every political study group got ingloriously stuck. Since this could not be explained by flaws or muddle in Dialectical Materialism itself or by obscurities in the author's exposition (the chapter was written by Lenin's Best Pupil and Friend), there were only two possible reasons: the difficulties of dialectical thinking for the backward and ignorant masses and the unstoppable onset of spring. In May, when the battle with chapter 4 was at its hottest, the toilers ransomed themselves by subscribing to the State Loan, and politics classes were discontinued.

When the study circles reassembled in October, in spite of the explicit and enduring wish of the Great Helmsman to move on quickly to the burning

* *Iskra*: The newspaper established in 1900 by Russian socialists abroad and initially managed by Lenin but seized by Mensheviks in 1903 and controlled by Georgy Plekhanov until the paper's demise in 1905, The Russian title means *Spark*.

questions of our own time, its deficiencies and determinant contradictions, they had to reckon with the fact that the toilers had forgotten everything during the summer and that chapter 4 was still waiting, and propagandists were told to begin all over again with the errors of the Populists, the errors of Plekhanov, the struggles with Economism and with Legal Marxism. . . .

So it went on, here, there, and everywhere, year in and year out. What made today's lecture at Marfino particularly important was that it was meant to finish off chapter 4, touch on the genius Lenin's dazzling *Materialism and Empiriocriticism*, break out of the vicious circle, and at long last launch the Marfino Party and Komsomol study groups along the high road of modernity, beginning from "the work and struggle of our Party in the period of the First Imperialist War and of Preparation for the February Revolution."

A bonus for the free workers of Marfino was that summaries of set texts were not expected on this occasion; those already written would keep till next Monday.

There was a further inducement to attend; the lecturer was no common or garden propagandist but Rakhmankul Shamsetdinov, who was on the staff of the Oblast Party Committee. Stepanov had gone around the laboratories before lunch to warn them that the lecturer was supposed to be hot stuff. (What Stepanov did not know was that the lecturer was a close friend of Mamulov. Not the Mamulov in Beria's secretariat but his brother, commandant of the camp attached to the Khovrin munitions factory. This Mamulov kept for his personal enjoyment a serf theater, in which prisoners who had once been Moscow artistes entertained him and his dinner guests, together with girls handpicked from the Krasnaya Presnya transit prison. Because he was so close to the Mamulovs, the Moscow Oblast Committee of the Party held the lecturer in such esteem that he felt free to soar on the wings of inspiration instead of reading from a prepared text.)

But in spite of the painstaking advance publicity for the lecture, the free employees of Marfino seemed resistant to its magnetic pull and found pretexts for lingering in their laboratories. One free worker was supposed to stay behind in every department—prisoners could not be left unsupervised—so the head of the Vacuum Laboratory, who never did anything, suddenly announced that urgent business required his presence there and sent his two girls, Tamara and Klara, to the lecture. Roitman's deputy in the Acoustics Laboratory did the same—stayed behind himself and ordered the girl on duty, Simochka, to go and listen. Major Shikin also failed to turn up, but his activities were so shrouded in secrecy that not even the Party could check up on him.

Those who did come arrived late and, out of a misguided sense of self-preservation, tried to find seats in the back rows.

A special room in the institute was reserved for meetings and lectures. A large number of chairs had been installed, irremovably nailed onto poles, eight at a time. (How else could the commandant deter people from carrying chairs around the whole site?) It was not a large room, so there was little space between rows, and knees were painfully jammed against the pole of the row in front. Those who arrived early tried to move their rows back to make more room for their legs. This provoked resistance, jokes, and laughter among the younger people sitting in neighboring rows. Thanks to the exertions of Stepanov and his whippers-in, all the rows were filled by 6:15 except the second and third, where no one could sit, because they were wedged tightly together and jammed against the front row.

"Comrades! Comrades! This is disgraceful!" Stepanov's glasses had a leaden glint as he urged on the laggards. "You are keeping an Oblast Committee lecturer waiting!" (The lecturer, so as not to lose face, waited in Stepanov's office.)

Roitman was the next to last to enter the lecture room. Finding nowhere else to sit—the whole place was occupied by green tunics, with here and there a bright dress—he walked all the way to the front row and sat down on the extreme left, with his knees almost touching the platform. Stepanov then went to get Yakonov; he was not a Party member, but it was only right for him to be present at such an important lecture, and anyway it should interest him. Yakonov squeezed his way forward close to the wall, bending double to squeeze his bulk past people who for the moment were not his subordinates but the Party and Komsomol collective. Finding no vacant place farther back, he sat down on the extreme right of the front row, so that he and Roitman were on opposite sides yet again!

This done, Stepanov led in the lecturer. He was a big man with broad shoulders, a large head, and an unruly mane of black hair flecked with gray. He was completely relaxed, as though he had come into the room simply to drink a mug of beer with Stepanov. He was wearing a light-colored worsted suit, somewhat creased, and a variegated tie with a knot as big as a fist. There were no exercise books or prompt sheets in his hands, and he got straight down to business.

"Comrades! Each and every one of us is interested in the nature of the world about us."

Looming massively over his audience from behind the red-calico-covered desk on the platform, he fell silent, and they all pricked up their ears. There was a general feeling that he was about to explain it in a few words: the true nature of the world about us. But the lecturer rocked back on his heels, as though he had been given a whiff of smelling salts, and exclaimed indignantly: "Many philosophers have endeavored to answer that question! But before Marx no one was able to do so! Because metaphysics does not recognize qualitative change! Of course, it is not easy"—with two fingers he plucked a gold watch from his pocket—"not easy to make it all clear to you in an hour and a half but"—putting away his watch—"I shall try."

Stepanov, who had installed himself at the butt end of the lecturer's desk, interrupted: "Take longer if you like. Feel free!"

Some of the girls were in a hurry to get to the movies. Their hearts sank.

But the lecturer, spreading his arms in a dignified gesture, acknowledged that he, too, was subject to higher authority.

"Let's stick to the time limit!" he said, putting Stepanov in his place. "What enabled Marx and Engels to give a correct picture of nature and society? The inspired philosophical system they devised, subsequently further developed by Lenin and Stalin, and known as dialectical materialism. The first major component of dialectical materialism is the materialist dialectic. I shall briefly describe its basic theses. The Prussian philosopher Hegel is usually said to have been the first to formulate the basic features of the dialectic. But that, Comrades, is radically—yes, radically—wrong! Hegel's dialectic was standing on its head—yes, on its head—that's indisputable! Marx and Engels set it on its feet, extracted its rational kernel, and threw away the idealistic husk! The Marxist dialectical method—that is the enemy! The enemy of all that is stagnant, all metaphysics, all superstition! And we distinguish, in all, four features of the dialectic. The first feature is . . . is that which . . . is interconnection! Interconnection, not an accumulation of isolated objects. Nature and society are not—how can I put it? Not a furniture store, where lots of things are on display, lots and lots of things, with no connection between them. In nature, everything is connected, everything—just make a note of that, and it will be a great help to you in your scientific investigations!"

Those who had not grudged an extra ten minutes but arrived early were sitting at the back in a particularly advantageous position. The stern gleam of Stepanov's spectacles could not reach them. There, a tall lieutenant, smart as a guardsman, wrote a note and passed it to Tonya, a Tatar girl from the Acoustics Lab, also a lieutenant but wearing a bright red knitted pullover, imported, over her dark dress. Tonya hid behind the man sitting in front and unfolded the note on her knees. Her black forelock slipped and hung down, making her more attractive than ever. She read the note, blushed slightly, and began asking her neighbors for a pencil or fountain pen.

". . . And the number of examples could be multiplied. . . . The second feature of the dialectic is that all things are in motion. All things move, nothing is or ever was at rest, and that is a fact! Science must study all things in motion, in their development, but at the same time we must get it firmly into our heads that motion does not take place in a closed circle; otherwise, the higher form of life we have today would not have emerged. Movement goes up a spiral staircase; that is self-evident, ever upward, ever upward, like this. . . ."

He showed them how, with a fluid wave of his hand; the lecturer's movements were as free and easy as his choice of words. Scattering the superfluous chairs on the platform, he cleared a space of some three meters square near the table, paced to and fro stamping his feet, and rocked backward and forward, leaning on the back of a chair that threatened to collapse under the pressure of his sturdy frame. "Indubitably" and "it goes without saying" rang out with special emphasis, challenging contradiction, as if he were standing on the captain's bridge, quelling a mutiny; and he pronounced these words not randomly but where arguments neat enough to begin with called for still further reinforcement.

"The third feature of the dialectic is the transition of quantity into quality. This very important feature helps us to understand what development is. You must not think that development simply means enlargement. Here we must point the finger at Darwin, above all. Engels explains this feature with examples from science. Take water, the water in this carafe, say; its temperature is eighteen degrees, and it is just water. But suppose you heat it. Heat it to thirty degrees, and it will still be water. Heat it to eighty degrees, still water. But what if you heat it to one hundred? What will it be then? Steam!"

The lecturer's cry of triumph made some of his listeners jump.

"Steam! But you can also make ice! So, then. That's what is meant by the transition of quantity into quality! Read the *Dialectics of Nature* by Engels; it's full of other instructive examples, which will throw light on your day-to-day difficulties. And now, we are told, our Soviet science has discovered that air, too, can be liquefied. For some reason, nobody had even thought of that a hundred years ago! Why? Because they didn't know the law of transition of quantity into quality. And so it is in all things, Comrades! I will give you some examples from the development of society. . . ."

Adam Roitman did not need, had never needed, a lecturer to tell him that *diamat* is as important to a scientist as air, that without it no one can make sense of life's phenomena. But at meetings, seminars, and lectures like this one, Roitman felt as if his brain were slowly turning, twisted out of true. He tried to resist but found himself succumbing to this hypnotic spin as an exhausted man surrenders to sleep. He tried to shake off his drowsiness. He could have spoken up and cited amazing examples from the structure of the atom, from wave mechanics. But he would never presume to interrupt or upstage a comrade from the Oblast Committee. His almond eyes simply stared reproachfully through his anastigmatic spectacles as the lecturer's gesticulating arms narrowly missed his head.

The lecturer's voice boomed on. "So, then, the transition of quantity into quality may happen explosively, and it may happen e-vol-ution-ar-ily; that is a fact! Development does not of necessity and everywhere require an explosion. Our socialist society is developing and will go on developing without explosions; that is indisputable! But social renegades, social traitors, right-wing socialists of every stripe shamelessly try to deceive the people, telling them that the transition from capitalism to socialism is possible without an explosion. Meaning what? Meaning without revolution? Without smashing the state machine? By the parliamentary path? Let them tell their fairy tales to little children, not to grown-up Marxists! Lenin taught us, and another theoretician of genius, Comrade Stalin, teaches us that the bourgeoisie will never give up power without armed struggle!"

The lecturer's shaggy locks jiggled when he tossed his head. He blew his nose into a big azure-bordered handkerchief and looked at his watch, not with the imploring gaze of a lecturer running out of time but doubtfully, uncomprehendingly, after which he held it to his ear.

"The fourth feature of the dialectic," he shouted, loudly enough to startle people all over again, "is that, which . . . is contradictions! Antitheses! The moribund and the new, negative and positive! It's . . . it's everywhere, Comrades; it's no secret! One can give scientific examples—electricity, say! If you rub glass on silk, that will be positive; but pitch against fur, that's negative! But only their unity, their synthesis gives energy for our industry. And you don't have to look far for examples, Comrade; they are here, there, and everywhere. Heat is positive, while cold is negative, and in society we see the same irreconcilable conflict between positive and negative. As you see, *diamat* has absorbed all the best achievements of every branch of science. The hidden internal contradictions of development laid bare by the Founding Fathers of Marxism not only were found in dead nature but were seen to be the fundamental motive force of all social formations from primitive communism to the imperialism now rotting before our very eyes! And only in our classless society is the moving force inarguably not internal contradictions but criticism and self-criticism without respect of persons."

The lecturer yawned and did not cover his mouth in time. Suddenly, he looked dejected; vertical lines appeared in his face; his lower jaw trembled in a suppressed convulsion. Struggling to remain on his feet, he spoke now in different, utterly weary tones.

"Oppositionists and defeatists of the Bukharinist persuasion grossly slandered us, claiming that we had class contradictions here . . . but. . . ."

Fatigue felled him. He blinked, slumped onto his chair, and finished his sentence in a feeble whisper: ". . . but they met with a crushing defeat at the hands of our Central Committee."

He went on to read the whole middle part of his lecture in the same manner. It was as if an insidious disease had suddenly sapped his strength, or as if he had lost all hope that this accursed ninety minutes of lecturing would ever end. He was a man lost in a maze, despairing of ever finding a way out.

"Matter alone is absolute, while all the laws of science are relative. . . . Only matter is absolute, while every particular form of matter is relative. . . . Noth-thing is absolute except matter, and motion is its eternal attribute. . . . Motion is absolute; repose is relative. There are no absolute truths; all truths are relative. . . . The idea of beauty is relative. Ideas of good and evil are relative. . . ."

Whether Stepanov was listening or not, his whole demeanor—sitting bolt upright, flashing glances at the auditorium—expressed his awareness that a political occasion of great moment was in progress and his modest pride that such an event should take place within the walls of Marfino.

Yakonov and Roitman were forced to listen to the lecturer because they were sitting so near. And one girl in the fourth row, wearing a cheap cotton dress, listened on the edge of her seat and was slightly flushed. She wanted to show off by asking the lecturer something but couldn't think what.

Klykachev was also watching the lecturer closely, his long, narrow head protruding from the uniformed throng. But he, too, was not listening. He conducted political education classes himself, could have given an even better lecture, and knew very well what teaching aids had provided the material for today's performance. Klykachev was studying the lecturer out of sheer boredom, calculating how much he was paid per month, then trying to determine his age and lifestyle. He was possibly about forty, but his ashen complexion, his hollow cheeks, and his spongy, purple nose made him look over fifty—or perhaps he was getting a good deal out of life, and life was taking its revenge.

The rest of them did not even pretend to be listening. Tonya and the handsome lieutenant had used up four pages of their scribbling pads in an exchange of notes, while another lieutenant was playing an absorbing game with Tamara: He would take her first by one finger, then by another, then by her whole hand; she would give him a little slap with her other hand and free herself; and then it began all over again. They were absorbed in their game; but, like crafty schoolchildren, they did their best to look serious—their faces were all Stepanov could see of them. The head of Fourth Group was making a sketch (on his knees, where Stepanov could not see it) for the head of First Group of an extension he thought of making to a circuit, already in operation.

Still, the lecturer's voice reached all of them in snatches. But Klara Makarygina, in a bright blue dress, had boldly planted her elbows on the back of the chair in front of her and, deaf and blind to all that was happening in that room, was wandering in that rose pink haze that is sometimes seen behind tight-shut eyelids. Mixed feelings of joy, embarrassment, and sadness had haunted her ever since Rostislav had kissed her. It was all such a hopeless tangle. Why had Erik entered her life? How could she slight him? How could she possibly "not wait" for Ruska now? But how could she "wait" for him? And how could she remain in the same group with him, meet his gaze, and go on talking where they had left off? Should she transfer to another group? Perhaps the engineer colonel had decided to transfer Rostislav? It was two hours since he had been summoned, and he had still not returned. She had hurried off to the politics class, glad that she could put off their meeting. As he left the room, he had turned around in the doorway and given her an unbearably reproachful look. It must indeed have looked like a shabby trick, making promises yesterday, then today. . . .

(She did not know that they were never to meet again. Ruska had been arrested and taken away to a tight little box of a cell in the prison headquarters. While back in the Vacuum Laboratory, in the presence of its head, Major Shikin was at that very moment breaking into and searching Ruska's desk.)

The lecturer had revived. He rose to his feet and, brandishing his big fist, demolished with ease the gimcrack formal logic created by Aristotle and the medieval scholastics, which now felt the full force of Marxist dialectic.

Marfino, by exception, received current American journals, and Rubin had recently translated for the Acoustics Laboratory at large an article that Roitman and several other officers had read on the new science of cybernetics. It was based on precisely those thrice-obsolete procedures of formal logic: "Yes" means yes, "no" means no, and *Tertium non datur.* (John Bull's *Two-Digit Algebraic Logic* had appeared in the same year as the *Communist Manifesto*, only nobody had noticed it.)

"The second main section of dialectical materialism is philosophical materialism," the lecturer thundered. "Materialism grew up in the struggle with the reactionary philosophy of idealism, of which Plato was the founder, and its most typical representatives subsequently were Bishop Berkeley, Mach, Avenarius, Yushkevich, and Valentinov."

Yakonov groaned so loudly that people turned to look at him. Whereupon he pulled a face and clutched his side. Roitman was perhaps the one person there with whom he could share his thoughts but also the last he could confide in. So he sat looking humbly attentive. To think that he had to waste on this the "one last month" for which he had begged!

"That matter is the substance of all that exists needs no proof!" the lecturer thundered. "Matter is indestructible; that is not open to dispute! And that, too, can be scientifically proved. Suppose, for instance, we plant a grain of corn in the ground; does that mean that it has vanished? No! It turns into a plant, into a dozen such grains. Take water, for instance. Say it has evaporated in the sun. Has that water vanished? Of course not! That water has turned into cloud, into steam! That's all! Only that base lackey of the bourgeoisie, that certificated hireling of religious obscurantism, the physicist Ostwald, has had the barefaced nerve to declare that "matter has disappeared." That is ridiculous, as anybody can see! The genius Lenin, in his immortal work *Materialism and Empiriocriticism*, guided by his progressive worldview, refuted Ostwald and drove him into such a blind alley that he didn't know where to turn!"

Yakonov thought: It would be good to drive a hundred lecturers like this one onto these close-packed chairs, give them a lecture on Einstein's theory, and make them go without dinner until they get their stupid, lazy heads around just one little problem: Where, say, do four million tons of solar substance vanish to in a single second?

But he had been made to miss his own dinner, and he ached all over. Only the hope that release would not be long delayed kept him going.

They all fortified themselves with the same hope: They had left home by trolley, bus, or electric train at 8:00, or some of them as early as 7:00, that morning, and they could not now expect to get home before 9:30.

One person looked forward to the end of the lecture even more eagerly than the others: Simochka, although she would be staying behind on duty, not hurrying home. Hot waves of fear and anticipation left her legs as unsteady as if she had drunk champagne. This was the very Monday evening on which she had arranged to meet Gleb. This was to be the most solemn, the supreme moment of her life. It must not be bungled or trivialized. That was why she had not felt ready for it the day before yesterday. She had spent all day yesterday and half of today as if preparing for a great holiday. She had sat with the dressmaker, urging her to hurry with the new dress, which was so becoming. At home, she had placed the tin basin on the floor of that cramped Moscow room and washed herself thoroughly. At bedtime she had painstakingly put her hair in curlers, and the next morning had spent just as long uncurling it, viewing herself in the mirror from all angles, trying to reassure herself that she would look attractive if she turned her head some other way.

She should have seen Nerzhin at 3:00 in the afternoon, immediately after the lunch break, but he habitually disregarded the rules for prisoners (must scold him for it today! he must be more careful!) and was late getting back from lunch. In the meantime, Simochka had been sent to another group to take delivery of apparatus and components, and it was nearly 6:00 when she got back to the Acoustics Laboratory, missing Gleb yet again, although his desk was littered with journals and folders and his lamp was on. So she had left for the lecture without seeing him, unaware of the terrible news—that after a twelve-month interval he had been visited by his wife the day before.

Now she was sitting in the lecture room in her new dress, with burning cheeks, apprehensively watching the hands of the big electric clock. Shortly after 8:00 she and Gleb should have been alone together. Simochka was so small that she fitted in easily between the cramped rows, and from a distance her chair appeared to be unoccupied.

The lecturer's pace was perceptibly accelerating, rather as an orchestra picks up speed in the final bars of a waltz or polka. They all sensed it and cheered up. Winged thoughts chased one another, foam flecked, over the heads of his listeners.

"Theory becomes a material force. . . . The three characteristics of materialism . . . the two special features of production . . . the five types of producer relations . . . transition to socialism impossible without the dictatorship of the proletariat . . . the leap into the realm of freedom . . . bourgeois sociologists understand all this very well . . . the force and vitality of Marxism-Leninism . . . Comrade Stalin has raised dialectical materialism to a new, still higher level! What Lenin had no time to do in matters of theory, Comrade Stalin has done! . . . victory in the Great Fatherland War . . . inspiring results . . . immense prospects . . . the wisdom and genius of our . . . our great . . . our beloved. . . ."

And now, to applause, he was looking at his pocket watch. It was 7:45. Still a smidgen short of the prescribed time.

"Perhaps some of you have questions?" the lecturer said half threateningly.

"Yes, if I may. . . ." The girl in the cotton dress called out from the fourth row, blushing furiously. She rose, uncomfortably aware that everyone was looking and listening, and asked, "You say that bourgeois sociologists are well aware of all this. And it is, indeed, all so clear, so convincing. So why do they write the opposite in their books? Does it mean that they deliberately seek to deceive people?"

"It's because it wouldn't pay them to say anything else! They get a lot of money for it! They are bribed with the superprofits squeezed out of the colonies! Their doctrine is called pragmatism, which means, translated into Russian, 'What's profitable is permissible.' They are all frauds, political prostitutes."

"Every single one?" the girl asked in a voice shrill with horror.

"Every single one," the lecturer said firmly, tossing his graying mane.

# 89

## Little Quail

SIMOCHKA'S NEW BROWN DRESS had been made with careful attention to her good and less good points. The bodice hugged her wasp waist but was loosely gathered into irregular folds over her breast. To give her a fuller figure, where the bodice met the skirt it was trimmed with two ruffles, one plain, one shiny, which bobbed up and down as she walked. Billowing sleeves concealed her thin arms. The collar, too, was a naively pretty novelty: A long strip cut separately from the same cloth, its dangling ends were tied in a bow over her breast and looked like the silvery wings of a brown butterfly.

These and other special features were inspected and discussed by Simochka's friends on the stairs outside the cloakroom when she emerged to say good-bye after the lecture. In the noisy, jostling crowd, men struggled into their military coats or civilian overcoats and lit cigarettes for the journey, while girls propped themselves up against the wall to pull on their overshoes.

In their suspicious world it might seem strange that Simochka had chosen an evening when she was on duty to wear for the first time a dress meant for New Year's Eve. She explained to the girls that after her shift she was going on to her uncle's birthday party, where there would be other young people.

Her friends admired the dress, told her that she looked "really pretty," and asked where that crêpe satin had been bought.

But Simochka's nerve faltered. She was in no hurry to get back. Her heart was pounding. When, at two minutes to eight, she finally entered the Acoustics Laboratory, the prisoners had already handed in their secret materials to be locked in the safe. The middle of the room was bare now that the scrambler had been transferred to Number Seven, and she could see Nerzhin's desk.

He wasn't there. (Couldn't he have waited a bit?) His desk lamp was out; the rolltop was closed; his secret materials had been handed in. There was one unusual feature: Gleb never left things lying around during the break, but an American journal lay on top of his desk, with a dictionary, also open, beside it. Could this be a secret signal—"Won't be long"?

Roitman's deputy gave Simochka the keys to the room and safe, together with the seal (laboratories were sealed for the night). Simochka was afraid that Roitman might want to visit Rubin again, in which case he could look in on the Acoustics Laboratory at any moment. But no, Roitman was right there, wearing cap and coat, pulling on his leather gloves, and urging his deputy to get ready quickly. He looked glum.

"Right then, Serafima Vitalievna, take over. All the best," he said, and left.

The prolonged ringing of an electric bell traveled down the hallways and through the rooms of the institute. The prisoners left as one man for supper. Unsmilingly, Simochka walked around the laboratory, watching the last of them leave. When she was not smiling, her longish nose with its bony bridge made her look plain and forbidding.

She was alone.

*Now* he could come!

She walked round the library wringing her hands.

It would have to happen today! The silk curtains that had always hung at the windows had been taken down to be washed. The three windows were bare, unprotected, and the blackness outside would conceal anyone keeping an eye on the lab. The depths of the room were invisible from the yard—the Acoustics Laboratory was on the first floor—but the perimeter fence was not far away, and she and Gleb would be in full view of the sentry on the watchtower facing their window.

Unless they put all the lights out when. . . ? The door would be locked, and everybody would think that she had left.

But what if they tried forcing the lock or looked for a spare key?

Simochka went over to the soundproof booth, ignoring the sentry, for whom the place was out of sight. On the threshold of this narrow little cell, she leaned against the stout double door and closed her eyes. No, she would not go in there without him. She wanted him to drag her in or carry her in bodily.

She had heard from other girls how it all happens but had only a vague picture of it. She became more and more agitated, and her cheeks burned more and more painfully.

That which it had once been supremely important to preserve had now become a burden!

Yes! She wanted very much to have his child and bring it up while she was waiting for him to be released! Only five short years! She went over to his yellow bentwood swivel chair and embraced its back as though it were a living person.

She glanced at the window.

The watchtower must be there, near the edge of the darkness, and on it—a black concentration of all that was hostile to love—a sentry with a rifle.

Gleb's footsteps in the hallway. Quieter than usual. Simochka flew to her desk, sat down, drew toward her the large amplifier, which was lying on its side with its valves exposed, and began inspecting it with a small screwdriver in her hand. Her heartbeats resounded in her head.

Nerzhin pushed the door shut gently, so that the sound would not carry down the hushed hallway. Across the empty space where the scrambler had been, Gleb saw Simochka crouching behind her desk like a quail behind a tussock.

"Little quail" was his pet name for her.

Simochka looked up at him with a bright smile, and her heart stood still. He looked worried, indeed deeply depressed. She had been sure that he would come right over and try to kiss her, and she would have to stop him because the windows were uncurtained and the sentry could be looking.

But he stayed at his own desk and spoke first.

"The windows are bare, so I won't come over. Hello, Simochka!"

He stood bracing himself with outstretched hands against his desk and looking down at her. "If we're not interrupted, we'd better talk things over right now."

Talk things over? Talk . . . things . . . over?

He unlocked his desk. The rolltop rattled open. Without so much as a glance at Simochka, Nerzhin assembled and opened books, journals, and folders—the camouflage she knew so well.

Simochka froze, screwdriver in hand, staring fixedly at his expressionless face. Had Yakonov's summons on Saturday spelled disaster? Were they giving him a hard time? Perhaps they meant to send him away soon? But why wouldn't he come over to her? Why wouldn't he kiss her?

"What's wrong? Has something happened?" she asked with a catch in her voice and swallowing hard.

He sat down. Planting his elbows on the pile of open journals, he gripped his head with the outspread fingers of both hands and looked at the girl, stared at her . . . but the look in his eyes was evasive.

There was profound silence. Not a sound reached them. They were separated by two desks, two desks lit by four lights overhead and a lamp on each desk and raked by the gaze of the sentry in his tower.

The sentry's gaze was like a barbed-wire curtain slowly lowered between them.

Gleb said, "Simochka! I would consider myself a scoundrel if I didn't tell you . . . if I didn't confess. . . ."

Confess?

"I haven't been fair to you . . . I didn't stop to think. . . ."

Think? Think about what?

"The fact is . . . I saw my wife yesterday. . . . We were allowed a visit."

Simochka shrank. The wings of her collar band trailed limply over the aluminum panel of the apparatus. Her screwdriver grated on the desk.

She forced herself to speak. "Why couldn't you . . . didn't you . . . tell me on Saturday?" she asked brokenly.

"Simochka!" He was horrified. "Surely you don't think I'd hide it from you?"

(Wouldn't he, though?)

"I wasn't told till yesterday morning. It took me by surprise. It's a whole year since we saw each other . . . as you know. Well, now we have seen each other, and. . . ."

His voice faded. He knew what it must be like for her, listening to this, but saying it was just as. . . . So much of what he felt was difficult to put into words . . . and it wouldn't help her if he could. In fact, he wasn't really sure himself what he felt. He had dreamed of this evening, this hour! On Saturday he had been in a fever of anticipation, tossing and turning in his bed. Now the hour had come, and there was nothing to prevent them. . . . The curtains didn't matter; they had the room to themselves; what more did they need? Only. . . .

Only yesterday he had left his soul behind. It had escaped his grasp, like a fugitive kite; it was a kite flapping in the wind, and his wife was holding the string.

Perhaps "soul" wasn't important here?

Strangely, it was.

He couldn't say all this to Simochka. But what could he say? He had to say something. He fumbled for excuses.

"You see . . . she's waited for me all the time we've been separated . . . my five years in prison and all through the war. . . . Other women don't wait. . . . What's more, she kept me going when I was in the camp, sent me extra food.

You said you'd wait for me, but that's not . . . not . . . I couldn't bear to cause her. . . ."

Gleb should have stopped there. His hoarse, hushed words had struck home. "Little Quail" was dead already, slumped over the desk, her head down among the complex array of valves and condensers that made up the three-circuit amplifier.

She sobbed quietly. Her sobs were no louder than sighs.

"Simochka, don't cry! You mustn't cry," Gleb said belatedly.

But still with two desks between them, keeping his distance.

While she wept almost soundlessly, showing him her straight part.

Seeing her helplessness, Gleb felt a pang of remorse.

"Little Quail!" he mumbled, bending forward. "Please, I beg you! I'm sorry!"

It hurt him to see her cry. But . . . the other one? It was unbearable!

"I don't understand myself why I feel as I do."

What would it have cost him to go over to her, take her in his arms, kiss her? But even that was impossible. He could not sully his lips and hands after his wife's visit!

It was lucky that the curtains had been taken down. Instead of jumping up and hurrying from desk to desk, he stayed where he was, feebly pleading with her not to cry.

She went on crying.

"Little Quail, please stop! . . . Maybe we can still . . . somehow. . . . Just give it a little time."

She raised her head and interrupted her weeping to look at him strangely.

He could not understand her expression and lowered his eyes to the dictionary.

She could hold her head up no longer, and it drooped again onto the amplifier.

It would be crazy . . . what did his wife's visit matter? What good were all those women outside to him while he was there in jail? It mustn't be today, but in a few days' time his heart would be back in place, and everything would be . . . possible.

And why not? If he told anybody, he'd be a laughingstock. It's time you woke up, they'd say, time to behave like the convict you are. Who says you'll have to marry her afterward? The girl's waiting; get on with it!

Besides—only don't say it out loud—you didn't choose this particular girl. You chose this place, two desks away, and you'd have gone for any girl who happened to be there!

But it mustn't be today.

Gleb turned away and leaned on the windowsill. With his nose and forehead pressed against the pane, he looked in the direction of the sentry. Eyes dazzled by lights nearby could not see into the watchtower, but farther away separate lights merged and became blurred stars, while beyond and above them a third of the sky was blanched by reflected light from the capital nearby.

Looking down from the window, he could see that it was thawing.

Simochka raised her head.

Gleb turned expectantly toward her.

Wet tracks gleamed on her cheeks. She did not wipe them away. In the lamplight her shining eyes and the feminine softening of her features made her almost attractive at that particular moment.

Perhaps . . . even now. . . .

Simochka looked hard at Gleb.

But said nothing.

He felt awkward. He must say something.

"And she's still . . . really . . . devoting her life to me. How many people could do that? Are you sure you could?"

The tears remained undried on her numbed cheeks.

"Didn't she want a divorce?" Simochka asked softly, deliberately.

How quickly she had gotten to the heart of the matter. But he was reluctant to admit that something new had happened yesterday. It was much too complicated.

"No."

Too pointed a question. If it were not so pointed, not so peremptory, not so sharp-edged, if we could stop calling things by their names and just look and look and look, then maybe you could get up, maybe you could walk to the light switch. . . . But pointed questions demand logical answers.

"Is she . . . beautiful?"

"Yes. To me she is," Gleb said cautiously.

Simochka sighed loudly. She nodded to herself, to the broken reflection in the mirror-smooth radio valves.

"She won't wait for you, then."

Simochka could not allow this invisible woman any of the advantages of a lawful wife. So she had once lived for a while with Gleb, but that was eight years ago. Since then, Gleb had fought in the war and done time in jail, while she, if she was really beautiful and young and childless, . . . had surely not lived like a nun. Gleb could never—not at yesterday's meeting, not in a year's time, not in two years, belong to her—but to Simochka he could. Simochka could become his wife that very day. That woman—no longer a phantom, no longer merely an empty name—why had she taken the trouble to get a visitor's permit? What insatiable greed made her clutch at this man who would never belong to her?

"She won't wait for you!" Simochka repeated mechanically.

It hurt more every time she touched that tender spot.

"She's waited eight whole years already!" Gleb said indignantly. But added, with his usual realism, that it would get harder before it was over.

"She won't wait for you!" Simochka said yet again, in a whisper.

She wiped her drying tears away with the back of her hand.

Nerzhin shrugged. If he was honest, Simochka was right, of course. They would grow apart—their characters would change; they would experience life differently. He had himself urged his wife over and over again to divorce him. But what gave Simochka the right to keep pressing on that sore spot?

"Anyway, suppose she doesn't wait. Just as long as she has nothing to reproach me with." This seemed to be the moment for a little philosophy.

"Simochka, I don't consider myself a good man. In fact, I'm a very bad man. When I remember all the things I did at the front, in Germany, the things we all did. And now this, with you. . . . But believe me, I got that way in the *free* world, the thoughtless, comfortable, free world. I let myself be deluded into thinking that . . . bad things are permissible. But the lower I sank the . . . it's strange. . . . She won't wait, you say? Well, she needn't wait. Just so long as I have nothing on my conscience. . . ."

He had hit on a favorite theme. He could have talked about it at length, especially as there was nothing else he could say.

Simochka had heard very little of this homily. He seemed unable to talk of anything but himself. But what was to become of her? She shuddered to think of herself going home, mumbling something to her tiresome mother, flopping onto her bed. The bed in which she had lain thinking of him for months past. How shameful, how humiliating! How eagerly she had prepared for this evening! All those lotions, all that perfume!

But if a one-hour prison visit with no privacy meant more to him than all the months they had spent side by side, what could she do about it?

There was no need to go on. They had said all they had to say, without stopping to think or to spare each other's feelings. She ought to walk away, shut herself in the soundproof booth, weep a little longer, and pull herself together. But she could not bring herself to dismiss him or to walk away. For the last time, some tenuous thread still held them together.

Gleb saw that she was not listening, that all his fine arguments were wasted on her, and said no more.

He lit a cigarette, relaxed a little, and looked through the window again at the scattered yellowish lights.

They sat there saying nothing.

He was beginning to feel less sorry for her. It wasn't as if her whole life depended on it. This was just a passing fancy. She would get over it . . . find somebody.

With his wife it was different.

The silence was becoming oppressive. Gleb's only companions for many years had been other men, and he had never needed to explain himself at length. There was no more to be said. The subject was exhausted. So why were they still sitting there like dummies? Women never knew when to let go.

He squinted at the electric wall clock without moving his head—he didn't want Simochka to notice. Roll call in twenty minutes. Twenty minutes of the evening recreation period left. But he couldn't just get up and leave. He didn't want to hurt her feelings. He would have to sit it out.

Who'll be on duty this evening? Shusterman, probably. And the junior lieutenant tomorrow morning.

Simochka sat huddled over her amplifier, idly wobbling the valves out of their sockets and putting them back in again.

She had never understood the first thing about that amplifier. And she understood even less now.

But Nerzhin's active mind needed something to occupy it. He had made a note of the day's radio programs, as he did every morning, and slipped it under his inkstand.

"20:30—Rs. s. & rm (Obkh)," he read, meaning "Russian songs and romances performed by Obukhova."

A rare treat! And in the quiet leisure hour. The concert had started already. But wouldn't it be a bit tactless to switch it on?

A receiver permanently tuned to the three Moscow stations stood within easy reach on the windowsill. A present from Valentulya. Nerzhin glanced at the motionless Simochka and furtively switched it on at the lowest possible volume.

The valves lit up, and suddenly the sound of accompanying strings, followed by Obukhova's low, hoarsely passionate, incomparable voice broke the silence in the room.

Simochka started. She looked at the receiver. Then at Gleb.

Obukhova was singing something painfully relevant: "No, you are not the one I burn for. . . ."

The last thing they needed! Gleb fumbled for the switch and could not find it.

Simochka sat slumped over her amplifier, head in hands, and wept uncontrollably.

He had not been satisfied with his own hurtful words in their last few minutes together.

Gleb was touched to the quick.

"Forgive me!" he cried. "Forgive me!"

He gave up feeling for the switch.

Impulsively he dashed across the room, around both desks, and with no further thought for the sentry took her head in his hands and kissed her hair near her forehead.

Simochka wept copiously, easily, no longer convulsively sobbing.

These were tears of relief.

# 90

## On the Back Stairway

WORRIED TO DISTRACTION and still reeling from the shock of Ruska's arrest (the buzz had gone around two hours ago, after Shikin had broken into Ruska's desk, and was confirmed at evening roll call when the orderly officer pretended not to notice Ruska's absence), Nerzhin almost forgot about his rendezvous with Gerasimovich.

Routine had inexorably brought him back fifteen minutes after roll call to the same two desks, the same open journals, and the upended amplifier still spotted with Simochka's tears. And now Gleb and Simochka were condemned to sit facing each other for another two hours (and tomorrow, the next day, and every day, all day long), staring at their papers so that their eyes would not meet.

But the minute hand of the electric clock jumped toward 9:15, and Nerzhin suddenly remembered. He was not really in the mood just at present to talk about the rational society, but maybe this was as good a time as any. He locked the left-hand side of his desk, where his more important records were kept, and, without tidying up his papers or turning off the desk lamp, went out into the hallway, cigarette in mouth. He sauntered over to the glass door that opened onto the back stairs and gave it a push. As expected, it was unlocked.

Nerzhin took a casual look behind him. No one to be seen along the hallway. He stepped briskly across the threshold, from wooden floor to concrete floor, keeping his hand on the door so that he could close it noiselessly, and set off up the stairs, into the gathering gloom, drawing on his cigarette occasionally to help him see his way.

The Iron Mask's window was unlit. A band of fading light filtered through one of the outer windows onto the upper landing.

After twice tangling with junk dumped on the staircase, Nerzhin called out from the top step in a subdued voice, "Is anyone there?"

A voice, which might or might not belong to Gerasimovich, called out, "Who's that?"

"It's . . . only me." Nerzhin pronounced the words slowly, in order to help the other man recognize him, and pulled on his cigarette so that the glow would light up his face.

A narrow beam from Gerasimovich's pocket flashlight indicated the block of wood on which Nerzhin had sat the day before, after the visit. Gerasimovich perched on one just like it.

A throng of invisible witnesses—the serf artist's paintings—lurked on the walls around them.

"There you are, you see, after all our years in jail, we're greenhorns when it comes to conspiracy," Gerasimovich said. "We omitted to take the simplest precaution. The newcomer hasn't given himself away, but the person waiting in the dark must not call out. We should have thought of some sort of password for you to use on the stairs."

"Ye-e-es," Nerzhin drawled, taking his seat. "We certainly have our work cut out. We're busy enough earning our bread and trying to save our souls, but we also have to learn to hold our own against the overfed apparatchiks of the KGB. How many of them are there? A couple of million? We have to live so many lives in one lifetime. No wonder we can't keep up! How do we know Mamurin isn't lying on his bed in the dark? If he is, we might as well be having this conversation in Shikin's office."

"I made sure before coming here; he's in Number Seven. If he comes back, we will be aware of him first. So let's get on with it."

His words were businesslike, but he sounded tired and distracted.

"Actually, I was going to ask you to postpone our talk. But the fact is that I'll be leaving this place any day now."

"Is that definite?"

"Yes."

"As a matter of fact, I will be leaving, too, though not quite so soon. I haven't given satisfaction."

"If only we knew that you and I will find ourselves in the same transit prison, we could have our talk then—plenty of time for it there. But prison history teaches us never to put off a conversation."

"Yes. I've learned that lesson myself."

"All right, then. You doubt whether it's possible to construct a rational society."

"I doubt it very much. To the point of total disbelief."

"And yet it's not at all complicated. But constructing it is a job for the elite, not the asinine hoi polloi. And the society to be constructed is not a 'democratic' one or a 'socialist' one; these are secondary characteristics. The society to be constructed is an intellectual one. It will of necessity also be rational."

"So that's it," Nerzhin drawled, disappointed. "You've outlined your plan in three sentences. But it would take more than three evenings to make sense of them. To begin with, how do you distinguish between 'intellectual' and 'rational'? We know all about the rational society. French rationalists have already made one great Revolution. Spare us any more of that!"

"They weren't rationalists, just windbags. The intellectuals haven't carried out their Revolution yet."

"And they never will. They're like tadpoles—big heads and nothing else. An intellectual society . . . how do you visualize it? It would obviously have nothing to do with ethics and religion?"

"Not necessarily. We can make provision for them."

"Make provision! But that's just what you're not doing. An intellectual society—what do we imagine it would be like? Engineers without priests. Everything functioning beautifully, a perfectly rational economy, everybody in the right job—and a rapid accumulation of all good things. But that's not enough, take it from me! Society's aims must not be purely material!"

"Adjustments can be made later on. But for the time being, most of the countries in the world. . . ."

"I don't want to talk about the time being! And later on will be too late! You talk about a rational social structure. Then you tell me it will be nonsocialist. Well, I don't give a damn about that; the form of property ownership is of minimal importance, and who knows which is best. But when you say 'not democratic,' that frightens me. What does that mean? Why?"

Out of the pitch darkness, Gerasimovich answered precisely, choosing his words as carefully as a fastidious writer.

"We have been starved of freedom, so we think that freedom should have no limits. But unless limits are set to freedom, there can be no well-adjusted society. The restrictions, however, must not be of the kind that shackle us now. And people must be kept honestly informed, not deluded. We think of democracy as a sun that never sets. But what does democracy really mean? Truckling to the uncouth majority. And that means accepting mediocrity as the norm, pruning the highest and most delicate growths. The votes of a hundred or a thousand blockheads set the course for the enlightened."

"Hm-m." Nerzhin seemed to be at a loss. "This is all new to me. . . . I don't understand . . . don't know . . . must think about it. . . . I'm used to the idea of democracy. What would we have in place of democracy?"

"Equitable inequality. Inequality based on talent, natural or cultivated. You can please yourself whether you call it 'the authoritarian state' or 'the rule of the intellectual elite.' It will be rule by selfless, completely disinterested, luminous people."

"Heavens above! As an ideal, that's just fine. But how is your elite to be selected? And, above all, how do you persuade the rest that this is the true elite? After all, a man's intellectual capacity isn't stamped on his brow, and honesty doesn't give off a glow. We were promised that it would be just like that under socialism; our rulers would be clad in light, like angels—and look at the ugly customers who crawled out of the woodwork. All sorts of questions arise. What about political parties? Or rather, how do we dispense with political parties, the old type and—heaven forfend—the new type? Mankind awaits the prophet who can tell us how to do without political parties altogether. Party membership always means leveling down to the majority, accepting discipline, saying things you don't mean. Every party warps the individual and perverts justice. The leader of the opposition criticizes the government not because it has really made a mistake but because—well, what else is the opposition for?"

"There you are—you yourself are moving away from democracy and toward my system."

"Not really! Just a tiny bit closer, perhaps. Authoritarianism, now. What are we to say about it? The state must exercise authority, of course. But what sort of authority? Moral authority! Power relying not on bayonets but on love and respect. Able to say, 'Fellow countrymen! You must not do this! It is wrong!' so that they are all conscience-stricken and know in their hearts 'This is bad! We will eschew it! We will do it no more!' What other way is there? What is called 'authoritarianism' is totalitarianism in embryo. I'd sooner have something on the Swiss model. Remember what Herzen says? The lower the authority, the more powerful it is: The most powerful is the village assembly, the most impotent man in the state is the president. . . . All right, I'm not really serious. Perhaps you and I are being a bit premature? Rational structure! It would be more rational to discuss how to escape from the irrational. We can't even do that, although it's a more immediate concern."

The voice from the darkness was unperturbed.

"That is, in fact, the main subject of our discussion."

And, as calmly as if they were talking about changing a fused valve in a circuit: "I think the time has come for us, the Russian technical intelligentsia, to change the form of government in Russia."

Nerzhin was taken aback. Not that he did not trust Gerasimovich; the very look of the man had inspired a feeling of kinship, although they had, as it happened, never talked until now.

But the quiet voice from the darkness, composed and somewhat solemn, sent a little shiver along Nerzhin's spine.

"Alas, spontaneous revolution is impossible in our country. Even in Old Russia, where those intent on subversion enjoyed almost unrestricted freedom, it took three years of war—and what a war—to stir up the people. While nowadays a joke at the tea table can cost you your head—what hope is there of revolution?"

"No need for the 'Alas,'" Nerzhin replied. "To hell with revolution: Your elite would be the first to be massacred. Culture and beauty would be eliminated; everything good would be destroyed."

"All right, forget the 'Alas.' But that's why many among us have begun to set their hopes on help from outside. That seems to me a profound and damaging mistake. What the 'Internationale' says isn't all that stupid. We look nowhere else for deliverance; let us win freedom with our own hands! You have to understand that the more prosperous, the more free and easy life becomes in the West, the less ready Western man is to fight for fools who have allowed themselves to be oppressed. And they are right; they haven't opened their own gates to the robber band. We have deserved our regime and leaders; we got ourselves into this mess, and we must get ourselves out of it."

"Their turn will come."

"Of course their turn will come. There is a destructive force in prosperity. To prolong it for a year, a day, a man will sacrifice not only all that belongs to others but all that is sacred. He will defy the dictates of common prudence. They fattened Hitler, they fattened Stalin, gave them half of Europe each; now it's China's turn. They'll gladly surrender Turkey, if that will allow them to postpone general mobilization by as much as a week. They will perish; of course they will. But we may perish first."

"Yes."

"The trouble with pinning our hopes on the Americans is that it eases our conscience and weakens our will; we win the right not to struggle, the right to submit, to take the line of least resistance and gradually degenerate. I do not agree with those who claim that over the years our people have begun to see more clearly, that something is maturing in them. Some say that it is impossible to oppress a whole people indefinitely. That's a lie! It is possible! We can see for ourselves how our people have degenerated, how uncouth they have become, how indifferent they are not only to the fate of the country, not only to the fate of their fellows, but even to their own fate and that of their children. Indifference, the organism's last self-preservative reaction, has become our defining characteristic. Hence also the popularity of vodka—unprecedented even by Russian standards. This is the terrible indifference of the man who sees his life not cracked, not chipped, but shattered, so fouled up that only alcoholic oblivion makes living still worthwhile. If vodka were prohibited, Revolution would break out immediately. But while he can charge forty-four rubles for a liter that costs ten kopecks to make, the Communist Shylock will not be tempted to enact a dry law."

Nerzhin did not react, did not stir. Gerasimovich could hardly see his face in the dim light from the lights around the camp, reflected from the ceiling. Although he knew nothing about this man at all, he had chosen to share with him thoughts that even bosom friends would not dare whisper to each other in that country.

"Corrupting the people took only thirty years. Restoring them to health will take—how long? Three hundred years? More? That is why we must hurry. Given the impossibility of a popular Revolution, the harm done by pinning our hopes on help from the outside, there remains only one way out: a palace revolt, pure and simple. As Lenin used to say, 'Give us an organization of Revolutionaries, and we will turn Russia upside down!' They threw together such an organization, and they did turn Russia upside down!"

"God forbid!"

"I don't think the creation of such an organization would be difficult for us, with the knowledge of people we have acquired in jail and our ability to pick out traitors at a glance; you and I, for instance, know that we can confide in each other, though we have never talked before. It would take only three to five thousand courageous and quick-thinking men able to handle weapons, plus a few intellectuals—"

"Like those making the atom bomb. . .?"

"We would establish links with the military chiefs—"

"Those puffed-up chickens!"

"To ensure their benevolent neutrality. And we would need to take out only Stalin, Molotov, Beria, and a few others. And immediately announce by radio that the whole of the upper, middle, and lower strata remain in place."

"Remain in place? And is that your elite?"

"For the time being! Temporarily. That is the peculiar feature of totalitarian countries; it is difficult to carry out a coup, but once you have, ruling them could not be easier. Macchiavelli said that the day after you expel the sultan, you can worship Christ in all the mosques."

"Don't jump to conclusions! We can't be sure who leads and who is led; does the sultan lead them, or do they lead him without realizing it? As for the supposed neutrality of those wild pigs of generals, who drove whole divisions onto minefields just to save themselves from the penal battalion. . . ! They'll tear anyone to ribbons to defend their sty! And then again Stalin will escape by a subterranean passage. . . . And as for your five thousand men of action, if they haven't been turned in by informants already, they'll be machine-gunned from listening posts. And anyway," Nerzhin said impatiently, "there aren't another five thousand like you, not in Russia! It's only men in prison, not so-called free men with families to care for, who can think so boldly, act so uninhibitedly, and contemplate such sacrifices. But, of course, prison is just the place from which nothing can be achieved! You invited me to pick holes in your scheme. Well, it consists of nothing *but* holes! Our overweening physicists and mathematicians need to learn that social activity also requires special study and special skills. You can't describe it in mathematical terms. But it isn't just that! It isn't just that!" (His voice was becoming too loud for the silence of the dark stairway.) "Alas, you've chosen the wrong person to advise you! I simply don't believe that anything good and durable can be constructed on this earth of ours. How can I set about advising you when I can't disentangle myself from my own doubts?"

Icily calm, Gerasimovich reminded him of Auguste Comte's assertion, before spectral analysis was invented, that mankind would never discover the chemical composition of the stars. Which they promptly did!

"When you stride along in the exercise yard with your army coat flapping," he said, "you seem quite different."

Nerzhin hesitated. He remembered what Spiridon had said yesterday—"Killing wolves is right, eating people isn't"—and Spiridon asking an airplane to drop an atom bomb on him. His naive wisdom could be overpowering, but Nerzhin resisted it as best he could.

"Well, I get carried away sometimes. But your plan requires serious thought, and I can't express myself fully all at once. Do you remember Anatole France's story about the old woman of Syracuse? She prayed to the gods to grant the island's hated tyrant a long life, because experience had taught her of old that each successive tyrant was more cruel than his predecessor. Yes, our present regime is vile, but how can you be sure that what you want will be any better? Maybe it will be worse. No, you say, just because you want it to be better. But maybe those before you wanted things to be better. They sowed rye, and what came up was goosefoot. Forget about our Revolution! You can look back . . . twenty-seven centuries! Over all those twists and turns in the meaningless journey, from the hill where the she-wolf suckled the twins, from the valley of olives where the wonder-working dreamer rode on an ass, to our own thrilling heights, our own grim gorges, through which only self-propelled cannons grind their way in single file, to our icy mountain passes where, at seventy degrees below, the freezing wind of Oymyakon blows through convicts' jackets. I can't see why we've struggled all this way, shoving one another over precipices. Poets and prophets have hymned through the centuries the shining heights of the future. Fanatics that they are, have they forgotten that on the heights hurricanes howl, vegetation is sparse, there is no water, and you can easily fall and break your neck? Shine a light, and you can see right here what may be the Castle of the Holy Grail."

"I've seen it."

"Where a knight galloped up and beheld . . . nonsense! Nobody will ever gallop up; nobody will behold anything! Give me my modest little valley where there's grass and water."

"Back to the past?" Gerasimovich rapped out.

"If only I believed that there is any backward and forward in human history! It's like an octopus, with neither back nor front. For me there's no word so devoid of meaning as 'progress.' What progress, Illarion Palych? Progress from what? To what? In those twenty-seven centuries, have people become better? kinder? or at least a bit happier? No, they've become worse, nastier, and unhappier! And all this thanks to beautiful ideas!"

"No progress? No progress?" Gerasimovich protested, forgetting the need for caution and sounding younger than his years. "That's unforgivable in a man who's had something to do with physics. Do you see no difference between mechanical and electromagnetic speed?"

"What makes you think I need airplanes? There's no healthier way to travel than on foot or on horseback! What do I need radio for? To murder the playing of great pianists? Or to send the order for my arrest to Siberia more quickly? Let them send it by post chaise."

"You must surely realize that energy will soon cost little or nothing, which means abundance of material goods. We will unfreeze the Arctic, warm Siberia, make the deserts green. In twenty or thirty years' time, foodstuffs will be as free as the air we breathe. Isn't that progress?"

"Plenty doesn't mean progress! My idea of progress is not material abundance but a general willingness to share things in short supply! But you won't achieve any of that anyway! You won't warm Siberia! You won't make the deserts bloom! It'll all be blown to bloody hell by atom bombs! And scattered to the winds by jet planes!"

"Try to look at it objectively . . . it hasn't all been mistakes—we have crept slowly upward. We have bloodied our tender mugs on jagged rocks, but nonetheless we are now at the head of the pass. . . ."

"On Oymyakon!"

"Well, we aren't burning one another at the stake anymore."

"Why bother with firewood when you've got gas chambers?"

"Still, the times when the folk meeting settled disputes with the cudgel have gone, and we have parliaments, in which reasoned argument prevails instead! Quite primitive people, after all, won the habeas corpus act! And nobody orders us to consign our wives to the overlord on our wedding night. You have to be blind not to see that manners are becoming gentler, that reason is prevailing over unreason. . . ."

"I don't see it!"

"That our conception of what it means to be human is maturing!"

A prolonged ring from an electric bell sounded throughout the building. This meant that it was 10:45, that all secret material should be handed in to be locked away and the laboratories sealed.

Both men raised their heads into the faint lamplight from the prison grounds.

Gerasimovich's pince-nez glittered like two diamonds.

"So, then, what's your conclusion? Should we just let the planet rot? Don't you think that would be a pity?"

"It would be a pity," Nerzhin whispered faintly, though there was no need to whisper now. "I feel sorry for our planet. Better to die than live to see that."

"Better to prevent it than to die," Gerasimovich answered calmly. "But in these crucial years of universal destruction or universal correction of mistakes, what other way out do you suggest? Front-line officer! Veteran jailbird!"

"I don't know . . . I don't know."

In the quarter light Nerzhin's distress was evident.

"Before the atom bomb, the Soviet system, the ramshackle, hidebound, vermin-ridden Soviet system was doomed; it could not have stood the test of time. But if our side gets the bomb, it's disaster. There is just one possibility—"

"What?" Gerasimovich pressed him.

"Perhaps . . . the new age . . . with its globalized information. . . ."

"You're the one who said you didn't need radio!"

"No . . . they can jam it. I'm saying that maybe in the new age a new means will be discovered for the Word to shatter concrete."

"Completely contradicts the laws of resistance of materials."

"Not to mention dialectical materialism. So what? Remember 'In the Beginning was the Word.' So the Word is more ancient than concrete. The Word is not to be taken lightly. Whereas your military coup is . . . just impossible."

"But in practical terms how do you envisage it?"

"I don't know. I repeat—I don't know. It's a mystery. Mushrooms, mysteriously, may not appear after the first or second shower, but sooner or later rain brings them out in profusion. Only yesterday we could never have believed that such monsters could emerge at all, but now they are everywhere. In just the same way, noble people will suddenly spring up, and their word will shatter concrete."

"Before that happens, your noble people will be carried away in hampers and baskets—weeded out, chopped up, short of a head. . . ."

## 91

# Abandon Hope, All Ye Who Enter Here

IN SPITE OF HIS FEARS AND FOREBODINGS, Monday was going well. Innokenty felt some lingering anxiety, but by early afternoon he had regained his equilibrium, and he did not lose it again. It was imperative now to take refuge in a theater for the evening so that he could stop fearing every ring at the door.

But the phone rang. It was almost theater time, and Dotty was just emerging from the bathroom.

Innokenty stood staring at the telephone, like a dog at a hedgehog.

"Dotty, answer the phone! I'm not in, and you don't know when I'll be back. They'll ruin our evening, damn them!"

Dotty had become even prettier since yesterday. She always became prettier when she was admired, and then she was admired even more and became prettier still.

Holding the skirts of her dressing gown together with one hand, she padded over to the telephone and gently but firmly picked up the receiver.

"Yes? . . . He's not at home. . . . Who, who?" Suddenly she was all affability; that little lift of the shoulders was always a sign of eagerness to please.

"Good evening, Comrade General! Yes, I'll find out right away. . . ." She quickly covered the phone with her hand and whispered, "The Boss! Sounds very friendly."

Innokenty wavered. The Boss, sounding friendly, calling in person, in the evening. . . . His wife noticed his indecision.

"Just a minute, I can hear the door opening; it could be him. Yes, it is! Ini! Don't stop to take your coat off; come quickly; the general's on the phone!"

However incorrigibly suspicious-minded the person at the other end of the telephone might be, from the tone of Dotty's voice he could almost see Innokenty hurriedly wiping his feet at the door, crossing the carpeted floor, and taking the receiver.

The Boss was in a good mood. His message was that Innokenty's posting had just been finally confirmed. He would fly out on Wednesday, changing planes in Paris. He was to hand over the last of his current work tomorrow and come along for half an hour right now to clear up one or two details. A car had already been sent for him.

Innokenty straightened up from the telephone a different man. He took such a deep breath in his happiness that the air seemed to have time to permeate his whole body. He breathed out slowly and, with the air, expelled his doubts and fears.

Incredible!

He had walked the tightrope in a crosswind without falling!

"Just imagine, Dotty, I'm flying on Wednesday! And right now. . . ."

Dotty, with one ear to the receiver, had heard it all for herself. But as she straightened up, she was obviously far from happy. Innokenty's departure alone, explicable and acceptable the day before yesterday, was hurtful and humiliating today.

"Do you think," she said, looking sulky, "the one or two details might possibly include me?"

"Yes . . . well . . . m-m-maybe."

"What did you tell them about me, anyway?"

Well, he had said something. Said something he couldn't now repeat to her, and it was too late now to play it differently.

But with the confidence she had gained yesterday, Dotty was able to speak freely.

"Ini, we've always made our discoveries together! We've always shared new experiences! You wouldn't go to see the Yellow Devil without me, would you? No, I simply can't accept it; you've got to think about the two of us!"

This was nothing compared to what she could come out with later. In the presence of foreigners, she would be repeating the most stupidly orthodox banalities, which would make Innokenty's ears burn. She would be vilifying America and buying everything she could lay her hands on there. But he was forgetting. It wouldn't be like that. He would come clean once he got there—and how much of it would she be capable of understanding?

"It will all work out, Dotty, but it takes time. Right now I have to go and present myself, complete the formalities, get to know people—"

"But I want to go right away! Right now is when I want to go! I can't be left behind!"

She did not know what she would be letting herself in for. She did not know what it was like having a twisted, round rope under slippery soles. And now he would have to spring from his perch and fly through the air, perhaps without a safety net. A second body, plump and soft and unused to hardship, could not fly beside him.

Innokenty smiled nicely and shook his wife gently by her shoulders.

"Well, I'll try. It isn't what was agreed before, but let's see how it goes now. In any case, you needn't worry. I will send for you very soon. . . ."

He kissed an unresponsive cheek. Dotty was not at all convinced. The harmony established yesterday was forgotten.

"Anyway, get dressed now—no need to hurry. We will miss the first act, but that won't spoil the whole thing. . . . We'll get there for Act Two. . . . Anyway I'll give you a tinkle from the ministry."

He scarcely had time to don his uniform before the driver rang the doorbell. It was neither Viktor, who usually drove him, nor Kostya. This driver was a lean, lively fellow with a pleasant, intelligent face. He went down the stairs jauntily, almost side by side with Innokenty, twirling the ignition key on its cord.

"I don't remember seeing you before," Innokenty said, buttoning his overcoat as he went.

"I even remember your stairway; I've picked you up twice before."

The driver's smile was genuine but vaguely mischievous. It would be good to have a bright fellow like this driving your own car.

They drove off. Innokenty had taken the rear seat. The driver twice tried to make a joke over his shoulder, but Innokenty wasn't listening. Suddenly the car swerved sharply and pulled up flush with the pavement. A young man wearing a soft hat and an overcoat pinched in at the waist was standing at the curb with his finger raised.

"A mechanic, from our garage," the amiable driver explained, and made as if to open the right-hand front door. But the door simply refused to open; the lock was jammed.

The driver swore without exceeding the limits of urban decency and said, "Comrade Counselor! Could he possibly sit next to you? It's a bit awkward, because he's my boss."

"Yes, of course," Innokenty readily agreed, making room for him. He was intoxicated, overexcited, mentally holding out his hand for his letter of appointment and visa, imagining himself boarding the morning plane at Vnukovo the day after tomorrow; but he would not begin to relax before he got to Warsaw, and even there a telegram might arrive to stop his journey.

The mechanic, gripping a long lighted cigarette with the corner of his mouth, got into the car with an offhand "All right by you?" and plopped down beside Innokenty.

The car jerked forward.

Innokenty scowled at him in disgust (What a boor!) but was soon absorbed in his thoughts again, ignoring the route.

Puffing at his cigarette, the mechanic had already half filled the car with smoke.

Time to put him in his place.

"Could you perhaps open the window!" Innokenty said, raising just his right eyebrow.

Irony was lost on the mechanic. Instead of opening the window, he lay back in his seat, took a piece of paper from his inside pocket, unfolded it, and held it out to Innokenty.

"Comrade Chief! Could you kindly read this for me? I'll shine a light."

The car turned sharply into a steep ill-lit street, possibly Pushechnaya. The mechanic shone a pocket flashlight on a scrap of pinkish paper. Shrugging his shoulders, Innokenty grudgingly accepted the sheet of paper and began reading casually, as if to himself.

"Authorized. Deputy Prosecutor General, USSR. . . ."

He was still too engrossed in his own thoughts to wonder whether the mechanic was illiterate, simply incapable of understanding the document, or perhaps drunk and anxious to confide in somebody.

"Warrant for the arrest . . ." he read, still not taking in what he was reading—"of Volodin, Innokenty Artemievich, born 1919"—and only then did a single great needle pierce his body from top to bottom and scalding heat envelop it. Innokenty opened his mouth, but before he could utter a sound, before the hand holding the pink page fell on his knees, the "mechanic" had gripped his shoulder in a painful hold and growled menacingly: "Easy now, take it easy; don't move or I'll strangle you here!"

He blinded Volodin with the flashlight, blew cigarette smoke into his face . . . and retrieved the document.

Innokenty had read that he was arrested, which spelled disaster and the end of his life, but for one brief moment what he could not bear was the man's insolence, his vise-like grip, the cigarette smoke, and the light shining in his face.

"Let go!" he cried, trying to free himself with his own weak fingers. It had finally sunk in that this really was a warrant for his arrest, but it might, he thought, be merely an unfortunate coincidence that he had landed in this car and given the "mechanic" a lift; he imagined that if only he could shake them off and get to his boss in the ministry, the warrant would be canceled.

He tugged convulsively at the handle of the left side door, but it would not give; it, too, was jammed.

"Driver! You'll answer for this! What is the meaning of this provocation?" Innokenty cried angrily,

"I serve the Soviet Union, Counselor," the driver rapped out, with an insolent glance over his shoulder.

Obeying the traffic regulations, the car circled the whole brightly lit expanse of Lubyanka Square as though it were making a valedictory round, giving Innokenty one last look at this world and the five-story bulk of the amalgamated Old and New Lubyankas, where he was to end his life.

Cars clustered at the traffic lights and then broke free, trolleys swished past, buses honked, people walked by in dense crowds, and no one knew or saw the victim being dragged to execution before their very eyes.

A little red flag, lit up by a searchlight from a recess in the roof, flapped in a gap between the columns of the tower above the Old Great Lubyanka. It was like Garshin's little red flower, which had absorbed all the world's evil. Two insensate stone naiads, semi-recumbent, gazed down scornfully at the miniature citizens pottering about below.

The car drove past the facade of the world-famous building, which levied tribute in human lives from all continents, and turned into Great Lubyanka Street.

"Let go, I tell you!" Innokenty was still struggling to shake free of the mechanic's fingers, which were digging into his shoulder near the neck.

The black iron gate opened as soon as the car pointed its radiator at them and closed again as soon as it had passed through.

The car coasted through the dark gateway into the yard.

The mechanic had relaxed his hold in the gateway. Once in the yard, he removed his hand from Innokenty's neck. "Out we get!" he said peremptorily as he scrambled from the car.

By now it was obvious that he was perfectly sober.

The driver also got out.

"Out with you! Hands behind your back!" he ordered. Could this icy voice of command really belong to the jester of a little while back?

Innokenty climbed out of the mantrap on wheels, straightened up, and, although there was no obvious reason for him to do so, obediently put his hands behind his back.

The arrest had been rough but not so terrifying as might be expected. He even felt a certain relief: no more need to fear, no need to struggle, no need to plot and plan. He felt the pleasurable numb relaxation that sometimes pervades the body of a wounded man.

Innokenty surveyed the small yard, which was patchily lit by two or three lights and lamps here and there in upper windows. Walled in by towering buildings, the yard was like the bottom of a well.

"No looking around!" the driver barked. "Move!"

With Innokenty in the middle, the three of them filed past uninterested MGB personnel, under a low arch, down steps into another little yard, dark under a low roof, turned left, and discovered a neat front door like the entrance to an eminent physician's office.

The door opened onto a short, very tidy corridor flooded with electric light. Its freshly painted floor seemed to have been washed very recently, and a strip of carpet ran down the middle.

The driver made a strange clicking noise with his tongue, as if he were calling a dog. But there was no dog.

The corridor ended at a glass door with faded curtains on the other side. The door was reinforced by a steel grille of the sort used to fence flower beds at railway stations. On the door, instead of a doctor's nameplate, there was a sign saying "Reception of Prisoners."

There was no line.

They rang. The bell was an antique with a handle to turn. After a while, someone peeked around the curtain, then opened the door: a guard with a long, blank face wearing sky blue epaulets with a sergeant's white stripes across them. The driver took the pink form from the mechanic and showed it to the guard. He scanned it indifferently, as a drowsy pharmacist disturbed in the night might read a prescription, and the two of them went inside.

Innokenty and the mechanic stood in profound silence outside the firmly closed door.

"Reception of Prisoners" made him think of another sign meaning much the same: "Mortuary." Innokenty couldn't even be bothered to take a good look at the smart aleck in the sharp overcoat who was playing this silly game with him. He should perhaps have been protesting, shouting, demanding justice; but he had even forgotten that he was clasping his hands behind his back and continued to hold them there. Thinking had come to a dead stop. He stared like a man under hypnosis at the words "Reception of Prisoners."

There was the sound of a key turning smoothly in an English lock. The long-faced guard nodded them in and went ahead, making those dog-calling clicks with his tongue.

Still no dog.

This corridor was just as brightly lit and just as clinically clean.

There were two doors in the wall, both painted olive green. The sergeant flung one of them open and said, "Inside."

Innokenty went in. He had scarcely had time to look around and see that the room was empty except for a large, rough table and a pair of stools, and that it was windowless, when two of them jumped on him, the driver from the one side, the mechanic from behind, held him with all four arms, and adroitly searched his pockets.

"What's the meaning of this thuggery?" Innokenty cried feebly. "What right do you have?" He resisted briefly, but the realization that this was not a mugging but men carrying out a routine duty robbed his resistance of force and his voice of conviction.

They removed his wristwatch and fished out two notebooks, a fountain pen, and a handkerchief. He caught sight also of the narrow silver epaulets in their hands and was struck by the coincidence that they, too, belonged to the diplomatic service and had the same number of stars as he did. They relaxed their rough embrace, and the mechanic held out the handkerchief.

"Take it."

Innokenty shuddered.

"After it's been in your dirty hands?" he said shrilly.

The handkerchief fell to the floor.

"You'll get a receipt for your valuables," the driver said, and they both hurried out.

The long-faced sergeant, however, was in no hurry. Glancing at the floor, he advised Innokenty to pick up the handkerchief.

Innokenty did not bend down.

"What have they done? Have they ripped my epaulets off?" He had only now realized, feeling under his overcoat, that they were no longer on the shoulders of his uniform. He was furious.

"Hands behind your back!" the sergeant said tonelessly. "March!"

He clicked his tongue.

Still no dog.

Rounding a sharp bend, they found themselves in another corridor, with facing rows of small olive green doors in close succession, each with a shiny oval number plate. A careworn middle-aged woman in army regulation skirt and tunic, and the same light blue epaulets with sergeant's white stripes, was walking between the rows of doors. As Innokenty and the guard appeared from around the bend, she took a quick look through the peephole in one of the doors. When they drew level, she let the flap fall back over the peephole and looked at Innokenty, as though he had walked that way hundreds of times before and she was not a bit surprised to see him walking there yet again. Her face was somber. She inserted a long key into the steel casing of the lock on a door numbered 8, unlocked it noisily, and nodded to him.

"Inside."

Innokenty crossed the threshold, and before he could turn around and ask for an explanation, the door was shut behind him and the key grated the lock.

So this was now to be his home! For a day? For months? For years and years? His quarters could not be called a room or even a cell because, as we know from literature, a cell must have a window, if only a little one, and room to pace the floor. Here, not only pacing the floor, not only lying down, but even sitting comfortably was impossible. A small table and stool occupied almost all the floor space. If you sat on the stool, you could not stretch your legs out freely.

There was nothing else in the cell. To chest height the walls were paneled and painted dark green. The upper part of the walls and the ceiling were whitewashed and glaringly illuminated by a big two-hundred-watt electric bulb enclosed in a wire basket.

Innokenty sat down. Twenty minutes ago, he had still been imagining himself arriving in America and, of course, reminding them of his telephone call to the embassy. Twenty minutes ago, his past life had seemed to him a harmonious whole, every event lit by the steady light of premeditation and welded to other events by white flashes of good fortune. But after the last twenty minutes, his whole past life seemed to him just as certainly an agglomeration of errors, a heap of meaningless fragments.

Sounds from the corridor reached him only twice, when a nearby door was opened and closed. Every minute the little disk over the glazed peephole was disturbed and a single inquisitorial eye observed Innokenty. The door was four fingers thick, and the spy hole ran right through it, a cone of which the optic was the apex. Innokenty surmised that it was made this way so that there was nowhere in this torture chamber for the prisoner to escape the guard's gaze.

It was hot and stuffy. He took off his warm winter overcoat and squinted miserably at the ragged holes where his epaulets had been torn from his uniform. Finding neither a nail nor any sort of protuberance on the walls, he laid his overcoat and hat on the little table.

Strangely, now that lightning had struck and he has been arrested, Innokenty felt no fear. On the contrary, his mind was released from its temporary paralysis, and he began going over the blunders he had made.

Why had he not read the warrant in full? Was it drawn up correctly? Did it have the official stamp? The public prosecutor's authorization? Ah, yes, of course, it invoked the public prosecutor's authority right at the beginning. On what date was the warrant signed? What was he charged with? Did the Boss know about it when he sent for me? He must have known. So his summons was a trick? But why this bizarre procedure, why this farce with the "driver" and the "mechanic"?

In one of his pockets his hand felt something small and hard. He took it out. An elegant miniature pencil, it had detached itself from a notebook. Innokenty was greatly cheered by this little pencil: It could prove to be very useful! Rank amateurs! Even here in the Lubyanka, they were rank amateurs, didn't even know how to search a prisoner! Trying to think of the best place to hide the pencil, Innokenty broke it in two and eased one half under the sole of each of his shoes.

Heavens, how careless! He hadn't noticed what he was accused of! Perhaps his arrest had nothing at all to do with that telephone call? Perhaps it was a mistake, a coincidence? What was the correct way to behave now?

Maybe there was nothing they could accuse him of? Probably not. Let's just arrest him!

He had not been there very long, but several times already he had heard the steady hum of some sort of machine beyond the wall farthest from the corridor. A disturbing thought suddenly occurred to Innokenty. What sort of machine would you expect to find in a place like this? This was a prison, not a factory. Why the machinery? Any man of the forties had heard so much about mechanical means of destroying people that something sinister immediately came to mind. A thought at once bizarre and yet highly probable flashed through Innokenty's mind: that this was a machine for grinding the bones of murdered prisoners. He felt frightened.

Yes—by now the thought stung worse than ever—what a mistake not even to read the warrant through, not to begin protesting his innocence then and there! He had submitted to arrest so meekly that they must be convinced of his guilt! How could he have failed to protest? Why, oh why, had he not protested? It must look for all the world as if he had been expecting arrest, that he was resigned to it.

He was cut to the quick by this fatal mistake! His first thought was to jump up, thump and kick, yell at the top of his voice that he was innocent, but second and wiser thoughts prevailed: None of that would come as a surprise to them; no doubt people were always banging and shouting here, and his silence in the first few minutes had complicated things anyway.

To think that he had let himself be taken so easily! A high-ranking diplomat allowing himself to be plucked from his apartment, from the streets of Moscow, carried off, and locked up in this torture chamber with no attempt to resist, without a sound.

There could be no escape from here! No escape from here!

Unless, perhaps, the Chief was still expecting him? Was there any way to get through to the Chief, if only under escort? How to find out?

No, his thoughts were becoming no clearer, only more confused and complicated.

The machine beyond the wall hummed and was silent by turns.

Innokenty's eyes, blinded by the artificial light that was too bright for this high but narrow three cubic meters of space, had for some time sought relief by resting on the single black square that broke the monotony of the ceiling. This square of wire mesh was to all appearances an air vent, though it was uncertain what it led to or away from. Then, suddenly, it was starkly obvious that this vent . . . was not a vent at all, that poisonous gas was gradually released through it, perhaps produced by that very same humming machine, that they had been pumping gas in from the very first minute he had been shut in there, and that such a hermetically sealed cell, with not even the narrowest of cracks between door and floor, could have no other purpose.

That was why they kept spying on him through the peephole—to see whether he was still conscious or already gassed.

And that was why his thoughts were so confused; he was losing consciousness! That was why for some time now he had been short of breath! That was why there was such a pounding in his head!

Gas was seeping in! Colorless! Odorless!

Terror! The primitive animal terror that unites predators and their prey in a single stampeding herd fleeing from a forest fire gripped Innokenty, and incapable by now of any other thought, he began hammering on the door with fists and feet, calling upon any living being.

"Open up! Open up! I'm suffocating! Give me air!"

That was another reason why the spy hole was conical: No fist could reach the glass to break it!

An unblinking eye pressed against the glass on the other side and gloated over the wreckage of Innokenty.

What a spectacle! The detached eye, the eye without a face, the eye that has concentrated all expression in itself! . . . now watching you die!

There was no way out!

Innokenty collapsed onto the stool.

The gas was suffocating him. . . .

# 92

## Keep Forever

SUDDENLY THE DOOR, which was always crashed shut, opened quite noiselessly.

The long-faced guard stood in the narrow opening and from inside the cell, not from the corridor, asked in a menacing growl: "What's all this banging?"

Innokenty was relieved. If the guard was not afraid to enter, there was no risk of poisoning yet.

"I'm not feeling well!" he said hesitantly. "Give me some water!"

"Well, just remember," the guard said sternly, "no banging, in any circumstances; otherwise, you'll be punished."

"But what if I feel ill? If I need to call somebody?"

"And don't raise your voice! What you do if you need to call somebody," the guard explained in his sullen drawl, "is you wait till the peephole opens and raise a finger without speaking."

He backed out and locked the door.

The machine beyond the wall started up, then fell silent.

The door opened again, this time with a clatter. It dawned on Innokenty that they were trained to open doors noisily or quietly as required.

The guard gave him a mug of water.

"Listen," said Innokenty, taking the mug. "I'm unwell, I need to lie down."

"Not allowed in the box."

"Where? Not allowed where?" (He needed to talk to somebody; even this blockhead would do.)

But the guard had already backed out of the cell and was closing the door.

Innokenty pulled himself together.

"Listen, call your superior officer! Why have I been arrested?"

The door was locked.

("In the box," he had said, using the English word. So that's their cynical term for this sort of cell? Accurate enough, I suppose.)

Innokenty took a sip of water. He lost his thirst at once. The mug's capacity was three hundred grams; it was enameled, greenish, with a strange picture of a cat wearing glasses, pretending to read a book, but furtively eyeing a cheeky bird hopping around nearby.

They couldn't, surely, have chosen this picture especially for the Lubyanka? But how apt it was! The cat was the Soviet regime, the book the Stalin Constitution, and the sparrow a thinking individual.

Innokenty could not suppress a wry smile, and this suddenly brought home to him the immensity of the disaster that had befallen him.

He would never have believed himself capable of smiling after less than a half hour in the Lubyanka's dungeons.

(It was worse for Shchevronok in the neighboring box; it would have taken more than that cat to raise a smile from him right then.)

Moving his overcoat to make room, Innokenty put the mug on the table.

The lock clattered. The door opened. A lieutenant entered holding a piece of paper. The sergeant's joyless face could be seen behind him.

Innokenty, in his dove gray diplomatic uniform embroidered with gold palm leaves, rose unhurriedly to meet him.

"Listen, Lieutenant, what is this all about? Is there some misunderstanding? Let me see the warrant; I didn't read it properly."

"Surname?" the lieutenant asked tonelessly, looking glassy-eyed at Innokenty.

"Volodin," Innokenty conceded, eager to clarify the situation.

"First name, patronymic?"

"Innokenty Artemievich."

"Year of birth?" The lieutenant kept referring to his piece of paper.

"1919."

"Place of birth?"

"Leningrad."

And with that, just when the time for explanations had arrived and the counselor, second class, was expecting them, the lieutenant withdrew and the door closed, almost pinching the counselor.

Innokenty sat down and shut his eyes. He was beginning to feel the power of those mechanical claws.

The machine started humming.

Then silence.

Things great and small came into his mind, all of them so urgent an hour ago that his legs ached to be up and doing.

Here in the box there was no room to take a single full step, let alone to run.

The flap of the spy hole moved. Innokenty raised a finger. The door was opened by the woman with blue epaulets and a stupid, heavy face.

"I want to . . . you know," he said meaningfully.

"Hands behind your back! Move it!" the woman snapped, and Innokenty, obeying her nod, went out into the corridor, which seemed pleasantly cool after the stuffiness of the box.

After a short walk the woman nodded at a door.

"In here!"

He went in. The door was locked behind him.

There was an aperture in the floor and two iron footrests. Otherwise, the minimal floor space and the walls of this little cell were covered with red tiles. Water splashed refreshingly in the depths.

Glad that here at least he would get a rest from uninterrupted surveillance, Innokenty squatted.

But he heard a click from the other side of the door, looked up, and saw that here, too, there was a conical spy hole and that the importunate eye was watching him closely, not at intervals but continuously.

Embarrassed, Innokenty stood up. The door was flung open before he could raise his finger to say "Ready."

"Hands behind! Move!" the woman said calmly.

Back in the box, Innokenty felt a sudden need to know the time. Unthinkingly, he pulled back his cuff, but "the time" was no longer there.

He sighed and began studying the cat on the mug, but before he got lost in thought, the door was unlocked, and someone new, a fat-faced, broad-shouldered fellow in a gray smock, asked him his name.

"I've already answered that!" Innokenty said indignantly.

"Name?" the newcomer repeated tonelessly, like a radio operator calling another station.

"Oh, well—Volodin."

"Pick up your things. Walk," Gray Smock said impassively.

Innokenty took his overcoat and cap from the little table and walked. He was pointed toward the room he had entered first and in which his epaulets had been ripped off and his watch and notebooks taken from him.

The pocket handkerchief was no longer lying on the floor.

"Listen, my belongings have been taken from me," he complained.

"Undress!" was the reply from the guard in the gray smock.

Innokenty was flabbergasted. "What for?" he asked.

The guard looked him sternly in the eye.

"You Russian?" he asked harshly.

"Yes." Innokenty, never at a loss for words, could think of nothing else to say.

"Undress!"

"Don't non-Russians have to, then?" A dismal attempt at humor.

The guard maintained a stony silence and waited.

Innokenty assumed a contemptuous smile, shrugged, sat down on the stool, took off his shoes, then his uniform, and offered it to the guard. He attached no ritual importance to uniforms, but nonetheless felt a certain respect for his gold-trimmed garments.

"Drop it!" said Gray Smock, pointing to the floor.

Innokenty hesitated. The guard wrested the tawdry uniform from him, flung it on the floor, and barked: "Naked!"

"What d'you mean, naked?"

"Naked!"

"But that's completely impossible, Comrade. It's cold here, you know!"

"You'll be stripped forcibly," the guard warned him.

Innokenty thought awhile. They had assaulted him once, and it looked as though they would assault him again. Shivering with cold and disgust, he removed his silk underwear and obediently tossed it onto the same heap.

"Socks off!"

Innokenty removed his socks and stood barefoot on the wooden floor. His legs were hairless and a delicate white, like the rest of his unresisting body.

"Open your mouth. Wider. Say 'Aah.' Again, longer—'Aaa-aaa-aaah!' Now raise your tongue."

As though Innokenty were a horse for sale, the guard's dirty fingers plucked at one of his cheeks, then the other, the pouch under one eye, the pouch under the other, reassured himself that nothing was hidden under the tongue, inside the cheeks, or in the eyes, tipped Innokenty's head back with a firm push, so that the light shone into his nostrils, inspected both ears, tugging at the lobes, ordered him to spread his fingers, ascertained that there was nothing between them, and made him flap his arms to check that there was nothing under his armpits either. Then, in the same unanswerable robotic voice: "Take your member in your hands. Turn back the skin. Farther.

Right, that's enough. Move your member to the right and upward. To the left and upward. Right, let go. Stand with your back to me. Legs apart. Wider. Bend over and touch the floor. Legs wider apart. Part your buttocks with your hands. Right. Good. Now squat. Quickly! Once more!"

Whenever he had thought about being arrested, Innokenty had visualized a furious intellectual dual with Leviathan—the state. He was keyed up, ready to defend heroically his life and beliefs. He had never imagined that it would all be so crude, so stupid—and so ineluctable. The people waiting for him in the Lubyanka, low-ranking, obtuse people were uninterested in him as an individual and in the act that had brought him there but had a zealous concern for trivialities that took him by surprise and left him helpless. And anyway, what form could resistance take, and where would it get him? The repeated demands they made on him seemed so insignificant compared with the great battle ahead that it was not worth digging his heels in—but the details of this nonsensical procedure taken together served to break the will of the newly arrested prisoner.

So Innokenty bore all these indignities in dejected silence.

The searcher silently indicated a stool nearer the door, on which Innokenty, still naked, was to sit. He disliked the idea of contact between his naked body and this new cold object. But as soon as he sat down, he was pleasantly surprised to find that the wooden stool seemed to impart some warmth.

Innokenty had experienced many acute pleasures in his life, but this was something new. Pressing his elbows to his chest and drawing his knees up higher, he felt still warmer.

While he sat like that, the searcher stood over the heap of clothing, shaking, probing, holding things up to the light. He was kind enough not to detain the underpants and socks for long. With the underpants he just felt along the ribs and seams, pinch by pinch, then tossed them at Innokenty's feet. The socks he detached from their elastic garters, turned inside out, and tossed to Innokenty. After feeling the seams and folds of the undershirt, he tossed that, too, in the direction of the door, so that Innokenty could now dress, making his body still more blissfully warm.

The searcher then took out a big pocket knife with a crude wooden handle, opened it, and got to work on the shoes. He disdainfully ejected the fragments of pencil and repeatedly flexed the soles with a look of intense concentration, searching for anything hard concealed there. Slitting the insole with his knife, he did in fact tease out a small piece of steel and placed it on the table. Then he picked up an awl and drove it right through one heel.

Innokenty watched him intently as he worked and was able to think how sick he must get of fingering other people's underwear, cutting up their footwear, and peering into their back passages year after year. That must be why the searcher had such a grim, forbidding look on his face.

But the misery and tedium of watching and waiting snuffed out these flickerings of ironic thought. The searcher began stripping the gold facings, the service buttons, and collar tabs from Innokenty's uniform. Then he slit open the lining and felt under it. He took as long again over the creases and seams of Innokenty's trousers. The winter overcoat gave him still more trouble; deep down in the padding he seemed to hear a rustle, not that of padding (a note sewn in there? addresses? an ampoule of poison?), and ripping open the lining, he searched lengthily, wearing a look of such concentration and concern that he might have been operating on a human heart.

The search took a long time, perhaps over an hour. At last, the searcher gathered up his trophies: braces, elastic garters (he had already told Innokenty that these were not allowed in prison), tie, tiepin, cuff links, the piece of steel from the welt of his shoe, two fragments of pencil, the gold facings, all the decorations from the uniform, and several buttons. Only then did Innokenty fully realize how thoroughly the man had done his destructive work. Of all the indignities heaped upon him that evening, the worst was not the slits in the soles of his shoes, not the ripped lining, not the padding sticking out from the armpits of his overcoat; no, the absence of almost all of his buttons when they had already deprived him of suspenders was the affront that Innokenty felt most acutely.

"Why have you cut off my buttons?" he exclaimed.

"Not allowed," the guard growled.

"What do you mean? How am I supposed to go around, then?"

"Tie yourself up with string," the man answered sullenly, already at the door.

"What nonsense is this? What string? Where am I supposed to get it from?"

But the door was slammed and locked.

Innokenty refrained from knocking and arguing. He had to think himself lucky that they had left him buttons on his overcoat and one or two elsewhere.

He was proving to be a quick learner.

He had not had long to enjoy the spaciousness of his new quarters, clutching his trouser tops as he walked around to stretch his legs, when the key grated in the lock again and a new guard appeared. This one wore a white smock—not, however, of the first freshness. He looked at Innokenty as if he were some long-familiar object that had always been in this room and abruptly ordered him to strip naked.

Innokenty wanted to answer indignantly, to sound threatening, but he was choking with resentment and could only utter a feeble squawk of protest.

"But I've just stripped once! Couldn't somebody have warned me?"

Obviously not, because the new arrival simply waited with a blank, bored look for him to carry out the order.

What surprised Innokenty most in those he met here was their ability to remain silent where normal people usually respond.

He was getting used to the rhythmic routine of implicit and automatic obedience. He took off his shoes and undressed.

"Sit!"

The guard pointed to the stool on which Innokenty had sat for so long already.

The naked prisoner sat submissively without wondering why. (The free man's habit of thinking over his actions before performing them was atrophying fast, now that others were thinking so effectively for him.) The guard's fingers gripped the nape of the prisoner's neck roughly. The cold cutting edge of a machine was pressed hard against the top of his head.

Innokenty winced.

"What are you doing?" he said, making a feeble effort to free himself from the clutching fingers. "What right have you to do this? I'm not under arrest yet." (He meant that he had not been formally charged.)

But the barber did not relax his grip. He went on shearing. The spark of rebellion fizzled out. The proud young diplomat, used to alighting nonchalantly from intercontinental aircraft, gazing absently through half-closed eyes at the daytime dazzle of bustling European capitals, was now merely a naked male person, all skin and bones, and with a half-shaven head.

Innokenty's silky light-brown hair fell as sadly and soundlessly as snowflakes. He caught one wisp and rubbed it gently between his fingers. He was full of love for himself and the life that was leaving him.

He remembered deciding that submissiveness would be interpreted as an admission of guilt. He remembered resolving to resist, to protest, to argue, to demand to see the prosecutor, but against all reason he was helpless, paralyzed by the pleasurable indifference of a man freezing in the snow. The barber finished shaving his head, then made him stand and raise his arms, one by one, and shaved his armpits. He then squatted and began shaving off Innokenty's pubic hair. This was a new sensation. It tickled. Innokenty involuntarily shrank, and the barber made an impatient noise.

"May I dress now?" Innokenty asked when the procedure was over.

But the barber left without a word, locking the door behind him.

A crafty inner voice told Innokenty not to get dressed in a hurry this time. He felt an unpleasant prickling in the newly shaved tender spots. Running his hand over a head that seemed unfamiliar (he could not remember being close-cropped since childhood), he felt a strange prickly stubble and bumps on his skull that he had not known about.

He decided to put on his underwear, after all, and was about to slip into his trousers when the lock rattled and yet another guard came in, one with a purplish fleshy nose. He was carrying a large piece of cardboard.

"Name?"

"Volodin," the prisoner answered. He had given up resisting these senseless, sickening repetitions.

"First name and patronymic?"

"Innokenty Artemievich."

"Year of birth?"

"1919."

"Place of birth?"

"Leningrad."

"Strip naked."

Scarcely realizing what was happening, he took off the rest of his clothes. His undershirt, which he had placed on the edge of the table, fell onto the dirty floor, but he did not stoop to pick it up.

The purple-nosed guard inspected Innokenty minutely from various angles, systematically recording his findings on his index card. His close attention to birthmarks and facial details told Innokenty that these characteristics were now a matter of record.

This one left in turn.

Innokenty sat limply on his stool and made no effort to dress.

The door rattled again. A stout, dark-haired woman in a snow-white smock came in. Her face was coarse and forbidding, her comportment that of an educated person.

Innokenty pulled himself together, reached quickly for his underpants and half concealed his nakedness. But the woman darted a contemptuous, utterly unfeminine glance at him and, thrusting even further her jutting lower lip, asked, "You—have you got lice?"

Innokenty, offended, looked straight into her black eyes and, still holding his underpants together in front of him, said, "I'm a diplomat."

"What's that got to do with anything? Do you have any complaints?"

"I want to know why I've been arrested! I want to read the warrant! I want to see the prosecutor!" Innokenty blurted out.

The woman frowned.

"You misunderstood my question," she said wearily. "No venereal diseases?"

"What?"

"Have you ever had gonorrhea, syphilis, or soft chancre? Leprosy? Tuberculosis? Any other complaints?"

She left without waiting for an answer.

The very first guard, the one with the long face, came in. Innokenty was almost pleased to see him. This one had not insulted or harmed him.

"Why aren't you getting your clothes on?" the guard asked gruffly. "Get dressed quickly."

Easier said than done! Alone and locked in again, Innokenty struggled to keep his trousers up with no suspenders and several buttons missing. Unable to draw on the experience of dozens of generations of prisoners, Innokenty knitted his brow and solved the problem unaided—as millions of his predecessors had done before him. He must use his shoelaces to tie around his waist and hold his fly together. (Only now did he look closely enough to see that the metal tips had been torn off his laces. Why did they go to such lengths? Unknown to Innokenty, the Lubyanka's standing orders allowed for the possibility that a prisoner might use one of these tips as a suicide weapon.)

He did not even try to tie the jacket of his uniform together.

The sergeant looked through the spy hole to check that the prisoner was dressed, unlocked the door, ordered him to keep his hands behind his back, and led him to yet another room. There, Innokenty found his old acquaintance, the guard with the purple nose.

"Shoes off!" he said by way of greeting.

This was no longer a problem; the shoes, now without laces, fell off unaided, and the socks, without their elastic garters, slipped down around his ankles.

A contraption with a vertical white gauge for measuring height stood by the wall. Purple-nose shepherded Innokenty toward it, lowered the movable bar onto his head, and recorded his height.

"You can put your shoes on," he said.

While the long-faced one at the door admonished him: "Hands behind your back!"

Hands behind your back! Although Box No. 8 was only two steps away, diagonally across the corridor.

Innokenty was locked up in his box again.

The mysterious machine on the other side of the wall was still alternately revving up and falling silent.

Innokenty slumped limply onto the stool, holding his overcoat. From the moment he had landed in the Lubyanka, he had seen nothing but blinding electric light, cramped rooms between tight walls, and silent, impassive jailers. The procedures, each more absurd than the last, seemed to him a cruel farce. He did not realize that they formed a logically calculated sequence: the preliminary body search by the operatives who arrested him; establishment of the prisoner's identity; receipt of the prisoner (not presented in person) acknowledged by the prison administration; initial prison body search on receipt; preliminary hygienic treatment; recording of marks on body; medical examination. These procedures had left him dizzy, robbed him of his ability to think straight and the will to resist. He was tormented now by one desire—to sleep. He decided that they were leaving him in peace for the time being. His first three hours in the Lubyanka had given him a new view of things, and he saw that there was only one way to make himself at home: by putting the stool on top of the table, throwing his exquisite overcoat with the astrakhan collar on the floor, and lying down on it diagonally across the box. This meant that his back was on the floor, his head raised and wedged awkwardly in one corner of the box, and his legs, bent at the knees, twisted to fit into the opposite corner. Still, for a little while, until his limbs became numb, it was bliss. But before he could sink into a deep sleep, someone flung open the door, deliberately making as much noise as possible.

A woman growled, "Get up!"

Innokenty scarcely batted an eyelid.

"Get up! Get up!" the voice overhead commanded.

"Suppose I want to sleep?"

"Get up!" the woman thundered, hovering over him like a Gorgon in a nightmare.

From his contorted position, Innokenty had difficulty rising to his feet.

"So take me where I can lie down and sleep a bit," he said feebly.

"Not permitted!" the Gorgon with the light blue epaulets snapped back and slammed the door.

Innokenty propped himself up against the wall and waited while she opened the spy hole—once, twice, three times—and studied him at length.

He took advantage of her departure to sink back onto his overcoat.

He was losing consciousness when the door crashed open again. Another big strong fellow in a white smock stood on the threshold. He would have made a heroic blacksmith or quarryman.

"Name?" he asked.

"Volodin."

"Bring your things!"

Innokenty scooped up his coat and cap from the floor and, with eyes glazing over, followed the guard on unsteady legs. He was utterly exhausted, and his feet were so numb that he could not tell whether the floor beneath them was even or not. He could hardly muster the strength to move and felt like lying down right there in the middle of the corridor.

He was led through a narrow opening bashed in the thick wall into another, dirtier corridor, where they opened a door into the anteroom to the shower room, handed him a piece of coarse soap smaller than a matchbox, and ordered him to wash.

Innokenty was reluctant to obey. He was used to tiled bathrooms with surfaces like polished mirrors, and this wooden dressing room, which might have seemed clean enough to most people, struck him as nauseatingly dirty. He forced himself to find a sufficiently dry place on the bench, undressed, and walked queasily over the wet grating that bore the prints of bare feet and shoes. He would have been glad not to undress and wash at all, but the door of the anteroom opened, and the blacksmith in the white smock ordered him to get under the shower.

A flimsy, unprisonlike door with two unglazed slits in it opened onto the shower room. There were four gratings, which Innokenty decided were also dirty, and over them four showers. The hot and cold water were just right, but Innokenty was not a bit grateful. Four showers for the use of one man! But Innokenty felt no happier. (He might have appreciated his sixteenfold advantage more if he had known that four men under a single shower was more usual in the zek's world.) The evil-smelling soap they had given him (he had handled nothing like it in his thirty years, indeed had never realized that such a thing existed) he had abandoned with a shudder in the dressing room. He splashed about for a minute or two, mainly to wash off hairs left behind by the clippers, which were prickling him in tender places, then, feeling that he had not washed but gotten dirtier, went back to dress.

Or so he thought. But the benches in the dressing room were bare. His splendid, though now mutilated, garments had been taken away, and only his shoes remained, hiding their noses under benches. The outer door was locked, and the spy hole was covered with its disk. All Innokenty could do was sit on the bench, statuesquely naked, like Rodin's *Thinker*, and meditate while he dried off.

After a while, he was given coarse underwear, the worse for frequent laundering, with the words "Inner Prison" stamped in black on the back and the belly, and a square rag with a crisscross pattern bearing the same stamp and folded in four, which he did not immediately identify as a towel. The buttons on the undergarments were of stiffened cloth. Some buttons were missing, and some of the tapes had been torn off. The skimpy drawers were too short and too tight for Innokenty and pinched him between the legs. The shirt, on the other hand, was very roomy, and the sleeves came down over his fingers. They refused to exchange these underclothes, arguing that Innokenty had already spoiled one set by putting them on.

Wearing his ill-fitting underwear, Innokenty was left sitting in the dressing room for a long time. He was told that his outer garments were still in the "cooker." The word was new to Innokenty. Even during the war, when the whole country was dotted with heat-sterilization rooms, he had never come across them. But the "cooking" of his clothes was perfectly in line with the senseless indignities inflicted on him that night. (He imagined a huge devil's frying pan.)

Innokenty tried soberly to consider his situation and what he should do. But his thoughts were kaleidoscopic: The tight drawers, the frying pan in which his tunic now lay, and the unblinking eye for which the lid of the spy hole frequently made way chased one another and merged.

The shower had driven sleep away, but a murderous weakness overcame him. He wanted to lie down on something dry and not cold, to lie there motionless, recovering the strength that was draining from him. But he could not bring himself to lie with his bare ribs against the wet, sharp-edged slats of the bench (they did not even run parallel).

The door opened, but not because they had brought his clothes from the cooker. At the shower room guard's side stood a girl with a big red face in civilian dress. Bashfully covering gaps in his underwear with his hands, Innokenty walked to the doorway. The girl ordered him to sign a copy and handed him a pink receipt—items received for storage this day, December 26, by the Inner Prison of the USSR Ministry of State Security from Volodin, I. A.: one yellow metal watch (number of watch, number of mechanism); one fountain pen trimmed with yellow metal and with matching nib; one tiepin with red stone inset; cuff links of blue stone, one pair.

Again, Innokenty waited, drooping. At last they brought his clothes. His overcoat was returned cold and undamaged, but his tunic, trousers, and shirt were crumpled, discolored, and still hot.

"Why couldn't they be as careful with the uniform as with the overcoat?" he asked indignantly.

"The coat has fur bits," the blacksmith informed him. "Use your head!"

After heat sterilization, even his own clothes seemed alien and disgusting. Clad from head to foot in strange and uncomfortable things, Innokenty was led back to his Box No. 8.

He asked for water and twice greedily drained the mug with the picture of the cat.

After this, another young woman visited him and, in return for his signature, gave him a bright blue receipt reading: "this day, December 27, received by the Inner Prison of the USSR Ministry of State Security from Volodin, I. A: one silk undershirt, one pair silk drawers, suspenders, tie."

The mysterious machine was still humming away.

Left locked in again, Innokenty folded his arms on the table, laid his head on them, and tried to go to sleep sitting.

"Not allowed!" The door was unlocked by a new guard who had just taken over.

"What isn't?"

"Laying your head down!"

Innokenty's muddled mind had expected worse.

Another document was brought, this one on white paper, acknowledging receipt by the Inner Prison of the USSR Ministry of State Security of 123 (one hundred twenty-three) rubles from Volodin, I. A.

Then another new face—a man in a blue smock over an expensive brown suit.

Every time they brought a receipt, they asked his name. This time was no exception. Surname? First name and patronymic? Year of birth? Place of birth? After which, the visitor ordered: "All right—without."

"Without what?"

"Without your gear. Hands behind your back!" In the corridor all orders were given in a low voice so that those in other boxes would not hear.

Clicking his tongue at that invisible dog, the man in the brown suit led Innokenty through the main exit, then along another corridor to a large room unlike the rest of the prison; blinds were drawn over the windows, there was soft furniture, and there were desks. Innokenty was made to sit on a chair in the middle of the room. This, he thought, is when they interrogate me.

Deny it! Deny absolutely everything! Deny with all your might!

But instead of that, a brown box camera was trundled out from behind a curtain, bright lights were switched on to left and right of Innokenty, and he was photographed once full face and once in profile.

The head guard who had escorted Innokenty took the fingers of his right hand one by one and pressed their tips against a sticky black cylinder that seemed to be coated with marking ink, so that all five fingertips were black. Then, parting Innokenty's fingers to leave equal spaces between them, the man in the blue smock pressed them heavily against a form and pulled them sharply away. Five black prints with white whorls were left on the form.

The fingers of his left hand were smeared and printed in the same way.

Written on the form above the prints was "Volodin Innokenty Artemievich, 1919, Leningrad," and above that in heavy black print, "KEEP PERMANENTLY."

Reading this instruction, Innokenty shuddered. There was something mystical in it, something that looked beyond the human race and the planet Earth.

They gave him cold water, soap, and a little brush to wash his fingers. The sticky dye was not easy to remove by these means; the cold water simply trickled off it. Innokenty scrubbed his finger ends vigorously with the soaped brush. He did not ask himself whether the fingerprinting should logically have come before the bath.

Exhausted and disoriented, his brain was in the grip of that overpowering cosmic formula: "KEEP PERMANENTLY"!

# 93

# Second Wind

NEVER IN HIS LIFE had Innokenty experienced such an interminable night. He was wide awake all night long, and a chaotic jumble of thoughts thronged his mind, more than would occur to a man in a month of untroubled normality. There had been time for reflection during the leisurely unpicking of the gold facings from his diplomatic uniform, then while he was sitting half naked in the shower room, and in the various boxes he had been moved to in the night.

"Keep permanently": apt words for his epitaph.

In fact, whether or not they could prove that it was he who had made the telephone call, now that they had arrested him he would never be released. Stalin's paw, he knew, let no one escape alive. He faced either execution or solitary confinement for life in some bloodcurdling place like the legendary Sukhanov monastery. It would not be a home for the aged, like Schlüsselburg. He would not be allowed to sit down in the daytime, not be allowed to speak for years on end, no one would ever hear of him, and he would know nothing about the world outside, even if whole continents changed their flags or people landed on the moon. And on the very last day, when the Stalin gang was rounded up for Nuremberg Mark Two, Innokenty and his voiceless neighbors on the monastery corridor would be shot to a man in solitary—as the Communists had shot people during the retreat of 1941 and the Nazis in 1945.

But was he really afraid to die?

Last night Innokenty had been glad of every little happening, every opening of the door to interrupt his solitude and the unfamiliar feeling of being trapped. Now, though, all he wanted to do was to concentrate on formulating an idea that had so far proved elusive, and he was glad that they had brought him back to his old box and left him undisturbed for so long, though he was under continuous surveillance through the spy hole.

Suddenly it was as if a fine veil had been lifted from his brain, and words he had read and thought about yesterday stood out clearly.

"Belief in immortality was born of the greed of insatiable people. . . . The wise man will find our allotted span long enough to make the round of all attainable pleasures."

But pleasure was not what concerned him now. He had enjoyed money, fine clothes, esteem, women, wine, travel—but to hell with all that; right now he longed for one thing only, justice! To live to see the end of that gang of crooks and hear their pathetic gibbering in the dock!

Yes, he had enjoyed so many blessings! But the most precious of blessings had never been his: the freedom to say what you think, the freedom to associate openly with your intellectual equals. There must be so many of them, unknown to him by name or sight, behind the brick barriers of this building! It hurt him to think that he could not share their thoughts and feelings before he died.

It was all very well philosophizing under shady boughs in stagnantly happy epochs!

Now that he was without pencil and notebook, whatever floated up from the black hole of memory was all the more precious. He remembered vividly: "You should not fear physical suffering. Prolonged suffering is always insignificant; significant suffering is of short duration."

But what if you sit for a day and night without sleep and without air in a box like this, where you can't straighten and stretch out your legs—is that prolonged or unprolonged suffering? Significant or insignificant? Or ten years in solitary, say, with never a living word?

In the room where photographs and fingerprints were taken, Innokenty had noticed that it was after 1:00 a.m. It might be after 2:00 by now. A foolish thought forced its way into his mind: His watch had been put in the storeroom; it would go on working until it ran down, then stop; nobody would ever wind it again; and it would await its owner's death, or confiscation together with the rest of his property, with its hands in that position. What time, he wondered, would it be showing?

Was Dotty still waiting for him to take her to the operetta? Had she called the ministry? Most probably not—they would have arrived to search the flat immediately. An enormous flat! It would take more than five men to turn it upside down overnight. And what was there for them to find, the idiots?

Dotty won't go to jail. Our year apart will save her.

She'll get a divorce and remarry.

But who knows, they may jail her. Anything is possible in this country.

My father-in-law's career will come to a halt. A black mark! I can hear him bellyaching now—"He has nothing to do with me, I tell you!"

All those who have ever known Counselor Volodin will loyally expunge him from their memories.

An insensate mass would crush him, and no one on this earth would ever know how puny, milk-and-water Innokenty had tried to save civilization!

He wanted to live! Long enough to know how it would all end.

In history one side always wins—but never only one side's ideas! Ideas merge; they have a life of their own. The victor always borrows something, sometimes a lot, sometimes everything from the vanquished.

All things will merge. . . . "The enmity of race against race will be no more." State frontiers will disappear, and armies with them. A world parliament will be convened. A president of the planet will be elected. He will bare his head before mankind, and say . . .

"Bring your things."

"Eh?"

"Bring your things."

"What things?"

"Your gear—what d'you think?"

Innokenty rose, holding his overcoat and cap, which were especially precious to him now because they had not been ruined in the sterilizer. Around the door, shouldering the corridor man aside, came the smart, swarthy sergeant major (where did they recruit these guardsmen? for what heavy duties?) with the light blue epaulets, who consulted a piece of paper and asked:

"Name?"

"Volodin."

"First name and patronymic."

"Innokenty Artemievich."

"Year of birth?"

"1919."

"Place of birth?"

"Leningrad."

"Bring your things. Walk!"

He went ahead, clicking as prescribed.

This time they went outside and in the dark, covered end of the yard, down a few more steps. Were they, he wondered, taking him to be shot? Execution by shooting, so people said, always took place in cellars and always at night.

His momentary anxiety was relieved by the thought that they would hardly have given him those receipts if they meant to shoot him. It wouldn't be just yet, anyway!

(Innokenty still believed that the Ministry of State Security's tentacles were cleverly coordinated.)

Still clicking his tongue, the dashing sergeant major conducted him into the building and through a dark lobby to an elevator. A woman with a pile of freshly ironed yellowish gray linen stood to one side and watched as Innokenty was installed in the elevator. This young washerwoman was unattractive, socially inferior, and looked at Innokenty with the same inscrutable stony indifference as did all the other clockwork-doll people in the Lubyanka, but Innokenty felt just as he had in the presence of the storeroom girls who had presented him with receipts pink, blue, and white—hurt that she should see him so stricken, so humiliated, and perhaps think of him with insulting compassion.

This thought, too, vanished as quickly as it had come. "Keep permanently!" After that, nothing mattered.

The sergeant major closed the door of the elevator and pressed the button. The numbers of the floors were not marked.

The moment the elevator started moving, Innokenty recognized the humming of the mysterious machine he had heard grinding bones beyond the wall of his box.

He smiled wanly.

But he was glad to have been mistaken and was somehow reassured.

The elevator stopped. The sergeant major led Innokenty onto the landing and at once into a broad corridor, where he glimpsed many guards wearing blue epaulets with white bars. One of them locked Innokenty in an unnumbered box, a roomy one this time, about ten square meters, dimly lit, with walls painted an unrelieved dark green. This box, or cell, was empty, looked not very clean, had a scuffed cement floor, and a chill in the air made it still more forbidding. There was the usual spy hole.

Many pairs of boots could be heard shuffling past outside. Guards seemed to be continually coming and going. The inner prison had a busy nightlife.

Innokenty had thought earlier that he would be permanently housed in narrow, overheated, blindingly lit Box No. 8 and had suffered agonies because there was no leg room, the light hurt his eyes, and breathing was difficult. Now he realized his mistake, realized that he would be living in this big, uncomfortable, unnumbered box, and he was suffering in anticipation: The cement floor would be cold to his feet; the incessant shuffling out in the corridor would irritate him; the poor light would be depressing. What a difference a window would make! Even the littlest of windows! A window like those in prison vaults on the operatic stage! But there was not even that.

The memoirs of émigrés would give you no idea of what it was like: the corridors, the stairways, the doors, doors, doors, the comings and goings of officers, sergeants, auxiliary staff—the Great Lubyanka was teeming with life in the middle of the night, yet there was no longer a single prisoner in sight; you could not possibly meet someone like yourself, could not possibly hear an unofficial word, and even official ones were few and far between. It was as if the whole enormous ministry were going without its night's sleep just for your sake, exclusively preoccupied with you and your crime.

During his first hours inside, a prisoner is at the mercy of a single murderous idea: The newcomer must be kept apart from other prisoners so that no one can encourage him, so that he feels in isolation the full weight of the brute force that sustains the whole many-tentacled apparatus.

Innokenty felt more and more sorry for himself. His telephone call no longer seemed like a great feat that would be recorded in all histories of the twentieth century but, instead, a thoughtless and—worst of all—pointless suicidal act. He could still hear the arrogantly casual voice of the American attaché mispronouncing the Russian for "Who are you?" Idiot, idiot! He had probably not even informed the ambassador. It had all been in vain. What fools they were! Prosperity breeds idiots!

There was room to walk about in this box, but exhausted and demoralized by all the formalities, Innokenty felt too weak. He made two attempts, then sat down on the bench with his arms dangling.

So many noble aspirations, locked away in these boxes, entombed within these walls, would remain unknown to posterity!

Accursed country! All the bitter pills it swallowed were medicine only for others. Never for itself!

Other countries were luckier. Australia, for instance, tucked away at the back of beyond, getting along nicely without air raids, without Five-Year Plans, without discipline.

Why, oh why, had he set off in pursuit of the bomb thieves? He should have headed for Australia and stayed there as a private person.

Today or tomorrow Innokenty should have been flying to Paris, then on to New York!

He imagined himself not just traveling abroad but setting out within the next twenty-four hours, and his heart sank; he would never be free again! He could have vented his frustration with his bare fingernails on the walls of his cell!

The opening of the door forestalled this breach of prison rules. Once again his "particulars" were checked (Innokenty answered as if in his sleep) and he was ordered out—"with his things." He had felt a little chilly in the box, so his hat was on his head and his overcoat was draped over his shoulders. He tried to leave the box like that, not realizing that he could possibly have been carrying two loaded pistols or two daggers under his coat. He was ordered to slip his arms through the sleeves and then put his bare hands behind his back.

More tongue clicking as he was taken to the head of the stairs near the elevator, then downstairs. Innokenty's main concern in his present position might have been to memorize how many turns he took and how many steps there were between them so that he could try to understand the layout of the prison when he had time. But he was by now so disoriented that he walked along absentmindedly, not noticing how far down they had gone; then, suddenly, another hefty guard emerged from yet another corridor to confront him, clicking just as insistently. The guard who had brought Innokenty tugged open the door of a green plywood booth, which blocked much of a smallish landing, bundled Innokenty in, and pulled the door closed behind himself. Inside, there was just room to stand, and a diffused light filtered down from above. The booth evidently had no roof; light found its way there from the stairwell.

The normal human reaction would have been to protest loudly, but Innokenty, who was getting used to senseless harassment and the Lubyanka's monastic silences, was mutely compliant, in other words, behaved just as the prison required him to.

Of course! That probably explained all the clicking: It was to warn people that a prisoner was being taken somewhere. One prisoner must not meet another. Must not be heartened by the fellow feeling in his eyes!

One man was led past, then another, and Innokenty was let out of the booth and taken farther.

Only here, as he descended the last flight, did Innokenty notice how worn these steps were! He had never seen anything like it in his life. Between the two sides of each step there was an elliptical hollow, and at the midpoint the step was worn to half its original thickness.

He shuddered: In thirty years how many feet, how many times, must have shuffled their way down to wear the stone away like that? And of every two walkers one would be a guard, the other a prisoner.

On one landing there was a locked door with a ventilation panel, shut tight, behind a grating. Here a new trial awaited Innokenty: He was made to stand with his face to the wall. He could still see his escort out of the corner of his eye, pressing a button. An electric bell rang, and the panel cautiously opened, then closed again. A key turned noisily in the lock; the door opened; someone came out and, unseen by Innokenty, began questioning him.

"Name?"

Innokenty naturally looked around, as people usually do when they speak to each other, and saw a face that was neither masculine nor feminine, a flabby, boneless face with a big red scald mark, and lower down a lieutenant's golden epaulets. Pausing only to yell "No turning around!" the man reeled off the sickeningly familiar questions, and Innokenty addressed his answers to the patch of white plaster in front of him.

Having verified that the prisoner still claimed to be the person designated on the card and still remembered the year and place of his birth, the flabby lieutenant rang the doorbell himself—the door had been locked behind him for safety. The panel slid open cautiously once more, someone looked through the aperture, the panel was closed, the key turned noisily in the lock, and the door opened.

"Walk!" the flabby lieutenant with the red scald mark said sharply.

They stepped inside, and the door was noisily locked behind them.

Ahead, a gloomy corridor branched out in three directions. It had several doors, and to the left, by the entrance, stood a desk, pigeonholes, and still more guards. Innokenty caught no more than a glimpse of all this before the lieutenant's voice, subdued but clearly audible in this hushed place, commanded, "Face the wall! Don't move!"

A ludicrous situation to be in—staring closely at the border between dark green paneling and white plaster, all the time feeling several pairs of hostile eyes on the back of your head.

They were obviously consulting his index card. The lieutenant then ordered, almost in a whisper but quite audibly in the profound silence: "Third box!"

A guard detached himself from the desk and, careful not to jingle his keys, set off along the strip of carpet in the right-hand corridor.

"Hands behind! Walk!" he said very quietly.

On one side of their path, the same dark olive green wall wound around three turns; on the other side, they passed several doors, bearing highly polished oval number plates: 47, 48, 49, and beneath them lids over the spy holes. Warmed by the feeling that friends were so near, Innokenty felt an urge to disturb the lid over one of the spy holes, put his eye to it for a moment, and take a look at the secluded life of the cell. But the guard drew him briskly on, and, anyway, Innokenty was already inured to prison discipline—though it was difficult to see what a man who had joined the battle over the atom bomb still had to fear.

Fortunately for governments, mere humans (unfortunately for them) are so constructed that as long as they live, there is always something to take away from them. Even a man imprisoned for life, deprived of movement, of the sight of the sky, deprived of a family and property, can be transferred to a damp punishment cell, denied hot food, and beaten with canes; and these minor punishments are just as keenly felt as his earlier dislodgment from the peak of freedom and prosperity. It is to avoid these vexatious later punishments that a prisoner duly complies with abhorrent and degrading prison regulations that gradually destroy his humanity.

The doors around the next turn were close together, and the glazed disks bore the numbers 1, 2, 3.

The guard unlocked the door of the third box and, with a hospitable flourish that looked rather comical in the circumstances, held it wide open for Innokenty. Innokenty noticed the humorous touch and looked closely at the guard. He was a short young man with smooth black hair and slant eyes like oblique saber cuts. He looked unfriendly, his lips and eyes alike were unsmiling, but after all the dozens of impassive Lubyanka faces seen that night, the mean face of this last guard was somehow rather likable.

Locked in his box, Innokenty took a look around. He had been able to compare several boxes in the course of the night and could consider himself an expert. This box was heavenly: three and a half steps wide, seven and a half long, with a parquet floor. A long and fairly wide wooden bench built into the wall almost filled the cell, and there was a small, free-standing hexagonal wooden table near the door. The box, of course, was windowless, with just a black grille for ventilation high up in the wall. The box was also very high, three and a half meters of wall, every meter of it whitewashed and reflecting the glare from a two-hundred-watt bulb in a wire cover over the door. The light warmed the box but hurt the eyes.

Prison skills are soon learned and not easily forgotten. This time Innokenty did not delude himself. He had no hope of staying long in this comfortable box. He realized as soon as he saw the bench, a long, hard bench—for the mollycoddled Innokenty was toughening up by the hour—that his first and most important object now must be to get some sleep. And just as a young animal, uninstructed by its mother, is taught by the promptings of its own nature all the skills it needs to survive, so Innokenty quickly contrived to spread his overcoat over the bench and bundle the astrakhan collar and rolled-up sleeves together to serve as a pillow. He lay down immediately. It felt very comfortable. He shut his eyes and got ready to sleep.

But he could not get to sleep! He had so longed to sleep when there was no possibility of it! He had gone through all the stages of tiredness and twice lost consciousness, dozing off for a single second—and now, when sleep suddenly was a possibility, he could not sleep! Whenever his overstrained nerves seemed about to relax, they suddenly became as tense as ever. Fighting off forebodings, regrets, and speculations, Innokenty tried breathing rhythmically and counting. It was most annoying not being able to sleep when his whole body was warm, his ribs were on a level surface, his legs were stretched out full length, and the guard for some reason was not keeping him awake!

He lay that way for about half an hour. His thoughts were finally becoming incoherent, and a drowsy warmth was stealing over him from his feet upward.

But suddenly Innokenty felt that he could not possibly go to sleep with that insanely bright light in the cell. The light not only filtered through his closed eyelids in an orange glare; it pressed upon his eyeballs. The pressure of light, which Innokenty had never noticed before, was now driving him to distraction. Tossing and turning in the vain hope of finding a position where the light would not be oppressive, Innokenty finally sat up and lowered his legs from the bench.

He had repeatedly heard the faint sound as the cover was displaced from the spy hole. Next time it was moved he quickly raised a finger.

The door opened noiselessly. The squint-eyed guard looked at Innokenty without speaking.

"Please, please switch off the light," Innokenty implored.

"Not allowed," the squint-eyed one answered calmly.

"Change the bulb, then! Put in a dimmer one! Why such a bright bulb for such a small . . . box?"

"Don't speak so loudly," Squint-eyes said very quietly. Behind him the main corridor and the whole prison were indeed silent as the grave. "The light is as ordered."

And yet there was some slight sign of life in this dead face! Left with nothing to say and expecting the door to close at any moment, Innokenty asked for a drink of water.

Squint-eyes nodded and locked the door noiselessly. Innokenty did not hear him walking away or returning along the strip of carpet outside the box. There was just a little jingle as the key was inserted, and Squint-eyes stood in the doorway with a mug of water. Like those on the ground floor of the prison, the mug was decorated with a picture of a cat, but this one was without spectacles, book, or bird.

Innokenty drank heartily and, in between swallows, took a look at the guard still standing there. Keeping one foot outside, he half closed the door, leaving just room for his shoulders, and, with a distinctly nonregulation wink, asked in a low voice:

"Who were you?"

How strange it sounded! Being addressed like a human being, for the first time that night! The natural tone of voice in which the question was asked (quietly, so that the man's superiors could not overhear it) and the unintentionally cruel word "were" seemed to involve Innokenty in a sort of conspiracy with the guard.

"Diplomat," he whispered. "State counselor."

Squint-eyes nodded sympathetically and said: "Well, I was a sailor once—Baltic Fleet!" Then, after some hesitation: "What are you in for?"

"I don't know myself," Innokenty said cautiously. "For no particular reason."

Squint-eyes nodded sympathetically.

"That's what they all say to start with," he said, and added coarsely, "Want to go for a . . . you-know-what?"

"Not just yet," Innokenty said. The unenlightened newcomer did not know that the offer made to him was the greatest favor in the power of a guard to give and one of the greatest blessings on earth, normally accessible to prisoners only at prescribed times.

After this absorbing conversation, the door closed, and Innokenty stretched out on the bench again, trying in vain to escape the pressure of the light through his unprotected eyes. He tried covering his eyes with one hand, but the hand became numb. It occurred to him that it would help a lot if he twisted his handkerchief into a sort of blindfold—but where was it? It had remained on the floor where it had fallen. What a stupid young pup he had been last night!

Such small items as a handkerchief, an empty matchbox, a bit of coarse thread, a plastic button are the prisoner's best friends! He never knows when one or another of them may become indispensable and save the day!

Suddenly the door opened, and Squint-eyes transferred a red-striped quilted mattress from his own embrace to Innokenty's. A miracle! The Lubyanka not only not preventing a prisoner from sleeping but doing its best to help him! Tucked inside the doubled-up mattress were a little feather pillow, a pillowcase, and a sheet—the last two stamped "Inner Prison"—and even a gray blanket.

What bliss! Now he'd be able to sleep! His first impressions of prison had been too gloomy! Enjoying his comfort in anticipation (and doing it with his own hands for the first time in his life), he pulled the pillowcase over the pillow, spread the sheet over the bench (which was so narrow that the mattress drooped over the edge), undressed, lay down, covered his eyes with the sleeve of his jacket and—nothing could stop him now—was just beginning to sink into a sweet sleep—"in the arms of Morpheus," as they say, when . . .

. . . suddenly, the door crashed open and Squint-eyes said, "Take your hands from under the blanket!"

"What for?" Innokenty exclaimed, almost weeping. "Why did you wake me up? I had such difficulty getting to sleep!"

"Get your hands out!" the guard repeated, unmoved. "Hands must be out in the open."

Innokenty obeyed. But it proved to be not so easy to fall asleep with his hands above the blanket. This was diabolically clever! Human beings, without even noticing it, have an inveterate habit of concealing their hands, pressing them to their bodies, while they sleep.

Innokenty tossed and turned, trying to adapt himself to yet another cruel humiliation. At last sleep began to get the upper hand. A sweetly toxic mist was flooding his consciousness.

Suddenly a noise in the corridor reached his ears. Beginning at a distance and gradually drawing nearer, they were banging neighboring doors. Some word or other accompanied every bang. Now they were next door. And now Innokenty's own door opened.

"Time to get up!" the man who had served with the Baltic Fleet announced uncompromisingly.

"What? Why?" Innokenty bellowed. "I haven't slept all night!"

"Six o'clock. Getting-up time. It's the law!" the sailor repeated and walked on to deliver his message to others.

And this was when Innokenty felt a more powerful need than ever to sleep. He collapsed on his bed and immediately lost consciousness.

But right away—he couldn't have managed more than a couple of minutes' sleep—Squint-eyes flung the door open with a crash and repeated: "Time to get up! Time to get up! Roll your mattress up!"

Innokenty raised himself on one elbow and looked blearily at his tormentor, who just an hour ago had seemed so amiable.

"But I haven't slept, I tell you!"

"That's not my business."

"Right, I roll my mattress up, I get up—and what do I do next?"

"Nothing. Sit."

"But why?"

"Because it's six a.m., you've been told."

"So I'll sleep sitting up!"

"I'll see you don't. I'll wake you up."

Innokenty held his head in his hands and rocked from side to side. What looked like a glimmer of compassion showed in the squint-eyed guard's face.

"Do you want a wash?"

"Oh, all right," Innokenty said absently, reaching for his clothes.

"Hands behind! Walk!"

The washroom was around a bend. Despairing of getting any sleep that night, Innokenty risked removing his shirt and washing in cold water down to his waist. He splashed water freely on the wide cement floor of the chilly washroom. The door was shut, and Squint-eyes did not disturb him.

Perhaps he is human, Innokenty thought, but if so, why did he so perfidiously fail to warn me that reveille would be at six?

The cold water rinsed the debilitating poison of a broken sleep out of Innokenty's system. In the corridor he started saying something about breakfast, but the guard cut him short. Back in the box he gave his answer.

"There won't be any breakfast."

"No breakfast? So what will there be?"

"At eight o'clock you get your ration, sugar, and tea."

"What do you mean, ration?"

"Bread, of course."

"So when is breakfast?"

"Nothing about that in regulations. Right through to dinner."

"And I've got to be sitting here all that time?"

"That's enough talk!"

Innokenty quickly raised his hand when the door was very nearly closed.

"Now what?" the veteran of the Baltic Fleet said, opening the door wide.

"My lining's been ripped open and my buttons cut off. Can I get somebody to sew them back on?"

"How many buttons?"

They counted.

The door was locked and unlocked again shortly afterward. Squint-eyes held out a needle, a dozen or so lengths of thread, and a few buttons of different sizes and materials—bone, plastic, wood.

"What good are these? D'you think the ones they cut off were like these?"

"Take them! They're about all we've got!" Squint-eyes said, raising his voice.

And Innokenty began sewing, for the first time in his life. It took him a little while to find out how to knot the thread at one end, how to draw the stitches through, and how to make sure the button was firmly attached. Not having a millennium of human experience to draw on, Innokenty discovered for himself how to sew. He pricked himself repeatedly, and his tender fingertips began to hurt. It took him a long time to sew up the lining of his uniform and stuff the padding back into his gutted overcoat. He had sewn on some of the buttons in the wrong places, so that his uniform was puckered at the edges.

But this unhurried, painstaking labor not only killed time, it calmed Innokenty down completely. He no longer felt afraid or despondent. Clearly, even this nest of legendary horrors—the Great Lubyanka Prison—was not so terrible. People could live even here (how he wished that he could meet them!). This man, who had not slept all night and had not eaten, this man whose life had been shattered in a few hours, had risen above it all; he was like an athlete whose stiffening body becomes fresh and tireless again with his second wind.

A guard, a different one this time, took away the needle.

Then they brought a five-hundred-gram lump of half-baked black bread, with a triangular makeweight and two lumps of sugar.

A little later they poured some hot, colored liquid into the mug with the cat and promised a refill.

All of which meant that it was 8:00 a.m. on December 27.

Innokenty dropped the whole day's sugar ration into the mug and unfastidiously tried to stir it with his finger, but the tea was too hot. He stirred it by revolving the mug, drank with relish (he felt no need for food at all), and raised his hand to ask for more. Shivering with pleasure, Innokenty imbibed the second mugful, too. There was no sugar this time, but he enjoyed all the more keenly the acrid aroma of stale tea.

Suddenly he was thinking more clearly than he had for a long time past.

In the narrow passage between the bench and the opposite wall, gripping the rolled-up mattress, he began pacing as if warming up for a fight. Three short steps forward, three short steps back.

He would have done no other. He could not have remained indifferent.

It had fallen to him to do it.

What was it Uncle Avenir had said? How did Herzen put it: "Where are the limits of patriotism? Why does a man love his motherland?"

Nothing was more important to him now, nothing more cheering, than his memories of old Avenir. He had met so many men and women frequently, year after year, made friends of them, shared their pleasures; but it was the old man at Tver, with the funny little house, whom he had seen only for two days, who meant most to him here in the Lubyanka. No one in his life had ever been so important to him.

Slowly pacing his cul-de-sac, seven steps there, seven steps back, Innokenty tried to remember what the old man had said. It was at the back of his mind. But for some reason what came uppermost was "Our inner feelings of satisfaction and dissatisfaction are the highest criteria of good and evil."

That wasn't his uncle. That was something stupid. Of course—Epicurus. He hadn't understood it yesterday. Now it was clear: Whatever gives me pleasure is good; whatever displeases me is bad. Stalin, for instance, enjoyed killing people—so that, for him, was "good"? Whereas we who are imprisoned for the truth get no satisfaction from it—so is that evil?

How wise it all seems when you read these philosophers as a free man! But, for Innokenty, good and evil were now distinct entities, visibly separated by that light gray door, those olive green walls, and that first night in prison.

His struggle and his suffering had raised him to a height from which the great materialist's wisdom seemed like the prattle of a child or perhaps a savage's rule of thumb.

The door opened noisily.

"Name?" barked a new guard, of Asiatic appearance.

"Volodin."

"Interrogation! Hands behind!"

Innokenty put his hands behind him, and with his head thrown back, like a bird swallowing water, walked out of the box.

"Why must love of country extend to. . . ."

## 94

# Always Caught Off Guard

IN THE SPECIAL PRISON, too, it was time for breakfast and morning tea.

The day began with no warning that it was to be in any way special. It was notable to begin with only for the captiousness of Lieutenant Shusterman; he was getting ready to go off duty and did his best to prevent prisoners from sleeping after reveille. The exercise period, too, went badly; an overnight frost had followed yesterday's thaw, and a thin crust of ice had formed on the well-trodden paths. Many of the zeks emerged from their quarters, made one circuit, slithering on the ice, and went back inside. In their cells, zeks sat on their bunks, those up above with the legs tucked under them or dangling, none of them in any hurry to get up, scratching their chests, yawning, making an early start with the usual dreary jokes against one another or about their wretched fate, and, of course, telling one another their dreams, a favorite prison pastime.

But although someone had dreamed of crossing a bridge over a turbid stream and someone else of pulling on high boots, no one's dream had foretold transportation en masse.

Sologdin, as usual, went out early to chop wood. He had kept the window ajar through the night, and he opened it wide before leaving for the woodpile.

Rubin, who lay with his head toward the same window, exchanged not a single word with Sologdin. He had gone to bed late the night before, had again been unable to sleep, and felt now a cold draft from the window, but not wishing to interfere with the offender's proceedings, he put on his fur cap with earflaps and his padded jacket, lay curled up with his head under the covers, did not get up for breakfast, and ignored the admonitions of Shusterman and the general noise in the room, doing his best to prolong the hours of sleep.

Potapov was one of the first to rise. He had taken his walk, was among the earliest breakfasters, had already drunk his tea and straightened his bed, and was sitting reading the paper—but secretly longing to get to work (he was going to calibrate an interesting apparatus that he had made himself).

Breakfast was millet mush. Many prisoners stayed away.

Gerasimovich, on the contrary, lingered in the dining room, slowly and carefully inserting small quantities of gruel into his mouth. A casual onlooker would never have taken him for the theorist of palace Revolution.

Nerzhin looked at him from the opposite corner of the half-empty dining room and wondered whether he had given the right answer the night before. To doubt is to be conscientious in the quest for knowledge; but was there a limit beyond which the doubter should not retreat? If free speech ceased to exist everywhere in the world, if the *Times* obediently reproduced *Pravda*, if the natives on the Zambezi subscribed to the State Loan, if collective farmers on the Loire bent their backs for kolkhoz wages, if Party hogs took their holidays behind ten fences in the gardens of California, would life still be worth living?

How long could you shirk decisions with a "Don't know"?

Nerzhin listlessly finished his breakfast and climbed into his upper bunk to spend his last fifteen free minutes lying down and looking at the domed ceiling.

What had happened to Ruska was still the subject of discussion in the room. He had not returned for the night and had obviously been arrested. Prison HQ contained a small, dark cell, and he must have been locked up there.

They didn't come straight out with it, didn't openly call him a double-crosser, but that was what they implied. The gist of what they said was that nothing could be tacked on to his sentence, but maybe they'd convert twenty-five years of labor camp to twenty-five years' solitary (that year new prisons were being built with single-prisoner cells, and solitary was becoming more and more fashionable). Shikin, of course, could not be charging him with double-dealing. But the charge brought against a man and his actual offense did not necessarily coincide; if he was towheaded, you could accuse him of black-headedness—and give him just as long a sentence.

Gleb did not know how far things had gone between Ruska and Klara and whether he ought to, or would have the courage to, comfort her. And if so—how?

Rubin threw off his blanket and, to laughter all around, appeared in his fur cap and padded jacket. Laughter at his own expense he never took amiss; ridicule of socialism was what he could not stand. He removed his cap but kept his jacket on and did not lower his feet to the floor to get dressed—there was little point in it now that he had missed exercise, ablutions, and breakfast—but asked someone to pour him a glass of tea and sat in bed, with his beard disheveled, absently popping bits of buttered white bread into his mouth and washing it down with the hot liquid, while with half-open eyes he lost himself in Upton Sinclair's novel, holding it with the same hand beside his glass. He was in the blackest of moods.

Morning inspection was now in progress. The junior lieutenant was deputizing. He counted heads while Shusterman made announcements. Entering the semicircular room, Shusterman called out, as he had in the others before it: "Attention! Prisoners are informed that after supper no one will be allowed into the kitchen to get hot water; the duty officer must not be knocked for and called out for this purpose."

"Whose order is that?" Pryanchikov yelled furiously, jumping out of a cave formed by placing two double bunks together.

"The commandant's," Shusterman answered importantly.

"When was it made?"

"Yesterday."

Pryanchikov raised his skinny arms and brandished his fists above his head as though calling heaven and earth to witness.

"That cannot be right!" he protested. "Last Saturday evening Minister Abakumov in person promised me that there would be hot water at night! It stands to reason. After all, we work till twelve at night!"

A peal of laughter from the prisoners was his answer.

"So don't work till twelve, you prick," Dvoetyosov boomed.

"We can't employ a night cook," Shusterman explained reasonably.

Then, taking the list from the hands of the junior lieutenant, he called out in an overbearing voice that reduced them all to silence: "Attention! The following will not report for work but will get themselves ready for transportation. . . . From your room. Khorobrov! Mikhailov! Nerzhin! Syomushkin! Have items of prison issue ready to hand in!"

With this, the inspection party left the room, leaving the four whose names had been called out as if a tornado had caught them.

People abandoned their tea and bread and butter and hurriedly formed little groups, some of them around those due to depart. Four out of twenty-five—an unusually large cull. They all started talking at once, excited voices, lowered voices, dismissively cheerful voices. Some of them stood upright on upper bunks waving their arms, some clutched their heads, some held forth excitedly, beating their breasts, some were already shaking the pillows out of their pillowcases, and altogether the room presented such a chaotic medley of grief, submissiveness, resentment, resolution, lamentation, and speculation—all of this crammed into a confined space and on several different levels—that Rubin rose from his bed just as he was, in his padded jacket and underpants, and yelled: "A historic day for the special prison! Morning of the execution of the streltsy!"

Spreading his arms out wide over the general scene.

His excitement certainly did not mean that he was happy to see men transported. He would have found it just as funny if he had to leave himself. If he saw a chance to make a joke, nothing was sacred.

TRANSPORTATION IS AN EVENT as momentous in the life of a prisoner as being wounded is in the life of a soldier. And just as a wound may be light or serious, curable or fatal, so transportation may be to somewhere close or somewhere distant; it may be a diversion—and it may mean death.

When you read about the alleged horrors of penal servitude in tsarist times as described by Dostoevsky, you are amazed to find how tranquilly men were allowed to serve out their sentences! They could go for ten years without being transported once!

A zek lives in one and the same place, gets used to his comrades, his work, his masters. However unacquisitive he is, he inevitably accumulates possessions; he finds himself the owner of a fiber suitcase sent from outside or one made of plywood in the camp. He acquires a little frame in which he puts a photograph of his wife or daughter, rag slippers that he puts on to walk about the hut after work and hides from inspection during the daytime; he may even have pinched an extra pair of cotton trousers or hung on to his old shoes instead of handing them in, and all this moves from one hiding place to another after every stocktaking. He even has his own needle, buttons sewn on securely, and a couple more in reserve. There is usually tobacco in his pouch.

If he is a "square," he will also have a supply of tooth powder and occasionally clean his teeth. This prisoner accumulates a stack of letters from his family and usually has a book of his own to exchange with others, so that he gets to read every book in the camp.

But transportation strikes like a bolt from the blue to destroy his little life, always without warning, always contrived to take the zek unawares and at the last possible moment. Then letters from loved ones are torn up and dropped into the hole of the latrine. And then the escort—if transportation is to be in red cattle trucks—cuts off all the zek's buttons and sprinkles his tobacco and tooth powder on the breeze, since they might be used to blind one of the guards in the course of the journey. If transportation is to be in locked passenger-train cars, the escort guard stamps furiously on cases that refuse to go into the baggage compartment, smashing the photograph frame while he is at it. In either case, they take away the books (not allowed on the journey) and the needle, which might be used to saw through bars and stab a guard; the rag slippers are thrown away as trash, and the spare pair of breeches confiscated for general camp use.

And purged of the sin of property ownership, of his predilection for a settled life, of his hankering after petit bourgeois comfort (justly stigmatized by Chekhov all those years ago), deprived of his friends and his past, the zek puts his hands behind his back and in columns of four ("One step to the right or one step to the left and the escort guard opens fire without warning!"), surrounded by dogs and guards, walks toward the car.

You have all seen him on our railroad stations at that moment but have faintheartedly lowered your eyes in a hurry, loyally turned away, in case the lieutenant in charge of the convoy suspects you of something and arrests you.

The zek enters the carriage or truck, and it is hitched on so that it stands alongside a mail truck. Tightly caged in on all sides, invisible from the platforms, he travels according to a leisurely timetable, carrying with him in that airless confined space hundreds of memories, hopes, and apprehensions.

Where are they taking him? They aren't saying. What awaits the prisoner in his new place? The copper mines? A lumber camp? Or a coveted reassignment to an agricultural working party where he may sometimes be lucky enough to bake a potato and can eat his fill of the cattle's turnips? Will the prisoner be laid low by scurvy or malnutrition after one month on "general assignment"? Or will he be lucky enough to grease a palm or meet somebody he knows and latch on to a barracks orderly's or hospital orderly's or even storeroom assistant's job? And will they allow him to write and receive letters in his new place? Or will his letters be intercepted year after year, until his loved ones write him off as dead?

But perhaps he won't even reach his appointed destination? Perhaps he will die in the cattle wagon? Of dysentery? Or because they are kept on the move for six days without bread? Or perhaps the guards will beat him to death with hammers because someone else has made his escape? Or maybe at the end of the journey in a freight car with an unheated stove, the zeks will be frozen stiff and their bodies slung out like so much firewood?

It takes the red trains a month to reach Sovgavan.

Remember, O Lord, those who did not arrive!

THOSE LEAVING WERE TREATED LENIENTLY, even allowed to keep their razors as far as the first prison, but all these questions tormented the twenty prisoners detailed for transportation during the Tuesday morning room inspection.

For them, the untroubled, half-free life of the special prison was over.

# 95

# Farewell, Sharashka

PREOCCUPIED AS HE WAS with preparations for his transfer, Nerzhin felt a sudden itch, which became a burning desire, to give Major Shikin a piece of his mind by way of farewell. So when the bell sounded for work, although his twenty had been ordered to wait in their quarters for a guard, he darted through the doors with the other nineteen. He rushed up to Shikin's office on the third floor, knocked, and was told to enter.

Shikin was sitting at his desk looking gloomy. Something had snapped in him since yesterday. One foot of his had hovered over the abyss, and he knew now what it would be like to have the ground cut out from under him.

But he could not vent his hatred of that young pup directly and at once. What Shikin could do, with least danger to himself, was to wear Doronin to a frazzle in the hole, then send him back to Vorkuta with a stinking report, ensuring that he was assigned to a punitive work team and would be checking out in a hurry. That would be just as good as putting him on trial and shooting him.

He would have called Doronin in for interrogation early that morning, but he was expecting endless protests and delaying tactics from the men who were to be transported.

He was not mistaken. In came Nerzhin.

Major Shikin had never been able to stand this lean, openly hostile prisoner with his imperturbable self-confidence and precise knowledge of the law. He had for some time past been trying to persuade Yakonov to transfer Nerzhin, and he was maliciously pleased to see the angry look on the man's face.

Nerzhin had a talent for putting a complaint into a few trenchant words. He could utter his protest in a single breath, while the food hatch in the cell door was momentarily open, or find space for it on a scrap of the absorbent toilet paper made available for submissions from prisoners. In five years of incarceration he had also perfected his own uncompromising way of talking to the authorities—"politely blowing them off," fellow prisoners called it. He never used improper language, but his loftily ironic tone, though there was nothing for his hearer to pick on, was that of a superior to an underling.

He began speaking as he entered.

"Citizen Major! I have come to reclaim a book unlawfully taken from me. I feel entitled to assume that communications in the city of Moscow being what they are, six weeks is long enough to ascertain that it is permitted by the censor."

"Book?" Shikin, taken by surprise, could think of nothing sensible to say offhand. "What book?"

"I likewise assume," Nerzhin rapped out, "that you know to which book I refer. The *Selected Poems of Sergei Yesenin.*"

"Ye-se-nin?" As if only just remembering and shocked by this treasonable name, Major Shikin rocked back in his chair. His grizzled crewcut seemed to express indignation and disgust. "How can you find it in yourself to ask about Ye-se-nin?"

"Why shouldn't I? He was published here in the Soviet Union."

"That makes no difference."

"Moreover, he was published in 1940, i.e., he does not fall within the prohibited period, 1917 to 1938."

Shikin frowned. "Prohibited period? Where d'you get that from?"

Nerzhin replied as succinctly as if he had memorized his answers in advance.

"A camp censor kindly clarified things for me. During a search before the holiday, my copy of Dahl's *Dictionary* was taken from me on the grounds that it was published in 1935 and therefore subject to the most rigorous scrutiny. When I showed him that the dictionary was a photomechanical copy of the 1881 edition, the censor promptly returned it and explained that there are no objections to pre-Revolutionary editions, since the 'enemies of the people were not then active.' And the unfortunate fact is that Yesenin was published in 1940."

After a moment's magisterial silence, Shikin said, "Have it your way. But have you"—he asked weightily—"have you read that book? Have you—read all of it? Can you confirm that in writing?"

"You have at present no legal grounds for requiring a signature from me under Article 95 of the Criminal Code of the RSFSR. But orally I confirm that I have a bad habit of reading those books that are my own property and, conversely, keeping only those books that I read."

Shikin threw up his hands. "So much the worse for you."

"So, then, let me summarize my request. In accordance with point 7 of section B of Prison Regulations, give me back the book illegally taken from me."

Cowering under this torrent of words, Shikin rose. When he was sitting at his desk, his head did not look like that of a little man, but when he rose, he became smaller, and his arms and legs were seen to be very short. Looking black, he went over to the cupboard, opened it, and took out a miniature Yesenin, with a maple-leaf pattern on its jacket.

There were markers in several places. Shikin made himself comfortable in his armchair, still without inviting Nerzhin to sit down, and began a leisurely inspection of the marked passages. Nerzhin calmly seated himself, leaned forward with his hands on his knees, and fixed Shikin with a hostile stare.

"Take this, for instance," the major said with a sigh, and read the lines with as much feeling as if he were kneading dough:

" '*Lifeless hands, alien hands!*
*These songs cannot live where you are!*
*But the ears of corn that are horses*
*Will grieve for their old master forever.*'

"Who, I ask you, is this master? Whose hands does he mean?"

The prisoner looked at the security officer's own puffy white hands.

"Yesenin had the limited vision of his class, and there were many things he did not fully understand, just like Pushkin and Gogol."

Something in Nerzhin's voice made Shikin glance at him apprehensively. What was to stop him from suddenly hurling himself at the major now that he had nothing more to lose? Just in case, Shikin rose and opened the door an inch or two.

"And what does this bit mean?" he said, returning to his chair.

" '*A rose all white and a crab all black*
*I tried to join in wedlock.*'

"Et cetera. . . . What is he getting at?"

The prisoner's taut throat quivered.

"It's very simple," he answered. "You shouldn't try to reconcile the white rose of truth with the black crab of wickedness."

The short-armed, big-headed, dark-faced godfather sat before him like a black crab.

"However, Citizen Major"—Nerzhin spoke rapidly, his words tumbling over one another—"I do not have time to enter into textual analysis with you. My escort party awaits me. You announced six weeks ago that you would refer the matter to the All-Union Censor's Office. Did you do so?"

Shikin shrugged and noisily closed the little yellow book.

"I am not accountable to you for my actions. I shall not return the book to you. And if I did, you would not be allowed to take it away with you."

Nerzhin stood up angrily with his eyes fixed on Yesenin. He remembered that his wife's loving hands had once held the little book and written in it: "So may all that you have lost be returned to you!"

Words like a hail of bullets sped effortlessly from his lips.

"Citizen Major! You have, I hope, not forgotten that over two years I repeatedly requested the Ministry of State Security to return some Polish zlotys improperly confiscated from me, and although it was converted to rubles at a twentieth of its value, I did get my money back through the Supreme Soviet. And I hope you have not forgotten how I insisted on being given five grams of Grade One flour? I was laughed at, but I got them! And I could mention many other instances! I warn you that I will not let you keep that book! If I'm sent to Kolyma, I'll wrest it from you before I die there! I'll stuff the letterboxes of the Central Committee and the Council of Ministers with complaints about you. So hand it over now, and save yourself trouble!"

The major in the State Security Service could not hold out against this doomed prisoner, stripped of his rights and on his way to a lingering death in a labor camp. He had, in fact, made inquiries of the Central Censorship and, to his surprise, been told that the book in question was not formally prohibited. Formally! Shikin's unerring sense of smell told him that this was a blunder on somebody's part and that the book certainly should be forbidden. But he needed to defend his name from the imputations of this indefatigable troublemaker.

"Very well, then, you can have it back. But we won't let you take it away with you."

Nerzhin walked triumphantly to the stairs, pressing his beloved shiny yellow volume to his breast. It was a token success at a moment when everything was collapsing around him.

On the landing, he passed a group of prisoners discussing the latest developments. Siromakha was holding forth (but taking care that his voice would not carry to their masters).

"What do they think they're doing? Sending guys like that off to the camps! What for? And what about Ruska Doronin? What bastard's informed on him, eh?"

Nerzhin made for the Acoustics Laboratory, in a hurry to destroy his notes before a guard took charge of him. Prisoners due to be transferred were not supposed to walk around the special prison freely. Nerzhin could enjoy this last brief interval of freedom only because so many were to be transported and because the junior lieutenant was as negligent and easygoing as ever.

He flung open the laboratory door and saw that the steel cabinet was wide open, and Simochka, now wearing her ugly striped dress again, and a gray goat-hair scarf around her shoulders, was standing between its doors.

She sensed Nerzhin's presence without looking and froze, as if she could not make up her mind what to take out of the cabinet.

Without stopping to think, he took refuge between the steel doors and whispered, "Serafima Vitalievna! After what happened last night, it's heartless of me to turn to you. But things I've been working on for many years are in danger. What shall I do? Burn them? Or can you keep them for me?"

She already knew that he was leaving. She raised sad eyes, red from lack of sleep, and said, "Give them to me."

Somebody came in, and Nerzhin hurried over to his desk, where he found Roitman.

Roitman looked dismayed. "Gleb Vikentich! This is most annoying!" he said. "Nobody warned me. . . . I had no idea. . . . Until today—too late to change anything."

Nerzhin gave the man whom until now he had thought sincere an icily pitying look.

"Adam Veniaminovich, this isn't my first day here. Such things aren't done without consulting the heads of laboratories."

He started emptying the drawers of his desk.

Roitman looked pained.

"Believe me, Gleb Vikentich, I didn't know, nobody asked me, I wasn't warned. . . ."

He said it loudly enough for the whole laboratory to hear. Beads of sweat stood out on his brow. He watched uncomprehendingly while Nerzhin collected his belongings.

It was true. He had not been consulted.

"Shall I give my notes on articulation to Serafima Vitalievna?" Nerzhin asked casually.

Roitman walked slowly toward the door without replying.

"Here you are, then, Serafima Vitalievna," Nerzhin said, bringing her the first load of files and folders, and loose sheets of graph paper.

He was about to slip his most treasured possession—the three notebooks—into one of the files. But an inner voice warned him against it.

Her outstretched hands were warm enough, but how long would she stay a virgin and faithful to him?

He transferred the notebooks to one of his pockets and gave the files to Simochka.

The library at Alexandria had burned down. Manuscripts in monasteries had been burned to keep them out of the wrong hands. And soot from the Lubyanka's chimneys—soot from countless bundles of burned paper—had fluttered down onto the heads of prisoners led out for exercise in the pen on the prison roof.

More great thoughts had gone up in smoke, perhaps, than had ever been made public. . . . He felt sure that if he survived, he could reproduce his work.

Nerzhin rattled a box of matches, ran out of the lab . . . and returned ten minutes later pale and expressionless.

Pryanchikov walked in.

"It's incredible," he said. "We've lost all sense and feeling! We don't even kick up a fuss! We're 'transported,' 'shipped,' 'forwarded.' You can transport luggage, but what gives them the right to 'transport' people?"

Valentulya's outburst found an echo in the prisoners' hearts. Disturbed by news of the transfer, not one of those in the laboratory was working. A transportation was always a terrifying reminder that "we may be next." A transportation made every prisoner, even if unaffected by it, reflect that his fate was in the balance and that the ax of the Gulag was poised to cut short his existence. Even zeks with no black marks against them were invariably sent away from the special prison two years or so before the end of their sentence, so that they would forget all they had done there and lose their skills before they were freed. Men serving twenty-five years would never see the end of their sentence, so the security services happily recruited them for the special prisons.

Prisoners surrounded Nerzhin, some of them sitting on desks instead of chairs, as if to emphasize the unusual importance of the occasion. Their mood was one of melancholy resignation.

Like mourners at a funeral recalling all the good things the deceased had done, they praised Nerzhin as a zealous defender of prisoners' rights. They remembered, among other things, the famous story of the fine flour. He had showered the prison authorities and the Ministry of Internal Affairs with complaints about the failure to issue him personally five grams of the best flour per day. (Prison rules forbade collective complaints or complaints from one person on behalf of others. The prisoner was supposedly being reeducated in the spirit of socialism, but he was forbidden to suffer for the common good.) At that time, convicts in the special prison were still underfed, and the fight for those five grams generated more excitement than any event on the international scene. The gripping epic had ended in victory for Nerzhin. The commandant's deputy in charge of stockrooms was relieved of his duties, and the flour allowance supplied the whole prisoner population with extra noodles twice a week. They remembered, too, Nerzhin's campaign for a longer exercise period on Sundays—which had, however, ended in defeat.

Nerzhin himself, however, hardly listened to these graveside eulogies. He was thinking that the moment for action had arrived. The worst had happened, and only he could do anything to improve matters. He had handed over his notes on speech tests to Serafima and all secret material to Roitman's assistant, burned or torn up all his personal papers, stacked all his library books in piles, and was now rummaging in his drawers and distributing what was left to his friends. It had already been decided who was to have his revolving yellow chair, his German rolltop desk, his inkwell, his roll of colored and marbled sheets of paper made by the Lorenz company. The deceased distributed his legacies in person, and beneficiaries gave him two, or sometimes three, packs of cigarettes in return. This was standard practice in the sharashka: In "this world" (their world) cigarettes were plentiful; in "the next world" (the Gulag) they were more precious than bread.

Rubin came in from his top-secret group. He looked sad, and there were bags under his eyes. Surveying his books, Nerzhin said, "I'd make you a present of Yesenin if you liked him."

"How ever did you manage to get him back?"

"Only he's too remote from the proletariat."

"You haven't got a shaving brush," Rubin said—producing from his pocket a brush with a shiny plastic handle, which any prisoner would find luxurious—"and I've vowed never to shave till I get my pardon, so take this one!"

Rubin never said "till I'm released," which might simply mean till he'd served his sentence, but always "till I get my pardon," never doubting that someday he would.

"Thanks, old man, but you've become such a 'special prison prisoner' that you've forgotten how things are in the camps. What makes you think they'll let me shave myself where I'm going? Will you help me take the books back?"

They collected the books and magazines into neat piles. The other prisoners drifted away.

"Well, how's your protégé?" Gleb asked quietly.

"I've heard the two main ones were arrested last night."

"Why two?"

"They're both suspects. History demands victims."

"How do you know you've got the right one?"

"I think we've caught him. They've promised to send us the interrogators' tapes by dinnertime. We'll compare them."

Nerzhin finished stacking books and straightened up.

"What does the Soviet Union want with the atomic bomb anyway? That fellow had his head screwed on right."

"A Moscow airhead, a no-good troublemaker, take my word for it."

Heavily laden with library books, they left the laboratory and walked up the main staircase.

In the window space along the upper corridor, they stopped for a rest and to get a better grip on their collapsing bundles of books.

Nerzhin's eyes, lit with feverish excitement while he was making his final arrangements, were now fixed in a lackluster stare.

"You know what?" he said. "You and I have been together less than three years, spent most of that time arguing and trashing each other's beliefs—and now that I'm losing you, forever, I realize clearly that you are one of those I most—"

His voice broke.

Rubin's large brown eyes, which many people had only seen flashing with anger, shone now with shy kindliness.

"I know what you mean. . . . Give me a kiss, you brute."

And he smothered Nerzhin in his piratical black beard.

After that, they went straight to the library, where Sologdin caught up with them. He looked very worried. He carelessly slammed the door so that the glass panes rattled, and the librarian looked round in annoyance.

"Well, Gleb, my boy! That's it, then!" Sologdin said. "It has come to pass! You are leaving us."

Ignoring the "Old Testament fanatic," Sologdin looked only at Nerzhin.

Rubin, equally disinclined to make peace with the "boring hidalgo," looked the other way.

"Yes, you're leaving us. A pity. A great pity."

They had found so much to say to each other across the sawhorse, argued so passionately in the exercise yard. Now it was too late, and not the place, for

Sologdin to teach Gleb, as he had always meant to, the rules that governed his own thinking and his life.

The librarian vanished among the stacks, and Sologdin said quietly, "But you really must stop being such a skeptic. It's just a facile excuse for refusing to fight."

Nerzhin replied just as quietly. "But what you were saying yesterday about this hopeless, cockeyed country—that's even more facile. I don't know what to think."

Sologdin's blue eyes flashed, and his white teeth gleamed in a brilliant smile.

"You and I should have talked more; you still have so much to learn. Remember—time is money. It still isn't too late. Tell them you're willing to stay here as a designer, and maybe I can get you kept on. In a group we've set up here." (Rubin darted a look of surprise at him.) "But I give you fair warning—you'll have to put your back into it."

Nerzhin sighed.

"Thanks, Dmitri, old man. I could have done something like that, but while I'm putting my back into it, would I ever have time for self-improvement? I've more or less made up my mind to try an experiment. There's a proverb that says, 'It's not the sea that drowns you, it's the puddle.' I want to try a dive into the sea."

"You do? Well, just be careful. It's a great pity, Gleb, my boy, a great pity."

Sologdin, looking preoccupied, was in a hurry but forced himself not to hurry away.

The three of them stood waiting while the librarian, herself a lieutenant in the security service, with dyed hair and heavily made up, lazily checked Nerzhin's library card.

Gleb, upset by the ill feeling between his friends, said, lowering his voice in the hushed library, "Listen, you two! You must make up!"

Neither Sologdin nor Rubin looked around.

"Mitya!" Gleb insisted.

Sologdin raised his piercing, cold blue eyes. "Why are you addressing me?" He sounded surprised.

Gleb tried again: "Lyova!"

Rubin looked at him wearily.

"Do you know why horses live so long?" He paused briefly and went on. "Because they never try to explain their feelings."

• • •

Once he had finished handing in the prison's property and his work notes, Nerzhin was ordered by a guard to go on to the prison and get ready to leave. As he went along the hallway clutching several packs of cigarettes, he met Potapov, hurrying somewhere with a box under his arm. Potapov at work walked quite differently from Potapov in the exercise yard; in spite of his limp, he moved quickly, head jerking backward and forward on his stiff neck, eyes screwed up, gazing into the distance, as if his head and eyes were trying to outpace his no-longer-young legs. Potapov was anxious to say good-bye to Nerzhin and the others who were leaving, but the moment he entered the laboratory that morning he was gripped by the inner logic of his work and had no thought or feeling for anything else. This capacity for total absorption in his work, forgetting all else that was happening in his life, was the basis of his success outside as an engineer, one of the Five-Year Plan's indispensable robots, and it had helped him to withstand the hardships of prison life.

Nerzhin barred his way.

"That's it, then, Andreich," he said. "The deceased was in good spirits and wore a smile."

Potapov made an effort, and his eyes lit up with ordinary human comprehension. The hand not holding the box reached for his neck as if to scratch it.

"Er . . . er . . . er. . . ."

"I'd give you my Yesenin, only apart from Pushkin you don't. . . ."

"We will all end up there," Potapov said sadly.

Nerzhin sighed.

"Where will we meet next? In the Kotlas transit prison? On the Indigir goldfields? Somehow I don't believe that we will ever meet walking freely down a city street. Do you?"

Half closing his eyes, Potapov declaimed: "I have closed my eyes to phantom joys. But distant hopes trouble my heart at times."

Markushev, beside himself with excitement, stuck his head out through the door of Number Seven.

"You, Potapov!" he shouted impatiently. "Where are the filters? You're holding up the work."

The coauthors of "The Buddha's Smile" embraced awkwardly. Packs of White Sea Canal cigarettes fell to the floor.

"You know how it is," Potapov said. "We're busy spawning—no time for anything else."

"Spawning" was Potapov's word for the rush and muddle prevalent in the Marfino Institute and in all the activities of the Soviet state, as newspapers reluctantly admitted when they spoke of "shock work" and "last-minute-ism."

"Write to me!" Potapov said in conclusion—and they both burst out laughing. Those words, so natural when people say good-bye, sound in prison like a cruel joke. There was no postal service between the islands of the Gulag.

Holding his box of filters under one arm, Potapov dashed off along the hallway again, with his head bobbing backward and forward. His limp was barely discernible.

Nerzhin, too, hurried off—to the semicircular cell, where he began assembling his belongings, acutely aware of the cruel surprises that might await him when he was subjected to body searches at Marfino and later on in Butyrki.

The guard looked in twice to hurry him up. The others had already left of their own accord or been chased out to Prison HQ. Just as Nerzhin was finishing his preparations, Spiridon came into the room, wearing his black, belted tunic and bringing a breath of outdoor freshness. Removing the ginger cap with the big earflaps, he carefully turned back the bedding (tucked into a white comforter) on a bunk close to Nerzhin's and lowered his dirty padded trousers onto the steel frame.

"Spiridon Danilych!" Nerzhin said, holding out the book to him, "I've got my Yesenin!"

"The snake gave it back, did he?" Spiridon's gloomy features, which seemed more deeply wrinkled than ever, brightened momentarily.

"What matters to me is not so much the book, Danilych," Nerzhin explained. "What's important is that they mustn't treat us like dirt."

Spiridon nodded.

"Here, take it. Something to remember me by."

"Don't you want to take it with you?" Spiridon asked, embarrassed.

"Wait a minute." Nerzhin took the book back and started looking for a page.

"I'll find it in a minute, you can read it for yourself. . . ."

"Better be on your way, Gleb," Spiridon said gloomily. "You know what it's like in labor camps; your heart wants to be working and making, but your feet drag you to the sickbay."

"I'm not new at the game, Danilych. I'm not afraid. I want to try a bit of real work. You know what they say: The sea won't drown you, the puddle will."

Only then did Nerzhin look closely at Spiridon and realize that he was very upset—more than he would be if he were simply parting from a friend. The events of the day before—the harsh new regulations, the unmasking of the informers, Ruska's arrest, the scene with Simochka, his discussion with Gerasimovich—had made him forget completely that Spiridon should have received a letter from home.

"What about your letter? Did you get your letter, Danilych?"

Spiridon was clutching the letter in his pocket. He took it out. The envelope was frayed in the middle where it had been folded.

"Here . . . but you haven't got time. . . ."

Spiridon's lips trembled.

That envelope had been folded and unfolded over and over again since yesterday! The address was written in the large, bold hand of Spiridon's daughter, Vera, acquired in the five years of schooling that were all she had received.

As he and Spiridon usually did, Nerzhin began reading the letter aloud.

"*My Dear Daddy!*

> *I don't know how I can carry on living let alone write to you. What bad people there are in the world; they tell you things, and then they let you down. . . .*"

Nerzhin's voice failed him. He glanced at Spiridon and met his wide-open, steady, almost blind eyes under their bushy red eyebrows. But he was not allowed a second to think and try to find a word of consolation that would not ring false. The door was flung open, and Nadelashin rushed in looking furious.

"Nerzhin!" he yelled. "If people treat you decently, this is what they can expect! All the others are ready and waiting—you're the last!"

The guards were in a hurry to get the transferees into headquarters before the lunch break so that they would meet none of the other prisoners.

Nerzhin embraced Spiridon with one arm around his unshaved neck.

"Get on with it!" the junior lieutenant yelled. "I'm not waiting a minute longer!"

"Dear old Spiridon!" Nerzhin said, embracing the red-haired yardman.

Spiridon sighed hoarsely and waved his hand.

"Good-bye, Gleb, boy."

"Good-bye forever, Spiridon Danilych!"

They kissed. Nerzhin picked up his things and rushed out, followed by the duty officer.

With hands from which washing would never remove years of ingrained dirt, Spiridon picked up from the bed the open book with the maple leaves on its jacket, put his daughter's letter in it as a marker, and went off to his room.

He did not notice that he had knocked his shaggy cap off the bed with his knee, and it stayed there on the floor.

# 96

# Meat

As the relegated prisoners were gradually herded into Prison HQ, they were frisked, and as the search was completed, they were shunted into an unoccupied room where there stood two bare tables and a crude bench. Major Myshin in person was present throughout the search, and Lieutenant Colonel Klimentiev looked in from time to time. Bending down to look into sacks and suitcases would have overtaxed the corpulent, purple-faced major (and anyway it was beneath his dignity), but his presence could be relied on to encourage the screws. They zealously undid all the prisoners' bundles and parcels and were particularly quick to pounce on anything written. There was a standing order that men leaving the special prison had no right to take with them the merest scrap of paper with anything written, drawn, or printed on it. So most of the zeks had burned all their letters, destroyed their professional notebooks, and given away their books in advance.

One prisoner, the engineer Romashov, who had only six more months to serve (he had chalked up nineteen years and a half), openly carried a fat file containing clippings, notes, and calculations accumulated over many years on the construction of hydroelectric power stations. (He was expecting to be sent to the Krasnoyarsk region and counted on being allowed to practice his profession there.) Although Engineer Colonel Yakonov had personally inspected this folder and authorized its release, and although Major Shikin had already sent it to the ministry, where they had also given their approval, Romashov's foresight and unremitting efforts over many months went for nothing: Major Myshin now announced that he knew nothing about this file and impounded it. It was seized and carried away, and Engineer Romashov's eyes, which had gotten used to everything, followed it unseeingly. In his time, he had survived a death sentence, transportation in a cattle wagon from Moscow to Sovgavan, and a broken shin down a pit at Kolyma—he had let a coal tub run over his leg so that he could rest up in the hospital and escape certain death as a general laborer in Arctic conditions. So the destruction of ten years' work was no reason for shedding tears.

Another prisoner, the small, bald-headed designer Syomushkin, who had put so much effort into darning his socks on Sunday, was, by contrast, a raw recruit. He had been inside barely two years, in prison, then at Marfino, and was now terrified at the thought of a labor camp. But scared and miserable as he was, he tried to hang on to a small volume of Lermontov that was a sacred object to him and his wife. He implored Major Myshin to return the little volume, wringing his hands—strange behavior in a grown man, which the old-line zeks found offensive. He was prevented from bursting into the lieutenant colonel's office but suddenly, with unexpected strength, snatched the book from the godfather (who recoiled toward the door in a fright), wrenched off the tooled green covers, flung them away, and began tearing the pages into strips, weeping convulsively, screaming—"Here then! Gobble it up! Gorge yourselves!"—and scattering what was left of Lermontov around the room.

The search continued.

When they emerged, the prisoners scarcely recognized one another. As ordered, they had made one pile of their blue overalls, another of their prison-issue underwear with the official stamp, a third of their overcoats, if these were not too threadbare, so that they were all now wearing either their own old clothes or a substitute provided for them. Their years of work for the institute had not earned them enough to buy clothes. Not because the prison authorities were spiteful or miserly. They were answerable to the bookkeepers—"the watchful eye of the government." So, in the depths of winter, some were left without warm underwear and had pulled on short pants and mesh undershirts that had lain moldering in their knapsacks in the stockrooms, as unlaundered as they had been on the day of the prisoner's arrival from some camp. Some were shod in clumsy prison-camp boots (if a man had camp boots in his sack, his "civvy" half boots with galoshes were confiscated), others now had boots with cloth legs attached to leather soles, and the lucky ones had felt boots.

Felt boots! The convict. That most desolate of earth's creatures—with less inkling of his future than a frog, a mole, or a field mouse—has no defense against fate's perversities. In the warmest and deepest of holes, the convict cannot rest assured that once night comes, he will be safe from the horrors of winter, that an arm with a blue-cuffed sleeve will not seize him and drag him off to the North Pole.

Woe, then, to feet not shod in felt boots! Two frosted icicles are what he will set down on Kolyma as he emerges from the back of a truck. A zek without felt boots of his own will make himself scarce all through the winter, lie, dissemble, put up with insults from the lowest of the low, or himself bully others—anything to avoid transportation in winter. But the zek wearing felt boots of his own is dauntless! He looks authority defiantly in the eye and accepts his marching orders with a stoical smile.

It was thawing outside, but Khorobrov, Nerzhin, and others with felt boots thrust their feet into them—partly to lighten their burden but mainly to feel that reassuring warmth all the way up their legs—and strutted around the empty room. This, although for the present they were going no farther than Butyrki Prison, where it was not the least bit colder than in the institute. Fearless Gerasimovich was the only one with no clothes of his own. The stockroom man had given him a "previously used" prison-issue jacket too large and loose to fasten around him and with long, dangling sleeves, together with a pair of blunt-toed, cloth-legged boots, also "previously used."

This costume looked all the more comical because he was wearing pince-nez.

Nerzhin emerged from the search pleased with himself. Anticipating an early transfer, he had equipped himself yesterday afternoon with two sheets of paper and penciled them over with a closely written text incomprehensible to anyone else—simply omitting vowels or using Greek words or a medley of Russian, English, German, and Latin words, often abbreviated. To make sure of getting them past the searchers, Nerzhin had torn each sheet slightly, crumpled it, as people sometimes crumple paper for its secondary use, and stuffed it into a pocket of his camp trousers. The guard searching him had seen these pieces of paper but drawn the wrong conclusion and left them with him. Now, if he didn't take them into the cell in Butyrki but left them with his belongings, they might survive even longer.

These sheets of paper contained in succinct form some of the facts and thoughts consigned to the flames earlier that day.

The search was over, and all twenty prisoners were herded into the empty waiting room with the things they were permitted to take along. The door closed behind them, and a sentry was posted outside it while they waited for the prison truck. Yet another guard was detailed to patrol the slippery patch under the windows and shoo away anyone who turned up during the lunch break to say good-bye.

Thus, all ties between the 20 departing prisoners and the 261 staying behind were severed.

The transferees were still there, yet they were there no longer.

At first, seating themselves randomly on the benches or on their belongings, they were all silent.

Their minds were still on the search, each man going over what had been taken from him and what he had managed to get through.

And on the institute: all the blessings they were leaving behind with it, how much of their sentence they had served there, and how much remained to be served.

Time checks are the prisoner's hobby: calculating how much of his life has been lost and how much is still destined to be lost.

They were thinking, too, of their families, with whom they would be out of touch at first and whose help they would need to seek again; the Gulag is a country in which a grown man working twelve hours a day cannot earn enough to feed himself.

And thinking of the blunders or deliberate actions that had earned them transportation.

Wondering where they would be sent, what awaited them in their new place, and how they would adjust to it.

Each of them had his own thoughts, but all were equally somber.

Every one of them was in need of reassurance, of hope.

So when some of them began discussing again the possibility that they would be sent not to a camp but to another special prison, even those who did not for one moment believe it listened.

Christ in the Garden of Gethsemane, though he knew for sure that he must drain the bitter cup, nonetheless hoped and prayed.

Khorobrov, trying to repair the handle of his suitcase, which kept coming away from its fastening, was swearing loudly.

"The bastards, the swine can't even make a simple suitcase in this country. The shift in honor of May Day takes up half the year, the shift in honor of October the other half. They have to do everything in a frantic rush. Look at this—some bastard's labor-saving idea—they just bend a bit of wire at both ends and shove it through the handle. It'll hold when the case is empty, but wait till you fill it! They've developed heavy industry—damn and blast it!—but the humblest old-time village craftsman would die of shame if he made this stuff!"

Khorobrov picked up two lumps of brick that had come away from a stove built in the same slapdash way and tried viciously to hammer the ends of the handle into the lug.

Nerzhin understood Khorobrov very well. Whenever he ran into a humiliation, a slight, an insult, a rebuff, Khorobrov was furious, but how could anyone be calm and reasonable about such things? Could a man under torture howl politely? At that very moment, arrayed in his prison-camp costume and on his way to the Gulag, Nerzhin himself felt as if he were regaining an important constituent of masculine freedom: the right to make every fifth word an obscene one.

Romashov was talking quietly to the novices, telling them by what routes prisoners were usually taken to Siberia, comparing the Kuybyshev, the Gorky, and the Kirov transits and highly recommending the first.

Khorobrov stopped hammering and angrily hurled his brick to the floor, reducing it to red crumbs.

"I can't bear to listen!" he yelled at Romashov, with an agonized look on his lean, hard-bitten face. "Gorky was never in prison in the place named after him, nor Kuybyshev in the other; otherwise, they'd both have been buried twenty years earlier. Be a man and call them by their proper names: Samara, Nizhny Novgorod, and Vyatka transit prisons! You've chalked up twenty years—why truckle to our masters?"

Khorobrov's vehemence was catching. Nerzhin rose, summoned Nadelashin through the sentry, and declared in a ringing voice, "Junior lieutenant! We can see through the window that it is now twelve thirty, and lunch is in progress. Why aren't they bringing us any?"

The junior lieutenant shuffled uneasily and answered sympathetically.

"You've been . . . taken off the ration strength today."

"What do you mean, taken off?" And encouraged by the buzz of discontent behind him, Nerzhin rapped out: "Report to the prison commandant that without lunch we go nowhere! And we won't let them load us forcibly!"

The junior lieutenant caved in—"All right, I'll inform him"—and hurried off guiltily to tell his superior officer.

No one in the room paused to ask himself whether it was worth getting involved. The niggling self-respect of the free and well-fed is alien to the zek.

"Good for you!"

"Keep them on the run!"

"Stingy bums!"

"Skinflints! I work three years, and they begrudge me one lunch!"

"We just won't leave! It's that simple! What can they do to us?"

Even those who were meek and docile with the prison staff day in and day out plucked up their courage. The free wind of the transit prisons was blowing in their faces. This farewell meal with meat was not only their last chance to eat their fill before the months and years of thin gruel ahead; it was an assertion of their human dignity. And even those whose throats were so dry with anxiety that they could not have forced themselves to eat—even they forgot their misery for a while and eagerly demanded that meal.

The path connecting Prison HQ with the kitchen was visible from the window. They could see, too, a truck backing toward the wood yard, carrying a big Christmas tree, with its boughs jutting out over the sides. The prison officer in charge of supplies and stores alighted from the cab, and a guard sprang down from the back.

Yes, the lieutenant colonel had kept his word. Tomorrow or the next day, they would put the tree up in the semicircular room; prisoners—fathers without their children transformed into children themselves—would trim the tree with toys (lavishing the state's time on their preparation), Klara's little basket, a bright moon in a glass cage; and men with beards and mustaches would join hands and dance around the tree with wry laughter and try to drown the wolf's howl of their own fate with their singing.

*A Christmas tree was born in the woods,*
*In the woods a tree grew. . . .*

They could see the guard on patrol outside shooing Pryanchikov away—he was trying to break through to the windows under siege, shouting something and raising his hand to the heavens.

They saw the junior lieutenant trotting anxiously to the kitchen, back to HQ, back to the kitchen again, back to HQ again. . . .

They saw, too, that Spiridon had been turned out before he could finish his lunch to help unload the tree, wiping his mustache and adjusting his belt as he went.

The junior lieutenant finally almost ran to the kitchen and shortly after led out two cooks carrying between them a large can and a ladle. A third woman followed them with a stack of deep bowls. Afraid of slipping and breaking them, she came to a stop. The junior lieutenant turned back and took some of the bowls from her.

Everyone in the room shared the excitement of victory.

Lunch appeared in the doorway. The women began ladling out soup immediately. Zeks carried their dishes to their own corners, to windowsills, or to their suitcases. Others stood, leaning over the table where there were no benches in their way.

The junior lieutenant and the soup dispensers went out. Silence reigned, the pristine silence that should always accompany eating. They were thinking—here's a soup with some fat in it, a bit watery, but you can smell the meat: first one spoonful, then another, then a third with little spangles of fat in it and shreds of meat boiled white. I'm pouring it all into myself; the warm wetness passes through my gullet, down into my stomach, and my blood and muscles rejoice in anticipation of replenishment and new strength.

Nerzhin remembered an old saying: "A woman marries for meat; a man marries for soup." He took this to mean that the man would have to find the meat and the woman would use it to make the soup. There were no pretenses and no lofty pretensions in the common people's proverbial sayings. The folk were even more frank about themselves in their huge stock of proverbs than Tolstoy and Dostoevsky in their confessions.

The soup was nearly finished, and the aluminum spoons were scraping the bottoms of the dishes, when someone sighed: "Ye-e-e-es."

And a voice from the corner answered: "Now comes the big fast, lads."

Some faultfinder chimed in: "They ladled it from the bottom of the pot, but it was pretty thin stuff. I reckon they fished the meat out for themselves."

But someone else called out dolefully: "Will we live to eat the like of it again?"

Then Khorobrov tapped his empty plate with his spoon and said, almost choking with resentment: "No, friends! Bread and water is better than tart and trouble!"

Nobody answered him.

Nerzhin started banging on his plate and demanding the main course.

The junior lieutenant appeared immediately.

"Finished?" he asked, surveying the transferees with a friendly smile. And satisfied with the amiable looks produced by being full, he made an announcement that his experience of prisons had suggested would be better not made earlier.

"There's no second course left. They're washing the pot now. Sorry."

Nerzhin looked around at the prisoners, wondering whether it was worth making a fuss. But Russians are easily mollified, and they had all cooled off.

"What was the second course?" a deep voice boomed.

"Stew," the junior lieutenant said, with a diffident smile.

They sighed.

They somehow forgot all about the third course.

Outside, an engine was sputtering. A shouted command set the junior lieutenant free. Lieutenant Colonel Klimentiev's stern voice could be heard in the corridor.

They were led out one by one.

There was no roll call with identity check because the prison institute's own convoy guards would be escorting the zeks as far as Butyrki and handing them over there. But they were counted, each of them checked off as he took that all too familiar and always fateful step from the ground onto the high footboard of the police truck, lowering his head so as not to bump it on the steel lintel, bent double under the weight of his belongings, and clumsily banged them against the sides of the doorway.

There was no one to see them off: The break was over, and the zeks had been shepherded back indoors from the exercise yard.

The truck had been backed right up to the threshold of the HQ building. The prisoners were spared the frenzied barking of guard dogs while they were boarding, but there was the usual crush, the usual jostling. The guards, as always, were eager to get it over with, which made no difference to anyone except themselves, but their haste inevitably affected the prisoners, so that they had no opportunity to look around and take stock of their situation.

Of the first eighteen seated, not one looked up to say good-bye to the tall, graceful lime trees that had shaded their sorrows and their joys for so many years past.

The two who did contrive to look about them, Khorobrov and Nerzhin, looked not at the lime trees but at the side of the truck itself, for a particular reason: They wanted to know what color it was painted.

It was as they expected.

They thought back to the times when lead-gray-and-black police trucks scoured the streets, striking terror into the citizens. There was a time, long ago, when this was judged necessary. But in the golden epoch that followed, even police trucks were required to mirror its smiling face. Some genius had an inspiration: Police trucks would be designed to look exactly like food delivery trucks, painted with the same orange and light blue stripes, and bearing the legend in four languages:

*Khleb*

*Pain*

*Brot*

*Bread*

or

*Myaso*

*Viande*

*Fleisch*

*Meat*

Nerzhin, as he climbed into the truck, managed to twist around and read the word "Meat"; then it was his turn to squeeze through the narrow door and the even narrower second door, walk over somebody's feet, drag his case and sack over somebody's knees, and take his seat.

Inside, this three-ton truck was not "boxed," that is to say, not divided into ten iron boxes, into each of which one single prisoner would be squeezed. No, this was a truck of the "general" type, meaning that it was meant for the transport not of prisoners under investigation but those already sentenced, which greatly increased its "live freight" capacity. In its rear section, between the two iron doors with their small ventilation grilles, the truck had a narrow space for the guards. They could lock the inner doors from the outside and the outer doors from the inside and communicate with the driver by means of a speaking tube running through the bodywork of the truck. There was barely room for two guards with their legs tucked up under them. The rear compartment was further reduced in size by a single small box to house any refractory prisoner. Otherwise, the rear of the truck was one single low-roofed metal box, a single communal mousetrap, and the prescribed number of men to be squeezed into it was, in fact, twenty. (If you kept the iron door latched by wedging two pairs of booted feet against it, you could squeeze a few more in.)

A bench ran around three walls of the mousetrap, leaving only a small space in the middle. Those who managed to find a place sat down, but they were not the luckiest; when the truck was crammed full, other people and other people's belongings landed on their cramped legs. Neither protests nor apologies had any point in this crush, and it would be an hour or so before they could change positions. The guards had put their shoulders to the door and locked it after shoving the last man in.

But they had not yet slammed the outer door of the guard's compartment. Someone else set foot on the rear step, and a new shadow obscured the view through the ventilation grille.

"Hey, guys!" Ruska's voice. "I'm due at Butyrki for investigation! Who are these? Who's being moved?"

There was an immediate explosion of voices: all twenty zeks answering him, both guards telling Ruska to shut up, and Klimentiev calling out from the doorway of HQ ordering the guards to keep their minds on the job and prevent the prisoners from calling out to one another.

"Be quiet, you. . . ," somebody said, using an obscene word.

It was quiet again, and the guards could be heard rearranging their legs so that they could stuff Ruska into the box quickly.

"Who told on you, Ruska?" Nerzhin called out.

"Siromakha!"

Several voices chorused, "The rat!"

"How many of you are there?" Ruska shouted.

"Twenty."

"Who's there altogether?"

But this was where they shoved him into the box and locked it.

"Keep your chin up, Ruska," they shouted. "We'll meet in the camp!"

As long as the outer door was open, a little light reached the interior of the truck. But then it was closed with a bang, and the heads of the guards prevented the last faint light from reaching them through the grilles in both doors. The engine rumbled, the truck shuddered and began moving, and now as it jolted along, only occasional gleams of reflected light played on the zeks' faces.

A brief exchange of shouts from cell to cell, like a hot spark leaping between flint and iron, always excites prisoners.

"What are the elite supposed to do in a labor camp?" Nerzhin spoke loudly but close to Gerasimovich's ear, so that no one else could hear him.

"The same as everybody else, only working twice as hard," Gerasimovich answered in another loud whisper.

The truck stopped when they had gone a little way. Obviously at the guardhouse.

"Ruska," a prisoner called out, "did they beat you up?"

A muffled reply came after some delay. "Yes, they did."

"Damn and blast all Shishkin-Myshkins!" Nerzhin shouted. "Don't let them get you down, Ruska!"

Several voices were raised at once, and no one could make himself heard above the hubbub.

The truck moved on again, past the guardhouse; then they were all rocked sharply to the right, which meant that they were turning left onto the highway.

Gerasimovich and Nerzhin swayed toward each other, shoulders touching, at the turn. They looked around, trying to distinguish each other's faces in the half dark. It was not just their cramped quarters that made them feel so close.

"I'm not a bit sorry I've left the place, men," Khorobrov said. "What sort of life do you have in a special prison? You can't walk along a hallway without bumping into some Siromakha. One in every five there is a snitch. If you fart in the bathroom, the godfather hears about it right away; we've had no Sundays for two years, the bastards. And a twelve-hour working day. You swap your brains for twenty grams of butter. They banned letters to and from home—damn and blast them! Just work, work, work. It's hell on earth!"

Khorobrov fell silent, overcome with indignation.

Nerzhin's voice rose in reply above the sound of the engine, which was quieter now that they were driving along the asphalt highway.

"No, Ilya Terentich, that isn't hell. *That* is *not* hell! Hell is where we're going. We're going back to hell. The special prison is the highest, the best, the first circle of hell. It's practically paradise."

He left it at that—no need to say more. They all knew, of course, that something incomparably worse than the special prison awaited them. They knew that, from the camp, Marfino would be remembered as a golden dream. But for the present, to keep their spirits up, and to feel that they had done the right thing, they had to curse the special prison, so that no one would feel any lingering regret or reproach himself with a rash act.

"When war breaks out, they'll kill off the zeks in special prisons with poisoned bread, like the Hitlerites did, because they know too much."

"Well, that's what I keep telling you," Khorobrov exclaimed. "Bread and water is better than cake and woe."

As their ears grew accustomed to the noise of the engine, the zeks fell silent.

Yes, what awaited them was the taiga and the tundra, the Cold Pole at Oymyakon, the copper mines at Dzhezkazgan. What awaited them yet again was the pickax and the wheelbarrow, a starvation ration of half-baked bread, hospital, death. They could look forward to nothing but the worst.

Yet in their hearts they were at peace with themselves.

They were gripped by the fearlessness of people who have lost absolutely everything—such fearlessness is difficult to attain, but once attained, it endures.

SWINGING THE COMPRESSED mass of bodies to and fro, the gaily painted orange-and-blue truck swished along the city streets, passed one of the stations, and pulled up at a crossing. A dark red car was held up by traffic lights at the same road junction. It belonged to the Moscow correspondent of the newspaper *Libération*, who was on his way to a hockey match in the Dynamo stadium. The correspondent read the words on the side of the truck:

*Myaso*

*Viande*

*Fleisch*

*Meat*

He had made a mental note of several such trucks seen in various parts of Moscow that day. He took out a notebook and jotted down in dark red ink:

"Every now and then, one encounters on the streets of Moscow food delivery trucks, spick-and-span and impeccably hygienic. There can be no doubt that the capital's food supplies are extremely well organized."

**"Best Nonfiction Book of the Twentieth Century."**
**—*Time* magazine**

**"It is impossible to name a book that had a greater effect on the political and moral consciousness of the late twentieth century."**
**—David Remnick, *The New Yorker***

**Available wherever books are sold, or call 1-800-331-3791 to order.**